The Hall Monitors of Ravencrest Academy

Rachel Joel

The Hall Monitors of Ravencrest Academy

ISBN 978-1506-911-62-5 PBK
ISBN 978-1506-911-63-2 EBK

B&N –
9781506911755 PBK
9781506911762 EBK

February 2024

Published and Distributed by
First Edition Design Publishing, Inc.
P.O. Box 17646, Sarasota, FL 34276-3217
www.firsteditiondesignpublishing.com

To Becca: my first reader, editor, and friend. I'm so blessed to have such a sweet, encouraging, and mischievous little sister in my life. You were the first to hear my stories, and I kept writing because of you. Thank you for everything.

Chapter One

On the same day Aiden opened his eyes for the first time he could remember in nine months, Ravencrest Academy was closed.

And after three months of pure physical and mental recovery, the academy was opened once more.

A new school year, Aiden knew. *A fresh start.*

It wasn't a normal fresh start. Ravencrest Academy was an elite residential high school on one of the Pacific islands. It almost took up the entire island, full of spacious dormitories, scientific laboratories, detailed simulators, college professors, strong security measures, and incredible food. Students spent their free time working in research labs, practicing sports, playing musical instruments, and designing jaw-dropping inventions.

This was no ordinary high school. It was considered one of the best schools in the world. The Academy produced diplomats, scholars, world leaders, artists, scientists, and more. Oh, and a master thief or two in the past several hundred years, but no one ever spoke about him.

The years of eleventh and twelfth grade at Ravencrest Academy could truly impact students for years to come. Gifted students excelled and flourished. Talented students who could handle the intense coursework and rigorous academic program were admitted. However, book smarts weren't the only requirement. Students really had to, as the school put it, "love learning."

Aiden did love learning very much. Nonetheless, he wasn't technically a student. He was the headmaster's son. This meant he was next in line to be the headmaster once his father expired. Of course, this made things a little awkward when the subject was brought up in front of the headmaster.

Which is why Aiden gasped, "Mengele!" at the faint sound of footsteps. He was sitting in his father's office chair, imagining himself as the headmaster. This wasn't the most logical move, since he had many years to go before becoming headmaster. After all, he was just fourteen. Father turned the corner as Aiden sat, frozen with guilt. He knew better than to run.

"Aiden Ravencrest!" Father snapped. "I forbid profanity in this school! You should be ashamed of yourself. This is the headmaster's chair, and you do not deserve to sit here unless you are headmaster!"

"Sorry, Father, I—"

"Welcome Dinner will begin any minute now. You will stay in your room. Don't expect dinner. I'll have a porter escort you."

"What? Father, it's Welcome Dinner!" Aiden protested. "I look forward to it every year!"

"You need to understand the consequences of your actions. You should be thankful your punishment isn't more severe. Now go." Father dismissed him with a wave of the hand.

Aiden frowned as Porter Jimmy grabbed his arm and, none too gently, half-dragged him to his room. Father had given more severe punishments for less criminal offenses in the past, yet this one in particular frustrated Aiden. *Welcome Dinner is my favorite! Really, Father, are you testing me to see how quickly I'll sneak out of my room this time?*

"I'm perfectly capable of walking there myself, Eliza," Aiden said in annoyance. He knew Jimmy hated to be called Eliza, the porter's unfortunate middle name.

Of course, Jimmy only tightened his grip and said with a nasty smile, "You shouldn't be so irritating to the person who saved your life, young man."

It was true Jimmy had supposedly saved Aiden's life. Yes, Porter Jimmy had always hated Aiden because of how Aiden tended to make his job harder. After all, the porters' job was to serve the Ravencrest students and give them the best experience possible, treating them with courtesy while answering all their possibly outlandish demands. No such protocol existed for the headmaster's son. In the past, the children of the headmaster either participated in running the school or in a profound field of study. Aiden had lived at the school all his life. This island was his home. Although he was disciplined enough to focus on his self-guided studies, he was also a bit mischievous. Thus, the porters were usually frustrated by Aiden's ability to make life more interesting at Ravencrest. Most of the porters were rather annoyed by Aiden's existence, though a few were kind enough to listen to his explanations, nurture his learning, and even help him. Porter Jimmy was the one porter who absolutely detested the boy, most likely because of the Frying Pan Incident seven years ago.

Then again, because of Porter Jimmy, Aiden had woken up three months ago with a splitting headache. He had suffered a terrible concussion due to a fall, a concussion that had made his memories for the past nine months disappear.

"I don't remember you saving my life," Aiden shot back. So what if Porter Jimmy was the one who had found Aiden's unconscious body and reported the incident? There had been no other witnesses available to confirm Jimmy's account. "If you had found me almost dead, no doubt you would have leaped for joy."

Porter Jimmy's scowl faded, and he looked away. A shadow crossed over his face. "Is that what you think, boy?"

"Are you going to lock me in my room?" Aiden sighed as he watched the porter enter the usual security precautions for the Ravencrest family room. Iris scan, fingerprint check, alphanumeric password, etc. "You know I'll find a way out. Why don't you save us all the trouble and leave the door unlocked?"

Jimmy smirked. "We'll see, young man. Remember your place. I'm on strict orders from your father. Maybe if I feel kind, I'll smuggle some leftover Welcome Dinner for you." Jimmy's laughter echoed down the hall as the door slammed shut and locked.

Aiden made a face. "*Maybe I'll smuggle some Welcome Dinner for you*," he mocked in the mirror. "*Maybe I'll see what it's like to get Welcome Dinner shoved in my face, which will be so much fun because I have nothing better to do with my time.*" Aiden paused, abashed. "How immature," he scolded his reflection. "You know better. Mother wouldn't have allowed you to act this way."

The mention of his mother brought weariness to his eyes. His childish grin faded, and his reflection's youth seemed to disappear. After receiving the news of his mother's death, the first month had passed in a blur. The next nine months were nonexistent in Aiden's mind, and the last three had been focused on recovery alone due to the severity of the brain damage. In total, Aiden lost over a full year of his life. It was as if he had suddenly woken up a year older, in more ways than one.

"Physically speaking, I've made a full recovery," he said, speaking to a person who was no longer present in the world. "I should be thankful. I just wish you were still here, Mother."

It wasn't healthy for him to pretend she was still alive. He had been doing it anyway, ever since he had woken up to the terrible reality that he had lost nine months of his life and, much worse, his dear mother. Finally, he slumped into a chair and closed his eyes.

"Mother, what would you want me to do?"

He knew the answer: *Remember that you are a Ravencrest.*

So he opened his eyes, hacked himself out of his room, shut down the security measures using the card he had swiped from his father, changed into Denver's old clothes, disguised himself as a student, and went down to Welcome Dinner, all in about half an hour.

As a young prodigy, Aiden tended to do things for multiple reasons at a time. He was not at Welcome Dinner just to enjoy the food. Nor was it to count the minutes his father could hold up a wide, unfaltering smile under the spotlight. Nor was it to help Chef Gaston by making each dish a little more special. No, there was another reason Aiden attended Welcome Dinner. It was a soft-hearted reason, true, but Aiden could be a soft-hearted person at times. He got it from his mother.

She had been the soft-hearted one, the surrogate mother for many Ravencrest Academy students. Mother had always attended every welcoming event. By the end of the year, she would know every Ravencrest Academy student by heart and would be greeted with, "Good morning, Mrs. Ravencrest!" every time she passed one in the halls. If a student showed up at her door with tears in their eyes, Aiden would be instructed to go to the smaller, adjoining bedroom while his mother spoke to the student. Every student knew Molly Ravencrest, the "kindest person to ever walk the halls at Ravencrest."

She had been an incredible mother with a beautiful smile. Her face used to light up whenever he entered the room. The excitement she held for learning was contagious, and she played no small role in his education. In fact, she taught him how to learn, then gave him the tools and opportunities to do so himself. It was how he had graduated middle school by six, high school by nine, and college before thirteen (when his mother had died). She had made his life the special treat it was, and nothing had been the same since she died.

Had he ever told her *thank you*? Or a simple *I love you*? She had told him many times how she loved him more than anything else in this world. He could still remember her distant voice, her gentle touch, and the sincere care in her eyes. He had taken her selfless love for granted. If only...

"'Scuse me," said a voice as an African American student—his name tag read *Everest Michaels*—brushed by him, eager to get to the food. The student's eyes were wide as he looked at the options and rubbed his hands together in anticipation. Aiden chuckled as he watched Everest consider his choices, eyes darting from option to option. It was obvious that the students appreciated the delicious food. If his mother had been present, she would've joked about Everest's clear excitement and sparked a conversation with him regarding the importance of good food. Instead, Aiden stayed silent and watched the excited boy rush to grab a plate.

Despite his reluctance to talk to anyone, Aiden was here to get to know the new students. In previous years, most students had become friends with Aiden's mother before Welcome Dinner was over, although they hardly noticed Aiden. This year was different.

Her death had been declared an international tragedy. Students from up to twenty years ago had arrived at the funeral and mourned. Aiden couldn't remember them all. He had been in a daze at the time. Drifting in and out. Never mentally present. He only remembered snippets of conversations.

I'm so sorry.

How did this happen?

They should sue the pilot. They should sue the airplane company. They should sue somebody! I can't believe she...

Didn't she have a kid?

Is that him?

Are you eating enough?

How are you?

You know I'm always here for you.

Listen to me...

You're not listening to me...

Aiden paused and clutched his head. At times, his memories became painful and confusing. Most of them were buried in a sea of vague understanding. Sometimes he remembered more than others. One day, he prayed, one day he would have all his memories back. No more headaches or hazy memories. One day, things would be clear. Every memory would have context, every thought meaning, and every blurry face recognition.

"What kind of cuisine would you like, sir?" RAVEN, an invention of an old Ravencrest student, asked. Aiden had been handed a RAVEN earpiece in line after ensuring the porters had extras.

Aiden deepened his voice and imitated an American accent. "Uh, somethin' Chinese, I guess?"

"Chinese food is to your left. Keep walking. Turn right. Yes, you have arrived at the Chinese food table. Would you like me to give you a recommendation?"

"Uh, sure."

"Do you enjoy spicy food?"

"Yeah!"

"I would recommend order #312. A porter will assist you." Already one of the porters was approaching him.

Aiden maintained his disguise, and soon he was comfortably seated with piping hot, spicy, traditional Chinese food. By the time Aiden had finished, he was both satisfied and curious. It was time to get to know the new class of students. Without moving more than his eyes, Aiden learned in about five minutes the backstory, personality, and aspirations of all twenty students seated at his table. He looked to the next table. By the end of the hour, he knew all one thousand students from around the globe sitting in the mess hall. Just by watching the way they ate, spoke, coughed, fidgeted, shone, chose their food, and more, he soon knew more about each person than their friends did.

"Hello, faculty, fellow Ravencrest alumni, and Ravencrest students!" boomed Father's cheerful, charming voice. Father had the gift of transforming his usual quiet, analytical self into someone who could shine in the spotlight. The porters had set up a small stage in the mess hall for Father to speak. At most events, speakers would give their speeches in the auditorium; however, just for Welcome Dinner, a stage was set up in the mess hall. "Welcome to Ravencrest Academy!"

Cheers followed this statement.

"Congratulations on your acceptance! A select five hundred high school juniors from all over the world are chosen each year to attend this prestigious school. Let's give a round of applause for all the new students!"

When the cheering had died down, Father continued, "Let's turn our attention to our alumni. Owls, please rise."

Every student who had previously attended Ravencrest rose to their feet and received plenty of awed clapping. Father continued, highlighting achievements these students had reached over the summer. These were not normal achievements. These were lifetime achievements most people hoped to accomplish one day.

While Father went on, Aiden multitasked. Rather than listening to Father, he formulated an assessment of possible allies. It would be beneficial to have a partner this year to help him make life at Ravencrest more exciting. A few years ago, he had been best friends with Denver Tennyson. Now Denver was off, working for NASA and landing a shuttle on Mars as a twenty-two-year-old. He didn't have time to hang out with Aiden anymore. Finding a new partner for his missions, Aiden thought, would be very beneficial—and only beneficial, nothing more. Surprised by the little boy's brilliance, Denver had been very kind to eight-year-old Aiden. The two had become fast friends, despite the eight-year age difference, and Aiden had been thrilled. Now they hadn't spoken in years, except for the awkward exchange at the funeral service.

Aiden understood. Friends were like that. Thus, he wasn't interested in friends, only teammates.

Perhaps the girl who was hacking into the security software on her homemade phone? Or the boy who was absentmindedly sketching PhD-level mathematical art on his tray? Or the girl over there, transcribing every word Father said in an undecipherable shorthand? Aiden noted these characters. Partners who had helpful talents would be preferable. The real question was, did they have a strong enough moral compass? It was a question his mother would have considered as a deciding factor. So, did they?

Hm. He'd have to find out later.

"...and now, of course, we must go over some ground rules," Father continued. "First, all electronics used on campus must download Ravencrest Academy software. This software provides security, unlimited data, and many more functions."

Aiden checked his watch. How many points did Father have left to cover? All this information would be sent out in a mass email later.

"You will each be given one day of rest. Every student is required to attend classes from Monday to Friday. As for the weekend, each student must choose either Saturday or Sunday as a day of rest. The other unchosen day will consist of asynchronous learning. All of you have been assigned schedules, yes?"

A general murmur of agreement greeted this statement.

"We here at Ravencrest believe in utilizing every moment of our lives," Father said. "Some may find this schedule demanding. We find it necessary to teach you everything in the Ravencrest curriculum. Our weekday schedule consists of the alarm bell ringing at 6:00 AM sharp, breakfast served right away, and classes beginning at 6:30 AM in Central Indonesian Time. Remember, you are all in a different time zone now. Since you participated in our two weeks of orientation to adjust to this time zone, you are expected to show up to class on time. Plan accordingly. You must be dressed in a Ravencrest uniform. You must also have brushed your teeth, showered, and eaten breakfast before coming to class. Do not attempt to 'wing' it. Should there be an issue with this, we will give you a tardy pass. Up to five tardy passes are allowed per year, and once they are all used, demerits will be given. Demerits do disqualify you from winning many recognitions and awards at Ravencrest Academy."

There were a couple of whimpers from the audience, most likely from those who took quite a while in the morning. One whimper came from the girl who was furiously noting everything down in that impressive shorthand.

"Every weekday, there are six class periods that will each run for 90 minutes. Ten minutes will be given between each class, and there is an hour-long lunch break. Classes will end at roughly 5:30 PM. Expect at least four hours of homework. Your in-building curfew is relatively early, at 10:00 PM."

Quite a few students seemed shocked by this rigorous schedule. *Hmm, it seems Father didn't do an excellent job of informing students of the demands of Ravencrest beforehand.* No, more kids than usual seemed to be on the verge of crying. Maybe a full three students. *Did Father have something else on his mind? One of his priorities is to make sure these kids know what they're getting themselves into before they apply.*

"However," Father said, "we do have quite a few bonuses you won't find at other schools. Each student has the opportunity to visit any country of their choice, within reason. You have all been given a RASIN card, which allows you to travel the world and purchase necessities such as food, shelter, etc. Keep in mind that you may not use your RASIN card for extravagant purchases. Also, Ravencrest is not liable for any injuries, accidents, or issues on your trip unless you apply to bring along a porter chaperone, in which case you must pay a fee ahead of time. Your RASIN card will track your purchases to ensure you are only paying for your own experience. Violations of these policies may result in your card being revoked. Be sure to use the money wisely. You can disable the card at any time to prevent someone else from stealing it. I trust you will all use this privilege well."

Father droned on and on. Finally, after quite a while, he finished with, "Once more, I congratulate you all. Best wishes, and welcome to Ravencrest Academy!"

Confetti sprinkled the stage. Students cheered.

Yet Aiden did not participate in this response. Instead, he sat there, blinking at Father in shock. He had seen a few reports on Father's desk, and he wondered—no mention of Mother? No mention of the new security additions installed in the required Ravencrest software? Or the newest developments in Campus Security with the new technology and guards? Or the construction workers installing extra security cameras around campus?

Was Father trying to hide something?

Students were chatting, finishing dinner, and traveling to their respective rooms. Father was smiling at the camera with his usual charm. Porter Jimmy was in the back, on the lookout for Aiden. Knowing this, Aiden got back to work. He slipped into the kitchens, then into one of the carts. He crawled into the dumbwaiter and let it bring him to the attic. Then he dropped onto the rafters, shifted along, and landed on the panels above Father's office. To Aiden's surprise, Father had installed new electric wiring, and an alert porter was standing outside the office door.

Aiden frowned. All he had wanted to do was look at Father's secret notebook. It would explain the lack of what Aiden considered to be necessary information. No need for Father to increase the security force so drastically.

By the time Father opened the door to Aiden's room, Aiden was propped up on his bed reading a book.

"Have you learned your lesson, young man?" Father stiffly asked as if speaking to his son was a dull formality.

"Why didn't you mention everything on your desk at Welcome Dinner?" Aiden asked. So what if he was grounded again? He could handle it.

Father scowled. "You were not to leave your room."

"Did you really believe I wouldn't?"

"I suppose you went right back into my office?"

"Perhaps." Aiden met his father's eyes.

Father frowned. "I should upgrade my security, even more so."

"You didn't answer my question!"

"Do not raise your voice at me, young man!" Father shouted. "I am your father, which means I am the authority figure here. You will do as I say, do you understand me?"

"Yes, sir," Aiden mumbled, momentarily intimidated.

"Regarding your inquiries, all I will say is...I have my reasons."

"What reasons?" Aiden said through narrowed eyes.

Father seemed tired as he sat down in a nearby chair. "You do not trust me?"

Aiden's eyes lowered to the floor. The reason why he had suffered a concussion in the first place was because he had fallen from a tree outside the server room. According to the porters, he had been trying to see limited information inside the server room, information Father had told him to forget about. Father hadn't said much other than his usual stern lecture on the subject, yet Aiden could still sense how hurt Father was.

"Aiden, I asked you a question."

I guess I do trust him, at least a little. Yet Aiden had to find some way to deal with this much-too-strong grief, and if it was proving he knew better than his father, then so be it. This was why he had been sneaking around much more often than usual lately.

Father sighed, then admitted at last, "We have received several threats to the safety of this school. Some people in the media claim we support an oligarchy and favor the rich. There are many who have attempted to take action against us, and thus I need to strengthen the school's security measures."

Aiden's heart quickened. "We have excellent security."

"Yes. However, several groups have formed solely to bring down Ravencrest Academy."

He couldn't help but feel a jolt of shock. "What? Why?" He knew the usual reasons people didn't support Ravencrest. Yes, it was a common name associated with "biased Admissions," "only accepting the rich," and "not enough diversity." In the past, Father had ignored those shouting crude remarks at him and, instead of responding, released lists of previous classes. Each year, the list included people from all over the world. Students came from all backgrounds, religions, races, classes, and backgrounds, united by one purpose: to learn.

It had been an institution considered noble for years, existing solely for the purpose of training the next generation of world leaders. Every Ravencrest headmaster had sighed and admitted that there were always going to be haters who yelled obscene things and published untrue articles. For years, Ravencrest leaders had put up with it. Yet full-on anti-Ravencrest terrorist groups?

"For many idiotic reasons, these groups do exist. I have done my best to increase security measures around here. Even so, I need to deal with all the hacking attempts and threats to student safety..." For a moment, the headmaster looked completely exhausted.

Not for the first time, Aiden realized how stressful it must be to care for a thousand of the smartest teenagers in the world, some of whom were children of world leaders.

"...and I do not need my son disrupting my plans to ensure this school is a safe, secure, and closely monitored system. Am I understood?" Ah, here was Father's infamous, stern glare.

Though Father was a stone-faced, strict headmaster, he was a kind and hardworking man. He had created the most scholarship opportunities any headmaster had created thus far. Also, he had made many gracious edits to the curriculum, keeping them challenging yet doable. Furthermore, while he was infamous for his terrifying glares, he never punished a student with anything more than a lecture or detention. Father had entirely devoted himself to this school; he was always giving students more opportunities to excel, whether it was organizing a new program involving world leaders or setting up a highly requested lecture from an admired professional. He was usually working late, juggling meetings, paperwork, and the overwhelming responsibility of being in charge of a thousand children at once. Somewhere underneath that stern glare was a man who loved his job. Somewhere very far underneath.

Aiden dutifully nodded when he realized his father was still waiting for a response.

"Since you've learned your lesson, you are free to roam about. Be sure to finish your courses this school year. How many did you finish last year?" Father rose to his feet, dusted himself off, and walked to the door.

"None."

Father paused, frowning. "None?"

"I lost the last year of my life, Father," Aiden said bitterly. "I only entirely finished my recovery yesterday."

He was still a self-guided student. Previously, Mother had homeschooled him. This meant that every dinner, she asked him for a progress report of what he did that day. She also offered educational opportunities, such as letting him "tag along" on one of her business trips. Though she worked for Ravencrest Academy, she was also a scientist with an interest in many different fields. She was always publishing fascinating research papers for one journal or another, and her research allowed her young son to come along occasionally. It was how Aiden had experienced so much of the world during his childhood; though most kids would have forgotten or underappreciated this blessing, he was a prodigy and understood more than most kids did. Perhaps it was why his mother enjoyed traveling together with him. Or perhaps it was because they used to have the most intellectually interesting conversations together; Mother would explain a concept he had never heard of, he would describe his thoughts on something he had recently learned, they would debate and discuss all sorts of—

"Your mother would've wanted you to—" Father began, breaking Aiden's remembrance of those wonderful conversations. The day he had realized he would never have a conversation with his mother again, Aiden hadn't moved from his hospital bed for hours and skipped two meals without noticing his hunger.

"I'll combine two years into one," Aiden interrupted. "Satisfied?"

"Do not raise your voice—"

"I know, I know, I get it."

"Aiden!" The sternness was back. For a moment, Father had dropped his defenses and confided in his son, something Aiden had never experienced before. Then again, something had been different between the two of them since Mother's funeral.

"Sorry," he lied, staring at the graduate-level textbook he had been reading before bed.

There was a nervous silence.

Eventually Father said, "A new archeological dig in Pampas is currently in the process of being approved. I plan on using the finds in my book, so I will be leaving in about two months. It should be a short trip."

"Your summer project?" Aiden felt a tinge of jealousy. One day he would be old enough to approve archeological digs. As it was, he was too young to do much other than publish scientific papers under a pen name. It was a large mystery in the scientific community who on earth the mysterious Mergen K. was who published such astonishing works yet cleverly avoided ever addressing themself.

"Yes, the book about Pangea."

"Will you include Biblical references?" Now Aiden's voice was taut. This was a low blow. Mother had been a devoted Christian. Father was an agnostic at best and an atheist at worst. So, indeed, religion was not a topic they ever casually discussed.

Again, another tense silence pervaded the room until Father said, in a voice stiffer than starch, "Would you be interested in coming along?"

What? Was his father reaching out to him? Offering a hand of friendship? Father had been saying these kinds of things, offering peace after fights, and trying to connect with Aiden ever since he had woken up. It was strange. In the past, their relationship had consisted of Aiden choosing what to tell Father and Father avoiding his only son.

So what had changed? Was it possible that somehow, in the aftermath of the death of his wife and the subsequent near-death of his son, Father was attempting to connect with him?

Aiden almost laughed out loud at the irony. Ever since waking up, he had been pushing himself as far away as he could from his father. He didn't like to think about why, about the cold emptiness that gripped him at night, about how no one understood him anymore, or about how strict his father had been toward him for years. For Aiden, it had taken his mother's death to break any lingering attempt at establishing a lasting relationship with his father—and yet the same death had caused Father to reach out to his son for the first time.

Yet Aiden was terribly soft-hearted, and as he looked into Father's eyes, he realized he could see his father's softer side. The man was worn out, stressed, and frustrated; despite this, he had made time to talk to Aiden, explain his reasons, break the silence, and invite his son along on a trip.

"Sure," Aiden said. "I'd love to come along."

Father smiled. It was a rare smile, not like the charming one for the cameras. It made Father look different. He seemed young and alive, not like the man who frowned so sternly. "Sleep well," Father instructed, with a warmth in his words Aiden did not hear often.

Aiden watched Father close the door behind him. He skimmed through the last page of his book in less than a second and threw it under the covers, eyes darting to the door in case Father stepped back in. He pulled out the secret compartment he had built under his bed. He didn't keep a notebook in case someone would try to read it; despite this, he knew all the plans he had for the upcoming year. Plans to make his life more exciting. Plans to make his mother proud. Plans to show his father how he could be a Ravencrest too. Plans he had created while recovering from the fall. Plans that would make up for losing so much of his young life.

He smiled his own genuine smile, though it was more of a mischievous smirk. For the first time in quite a while, a light sparkled in his eyes.

It was time for a new school year at Ravencrest Academy.

Chapter Two

A gentle yet firm alarm bell rang through the school, similar to the ringing of London's Big Ben. It was to ring six times, clear and loud, in order to wake up each student at 6:00 AM sharp. This was how it had been for years. Years before Aiden was born, that is.

"What's up, Ravencrest Owls?" Aiden said in the best American accent he could muster. He played a recording of owls crying out "*Hoo hoo*" for a good two seconds, then switched to his own voice (and British accent) once more. "It's time to rise and shine for your first day here! I know owls are nocturnal, but we Ravencrest Owls are the exception! If you need more encouragement, Chef is making a full-on breakfast menu. He's got recipes loaned from the best breakfast restaurants in the world. So go on and hurry up, or else I'll be eating them all myself. Have a great first day!" Aiden finished the recording in the nick of time. If he had been a few seconds longer, the recording wouldn't have been the right length of time, and his plan couldn't have worked.

Got it. Now that he had the recording, it was time to slide it near the intercom.

This was the hard part. Porter Jimmy was always on the lookout for him, and every year Aiden had played a similar recording at the beginning of the year. Students had always assumed the unique alarm system on the first day of school was merely a fun Ravencrest tradition. In reality, Aiden was starting the year with a nice way to outsmart Porter Jimmy and to let him know it wasn't a good idea to treat the headmaster's son like trash. And, on Porter Jimmy's end, it was an attempt to teach Aiden a lesson before the school year began. Besides, the rest of the year continued with the normal bell ringing at the beginning of the day—a little more boring, yes, but certainly traditional and comforting for many, including Aiden.

This little tradition of frustrating Jimmy had never been brought to Father's attention because everyone else besides Mother assumed the intercom truly was Father's fun idea to make the first day a little more festive. Aiden had only been caught once when he was nine, which had done two things. First, it had fueled Porter Jimmy to pursue Aiden every first day of each Ravencrest school year in order to catch him again. Second, it had taught Aiden to do this tradition every year from then on to set the record straight.

Though Aiden hated to admit it, Jimmy was highly intelligent. All the porters were. Intelligent, fit, polite, respectful, mindful of manners and customs, and could speak at least three languages. Those were the requirements to be a Ravencrest Porter.

Yet today, Aiden was glad Jimmy was so clever. It made Aiden's work all the more fun.

"Let's see what you've got, Eliza," Aiden hummed as he used his mother's old computer to hack into the software. She had designed most of the software years ago and thus had direct access to the code. Therefore, it was very easy for Aiden to keep her account active and secretly change the security software whenever he deemed necessary, which was much more often than healthy. The hard part was covering up his actions. Father had enlisted a greater security team recently.

Aiden gasped, despite himself, as he looked through the security camera footage. He questioned what his eyes were witnessing: six porters in the hall, locks that would shock people attempting to break in, lasers, and more. This was overkill. *Father, how much money are we spending on security this year? Is the threat really as bad as you're making it out to be?*

Back to his mission.

He considered the variables. Hmm...a baffling locked-room mystery. His favorite kind.

Smiling, Aiden glanced at the time. 10:42 PM. Welcome Dinner had long since ended, and the chatter in the halls had settled at last. All of Ravencrest was asleep except for a few night porters.

Time to get to work.

Having snuck out of his room past a sleeping Jimmy, Aiden crept down the hallway in socked feet. He was surrounded in pitch-black darkness but had the route memorized.

He paused for a moment and listened to the breathing.

A porter at the intersection of the next hallway. Breathing heavier than usual. Porter Craig?

Aiden relaxed. Porter Craig was the oldest and friendliest of the porters. He was the closest to retirement yet had chosen to work anyway. No doubt he would, as usual, turn a blind eye.

Aiden's socks lightly brushed the mat. The next morning, one of the porters would vacuum the area, effectively covering his tracks. After returning from a quick detour, Aiden drew near to Porter Craig. Another porter, possibly Nikolai (an older Russian man who rarely spoke), was patrolling the hallway as well.

Rather than whisper *it's me,* Aiden tapped the message in Morse Code on Craig's shoulder.

Craig jumped a little at first. *He's getting a bit rusty, isn't he?*

Then Aiden felt a small key pressed into his palm. Craig squeezed the boy's hand, and in the silence, Aiden felt a rush of warmth. Craig knew why Aiden was there. That little squeeze was his way of saying, *Go get 'em.*

Aiden smiled in the darkness. When he was headmaster, only porters like Craig would be given the privileges all porters had now.

It was time to get into the room. While he had the key, the porter on night watch pacing back and forth down the hallway outside the door—Porter Keil, by his gait and light humming—was certain to catch him. *Unless...*

With the precision of a bullet, Aiden shot in the darkness swiftly, diving past Porter Keil and standing in front of the door. He climbed so he was standing on the doorknob and flattened himself against the door. *Silence.* He held his breath as Keil walked by and, like a pendulum duly returning, turned and walked back down the hall, still lightly humming an Irish jig.

Aiden slid the key in and held the doorknob in place. Moments before it would click, he visualized Keil's position and flicked a piece of paper so it brushed the man's nose. Keil stopped humming and shouted, "Who's there?"

Silence.

Since Ravencrest protocol was to turn on the lights only when a serious issue was suspected, Aiden knew Keil wouldn't turn on the lights. But he did have a flashlight. Keil clicked on the flashlight and shined it around the hall, resting the beam of light on the doorknob.

Nothing.

Keil frowned, looked down at the little indents in the carpet, and followed the feet shapes. He would soon land in the kitchen, where one of the maids (Maratha had a soft spot for Aiden; in his detour, he had explained everything to her) would take the blame.

Ah, it did make Aiden, who was pressed up against the ceiling, smirk a little. Walking backward was an old trick. Keil shouldn't have fallen for it. The newer porters were a bit dafter than the older ones, he supposed. Then again, they probably just had less experience.

Parkour does come in handy. It had helped him keep his feet off the floor as he had returned from the kitchens to the hallway. Counting his blessings with his full physical recovery, he swung the door open silently and slipped in. The cool of the damp programming room greeted him. He walked in, felt the sides of the computer with gloved fingers, and pulled out the little drive with the original bell ringer program. He replaced it with an identical-looking flash drive from his room, grabbed the old flash drive case in the drawer, and snuck back out

Soon the old drive was in its rightful place in Aiden's pocket, and Aiden was on his way back to his room. He was grinning broadly because he couldn't wait to see the look on Jimmy's face in the morning.

"Hello, Porter Jimmy," Aiden said as he walked down to the kitchens, yawning a little. "Pleasant day, isn't it? May I ask why you were standing outside my room this morning? To escort me? Oh, how kind."

"You know perfectly well why." Jimmy's narrowed eyes were fixed on the young boy. "How did you like your stay last night?"

"Oh, it was wonderful. I had a delicious Chinese dinner—I mean, novel." Aiden fake-stammered over his words. "And I could imagine Father's speech, what, with his gold tie and dark tuxedo? The one he had tailored this year? Ah, how nice."

"How did you get out?" Porter Jimmy shouted. "I don't get it! How do you keep doing that?"

Aiden smirked. "It takes brilliance. I'm afraid it might not be possible for you to understand, sir."

Jimmy smirked right back. "Well, however you're doing it, it's going to stop soon. The new security expert's implementing this foolproof software."

This wiped the smile right off Aiden's face.

"That's right," said Jimmy. Now he was the one grinning broadly. "The old software keeps getting edited. Seems the old creator's account wasn't deactivated. They're going to erase the whole thing and try a new one. Sad, seeing we've had that software for almost thirty years now, huh? It was even designed by your mother. And it's all because some nosy young boy couldn't keep his nose out of trouble."

"*Nosy young boy keeping his nose out of trouble?* Ah, yes, brilliance is definitely only an illusion for you, sir," Aiden said fake-politely, even though he knew his face was hot. "I suggest a career in perhaps counting sheep. It seems perfect for your intelligence level."

"Insult me all you want. You're not the headmaster yet. You might never be. And if you ever are, I'll be long gone by then." Jimmy's voice grew nastier and nastier. "You can play your tricks and games with me all you want, Aiden Aubrey Ravencrest, but you're not going anywhere anytime soon."

"Nice try with Aubrey." Should Jimmy ever get hold of Aiden's embarrassing middle name...he tried not to think about the teasing.

"Shut up. Let's sit together, shall we? Until we hear the bell ring."

Aiden kept his gaze still and imitated Jimmy's smug tone as he said, "We'll see, Eliza. Perhaps the bell ringer might mix it up a bit."

Porter Jimmy chuckled. "There's no bell ringer. It's all electronic, as always."

Aiden feigned a yawn. "How fascinating."

Jimmy stayed by Aiden's side as Aiden slowly walked to the kitchens. It was only five forty-five, but no doubt Jimmy had been up earlier than that, possibly since four-thirty. A streak of sympathy reverberated in Aiden's heart until he remembered Jimmy's nasty smile. It was time to show who was going to win this thing.

"How long have you been outside my room?" Aiden said sweetly. "You didn't camp out there, did you? I mean, I'm sure the sleeping bag you hid in the storage closet was only a mirage."

"If the bell is different this year, boy, I will not stop until you are in detention for a full week," Jimmy threatened.

Aiden chuckled. "Have you ever thought about being a comedian, Eliza? Father wouldn't let you touch me for a minute."

"Not your father. The new Dean of Education who'll arrive here soon. He issues the punishments and warnings now. What, you didn't know?"

What? No, he hadn't known. Still, for the sake of appearances—

"No, I was wondering how you knew, considering your inferior position." He considered his breakfast options. The dining team was working furiously, preparing an amazing breakfast for the first day of school. Aiden picked a small plate with a fruit salad and bagel, just to stay out of the dining team's way. He took his sweet time putting the bagel together and savoring his salad. He knew Jimmy was going crazy just watching Aiden leisurely eat, but he was having too much fun to stop.

Soon, it was a few seconds until six o'clock. Both of them knew this and grew silent as the seconds ticked closer and closer. Jimmy's foot tapped, and he suddenly clutched Aiden's arm and pinned it to the table.

Aiden's watch signaled it was now six o'clock.

His DJ-like voice came over the loudspeakers: "What's up, Ravencrest Owls?"

Jimmy sputtered. "What—how—you've got to be kidding me! You were here!"

"So I was. Your point being?"

"How did you do this? I did everything! You couldn't have—it doesn't make—"

"What, you think I had something to do with this?" Aiden said, pretending to be shocked. He held back laughter and adopted a grave expression. He hadn't had this much fun in a while. "Why would I outsmart you oh so easily?"

"I'm going to make you pay for that! Just wait until next term! You're going to get in trouble for breaking and entering! And—"

"Shh," Aiden said. "I'm trying to listen."

Jimmy stammered and growled until his phone buzzed. Aiden listened in and noticed Jimmy's eyes narrow. "You found the old flash drive case in his room?"

Aiden was genuinely shocked. "You looked in my room? Isn't that illegal? There are privacy laws for my things!" Despite his surprise, a part of him had expected this. Jimmy could get desperate. It was a good thing Aiden had kept the flash drive with him and hidden the too-big old flash drive case in his room.

"Not if you have the new security clearance," Jimmy said. He spoke back into the phone: "Got it. I'll search him and get the flash drive as proof. He's going to be in detention soon." His smirk was creeping back.

Not on my watch. Aiden licked his fingers, then quickly twisted out of Jimmy's grasp. He used his years of self-defense training to knee Jimmy in the stomach and run. Jimmy gasped in pain (perhaps it hadn't been necessary to knee him so hard?), and soon furious footsteps were behind him. He dodged sleepy yet alert porters on their way to rooms that had forgotten toothpaste or a special suitcase in the lounge. Aiden zipped upstairs in a chase that didn't tire Jimmy as Aiden had hoped. *Seems he's been working out.* No problem. Aiden had endured months of boring recovery when he imagined doing heists like this. Jimmy was still lunging for him when Aiden skipped stairs and ran up the spiraling staircase. Behind him, he could hear shallow breathing. *Jimmy must be getting tired from all the running.* Aiden kept a close tail until he had made it to the highest floor of the stairwell. Porter Jimmy finally made the last few steps, wheezing.

"I warned you..." he said, stepping toward Aiden. He was breathing heavily. "I needed the exercise. You're going to want some in detention. Let's make it two weeks?"

"What about never?" Aiden suggested. He flipped over the staircase railing and, to the jaw-dropping amazement of Porter Jimmy, half-slid and half-jumped his way straight down, using the sides of railings to break his fall. As Jimmy stammered, Aiden couldn't keep the grin off his face. *Looks like old Jim thought I wasn't in shape. Well, I'm probably in better shape than I've ever been, what with the exercise I've put myself through.*

That didn't mean Jimmy wasn't relentless. No doubt, the man was still coming for him. Aiden knew he needed to avoid the porters. All of them. Now.

Aiden had been raised in Ravencrest Academy, so he knew the school's layout like the back of his hand. Soon he was skidding to a stop outside the dormitories. To his left was the door to the girls' main hall. To his right was the door to the boys' main hall. And on the ceiling above him was a security camera.

Now he faced a dilemma: the boys' hall or girls' hall? The camera was focused on him, and getting caught in the girls' hall was a very good way to end up in detention. On the other hand, the boys' hall would be more closely scrutinized by the porters. Plus, Aiden kind of wished Ravencrest had kept its old wooden floors. These carpet fibers gave away so much information about where he was, the direction of his footsteps, everything. No doubt that was why it had been installed recently.

Then again, these troublesome carpet fibers were an excellent challenge.

Aiden pushed the girls' door open, backed up with an exaggerated "Oops!", turned, and pushed open the boys' hall door. He took a few steps in, calculating in his mind the area where the dormitory hall's camera and the boys' hall camera overlapped the least. Then it was showtime. With stunning parkour expertise, Aiden backed up and ran up against the wall. To the cameras, it was as if he had stepped out of the sight of both cameras and disappeared. He manipulated his center of gravity and clenched the upper side of the wall, head brushing against the ceiling.

More porters were coming soon. He had to hurry.

He crawled out of the room and maneuvered around the cameras while keeping his balance through little indentations and the large metal crest on the wall at the fork in the hallway between the girls' and boys' halls. Then he slipped into the girls' hall, shifted the camera ever-so-slightly with the back of his knuckles, and dropped down onto his toes right outside a dormitory door. The lounge was too big and in the open, so he was left with no choice.

Aiden grimaced. This was his least favorite part of the plan. He knocked on the door, dreading what was about to come next.

There was a commotion, and then the girl who had been taking undecipherable shorthanded notes at Welcome Dinner—Layla Writcroff, from the student registry—opened the door. "What are *you* doing here?" she said, her voice rising. "I thought no boys were allowed in the girls' hall!"

"What? There's a boy there?" said another voice. The door was thrust more open, and a curly-haired Indian girl—Ruthie, was it? Ruthie Jocelyn—gaped at him. Both girls were dressed in nightclothes, Ruthie in owl pajamas and Layla in a cami and shorts. The two yawning adolescent females glared at him with suspicion, confusion, and curiosity. *Not good.* Again, there was a reason this was his least favorite part. He hadn't had much experience talking to adolescent females or any females his age, for that matter.

This is no different than a simulation, Aiden lied to himself. *People's main motives for participating in illegal deeds are money, power, and love. I'll use an appeal to each.*

"I've eighty thousand dollars from the stock market last week. I'll split it with you two if you keep your mouths shut and help me hide," Aiden said rapidly. He could hear distant shouting.

Ruthie looked offended. "Bribery?"

Aiden tried to push himself inside, but Layla blocked him and pushed him back outside. He stumbled slightly.

There goes money.

"I have connections. I can upgrade you both to any room you want or give you automatic acceptance to any program here. Just let me hide under a bed for a few minutes."

Ruthie looked even more offended. Layla opened her mouth as if she was about to call one of the porters. He was incredibly thankful porters didn't enter dormitory halls unless they were called, either by shouting or by the buttons inside the dorm room.

Non-deterministic polynomials...looks like I'll have to resort to love. He was most reluctant to try this one out as he had the least experience with it. It was time to rely on his limited movie expertise.

He leaned against the door, winked at Layla, and tried his most suave voice: "So, what do you say if I take you out for dinner? I'll take you to any restaurant of your choice. Maybe get you something you'd like. An expensive perfume? A designer outfit from—" He was rudely interrupted by both girls. They had gone from looking surprised to annoyed to disgusted and were now shouting for the porters.

At least now I know love causes the most explosive reaction.

Panic exploded like firecrackers. No, no, Jimmy couldn't win. This was supposed to mean that Aiden was back on his feet, that everything was back to normal, that nothing had ever happened, that he was still the mischievous young prodigy racing down the hallways eluding Jimmy's grasp, not the young teenager who had lost nearly everything overnight. He had to win this to prove to himself that he was going to be okay. Oh, why were people such variables? And adolescent females were the most confusing variables of all. He was charming with people, yes, but he didn't remember speaking to anyone his age (especially a female!) since Mother's funeral, which was still a painful, hazy blur. He didn't want to think about her amid a possible failed scheme—yet what if thinking about her would help him the most?

What would Mother do?

"Please," he said, choosing to be honest, "I was the voice on the intercom. It was harmless fun, and I thought it would make the first day more special. The porter who's chasing me is on a power trip; he has it out for me. I just need to hide for five minutes. Please?"

Both girls glanced at each other. Aiden held his breath. *Does human compassion count as a motive?*

The exact moment the door to the girls' hallway swung open, Layla grabbed Aiden's arm and pulled him inside. Ruthie locked the door from the inside. "Hide him under my bed!" Ruthie frantically whisper-shouted across the room. "I'll take the blame if we get caught!"

"No, we'll hide him under mine! I have more suitcases!" Layla whisper-argued back, firmly shoving Aiden toward her bed. He dropped to his knees and crawled under the bed as she pulled the suitcases around him, hiding him from view.

Through the cracks between the suitcases, he saw Ruthie's socked feet near him. "This was a harmless prank, right?" Ruthie repeated nervously. "You weren't trying to hurt anyone or anything?"

"Ruthie, shh!" Layla hissed.

"Because if it was, I have your face memorized," Ruthie warned. "And I'll turn you in. I'll ask a porter about the recording, and if you did something wrong, you are going to get caught." She was still speaking when a porter knocked on the door.

Ruthie screamed and jumped, then awkwardly stammered.

Aiden could almost hear Layla roll her eyes. He squirmed a little as Layla opened the door. "Good morning, sir," she said with a yawn that didn't sound fake at all. "Do you need anything? We only have a few minutes to get ready."

"I thought I heard some shouting. You see, I'm looking for a boy, a bit of a prankster." *Porter Jimmy.* "He might be running around here. Did you see him?"

"A boy? In the girls' dorms?" Layla feigned surprise. Aiden could imagine her large brown eyes widening in innocence. "They allow that here?"

"Of course not. Didn't you request a porter? I heard shouting," Jimmy said politely.

Ruthie stuttered, "No, I mean, yes, but...it's...it's because...I thought I saw something."

"You did?" Jimmy asked.

"I...uh..." Ruthie seemed to be struggling to find her words. *She's a bad liar.* How disappointing yet admirable, he supposed. It was also a bit frightening, considering his possible detention depended on if she lied or not.

Layla smoothly covered for her: "We thought we saw a boy in the girls' hall, but it was just the girl from across our dorm. It's no big deal, really. Sorry to bother you." She began to close the door.

Porter Jimmy stopped her. "Young lady, I would like to remind you that if you are found lying to a porter, there *will* be severe consequences, am I understood?" His voice was authoritative and commanding, and Aiden heard Ruthie's breathing tremble slightly.

While Ruthie seemed to be quietly having a small panic attack, Layla paused.

Oh no. Perhaps these females weren't so reliable. He should have taken his chances with the lounge room. Aiden already dreaded the idea of staying in the detention room, forced to endure Jimmy's smirk.

Then Layla said in a low, dangerous tone, "Are you *accusing* me, sir?"

Porter Jimmy stammered, "No, of course not—"

"I will have you know that my father is a senior United States diplomat, my mother is a London anesthesiologist, my sister is a top-scoring Owl, and my brother is a leading neurosurgeon! None of those four will be happy to know that I was accused of harboring a boy in my room. A *boy*, of all things! Who do you think I am?" Layla was the authoritative one now, bellowing in dignified rage. "How dare you accuse me! Search my room. Go right ahead! The press *will* be hearing about this!"

"No, ma'am, I'm very sorry," Jimmy apologized, already backing away from the door. But Layla wasn't finished.

"And what are *you* doing in the girls' hall? Shouldn't a girl porter be checking on me and looking in my room over my shoulder? Are there any girl porters in this school? *Are* there?" she demanded with righteous fury.

Now Aiden was beginning to feel a little sorry for Porter Jimmy. "Ah, yes, there are," Jimmy started, but Layla cut him off again. "Then why are *you* barging in here and interrogating me?"

"It was just the urgency of the chase—" Jimmy began.

"If this happens again, I *will* let Daddy know! And he won't be happy." Layla's nose stuck up in the air. "Goodbye and good riddance!" She slammed the door shut. "Humph!"

Aiden didn't emerge yet. They all listened as Jimmy's footsteps receded. Layla opened the door a little, peeked outside, looked both ways, and closed it again. "The coast is clear," she whispered, and a little shiver of excitement passed through her. "Oh, I've always wanted to say that."

When enough time had passed, Aiden emerged from under the bed and dusted himself off. For a moment, they all stood and let out a collective sigh of relief.

Layla twirled as if she was a model. "So? How'd I do? Five-star performance?"

"You could have been more polite," Ruthie argued.

Layla rolled her eyes. "Grow up, Ruthie."

"It never hurts to be nice," Ruthie persisted.

Layla frowned. "Now you know he'll leave us alone. I'll be nicer next time, okay?"

Ruthie sighed in relief. "Deal. Wait, what do you mean by *next time*?"

"What's your name, weirdo?" Layla asked Aiden, ignoring Ruthie.

"It's not weirdo," Aiden said, already reaching for the door. "I owe you two. That was a brilliant, well-acted, and kind favor. I'll upgrade your rooms—"

"We don't want anything," Ruthie called, stopping him.

"Why not? I have practically unlimited resources at my disposal to make your lives—"

"No," Ruthie said firmly. "That would be wrong."

Aiden glanced at Layla. She nodded. "Ruthie's right. We don't accept bribes. And if you actually did something wrong, we'll go straight to that Porter Jimmy guy. Got it?"

"Of course. I won't forget this," Aiden said gratefully as he stepped outside. Perhaps adolescent females weren't so confusing after all. In many ways, they seemed a lot like him. Behind his shoulder, he softly called, "You both better forget about this for now."

As he closed the door, he heard Ruthie quietly say, "I wish I could."

There was no time to dwell on what she could mean by that. Aiden jumped up the wall, clung to the crevices, and made his way to the boys' hall. A porter was in one of the rooms, and another was strolling briskly down the hallway. He jumped down near the entrance as a boy stumbled out of a room, clearly having shoved everything on as fast as possible. The boy—those muscles must have meant he was that athlete kid, the same kid who had been so excited about the food at Welcome Dinner: Everest Michaels—glanced at Aiden and raised an eyebrow.

Aiden put a finger to his lips. The boy nodded and went on his way, pretending not to have noticed.

The new students seem quite promising already.

Aiden strolled out into the main hall. He confidently nodded to a porter who was too absorbed in checking the hallways. Poor Porter Keil, who hadn't gotten a good rest, barely registered that he had mumbled "Good morning" to the very boy he was looking for. Ah, well, all porters eventually adjusted to how Ravencrest worked. It would take time. And perhaps one day Porter Keil would turn out to be just like Porter Craig.

Or he could turn out to be just like Porter Jimmy.

The thought made him shudder. He picked up the pace, breaking into a speed walk, then a jog, and then a sprint. He turned the corner and ran right into Porter Jimmy.

He barely had time to gasp before Jimmy wrenched Aiden's arm behind his back and shoved him up against the wall. Aiden frowned with dignity, his heart pounding. "Eliza, let go of me."

"I've got him. Resume your normal positions," Jimmy barked into his phone.

"I said, let go of me. You have no right to grab me like this."

"Yes, I do. I have reasonable cause to search you right now, and considering how you evaded me—"

"I was simply frightened," Aiden lied. Both of them knew he was lying; he was really saying, *I'll pretend I ran because I was scared. You still have no reason to search me.* "Let me go!"

"Let's see if the flash drive is on you. And if it is, you're toast." Porter Jimmy began to pat him down, none too gently.

Aiden did his best to appear unfazed, confidently looking into the man's eyes as Jimmy checked Aiden's pockets, jacket, shoes, hands, and everything. He even scanned Aiden with a metal detector. Still nothing.

"Am I free to go, office?" Aiden smirked.

Jimmy growled. "Where did you hide it?"

"Hide it? Hide what? I don't know what you're talking about. You shouldn't accuse innocent people, Eliza. Now you had better let me go if you don't have any proof."

Jimmy clenched the metal detector so hard that his knuckles turned white. "We'll see," he spat. "I'll call you if we find anything. I'm sure it'll be soon."

"We'll see," Aiden agreed with a stiff nod. "I'll see you around, Eliza."

Jimmy said nothing and watched, seething, as Aiden strolled away.

Thank God Layla has so many suitcases and purses. No doubt it would take her quite a while before she noticed the tiny flash drive hidden in her special perfume purse, the one he had squirmed against while hiding under her bed. A slow smile broke out on his face. He had done it. Now it truly felt like the beginning of a Ravencrest school year. Right?

Something was different this year. Something he didn't want to think about.

He locked himself in his room. It was time to focus on his work. He wouldn't let himself think about what was missing this year. No, he was going to think about what he had left to do. He was going to *focus*.

Silence for a while as he tried to work, until—

"I outsmarted Jimmy," Aiden said out loud. "I won. It's a new year at Ravencrest. What's wrong with me?"

He already knew the answer.

He closed his computer. His smile was gone, and his features were haunted. Couldn't he even enjoy a small success without thinking of Mother?

He briskly pulled on a jacket and stepped outside. Perhaps a walk would clear his mind.

Perhaps.

Chapter Three

Seven years ago, Mother had been ambushed in Italy.

He had been a curious seven-year-old with a sweet tooth; Mother had thus treated this sweet tooth with some gelato ice cream while they dined at an Italian restaurant. Shortly after, while they were drifting down the Venice Canal, Mother noticed a suspicious passenger on the boat. Aiden watched as she yawned and checked her watch. The passenger, though pretending not to notice, also subconsciously yawned and checked his watch. The moment the boat stopped moving, Mother grabbed Aiden and ran.

He remembered the chase; she had been holding him, his head resting on her shoulder sleepily while they darted through the streets of Italy. Though she must have been terrified, she kept a calm composure with an easygoing smile every time he murmured a question. He was half-asleep when suddenly, a nearby woman grabbed his mother's arm just as their pursuer turned the corner. Behind them, a man sitting on a bench pulled out a previously hidden gun from under his jacket. Drowsily, he watched as his mother twisted the woman's arm swiftly and twirled her in front of the man on the bench, shielding Aiden from his gun. As their pursuer from the boat pulled out his own gun, she kicked his wrist, sending the gun flying. Still keeping the woman in front of her, Mother screamed when the man on the bench pointed the gun at her. A policeman rushed over as the other woman fought back and managed to get away. Mother immediately pulled Aiden behind her; there were multiple gunshots, but she received the brunt of the blows. She staggered back, bleeding and dazed, just as the police officer made it to the scene. By now, Aiden was awake and crying. A bullet had nicked his side.

"*You shot a child!*" shouted Mother in Italian as the criminals scurried away. "*You shot my son!*" The police officer shouted for backup, but of course, the assassins escaped. He turned to Mother, insisting she go to the hospital while the other policemen chased after the almost-murderers; in response, she revealed that she was wearing a bulletproof vest. While she was in pain, she was not dead. She was more worried about her son than anything else.

Since Aiden had slept through most of the incident, the only scary part had been when the mean-looking man on the bench pointed a gun at Mother. She later disinfected and treated the wound where the bullet had grazed him so the cut healed quickly. After his mother's gentle coaxing and loving promises, he fully believed that she would always protect him. As long as he listened to her, everything would be okay. As long as she was there, no harm would come to him—or her. Now, he was older. He knew better.

He walked briskly down the halls of Ravencrest Academy. Classes were in session, and he could sense the concentration in each room. Students were studying in classes that would be sure to stretch them to the limit. There was a porter at the corner of each and every hall. Each one tipped his hat to Aiden automatically. He tipped an imaginary hat back. It was the code between the Ravencrest family and the porters.

Mother had done the same thing once upon a time. But she wasn't coming back.

Would she have known the plane was going to crash? She would have heard the difference in the mechanical hum. She would have sensed that something was wrong. She would have known before any of the passengers did. She would have thought of him in those last moments.

What had she thought? What had been flying through her mind? Her little boy waiting at home, her husband she hadn't spoken to in months, her work?

Your mother loved you very much...

Your mother...

Mother...

MOTHER!

Aiden grabbed his head as another splitting headache rose. Confusing voices, some perhaps his own, twisted in him. They were coming randomly now, fragments of the past he couldn't place:

Let me go!

You have to understand me—

You're not listening!

I know what's best.

He couldn't remember who said what. His broken memories were bewildering, floating around, zipping by, and he was lost in the labyrinth of it all. Sometimes his own mind was what caused him the most anguish. Nothing had been the same since he woke up to a grim-faced Father. He'd tried everything to make it the same, but it just wasn't. Everything was different. His mother, his father, the porters, and even the fun he used to have. It was all so...numb. Distant. Cold.

Everything was different now. He wondered if he could ever go back to the way things had been for the first thirteen years of his life.

But he wasn't walking down the halls of Ravencrest to dwell on the past. He was walking down the halls of Ravencrest to compose himself. He had great learning to do, with his self-guided studies patiently waiting for him in his room. First, he'd—

Every porter around him suddenly grabbed their earpiece, rushed into the nearest classroom, and locked the door behind them. An announcement came over the loudspeakers: "Students, please stay in your classrooms until we tell you it is safe to leave. Resume your learning activities and stay calm. This is a lockdown. It is not a drill. Please remain in lockdown."

Porter Craig grabbed Aiden's arm and half-dragged him into a classroom. "What's happening?" Aiden whispered, though he already knew. His heart pounded. A threat had made it into the school.

He was shoved into a chemistry classroom. Students wore lap aprons, goggles, and gloves. Many were shocked and terrified. He recognized Layla, Ruthie, and Everest, though it was a little hard to tell under all the equipment. The chemistry professor was shouting instructions on handling all the dangerous chemical substances. Aiden pressed himself against the door.

Porter Craig locked all the doors and windows. He was still at a window when a man pushed aside a ceiling panel, slid through, and dropped into the room, briskly knocking Craig out the window down the two-story drop. Ceiling panels fell onto the floor, and kids screamed as a group of masked figures dropped into the room. There were eight in total. One pulled out a gun. "Line up against the wall!" he shouted in English. He had a masculine voice with an American accent.

The smartest students in the world compiled. The chemistry teacher jumped protectively in front of his students, but one of the men (or women?) handcuffed him. The person with the gun turned to the students, unaware that Aiden was behind him.

He counted down: *three...two...now!*

Aiden tackled the man from behind, fought for and grabbed the gun, shot it at a closed window, and threw it outside. The glass shattered, alarms wailed, and now the leader was disarmed. Radiating fury, the man managed to grab Aiden's wrists.

Immediately a girl he recognized—fierce and brilliant, with a smirk just like his—grabbed a piece of equipment and slammed it over the figure's head before Aiden could kick him in the face. She grabbed another piece of chemistry equipment and, as Aiden twisted free, stuck the man's finger in it. He screamed as bolts of electricity jolted through him; then, too dazed to fight, he slumped to the floor.

More students jumped into action. A Chinese boy—the analytical one at Welcome Dinner, who had been absentmindedly sketching PhD-level theorems on his tray—grabbed two glass beakers, poured one into the other, shook the container, and slammed it on top of another intruder's head. The man screamed as the glass shattered. The chemicals made him grab his head and crumble to his knees, completely incapacitated. Everest slammed a chair over the same man and pinned him to the ground firmly. Layla grabbed a fire extinguisher and sprayed it in a different intruder's face, blinding them, while Ruthie ran to the emergency lock and typed in the twenty-digit alphanumeric code.

Wait, how does she know the emergency code? It changes every week. He didn't have time to think about it too deeply as chaos reigned. The figures seemed to finally realize that they were dealing with students who would fiercely fight back. Most students pressed themselves against the wall. The few who had begun fighting continued.

By the time the proverbial dust had settled and Ruthie had let the porters in, all eight intruders were on the floor, drifting in and out of consciousness. Some looked badly burned while others were severely injured; one was still trembling from electrocution, and another brokenly cried out in delirium, "You're all in danger you just can't see...we've come to save you...you have to understand..." and other ridiculous things no one paid any attention to.

"It seems you have it under control," Porter Keil joked as the unhurt and overly prepared porters took the men out.

Aiden rushed to the window and looked down. Porter Craig was hanging onto a ledge about three yards down and was quickly climbing up. Aiden opened it to help and—

"What do you think you're doing?" Porter Jimmy scowled in Aiden's ear. Jimmy shoved Aiden out of the way, helped Craig up, and reported the incident on a walkie-talkie. He finished with, "...all students seem unhurt, although the intruders are badly injured. We'll send them in for an interrogation and contact the authorities."

Porter Craig traveled from student to student and checked to make sure every kid was alright. "We'll have physical and psychological check-ups for each one of you," he promised. "You are all safe and secure, I promise. This will never happen again."

Now that the adrenaline had worn off, the kids were beginning to, well, act their age. Everest was excitedly re-enacting the action of slamming the chair down, making each re-enactment more dramatic than the last. The Asian kid was quietly putting the chemicals away while others applauded his actions in admiration. Layla was polishing the fire extinguisher. Ruthie was helping the porters. And the girl who had saved Aiden's life—though he hadn't exactly asked for the favor—was wiping her hands with satisfaction.

"You go, Ken," said one of the girls.

Ken glanced at Aiden. "I woulda jumped into action first if this guy hadn't startled me. He's not in our class. You supposed to be wanderin' the halls in the middle-a first period?"

Interesting. She spoke quickly with a slight New York City accent—the rarer, old-school, rushed Manhattan kind. Aiden was tempted to pause and ask her where exactly in New York City did she come from, just to confirm if his guess was right. Instead, he winked at her and said, "I'm not a student here, kiddo."

"Kiddo? We're the same age! And who are ya, some kinda teenage security guard? James Bond, is it? Shaken, not stirred?" she teased curiously.

He chuckled. "I appreciate the compliment. Good luck with your classes, and enjoy your first day of school." With that, he crossed briskly to the door. He could hear her sputtering behind him. Was she attempting to follow him? He chuckled again. She'd have to get past the porters if she truly wanted to talk to him, and no one could possibly get past the highly-trained men behind him—

"Ha!" said a voice behind him as Ken ducked under a porter's arm and stepped out into the hallway, pulling the door shut behind her.

Aiden turned so he was facing her from a few feet away. His trademark smirk surfaced. "If I were you, kid, I'd step back in there."

"Why?" Ken argued, taking a tentative step forward. "So you can disappear into the night? If you're not a student 'ere, then who are ya?"

Maybe he was having too much with this girl who reminded him way too much of himself. But he couldn't help it: "Are you sure I'm not just in your imagination?" He winked again as Porter Craig burst through the door, strictly took Ken by her arm, and pulled her back inside as she protested. Never once did he even glance at Aiden.

As a student, her safety was deeply valued. Because he wasn't a student, his safety was ignored by all except his parents. Mother wasn't there to check on him, and Father was much too busy. So he strolled away and snuck into his hidden labyrinth in the ceiling one last time, this time through a closet with a weak panel in the ceiling. Clearly, his little secret pathway throughout the school had been discovered at last. He sighed and ran his hand over the cracks around him. It was supposed to be too dangerous to come up here, but Aiden had fixed it up well. Now the highest floor would be guarded with cameras and such to prevent entry.

One last trip to his room through the secret pathway. Then he'd simply act innocent about the whole affair.

"Don't simply act innocent about the whole affair!" Father shouted, his eyes flashing.

Aiden drummed his fingers on the armrest and planned what to do once he could return to his room. Do some leisure reading on the most recent wormhole theories, brush up on his Mandarin, and possibly—

"Did you know about the ceiling pathway through the school beforehand?" Father repeated angrily.

Aiden stared at him, straight-faced. "There was a ceiling pathway through the school?"

Porter Jimmy stepped forward. "After the incident today, Porter Ramona saw Aiden enter a closet and never come out. When she came to check on him, no one was inside. Instead, she discovered a way to get into a ceiling pathway from the closest. It was as if Aiden had known about this pathway beforehand but hadn't told us anything about it."

"I was exploring new territory. Nothing wrong with curiosity. Isn't that one of Ravencrest's main principles?" Aiden said, seeming bored by the whole conversation. "Seriously, there was a ceiling pathway *through the whole school*?"

"His knowledge of this pathway would explain how he made it into and out of the room where the announcements were broadcasted," Jimmy continued.

"There was a room where the announcements were broadcasted?" Father frowned. "Jimmy, I told you not to invest too much security into it. We need to conserve our security resources, especially after what happened today."

"But it wasn't enough!" Porter Jimmy sputtered. "He somehow found a way in!"

His voice was too raised. Father arched an eyebrow. "Mr. Jimmy Gonzalez, I would advise you to lower your voice and never again speak to me like that if you wish to remain employed."

"I apologize, sir," Jimmy said in a rush and stepped back.

Father turned to Aiden. "Aiden, look at me. Tell me. You won't be in trouble if you just tell me the truth. Did you know about the ceiling pathway beforehand?" He was asking Aiden to make a choice. To lie or tell the truth. He was giving Aiden one last chance.

Maybe in the past, Aiden would have told the truth. But today, he was recovering from the loss of his two upper hands: his ceiling pathway and his security software. He was vainly trying to be his old self again, to pretend he hadn't lost the one person who meant more to him than anything else. He was still struggling to find something—anything—that would replace the large, missing part of himself. And if that was rebelling against Father, like old times, then so be it.

"No," lied Aiden.

Father sat back, shocked and hurt. He knew Aiden was lying. For a moment, he seemed vulnerable enough to ask *Why would you lie to me?*—and then he was his usual strict self. "I find that hard to believe. Many of your previous stunts require knowledge of a hidden pathway around the school, and the newly discovered ceiling pathway is the only previously abandoned path accessible to you, according to the school blueprints and past history. It was restricted and ignored due to more pressing concerns. To be honest, the fact that such a large, hidden piece of this school was re-discovered and secretly used all this time...it's quite surprising. Clearly, a very clever and resourceful person such as yourself might have known about it."

Aiden shrugged. "I'm smart. You know that." There was neither arrogance nor modesty in his voice. It was an undeniable fact. "That doesn't mean I knew about this."

"You are, in fact, brilliant," said Father emotionlessly. "Now, I have a position on my team for a brilliant, young security expert. If you had known about the ceiling pathway beforehand, I could have recruited you to find other such weaknesses in our school's security."

Recruit me? Aiden's heart softened. His father hadn't been trying to lecture, scold, or punish him for the school's security failures. No, he hadn't deserved Aiden's cold exterior, lies, and quiet rebellion. "I'm sorry, Father," he said at last with genuine sincerity. "I was lying earlier. I did know about the ceiling pathway."

Jimmy scoffed at the apology.

"I know I don't sound very believable," Aiden continued, "but I give you my word that I truly am sorry. I do know many areas around the school that could use an upgrade. After the attack today...I was planning on forming my own security team to assist in protecting Ravencrest Academy from such future incidents." His earnest brown eyes pleaded with Father.

Father paused, then quietly said, "Gonzalez, you have been very helpful in extracting the truth from my son. I need to speak to him alone."

Jimmy nodded and respectfully left the room.

Father was silent for a long moment as Aiden stared at his scuffed, black Converses. He owned finely polished dress boots in his closet, sneakers for expeditions, and now donned his usual wear—perfect for parkour attempts while pretending to be a Ravencrest student.

"Aiden, I know I haven't been the best father," said Father unexpectedly, startling his son. "I'm not very good with…these sorts of things. Sentimentality. Do you understand?"

"Yes," affirmed Aiden. He said nothing more as he stared at Father, observing this new man with noted interest.

"I promise to do better—to *try* to do better. You don't have to lie to me. Please, from now on, just tell me the truth." Father's earnest dark brown eyes pleaded with Aiden. *I really do have my father's eyes.*

Aiden nodded. "I give you my word, Father; I'll tell you the truth from now on." He had impulsively shoved himself into this new challenge. It wasn't a rational, logical decision, but it was the right thing to do. Perhaps he had needed to lie to the old Father, but he had to tell the truth to this new one who actually seemed to care. *I truly must work on my soft-heartedness.*

"Thank you," said Father. He seemed to not know what to say next, having put himself in an uncomfortable position. "Ahem, should I, uh…perhaps…"

"Dismiss me to my room?" Aiden offered.

"Yes," agreed Father. "That's it. I'll see you later…son."

Aiden fought against the rising warmth. Father *was* trying. More than ever before. Aiden respectfully nodded at the headmaster, rose to his feet, and left the room—then ducked his head back in. "May I have a toffee from your desk?"

Father frowned. "I saw your recent dietary report, Aiden. Chef reports directly to me. I believe you bribed him not to?"

Aiden blushed, feeling betrayed. "Chef has always been trustworthy before."

"Yes, but your fall seemed to make him rather protective." Aiden privately wondered if his fall had similarly affected Father. "He will not give you any more desserts for the rest of this week."

"Father!" protested Aiden. It was only Tuesday. "I've measured my metabolism and factored in my daily exercise, and I assure you a few desserts will be relatively innocuous!"

"Aiden," said Father very sternly, "be grateful I am not sending you to detention."

"Yes, Father," Aiden said right away and disappeared from the doorway as quickly as humanly possible.

He bumped into an eavesdropping Jimmy, who gave him a nasty glare. No doubt the man was disappointed Aiden hadn't received a more severe punishment. Porter Jimmy was always muttering about how spoiled Aiden was, and Aiden was always wondering how on earth anyone could hold a grudge for that long. It had been seven years since the Frying Pan Incident, and it seemed Jimmy *still* couldn't forgive the young boy for the slight miscalculation.

That night, as Aiden showered, he calculated new security plans. And as he snuggled in his cold and empty bed, a little embarrassed by how he had slept next to Mother until she had passed, he considered the day's events.

"Eventful day," he said to a woman who was no longer there to ask him how his day had been. "Physical attack on Ravencrest. First time in seventy-three years and five months. First security breach on Ravencrest in eighteen years, besides the one I must've caused before I fell. Today was certainly *very* eventful."

He imagined what she would say next.

"No, I was unhurt. Porter Chan has been truly beneficial in developing my self-defense abilities. He says I'm a natural. Exciting, right? I've been practicing every day."

He paused with some guilt.

"I might have lied to Father," he admitted into the darkness, feeling more and more silly by the second. "He was actually hurt by it. I think he might be changing, Mother. Perhaps he really does care about me now. I have to give him marks for effort." He rolled over, facing the ceiling, staring at the highly realistic planetarium in his room. Mother had meticulously designed it with him. Even now, he could make out the constellations and see the vivid details of the different planets with their moons. "I promised to tell him the truth from now on, and would you believe it? He recruited me for the security team! I'm quite excited, and I have all these ideas."

Idiot. Not a single word came in response. It was illogical to pretend otherwise. Last night, Jimmy had been listening. Now, no restraint was holding him back from the childish side of him that refused to listen to reason.

"I miss you, Mom," he mumbled, sounding rather babyish.

Then Aiden lapsed into a silence that stretched on for the rest of the night as he wondered when the cold darkness would ever end.

Chapter Four

At some point, Aiden finally acknowledged that he was not getting a good rest. Thus, he decided to do something relaxing so he could fall asleep faster. He pulled out his leisure reading on wormhole theories, then paused and put the book back.

He got dressed quickly. Normally, he would have disabled the security cameras or slipped into the ceiling. Now, neither option was available. Besides, some porters were stationed near his hall, equipped and probably more experienced than Porter Keil. Aiden frowned. Many of his usual pathways had been cut off.

His eyes rested on the windows. *There.* If he couldn't get *in*, he could still get *out*.

He traveled across the side of the building, far above the security cameras stationed at the entrances, and maneuvered his way onto the roof. It was slippery and dangerous, yet he knew how to manipulate his center of gravity and thus keep himself from falling. Though the Ravencrest family room was in the less occupied area above the Staff Residential Hall, it was still on the highest floor, and thus was closest to the roof. He carefully made his way across the flat roof, stepped across the arch-like exterior of the Performance Hall, climbed over the Academy's dome-like roof, walked across the top of the Walkway bridge, and made it onto the roof of the Student Residential Hall at last. He pried open a small crack until it was big enough to slip through. Soon, he found himself crawling into his old ceiling pathway. He clicked on a flashlight and gingerly stepped onto the creaking floor. *Looks like I get to use my usual path one more time.*

He found the little rope coiled in the corner and opened the trapdoor at the top of the stairwell. It was a tight fit but just big enough for him to slide through. He threw the rope down, ensured it was securely fastened, checked his thick gloves, then slid down the rope until he was far enough down to jump off. Still in darkness, he grabbed the side of a stairway railing, then pulled himself over it until he was standing on the stairs. As of now, there weren't any infrared lights in the stairwell, only normal security cameras (which Aiden made a mental note to fix) since entry into the stairway required a student, faculty, or security pass. Thus, the darkness obscured all of Aiden's movements. He silently ran down all five floors until he was at the single underground floor of the Residential Hall: the basement.

Ravencrest had a basement that functioned as a server room, a temporary storage area for malfunctioning or outdated equipment, and Campus Security headquarters. Thus, extremely high security was necessary for entering it. Normally, this would have been a problem. Now, using an identification card he had swiped from Porter Jimmy, Aiden easily bypassed the security controls and entered the basement. As he had expected, a porter or two paced near the staircase areas and exits. Aiden hid in a closet and listened to the quiet murmurs of the porters.

There was Porter Shyla, her voice lowered as she said, "Some are in the holding cell, but one of them was badly injured. He's cooling off in the clinic."

Thank you, Porter Shyla. I do appreciate your help.

So he snuck back into the stairwell, climbed the rope up to the top, and rummaged around in one of the old boxes of supplies. He pulled on Porter Craig's old uniform and checked his reflection in a small mirror from the supply box. With his tailored-enough uniform and polished boots, in the dimness, if no one looked too closely at his face, Aiden looked like a porter on night duty as he stepped out into the main hall. He calmly walked down the hall, never flinching as he passed other porters.

"Not bad." He would have congratulated himself if a porter hadn't slapped a hand over his mouth. Aiden didn't tense. From the breathing, he could tell right away that it was Porter Craig.

Best possible outcome.

"This is the worst possible outcome!" whispered Porter Craig into Aiden's ear. "What are you doing up here?"

"Wanted to interview the intruders."

"Couldn't you wait until morning? I heard about your recent promotion."

"Couldn't sleep. Thought I'd get an early start."

"How'd you get here from your room?"

"A magician never reveals his secrets."

Yet Craig wasn't smiling. "Aiden, you will get in serious trouble if you're found here, though I will say it's impressive you made it this far. What were you planning to do?"

"Get to the clinic," Aiden admitted. "Sneak past the nurses, then begin an interrogation. I might have new security status, but Father wouldn't want me to interrogate these criminals alone. Still, I couldn't sleep; what else was I supposed to do?"

"What else?" sighed Craig. He put a firm arm around Aiden's shoulders and said, "Better idea: why don't you let me walk you there?"

Aiden frowned. "Seems not nearly as exciting."

"Yes, but it's *safer*. I need to know the whereabouts of every student on campus at all times from now on. All the porters do." They walked to the clinic together, Craig's arm still around Aiden's shoulders.

"I am not a student," Aiden pointed out.

Craig scoffed. "Don't be ridiculous. Maybe the other porters feel that way, but to me, you *are* a Ravencrest student. More so than any other kid here."

Aiden smiled. Craig was like an uncle to him, and at times like these, he needed him more than ever.

Soon they were in the hospital room. Craig endured all the security procedures and, without Aiden's consent, agreed to act as Aiden's unofficial bodyguard. They entered to see one of the intruders lying on the bed and staring at the ceiling. He didn't seem to be asleep or awake.

"Sir," said Aiden with no sympathy in his voice. "Wake up."

The figure on the bed turned. "I'm awake," he said with a raspy voice. "Why are you here? Time for the interrogation, torture, threats?"

Aiden scoffed. "I'm here for an interrogation, but no one here is going to torture or threaten you, no matter how tempted they might be to do so."

The lights flickered on, and the patient took in the scene of Aiden a safe distance away with Craig behind him. The intruder's eyes traveled behind Aiden to the needles, drugs, and many other items Aiden could use to extract a confession.

Aiden refused to soften at the man's obvious terror. This jerk had attempted to kidnap a class of Ravencrest students. He had been armed, with no qualms about handcuffing the chemistry professor or terrifying the children huddled against the wall. Aiden stepped forward, causing the patient to draw back in fear.

"Let's start at the beginning," said Aiden. "Who hired you?"

The patient looked at him with hazy eyes. "Now, why would I tell you that?"

"You were going to kidnap the smartest teenagers in the world, weren't you?"

"Yes." He didn't sound very sorry.

"Why?"

The patient laughed bitterly. "Good question. You're the kid, aren't you?"

"I am a child, but I hardly see how—"

"You're Molly's kid?"

A shiver pierced through Aiden's heart. "You'll have to be more specific. Molly who?"

"So it is you," the patient said with a sigh. "I knew your mother. Kid, you want to know what's really going on? Or are you just looking for a good story?"

"I think it's obvious."

"Then ask your daddy. Ask him who the heck Vladimir Damon is. Watch him squirm, then ask him if he's taking a trip out of town in the next month." The patient's voice grew raspier. "And when he's all out of excuses, tell him you know about Operation Injection. Oh wait, then you might end up as a martyr like me."

"You think you're a martyr?" scowled Aiden furiously.

"I didn't want to be one, but it wasn't like I had a choice. Not everything's black and white, kid. You've got to dig deeper sometimes." The gray eyes fixed on him. "Ask your daddy about what the heck really happened to your mother."

Another shiver went through Aiden. Craig stepped forward and put a hand on Aiden's shoulder, but Aiden pushed it off. The teen prodigy growled, "Who do you think you are? You don't know anything about my family!"

A raspy laugh. "I know more than you do, kid. You don't think your mother—who survived attacks, ambushes, betrayals, crashes, drugs, assassins, kidnappers, and more action than an R-rated thriller—died from a dumb plane crash, do you?"

Aiden lunged for the patient and pinned him to the bed. His eyes were wild. "You never speak about my mother," he snarled. "Do you understand me? You crossed the line implicating that my father is part of some secret operation. Operation Injection! Like I'd fall for that."

His hands were gripped by a dark, subliminal urge to rip the IVs out of the man and watch him die. How dare he! Almost kill a bunch of teenagers, slander Mother, try to confuse him—Aiden's head swarmed with fury until he nearly ripped the IVs out.

But he didn't. Even he had his limits.

"I'll ask you one last time," he said, resisting the urge to add *you piece of human garbage*. "How did you break into Ravencrest Academy?"

The patient tried to pull away, but Aiden's grasp was much too strong for limbs that had been rendered useless with drugs. The man looked into Aiden's eyes, and Aiden saw the struggle in them. Finally, the patient spoke with resignation, "I'm going to die or end up in prison anyway. What does it matter?"

"Tell me!" shouted Aiden, and he twisted the patient's arm painfully.

"You're too much like your father," muttered the patient, wincing at Aiden's wrenching of the man's arm. "There was a security breach three months ago. Leaked some information. Our men grabbed as much as we could and assembled blueprints. We compared a new and old copy of the blueprints and discovered an old ceiling pathway. It seemed ignored and dangerous, but we trained for that. It wasn't as bad as we expected it to be, honestly. It seemed like someone had fixed it up for us. Anyway, we also used the information from the breach to figure out how to get onto the island and hide here until the first day of classes. We'd grab at least one class and hold the kids as hostages to force the rest of the Academy to move out. We were so close to getting the kids out. We just didn't count on them fighting back."

"Why were you 'getting the kids out'?" repeated Aiden.

"It's a long story. You wouldn't believe me. I wouldn't know where to start." The tired eyes fixed on Aiden. "But believe me when I say this: we were trying to protect Ravencrest Academy. It's not safe for those kids to be here."

"Ha! Not safe because of people like you!" He resisted the temptation to use stronger wording. "Believe *me* when I say this: our top-notch security team will make sure those kids are safer than ever."

"They'll be in even more danger if you don't listen to me."

"Why would I listen to you? You make it sound like my father is an evil mastermind, my mom faked her death, and you've got a good reason to kidnap and hold hostage a bunch of kids. There are whole teams of you people, just waiting to terrorize the leaders of the next generation." Aiden shuddered. "Father's going to make you pay, believe me."

"That's the only true thing you said, that your father will make me pay." The patient turned away, but not before Aiden saw the weariness in his eyes. "Your father is not evil and your mother is dead. That's the only true information you'll believe me in saying."

"What other information are you trying to say? Who are you working for?" Aiden shouted.

"I can't tell you." The patient began to tremble. "If your people are going to kill me, tell them to do it quickly. Please." His eyes were so haunted.

Aiden's hands trembled from rage. He coldly picked himself up, dusted off his hands, and said with disgust, "I'm not going to get any information from you, am I? Thank you for the complete waste of my time." This wasn't entirely true. One bit of information had come out of the whole fabrication that the patient was implying: the security breach.

"Wait! What will happen to me? I...I need to know," the man begged as Aiden turned to leave.

The dark side of Aiden that had briefly emerged pushed him to ignore the patient as he walked out of the room with Craig at his heels.

Yet the look in the patient's eyes haunted him.

He really was becoming too soft-hearted. He sighed, turned, opened the door, and said, "You're going to prison for the rest of your life. Father's not going to kill you. He wouldn't, and even if he wanted to, the legal course of action is to lock you away for the next fifty years or so for the attempted kidnapping."

"He's not going to kill me?" gasped the man with childlike relief.

Aiden scoffed. "If he tried to, he'd be arrested. Honestly, who do you think my father is? He's scared of *moles*. The animal, not the unit of chemistry." Turning away, he began to leave.

"Wait!"

Aiden stopped, his hand on the doorknob.

"Kid, I..."

Aiden held his breath. Perhaps he would finally get some answers?

"Your mother thought of you in her last moments. She wrote a letter when the poison was working in her system. Her hands were shaking, but she wrote it and held onto it until she was found. Our guys have it." The man's voice was getting raspier. "They'll get it to you when it's safe. Her last wish was that you'd read it."

Aiden's knuckles were white. He left wordlessly.

"Do you want to talk about what just happened?" Craig asked. They were walking down the main hall. Jimmy scowled when he saw Aiden, but Craig glared at him and barked something threatening under his breath. Porter Jimmy backed off as Aiden stormed down the hall without looking anyone in the eye.

"The man was insane," Aiden said. "Mental. Serious problems."

"Of course," agreed Craig.

"Not one word was true."

"Right."

Aiden's footsteps dug deep into the carpet. "He had no heart and tried to manipulate me every chance he got. Father should have locked him away the first chance he could."

"Correct."

Aiden's eyes stung. "Everything he said about Mother and Father was meant to get to me."

"Yes."

"I shouldn't have even talked to him. I should have let the security interrogate him instead. I shouldn't have told him he wasn't going to die, either. Let him feel as miserable as I do."

"Affirmative."

They walked the rest of the way across the courtyard and up the elevator in the Staff Residential Hall. Now he was in front of his room, the room for Ravencrest family members, the room his mother and him had shared. Now he was looking into the doorknob's reflection from the flashlight, his anguished eyes staring back at him. Now he was stepping into a room that he had lived in since birth.

And now he was crying. Because for the first time in a long time, he was lying to himself and refusing to do what was right.

The patient hadn't been lying.

Aiden had trained himself to recognize deception with an extremely high accuracy rate. From what he could tell, the patient had been telling the truth. Aiden had searched with earnest desperation for any sign of lying or trickery but had found only honesty.

This meant Father really was hiding things from him.

Mother had a life she never told him about.

Aiden's fall had caused the security breach. He had caused the first attack on Ravencrest in nearly a century.

And something ominous called Operation Injection was about to happen.

Aiden may have been a brilliant teenager. He may have had the IQ of a genius, the mischievousness of a prankster, his mother's heart, and his father's charm. Yet he was also a human. A human with flaws that could override logic and reason. So he curtly thanked Craig, closed the door, robotically changed, and went to bed. He did not write any notes or speak to his mother that night. He slept fitfully, hoping his dreams would drown out all he had learned. He was going to pretend he had never spoken to the patient and that all this information was false. Over time, he would teach himself to believe it until his conscience no longer bothered him so. For once, he was choosing to believe deception over the truth.

And that was the end of the matter.

Chapter Five

Aiden woke up early, as usual. He knew better than to disrupt his sleep schedule and sleep in. Though he was exhausted and knew his cognitive abilities would be impaired due to the sleep deprivation resulting from his late bedtime, he was not willing to throw the day away.

Every day mattered. Every day a person could change the world.

No one at Ravencrest suffered from procrastination or time management after the first month of learning. No one kept themselves from living life to the fullest and making the most of the time they had. If they struggled with time management previously, the rigors of Ravencrest drummed it out of them over time. Thus, Aiden was extremely reluctant to let even a single day go to waste.

Still, he gave himself relatively easier work with his self-guided studies. He conferenced with security experts and gave the construction team suggestions to improve certain parts of the school. He privately gave himself a stern, angry lecture that there was to be no more sneaking around unless absolutely necessary. Look at what had almost happened to a bunch of innocent teenagers.

All in all, by the time Aiden walked into the gym's training room, he was ready for a break.

Porter Chan was patiently waiting for him. "Are you ready, Aiden?"

Aiden stretched and stood alert. "Ready, sir."

They ran through drills, practice, and then actual fighting. Soon, he was drenched in sweat and exhausted as Chan shouted orders at him in his thick Chinese accent: "Keep your fists up! Knees bent! Focus on your enemy's weaknesses!"

Aiden delivered a powerful roundhouse kick.

"Impressive. But you fight to defend yourself, no? Not to impress a girl." Chan didn't seem even the least bit proud of Aiden's progress. "That kick won't do anything unless your opponent is impaired enough to watch you spin around. Be faster so they won't see it coming."

Aiden wiped the sweat from his eyes to see better and pushed through the exhaustion to send a devastating punch Chan's way.

Chan simply grabbed his arm and flipped him over so Aiden was facing the ceiling.

"I need some water," Aiden gasped. He started to rise, but Chan held him down. "Hey!"

"Try again."

"May I please have some water?" Aiden politely asked.

"Try again."

Aiden tried to squirm out of the iron-like grip pinning him to the ground. "Let me go!"

"Try again." Chan smiled at him with an infuriating patient look.

Finally, the crescendo of frustration over the past hour exploded. Aiden relaxed and let the pressure on his back loosen slightly, just enough for him to snap his head back and catch Chan in the face. He slid out of Chan's grasp like a snake and rolled to his feet, face blazing in anger. Then he froze, remembering the ferocity of his attack.

Yet Chan was smiling. He had brought his hand up in time before Aiden's skull had hit Chan's nose. "You have great potential, Aiden, more than some of the best men and women I have trained with." Chan rose and gave Aiden his water. "Keep practicing."

"Yes, sir," said Aiden. "Thank you."

Everest—the boy who had kept quiet about Aiden's escape earlier—caught Aiden as soon as he stepped out of the training room. "Hey, Karate Kid!"

Aiden gave him a questioning look.

"I watched from the doorway 'cause you left the door unlocked by accident," Everest admitted with a strong American accent. "You've got some *skills*, man! You wanna challenge me?"

"I don't believe I'm qualified enough to fight without seriously injuring you."

"You know how to fence?"

Aiden chuckled. "Mastered it years ago."

"Then come on."

Aiden raised an eyebrow. "*You*, an American, know how to fence?"

"Dude, I can play like every sport you can think of." Everest handed him the uniform, helmet, and sword. "Let's do this."

"Why me?" Aiden asked, though he already knew the answer.

"You're good. The trainer starts next week. I need to practice." Everest motioned. "Hurry up. I got homework."

True. Homework equaled nearly the full amount of classwork, which was a hefty amount. Add extracurriculars, and Aiden could tell this kid really wanted to fight. The Chinese kid who had fought back during the attack—Ming Xingshi, according to the registry—watched in silence as Everest and Aiden pulled on their practice uniforms.

The first match ended quickly. Everest swiftly recovered from the shock of losing so drastically with a "best out of three!" cry.

The second match was only a little longer. Everest was still picking up his sword when Ming Xingshi walked over and quietly spoke something in Everest's ear. Ming returned to his seat as Everest slipped on his visor.

The third match surprised Aiden. Everest had considerably improved. Nonetheless, Aiden easily won within minutes.

"Good game," agreed Aiden, shaking Everest's hand firmly. He turned to leave.

Everest stopped him. "Come back here as often as you can and train me, please!"

Aiden frowned. "I can't. I have work to do."

"You're *killer* at this! Seriously, dude, please."

"You're not sore over losing?" *Curious.* Perhaps that was only another American stereotype.

"No, I want to get better so I can win next time."

"How very American of you."

"What, are you English then?" imitated Everest in a thick London accent. "Come straight from the heart of London, eh?"

Aiden laughed. "English? *Me*?"

"Well, where *did* you come from?"

"I've lived here all my life. Traveled around the world a few times. Ravencrest is my home, my family, and my life." Aiden's voice was tinged with bittersweetness. He used to say those words with pride, his chest puffed out. Now, he only smiled sadly and moved to leave.

"You're only a student," Everest pointed out.

Aiden winked at him. "Actually, I'm not."

Before Everest could come up with a further line of questioning, Aiden had disappeared out the door.

It was evening, and the mess hall was crowded for dinner. Aiden kept his wig and glasses firmly adjusted, wearing jeans and a Ravencrest jacket in order to blend in. No one gave him a second glance.

He sat by himself with a hot meal, propped up his astrophysics book (physics was his favorite leisure reading), and listened to the girls' conversation behind him. Ken starred in the spotlight, clearly having become the most popular girl in school in the past twenty-four hours.

"...and then he just disappeared!" Ken was saying, munching on a salmon salad. *Health-conscious. Interesting. Oh, and I see that brownie—it looks like she still has a sweet tooth, just like me.* "And no one here knows who he is!"

"You should ask some of the boys," said one of the other girls, with short blond hair and green eyes (Darlene Dickens, most likely). "If you really like this guy, they can help set you two up on a date."

Aiden choked on his food.

So did Ken.

"What?" shrieked Ken once she had stopped coughing. "On a *date*?"

"Well, you do talk about him a lot," giggled Darlene.

Ken wiped her mouth, her eyes flashing. "That's 'cause he's such a *mystery*! I love mysteries and puzzles and that sorta thing."

"Well," Darlene continued, "I can talk to some of the guys for you."

Ken regained her composure. "You do that, but don't ya dare say or imply that I like him! I just find him intriguing, that's all."

"What are you, Sherlock Holmes?" laughed another girl with a vague French accent, straightened hair under a fashionable beret, and perfect freckles. *Veronica Lafayette.* The daughter of France's ambassador.

"I happen to *love* Sherlock Holmes," sniffed Ken.

Another girl—Layla—plopped her lunch tray down next to Ken and spoke in an aristocratic yet playful tone, "Are you serious? So do I!"

Veronica frowned. "Bit rude of you to interrupt us," she said a little smugly.

"Bit rude of you to say that," Layla retorted without missing a beat.

Ruthie shyly sat down in the empty seat near Darlene. The contrast between her and Layla was striking.

Not seeming bothered by the casual tension between Veronica and Layla, Ken continued, "I just love solvin' stuff, ya know?"

"Interesting. What's your schedule?" Layla briskly tucked in her napkin with an air of expertise, as if that was how she had eaten her whole life (*probably true, knowing her background*), and picked the right fork out of the three options to eat with.

"Well, I've got the required ones: RA Chem, RA Calc, RA English, and next year, RA Physics and RA Bio. Oh, and World Basics this semester and Spanish Basics the next semester. Then—"

"Why Spanish Basics?" Layla interrupted.

"We have to choose a language to study if we can't test out of it," Ken grumbled. "And Spanish seemed the easiest. I'm not very good with languages."

"Obviously. You're American." Layla grinned mischievously as she said this.

Ken snickered. "Fair enough. Other than the ones everyone's taking, I'm double majoring in Engineering and Computer Science. I'm taking the RA Engineering and RA Computer Science prerequisites this year, then a bunch of online summer classes for both, *and* I'm taking RA Mastery in Engineering plus RA Mastery in Computer Science. Then I can graduate with a degree in Engineering and Computer Science. Oh, and I'm taking a problem-solving class over the summer, too. It's just for fun since it's all about puzzles and riddles and stuff."

"Nice," said Amika appreciatively. "Good for you."

"Thanks. What about you guys?" Ken took another bite of her food.

Layla answered first: "I tested out of RA Calculus and all the language classes, so—"

"Wait, what?" Ken interrupted. "I get Calc since it's basically just advanced calculus, but *all* the language classes?"

Layla shrugged modestly. "I know fourteen different languages."

Everyone coughed or choked on their food, even Aiden. Ken sputtered, "How—"

"I don't know. It's weird. My sister and brother both only speak one language fluently, but my parents speak a lot of different languages. Anyways, I tested out of RA Calc, all the language classes, and most of the required science classes. Since my mom's an anesthesiologist and my brother's a neurosurgeon, they made sure I was taught a lot of science even before I applied here. After I talked with the counselor, she said I could fulfill my science requirement by being a teacher's assistant in RA Chemistry for the first semester and RA Biology for the second." She frowned. "I still have to take a full-year RA Physics course, though. And being a teacher's assistant involves a lot of actual work. I have to make answer keys and grade tests—and not the multiple-choice questions, since the computer does that. I have to grade the free responses and organize review activities and make cheat sheets and help with running class and everything. To say the least, I'll be an expert in chemistry and biology by the end of this year."

"That is so cool," said a girl named Christine. Other girls voiced their agreement.

Layla shrugged. "I guess. Anyways, since I cleared a lot of classes ahead of time thanks to my tutors, the rest of my schedule is focused on what *I* want to do. I'm taking RA English, RA Political Science, RA Psychology, RA Master in World History and Cultures, Cryptography

Basics this semester, and Linguistics Basics the next. I'm also taking a problem-solving class over the summer, just for fun. I'm majoring in social sciences, though I haven't figured out what I'm taking next year. Oh, and I'm going to intern as a UN translator over winter *and* summer break! I'm so excited."

Everyone could only stare at her.

Veronica laughed. "Living up to the Writcroff legacy, aren't you?" It was clear she thought Layla was a snobby braggart. She added, "Well, you should hear what *I've* got on my schedule." She went on, and eventually, the other girls began sharing their plans as well.

Somehow the group of girls had bonded over the break-in. For the rest of the lunch period, they all vividly recreated the events of what had happened until Aiden grew bored enough to get up and leave. He relocated to another area, where he could listen in on some of the boys' conversations.

Everest was seated next to Ming and a few other boys. "Dude, I've heard at least five different theories about the guys who broke in. Some people think they were members of the Mafia and some people say the whole thing was an IQ test. It's *ridiculous*."

"What do *you* think happened?" Rajesh Gollapudi, an Indian boy who had been in a different classroom during the attack, retorted.

"I dunno, but I'm not gonna make up a bunch of dumb rumors about it! Those guys were wearin' masks, so it's kinda hard to figure out anything about them." Everest paused. "Does this school have a newspaper?"

"Yeah," said Matthew Welsh, a friendly chemistry nerd with large glasses. He always wore a lab coat.

"Then I can pretend I'm part of it and investigate," Everest finished. "I could ask Campus Security stuff, too."

"They'll know you're lying about being part of the newspaper team," Norton Russel, a young athlete who specialized in biophysics, pointed out. "Ask someone who *is* part of the team."

"Like who?" argued Everest.

For the first time, Ming spoke up: "Presumably, they will publish the reason behind the attack in the next edition of the newspaper if the information is safe for us to know. Until then, we should wait rather than speculate over rumors."

That ended the conversation concisely, and there was an awkward pause before Everest started discussing science topics with the others.

Aiden smiled. He had observed the most notable members of the new class—the ones who had fought back—and had constructed a team. The old class would graduate before they could pledge their loyalty for two years; thus, he had chosen a team from the new class. He would soon recruit them to create a student security team to protect Ravencrest.

I'll call them the Hall Monitors of Ravencrest Academy, he decided as he finished his lunch with satisfaction.

Perfect.

Chapter Six

Aiden gave his team time to acclimate. The rest of the week passed uneventfully. Aiden didn't sneak around the school, continued his studies, and drastically improved the school's security measures. He even managed to obey his sugar-less orders despite Chef's newest dessert concoction.

Well, perhaps he had taken a bite. Or two.

He still frequently took walks, more so than ever before. There was something comforting about the glimpses of students milling about the café, kids savoring the food in the mess hall, athletes working out in the gym, and girls giggling together in the hallways. He didn't see Everest at all in the next few days, knowing that the boy would pummel him with questions. Instead, Aiden met with Porter Chan at a different location.

Finally, on Monday of the second week of school, Aiden made his move.

Three rooms were snuck into. All five recipients found an encrypted note under their corresponding door. Each note was easily and quickly decoded.

Earlier, Father had agreed to Aiden's plan, commenting with amusement on his son's "little team," much to Aiden's frustration. Father did, of course, grow a little stern in reminding Aiden to make sure no child would be put in danger. Aiden agreed to do his best to prevent that. In doing so, he kept his promise to tell the truth. Thus, these five chosen children were given signed hall passes which allowed them to be out of their rooms after curfew. The porters were not informed of this, and thus all five students had to hand over their hall passes and explain before the porters reluctantly let them continue.

In the end, all five students followed their note's instructions and grouped outside of Aiden's room.

"You guys got a note too?" Layla said, surprised at seeing the others.

"Yeah," Ken said thoughtfully. "What do we all have in common?"

"We were all involved in the attack," Ming said quietly.

"We all fought back," agreed Ruthie.

Everest chimed in, "Yeah, and who do you think this guy is?"

Ken pointed out what they had all been thinking: "It has to be the James Bond guy. The kid who's not a student at this school but randomly shows up around campus. He's only directly spoken with Everest and me."

"I did pressure him into it," Everest admitted. "And I haven't seen him since he told me he wasn't a student."

Ruthie paused. "Should we knock? I didn't know this room was used for the Ravencrest family." She shivered. "If it wasn't for the hall passes and the fact that I'm a very curious person, I'd stay in my room. We could get in trouble for being up here. It's a restricted area, you know."

"Wait, back up. Ravencrest *family*?" Layla said.

Ruthie shrugged. "Yeah. Your mysterious James Bond guy is the headmaster's son."

There was silence.

"Why didn't you tell us this earlier?" Ken hissed at the same time Ming questioned, "Why would you think that?"

Ruthie shrugged again. "Ken, you never asked. And Ming, it's kind of obvious. Their facial structures are similar, and you all heard about the headmaster's wife's death thirteen months back, right?"

"Of course," Everest said.

She continued, "Well, about twelve months ago, I read an article in a TIME magazine, page eight, under the title, *An Academic Tragedy*. It said, and I quote, '*Reports of a son running around the school and performing quite a few stunts over the years have been confirmed by previous Ravencrest Owls, though his presence has been hidden from the public for years. One can only assume that father and son will grieve together over the loss of this visionary who once graced our world.*' I did some research around six hours ago, and I discovered the son's name is Aiden Ravencrest. He must be roughly our age, but that's all I know about him. He's only befriended a few kids before, including a man who's now a NASA scientist. Other than that, he keeps to himself."

When he had recovered his voice, Everest managed to say, "What, did you study this on top of everything else?"

"Not really," Ruthie said modestly.

Layla spoke up for her: "She has SAM, or Superior Autobiographical Memory. It's this super rare condition where she can remember every event in her life and basically memorize everything she sees. Only seven people in the world have it. But for some silly reason, she doesn't like to talk about it."

"Layla!" Ruthie cried, anguished. "I told you not to tell anyone about that!"

Layla shrugged. "What? It's dumb that you want to pretend you're just really, really good at memorizing things."

Ken gasped.

"It's not *that* big of a deal," Ruthie mumbled, blushing furiously.

"No, not that," Ken said. "I found it!"

"What? You found a way in?" Layla said eagerly, rushing to Ken's side. Her elbow accidentally hit Ming, and he silently moved out of the way. She had forgotten he was there. It seemed to be a talent he had.

"While you guys were talking, I found a camera! I just disabled it, but this confirms what I suspected: this is a test. He's watching us. Well, he was."

"So we each have to find a way in," Ruthie confirmed.

There was a silence, and then immediately all five leaped into action.

Ken secured a way in by using some metal tools she always carried around, getting past the high-tech lock within a minute. She adjusted it so the lock wouldn't appear tampered with, then stepped inside.

Everest took a few steps back, ran up the side of the wall, grabbed onto the ceiling, pushed the panels aside, and pulled himself up. He crawled over to where the room was and jumped in, right next to the others.

Layla found a vent in the hallway. She grabbed a diamond—the hardest substance on earth—necklace and sharpened it with her nail sharpener before using it as a screwdriver. Within a few minutes, she had taken the vent off the side of the wall, climbed through, and followed the path to the vent in the ceiling of Aiden's room. She used a scarf as a rope to break her fall when she jumped down.

Ming ran his fingers over the building material. *Plaster*. He mixed some chemicals he always carried with him and created a strong concentration of acid. Yes, it was dangerous, but he was a very precise boy and didn't make mistakes often in calculations...or in life, really. He used the acid to burn through the plaster, managed to extend the hole so it was big enough for him to slide through, and then he was inside.

Ruthie closed her eyes and remembered an old blueprint of Ravencrest. As she had explored the building before, it wasn't hard for her to estimate the size of the room. She realized this room had to be on the side of the building. Thus, she strolled outside into the darkness, bypassing all interrupting porters with her pass from

Aiden, and borrowed a ladder from a porter. She climbed through the window onto the fifth floor, panting a little and arriving a bit later than the rest, but there nonetheless.

They met again in the room, which was evidently the Ravencrest family room. There was a restroom, a perfectly made bed, a small kitchen and table, large bookshelves, and a desk. It was cozy and comfortable. A television screen flashed one word over and over: Wait.

"Wait until *what*?" complained Layla in exasperation, as Ruthie entered the room.

"Why would he invite us to his room?" mused Ken. "He must have been testing us to see if we could get in."

"Why is this person playing with us?" Everest shouted. He glared at the room around him. "You can come out now, or else I'm leaving!"

"Please don't," Aiden said, briskly stepping into the room. "Apologies for keeping things confidential, but I'm sure you all can wait a little longer for explanations. By the way, congratulations on passing the test." He chuckled good-naturedly. "To say the least, the porters will definitely have to fix your rather creative modes of entry."

"Dude, what's with all the tests?" Everest scowled, walking toward Aiden like he was going to pin him to the wall and demand answers. "It's not cool."

"Stop, Everest!" Ruthie commanded, though her nervous voice wasn't much of a command. "This might be another test. Be patient."

Aiden winked at her and said nothing. "Come on, follow me," Aiden called, and he led the party down the elevator, outside through the courtyard, and into the academy. They entered an elevator on the other side of the academy.

"Which floor is it?" Ken asked, her hand poised over the buttons.

"Fifth."

Ken frowned. "There's no fifth floor."

"Good to know." Aiden pressed twice the blank button above the fourth-floor button. It flashed briefly, taking in his fingerprint, and then they were steadily traveling up the floors.

"No way," breathed Layla, and even Ken's eyes widened eagerly, despite herself.

"Before you ask," Aiden added as the elevator doors soundlessly slid open, "Ken, you are not allowed to take apart the button and see how it works."

"How did you know—"

"I've read your file. This way, everyone."

Aiden and Everest kept the doors open as the others walked out onto the highest floor of the building. Aiden had spoken with Father and the construction workers, and together they had come to an agreement on portioning out the previously-restricted area so his new security team could station a headquarters there, away from prying ears. While he wasn't complaining, he was a bit annoyed by how Father had treated Aiden's request as if he was asking for a treehouse to go play with his friends.

"Wow," breathed Ruthie. "I never thought I'd get to see this part of the building."

"I know, right?" Everest agreed. "I knew Ravencrest was big since it's got the whole island to itself—"

"Not the whole island," Ruthie interrupted. "A forest full of wildlife stretches over more than half of the island. We get the other half, though it's more of a third."

Everest frowned, displeased at being corrected by a petite girl with big glasses. "Did you get that from the brochure, Ruthie?"

"No," mumbled Ruthie, retreating into herself again. "I got it from the website."

"Impressive," Ming commented.

Ken's face was aglow with excitement. "I know, right? This whole area has so much potential! I could totally make this the coolest tech room *ever*!"

Ming said nothing, and only Ruthie caught that he had been speaking about her, not the attic they were in.

"And now for the answers I promised." Aiden motioned for them to sit down. "Make yourselves comfortable."

"Approximately how long?" Ruthie asked.

"Geez, Ruthie, you talk too much," Layla impatiently snapped at the same time that Everest interrupted, "Ignore her and just tell us."

Ruthie fell silent and didn't say more than a word for the rest of the night. She was used to being considered annoying, but it still hurt to be ignored and have someone roll their eyes at her every time she opened her mouth. She did talk too much, she knew, but it wasn't a fault she could always control. She was simply an inquisitive, curious girl who was either too shy or too talkative around others, at least with most people. In general, Ruthie struggled socially. She may have had an astonishing memory, but she had a terrible grasp of social skills in return. She snapped out of her daze when Aiden began speaking:

"I've recruited you five because you all fought back during the attack. I'm starting my own security team at Ravencrest Academy.

Your responsibilities will be relatively light, as I'm sure you all have enough going on as students here."

Layla coughed under her breath, "You're right about that."

Ken sat up straight. "Does this mean I can design security gadgets?"

"Of course," Aiden agreed. "You all are my eyes and ears around campus. Layla, you're one of the most popular girls on the girls' side, and you know everything about everyone. Everest, it's the same with you for the boys. Ruthie can memorize anything and Ming can seem invisible anytime he wants."

"He's still here?" Ken said blankly.

"Exactly. And you, Ken, are our security gadgets person, if you know what I mean." He looked at all of them solemnly. "You are all now officially part of the Hall Monitors of Ravencrest Academy. I also hope you all will keep this a secret."

"Why the secrecy?" Everest asked.

Aiden sighed deeply. "There are groups forming to attack the school. This year's class is the least safe class in all of Ravencrest history. I need your help, but I don't want to endanger any of you. Will you all promise to keep everything said here secret, to the best of your ability?"

They all nodded and gave murmurs of agreement, excitement sparkling in their eyes. Even Everest said, "*Dude.*"

"Should you see anything *you tell me right away,*" Aiden instructed, pretending not to have heard. "Keep your eyes and ears open. In the best-case scenario, I won't see any of you again for months, as hopefully there won't be a need to."

Everest asked, "Can we keep our fencing matches? Like I said, I need the practice, and you're tough to beat."

Aiden sighed. "Sure, why not?"

"Will I ever need to go undercover?" Layla hoped.

"No," Aiden said firmly. "Never."

"So wait a minute," Ken blurted. "You *are* the headmaster's son?"

"Yes, I am."

"And you were just bein' mysterious *for fun*?"

"Perhaps." Aiden grinned. "Adds some flavor around here, huh?"

Chapter Seven

A little over a month passed without incident, which was preferable to some of the Hall Monitors and disappointing to others. The students worked tirelessly in their courses. Aiden completed his plans and finished an advanced security system (the look on Jimmy's face when he had discovered that the new security designer was Aiden...it was a very fond memory, to say the least). Life continued on.

The only difference was that the Hall Monitors had become a unique group of friends. After the little nighttime meeting, Layla actively sought out the others and brought them together. They became their own little group with knowing looks and secrets. Nonetheless, they didn't hang together as often as they did with their other friends, and most of their conversations consisted of speculation.

One afternoon in the sixth week of school, there was a test in RA English. The first thirty minutes were occupied writing a literary analysis on a Shakespearean text. The second thirty minutes were spent answering difficult multiple-choice questions about the same text.

Ruthie was concentrating on a particularly difficult question. Her memory was not always useful at Ravencrest, though it did come in handy often.

Come on, think, she was saying to herself. She squeezed her eyes shut and massaged her temples. *Which answer choice is best?* She was finding it difficult to focus; despite the pin-drop silence, there were the usual test-taking sounds RA tests were not immune to: coughs, sighs, feet swinging, bouncing, and fingers tapping.

Behind her, Veronica's fingers were drumming loudly. Ruthie frowned, debating if there was anything she could say to Veronica without breaking test protocol. Since she couldn't, she tried to focus, but the tapping didn't cease. *Tap tap tap-tap tap tap tap-tap tap tap-tap—*

Is that in any particular pattern? It almost sounds like...

Morse Code.

She listened to the tapping again: *tap tap-tap tap-tap tap tap-tap tap tap tap tap tap*. She experimented with dots and dashes and found...

Nonsense.

Ruthie scolded herself; what was she doing analyzing others like that? She had to focus on her test, not try to get an innocent student in trouble.

She focused, finished, and as she fell back, exhausted...

It hit her: the Baconian Cipher!

Groups of five noises at a time would be—without thinking, Ruthie pulled out a spare sheet of paper and scribbled down what it would all be from her perfect memory with all the *taps* being *A*s and the *tap-taps* being *B*s. When that produced nonsense, she tried again with the letters switched.

She looked at the list:

AAAAB AAAAA AAABA AAABA AAABB AAABB AABAA AAAAB AABAB AAAAA...the list stretched on and on and filled up the entire page. Utter nonsense—unless one knew what one was looking for. It took five minutes to switch every other group of five into 1s and 0s. If the 1s and 0s listed numbers in binary and the As and Bs were letters in the Bacionain alphabet, the list read:

1A 2C 3D 4B 5A and went on.

Ruthie sat back in astonishment. She compared the answers on her sheet of paper to her own: they matched, save for a few, which she didn't dare change. *These are the test answers!*

What were the chances that Veronica's finger-tapping methods tapped out the answers to the multiple-choice portion of the test in a combination of binary code and a Baconian cipher? It was clever—no wonder Veronica had started her tapping at the beginning of the test, even during the free-response portion. Ruthie tried to look around to see if there was anyone scribbling down letters or running through the free-response quickly, but the dividers between the tables prohibited her from continuing further. She tried to peer around them yet noticed the teacher watching her intently. She fell back in her seat, looked as innocent as possible, and did her best to calm down.

Veronica was cheating. Cheating! An offense that could lead to expulsion!

What to do? She wouldn't turn Veronica in, poor girl! She'd talk to her, yes, that was the best option. She'd talk to Veronica and maybe she could at least convince her to never do it again.

She was so frazzled about this discovery that she couldn't help but look a little nervous, biting her lip and tapping her foot. The moment the test was over, she bolted for the door, ready to ambush Veronica outside. She didn't notice the teacher's suspicious glare watching her, and was too lost in her own thoughts to put her scrap paper on the teacher's desk. Instead, she held it neatly folded in her fist.

The moment Veronica stepped outside, Ruthie blurted, "We need to talk," grabbed Veronica by the arm, and dragged her into the nearest closet.

"Ruthie, what are you *doing*?" scowled Veronica. "I'm going to be late! We only have a few minutes to get to our next class! Let go of my arm! *Wow*, you're strong. Why—"

"You cheated."

The accusation silenced Veronica. Her face paled and shock flashed in her eyes. Then Veronica seemed calm and collected again. "I don't know what you're talking about."

"I heard your finger tapping." Ruthie unfurled the paper. "See? You used binary and Baconian and tapped out all the answers to the test. It's right here."

Veronica read over the list, her face growing paler by the second. "Really, Ruthie?" she said. "You're so dumb that during the test all you could do was listen to random noises? You're pathetic." But her voice was on the edge of cracking, her breathing grew more rapid, and Ruthie could sense that Veronica was growing more and more frightened.

"Listen, Veronica," pleaded Ruthie. "I won't tell anyone. Ever. You have my word. But only if you never do this again—*never*, okay? You could be expelled! Besides, I'd rather have a surgeon who passed his classes honestly, not a surgeon who cheated on his tests."

"What?" scowled Veronica. "Ruthie, look, you can take any combination of sounds and twist them around enough to make out a code. You're just trying to get me in trouble. Is this about what I said to Layla last week?" Suddenly, Veronica went still. "Oh my God. You're friends with Layla, aren't you?"

Everyone knew Veronica and Layla were mortal enemies. From outright insults to glares behind people's backs, they were definitely not friends. Most of their animosity was due to the fact that they shared classes and extracurriculars, meaning they were always competing.

"Well, yes," Ruthie stammered, her lack of social skills showing, "but I wouldn't tell her if you didn't want me to."

"You want to get me out of here, don't you?" snapped Veronica. "You think you're so high and mighty. I bet you've got it so easy."

Ruthie blinked, not knowing what to make of this. "So you won't do this again?"

"I told you," said Veronica, turning and tossing her hair over her shoulder, "I don't know what you're talking about."

She opened the door and ran right into their English professor.

"Sir?" she said, her voice coming out as a squeak. Her face was turning different colors: white, then red, then pink, then white again.

Ruthie's face administered sympathy. Justice was about to be served.

However, the professor wasn't looking at Veronica. "Ruthie Jocelyn?" he said sternly.

"Yes, sir?" she said, anticipating her testimony in court and already feeling sorry for Veronica.

"You never turned in your scrap paper. Would you please give it to me now?"

Ruthie froze. "Um, well, didn't you, um, hear everything that just happened? I mean, did you hear Veronica and me talking?"

"No. These closets are soundproof. Your paper, please, Ms. Jocelyn." He held out his hand, still frowning. His eyes were narrowed at her.

Ruthie bit her lip, debating whether to say anything. She saw Veronica's face, hardened, waiting for the ax to fall.

But Ruthie was too noble a person.

She said nothing and handed him the paper in her hand without thinking. She turned to leave and then froze, suddenly paralyzed as her actions caught up to her. "Wait!" she shouted as he began to unfold it. "Don't—don't read that, please!"

"Why not?" asked the professor. His eyes were on her.

"Because, um..." Ruthie said desperately, at her wits' end, "um..." Her eyes rested on Veronica, pleading for help.

Veronica acted first. "She cheated."

Ruthie gasped. "What? No! No, Veronica cheated! See, I caught her! Look, here's the paper!" Ruthie opened the paper and showed the professor. "See? These dots represent her finger tapping. I recorded it—I have a perfect memory—and I could tell that she tapped out all the answers! Didn't you notice her tapping?"

Unfortunately, Ruthie's stammered explanation was nothing compared to Veronica's composed yet outraged response: "She's friends with Layla, Professor. They've been treating me horribly all week, and now she just tried to frame me for something I'd never think of doing. I didn't do anything wrong! My fingers always tap when I'm nervous. How was I supposed to keep track of all these dots and dashes?" She shook her head in amusement. "It's ridiculous."

Now Ruthie's face was turning colors as the professor looked at Ruthie sadly. She had been one of his best students. "Come with me, Ms. Jocelyn."

"But I didn't do anything!" Ruthie shouted, almost screaming. "I've never cheated, ever!"

"She's lying! Ask anyone, and they'll tell you what a jerk she and Layla have been to me. Ask anyone!" shouted Veronica right back.

The professor clutched his head. "That's enough from both of you. Come inside, and we'll get this all sorted out."

Ruthie started to cry as Veronica's voice rose. "And now I'm going to miss the rest of my classes. Look what you've done—are you happy now, Ruthie? You're getting exactly what you wanted. I'm going to have to spend all weekend doing makeup work—thanks a *lot*!"

After they walked back into the classroom, Layla entered briefly. "Ruthie, are you coming?" she asked. Her voice faltered when she saw Ruthie in tears and Veronica swollen with rage. When she found her voice, she managed to say, "Um, what happened?"

"This doesn't involve you," said the professor wearily. "Does it, girls?"

"Yes," Veronica replied instantly.

"No," sniffled Ruthie.

"What?" Layla said, her brow furrowed. "Ruthie, what's going on?"

Veronica shot her a look. "You know exactly what's going on."

"No, she doesn't," cried Ruthie. "This doesn't concern her, just me."

"So you did cheat?" asked the professor.

Ruthie caught herself. "No, I'm just saying that Layla had nothing to do with it, I mean, my not cheating. Please, leave her out of this."

"You think Ruthie cheated?" Layla said in astonishment. "Are you *kidding*? She's the nicest person and the strictest rule-follower I know! She once said I need to improve my work ethic, and when I got mad, she bought me apology books on the Mayan language! First edition!"

The professor was so swayed by this that he looked at Veronica with uncertainty.

"She's lying," Veronica said. She was the sort of girl who could inject enough authority into her voice to make it a reality.

The professor massaged his forehead. This was not in his job description, although he knew a person for whom it was.

"I'm taking you girls to the Dean of Education," he said at last, and rose to his feet, clasping the incriminating scrap paper in his hand.

"And me?" Layla asked.

"I'm not sure, Miss..." the professor began.

"Writcroff." She wondered how a man who knew *Romeo and Juliet* better than his own birthday could forget his students' names so easily.

The professor's eyebrows shot up. "Are you related to Melanie Writcroff?"

"Yes, she's my sister."

Those words were magic. "Ah! She was an angel, that one."

"So can I go to my class?" asked Layla respectfully. Her perfectly tailored Ravencrest uniform helped her look like any law-abiding student. The mention of her sister made her seem even more innocent and angelic.

"Of course," the professor said at last. "Run along or you'll be late. I'll write you a pass."

The tears were still drying from Ruthie's eyes as she and Veronica stiffly made their way to the Dean's desk. Ruthie's stomach twisted. *I didn't do anything wrong! I'm innocent—why won't they believe me?* Both girls sat at the Dean's table in silence. Veronica folded her arms defensively and Ruthie rocked herself back and forth, unable to sit still. She was relatively calm when the Dean entered.

"Hello, girls," said the Dean with a sigh. He was an imposing figure of authority, with a crisp suit and dark, disappointed eyes. "I was hoping I wouldn't be needed in this way my first month here."

That was all it took for Ruthie to start crying again. Through her sobs, she tried to explain how she didn't do anything wrong.

"You're so dramatic," Veronica muttered. "She's putting on a show so she doesn't get expelled."

"One of you," said the Dean, "will no longer be at Ravencrest by the end of today, I'll tell you that much. Our school goes against all dishonesty in our students. It seems our Admissions team is getting a little rusty, recruiting students who cheat."

Veronica and Ruthie looked at each other. One of them would be leaving Ravencrest forever by the end of the day in disgrace, all hopes and plans for the future dashed. Above their heads, the tiny bug Ken had implanted recorded the following conversation full of accusations, denials, and tears.

Chapter Eight

After listening to the record, Aiden sent emergency messages to all the Hall Monitors to meet in the headquarters the moment classes ended.

"What happened?" questioned Everest. Ming was behind him, as usual.

Aiden put the recorder on the table, and all of them listened to the Dean recount the story, sort through the accounts, interrogate both girls, and try everything he could to get the truth out. Both stuck to their stories—Ruthie emotionally and a bit hysterically, Veronica frustrated and annoyed as if she was sure that she'd be found innocent. At the end of the conversation, when the Dean lost patience and it was unclear who was lying and who was telling the truth, both girls were sent to a holding room while he spoke with the headmaster.

"Wow," said Ken at the end of it all. "That's ridiculous. She's literally the sort of person who thinks stealing an extra cookie from someone is the end of all law and order. She'd never cheat."

"We need to prove she didn't," said Ming. It was odd he had spoken; usually, he was invisible.

Layla rubbed the sides of her arms. "How? We can't exactly prove Veronica was cheating; Ruthie has the proof and see how far it got her."

"We can testify as character witnesses," Everest offered. "Vouch for her honesty."

Ken shook her head no. "Veronica has girls who would vouch for *her* honesty. *I'd* vouch for Veronica's honesty until now. I mean, she can be a little arrogant, but I never thought she was this rotten. She's not a saint or anything, but she's honest, y'know? I guess the stress got to her."

Aiden spoke up, "Think logically, all of you. What does Veronica need in order to cheat?"

"The answers," Ken realized.

Layla's brow furrowed. "So, we need to find a way to prove that Veronica has access to the answers. But what if she didn't? What if she figured out the answers and broadcasted them to everyone?"

"Easy. You could compare the notes on Ruthie's sheet to what Veronica scored," Everest said.

"But what if she intentionally messed up some of her answers to pretend she didn't cheat?" Layla pointed out.

"Why would she do that?" Ken said. "It's a tough enough test."

"True." Layla's brow furrowed. She was quieter than normal, mainly because her roommate's absence was making her feel a little lonely and perhaps a bit guilty. Maybe if she had waited for Ruthie, who had been lingering near the doorway, she could have prevented this from happening. Either Veronica or Ruthie was going to get expelled, and while there may have been plenty of alternative options for the daughter of an ambassador from France, Ruthie came from a middle-class family who had invested all their savings in their eldest daughter's tuition fees at Ravencrest Academy.

"I acquired photos of the document Ruthie wrote," Aiden went on, and passed it around the room. "Also, here are printed versions of both girls' tests. Notice anything?"

Ming spoke first: "The frequencies of Ruthie's answers vary evenly. She has the usual number of changed answers and made a few errors due to careless mistakes. Judging from her online annotations, she most likely took the test honestly."

"Good," said Ken. "Any expert could look at her test and see that she's probably telling the truth."

Ming paused. "Veronica's test varies more. She consistently scored incorrectly on lengthier questions that looked difficult but were easily answered by most of the class. Look at these standardization notes."

"You're right," Everest realized. "Veronica got questions that *looked* hard wrong and got the rest right."

"It's almost as if she messed up a little on purpose." Layla *humph*ed. "Makes sense that she'd cheat. She's not the best at that class anyway."

"If she wasn't the best at that class, how could she have figured out the answers on the fly?" Ken questioned. "She had to have received the answers from someone. But from whom?" She paused. "We need to—"

They all spoke at once:

"Hack her Ravencrest account," Ken said.

"Interrogate her with threats," Layla said.

"Retrace the path of the answer key from the moment it was produced," Everest said.

"Compare the answer frequencies of all the students in the classroom to analyze who most likely used Veronica's code to cheat," Ming said.

Aiden chuckled. "Since you all seem to know what to do, let's get to it, shall we? I suppose this is our first Hall Monitors case. Not what I expected, but it'll have to do. Now, let's find out who can prove Veronica's guilt or Ruthie's innocence first."

It was the perfect thing to say. Layla and Everest were both extremely competitive and left immediately. Layla found Veronica right away and interrogated her as best as she could. Everest talked with the professor and tried to retrace the path of the answer key, hoping to find a point where someone could have stolen the answers. Ken seemed ruffled by the injustice and went out to set it right, spending a lot of time trying to hack into Veronica's Ravencrest account. This turned out to be much more difficult than she had anticipated. And Ming...his reasons were more obscured. Whatever they were, he set aside twenty-eight minutes of his precious time to analyze each test meticulously.

While her friends were setting the record straight, Ruthie was sitting on a bed in the holding room, which had been put together by some porters a few hours ago. The two girls were only allowed to communicate with other students under supervision. While it wasn't exactly solitary confinement, Ruthie felt as if it was.

She had been punished unfairly! Naive or not, she felt a righteous sense of justice. It wasn't fair. She shouldn't have her future dashed just because Veronica was a good liar. She was the sort of person who tried really hard not to dislike others, but it was difficult not to dislike Veronica. Neither girl spoke a word to the other when they arrived at the holding room. Neither made eye contact. They each pretended the other person didn't exist.

Ruthie crawled into bed and updated her journal. Veronica crawled into her own bed and updated her own journal.

Both girls looked up at each other, quickly looked away, and then put their journals away.

There was a knock at the door. "Layla has come to see you, Veronica," said a porter. Veronica frowned, got to her feet, and crossed to the door. She paused in the doorway and glanced back at Ruthie, who was curled up in her owl pajamas on the bed. Veronica began to say something, stopped herself, and left.

Ruthie squeezed her eyes shut and fought the conflicting emotions. Had there been *remorse* in Veronica's eyes?

No. It was her or Veronica. *Her or me.* It was the rhythm in both girls' minds now. Both futures were at stake, and only one of them was going to make it.

I deserve it, Ruthie thought grimly. *I did the right thing.*

She decided to finish some homework to get her mind off what had happened. It wasn't until she checked her email that she found—

Hello Ruthie Jocelyn,

It's terrible what happened, isn't it? Accused of a crime you didn't commit.

Unless you did commit it. Then you'd lose everything.

No, you wouldn't lose everything. You'd still have your eleven-year-old sister, Bella Joelle Jocelyn, who attends Rangers Middle School. Oh, and your eight-year-old brother, Reuben Lionel Jocelyn, who attends Levine Elementary School. And your parents—and that house they work from home in, on 4329 Ridge Parkway. No, you'd still have them, wouldn't you?

What if you didn't have them anymore? What if I sent one of my friends over? What if your little sister was suddenly killed on her way to school tomorrow, or your little brother was accidentally run over in the street, or your parents were murdered? It's horrible, the things that happen to people when they're not careful. All it would take is a call and they would be gone. Just like that.

You have forty-eight hours to ensure Veronica Lafayette is not expelled. Otherwise, I will make that call.

—VD

Ruthie couldn't breathe. She trembled uncontrollably and grabbed her phone, immediately calling her parents. Only her father picked up.

"Daddy! Be careful, I got this email—"

"Keep your mouth shut or you'll never hear from your daddy again," snarled a distorted voice on her father's number.

She gave a short scream and hung up, terrified. Then, after a shuddering breath, she tried again. "H-hello?"

"Hi, Ruthie, how's it going at Ravencrest?" said the friendly, teasing voice of her father. She hadn't told anyone in her family what was going on.

"G-good," she stammered. "I, um…I just called to say hi. I've got to go. Bye." Before her dad could ask any more questions, she hung up, her heart pounding. Her eyes burned, and suddenly she felt like crying. She was absolutely terrified. Terrified out of her mind. She was too scared to even call her father back.

When Veronica returned, she found Ruthie staring at the wall with tears in her eyes. "Hey, don't be such a baby," Veronica said. "We'll be fine. They'll figure something out."

Ruthie rubbed her eyes and blurted out sorrowfully, "Whatever happens tomorrow, someone's going to lose. It's either going to be me and my family or you and yours. Oh, I wish none of this had ever happened."

Veronica muttered, "Should've kept your nose out of things and it wouldn't've."

"Why did you cheat?" Ruthie asked. "You're not the sort of person who would. I can tell. I know Layla and you don't get along but...both of you are good, honest people. You're not someone who would cheat."

Veronica sighed. She slumped onto her bed and stared at the ceiling. Perhaps Ruthie was mistaken, but it looked as if Veronica was on the verge of tears herself. "You're right about one thing. I'm not a cheater."

"But you cheated on this test! Why?"

"I didn't cheat." Veronica didn't sound convincing. Now it seemed that she was crying a little herself. "Okay? End of story. It's late. Good night."

Ruthie and Veronica didn't speak again as they both focused on their homework, sitting on their respective beds. They brushed their teeth and slipped under the covers. Ruthie turned off the lamp by her bedside and glanced at Veronica once more in the dim light. Their faces looked oddly similar in the growing darkness. In different circumstances, their roles could have been reversed.

Things used to be easy when she was younger. The choices were always black and white. One right, the other wrong.

Now things weren't easy anymore.

Veronica placed a bookmark in her journal, neatly tucked it away, and turned off the light, plunging the room into total darkness. Her breathing remained steady, then grew tighter, as if she was fighting her own battle. She tossed and turned restlessly. Ruthie couldn't sleep either. The nightmares of a monster hunting down her family plagued her until it was well past midnight and she found herself still awake. She cried all her terror out onto a pillow, and then she was fast asleep.

Chapter Nine

The morning came, and with it, rising feelings.

The Hall Monitors were discouraged, except for Ruthie, who was more frightened than anything else. Layla's clever line of questioning had been outwitted, and she hadn't found any incriminating confessions. Everest traced the path of the answer key from the professor and hit a dead end; it seemed impossible for anyone to get their hands on it. Ken did her best, but the Ravencrest account security was excellent (Aiden had designed it), and it was impossible to hack into Veronica's account. Ming didn't exactly fail—he did use those 28 minutes well to create a folder with data that outlined the possibility that each child cheated on the test—yet he seemed discouraged when its presentation to the headmaster did nothing for Ruthie's innocence. It only gave him a recommendation letter from the headmaster should he apply for the Data Science Analyst Award position.

Ruthie numbly went through the motions of getting out of bed. Neither Ruthie nor Veronica had told their family, and the Dean had agreed not to do so until the guilty girl had been found out.

The girls walked with the porters to the Dean's office, waiting for him to arrive. A boy named Rajesh Gollapudi stopped Ruthie on the way there. "Hey," he said, surprising her. "Sorry, I know you don't know me that well, but I just want to say…good luck. We all know you didn't cheat, and we're all rooting for you."

"Thanks," Ruthie said a little shyly.

He nodded and walked away. Veronica cleared her throat, and the porter ushered for them to hurry. The room was empty except for the two girls, with Porter Melissa standing outside the door. Both girls were still, refusing to look at each other.

The Dean finally entered. He looked tired as he sat down. "Well, girls, I'll have you know I've spoken to the headmaster."

"What did you decide?" Veronica asked.

"After speaking with a security expert and after looking at some *very* detailed data folders, I believe I know which one of you cheated." The Dean's eyes rested on Veronica. "As you both know, the consequences of cheating include expulsion. Harsh—and the headmaster's son tried to convince me otherwise—but I find it absolutely necessary. He was very persuasive and insistent, but we need to show future classes that we do not tolerate cheating here."

It was obvious who he was speaking to since he stared directly at Veronica, whose face was turning white and rigid.

So Aiden's plan to convince the Dean to deliver a lighter punishment had failed. Ruthie had no doubt he was in the ceiling above them, ready to convince his father to forcefully persuade the Dean to give Veronica a lighter punishment. Unfortunately, the damage would already be done. Cheating would prohibit Veronica from extracurricular activities, competitions, awards, and certain courses. When she wanted a job in the future, she might have to explain the black mark on her permanent record. Arguably worse, she would forever be known as the only student to cheat in quite a few years of Ravencrest history.

"I'm very determined to keep the punishment as traditional as it needs to be, and I have convinced the headmaster to agree with me. This student not only cheated but tried to destroy the future of another student. The cheater *will* be expelled and punished to the fullest extent, do you understand me?" He glared at Veronica.

Ruthie thought Veronica might cry, but the wealthy daughter of a French ambassador kept her collected composure and superfluous glare. Suddenly, Ruthie realized that Veronica was trembling as if she was on the verge of tears again. It was all so horrible—

"I cheated," Ruthie lied.

It was as if she had dropped a bomb. The Dean turned and looked at her in disbelief. Veronica broke her dignified stance and dumbly blinked, staring at Ruthie in shock. Above their heads, Aiden nearly dropped the cables that were holding him in place.

"I cheated. Veronica's innocent and I'm guilty."

Ruthie hadn't said a lie in years, and thus she was a very bad liar. Her face, growing redder by the minute, gave her away. She fidgeted uncontrollably.

"You know what this means for your future?" the Dean asked.

She closed her eyes as if preparing herself for the punishment. "Yes." Her voice quivered slightly.

The Dean sighed. "We'll need a written statement from you, and then I'll give you 24 hours to take your things and leave this island. You are not permitted to return until your high school education is over. Am I understood?"

To Ruthie, he looked very blurry. "Yes," she said, fighting a tsunami of despair as tears rolled down her face. At least now, her family was safe.

Veronica, who had been getting redder and redder, couldn't take it anymore. She shouted at the Dean, "I cheated! She's innocent. She's just trying to be the hero."

"What?" Ruthie gasped. "Veronica, stop—"

"I cheated, okay?! I cheated and she caught me. End of story."

The Dean looked from girl to girl like he couldn't believe what he was hearing. Both fiercely protested their guilt and the other's innocence. A few minutes ago, he had been convinced who was lying and who was telling the truth. Now he wasn't sure of anything.

"So both of you cheated."

"No! I cheated, *she* didn't!" they both shouted.

"Do you both want to be expelled?"

"No," they both said, seeming troubled.

The Dean grit his teeth in frustration. "This is ridiculous."

There was a knock at the door, and Aiden walked in. "My apologies for being late," he said briskly. His timing was slightly off; he had wanted to step in the moment Veronica confessed, but he had been stopped by a certain porter whose middle name was Eliza and who was currently locked in a closet.

"Ah! My security expert." The Dean rose to his feet in relief. "Both students claim that they are guilty and that the other student is innocent."

"Interesting. So now we either expel both of them—"

"Which would damage the school's reputation," interrupted the pale-faced Dean.

"Or..." Aiden let his voice linger. "...with the headmaster's permission, of course, we could let them both go and keep this as a side note in their permanent record. We'll write that they may have been involved in a cheating scandal, but the extent of involvement was never determined. Should they ever be caught cheating again, they will be immediately expelled."

"Yes," said the Dean slowly, warming up to the idea. "Did you girls hear him?"

"Yes, sir," they chorused. At the same time, they both found that they could breathe again. Ruthie looked at Aiden and mouthed *Thank you.* He kept his face stoic yet winked once.

On the way out, Veronica grabbed Ruthie's arm and shoved her against the wall. "You were going to take the blame for it, weren't you?"

"Maybe," Ruthie admitted.

"Why?"

"I...can't say."

Veronica stepped back. "Did VD email you?"

Ruthie's eyes widened. "Did VD email *you*?"

There was a moment of silence.

"I'm…I'm sorry," said Ruthie, her hands in her pockets. "That's awful. Is he the one who made you cheat in the first place?"

Veronica nodded. Tears built up in her eyes.

"Oh, Veronica!" Ruthie hugged her. "I'm so sorry."

Veronica chuckled through her tears. "Why would you be sorry? It's not your fault we were both coerced into doing stuff we didn't want to do." After a moment, she pushed Ruthie away, though not roughly. "Take care of yourself, Ruthie. I'll see you around."

Ruthie watched Veronica walk away for a moment. Then she called out, "Hey, Veronica!"

"Yeah?"

"Let's get some ice cream before getting back to class."

"Ice cream?"

"We can eat in our rooms. No one has to know."

"Why ice cream?"

"We've got to stick together," Ruthie said. "If there's someone like VD out there, and we're caught up in whatever he wants us to do…well, we've got to stick together. Consider it a peace offering."

Veronica hesitated. "It's Madagascar vanilla with chocolate sprinkles. Medium size," she said at last.

"I'll meet you in the holding room with both of our orders."

"Don't be late."

From Veronica's rare smile, it was clear there were no hard feelings.

"…and so everything was resolved," Ruthie finished. "Again, thanks for everything, guys. Oh, I'm so relieved it's all over. Thank God no one got hurt." She had explained all that happened, except for the parts with VD. The creepy voice on her father's number had told her to keep her mouth shut, and that was what she intended to do.

"Veronica's still a jerk," Layla muttered. It was fair enough, considering that Layla didn't know Veronica had been blackmailed.

Ken gave Ruthie a hug. "We're so glad everything turned out alright," she said. "I wish I could have been a little more help."

"Well—" Layla began.

"No, Layla, I will not use my hacking abilities for evil."

Layla pouted.

"So, who won?" Everest asked. "Probably Ming; he's the only one who actually found something useful. The rest of us Hall Monitors didn't do much, huh?" He sighed, clearly disappointed in himself.

"Not true," said Ken. "I broke into Veronica's room while you two were talking to the Dean this morning, and Veronica's roommate helped me check her email account, just in case someone emailed her the answers. I found an email in her inbox. The subject line was blank, and it was this horrible threatening email that forced her to cheat. The answers were attached to the email in a pdf. It looked like she sent it to herself. Someone must've hacked into her account."

"That's impossible," said Aiden sharply. He had designed the code.

"Or she gave someone her account information," Everest pointed out. "Did the guy who emailed her the answers have a name?"

"And why would someone ask her to broadcast the answers if they already had the answers?" Layla questioned. "There has to be someone who gave her the answer key. But why doesn't the person with the answers just broadcast them instead of asking her? And why didn't we find anyone else with a perfect score if someone else cheated off Veronica? Ugh, this whole thing is baffling."

"The only correspondence in the email was a dash and *VD*," Ken said. They were in the headquarters, curled up in the comfortable chairs and beanbags Layla had decorated the room with. "Does anyone know what VD could stand for?"

"Valentine's Day, Ven Der (a prefix in Dutch surnames), or the number 495 in Roman numerals," Ruthie said immediately. Only Ming noticed that Ruthie was fidgeting, a clear sign that she was hiding something.

Vladimir Damion, Aiden thought and felt a shiver go up his back.

"Aiden, did you think of someone?" Ming said. He had been silently observing.

"I think we should all head to bed," said Aiden. "It's a school day tomorrow, and we all need our rest."

"Why does Ravencrest angst so hard about sleep?" Layla grumbled.

"What?" Ruthie said.

"Why does Ravencrest care so much about sleep?" Everest translated. "I mean, we have strict curfews and the porters are always telling us to get some rest."

Aiden raised an eyebrow at them. "You are all very intelligent people. I'm sure you can figure it out."

He was right. They all knew how important sleep was. Ravencrest didn't ever let its students stay up late on school nights. The only nights that kids could pull all-nighters on were Friday and Saturday nights, though most kids didn't venture that far. They usually fell asleep before midnight, even when they tried not to. Those were just the lingering effects of being a Ravencrest kid.

Totally worth it, Aiden thought. He hesitated as he rose to his feet, debating whether he should tell the others about Vladimir Damon.

"What?" Ken said, interpreting his silence correctly.

"Nothing." Aiden turned away. "I'll contact you all if I need anything again. Good work. I know it feels like we accomplished little, but we worked together as a team for the first time, and it all worked out in the end." *I might not have needed your help for this one, but I definitely learned that you all can be resourceful, clever, and inventive in getting what you need.* Besides, they had discovered that someone named VD forced Veronica to cheat.

"Wait! Aiden, you should join our group chat," Ken suggested.

"No. You shouldn't need to hear from me unless necessary."

"It's easier than slipping notes under doors," Ken hinted.

Aiden was already stepping onto the elevator. "I need the exercise."

"I doubt it," grumbled Everest as Aiden left the room. "I bet he just likes to be mysterious."

Chapter Ten

A few weeks passed before the drugs were found.

The island that held Ravencrest Academy also had its own runway for planes to land and take off. These planes dropped off students at airports of their choice, since the students came from all over the world. Recently, the planes had been used for quite a few field trips. Even more recently, a small container of drugs had been found on a plane under an unoccupied seat (seat 3A). The medical team at Ravencrest confirmed that these drugs were not prescribed to any student or allowed at the academy. Campus Security brought in dogs that could sniff out drugs and interrogated the students who had been seated near seat 3A. How exciting and perfectly planned.

Except no drugs were found.

"Clearly the drugs found in the plane must have come from a Ravencrest student," Aiden explained after he called them in for a meeting. "We're going to have every athlete undergo drug testing."

"What drugs were they?" questioned Everest. His major was biology, but he knew Ming's was chemistry (and physics, but that wasn't relevant here).

"Anabolic-androgenic steroids."

"A class of performance-enhancing drugs for athletes," noted Ruthie. "Interesting..."

"Has Campus Security questioned all the athletes and searched their rooms?" Layla asked.

"Yes. Nothing incriminating was found. The drug dogs went through all the dorm halls and didn't find anything. We didn't let them in any rooms for privacy reasons. Besides, if there were drugs in any of the dorm rooms, the dogs would have detected them from the hallway. Furthermore, every interrogated athlete claimed to be innocent." Aiden was multitasking, both speaking and perfecting a paper he'd publish that weekend.

"Do you know where the drugs came from?" Ken asked. "Can't we perform a chemical analysis? We learned about this in class."

"We have, but all we can determine is their chemical makeup. They're simply performance-enhancing drugs. Nonetheless, it would be good for one of you to take a closer look at the chemical analysis, to see if they missed anything," Aiden said. "The blood tests will reveal whether a student is consuming these drugs."

"I don't get it. I thought Ravencrest's Admissions were impeccable. How could they let in a drug dealer?" Ken asked. "And weren't all the athletes tested at the beginning of the year as standard protocol?"

"To answer your second question, they were," said Aiden with a sigh. "To answer your first...well, it raises two possibilities: either the Admissions team is recruiting not-so-great candidates for the first time in Ravencrest history instead of performing their usual thorough background checks or..."

"Or?" Ruthie prompted. "I can tell you have a really good idea."

"Keep in mind this is only a theory, but what if there is an external factor that is compelling these students to cheat, to steal, or to distribute drugs?" Aiden asked. "Ravencrest Academy misbehavior has increased dramatically this year. Most students are fine, but more than usual are participating in minor infractions and seem distressed. Father's hiring a psychologist to stop by and speak to some of the students who have acted out recently."

"Let me get this straight. You're saying there's a conspiracy trying to brainwash these perfect students to turn them into criminals." Everest scoffed. "Some theory."

"There are many factors that can lead to misbehavior," Ruthie cut in. "And there could very well be an external factor influencing all Ravencrest students." She paused. "Like...VD?"

"Do you think the person behind the cheating is the same as the one behind the drugs?" Ken asked.

"I don't know," Ruthie admitted.

"Perhaps," said Aiden. "Or perhaps not. Maybe VD is a student who is acting out as well. I need you all to investigate. Law enforcement can only do so much. Layla, could you speak with Madeline Woodrow, Sophia Manchester, and Isabel Garcia? You've conversed with them numerous times, and they might be willing to trust you with the truth if anyone is bothering them."

"On it," Layla agreed, her fingers flying over her phone. "I'm already organizing a study session with them. They're smart kids, from what I can tell in English class. I don't understand why they've all gotten detentions for talking back to teachers in the past few months."

"English?" Ken interrupted. "The same English class where the whole cheating thing happened?"

Layla frowned. "Yes...? Oh, come on, Ken, they had nothing to do with that."

"I'm not saying they did. I'm just saying it's a correlating factor," Ken pointed out. "And, Aiden, what do you want *me* to do?"

"Or me?" Everest spoke up, eager to compete.

"Ming, analyze the chemical makeup of the drugs and work with Everest to find out how the drugs were made. Normally I would ask Everest to ask his friends as well, but as they are athletes and have already been interrogated, there would be no point. Ken and Ruthie, try to find out how the drugs were distributed without raising suspicion." Aiden promptly closed his laptop. "This meeting is adjourned."

"Aiden," Ken called. "Before you disappear into the night, I have two questions."

"Yes?" Aiden paused, already halfway into the elevator.

"First of all, do you know something about VD? You get this weird look on your face every time someone mentions him. Do you know who he—or she is? And if so, why haven't you told us?"

"You asked three questions."

"Aiden!"

"Are those all your questions?" Aiden said rather than answering them.

"No," Ken admitted. "I was also asking if you could join our group chat."

Aiden sighed. "You're not going to stop asking me about it, are you?"

Ken smirked.

"I don't see a need to," Aiden said briskly, and just like that, he was gone.

"Of course you don't," Ken muttered. "One day, Aiden Ravencrest, I am going to make you join our group chat."

"Mesterolone, Methandienone, Methyltestosterone, Oxandrolone, and Stanozolol," said Ming. "Five different oral medications. Unmarked and mixed together."

"No identification?"

"None. Chemical tests were necessary to determine their identities."

Everest thought. "How could you manufacture them?"

"Only a facility that specializes in producing drugs would," Ming said.

Everest paced. "So someone must be receiving these drugs from the outside. They could have smuggled these drugs in, then used Ravencrest planes to distribute them across the world. Or they could just sell them to their friends here."

"You're an athlete," Ming pointed out. "I find it unlikely that you would take that option, at risk of your health and career."

Everest bitterly laughed. "I find it unlikely that *any* Ravencrest athlete would take that option. Whoever owns these drugs must be distributing them across the world using Ravencrest planes."

"How long has this been happening?" Ming asked. "Perhaps these drugs were distributed previously."

"No, the porters would have discovered it earlier. They do a clean sweep each month."

"How do you know that?"

Everest shrugged. "I travel a lot for sports. I lost a watch there once. The porters told me they'd let me know if they found it when they did their monthly sweep."

"Is it common knowledge that they clean the plane once a month?"

"No," said Everest slowly, "but it's no secret either. Whoever is distributing these drugs doesn't know how often the porters clean the plane. I'll slip a note under Aiden's door asking when the last sweep was, though it was probably the first week or so. It's only two months in." Everest began his usual evening exercise routine, starting with stretches. "What else can we do? We have a time frame, and we know the person couldn't have known about the sweep. That's not much. I guess we better rely on the drug test."

"I don't understand how the drugs were undetected," Ming said. "If they were in the building, the drug dogs would have found them."

"I'll ask Aiden to include a map showing where the drug dogs looked," Everest agreed. "From what he told me, they looked practically everywhere—in every single hallway in the Residential Hall, the Performance Hall, the Staff Residential Hall, and Student Life. Plus all the classrooms. The dogs would have noticed if it was within a fifteen-foot radius."

"That's for marijuana," Ming corrected.

"What?"

"I don't know about steroids, but drug dogs can sniff marijuana within a 15-foot radius."

Everest raised an eyebrow, beginning lunges. "How d'you know that? Do you have a photographic memory like Ruthie?"

"No, but almost. I can forget what I want to, unlike her."

Everest scoffed. "Why would you want to forget memories? I'd want a perfect memory like that."

Ming glanced at him. "It's not pleasant to never forget anything, Everest. There is a reason Ruthie wishes we did not know of her memory."

"How do you know? Did she tell you?" Everest transitioned to pushups.

"Yes."

"When?"

"After the last meeting."

"You talked to Ruthie?" Everest chuckled. "What, did she bore you to death with facts about the first thing that came to her mind?"

"I take it you don't like her?"

"I think she's annoying and talks too much," Everest said, performing burpees now. "I don't know why Aiden asked her to join. You have her memory, and she's just going to slow us down."

"She could be helpful," Ming said quietly.

Everest rolled his shoulders back, then began jumping jacks. "I doubt it. But if we measure ourselves in terms of ability, Ken's got the puzzle-solving genius we need, and she does best in a crisis. I can tell why Aiden recruited her."

Ming seemed surprised. "I thought you would speak about Layla first."

"Huh?"

"You seem quite taken with her."

"*What?*" Everest missed his landing on the jumping jack, tripped, and nearly fell. "You think I like Layla?"

"No need to hide it from me."

"That's...that's..." Everest fumbled for the word.

"Correct?"

"How did you know? I didn't even know!" Everest snapped. He took a swig of water, then began jumping jacks again. After a pause, "Is it that obvious?"

"No," Ming said. "I'm simply very observant. As is Ruthie."

"How d'you know all this? I mean, you already knew how I think Layla is..."

"Bold, daring, adventurous, uncaring of what others think of her, someone you stare at admiringly when you think no one is watching—" Ming began, but Everest cut him off with, "I get the picture. Geez, Ming, you really get people, don't you?"

Ming's eyes focused on his computer. "It comes naturally."

"Okay, Ruthie, read out everything we know," said Ken, curled up on Layla's bed. Her room was across the hall, but she had a room to herself since her father had paid an extra hundred dollars for it.

"Somehow this student was able to transport a small bottle of pills via Ravencrest airplanes that are used to transport students to parts of the world for sports and competitions," Ruthie said in one long breath. She paused to breathe, then continued, "This student somehow acquired these pills, hid them in the plane, then presumably transported them to the places where the planes traveled."

"Our job isn't to find how this student got these medications," Ken reminded them. "It's to find out how these pills got on that plane."

"We've both traveled on the planes before," continued Ruthie. "You've traveled for Junior Varsity soccer competitions, right?"

"It'll be Varsity soon," Ken said. "But yes."

"Do you remember the security procedures?" Ruthie asked.

"Yes, but list them anyway. You have a perfect memory."

Ruthie blushed a little. "I wish Layla hadn't told you that."

"Why not?"

"I wish I didn't have a photographic memory," Ruthie sighed. "I know it seems like a first-world problem, but no one knows what it's like not being able to forget things." She shuddered. "To forget nightmares, or bad thoughts, or things people say to you, or..." She couldn't finish and looked sick.

"Are you okay?" Ken said, momentarily worried.

"Yeah, I'm fine."

"You're right; that doesn't sound fun. Have you told Layla? She wouldn't tell everyone about it if you asked and told her why."

"I have asked, but I haven't told her that stuff," Ruthie confessed.

"Why not?"

"I don't think she likes me very much."

"What?" Briefly, Ken pushed aside the puzzle that was waiting to be solved. To her, her little friend was more important. "Why not? Layla's awesome."

"She is! She's the coolest person ever. She's funny and smart and pretty and can speak fourteen different languages...but she thinks I'm annoying." Ruthie sighed. "Everyone does. I don't *mean* to be that way. Do you think I'm annoying?"

"No," Ken said immediately.

Ruthie studied her face. "I don't *think* you're lying."

"You're a psychology expert, aren't you?"

Ruthie looked at her feet modestly. "Well, I am trying to get a degree in it. I like understanding people."

"You're right about me not lying. I think you're pretty cool, and I don't just mean your memory."

"Really?" Ruthie's eyes shone.

"You always see the best in everyone, and you're the most loyal and kindest person I know," Ken said. "I promise you I'm not lying when I say that. You forgave Veronica faster than anyone I know would have, even after she tried to get you expelled. You were willing to give up your time and space to help as a tutor here. And I read about all the nonprofit organizations you helped. I'm pretty sure you even started a nonprofit yourself." She reached over and squeezed Ruthie's hand like an older sister. "Just don't let people stomp all over you, all right?"

"What do you mean?"

"Layla's awesome, but if she treats you like a pest, you don't have to keep acting like her servant and hoping she'll like you one day," Ken said.

Ruthie blushed again. "It's that obvious?"

"No, but I can tell you wish she'd like you. Don't care about what other people think. You can't please everyone, you know. Just be yourself." Ken swung her heels back as she sat on Layla's bed. "Got it?"

"Yeah, thanks," said Ruthie rather awkwardly.

"No problem. Now, back to security procedures with boarding Ravencrest planes."

"Right." Ruthie straightened, then began, "Well, I remember signing a form about being responsible for any illegal activities that involve this plane—"

"Who knew those forms would actually be helpful?" Ken muttered.

"—and some other legal stuff about passports and everything at the beginning of the year. Because of how frequently those planes are used, they don't perform lots of security procedures before the day of boarding. When boarding, porters make you pass through a metal detector, sign some forms promising you're not going to do anything illegal, and scan the contents of your bag. They even have airport scanners that flag the porters if they find anything suspicious—"

"Like illegal drugs?"

"Exactly. After all those security procedures, the porters put your bags in the back and look through the contents of any carry-on. Then you sit in your seat and enjoy the trip." Ruthie frowned. "That's all the security I know about."

"Do they repeat these procedures on the return trips?"

"Not at the school, but they repeat them at the airports before the students return," Ruthie said.

"Is there any communication between the porters and students *after* these security procedures?" Ken asked. "I mean, if you forgot a jacket, could you send a porter to grab it for you?"

"You'd have to miss the flight since they'd go through all those procedures again for that jacket. And we all know how no porter ever deviates from protocol."

"The question is, how'd they get the drug into or outta Ravencrest?" Ken murmured to herself. Her eyes glazed over and she remained deeply lost in thought. This was her puzzle-solving face, and Ruthie knew better than to disturb her.

Ruthie checked her phone. She had received a text from Rajesh Gollapudi, who was her partner in RA Calculus. He wanted to get together for their math project at the study booth in the back of the café. Please? I want to get it out of the way. Sorry for the late reply, he had texted with some sad faces.

Her fingers poised over the keys. Can't we meet up online? Ruthie hesitated. It was odd how Rajesh kept asking to hang out with her. She was beginning to suspect there was something off about him. Still, she decided not to send the message and instead grab her backpack. "I'll be right back," she told Ken. "This should be quick."

"Yeah, okay," said Ken, staring at the carpet intently.

Layla giggled. She was curled up with Madeline Woodrow, Sophia Manchester, and Isabel Rodriguez in the girl's lounge room, snacking on bagels and cream cheese. "You want some cream cheese with all that jam?" Layla teased, glancing at Madeline's bagel.

Maddy grinned. "What can I say? I love strawberry jam."

"I never even had bagels before coming to Ravencrest," Isabel said dreamily as she took another bite. "I was really missing out."

Sophia laughed. "I had bagels every day. My brother's a professional soccer player and my parents give him *everything*. He loves bagels, so naturally, I got a lifetime supply."

"You're so lucky," said Isabel enviously.

Sophia chuckled, smile fading. "I don't know about that. I think they expected me to be a pro soccer player too, and when they realized I'm not naturally talented like him, they basically stopped caring about me."

"I'm sure that's not true—" Madeline began.

"You know what my dad said to my mom when I got in here?" Sophia said bitterly. "*Well, one kid off our hands. It's good for us; we can focus on the talent now.*"

Layla's heart dropped. "Oh, Sophia, that's horrible."

"Do you like it here?" asked Isabel, her legs crossed and her laptop closed. "I mean, do you like Ravencrest?"

"Are you kidding?" said Sophia, brightening again. "It's *awesome.* I love this place."

Madeline grinned. "Agreed. This is like my dream school."

"I know, right? We're living like kings and queens," said Isabel dramatically. "*And* we get to learn the coolest stuff ever. I mean, just yesterday, I wrote a detailed report on how to create a nuclear bomb—from a purely scientific perspective, of course."

"That's so cool," Madeline agreed. "And speaking of dangerous stuff, did you hear about the drugs?"

Layla was an incredibly talented actress. Her eyes widened when she asked, "What drugs?"

"Some porters found drugs on a Ravencrest plane!" said Sophia. "I heard all about it from Angel. She said she heard some porters talking about it. They think someone has been transporting drugs to and from Ravencrest."

"No," gasped Layla. "*Drugs*?"

"I know, right?" said Madeline. "Here at school! Who would do something so idiotic?"

Isabel cut in, "I get it, though. The pressure's been hard on a lot of freshmen, and if some athlete wants to smuggle in steroids so he can get better at his sport, I don't blame him. Not saying it's right, but I understand why, you know?"

Alarm bells rang in Layla's mind; how did Isabel know about the steroids specifically? No one knew exactly which drugs had been found, except for the security teams. Everyone had been very tight-lipped about it. Moreover, why did Isabel refer to the athlete as *he*? This prompted Layla to ask, "Do you know which drugs were smuggled in?"

"No," said Isabel. "This is the first time I've heard of it."

"How'd you know they were steroids?" Layla asked innocently. "And that it was a guy doing all this? Did you hear something about it?"

Isabel stammered, then said, "I mean, what other illegal drugs would be distributed here? And those kinds of drugs act like testosterone, right? So I guess my mind automatically thought guys would use them. If they're steroids, I mean. It could be any kind of drug. I was just guessing, that's all."

Madeline yawned. "Yeah, makes sense." She stretched, then said, "Layla, thanks for inviting us. The bagels were the best, and I got a lot done. I gotta go, though. The curfew's starting soon, and I need to shower before bed."

"Sure," Layla said. "But before we go, could I ask you all something?"

There was a general myriad of agreements.

"Have any of you gone to detention recently?" Layla asked.

"Yep," sighed Sophia. "That was my fault. My roommate was being a jerk so I shoved her, but I did it in front of the teacher. When he got mad at me, I talked back to him...and then I got detention. I guess I was pretty mean. It had just been a really bad day."

"The same thing happened to me," Madeline said. "I didn't shove anyone, but I talked back to a teacher. I was just really annoyed and frustrated. It hadn't been my day, y'know?"

Isabel looked up. "That happened to me, too. I lost my temper two days ago, and yeah, I ended up in detention."

Layla's brow furrowed. "You guys are all A-honor-roll, perfect-record students! How—"

"I know, it's just that things have been kind of rough," Sophia interrupted. Her face seemed a little flushed as she hesitated. "Have any of you guys been getting...I mean..."

Madeline went still. "Wait, you've been getting them too?"

"Getting what?" asked Layla.

Sophia and Madeline were now looking straight at Layla. They all were. Isabel was the first to speak: "Layla, have you gotten any weird messages lately?"

"No," said Layla. "What do you mean by weird?"

"Rude," said Sophia.

"Blackmail," said Madeline.

"Scary," said Isabel.

Layla gasped. "Guys, you should report stuff like that!"

Sophia bitterly laughed, though she seemed on the verge of tears. "Hard to do, if the emails are being sent to yourself."

"Why haven't you told anyone?" Layla said gently.

Madeline hugged her knees. "The emails I get always threaten to do some awful stuff if I tell anyone."

"It might have happened to a lot of other kids," said Isabel. "I think no one talks about it because they don't know what's happening. But it's not that bad. It's just a creepy email once a month, and it doesn't happen to everyone."

"That's so weird," Layla said. "But it explains why everyone keeps ending up in detention. I should definitely report this."

"NO!" all three girls shouted.

Layla blinked.

Isabel tried to explain: "If you do, he'll find out. He finds out about everything. And he doesn't bother us that much anyway. It's fine, really. Just to be safe, *please* don't tell any of the staff here. *Please*, Layla, promise us that!"

"I won't tell any of the hired staff," Layla promised, knowing Aiden (who wasn't technically a hired staff member) was going to flip after hearing this. "And how do you know it's a guy?"

"We don't," said Madeline. "But the emails always have the same signature, at least for me."

"So do mine," said Sophia. "They're always signed *VD*." She whispered the initials, and the other girls' eyes widened.

Despite herself, Layla gasped again. "*VD*?"

VD—the same name that had emailed the answers to Veronica. She wondered what Aiden would say when he found out.

While Layla was casually probing her ever-widening group of friends for answers, Ken was solving a tricky puzzle, Everest was finishing his routine, Ming was submitting the rest of his assignments, and Ruthie was off to meet Rajesh.

He was sitting in the back study booth of the café, just as he had said. It looked like he had brought snacks—his chips and Ruthie's favorite raspberry-cheesecake Danish pastries with extra raspberries.

"Woah, you remembered my special order?" said Ruthie in amazement. "Thanks."

"No problem."

She slid into the seat across from him and set up the laptop, all the while nibbling on the pastries. "So, for our Calculus presentation, I finished the outline and my part of it. Just send me what you finished and I can combine the two. Then we can practice presenting it, which should take, like, ten minutes. Does that sound good to you?"

"Sounds great."

Ruthie turned to him expectantly. "Did you email your part of the presentation to me?"

For the first time, she noticed how startled he seemed by the question. *Odd*. He seemed like the sort of person who was always on top of things. It was weird how he kept looking at her like that. He stammered and answered, "Yeah, sure. Here it is."

She typed away, combining both of their work, then pulled up the resulting presentation. "Okay, let's divide up the slides. I'll cover all the odd-numbered ones and you the even."

"Great."

"Except for the title side. I'll read the title, and we'll each read our name."

"Of course."

She squinted at him. "Are you even listening to me?"

He coughed. "Of course. I'm listening. We're both doing the title slide."

"Are you feeling alright?"

"I'm fine."

"Okay, then." She stared at her food for a moment. "Also, Rajesh..."

"Yeah?"

"I never did say this, but thanks for not thinking I was a cheater during the whole Veronica-and-me cheating thing a few weeks ago. I really appreciate it."

Rajesh smiled back, relaxing a little. "Yeah, well, from what I've heard, you don't seem like someone who would cheat on a test. I just...wanted to talk to you. Felt kind of weird about the whole thing, I guess." He hesitated as if he was about to confide in her. "Ruthie, I—"

"I don't really want to talk about the cheating incident," sighed Ruthie, still mentally reliving what had happened. "It was awful, and I'm glad it's all over. Anyways, let's go over the presentation a few times."

"Right," Rajesh stammered. "Of course."

After they ran through their presentation enough times, Ruthie said, "We should go back to our rooms; it's getting late. I think we should practice this one more time tomorrow, but we should be good after that." Rajesh agreed robotically. She received the distinct impression that he was too nervous to do something, but what? Why did he keep looking at her and hesitating, then changing his mind and saying something else?

They walked back in awkward silence. To fill the silence, Ruthie asked, "So, Rajesh, what's your major?"

"Astrophysics. You?"

"Biological sciences." She glanced at him, her face peeking over the edge of the huge binder clutched to her chest. "Astrophysics? Wow, that's kinda hard. You want to be an astronaut?"

"Definitely. It's my dream." His eyes went far away. Every Ravencrest student had something—some field or topic they wanted to dedicate their life to, something that could make them teary within sixty seconds of talking about it. For Rajesh, it was clearly astrophysics. "I mean, humanity has accomplished so much, but just think about the wonders of space. We're only a stray planet floating through the universe. There are all these galaxies and undiscovered worlds. I want to find what's out there, y'know?"

"That's so cool," said Ruthie honestly.

"You mean it?"

"Rajesh, trust me when I say this: I never lie." She paused. "Well, except for surprise parties and not spoiling books and the whole cheating thing, but that was complicated."

He laughed. "I'd love to hear the whole story from you someday. There are so many versions floating around about what happened. I'm sure it was awful. And it makes sense it happened in RA English. I've always hated that class. So what happened?"

"It's all so crazy and complicated," sighed Ruthie. "I'm not even sure I'm allowed to talk about it."

"Of course," said Rajesh automatically. "If you're not supposed to talk about it, I'm not going to get you in trouble."

"Well, thanks." They reached the part of the hallway where it split into the girls' and boys' dorms. Ruthie thanked Rajesh and said goodbye to him, walking to her room. She was still a little confused about the whole encounter. There was something Rajesh was hiding, that much she could tell. Why was he so nervous around her? At least he was a nice kid, even if he was kind of perplexing. It was surprising he remembered her favorite snack and ordered it for her. Maybe she was overthinking everything. He was probably just a normal, friendly guy.

Layla was rushing back from the lounge room and met her in the hallway. "Ruthie!"

"What?" said Ruthie, forgetting about Rajesh and the Calculus project. "You found something!"

"Did I ever! I'll tell you all about it in our room—and hey, was that *Rajesh Gollapudi* I saw?" Layla giggled at her knowingly.

Ruthie stared at her with genuine confusion. "Yeah, he's my math partner."

Layla waited for the punchline. On seeing none, she sighed. "You really are clueless, aren't you, Ruthie?"

"About what?"

"Oh, never mind. I'll tell you later. Look, I think the same guy behind Veronica's cheating was behind the drugs." Layla had lowered her voice by now, and she had already used her student card to enter their room. "The same initials—*VD*—are cyberbullying kids the same way they forced Veronica to cheat."

"How do you know that has anything to do with the drugs?"

"*Think* about it, Ruthie. Whoever has access to these drugs must have access to the outside world, right?"

"Yeah, so?"

"So who might be pressuring this student into distributing drugs the same way they threatened Veronica and bullied other kids?" Layla urged. "The same initials: *VD*."

"I don't know, Layla," Ruthie said at last. "You don't know for sure they're connected."

"Well, we might as well tell Aiden," said Layla. "He might know what to make of everything."

Ruthie bit her lip. "Yeah, and did you see his face when Ming asked him if he remembered anything about VD? I think Aiden's hiding something. He knows something about VD."

Layla rolled her eyes. "I don't think Aiden's hiding anything. You just see a lot of things that don't really exist."

"What?"

"You're *paranoid*, Ruthie. You've always got your head up in the clouds, making up conspiracy theories and mentioning whatever pops in your head." Layla shook her head, amused. "Sometimes it's kind of annoying, actually."

"Oh, sorry," mumbled Ruthie.

"Come on, let's go tell Aiden. I'll slip a note under his door." Layla swung her feet and tore out a clean sheet of notebook paper to write on. "We have to hurry so we don't break the curfew. Maybe we can ask Aiden for some more hall passes so we don't get in trouble with any porters in case this happens again."

Ruthie sighed, watching Layla write. "It would be so much easier if he just joined Ken's group chat."

"Seconded," Layla agreed, and then they were off.

Chapter Eleven

While all his fellow team members were following their orders, Aiden was fast asleep.

He was neither lazy nor ill. Tomorrow, Father was leaving for Pampas, Argentina to use the findings of his new archeological dig in his book. Aiden was coming along to explore. They were leaving Tuesday morning and would hopefully be back by Thursday night. The plane left quite early, so they both were in bed much earlier than usual.

Due to the discovery of the drugs, Father had considered canceling the trip, but Aiden had persuaded him that they had the entire matter under control. Privately, he had been looking forward to this opportunity. He hadn't been to Argentina in years, not since he and his mother had enjoyed slices of *Postre Balcarce* at a small plaza. She had arrived for an archeological dig herself and brought Aiden along for the same purposes: to explore, to learn, and to sample another culture. Mother took these trips frequently and usually asked Aiden if he wanted to come along. Aiden always said yes.

Now, he felt a tinge of bittersweetness as their plane landed on the small airstrip in the Argentinian airport. Who would have known he'd be here again, this time without Mother?

He shared Mother's sweet tooth as well as her love of exploring the world. The moment he stepped into the slightly chilly atmosphere of Pampas, the grass tickling his ankles, he remembered her smile, her touch, and her excitement here in Pampas. Suddenly, he longed to share a cup of *dulce de leche* with her.

"Come along now," said Father once they had passed through the terminals. "We don't want to be late. You need to stay close by until we get to the city, and even then, you need to keep your security tracker with you at all times, understood?"

"Yes, Father." He fingered his tracker and stealthily disabled it.

"Good. And Aiden?"

"Yes, Father?"

"Turn the tracker back on. Don't make me regret bringing you along, young man."

Aiden sighed and obeyed. Father was getting to know his son better and better. Aiden wasn't sure he liked the change. There was less freedom and independence, yet it showed that Father cared, enough for him to add, "Tell you what, Aiden—I won't check it unless I don't see you by sundown. Here's some money. I know you can take care of yourself."

Father really was learning. Aiden smiled, nodded, and for once chose to obey his father.

Why am I doing this? Aiden understood many things, but sometimes he didn't understand himself. He understood how nice it was to sit on the plaza under the warm sun on a chilly day, watching the younger children play. He didn't understand why he was trembling so much when he ordered his food in Spanish. It wasn't until the waiter had turned away that Aiden realized he had ordered the exact same food he and Mother had enjoyed together.

Breathe.

He took a few deep breaths. *I am here to enjoy Pampas, not to remember Mother.* This was a vacation, not a funeral.

Pampas was famous for its delicious beef, golden wheat, and beautiful sunflowers. Farmland stretched around them as far as the eye could see, at least until one reached the city. Mother's eyes had danced when she tried the meals at this same restaurant. And her eyes had filled with tears when young Aiden had picked a sunflower and given it to her with a poem he constructed on the spot. She had hugged him tightly and given him his first spoonful of *dulce de leche.*

Stop it!

He didn't want to think about her. But she was everywhere, coming back to him.

Don't think about it—

And then the flashbacks were back.

Not Mother! You're lying!

Don't lie to me.

Who are you?

Liar, liar, pants on fire.

Lies and lies and where's the truth?

How dare you!

Tell me the truth.

Disorienting emotions and feelings and words overwhelmed him in a flood. He clutched the side of his head as the world faded around him and the screams rose:

You're lying!

Stop, please!

I hate you!

How dare you!

Come back!

NO!

He didn't know if he was the one screaming or if someone was screaming at him, yet he remembered the scream. It had been a guttural cry, ripped from the depths of his soul. He remembered falling into the blackness and finality of grief.

He tried to breathe again, but he was drowning.

She's gone.

Dead.

Passed away.

Left.

No longer here.

You're next.

Nothing made sense. The world was tilting, he was falling, it was going too fast—

Please!

Never again.

Come back!

You'll be sorry.

Sorry.

I'm so sorry.

It's not your fault.

It's all your fault.

All your fault.

Your fault.

MOM!

"Are you all right?"

Slowly, his vision focused. The world regained its color. The haziness became defined and the rushing in his ears slowed. Pale and breathing heavily, Aiden found himself facing the concerned waiter.

Aiden nodded weakly. He hated being seen like this. He cleared his throat. "I'm perfectly fine, thank you."

"¿Discúlpame?"

Then he realized the waiter had spoken to him in Spanish with a thick Argentinian accent while he had responded in his usual English.

"Estoy bien, gracias."

The food was delicious, just as he remembered it. By now, he had recovered enough to eat it and banish all thoughts of Mother from his mind. He savored each bite. This was his own memory, unpolluted by all that had happened since the last time he had enjoyed this meal.

He let his thoughts wander to the others back home. He refused to acknowledge them as friends; to do so would risk the pain he'd suffer once they graduated. Denver had once been his friend, and look where that got him. Ravencrest students never looked back. The moment they left the Academy, they had more important things to do in life and more beneficial relationships than a two-year friendship with a mischievous young boy.

Still, he found himself enjoying their company. Besides, one of them, a particularly nice-looking and ingenious girl named Ken, kept reappearing in his mind for reasons he wished didn't exist.

He was furious at himself now. He was *Aiden Ravencrest*! He simply did not have crushes. He banished all thoughts of her from his mind and focused on the issue of the drugs. Should he return to Ravencrest as planned and take the reins of the mission to find the drugs? Or should he extend his stay in Pampas? Father would be easily convinced.

He savored his meal. *Stay in Pampas.*

Aiden could return to his work once he returned. Furthermore, his informal security team back home was doing their jobs well. He had responded to their notes in the morning by sending them replies under their respective doors. They must have been making progress, and he had no doubt they would soon have the criminal student(s) in custody. He had been working hard recently; he deserved a break.

There was another nagging reason: he wanted to savor this memory of Mother. It was a clear memory, unlike the flashbacks that had tormented him moments ago.

He'd return to Ravencrest when he was his confident, suave self again. When he wasn't scrambling for answers, trying to sort out the past, or fighting his mind for clarity. When he wasn't pushing away the conversation with the patient that implicated—never mind what it implicated. When he had fixed the broken part of him that needed his mother.

He stood up, paid for the meal, and briskly crossed the plaza. He'd take a walk, clear his mind, and forget about the security team for now. By sunset, he'd have Father convinced to let them stay an extra day. Before he returned to Ravencrest Academy, he'd be all right.

Again, he chose to lie to himself. He knew he'd never be the same again. Too much of his world had been destroyed because of Mother's death, his amnesia, and this VD.

VD...

Vladimir Damon?

It couldn't have anything to do with the drugs, or the increases in misbehavior, or even Mother's death, could it?

Right?

A hand covered Ruthie's mouth, stifling her scream. In her ear, a voice whispered, "Ruthie, it's me! You awake?"

"Wha?" mumbled Ruthie, barely conscious. Her sleepy eyes traveled to the clock. She turned on the lamp next to her bed, checked her watch, and groaned. "One AM? Ken!"

Ken shrugged, bright-eyed. "Ruthie, I solved it! I know how the person is smuggling the drugs outta Ravencrest and onto the plane!"

Ruthie yawned. "I had this amazing dream where I found the newest book in my favorite series, and I was about to open it to the first page when you woke me up. Couldn't this have waited until morning?"

Layla rolled over in her sleep, murmuring in agreement.

"It *is* morning," said Ken dismissively. "Now listen. I was rackin' my brain trying to figure out how a student could smuggle drugs onto the planes. I mean, porters have *drug dogs*, and I know dogs would bark at the smell of anything illegal. And we all know how strict the porters are."

"Of course," Ruthie said, groggily rubbing her eyes.

"So what if the porters *knew* there were drugs?"

"What? Are you saying the porters were *helping* smuggle drugs?" Ruthie frowned. "Ken, that's like bribing a judge; although it's theoretically possible, it's highly unlikely."

"No, I'm saying they were unknowingly helping smuggle drugs."

"*What?*"

"Look, what's the protocol for medication?"

"Medication? That's simple. You put it in a small pouch with a note from the nurse and carry it on board...." Ruthie realized what Ken was saying. "Oh, so our criminal switched their medication with the pills? But then the medication would have been monitored. I mean, if he kept it on the plane or took it off the plane, the porters would know."

"So what?" Ken asked.

"I don't know," Ruthie yawned. "It might be a problem, I guess."

Ken huffed impatiently. "Ruthie, *think*. If I carried an unmarked bottle of illegal pills with me, I'd be caught, right?"

"Yes...?"

"So...?"

Ruthie waited, then gave up. "Ken, it's too early in the morning for this!"

"There was a decoy bottle of real medication and a bottle of illegal pills *mixed with* real meds, both labeled as if they held the real meds. I think our criminal got the nurse's approval to take his meds in two bottles—"

"Their meds."

"What?"

"It could be a girl or boy," Ruthie reminded her. "We don't know."

"Whatever. Anyway, they took both bottles of pills, right? The fake medication, mixed with his actual medication pills, would be in the medication pouch with the nurse's note. It would be right next to a bottle of real meds. The dogs might notice the prescription drugs in there, as technically none of those are illegal unless they're used without a prescription, but the porters won't care since he has a note."

"Go on," said Ruthie. She was beginning to get into the story.

"So he sits down on the plane and hides the real meds on the plane while keeping the mix of real and fake medication in his pouch with the note."

"It could be a she—"

"*Then*," concluded Ken triumphantly, "when the plane lands, he goes out with the mixed real and fake meds in his pouch and trades it with whatever drug dealers he's working with. Then he adds the new fake meds to his mix of real and fake meds. When he's back in the plane, he transfers most of the fake meds to the hidden bottle on the plane and moves all the real meds from the hidden bottle back into his pouch. The porters check him when he gets back, and since he mostly has the real stuff mixed in, plus he has a note, he's fine. He probably thinks he hid the illegal stuff on the plane well enough, since he clearly didn't expect them to find it. The next time he gets to the plane, he keeps a mixture of real and fake medication in his pouch. While he's there, he adds the illegal stuff to his pouch and returns the real meds to the hidden bottle. He lands with a mix of real and fake meds, trades the fake meds, returns to the plane, puts most of the illegal stuff into the hidden bottle, and puts the real meds back into his pouch. This way, he can take drugs from wherever he goes and transport them to other places. Plus, he can keep some of the drugs with him in Ravencrest and sell them to anyone who's interested."

"So he operates the entire drug ring right under the porters' noses," breathed Ruthie. "Wow. Good job figuring it out, Ken!"

"Thanks," glowed Ken. "Now we need to tell Aiden and everyone else."

Ruthie continued, "We should tell the security team and the porters, and we should probably check the nurse's record so we know who asked for notes as excuses to bring medication on board. I'm guessing our guy—or girl—hides some of the fake meds here at the school somewhere and keeps most of them in the plane just in case the ones in the school get caught. After all, if he's going through all this to transport these drugs, he must be transporting even more drugs than the one bottle found on the plane."

Layla spoke up, "Really, it could be anyone who's asked for medication onboard since the last sweep."

"And Sleeping Beauty awakens!" Ken joked.

Ruthie stretched. "It's a long shot, but it fits. We'll let everyone know in the morning. Now, we all better get some sleep." She stretched again, her eyes bloodshot and exhausted.

"Yeah, got it," sighed Ken. "On my way to bed now." She rose and crossed to the door.

"Hey, Ken?" called Layla. "How'd you get in here?"

Ken explained, "I took a page out of Aiden's book and snuck in here right behind the porter's backs. I manually opened my room door and adjusted the security lock so they wouldn't know I left my room. Then I used Layla's spare keycard to get into your room, and then I used my new security clearance account and erased the last account of me entering your room."

"The porters are still outside?" said Ruthie nervously. "Oh, we need to whisper."

Ken shrugged. "Don't worry. These walls are pretty thick. Still, you guys needa sleep. *Now.* I'll get out of here. And if I get caught, I'll just say I needed water or somethin'." Due to her New York accent, she said *water* as *wahter*, causing Ruthie to chuckle.

"Mm," said Layla. She was already fast asleep.

"Here's the list the nurse gave me," said Ruthie, entering the closet where the Hall Monitors had convened for a quick meeting. They had all finished lunch quickly. Earlier, using the security clearance Aiden had given her, Ruthie had stopped by the nurse's office in the morning to ask for the list of all the students who had requested medications for any flight. By using her photographic memory, Ruthie could recreate the list while eating lunch, keeping them from having to take photos of classified information.

"Hurry," said Layla, rocking back and forth and glancing at the closet door nervously. "Class starts in ten minutes."

Ken examined the list. "There are more students than I expected."

"Isabel was the girl you said knew more about the drugs than she let on," Everest informed Layla. "And she's on here."

"So is Rajesh," noted Ming, remembering his arrogant friend from lunch.

"It's not Rajesh," said Ruthie. "He's too nice to do something like this. He's not athletic either, so why would he have anything to do with performance-enhancing drugs?"

"He doesn't have to be athletic to be distributing drugs," said Ming.

Ken scanned the list. "There are eight students who asked for medication since the sweep. D'you want to split up and investigate each of 'em?"

"Or I could investigate the chemistry lab supply closet," offered Everest.

"What?" asked Ruthie.

Everest explained, "Ming and I were talking this morning—where could our dealer store the drugs while they were here? The drugs weren't found in their room and the nurse wouldn't take care of illegal drugs, now would she?"

"We found a blueprint of where the dogs searched, and we noticed they didn't search the chemistry lab or its adjoining supply closet," said Ming.

Ruthie snapped her fingers. "Of course! That area of the school has enough dangerous chemicals as it is. But how would the student be able to sneak in and out of the lab? It has really high security."

Layla grinned. "Oh, Everest, you're brilliant. You're the person who's supposed to clean up the lab after school, aren't you? You're going to go on a stakeout!"

"In a manner of speaking," said Everest, also grinning. He was proud of thinking up such an exciting plan. "I'll clean up and hide in the lab. I'll need a double—maybe Ming—to leave as me. He can stay after."

"I could be your double," Layla said with excitement. "I'd love to go on a stakeout!"

Ruthie sighed and bit her lip. "I don't know. What if you get caught by the porters? And why does this have to be so cloak-and-dagger? We're the Hall Monitors, remember? We have security clearance so the porters are on our side. We can simply ask the porters to hide in the lab, or Ken can install some security cameras, and we can find whoever comes in. We don't need all this secrecy, and frankly, it's kind of dangerous. The student who gets caught won't be happy. And we don't even know if they'll stop by today. And—"

"Oh, shut up, Ruthie," said Layla, annoyed.

Ruthie did shut up, her face burning.

With sympathy, Ken interrupted, "I think Ruthie's right, but I also think Everest has a great idea. He already stops by the lab every night to clean up. He could—"

"Not every night," interrupted Everest. "Only Tuesdays. Isabel cleans it on Mondays, Ming on Wednesdays, Rodriguez on Thursdays, and Norton on Fridays."

"Make it every night," said Layla suddenly.

"What?"

Layla grew excited. "Stop by the lab every night this week, and watch whoever comes in. You can hide in a closet and use one of Ken's gadgets to spy on them. If you catch them revealing hidden drugs, you have video evidence *and* you can confront them in the act!"

"There's a flight this weekend," said Ming, catching on. "This is an opportune time for this student to smuggle drugs."

"Guys?" said Ruthie. "We're forgetting something."

Everest wheeled around to face her. "Oh, what now, Ruthie? There's a bug in our plan? Some random inconsistency that's going to send it all crashing down? Or maybe it's not fun enough for you? What problem do you have now?"

For a moment, no one spoke.

Then Ruthie said quietly, "I was only going to say that the bell's about to ring. But if I'm going to ruin your fun, then by all means, go ahead and get yourselves caught!" Her face burned again, and now she was fighting back: "At least I care about the Hall Monitors and I'm not some adrenaline-seeking jerk looking for a thrill!"

Everest sputtered, and his eyes took on a darker edge. Before he could say a word, Ming put a hand on Everest's arm and pulled him outside. At the same time, Layla wheeled around to Ruthie and shouted, "Ruthie! How could you say that?"

"He *was* being a jerk," muttered Ruthie, her dark eyes flashing.

"*You* were being a jerk," Layla said angrily. "Everest cares about the Hall Monitors too, and you didn't have to insult him like that!"

"Oh, so now you're taking his side?" said Ruthie, tears building in her eyes.

Ken tried to mediate: "No one's taking *any* side—"

Maybe it was from the lack of sleep, the mounting pressure, or even her own emails from VD, but Ruthie finally snapped. She shouted at Layla, "You're always against me, aren't you? I'm always too annoying, too logical, or too talkative. Why do you always have to shut me down like that? Sometimes you're the real jerk."

Layla couldn't see past her rage. "*I'm* the jerk now? Ruthie, I don't know why Aiden recruited you. I wish you weren't part of the Hall Monitors, and I wish you weren't my roommate! You're just so annoying and you're always holding me back. I'm going to request a roommate referral, that's for sure." She shoved past Ruthie, head held high.

Ruthie's bottom lip quivered as she glared at Ken fiercely. "What about you? Whose side are *you* on?"

"I'm not on any side," said Ken, not sure how she found herself in the middle of this argument. "Though, honestly, I didn't think you had it in you to yell at Layla and Everest like that."

"So you think I'm a jerk too?" Ruthie couldn't see past the burning tears. "Well, fine then, see if I care!" She stormed away.

Ken sighed. "That went well. Nice going, Ken."

Ruthie focused on walking to class, too flooded with emotion to see clearly. How dare Layla and Everest treat her like garbage! *Well, you did call them both jerks,* a little voice reminded her. *And you didn't handle the situation very well. Layla probably didn't intend to be so mean to you. Everest...well, you still could have been nicer to him.* She slumped at her desk, staring at the wood. Behind her, there was a tap on her shoulder.

Rajesh? She wiped her tears swiftly and turned around.

"Hey, Ruthie, is everything all right?" asked Rajesh. A few seats away, Ming seated and watched this exchange.

Ruthie shrugged. "I'm fine."

"Oh, okay." Rajesh hesitated, then asked, "Are we still meeting after school today to practice the presentation one last time?"

"Yeah."

"Great! Same place as last time, right?"

"Yep." She tried to smile.

"Great. I'll get the same pastries for you."

Now, she brightened a little. "Oh, you don't have to do that."

"I don't mind. And you like coffee, right? Chai tea with double sugar and extra milk?"

"Yes, but you don't have to—"

"It's no problem. You look like you've had a rough day, and I'm sure you deserve it." He looked almost as nervous as before.

"Well, thanks," she said, a little flustered by his kindness. "And you're right, I have had a rough day. But I'll tell you all about it later. Class is starting."

"Of course," he said, and she turned back as the teacher entered the room.

Silently, Ming turned away, his withdrawn face not betraying a single emotion.

Chapter Twelve

Ken was still trying to figure out what to do. She felt as if the Hall Monitors were falling apart, and in the absence of Aiden, it was her job to keep them together. *Where* is *Aiden?* she thought miserably. She liked all the Hall Monitors; did she really have to take sides and make permanent enemies?

The day passed uneventfully with the Hall Monitors all avoiding each other. Ken debated using the group chat but decided against it when she discovered that everyone was too angry to talk. *Are they ever going to cool down?* she mourned.

I'll stay neutral, she decided at last. Her opinion that Ruthie was right to finally speak up for herself was irrelevant; she still cared about Layla and knew better than to alienate Everest and Ming. So, once classes were over, she ambushed Layla and walked with her to Layla's gymnastics practice. "Hey, Layla!"

"Ken?" Layla glanced at her. "Oh, I thought you were Ruthie."

"I just wanted to stop by and watch gymnastics practice. I'm thinking about joining," Ken fibbed.

"Oh, interesting. Yes, I can help out." Layla picked up the pace. "Hurry. Madame Kate is a stickler about being on time."

"Madame Kate?" Ken winced. She had had a bad encounter with Madame Kate when she had called her "Mrs. Kate" and received a lengthy lecture in response. Since then, she had actively avoided the short-tempered and ever-watchful woman. While Madame Kate might have been an excellent coach and a wonderful trainer, she was a rather scary woman to be alone in a room with.

They were running by now. Layla wasn't panting; due to her workouts, she was a talented athlete and thus wasn't out of breath as easily.

"Layla, wait, I wanted to talk to you in private!"

"Can this wait until later?" Layla pushed open the door, and Ken instinctively froze at the sight of Madame Kate, even if it was only a side glimpse of her.

"Um, no. We need to talk *now*."

"Why?" Layla groaned, suddenly pausing in the doorway. "Oh, this is about Ruthie, isn't it?"

Ken took her arm and pulled her out of the room. Due to all the adrenaline and Layla's impatience and Madame Kate on the other end of the door, she decided to cut to the chase and tell Layla bluntly, "You need to apologize to Ruthie."

Layla's face darkened. "Not until she apologizes first."

"Do you like Everest?"

"*What?*"

"Either you really like Everest to avenge his honor for him or this isn't about him at all. I think it's about you and Ruthie."

"It is. I do dislike her."

Ken frowned. "Get real, Layla. You don't dislike her. You dislike how she doesn't go along with whatever you say."

"*What?*"

"Whenever she doesn't say much, you're your usual fun self. But whenever she says something you wish you'd thought of or if she contradicts you, you get so mad at her, especially when she's the voice of reason and you want to do something risky." Ken kept a firm grip on Layla's arm. "Am I right?"

Layla growled. "Let me go, Ken, I don't want to be late." She tugged her arm free and turned.

"Did you know Ruthie thinks you're awesome?"

Layla hesitated, her hand poised over the doorknob.

"She thinks you're really cool, Layla. She told me so herself."

"Then why did she call me a jerk, huh?" Layla turned, her face bright red and angry. "You make it sound like I'm totally cruel and she doesn't know any better, but honestly, I've never had anyone ever talk back to me before. She's always making my ideas sound like trash, and sometimes she right out embarrasses me in front of other people! And she's always tagging along like...like an annoying little sister!"

"That doesn't mean you should be so mean to her! You should tell her how you feel, and I know she'd do her best to stop frustrating you so much!"

Layla was quiet for a moment, then finally said, "Ken, are you really here to watch gymnastics or to convince me to apologize to Ruthie?"

Ken growled, getting frustrated. "Layla..."

"Ken, answer the question."

"Fine, I was lying about joining gymnastics, but only because I'm not flexible at all and I'm way better at soccer," Ken said in one breath. "Look, you're missing the point! I want to get the Hall Monitors back together—"

"Ruthie needs to apologize first," Layla said stiffly. "I've never apologized first before, and I'm not breaking my record now."

Ken was tempted to say something nasty about how spoiled Layla was, although she controlled herself. The last thing the Hall Monitors needed was for the only peacemaker to start fighting too. *You'd think a group of teenage international prodigies wouldn't have high school drama,* she thought grimly. "Fine, but can you not request a roommate referral? It would break Ruthie's heart. She really likes you, and I know she's probably going to apologize soon anyway."

Layla sighed. "Fine. I won't change rooms." Under her breath, she muttered, "I wasn't going to, anyway. Hall Monitor meetings with you two would be much harder otherwise."

"So you do care about the Hall Monitors!"

"Of course I do! Why wouldn't I?"

"Because your argument with Ruthie is literally tearing the entire group apart! Please, Layla, just apologize to Ruthie and forget the whole thing ever happened! If you're honest with her, she'll try to get along better with you, really!"

Layla pursued her lips. "I'll let you know how things go after she apologizes to me. Now I have to go or else I'll be late." With that, she spun around, her hair flipping over her shoulder.

Ken grit her teeth. Who knew the wealthy daughter of the famous Writcroffs, the spoiled sister of two incredible people, and the most popular polyglot at school could be so bratty sometimes?

Yet, as she turned away, she sighed. She had seen real regret in Layla's eyes. Layla was used to being the youngest and most spoiled person in the room, and if even she was being selfish, it was debatably more because of her upbringing rather than her character.

Of course, she wasn't sure if Ruthie was ready to apologize either....

"So what were you so upset about earlier?" asked Rajesh. He handed Ruthie a steaming mug of hot tea.

She breathed in the smell of the tea. "It's complicated, but the short version is that Everest was kind of mean to me—"

"Everest Michaels?"

"Yes, that's him. He was kind of mean, and so I sort of snapped at him—"

"You *snapped* at him?"

Ruthie stared at her tea. "I was kind of a jerk myself, now that I think about it. Layla got defensive for Everest, then criticized me, and so I got defensive and criticized her." Her face grew warm. "I sound like a total jerk, don't I?"

Rajesh laughed. "Oh, Ruthie, you're too hard on yourself. Honestly, you should be glad you're speaking up for yourself."

"Speaking up for yourself doesn't mean bringing other people down," Ruthie muttered.

"I'm sure you didn't do that—"

"I called them both jerks, but *I* was the real jerk," she sighed.

Rajesh cocked an eyebrow. "A moment ago, you were convinced they were the antagonists."

"No, I am," Ruthie said dejectedly. "Me and my big mouth. No wonder Layla doesn't like me and Everest thinks I'm annoying." She brushed some hair out of her face, then said, "Never mind me, we should get to the Calculus project—"

"Ruthie, don't care what Layla or Everest thinks," said Rajesh. "Seriously. I don't think you're annoying at all."

"You don't?" said Ruthie. Curiously, she asked, "What *do* you think of me?"

Everything turned awkward. Rajesh froze, stammered, then finally tried to say, "Well, I think you're—"

"I mean, you're only my math partner, but at least you don't hate me like Layla." Now tears pooled in her eyes. "I really do like Layla, but I guess she just doesn't like me. I don't know if it's my fault or hers. Maybe it's both. And I never really cared much for Everest anyways. He's too arrogant and impatient and just plain mean."

Rajesh, wounded (as he had been both arrogant and impatient in the past), stuck up for his friend: "Everest isn't so bad. Give him another chance."

"I guess I should." Ruthie slumped back in her seat, staring at her tea. "But only after I tell Layla that I'm sorry and that I was the real jerk. But seriously, enough about me. We're here to do a math presentation."

"Of course," stammered Rajesh. Gathering all his courage, he ventured to ask, "Ruthie, so, um, are you free anytime soon?"

"Rajesh, we can't reschedule this!"

"I don't mean rescheduling."

"Then what?"

With truly innocent eyes Ruthie looked at him, completely clueless about what was obvious for any observers—particularly another mathematics project behind them. Ming held his breath, unaware of how tense he was as he listened to Ruthie and Rajesh's conversation.

"I mean..."

"Yes?" prompted Ruthie.

"I mean...to work on that extra credit group project," finished Rajesh lamely.

For an arrogant, loudmouthed astrophysicist, Rajesh seemed to be rather flustered when it came to girls. Somehow Ming was relieved by this.

"Sure, I guess. I wasn't going to do the extra credit because of how much homework I have, but it's fine," yawned Ruthie. "Sorry, I haven't slept very well lately."

"We can finish this another time—"

"No, it's okay, the tea will help. Anyway, let's run through this a few times...."

At around 4:30 PM, Ruthie said goodbye to Rajesh and went to the lounge room to curl up on the comfortable seats and finish her homework. Layla went to the lounge room to stretch after an intense workout and to listen to French audio dramas (she listened to audio dramas in many different languages to keep her linguistic skills sharp). It took ten seconds for Ruthie to notice Layla and for Layla twelve seconds to notice Ruthie. Both had assumed they wouldn't accidentally see each other again.

Ruthie bit her lip, then went for it: "Layla, I'm—" Then she saw Layla's smug, self-assured expression and couldn't finish.

"What?" Layla said impatiently. "You're what?"

"Never mind," muttered Ruthie.

And that was the end of it. Ruthie picked up her backpack and left the room with quiet dignity. Layla watched her go, her heart hardening.

In the hallway, Ken was tempted to bang her head against the wall.

Ming "accidentally" found himself walking beside Ruthie on her way to the music hall. She had reserved an hour-long time slot in a practice room in order to practice her violin. "Ruthie," he said abruptly, surprising her, "Everest has planned a stakeout every night this week. I presume Layla will do something risky of the same nature. Ken is focused on uniting us back together. I propose an agreement; I'll keep an eye on Everest and you keep an eye on Layla."

"That's what we always do, don't we," said Ruthie bitterly.

Ming glanced at her. "Everest is more good-natured than he seems. He will come around eventually."

"I hope so."

"As for Layla, I refuse to get entangled in the lives of fighting teenage girls," said Ming with a teasing smile. "Whatever you two decide to do, do it. Just know that you have as much of a right to speak up for yourself as Layla does. You also deserve as much respect as she does. However, remember that Layla is human." Ming hesitated, then added, "Whatever happens, I will loyally support the Hall Monitors and will always do my best to protect this school, and I hope you will as well."

"Of course I will," promised Ruthie.

"Then we are a team."

Ruthie smiled.

"All of us," continued Ming, with his usual emotionless expression. "Including Ken, Layla, and Everest."

Ruthie's smile turned into a scowl.

"I have said all that I needed to say," Ming simply said, and then he was gone.

At 6:00 PM the next day, which happened to be Wednesday, Ming was practicing his violin in a practice room while Everest was finishing his routine early. Ruthie was curled up in the study café while Layla was listening to Italian music and working on her homework. Ken was practicing indoor soccer with some other students. None of them had spoken to each other since yesterday, and none intended to do so just yet. Things were tense between them all.

Meanwhile, Aiden was fighting for his life.

He hadn't expected to be mugged on the streets of Argentina. While he knew there were high crime rates in certain areas of the town, he was intelligent enough to stick to more public, safer areas. It was why it was such a shock when the man behind him in line at a local market suddenly wrapped an arm around Aiden's neck and whispered in Aiden's ear, "Don't shout or I'll kill you, Ravencrest" in English.

How did he know my last name? Aiden hadn't worn a single identifying item on him; his clothes were standard for a fourteen-year-old Argentine boy. Right away, Aiden knew someone had sent this man after him.

Had he not been a Ravencrest, he would have elbowed the man in the stomach, twisted free, spun around, and delivered a series of punches and kicks that would have left his attacker speechless. Then he would have called the police, endured hours of legal procedures, and gone on his way to enjoy the city, perhaps with Father this time.

But he was a Ravencrest. He was curious. Who would send a hitman after a fourteen-year-old kid? Was someone targeting his whole family now? Maybe the patient had been right—his mother's death might not have been an accident after all. If so, he'd get more answers if he sought to learn more instead of fighting back.

So instead he flicked his fingers slightly and pressed a button on his security tracker, alerting Father that he was in trouble. He remained absolutely motionless as the man—a muscular Hispanic adult with sunglasses and no expression—guided him to a remote place with a motorcycle. He showed little resistance, faking an attempted escape when the man pulled out handcuffs. He made it two steps before the man tackled him rather brutally and handcuffed his arm to Aiden's. Then the man briskly pulled Aiden up with one hand, the other strong hand over Aiden's windpipe, and dragged him back to the motorcycle. One hand holding Aiden in place, the other hand frisked Aiden briefly, checking his pockets and patting him down for weapons.

When the hand traveled to Aiden's pocket where the security tracker had been, Aiden stiffened slightly. The man found Aiden's watch and—much to Aiden's dismay—pocketed it. Thankfully, his attacker never noticed the security tracker that wasn't with Aiden but rather under the attacker's sleeve. The kidnapper said coldly, "Get on the motorcycle." It wasn't a polite request. It was an ultimatum.

"No, thank you," said Aiden. He didn't have a death wish; he just wanted the kidnapper to show his cards—how many weapons did this guy have? And how far was he willing to go? He waited for the threats.

The kidnapper slammed a fist into Aiden's chest, knocking the breath out of the young boy. The handcuff twisted around Aiden's arm and jerked him back to his feet. His kidnapper brought his fist up to send another punch.

"Yes, sir," Aiden nearly shouted, scrambling onto the motorcycle.

The kidnapper displayed little with his body language when he deftly placed duct tape over Aiden's eyes; all Aiden could tell was that his kidnapper was right-handed, observant, experienced, alert, and confident. There was no sign of nervousness or anxiety present from the kidnapper's heartbeat or breathing when he revved his motorcycle, forcing Aiden to hang on.

This is rather risky, Aiden thought, arms wrapped around his captor's stomach as the motorcycle picked up speed. There was a heavy chance he was dealing with a professional criminal.

He memorized the directions they had taken and traced the route in his mind. He was headed for...

There were multiple options, yet one was the most threatening. He forced himself to breathe normally when he felt his kidnapper make the turn that made his intentions clear: Aiden was on his way to an airport.

Images of being gagged and smuggled across the country shook him. It was time to get out, now. There was a fine line between taking chances and intentionally putting himself in too much danger; being smuggled somewhere in the world was not a worthy risk for meeting whoever wanted to kidnap him. To go any further would be suicide.

So he acted.

In his current position, he had to keep both arms wrapped around the man's midsection, or else he would fly off the motorcycle. However, as he let out a groan and slumped forward, it didn't mean he had to hold it too closely. As long as his arms were connected around his kidnapper's torso, he'd be safe. When his arms relaxed, his captor immediately pulled over. "Don't try anything," he said as he shook Aiden a few times. "Wake up or I'll throw you onto the road."

Aiden remained motionless and limp, but he was waiting. Once he had detected enough of his surroundings, he visualized where he was in relation to the man, the motorcycle, and the ground. Though unable to see, he suddenly flipped out of the man's arms and adopted a fighting stance.

He knew right away he was at a disadvantage. Being unable to see his enemy was deadly. Yet he could still use his other senses.

He heard his opponent's breathing, processed the swish of air that accompanied another attack, and used his imagination to paint a picture of what his enemy was doing. As he dodged blow after blow, protecting his face all the while, he was able to punch his attacker in the nose, hit him strongly in the stomach, and kick his legs out. One might say he did fairly well, considering his predicament. That isn't to say he didn't suffer some blows himself, simply that he recovered quickly and fought well for a blindfolded boy. He even heard his opponent go down, and so Aiden turned to run, dragging his captor by the handcuffs.

Then he was tackled again, more brutally than before. This time, he felt the blood from his nose drip into the ground while the agony of his bruised ribs shuddered through him. Vividly, he felt the pain. *Good,* he thought, despite the anguish. If he was still feeling such strong pain, he hadn't yet reached the point where his body would need to send out natural painkillers. So he tried to crawl away.

It didn't work.

The man holding him down was cruel enough to roll the boy over onto his stomach, grab his head, and slam it against the ground. The agony reverberated through Aiden's head, sending a subconscious warning that things were getting worse. Aiden clutched the hand and tried to pry the fingers off.

"Are you trying to kill me?" Aiden screamed. "You need me in one piece!"

"I need you alive, but you don't have to be in one piece," said the man calmly, then punched Aiden's nose, sending explosions of pain through the boy's face. The next blow was for his stomach, breaking his ribs. Three more shook him, broke him, terrified him. Then a hand pressed down on his neck.

All at once, Aiden knew he had no choice but to shout, "FINE! I'm coming, just stop!" He had hoped to at least stall the man for a little longer, to give Father more time to find him. Yet he didn't know if his body could take much more before permanent damage resulted.

For good measure, the man did it again—he slammed Aiden's head down so hard he saw stars. Aiden yelled once in shock and pain, and at that moment, he felt...odd.

Déjà vu, perhaps? No, it was something else...

Stop it!

Stop, please!

He wasn't screaming those words. These were memories, flooding him again.

You can't do this!

Please, don't kill me!

No, not another flashback now—

I don't know anything!

I'll keep my mouth shut, just stop!

Dimly, he was aware of his kidnapper bringing him to his feet, taking him by the elbow to the motorcycle, seating him in the right position, handcuffing his other arm to the attacker's free arm...

Don't hurt me!

Please, I'm just a kid!

He remembered screaming. He wanted to scream now, but no sound came out as he slumped forward, his face against his captor's back.

You won't get away with this!

You'll be sorry, I mean it!

His strength was evading him. His senses were deserting him. He was drowning, something pulling him under, under so deep the light was becoming murky—

Please!

No, don't—

Then he wasn't slumped in the back of a motorcycle, kidnapped, bleeding, and half-dead. He was on the floor, crawling, trapped, as a figure stood in front of him. The figure chuckled. Taunted him. Pulled out a gun.

It was so vague yet so specific. He knew nothing of his location, of the figure, of even himself. Yet he perfectly remembered the figure's words: "Don't get too sad about me killing your mommy, little boy. You'll be joining her soon." The figure pointed the gun at Aiden.

Aiden remembered screaming, the sound of the gunshot, the pain, and then the bliss. The silence that could've stretched on for eternity.

He hadn't fallen from a tree.

He had been shot.

And he had been shot by the same person who had killed his mother.

The truth was electric, shocking him and plunging him back into reality. He was barely present, shaken, torn, by the revelation of this buried memory. So many questions raced through his mind: *Who shot me? And why?*

Practical questions arose, such as, *Why did Father keep this a secret from me? Did he know the truth and want to protect me, or was he trying to hide something?*

But the greatest question that jolted him was, *Who?*

And, as the motorcycle raced closer to the airport and Aiden lay captive against his will, he knew that one day, he would have his revenge.

Chapter Thirteen

"I know none of you want to be here," said Ken, seated comfortably in the little plush chair Layla had given her. "We've been mad at each other for like three days now. I mean, it's Thursday. It's been nearly a week and you guys can't even talk to each other?"

Everyone had their own "corner" or "side" in the room. Aiden had put a few boards up over the entrance to the restricted area pathway. Ken had minimally decorated her side with a few of Layla's lends. All she had brought was her laptop, a toolbox, a swivel chair, and some technological appliances. Ruthie was curled up in a plush beanbag in her corner, which held a small desk with some stationary and a laptop. Layla had her own beautifully decorated corner with a small area that contained an exercise mat, plenty of CDs and audio tapes with headphones, some sketchbooks, and an entire audio-taping area for her linguistic teaching podcasts, plus a chair-and-desk workspace. Everest had a small exercise set, a mini chemistry lab in the corner, some science books he read in his free time, and a small desk and chair. Ming had nothing besides a relatively comfortable chair and desk. Layla had offered him more decorated options, but he had declined. Even Aiden had his own "corner" to himself.

...which was empty, much to Ken's frustration. Everyone was seated in their corner or side, glaring at each other.

"But we still have to focus on what Aiden wants us to do," Ken went on. "I know we're all mad at each other and everything, but come *on*, guys. We're Ravencrest Academy students. Aiden chose *us* to be part of the Hall Monitors, and I'm honored that he did. Every one of us has to fulfill our responsibilities to be part of this."

Layla and Ruthie avoided looking at each other. They had ignored each other as much as possible. From what Ken could deduce, both were sorry, but neither was willing to apologize first. It had annoyed Ken until she finally gave up on the matter and decided they could work it out themselves.

Ken crossed her arms and leaned forward. "So if any of you are too stubborn to uphold being a member here and you don't want to stop the distribution of addictive drugs across the world and you don't care about this school enough to want to help it, then leave. Now."

No one budged.

"We owe it to Aiden and the school to do this," Ken said with determination. "Even though *some* of you need to act like adults." She glared at Layla, Ruthie, and Everest.

Everest snapped, "Can we get to work? I'm tired of you being my mom."

Layla frowned. "That wasn't very nice, Everest."

Everest crumbled a piece of paper in his fist. "I'm tired of being nice and polite and not getting anything done."

"Shut up!" Ken yelled. Her temper was flaring now. "Seriously, what is Aiden going to say when he gets back? He's gone for three days and we all fall apart!" Silence answered her fury. Indignation (or was it shame?) sparkled in the eyes of all the members. Encouraged, Ken went on, "So, about the drugs—"

Ruthie interrupted with, "Where *is* Aiden?"

It was a valid question. Five pairs of questioning eyes turned to Ken.

"I don't know," Ken admitted. "I slipped a note under his door, but he wasn't there. One of the porters said he'd be away for a few days on some trip, but that was yesterday, so maybe he'll be back tonight or tomorrow night. I was hoping we'd have the criminals busted by then," added Ken rather sadly. "But it doesn't look like that's going to happen."

Another solemn silence fell on the group, and now Ken could see that there really was regret in the others' eyes. Although they might not have been willing to apologize yet, they were ready to move on, at least for the sake of the Hall Monitors.

"So," said Ken abruptly, "what *do* we know about the drugs?"

Everest went first: "We know where the drugs are being stored. Ming and I investigated and located them in some unmarked bottles in a small area behind the sink. It had a lock, but after taking fingerprints, Ming poured something on the metal that made it deteriorate by the next day so I could bust it open. With gloves, of course. The fingerprints appear to be blank—"

"We believe the suspect poured glue on his fingers so he wouldn't be tracked," said Ming.

"The drugs were inside," continued Everest. "We put it back, just as it was before, and I borrowed a sensor from Ken—"

"You stole it from my bag," interjected Ken.

"It was for a good reason," Everest defended himself.

Ken gave him a long, hard look. "Just ask next time, okay?"

"Fine," said Everest dismissively. "Anyways, I installed it in place of the lock, so if someone reaches back there and tries to open it, the sensor will detect them and send me an alert. One of us was near the lab at all times the past few days, but so far, no one has come in after hours. I also kept a close eye on anyone who came near the lab during class, even though the teacher's pretty good about keeping an eye on what's happening in there."

"Doesn't Rodriguez clean the lab on Thursdays?" Ruthie asked. "He'll be in there today."

"Yes, but he had no reason to look behind the sink," Everest explained, temporarily forgetting his fight with her. "So far, no one has tampered with the lock, but it's only Thursday. Ming and I think our criminal will try to break in on Friday night."

"You should talk to Norton," offered Layla. "He cleans the lab then. Don't tell him why, just ask him to let you know if he sees anything out of the ordinary."

"No, that's too suspicious," Ken said. "There's a porter stationed in that hallway during the night since all the dangerous chemicals and stuff are there. Tomorrow, during chemistry, one of us should leave something under a desk, like a jacket or something. One of us will be near the chemistry lab at all times. I'll send the monitoring camera link over the group chat, and we can all keep an eye on what's happening. When the alert comes, whoever's nearest will run in to grab the jacket—"

"The scarf," Layla said.

"What?"

"I'll leave a scarf there. I'm always losing them anyway."

"Right," said Ken. "We'll run in to grab the scarf and the porter will come in too since none of us are allowed near the supply closet in the lab without supervision—"

"And we'll catch the bad guy in the act!" Ruthie finished triumphantly. "Er, bad person. Could be a girl."

"We'll need to bring a camera," Everest said, already itching to get started.

"Furthermore," Ming said, instantly silencing everyone. He rarely spoke, but when he did, it was something important. "I implanted a tracker in the pills."

Everest snapped his fingers. "Oh, yeah, I forgot about that!"

"It was nice that you actually asked me for help that time," Ken said. "I was able to modify the tracker so we can always see where the pills are without the criminal ever knowing. Just always *ask me for help instead of stealing my things.*"

"Right, I just didn't want to bother you," Everest said, a little concerned by how fiercely she was glaring at him. As the technology expert on the team, she took her job very seriously.

Before another fight could break out, Ruthie spoke up: "So we have a plan? I can work out a schedule so that one of us is near the lab at all times. I'll pass around the paper, and everyone, please check off the time slots you're available."

"I'll send a picture of the final schedule over the group chat," promised Ken. "I think we have a great plan, guys! See what happens when we don't argue all the time?"

At this reminder, they remembered not to look so excited as if they were a team again. It was back to bored, annoyed, and frustrated expressions on everyone's faces. Ming silently sympathized with Ken. He had tried to speak some sense into Everest, but Everest had been resistant to hearing any opposition ("So you're against me too, Ming?").

"Are we done?" yawned Layla. She pulled on her headphones and opened up her laptop. "I've got homework."

"Wait, we're not finished," Ken said, stopping her. "There's more. I have a theory."

"You mind sharing it with us?" Everest said sarcastically.

"Everest, let her speak," said Ruthie. Then she froze, expecting Everest to yell at her again.

To her surprise, he muttered, "Fair enough." He actually seemed apologetic.

Ken hesitated. "I know this is only a theory, but do you think there may be more than one student involved in this?"

"You think there's a secret conspiracy working to deal drugs," scoffed Everest.

"Even *I* think that's far-fetched," Layla said. "No offense, Ken."

Ken pressed on: "No, I mean, there might be two students involved. One to hide the drugs in the school and the other to take them on the plane. Or maybe one to take it out of the school and one to take it back in. That way, there's less suspicion on either person. I dunno, it's just a theory. Multiple kids might keep Campus Security from catching any one of them."

"It's a good theory, really," said Ruthie. "We should look out for more than one kid. Maybe ask the Dean to offer a lighter sentence if the caught student mentions anyone else involved."

"Great. We all have our orders. Let's get to work."

Ten minutes later, as Ruthie left the room, still jittery from excitement, Everest met her alone in the elevator.

"Ruthie?"

She tensed. "Yeah?"

"I just want to say…sorry. I'm usually a pretty nice guy, but I guess I yelled at you for no good reason. I got really annoyed when Ming acted like I was some criminal, but I did feel bad about it later. You do make good points and raise interesting possibilities, and I'm sorry for treating you so badly." He shifted his weight. "Just because we don't see eye-to-eye doesn't mean I have any reason to treat you like I did. So I'm sorry."

Ruthie nodded. "Yeah. I'm sorry too."

"For what? Speaking up for yourself? You don't do it nearly enough." Everest seemed genuinely relieved she wasn't holding a grudge against him. "I would have been a lot worse, trust me."

Ruthie cocked her head. "Did Ming tell you to apologize to me?"

"He did, but I ignored him. I only apologized because I wanted to. It had nothing to do with him, I swear." He offered her his hand to shake. "We might not be friends, but we may as well be teammates. Deal?"

"Deal," she agreed and shook his hand firmly.

Still in the attic, watching through the camera Ken had set up, Ming finally cracked a relieved smile for a solid half-second. Then it was back to his usual, withdrawn, emotionless face.

Also watching the entire scene on her phone, Ken silently cheered. One battle down, one to go.

Aiden mapped out several escape routes in his mind yet didn't dare risk a single one. He had been beaten badly and could tell that this man didn't care if Aiden was left barely alive. What did this guy have against him? Whatever the case was, he needed to escape. The motorcycle was racing quickly. Would Father be able to find him in time?

A sudden flash of horror struck him. What if Father didn't have his phone?

When had Aiden become a damsel in distress? He had always been able to take care of himself in the past. If Father did find him, he'd be very disappointed in Porter Chan, who would be *very* disappointed in Aiden. And Mother would be…

Forget Mother. Right now, he wouldn't dare think about her.

Think.

His mind felt too fuzzy. His body ached.

You are a teenage prodigy. Forget the pain and focus.

This was only an escape room. A realistic simulation. He knew how to beat the odds. Father was coming for him, he had to be. All he could do now was stall.

How to stall without getting myself killed?

He had hardly finished the thought when he heard his driver swear under his breath. His captor pulled over and slapped Aiden hard across his face. "What did you do!" the man shouted. Aiden was beginning to see hallucinations through the darkness of the duct tape; being deprived of his sight was messing with his mind.

Aiden gasped, overwhelmed with agony. "I didn't do anything," he said, then threw up at the next blow to his stomach. "You're going to kill me!"

"I will kill you one day," said the man, and now it sounded like he was smiling. "One day, Ravencrest, I swear I will finish off your bloodline—or die trying."

"What do you have against my bloodline? What did we ever do to you?" Aiden shouted.

The grip around his neck tightened. "Ask your mommy when you see her again. It'll be soon."

Aiden couldn't breathe. He constricted in the man's grip and convulsed from the pressure in his lungs. He tried to say *Please* as he felt the darkness dimming further. He struggled in the man's grasp, slowly suffocating.

His captor laughed once more. "Tell her that my friend Vladimir Damon said hello. She'll love to hear how her killer had so much fun with her son." He let go of Aiden, letting the boy collapse onto the grass. The man approached Aiden again, who brought up his hands to defend himself. His arms were grabbed. "Have mercy," he begged. "I'm just a kid."

"This, boy, is not mercy," the attacker replied. Aiden felt the metal clasps around his arms come free.

Trembling, Aiden rubbed the circulation into his arms and started to get up. He was shoved back down to his knees. The man grabbed Aiden's wrists as he whimpered, "Please..." For once, he abandoned his pride and allowed himself to be the helpless boy on his knees, begging for mercy.

"It's revenge." His kidnapper offered one last kick, this time to Aiden's nose. The world was red, then black, then gray, and then fuzzy darkness. Aiden clutched his nose, cool blood on his palms.

Aiden protected his head, awaiting the next strike.

Terrible seconds ticked by. Then he heard the voices. A shout for his name. Spanish about the missing boy. Father was there, somewhere in the hazy distance, gently removing the tape from Aiden's eyes. Police officials were asking him questions. Someone was taking his pulse. He thought he saw his mother, running to him. He opened his eyes and she disappeared.

The sudden light burned his eyes, and he closed them again tightly.

Perhaps it was the blinding sun, but Aiden thought he had seen a glimpse of tears in Father's eyes. No, it must have been a mirage.

"I don't feel very well," Aiden murmured. "There was some Contrecoup brain trauma to the back of my skull, thankfully higher than my medulla, so please ask the doctor to check it out...."

"Of course," Father promised, his voice near yet far at the same time. "Whatever you want. Just stay awake." *Are we in an ambulance?*

"I apologize, Father, but I think I'm about to collapse." Then Aiden passed out, his father's strong arms tight around him, sirens his lullaby.

Chapter Fourteen

It was Friday evening. Ken was packing. She was going to visit her mother that weekend. By now, Layla's scarf had been deftly misplaced and the time slots had been distributed. Ken had given everyone instructions on what to do.

The plane left at six. It was five o'clock.

"Maybe we put the sensor on wrong," suggested Ruthie. "I mean, Everest did it without asking for Ken's help, so maybe the criminal already took the pills and is on their way out of here."

"I didn't put it on wrong," Everest said without much conviction. They had eagerly waited for alerts all day long but hadn't received anything yet. The excitement of the plan had faded by now, and he was beginning to doubt their idea.

"I don't get it," sighed Layla. "The whole school was searched last weekend. The pills haven't been tampered with since, as far as I know. And yet our criminal hasn't done anything."

Ken wasn't present at the meeting, so Ruthie tried to offer her support: "This is the last hour before the plane leaves, so our student might make his—I mean, their—move now."

"Isn't Norton supposed to clean the lab at 5:15 PM?" Ming asked when a sufficient amount of time had passed.

Everest slumped back in disappointment. "True. Our student couldn't come from 5:15-5:45 PM because Norton's there, and Norton would've alerted the porters right away. That boy is very passionate about chemistry."

"He's kind of cute," Layla said offhandedly.

"Norton?" Everest said, trying to sound disinterested.

Ruthie tried again to get them on track: "So if something is going to happen, it's going to happen in the next fifteen minutes or in the last fifteen minutes before six."

"Ruthie and I are the only ones who are supposed to be here," Layla said, glancing at Everest. "That's what it said on the time slot."

"Nothing's happened yet, and I've been covering this place all week whenever I wasn't in class or practicing," Everest said with a sigh. "Thought I'd stay here for one last hour."

They were in one of the classrooms near the chemistry lab; all four of them were sprawled across the room in different positions. Ming and Ruthie were the only ones sitting in the student's chairs as they worked. Layla was spinning in the teacher's chair with earplugs in, reading a book for English class while following along with the audiobook version, which was narrated in a different language. Everest was leaning against the wall and wrote on the whiteboard some equations for Biocalculus, the unit they were on this week in RA Biology.

Five minutes passed, then ten, then twenty. Layla put down the book and just listened to the audio version of the story, as she had dyslexia and was starting to get a headache.

Eight minutes later, Everest began to pack up. "Well, see you guys later. I skipped sports practice yesterday, so I'll make up for it now."

"You're leaving?" Ruthie checked.

"That alarm isn't going to go off anytime soon," Everest said. At the exact same time, the sensor alarm went off.

Everest dropped everything and bolted, Ming on his heels. Layla immediately checked her watch—5:43 PM. She looked at Ruthie. "Norton's still in there! Which means there isn't a porter around!"

"Oh shoot," Ruthie said nervously. They had sworn to keep the Hall Monitors a secret and now the guys were about to give all that up. "We need to stay here—we can't be seen with the other two."

Layla frowned as she jumped to her feet. "*I* wanted to bust the bad guys. I had all these dramatic scenes planned!"

"You suspected Isabel, right?" Ruthie said. "You could go check on her, just to give her an alibi."

"Maybe I will," Layla admitted, gathering her books and papers. "Don't follow me." In the next moment, she was gone.

"She always moves so quickly," sighed Ruthie, slumping in her seat. She had plenty more homework to do and she was feeling rather homesick. At least this was a comfortable place to finish her homework. She debated going after Layla as backup. Then again, Layla had specifically told her not to follow her. They weren't exactly friends, but they were teammates. Besides, Ruthie would only slow her down. It hurt a little, but Ruthie understood and stayed focused.

Still, part of her wished Layla good luck—as a teammate, she reminded herself. Not as a friend.

Everest ran to the door, secretly used his security clearance from Aiden to slip in, and dashed to the chemistry lab supply closet. He leaned against the wall next to the closet door and motioned for Ming to get behind him. Then, triumphant music blaring in his mind, he spun around, kicked the door open, and snapped a picture of the student on the floor with the kid's hand still reaching into the secret compartment for the pills. The picture was well-defined and incriminating. It was immediately sent to all Hall Monitor members, thanks to some of Ken's technology.

He was supposed to take multiple pictures, but it only took one for his hands to go numb. "*You*?" Everest gasped as he looked at the shocked figure on the floor.

"*Norton*?"

Layla called Isabel as she strode down the halls. "Hey, Izzy?"

"Hey, Layla! Um, is this urgent?"

"Not really, why?"

"I'm at lacrosse practice right now."

"Oh, I didn't know you took lacrosse!" She received the notification from Everest and held back a gasp when she saw the picture. Like the others, she immediately downloaded it.

"I don't, but Madame Kate thinks I'd be good at it. She wanted me to give it a try. According to her at tryouts, I have a strong arm and an excellent swing." Isabel made a face, as present in her tone. "I think it's kind of boring, honestly, but I'm okay at it and I want to get better."

"I guess it's not going so well so far?" Layla said sympathetically.

Isabel laughed. "Is it that obvious? Yeah, I forgot my lacrosse uniform."

"You need a lacrosse *uniform* for practice?"

"Yep. It's a fancy shirt and shorts," Isabel sighed. "Typical school stuff."

"Wow. We only wear fancy uniforms for gymnastics competitions. Speaking of which, are you going to the one this weekend?" *She already has an alibi, but I may as well get as many reasons as possible for her to be innocent.* Layla was nice like that.

"Don't I wish!" said Isabel. "I've got *so* much work to do. Why'd you call, anyway?"

"Just wanted to get together for a fun Friday night, because why not?" Layla watched her sandals sink into the carpet. "Though if you're busy, I can go."

"Thanks, Layla. Sorry I can't come."

"It's no problem." Layla nearly hung up. On second thought, she said, "Wait, Izzy?"

"Yeah?"

"I can stop by your room and pick up your uniform."

"Oh, no, you don't have to," Isabel began.

"No, no, it's fine. Seriously, it's no big deal." Layla paused as she ran across the Walkway bridge into the Residential Hall building. When she spoke again, she was near Isabel's door. "It's funny, my room's across from yours but on the floor below yours. Can you open the door for me?"

"Well...okay. I'm opening the door now on the app. But make it quick! Just grab my uniform—it must be on my bed—and get here quickly. And thank you *so* much. I totally owe you one," Isabel gushed gratefully, and then her dorm door swung open.

Layla stepped in, hung up, and scanned the somewhat-neat room for Isabel's uniform. There it was, on Isbael's bed. Layla grabbed it and was about to step outside when she suddenly realized there was only one bed. *She must have ordered a single room,* Layla thought. Only a few kids paid the large fee for a room to themselves rather than sharing a dorm with another. Odd, but so what? She turned again to leave.

It was then she realized that both parts of the uniform did not match. Either Isabel was color-blind or she had lost part of her uniform somewhere in her room. *She must have been in a hurry,* Layla surmised as she began to search the room. It had to be here somewhere. She lightly searched the bedroom, not wanting to invade her friend's privacy.

She stepped into the bathroom and cautiously looked around, still hesitant. Finally she decided to go. It was better to not show up with anything than to tell Isabel she ransacked her room and found it. It was simply respect. Layla turned to leave, then caught her reflection and frowned. Was her hair really that messy?

"That's what I get for reading with terrible posture," Layla muttered. She reached through her handbag for her comb or brush and, too late, remembered how Ruthie had borrowed them this morning to attempt to handle her wild hair. Sighing, Layla checked the topmost drawer, having to yank it out all the way. That was where all girls in their dorm kept hairbrushes and combs. She had spent enough weekend sleepovers with the girls in her dorm hall to know this. She combed through her hair, not stopping until it was nice, straight, and neat.

"That's better," Layla decided, put the comb away, and pushed the drawer back in. Unfortunately, it wouldn't go in all the way. She gave it a hard shove and smiled in satisfaction when it finally hit the hollow wood.

She turned and—

Hollow wood?

Something might be behind the sink.

Guilt pricked her conscience; was she really betraying her friend's trust if she looked behind the sink? Layla knew she wouldn't be comfortable if some girl looked around in her bathroom and bedroom, and yet here she was, doing it to Isabel. *I'll get out of here, right after I check this.*

It's my duty as a Hall Monitor.

That was her propelling thought as she opened the cabinet door and checked under and behind the sink. There was a small latch door with a high-security combination lock. She snapped a picture and texted Ken: How do I open this?

Ken responded quickly: You don't. It would take hours to crack through that kind of lock.

Layla frowned, then gave her best karate chop to the surrounding wood. Her arm ached, but the wood splintered enough for her to kick through. Now the guilt rose; she had *broken* the wood?

She'd pay for it later. She made a wide enough hole and used her phone light as a flashlight.

Layla groaned.

Pills.

Similar to what Aiden had shown her. They were the same pills Ming had described: performance-enhancing drugs.

Miserably, she snapped a picture. "Oh, Isabel," she mourned out loud. "I was hoping you wouldn't be involved in this."

She straightened and was about to send the picture to Ken when—

"Drop it." The words came from behind her. Layla looked up in the mirror to see the reflection of Isabel standing in the doorway, eyes furious, voice cold, and threateningly clutching a lacrosse stick.

Ken was finished packing. She stepped outside her dorm, relieved that in the last moments, the Hall Monitors had pulled through and caught their criminal. Norton? Although she wouldn't have suspected him, it made sense. He cleaned the lab on Fridays, so he could've taken the pills from the lab's supply closet and brought them onto the plane.

And yet...something still nagged at her. Norton wasn't allowed unsupervised in that area of the lab any time outside of 5:15-5:45 PM on Fridays, as was his lab cleaning time. No other time was open for a student to sneak in. If Norton had taken the pills from the lab, gone on the plane, and received more, where would he have kept the pills he received? The rooms had been searched.

That's why they were found on the plane, Ken thought in satisfaction.

Excellent. She'd pulled the team together through high school drama to stop an international drug ring that had been operating in one of the most elite high schools on the planet.

And yet…

She was missing something. There was a feeling, an itching nagging her. Someone or something else was involved, and she was missing it.

Ken sighed out loud. "What am I *missing*? It's an open-and-shut case. We did it."

It wasn't convincing enough.

She tried again, this time in her head, as she paced down the girls' dorm hall. *Norton took the pills from the lab during his lab cleaning time, used his medication as an excuse to smuggle them on board, and distributed them around the world.* What an awful thing to do. *Then he—*

How had he received the pills in the first place?

How had the pills made it to that area of the chemistry lab? If he had stored the drugs in his room, the drug dogs would have found them. Yet how had he taken the drugs from the chemistry labs on Fridays, received new ones on Saturday or Sunday, and kept the drugs somewhere undetectable on campus until Friday came around again?

He had to have an accomplice. Someone who could store the drugs in the lab before the search began. Someone he could brush by in the hallway and hand over the drugs to.

Ken whipped out her phone and immediately texted Ruthie her theory. She knew calling would lead to eavesdropping, which would make the Hall Monitors less of a secret.

Ruthie texted back: The search was on Monday night and all students were in their dorms.

So our accomplice has to put the drugs in the lab sometime between Norton's return on Sunday morning and the search on Monday night, Ken agreed, her fingers flying. Who was assigned to clean the lab on Monday night?

For a moment, Ruthie did not respond, even though Ken could tell she was active.

By now Ken was nearing the security gates. The plane was leaving in ten minutes and the security procedures didn't take very long. Ruthie, r u there? Ken texted in a rush. Ive gtg.

It's Isabel.

The text surprised Ken. Isabel? Layla was right. K, send a note under Aiden's door for when he gets back.

"Could you please give me your phone, miss?" asked a porter, and Ken quickly texted a Sry, gtg! to Ruthie before handing it over. Then Ken stepped through the metal detector, knowing that she would be unable to access her phone for the next ten minutes or so.

She was a moment too soon to see Ruthie's next text: Ken—Layla's with Isabel!

"Isabel, how could you?" said Layla, not moving. "Distributing *drugs*?"

"I said put the phone down." Isabel brandished the lacrosse stick threateningly. She locked the door behind her.

"What, you're going to hit me with it?" Layla didn't put the phone down. "Your parents are going to be shocked when they find out."

It was the wrong thing to say. Isabel's eyes flashed fire as she shouted, "You're not telling my mom!"

"I will if you hit me with that thing," said Layla. Another wrong thing to say. Isabel might have looked calm, but her hands were trembling. From rage, Layla knew.

Isabel shouted, "You think you're so smart, don't you, Layla? With your rich kid clothes and hair salon visits and getting in here and upper-class family." She spoke with a snotty accent, then returned to her usual voice. "You have it all so easy for you, and I bet right now, all you care about is all the fame you're going to get from this."

"Are you kidding me? I'm not doing this for the fame. I'm doing this because you are distributing dangerous drugs that skew athletes' performances," Layla said back, her voice rising. "It's morally wrong, and I can't believe you'd do this."

"You think I *wanted to*?" screamed Isabel. "You think I had a *choice*?"

"To not be part of a drug ring? Yes, Isabel, I think you had a choice."

Isabel kicked something. "See? What did I tell you, Layla? You're rich and soft and it's all black and white to you. Have you ever *worked* for something? Ever been forced to be someone you're not just to keep your family safe?"

"I have no idea what you're talking about, and frankly, I don't care," said Layla. "I'm sending these pictures to Campus Security, so you can stop your sob story act."

Isabel threw the stick at Layla. It bounced off the tile above Layla's head sickeningly hard. Isabel didn't even seem human when she screamed, "I'm not letting you tell anyone!"

"What are you going to do?" taunted Layla unsympathetically. She waltzed past Isabel's lunges. Confidently, Layla grabbed the door handle and—

Oh no. It was locked.

Layla's confidence withered. She reached for her phone and—

Isabel held it up. "Looking for this?"

Layla crossed her arms. "Fine. What are you going to do to me? Kill me or hurt me over the head with something sharp? Oh boy, your parents are *not* going to like that. Not to mention your criminal record or your future. So what's it going to be?"

Isabel was chagrined. "I—I don't know. I can't let anyone find out. Or else he'll…" She was lost in thought now.

"Who's *he*?"

"VD, who else?"

"Wait. He told you to do this?"

"No, I thought it up on my own." Isabel glared back. "Yes, Layla, VD told me to do this."

"And you *agreed*?" Disgust was clear in Layla's voice.

Isabel clenched her fists. "Will you at least *listen* before you judge me?"

Layla leaned back. "Fine. I'm listening."

"My stepdad pays for my tuition. He paid for my single room, my clothes, everything. And he looks after my sister and mom at home."

"How cute," said Layla sarcastically.

"He's not a good person, Layla. He hits my mom and the only reason he pays these things is so I can send him money. He says I owe him for not tossing me out on the streets. He's not my real dad, and I hate him!" Tears filled Isabel's eyes. "He's terrible, but he's the only thing keeping my sister and mom from starving. My mom doesn't know how to speak, read, or write English, and she doesn't want to leave my sister alone with my stepdad, so she's stuck at home. So I left, studied really hard, took the entrance exam, and worked on my application to get into this school. Coming here was the only way I could leave home and work out an arrangement to take care of my family until I was legally old enough to grab my mom and sister and run. I've skipped a grade or two, so I have until I graduate to worry about them. I was hoping to grab a job with these credentials and get a place for us to stay so we'd never have to worry about my stepdad again. Right now, my neighbor checks on them daily and texts me to make sure they're okay. I've *got* to do well at this school for them. I *have* to."

Layla felt a little sorry for Isabel, but not enough. "And this is relevant because..."

"VD threatened me. Said he'd talk to my stepdad and let him know some interesting information about my mom and sister. He said he'd get my family killed!" Isabel started crying. "I didn't believe him, but he had a picture of my mom and sister sleeping in the basement. He said if I told anyone, he'd shoot them next time."

Layla eyed Isabel's phone. If she could get her hands on that thing, she could text Ken and get the door open.

"All you care about is getting famous, isn't it?" said Isabel between sobs. "You're such a jerk, Layla."

"Isabel, if I get out of here and tell everyone the truth, you'll get the help you need. You *and* your family. I...I really do want to help you, I promise." To her own surprise, Layla found that she was sincere in telling this. Layla took a hesitant step toward the younger girl.

Isabel didn't believe her. She took a big breath and finally worked up enough coherence to say, "I don't think so. You can't tell anyone about this, and if you do, I'll—I'll email VD. Tell him *your* name, and what you're doing."

"You wouldn't." Layla felt cold.

New pools of tears sprung up in Isabel's eyes. "I don't want to."

To know that Isabel wouldn't wish VD's threats on a girl she was furious at...it made Layla's heart ache, despite herself.

"So are you letting me out of here?" Layla said hopefully.

"You won't tell anyone?"

Layla crossed her fingers behind her back. "Nope."

"What's that you're holding?"

Uh-oh.

Layla tried to cover it, but Isabel wrenched it free in one stride. "A recorder! You had it in your sleeve!"

For once in her life, Layla couldn't say anything. She just stammered.

Isabel's eyes narrowed. "So you *were* going to tell someone. I knew I couldn't trust you."

"So what are you going to do?" challenged Layla.

Isabel bit her lip, thinking. Then she grabbed her phone.

"What are you doing?" Layla asked as Isabel texted something. A shot of fear raced through Layla. "Are you texting VD?"

"No," said Isabel. Her face paled slightly, then she swallowed hard as if steeling herself when she looked up at Layla. "You're not going anywhere just yet."

"What are you waiting for?"

"You won't remember any of this soon."

For the first time, Layla remembered how skilled Isabel was at chemistry. With a student like Norton on her side, there was a good chance the two of them would whip up something that could make Layla forget the past hour. Layla glared back at Isabel, a sliver of fear dancing in her heart. "So," Layla said. "What are the side effects?"

"Only stuff you deserve," Isabel said, but Layla saw how tightly Isabel's fingers clutched her phone. Layla could see the pain in Isabel's eyes as she said, "I don't want to do this, but I have to."

"If I suffer permanent brain damage, whose fault is it going to be?" Layla sounded calm and not the least disturbed.

She was only making this worse for Isabel, whose face turned even paler. "Shut up!"

Layla smirked and took a step closer. "Really, Isabel? If I end up in the hospital forgetting my own name, whose fault will it be?"

"I said to *shut up*!"

Layla was only a few feet away from Isabel and glared directly into Isabel's eyes as she said, "The human mind isn't meant to be turned on or off. Drugging me isn't going to help matters. In fact, it might make things worse. Raise even more suspicion. As far as I see it, you only have one choice: to turn yourself in."

"You're really enjoying this, aren't you?" screamed Isabel, fiercely looking into Layla's eyes. At that moment, as Isabel was too angry to even speak any more, Layla made her move.

She lunged for the phone and pulled it out of Isabel's grasp, shoving the other girl aside and immediately dialing Ken's number as swiftly as she could. Yet Isabel had quick reflexes, and as she reached to get the phone back, she sharply jabbed Layla in the stomach.

In a moment, both girls were wrestling for the phone. Layla barely reached it in time, dialed, and called, shouting, "Ken?"

No one answered.

(Ken was going through boarding security procedures right now and didn't have the opportunity to answer her phone. Of course, Layla didn't know this.)

In the next moment, the phone was knocked out of her hands. They were both reaching for it, fighting and pushing each other aside in a flurry of panic, and so neither noticed as the door swung open and a figure stepped inside.

Everest was too shocked to do anything other than gape at the guilty boy on the floor. "Norton? *You're* the drug dealer?"

"I'm not a drug dealer!" the younger boy insisted. "I'm only distributing them and—and how did you—"

"It's a long story," sighed Everest. "Are you working alone?"

"Yes," Norton said, trying to pull his hand out. He had gotten his fingers caught between the secret compartment door and the inside of the cabinet. His face was twisted in pain. "I'm stuck! Everest, come over here and help me."

"You know you're in serious trouble, right?" Everest said, walking over and kneeling beside him. Despite himself, all he could ask was, "Why would you be part of this?"

"I didn't have a choice," said Norton, staring at the floor. "Seriously, Everest, my fingers are going numb!"

Everest reached over to help him, grimly accepting the fact that his little chemistry-obsessed friend was a criminal. They definitely needed to talk. He wanted answers. As he helped free Norton's fingers, he asked, "Tell me, why did you do this? What did you mean when you said you didn't have a choice?"

Norton rubbed the feeling back into his fingers. He looked up at Everest and quietly said, "Everest?"

"Yeah?"

"Sorry about this."

Everest barely had time to react as Norton slipped something out of his sleeve, inserted a needle into Everest's arm, then sprang to his feet and ran. Leaping into action, Everest grabbed Norton's arm, then stopped in confusion as he felt his powerful grip go slack. He looked up at Norton, but the world was already turning blurry as he slumped to his knees.

The chemistry storage closet door swung shut, and he thought he heard Norton's breathing catch as if the younger boy was holding back tears as he ran. The footsteps echoed away as Everest mumbled, "Wait, Norton..."

But it was too late. The world grew hazier and his eyes grew drowsier until he was drifting, lying on his back on a light raft in a never-ending ocean, confused, content, and oh-so-sleepy....

Ken impatiently bounced on her toes. Her mouth was already watering at the thought of the delicious food waiting for her at home; her mother was an amazing cook who had promised to cook her daughter plenty of welcome-home dishes every time she visited. "Am I good?"

The Porter reviewing her documentation nodded. "You're fine."

The alert, focused dog sitting by his side stared at her. She gave it a friendly wave and tried to pat it on its head. Porter Craig stopped her. "Don't." The dog glared at her suspiciously, barked once, and growled threateningly. Ken stepped back. *So much for the cute puppy Mom never let me have.*

Finally, the porter gave her papers and phone back to her. She started to walk away when the same porter stopped her again and said, "Mackenzie, is it?"

"Um, yes. It's me. I'm going to be late—"

"The headmaster wants to see you."

She stopped, startled. "*Now*? But I'm about to get on a plane!"

"The headmaster wants to see you...in Argentina."

"In *Argentina*?" Now she was bewildered. "But I was going to see my mom! Why didn't he tell me this earlier?"

"It was, uh, abrupt. Something to do with his son."

Ken growled. Aiden could have emailed her, could have called her, could have left a note under her door, could have frickin' joined her group chat, but *no*, he had to take away her trip to her mom and get the headmaster to—

"He thinks Aiden Ravencrest is about to die."

Well. That changed things.

Ken stumbled and stammered. "Are you *sure*? But...why me?"

"The headmaster knows about what happens in Ravencrest, miss," said Porter Craig. "And recently he's been keeping a close eye on his son, though he does his best to stay out of things. He's more of a father than he's ever been, I'll tell you that much. He knows about the security team Aiden put together and he knows that you have taken over since Aiden left. Furthermore, he suspects..."

"What?" Ken asked.

"Ah...never mind. My point is that he requests your presence in Argentina as soon as humanly possible."

"Okay," Ken agreed, trying to catch her breath. Aiden was *dying*? That was ridiculous! The kid was invincible! She had seen his self-defense and it was clear he basically knew everything—

Maybe his invincibility is what got him. He thought he could handle something he couldn't.

For now, she agreed to get on the plane to Argentina. Ken glanced mournfully at her phone. *Looks like I'm not getting Mom's home-cooked meals any time soon.* Then her gaze turned to the outside. *Am I really the only person at Ravencrest who was called about this? The headmaster and me—that's everyone who's coming? No one else is alerted about this kid's possible death?*

For the first time, she remembered Aiden's mother. Did he miss her? Aiden was incredible, but he was still a kid. He had to miss his mom. There were a lot of things he hadn't told her, things he hadn't told any of them.

Her heart ached. *Oh, Aiden, what have you gotten yourself into?*

"What is going *on*?" said Ruthie.

Layla jumped to her feet and pointed at Isabel. "She did it, Ruthie! She's working with—"

Isabel shoved a hand over Layla's mouth and said to Ruthie in a deadly cold voice, "Get out of here now or you'll regret it. I don't want to hurt you, Ruthie."

Ruthie blinked slowly. Then she turned to leave.

And instead closed the door behind her.

"What do you think you're doing?" growled Isabel.

"I promise I'm not here to get you in trouble or to blame you," swore Ruthie. "I'm here to find out the truth. We can work through what to do about it together. I *swear*, Isabel, I'm on your side." She held her hands up in surrender, showing open palms, and looked at Isabel with large, trusting eyes. She tilted her head, kept eye contact, and mirrored Isabel's body language, all sending subconscious body language signs that she was trustworthy.

Isabel hesitated yet stood firm, her hand over Layla's mouth. "Seriously, get out of here!"

"It'd be worse for you if I did," said Ruthie sadly. "If I kept my mouth shut, you'd keep doing this, and you'd just lose more of yourself and have to spend the rest of your life looking over your shoulder. I wouldn't wish that on anyone. Please, Isabel, I know there's more to the story. I won't tell anyone if you want me to, but I think it's best if we sit down and talk. I'll try to help you, but I won't do anything without your permission. I *promise*."

Isabel knew Ruthie's reputation for never lying. Ruthie didn't make promises lightly. A moment passed, and then Isabel asked quietly, "What about Layla?"

"What about me?" Layla said, shoving free.

"Are you gonna keep your mouth shut?" Isabel said, her voice rising again.

Ruthie quickly spoke up: "She will unless you tell her otherwise. If she doesn't, you can tell Madame Kate not to put her on the Varsity Dance team."

Layla's mouth dropped open in protest, but a glare from Ruthie silenced her.

Isabel looked between both of them. Her face crumpled. She put her phone on her desk, sat on her bed, and hugged her knees. "Fine."

Norton raced to the door and reached for it, his mind spinning. He had to warn Isabel, delete all his contacts from his phone, and pretend to have been in his room the whole day. He'd never forgive himself if Isabel got hurt because of this. One day, he'd find VD, and he'd be the hero. He'd bring him to justice, and then all that he'd done wouldn't matter anymore. It wouldn't matter that he had locked away a boy who had befriended him and hadn't treated him like some boring nerd. What he'd done wouldn't matter one day. He fought back the tears that dared to defy him. He had to get out of here.

He never saw it coming.

A silent figure stepped out of the darkness like a phantom. There was a swift motion, and then somehow Norton was on his back, confused, the breath knocked out of him. His senses returned as the figure grabbed something from the wall—a *fire extinguisher?*—and with perfect aim, strength, and velocity, threw it at the window. The alarm went off as a porter rushed inside. Before Norton could move, the porter grabbed his arm while the silent figure slipped into the darkness behind the porter. As Norton stammered out explanations, he realized that he was holding his key to the chemistry lab supply closet. The porter's eyes shot to the supply closet.

In the closet, Everest stirred and yawned. When the door swung open, he mumbled something in confusion, unaware of the incriminating picture dimming on his phone.

In the silence that followed, Norton quietly began to cry.

Chapter Fifteen

"You're going to be late!" Mother called from the docking area. "Hurry, Raisin!"

Aiden groaned. Did she have to call him that in front of everyone? Despite his embarrassment, he darted past the people streaming by, expertly maneuvered his bag around, and slid next to Mother like an athlete sliding into home base. "Made it!" he said as she wrapped an arm around him, holding him close as the captain called some announcements and the boat began its journey.

"Did you get all the science equipment?" Mother said, her long hair flying in the breeze. Usually she had it tied back somehow, but today, it was as wild and free as she was.

"All of it." Aiden's eyes were bright as he bounced. "This is going to be the best birthday ever! Thank you so much, Mother!"

"Well, I knew you'd like this cruise," laughed Mother. "Just steer clear of the rest of the scientists and I'll make sure you can come along on all the dives."

Aiden was too excited to stand still. "Let's play hide-and-seek! I want to practice recall to strengthen my cognitive map. Latent learning can be very helpful, like you said."

"More than you know. It's saved my life on a couple of occasions." His Mother was always saying mysterious things like that.

"When?"

"That, my boy, is a story for another time." Mother swung him around as they headed for the side of the ship facing the sunset. "Right *now*, let's get some Italian ice cream and watch the sunset. I have seen many marvelous things before, but the view of the sunset from the ocean is something else."

Aiden agreed. He didn't see any other nine-year-old boys on the ship, but he didn't mind. This time with his Mother was better than playing Legos with some other child on board. No one his age seemed to be as interested as him in science or math or art or history or—

"Mother?" he asked abruptly while he was licking his ice cream.

"Yes, Raisin?" Mother said affectionately as she dabbed some ice cream off his chin with a napkin.

"Do you love Father?"

Mother was caught off guard, he could tell, but she just finished wiping off the ice cream dripping down his chin and sat back with an, "Of course, dear."

"Then why do you both fight so much?"

"We disagree often," Mother said with a sigh. "And I'm sorry we argue so often." Although his parents both tried to refrain from arguing whenever Aiden was around, he was a smart boy. He knew.

"Then why did you get married?"

"Your father charmed my father, who was the headmaster at the time. My father and I were quite close, and he thought your father was the only man alive who was good enough for me. And I must admit, your father charmed me as well. My mother was skeptical but considered him barely good enough." Mother closed her eyes as if transported to another time and place. "This was years ago, mind you."

Aiden understood. Father could be charming when he wanted to be. Aiden had seen enough photographs and old videos to know how handsome, good-natured, and perfect Father had seemed years ago. Now Father was reserved, strict, and focused, and wasn't much of a father. He and Aiden had a mutual understanding: they would stay out of each other's way unless necessary. Father provided Aiden's food, water, tuition, and spending. Aiden gave Father his stellar grades, incredible contributions to the world, and a promise to stay out of Father's way.

In the early days, Aiden vaguely remembered Mother and Father spending much time together. Father always knew how to make her blush.

"It mattered who I married. As I was thought to be the only daughter of the Ravencrest family, I was to become the headmaster of Ravencrest, which I disliked since I didn't want to always be in the spotlight. I wanted to dedicate my life to science, not focus on the very large responsibility of running Ravencrest Academy. Thus, the man I married would be the new headmaster. I really did hate the unofficial tradition of keeping the Headmaster in the Ravencrest family." Mother's face twisted, almost in pain. "Some of my friends were only friends so they could be the next headmaster. Yet your father was different. He...he loved me before he knew who I was. He understood me. He really cared. My parents liked how he took care of me, back when they were deciding who would be the next headmaster—and, more importantly to them, my future husband."

"What do they think of him now?" Aiden said. He thought back to his grandparents, graying, frail, yet always gentle and loving.

Then he remembered.

"Oh," he said quietly. "Sorry, I forgot."

His mother smiled at him kindly, yet Aiden saw the pain she hid. "That's alright. I forget sometimes too."

"Does Father miss them?"

"Oh, very much. He was so sad when they passed. He hid it very well, but I knew how sad he was. I believe he was very close with them." Mother pursed her lips. "But it doesn't hide how different he became when they left. Once he was secure in his role as headmaster, married to me and father of you, he buried himself in his work and considered it more important than either of us. He does care about you and me, Aiden, but I just *hate* how he considers his work to be more important than spending time with either of us! He may be a headmaster and academic scholar, but he is also a husband and father!"

Aiden was shocked at the ferocity in his mother's voice. She rarely used the word *hate.*

Mother saw Aiden's face and sighed. "I'm sorry. I shouldn't have yelled or said those things about your father. I promise you that your father loves you. You should have seen him the day you were born. It was the closest he ever got to crying. He loves you very much but doesn't know how to express it. The two greatest loves of his life are us both and his work."

"That's three," Aiden pointed out.

"True. But your father and I fight often about so many things that sometimes I wonder if it's just you and his work. Nonetheless,"—here Mother seemed to remember something—"I was very wrong to speak about him behind his back. He loves us and works very hard for us both."

Aiden was motionless as he absorbed this information. "So...*do* you love him, Mother?"

"Love him?" Mother laughed. "I love you both more than anything else in this world." With that, she grabbed him and shook him playfully. "I promise you that, Aiden. You two matter most to me in this world."

It was odd for Mother to say so. She was wealthy, successful, and a respected scholar. Yet it was clear she was willing to give everything up for her family.

"Mother?"

"Yes, Raisin?"

"Can I get more ice cream?"

"Of course!" Mother laughed again, bouncing to her feet. She gave her son a hug and together they walked to get more ice cream.

Her phone buzzed while they were waiting. She glanced at it and a shadow of something crossed over her face for a moment. Then it was gone. Putting her phone away, she looked at the flavors. "Do you want something new or something old?"

Aiden thought about it. "Something new."

It was ironic because right then and there, he wanted to forever keep this something old, this moment of being together with his mother, enjoying the world, sampling it all, and leaving things better than they were before.

He never wanted things to change.

Never.

And as he snuggled close to his beloved mother, he knew that as long as Mother was there, things would always turn out all right.

He was drowning. There was no lifeguard, no life preserver, nothing to help him. She had been taken, and he was left alone, suffocating in grief.

He tried to swim. He kicked his legs and arms, but the water was too strong. It was dark and murky, and as he thrashed in its grip, the shadows tightened around his throat, squeezing his heart until he never thought he'd breathe again. He felt so lifeless, hopeless, alone.

He tried to scream, but no sound came out. The pain, the grief, and the frustration were overwhelming as he was pulled lower and lower into the depths.

There was nothing left. The darkness was too strong. The light was gone.

All gone.

He couldn't scream as the flashbacks descended.

All gone away.

Passed away.

Never coming back.

No longer here.

Gone.

Finished.

He was reading a book and he couldn't turn the page. His fingers were lead. The book dissolved in his hands and a mirror shimmered so he was face-to-face with himself. His grief and haunted features shook him. He looked wild, like a monster.

I want to go home, cried Aiden in the silence. *I want my mom.*

But there was no home to go to and no mother to comfort him. He was drowning and there was no one to help him. Where was up and where was down? He couldn't breathe, his lungs were burning, he was burning in grief, blazing, falling, and there was nothing left.

Nothing.

Never again.

Lost.

Never coming back.

No longer here.

Gone.

Finished.

Aiden died that day.

The innocent, naive boy who played pranks and games in the halls and experimented with the world and took it all in with wide, trusting eyes was no longer here. The child called Raisin who watched from the sidelines and cheered on the good guys was gone. The little boy who was once Aiden was finished.

That same day, Aiden Ravencrest was born.

A vague reality pulled from a distance. He couldn't see it. It was too cold, too dark.

A sliver of light danced, a glimmer of warmth. He followed it.

It was moving up. He followed it, the darkness curling around him, trying to pull him down as he swam up, the light his only solace as he was closer and closer and—

He broke through the surface and gasped.

Aiden Ravencrest woke up and gasped.

His father was holding his hand and standing very still. When Aiden opened his eyes, Father gasped as well. Father took a shaky breath and said in a rather weak voice, "How do you feel?"

"Odd."

The memories filtered in, slowly refilling his mind. He closed his eyes to speed up the process. His reasoning, skill, talent, and memory all returned to some extent. "I'll get the doctor," Father said, already on his feet. He squeezed Aiden's hand once and disappeared into the corridor. Aiden remained listless and waited for his body to recover.

When Father returned, his son was lying in the bed with dark, almost unrecognizable eyes. The doctor and some nurses began fussing over the boy as his father watched from the corner with concern.

His son looked at them all in bewilderment. "Father? What happened?"

"You had a car accident," said Father after a pause. "I'm sorry, my son."

"Where's Mother?"

Father looked stricken, then cleared his throat. "She, um, she's…she's not quite here."

"Where is she?"

"I'm sorry, Aiden, but your mother died over a year ago."

"What?" Aiden gasped. His eyes widened and tears filled them. "How? I—I don't remember anything!"

"What do you remember?" Father said gently yet firmly.

"I remember Ravencrest and everything," Aiden said impatiently. "But I don't remember how I got here. My most recent episodic memory was injured, so I must have injured my hippocampus. The lights in here are much too bright." He winced. "I must have a concussion."

"You do," sighed the doctor in Spanish with an Argentine accent.

"Father, why am I in Argentina?"

"It was a research trip," Father said solemnly. "I wish I was in your place, my son. We shouldn't have taken the car—we should have walked, as you suggested."

"I don't remember any of this," groaned Aiden. His head ached mercilessly. "When we get back to Ravencrest, I'm going to write out a recovery plan to stimulate my mind and keep it working while it recovers. I've already got some ideas for rehab, judging by which parts of my body hurt the most. I shouldn't see a computer screen while my mind recovers, so could you please order some paper and pencils for me to write this out?"

"Store it in your memory for now," said Father briskly. "We'll be home soon." He said some things to the doctor in Spanish while Aiden tested his strength.

Soon they were in a hotel while Father made some calls. "You're probably not up to traveling just yet," Father said. "I'll give you some time to rest and we'll get you home soon."

Aiden stretched and began to write out his plan.

Father hesitated, lingering in the doorway. "Do you remember this happening…before?"

"Of course. I had an accident before, right? Fell from a tree and received a concussion. Repeated brain trauma can be very serious," Aiden said as he continued writing. "I'll be careful from now on."

Father agreed half-heartedly and left.

Aiden didn't stop writing until he heard the footsteps go far enough away. Finally, after Father was long gone, he allowed himself to let out one long breath.

Father had lied to him.

Again.

His curious experiment had succeeded. Pretending not to remember his accident had reinforced what he wanted to know: whether Father would lie to him or not. But why lie? Aiden had not discovered any incriminating information. Yet what if Father thought Aiden had? Right away, Aiden knew Father couldn't be trusted. The man was clearly hiding something.

It was sad. Heartbreaking, even. For the first time, he had felt a connection to his father. And now VD had taken that away from him.

VD. Vladimir Damon.

He was the man behind the kidnapping. He must have been the man who caused the first concussion. Most of all, according to the man who had nearly killed him just now, VD killed his mother.

VD killed Mother.

A measure of hatred ran through Aiden's body; how he detested the very name of Vladimir Damon. Revenge swarmed Aiden's mind and ate at his heart. He would hunt down the man who had murdered Mother. He would make him pay.

Aiden Ravencrest swore revenge that day. His dark eyes burned. He knew the truth now. He would avenge his mother's death. He would let no one stop him. This was what VD had done to him.

And Vladimir Damon would pay for it.

Chapter Sixteen

"Knock, knock," said Ken at the door.

Aiden jolted. It was late by now, and some Spanish movie was flickering on the screen while he was practicing some mental exercises. "Ken! Why are you here?"

"Your dad wanted me to come. I missed visiting my mom because of it." Ken frowned. "But forget about that. You feelin' alright? I was told you almost died." She took in the cast, the gauze, and the bandages. "Wow. When your dad says you got beaten up, he's not kidding."

"Fencing match went awry," lied Aiden.

Ken raised an eyebrow.

"I prefer that myth," Aiden admitted. "It was a car accident."

"Car accident? With all those bruises?" Ken asked.

"Glass flew everywhere, I'm assuming. Ironically, I have no recollection of the accident." One day, he'd tell her the truth. It wouldn't be today, since he knew Father must be listening. How else would he know to invite this girl, out of all the other people he could have invited? Father must have been watching him, keeping a close eye nearby. He made a mental note of this.

For now, he kept his voice casual and pretended to be his usual self as he spoke: "Now, tell me about the drugs."

"Well, we had some...complications."

"Explain."

"An argument or two. Or three. Or an entire breaking up of all five of us, three refusing to speak to one another."

Aiden sighed. "I'm disappointed, but I suppose this was to be expected—"

"We still found the drug dealers though," Ken interrupted.

"Oh." Aiden paused. "Are things still rough between our team members?"

"No," Ken assured him. "We got it all straightened out." *Almost, anyway.*

"Excellent! I'm open to hearing the names of our caught criminals." Aiden sat back and gestured. "Please, take a seat."

Ken obeyed, yet she was hesitant. "You sure you're alright? There's something different about you."

"What do you mean?"

"You're...kind of dimmed somehow. Darker. I don't know how to explain it, but you've changed. I mean, you're not as *you*. It's all like a mask now." Ken squinted. "I don't know how to explain it, just...are you sure you're alright?"

It was odd how well she understood him. He usually hid himself pretty well. Nonetheless, he focused on the situation. "I'm perfectly fine, and I'd prefer you'd stick to the point instead of trying to psychoanalyze me," he said with uncharacteristic sharpness.

Ken could only blink in surprise in the silence that followed this statement.

Without apologizing, yet in a softer tone, Aiden spoke again: "So, tell me. Who were our criminals?"

Ken answered, "Isabel Garcia and Norton Russel." Over the ride here, she had been fully updated on the entire story. "Norton received the drugs and hid them in the chemistry lab supply closet. He smuggled them onto the plane by mixing them with his real medication and transporting them from the supply closet during his lab cleaning times. When he returned from the weekend trips, he'd give his drugs to Isabel, who would store them in her room until it was her turn to clean the chem lab on Monday evenings. Then she'd transfer the drugs to the supply closet there. Norton said he gave her some of the drugs after they searched everyone; he wanted to make sure they had a backup plan in case the drugs in the supply closet were found, and he knew they wouldn't search everyone again, at least for a while."

"Both students confessed to everything?"

"Yes. Isabel and Norton gave a full confession. And here's the clincher: they hadn't been doing it of their own free will."

"Someone forced them to distribute drugs? Let me guess: VD?"

"How did you know?"

"Don't ask questions," Aiden said briskly. "How did you all figure this out?"

Ken continued, "Well, I figured out how Norton was smuggling the drugs to and from campus, though I didn't know how he received them or that it was even him. Everest and Ming found the drugs in the chemistry lab. Then we figured out a plan to trap the bad guy. It was kind of risky, so we all met up and worked together to capture them. In the process, while Everest confronted Norton and Ming got a porter when Norton knocked out Everest."

"Norton knocked out Everest? It must have been with a drug or chemical mixture. Aren't the side effects usually dangerous?"

"Maybe, but the doctor's making sure Everest will be all right. Besides, Norton was crying about it. He's one of the youngest kids here; I'm sure he didn't want to hurt Everest."

"Everest is a survivor. He'll make it."

Ken squinted. "Why do you say that?"

"I know of his background. Now please continue. What happened after Norton was caught? Isabel was also caught, I presume?"

"Layla went to find an alibi for Isabel but ended up finding the pills instead. Isabel and Layla had this big confrontation, which is when Layla found out that Isabel was being forced by VD to play her part or else her family would suffer. Isabel was trying to keep Layla from talking—she was going to use the same drugs that Norton did, I think—when Ruthie stepped in, calmed her down, and even got Isabel to trust us and tell us everything. We got full confessions from both of them, and the Dean of Education is figuring out their punishments right now. Since he knows about the VD person, Campus Security's gonna try to figure out who that is. I found out about all this on the plane ride here." She paused. "My dad paid for the WiFi on the plane, by the way. He gave me his credit card."

Aiden's face was expressionless. "Admirable."

"What is? My dad's credit card? I mean, it does have a *lot* of money on there—"

"No, that you all managed to work together so well despite your arguments. It's admirable."

"Thanks. I'll tell them you said that." Ken hesitated. She wasn't sure how to act somehow. Things felt awkward between them. "Is there anything else?"

"No. I'll be back home soon, so I'll see you then," Aiden said. "I would see you out, but I need to rest to heal faster."

"Of course." *She sounds like Father: all hesitant and unsure of what to say or do.* Ken walked to the door, placed a hand on the door handle, then stopped and turned back. "Aiden?"

"Yes?"

"What *really* happened to you?"

"Nothing. I'm perfectly fine."

"You're lying."

"What makes you say that?"

"I just have this feeling."

"Perhaps one shouldn't rely on feelings so much," Aiden muttered under his breath. "They tend to be one's weakness."

"Are you talking about me?" She sounded more concerned than confused.

"No." Aiden looked at her with an unnerving, emotionless expression. "Now leave, before Father gets suspicious."

"He's watching us?"

"He may be if we keep talking for so long," Aiden lied; he knew Father was watching them. To humor Father, Aiden had ignored the tiny camera in the television antenna. "Now leave or else I will call a porter to forcefully escort you out."

"You never used to say things like that before," Ken said, sounding a little hurt. "Are you *sure* you're alright—"

"What are you, my *mother*?" Aiden scowled. There was a bitterness in his voice that Ken had never heard before. "Leave! Now!"

She left wordlessly. As she walked down the halls, Aiden heard her quietly say to herself, "What just *happened*? Is he okay?"

He wasn't entirely sure himself.

And honestly, he didn't care anymore.

He remembered to apologize when he saw her again. He hadn't meant to be so rude to her, he hadn't been feeling very well, and she had kindly given up her trip to her mother to make sure he was all right. Logically, if she was to be a good investment—and that was all he let himself think of her as—he had to maintain a good relationship with her. All these reasons combined, as well as a reason he refused to acknowledge, pushed him to apologize to her. She forgave him easily, seeming more concerned than angry. He called a Hall Monitors' video conference and briskly congratulated them all on a job well done. He agreed to speak to the Dean and ensure Norton and Isabel got off with fair punishments, considering how they acted under duress. Besides, it was better for the school's reputation. Finally, he mentioned that they'd certainly have to keep an eye on this mysterious VD.

He hung up, sat back in his plane seat, and did some of his self-prescribed exercises. *The security software I'll install will track any suspicious activity, not stop it from happening,* he decided. He wouldn't stop VD just yet; instead, he would use VD's activity to find him. The Hall Monitors could deal with the rest, such as stopping VD from hurting any more students.

From now on, he would devote as much time as possible to finding this VD, to finding the truth about Mother, and to finding what Father was hiding.

Then he would strike.

Ruthie opened the door to her dorm as Layla sang, *"I know a place where no one's lost...I know a place where no one cries..."*

"*Les Misérables*, the song *I Dreamed a Dream* as sung by Cosette," Ruthie recited automatically. Her eyes brightened. "Is our school play going to be *Les Misérables*? I love that play!"

Layla grinned. "It's one of my favorites. I'm trying out for Cosette!"

"Go, Layla!" Ruthie cheered. "I've got the lines memorized, but I'm a terrible actor and you've got some amazing talent. You're going to do great! I'll definitely help you practice." Then she hesitated. They hadn't apologized to each other yet. "I mean, if you want me to."

"Of course I want you to." Layla paused and stared at her feet. Either they were going to apologize now or not apologize at all. Layla quickly glanced at Ruthie, who seemed wary of what Layla was about to say. *Ruthie's not going to apologize first,* she realized with a tinge of disappointment. *It's either now or never.*

So much for her record. Her friend mattered more.

"I'm sorry—" both girls started at the same time.

They both cut off abruptly, glanced at each other, and began laughing.

"All this time I didn't want to break my record!" Layla said between giggles. "I was so dumb. I should've just said sorry from the start and moved on."

"I just kept imagining you being so smug about how I apologized first," Ruthie said, still chuckling. She took a deep breath. "Layla, I'm—"

"I'm sorry," Layla said triumphantly. "There. I broke my old record. And I'm starting a new one: I'll be the one to apologize first from now on."

"I shouldn't have yelled at you like that or waited so long," Ruthie said.

"I shouldn't have been so impatient and mean to you, or so stubborn," Layla said. "I really was a jerk. You were right. And I'm honestly glad you're my roommate. You're the best roommate I could have asked for."

"Really?" Ruthie asked, despite herself. Her eyes shone.

"Really." Layla curled up on her bed. "Honestly, when you first stepped through Isabel's door, I wanted to throw you out the window. I knew I could handle myself, but I didn't think you could, and I really thought she was going to hurt you. It kind of made me realize that you're one of the best friends I have. There aren't many people who confront angry Isabels with lacrosse sticks just to make sure their mean roommate doesn't get hurt."

"*Throw me out the window*?" chuckled Ruthie. "That's a little dramatic."

"I'm getting in the mood for the play," Layla said. "The tryouts are this weekend. Ken wants to do the lighting and tech and stuff, and I think Ming is part of the musical pit—"

"I want to try out for that," Ruthie said to herself. "Or maybe I could help with set design."

Layla continued, "I wouldn't mind helping with set design or costume design, since that would be a lot of fun." She hugged her knees as she sat on her bed. "But I think it'd be more fun to be the main character. The cast travels the world every weekend for a month, you know. We perform on stages all over the world every Friday, Saturday, and Sunday in April."

"That sounds awesome," Ruthie said dreamily. "I just wouldn't want to get up in front of everyone."

"You're a musician, though, aren't you?"

"I play the violin and can sight read a little piano," Ruthie said modestly. "Tell you what, let's practice your lines right now, and I'll attempt to improvise some music to set the mood."

What happened next was an ensemble of much giggling, lines cut off in laughter, and quite a few hilarious remarks. Soon the discussion turned to costume design, lighting, what it would actually be like to live during that time period, and finally a sort of fanfiction of *Les Misérables* that the girls created during what became a fun sleepover.

At last, the Hall Monitors were back together.

Many miles away, VD pointed a gun at a figure and shot. The cardboard figure fell to the floor. VD dropped the gun and held his hands to his face in anguish. "So close," he muttered. "I was so close. I won't let it happen again. I won't. I'll finish off that family if it's the last thing I do." His foot kicked over the cardboard figure, revealing the face of Aiden Ravencrest pasted to the figure's face. Face contorted in rage and hate, VD gave the cardboard one last kick.

Chapter Seventeen

Aiden was stumped.

He had polished the security system to perfection, cut off every little nook and cranny a hacker could sneak through, and employed every talented security expert he had to perfect the system. He himself had tried to hack in through multiple attempts and hadn't stopped until he failed. His brilliant mind had examined the system as cautiously as possible. He had even spoken with Father and worked with Campus Security to employ higher levels of authentication to ensure each student was safe.

So how had the results of the survey come back to say that over half of the student population was receiving emails from VD?

"I don't get it," groaned Ken. Over a week had passed since Aiden had returned to Ravencrest to work on his recovery. He had been so focused and disciplined that he had left her in charge of the Hall Monitors, with him only checking in for updates and progress reports as needed. "I've checked *everything*. How is VD hacking into these kids' accounts?"

"I've got a list of the kids here," said Ruthie, the pencil's eraser prodding her chin as she thought. It took thirty seconds for her to remember all the names and scribble them down. "I'm making a mini-profile for each targeted kid to figure out what they all have in common. Maybe VD is only targeting certain students."

"Maybe make a chart of the kids who *weren't* targeted," suggested Everest.

"Can I see the list? I can help," Layla offered.

"Um, I think I've got it," Ruthie said, stammering a little. She covered some of the names with her thumb and kept writing the other names down.

"Try an online document," suggested Ming, stepping forward until he was by her side. The others were jolted by his presence; except for Ruthie, they had all forgotten he was there. Ruthie nodded and raised both hands to type in her password. Slyly, Ming snatched the paper away and scanned it.

"Ming, give it back!" Ruthie shouted, but Ming had found it.

He looked up at her in horror. "Ruthie, *you've* been receiving these emails?"

Ruthie's face turned red as the entire room went silent. She mumbled, "It's not that big of a deal."

"How long has this been happening?" Aiden quietly asked at the same time that Ken and Layla both shouted, "Why didn't you *tell* us?" Neither Everest nor Ming said anything, but Everest looked at her with clear sympathy and Ming clenched the paper in his fist with unusual ferocity.

"Seriously, forget about it," she said, hating her voice for how small it sounded. She forced herself to speak up: "Come on, guys, we need to focus. What do these targeted kids have in common?"

"Have you been dealing with this the whole time?" Layla said, horrified. "*Even during our argument?*"

"Guys!" Ruthie said angrily. "We have one job to do, and this has *nothing to do with it*! Please, can we just not talk about it again? Ever?"

Everyone mumbled something close to the word *yes* but not quite there, except for Ming, who remained silent as always.

Aiden picked up their conversation from the silence and continued, "I know this week is going to be busy, and we're all still congratulating ourselves on our last successful job. However, we need to focus and prevent this VD, whoever he is, from striking again. I'll give you all jobs to do, and I expect you all to fulfill them to the best of your ability."

Now this received a firm agreement from everyone.

"I need someone to monitor how often this is happening. I also need someone to set up a platform for people to report these messages to us, preferably with a screenshot. We need to do this in a way that assures people that, despite whatever VD says, they will still be safe if they report these incidents to us," Aiden said.

Ken interrupted, "What if people aren't reporting because they think VD will go after them? There may be a lot of people getting these emails who didn't report it."

"That's why we need to monitor the levels of how many people are receiving these emails," Aiden said. "Layla and Everest, you both are well-known among the girls and boys, respectively speaking, as someone to go to in a crisis."

Both kids blushed a little at hearing this, though it was true. They were among the most popular kids at Ravencrest. Not much went on that Layla and Everest didn't know about.

"I need you two to set up this platform and monitor the levels of VD activity. Campus Security needs constant updates. Are you willing to do this during all of this week, the next, and however long it will take until we catch VD?"

Layla and Everest said they would.

"Ming and Ruthie, I need you two to use all your powers of math, logic, observation, organization, memory, and psychology to look through every student's profile and compile what factors VD may be targeting. We will keep you both updated on all changes. You also may have to do this for however long it takes. Ken, could you help them set up an algorithm to do this more often? A computer would be excellent at detecting patterns that we may not be able to."

They all agreed.

"And finally, Ken, I need you to analyze everything Ming and Ruthie send you. You've solved quite a few puzzles before, so I know you can do this. Find out how VD is getting past Campus Security and who specifically he's targeting."

"He?" Ruthie caught Aiden's slip-up.

Aiden stammered, "I mean, he or she. It could be anyone. VD could be a faceless computer for all I know."

Everyone except for Ken and Ruthie was convinced by this.

"Finally..."

They all attentively listened, leaning in to hear better.

"I wish you all the best of luck with your auditions." Aiden winked at them, displaying a trace of his old self. For once, his face relaxed as he smiled at them.

Ken was relieved while everyone else was encouraged, just as Aiden had intended. They all left, chattering away in excitement. He stayed behind in the attic, still typing. He waited until they were gone to let his face relax from that smile. It was his way of rewarding them, by letting them think he was still the same old Aiden. That was all they needed to think about him. They were friends, after all. Good investments for the future. *That's all friends are.* The thought felt alien to him. He brushed it aside.

He did care for his friends. He wished them well in life and would help them with anything they needed, as long as it didn't interfere with his plans. He wouldn't let himself grow attached to them or anyone. He could see now how that was what made people weak and opened them up to attacks.

Take Mother and Father.

He had confronted Father this morning. Before the morning bell, Aiden had strolled into the headmaster's office and sat in Father's seat, his hands folded, his eyes alert. He didn't move for a full ten minutes as he listened to the porters greet each other and move to their morning shift positions. He noticed the many curious-looking weapons his father hid under his desk; there were also plenty of official-looking documents. Finally, the door swung open as Father stepped inside, straightening his tie. Father's eyes widened at the sight of Aiden, perfectly calm, sitting at the headmaster's desk and looking straight at Father rather unnervingly.

"Is this some kind of joke?" Father scowled. "Aiden, I'm quite busy, and I don't have time for—"

"Tell me how Mother really died."

Father was suddenly very still. He opened his mouth and then closed it again.

Aiden repeated the same statement. It was almost disturbing how still he was and how cold his voice sounded as he said, "Tell me how my mother really died. *Now.*"

Father stammered, "I—I told you, it was a plane accident—"

"Show me the documentation. I want to see the plane ticket, the crash, and the medical examiner's report. Now."

"I have them all, it's on a file somewhere—" Father said, still stammering, as he took out his phone. Quick as a lynx, Aiden rose to his feet and struck the phone out of his father's hands. "Actually, I don't want to see the documentation. It's entirely fabricated, isn't it?"

"Aiden, I don't know what you're talking about," Father said desperately. "Please, son, I need to—"

"Don't call me your son!"

The enraged shout shook Father. For a moment, Father looked like a frail oil man, terrified of his own son.

Aiden was breathing heavily now. He barely looked like himself. "Answer the question. How did my mother die."

It wasn't a question.

His father carefully answered, "She was poisoned."

Aiden accepted this as a fact. The man who had broken into the school had said the same thing. "By whom?"

"We don't know." *He's lying.*

Aiden was very calm. He was so still that it scared his father. Father watched as Aiden reached over and pressed a button on his father's computer. The headmaster's monitors flashed a color, then went blank again. "Wh—what are you doing?" Father said. He reached for his wristwatch to alert the porter standing outside but found that it was missing.

"Looking for this?" Aiden said, holding it up. "Interesting, isn't it? You don't trust me. You don't even trust your own son." The words were mocking, imitating Father's exact words to Aiden weeks ago.

Headmaster Ravencrest breathed in deeply and closed his eyes. When he opened them, there was the same dangerously still calmness Aiden possessed. "Tell me, Aiden," said Father, "what did that man tell you?"

"Enough."

"I don't know what he brainwashed you into thinking, but I promise I only had your best interests—" Father took a step forward. He was now entirely too close to Aiden, so of course Aiden grabbed the high-tech weapon Father hid under his desk and pointed it at his father.

Father froze in his place as a flash of panic ran through his eyes. "Son, please—"

"Don't call me your son," Aiden said through gritted teeth. "Now tell me who killed my mother or else I will shut all of Ravencrest down. I just ran some new software on your computer. I now have the ability to shut down every electronic device on the routers provided here *with the touch of this button.* If you don't believe me, I'd be happy to show you what it looks like for a second." Aiden reached for the button as Father screamed, "Don't!"

Aiden let his hand dangle in mid-air as Father gasped repeatedly and begged, "Aiden, please. You wouldn't destroy your school, your home."

"I would if you lied to me one more time." Aiden looked at Father, his eyes hardly recognizable. "Now answer my question. Who poisoned my mother?"

"Please, son—"

"DON'T CALL ME YOUR SON!"

The words rang through the air, echoing dimly in Aiden's ears. It didn't like his own voice. It sounded like the enraged cry of a monster.

Father swallowed hard, closed his eyes, and said in a very weak voice, "Me."

Aiden's grip went slack. His hands fell limply to his sides. "You," he repeated once in disbelief. "All this time, it was you."

"It's not what you think—"

"You murdered my mother."

Father's voice was choked. "It—it wasn't like that—" His eyes were haunted.

"You killed her," Aiden said numbly, in shock. He laughed once without humor. Then he grabbed the button and clenched it in his fist without pressing down, a terrifying look in his eyes. "You have two minutes to explain before the school shuts down."

Father spoke rapidly: "I was forced to make a choice. Either kill your mother or start a world war."

"How?

"A man forced me to choose. He told me to either kill my wife or he'd start the war. To prove this to me, he kidnapped me and took me for a tour of his arsenal of nuclear weapons. Then he set me free. I had forty-eight hours, he said." Father trembled. "A poisoning was the most painless option. Because of me, the war never began."

"Who was it?"

Father swallowed hard. "A very bad man. I don't want you to know since it's too dangerous—"

"Vladimir Damon?"

Father was temporarily speechless. Then he stammered, "How did you—"

"Had her life been in danger before this happened?"

Father regained control of his composure. "Yes. He had tried to kill her many times but failed each time. She was a crafty one, your mother. The only way he could accomplish his plan was to use someone she trusted. In this case, me." His voice trembled.

"Why did he want to kill her?"

Father did not answer right away.

"Tell me," Aiden's voice rose. "Or you can say goodbye to Ravencrest."

Father closed his eyes and clenched the sides of the desk. "There has to be another way. Aiden, do not make me choose between your safety and Ravencrest Academy."

"I'm not safe as it is!"

"You can be. I don't want you to be involved in any of this, and if I tell you why he wanted to kill her or why he attacked you, your life will be over. In asking me this, you're asking me to choose between your life and this school."

Aiden's face was hardened and expressionless. "You have ten seconds to make your choice." Personally, he knew what Father would choose, even as the anguish danced on Father's face. The Academy was his father's life's work, Father had sworn to dedicate his life to Ravencrest, and Aiden knew how Father had revered the generations of headmasters who had run Ravencrest. Besides, Father had always chosen Ravencrest over Aiden in the past.

Finally, Father said, "I choose you, my son. Destroy Ravencrest if you will. But I will not kill my only son." Father's face crumpled. "I've already killed my wife." He slumped into the chair, put his hands over his face, and silently sobbed.

Aiden had never seen Father like this. Something flickered in his heart. He saw a mirror of himself, sobbing, haunted by his destroyed past, pushed to unspeakable ends. He saw Father as he really was:

what was left of an old man who hadn't realized what mattered most until it was gone. For a moment, only a moment, Aiden's heart softened. Then he was angry because of the reason behind all this pain: VD. He'd kill VD. He'd make him pay.

Revenge and hatred consumed him again as he let go of the button and quietly walked out of the office. Father looked up with tears glistening on his face. "You're not going to destroy Ravencrest?"

"Why would I destroy what's left of my home?" Aiden said. "I would rather die than destroy this place."

Then he walked out, leaving his broken father softly crying behind him.

He stopped. Perhaps some of Mother's weakness was still left in him. He turned, opened the door slightly, and gently said, "Do not fault yourself for what you could not control. VD is the murderer, not you. If you hadn't killed her, he would have, sooner or later."

Then Aiden left. One day, he would ask Father what his last words to Mother had been. For now, he'd let Father heal. He would search for the truth himself, no matter what Father said.

After all, he was a Ravencrest.

Chapter Eighteen

"*Rajesh*?" said Everest as they were leaving the Hall Monitors meeting. "Ming, Rajesh has been receiving this stuff! I can't believe it. The guy brags about himself so much and pretends he doesn't have a problem in his life, but he's been dealing with these emails this whole time too."

"Rajesh doesn't brag about himself at all!" Ruthie said. "He's quiet and nice and he stammers a lot. He doesn't talk about himself unless you ask him."

"What are you talking about, Ruthie?" Everest said pointedly. "Rajesh has always been a huge braggart."

"He's never been like that to me! He's always been really nice!" Ruthie defended him.

Layla stopped in her tracks. "He *has*?!"

"Yeah! He's done all these nice favors for me and he's always really friendly and he's just super nice in general...." Ruthie's voice trailed off because of the way Ken and Layla were looking at each other. Everest frowned and began to say something, but Ming grabbed Everest's arm with surprising strength and walked away. Ruthie frowned. "What? There's something you all aren't telling me."

"What makes you think that?" Layla asked as the girls walked into their dorm hallway. It was Monday night and curfew began in a few minutes, so they walked quickly.

Ruthie swiped her keycard against the sensor and the door swung open. "I have plenty of your facial expressions accompanied by your corresponding moods in my memory, and that's the face you use when you're hiding something from someone."

"That's...kind of creepy," Ken admitted, walking in behind them. "Are your parents okay with that? I mean, do you know when *they're* hiding something?"

"Yes, but it's never been that big of a problem," Ruthie explained. "My parents are experienced enough to hide surprise parties from me by avoiding me in general, and I've done my best to pretend I didn't know when they were worried about bills or their jobs or my grandparents or anything." For a moment, there was some sadness in her voice. Then she was spinning around and saying, "Hey, you didn't answer my question! Why do you guys keep looking at each other like that? I mean, what are you guys hiding?"

"Ruthie," Ken said carefully, "do you like Rajesh?"

"I already told you I do—"

"No, we mean," Layla said, attempting again, "do you *like* Rajesh? As a possible boyfriend?"

There could not have been a more explosive "No!" that came from Ruthie. "Of course not!" she practically shouted. "What—what even made you *ask* that? He's my friend!"

"Don't be ridiculous, Ruthie. It's normal to have a crush on someone." Ken rubbed her little friend's back. Having a friend like Ruthie was a lot like having a little sister, something she had always wanted. "It's not wrong or anything, it's just how you deal with it that matters."

"But I'm not—"

"That's another thing," Layla said. "You're a sweet, naive kid, and you're completely unprepared for the world of boys."

"*What?*"

"What we're trying to say is," Ken interrupted, "we don't want you to get hurt. You're really young, and first crushes almost always crash. Don't get your hopes up, okay?"

"But—"

"And if he does say or do anything to you, *tell me*," Layla emphasized. "Because he can be a jerk sometimes, and if he is one to you, I will murder him."

"You guys are crazy!" Ruthie bounced to her feet in indignation. "Listen to me! Rajesh is my study partner and friend, and I promise you that I don't like him in that way at *all*!"

This changed things. "You promise?" repeated Layla in surprise. Ruthie never made promises lightly.

"I swear!" Ruthie said, exasperated. "Look, I'm not interested in guys until after I finish graduating and stuff! I've got bigger things to worry about right now."

"That's definitely the smart way to go," Ken admitted.

"But...he's obviously interested in you," said Layla slowly.

"He *is*?" Ruthie slumped in her seat. "That's what he's been hiding this whole time! I thought he was just naturally a really nice and nervous person. Then...what am I going to tell him the next time we talk? I mean, how do I tell him that I'm not interested without hurting his feelings?"

Layla blinked. "I guess you should be super honest and really nice about it and, um, hope he takes it well?" She sighed. "Who am I kidding? This is Rajesh. He's not going to take it well."

Ken also sighed. "And here I thought we were finished with all the high school drama."

Suddenly, there was a knock at the door that startled them all. Immediately, Ken dove under the bed while Ruthie rolled over and buried herself under the covers. Layla kicked off her shoes, ran a hand through her hair to make it wilder, threw on a crumpled nightgown over her clothes, and drowsily stumbled to the door. Random curfew room checks were all well and good, as long as porters had reasonable suspicion that another person was in the room. If there was, they all might end up in detention.

Ruthie internally kicked herself. Usually, she would've kept track of the time by checking her watch; this time, however, she hadn't noticed that it was now a few minutes past ten o'clock and thus past curfew. Despite being strict, the porters were also merciful at times. They would probably let them all off with a warning. Nonetheless, none of them wanted to risk a possible detention.

Ken crouched under Layla's bed and eyed one of Layla's suitcases. She could crawl in if necessary. It was certainly big enough.

With an Oscar-worthy performance, Layla yawned, rubbed her eyes, and mumbled, "Yes, sir?" as she cracked the door as little open as possible.

There wasn't a porter at the door.

Instead, Sophia stood at the dorm door with tears in her eyes. "I need to talk to you, Layla," she said, holding back a sob.

"Oh, Sophia," said Layla, dropping her act. "I thought you were a porter. What are you doing here? It's after curfew. If a porter hears us talking, they'll stop by and we could get detention. Can this wait until tomorr—"

"Please?" Sophia said, a tear tracing her cheek.

Layla didn't hesitate. She pulled Sophia in and locked the door behind them. "Keep your voice down," she warned.

"Don't worry about that," Ken said, easily rolling to her feet. "These walls are really thick. I bet you didn't know I was in here."

"I didn't, but..." Sophia started crying. "You can't tell anyone, both of you."

"I won't either," Ruthie said, sitting up and looking at them earnestly.

Sophia sobbed harder. "Great! Is anyone else here?"

"No, just us," Ruthie said gently. "What's the problem?"

Finally, through her tears, Sophia said, "I have a secret, and I can't tell anyone except you guys. You have to promise me you won't tell anyone, all of you!"

"I promise," said Layla and Ken simultaneously.

"I promise," Ruthie said after a pause. "Unless someone is in danger, I won't tell anyone."

"My parents are getting divorced," Sophia said in a choked voice.

Ken was sympathetic. "Oh, Sophia—"

"There's more," Sophia said, taking a gasping breath. "My dad's leaving and he said he doesn't want any communication from us. He said that if my mom thinks she doesn't need him, she can pay for everything herself! And since my mom said she already paid for my tuition this year—"

"She won't pay for next year?" gasped Layla.

"She won't!" cried Sophia. "My parents are such *idiots* that they don't even care about me! My brother's going to save up for it, he promised me, but he'll barely muster up a couple thousand. He can't earn enough in a year—he just got fired! That's why my parents are fighting in the first place!"

"So you won't be here next year?" Ken said. She enveloped Sophia in a hug. "Oh, Sophia...listen, I'll get my dad to hand over some money. He has enough to spare."

"I can't take your dad's money! And I definitely can't earn it all in one summer," wept Sophia. "What am I going to *do*? My Ravencrest credits aren't going to count if I don't complete two full years here. I hate my parents! I hate them, hate them, hate them!"

Ruthie spoke up: "There's a clause in the Student Code of Conduct, on page 122, under Section 4B of student fees. It says you can request a long-term payment plan with the headmaster should your situation be dire enough for him. There's a Ravencrest financial assistance expert, and I memorized—I mean, I have—his phone number. I'll give him a call tomorrow. Don't worry; we'll sort this out. You'll be here next year."

"We *promise*," said Ken as she continued to hug Sophia.

Sophia pulled away and wiped her eyes with the palms of her hands. "Thanks, guys. Please, please, *please* don't tell anyone about my parents, and especially about my dad."

"We promise," Layla said before anyone else could say anything. "We'll get this sorted out, and no one has to know—"

Ken gasped. "Does VD know?"

Sophia jolted like she had been electrocuted. "VD! Oh God, I didn't even think about him. What if he finds out?"

"Why do you think he'll find out?" Ken asked.

Sophia shivered. "He knows everything. Even things you've never told anyone. I love Ravencrest, don't get me wrong, but he's the one thing that makes this place terrifying. I've even heard some kids are thinking about dropping out because of him."

"From *Ravencrest*?" Ruthie said incredulously. No one dropped out from Ravencrest. It simply didn't happen.

"These emails...the fact VD is someone Campus Security can't handle..." Sophia tried to explain, then finally said, "VD knows everything and can threaten us and can make even the nicest students turn into criminals just because they're Ravencrest students. A lot of kids feel trapped by him. And Campus Security can't do anything except identify the problem—weeks after it started! Some of us just want to get out of here because of him, no matter how nice everything else is."

This grim warning cast a somber mood in the room. Finally, the three Hall Monitors present realized how deep this issue was. It threatened not only the reputation of Ravencrest but Ravencrest itself. If students didn't feel safe here, if many were driven to terror and constant anxiety, and if Campus Security could do nothing about it, then Ravencrest wasn't the safe, beautiful learning environment it had been for centuries. It was a prison, caged by expectations to rise to the top without letting the monster who knew everything get to you. These emails were putting the very heart of Ravencrest in danger.

The worst part was that no one knew what VD would do next.

Aiden smiled. He now knew what VD would do next.

VD had hacked into three students' accounts—Charlotte Brenson, Samuel Rao, and Maribel Dwyer—and sent instructions to all three. Charlotte, who was threatened to have her older sister disappear, was told that she would receive a flash drive in the next box of sweets from her parents. She was to give Maribel Dwyer the flash drive at the end of her second period when she passed her in the hallway to grab an extra macaron from the mess hall, as they both did with their friends every Thursday morning (the fresh macarons were legendary at Ravencrest). Samuel Rao, who was threatened to have his parents' visas rejected indefinitely, was told to use his Cybersecurity Research clearance to engage the Head of Campus Security in a conversation at exactly 5:07 PM that Thursday. He was to guide the man away from his desk until they were near the window, with the man's back to the desk. At 5:07 PM, Maribel Dwyer, who was threatened to have the press find out the truth about her unmarried father still in prison, was to use her sleight of hand prowess (she was excellent at magic tricks, something only a few friends knew) to switch the flash drive

Charlotte had given her with an identical-looking one from the second drawer of the Head of Campus Security's desk. The collected flash drive from the man's desk was to be sent back in the same box of sweets, under the chocolate in the top left corner.

It was a very detailed plan. Each student only knew of their part in the plan and nothing more. Despite this, all three could easily surmise what the collected flash drive might do. Two of the students hadn't yet checked their emails yet, though Samuel—who had been running his own software to check for emails sent to himself ever since he heard about VD—read it ten minutes after receiving it in class.

No one had mentioned it yet. Aiden and Ken's little software update had caught the email marked *VD* quickly. Furthermore, Aiden's personal software detected that the email had been sent from a location on the island.

On learning of this, Ken raised an interesting possibility: "So if one of the computers at the school is sending these emails, what if it's a student writing these emails?"

"Are you saying that VD is a student?" Aiden asked sharply. He knew VD was *not* a student. If he was only a student, would it change anything?

Yes, it would. Even Aiden's fiercest anger held him back from hurting another kid.

Unless that person had killed his mother.

"No," Ken corrected hastily. "I think a student is given login information and messages to send, and *they're* the ones sending emails to other people."

"Great," groaned Everest. "So there's no tracing them."

"We can still trace them," said Ruthie, neatly rearranging her little workspace in the attic. "If we find the student or students VD is using for these emails, we can find other ways VD is getting to these kids and hopefully find VD. We can retrace his steps and maybe we can find him. Or her."

"Do we want to find VD?" Layla asked. "Or just stop what he's doing here?"

"Both," said Ken at the same time that Aiden said, "Just to stop him. Let Campus Security handle the rest."

"But, Aiden, *you're* Campus Security," Ken pointed out.

"True," Aiden admitted.

Ruthie frowned. "I thought *we* were part of Campus Security."

"To an extent," agreed Aiden.

Layla bit her lip. "So why can't we go after VD?"

Aiden didn't smile. "I'd rather you asked less questions and focused on preventing VD from doing any further damage to Ravencrest."

"If we stop him, we can stop all future—" Ruthie started.

Aiden cut her off, "If you try to find him, I will personally ensure you are expelled from Ravencrest with all your credits removed."

There was a stunned silence. Aiden spoke much more sharply now; he was getting exasperated with all the superficialities he had to constantly display, such as smiles and politeness. He preferred to be curt, crisp, and to the point.

Aiden continued in a gentler tone, "Your jobs are to reduce VD's influence on Ravencrest students here. For this next mission—"

Ruthie had been getting bolder and bolder lately, possibly due to Layla's influence, and now she was bold enough to interrupt, "Why can't we find VD? It would solve everything. If we work together, we could maybe find him."

"I said to stay out of it," Aiden said sharply.

"We've been doing so well," Ruthie went on.

Layla muttered under her breath, "Ruthie, stop, Aiden's getting mad. Don't ask any more questions."

"I *will* ask more questions," Ruthie insisted. "If we find VD, we can stop everything he's doing here."

"Ruthie—" Ken tried to warn, but now Ruthie couldn't stop: "Haven't you guys seen what he's doing to Ravencrest? This is an amazing place, and I *hate* seeing kids always angry and scared because of this horrible person! If we really care about Ravencrest, we need to target the source and get VD out of the way as fast as possible before he hurts more kids. Don't you guys care at all? We could totally do this. Aiden, don't *you* care about Ravencrest? Your mother even said once in an interview—"

"Shut up!" Aiden suddenly shouted.

Ruthie froze. Once more, a stunned silence stilled the room.

Ming stepped forward in front of Ruthie, his dark eyes flashing dangerously. "There is no need to shout." For a moment, he fiercely glared at Aiden as if challenging him.

There was a need to shout. Blood rushed to Aiden's face, his head ached, and his heart pounded. His conscience twisted. He *was* allowing VD to hurt Ravencrest, just so he could find and stop VD by himself. Perhaps the Hall Monitors could find VD, but then Aiden would never get his revenge. There was a certain class of revenge reserved for people who killed mothers and attacked young boys and manipulated men into murdering those they loved. Imprisonment was not enough. No, VD needed to feel every stab of pain, every moment of grief, every second of loss, and every anguish-filled bit of recovery that Aiden had suffered.

He would never let the Hall Monitors be a part of his revenge. They had to stay out of it. He would not let VD hurt them as well. He had already placed restrictions on Ruthie's email account should VD attempt to contact her again. He had also kept certain softwares running on the other Hall Monitor accounts to monitor every email composed. The others were becoming his friends, which was a problem. He was beginning to care about them; thus, he'd keep them out of his plan for revenge. There was no need for them to be involved in how he settled the score.

So he had to ensure they would not hunt down VD. They could only focus on limiting VD's damage until Aiden had made VD disappear.

Aiden noticed Ruthie's eyes well up with tears. Rather angrily, he snapped at her, "Don't be so sensitive."

"Speak to her like that again," warned Ming furiously, stepping forward once more so he was within a foot of Aiden. His usually withdrawn face was now alight with blazing anger. Next to him, Ken squeezed Ruthie's hand in comfort.

Aiden knew better than to lash out at Ming. It was not a good idea to make Ming an enemy. So Aiden mumbled some apology and Ruthie mumbled back that it was no big deal, and they returned to business.

"From what I can tell," Aiden went on, "we have two issues to deal with. First and foremost is the immediate threat of unauthorized access to our security systems via this flash drive. Secondly, we need to expose how VD is contacting the students who are hacking into these accounts to send these emails. For now, let's focus on the most immediate threat: the first one.

"This is how we'll do it...."

Chapter Nineteen

Charlotte Brenson paced back and forth at the island's airport with dark circles under her eyes. She was sweaty and fidgeting, clearly having dressed in a hurry. She seemed to constantly alternate between being on the verge of tears and displaying little signs of angry defiance. The porters didn't ask questions when she snapped at them about why it was taking so long, or when she groaned in frustration when she was informed that the shipment from her parents was slightly delayed. They simply remained patient and allowed her to continue pacing around for the next half hour, muttering to herself.

Finally, when the shipment arrived, Charlotte ran to it. She tore open the packaging, found the box of sweets, and shoved the rest of the package from her parents into her bag.

She was on her way to her room when Ruthie bumped into her "accidentally" and asked, "Hi, Charlotte, where are you going?"

"Back to my room, that's all," said Charlotte, looking very pale.

"I know Layla always mentions this," Ruthie said in her lighthearted way, "but your British accent is *so* nice. It's so charming and perfect. I wonder if I could learn it."

"Layla can speak in any accent, so I'm sure she thinks they're all charming. Besides, there's no such thing as a British accent. The UK is huge, and there are plenty of different dialects. The Glaswegian dialect is very different from the Cockney dialect," Charlotte said, speaking rapidly. "Anyway, I have to go, I'm going to be late."

"Late to what?"

"Uh, practice starts in, um, half an hour."

"Practice for what?"

"None of your business!" Charlotte snapped. She shoved Ruthie aside and began to walk away, hands visibly trembling.

Ruthie called after her, "Is everything okay, Charlotte?"

Charlotte stopped, sighed, turned, and admitted, "Yes, everything's fine. I'm alright. Sorry for yelling; I know you didn't mean any harm."

"Of course not," Ruthie said. "I was just curious. I'm here to pick up something from my parents too."

"Sure—wait, how did you know I was here to pick up something from my parents?" Charlotte said with narrowed eyes, suddenly alert.

Ruthie blinked. "You're holding a package with your parents' names?"

"Oh. Of course." Charlotte exhaled. "I'm sorry, Ruthie, it's been a long day."

"That's all right," said Ruthie, always easy to forgive. "Tell you what, we can stop by the café. I'll pick up some chocolate cake, and you can have your favorite macarons."

"How did you know they're my favorite?" Charlotte accused.

"You told me."

"When?"

"The last time we got some. It was last Thursday morning, I think."

"Do you know if anyone else was listening?"

It was an odd question, but Ruthie complied. She closed her eyes and focused. "We were standing near the counter...your back was to Maribel Dwyer and a few guys she was talking to...you were jumping up and down because they had a new flavor...and you were telling me that macarons were your favorite. Then we started talking about failed baking attempts from when we were younger." She opened her eyes. "I guess anyone around us could have been listening. Why?"

"Uh, nothing."

"So, about the café...?"

"Yeah, I've got homework—"

"It'll only take a minute! Also," —here Ruthie lowered her voice— "You mind helping me pick the right dress for Layla? Her birthday's coming up and I want to surprise her, and I know you're super into fashion."

Charlotte lingered. "Uh, I've got to do something in my room first, so I'll be there in a moment—"

"I'll come with you!" said Ruthie cheerfully. "Come on, it'll be quick. The snacks are on me."

Charlotte sighed. "Sure, why not?"

Samuel was staring at his notebook when Everest surprised him. "Heya, Sam!"

In shock, Samuel jerked his head back. "Everest? What are you doing here?"

"I came here to spy on you and keep you from making the school explode," deadpanned Everest. Samuel froze and couldn't breathe. Everest laughed awkwardly as he said, "You know I was joking, right?"

"Oh," breathed Samuel, forcefully laughing a little as he added, "Right."

"You okay? You look a little nervous."

"Why would I be nervous?" Samuel said. He seemed to pull himself together as he added, "Sorry, I'm just worried about the test tomorrow."

"Yeah, I hear it's killer."

Everest dropped into the seat next to Samuel, holding a plate full of hummus and chips. "Want some? I'm not going to double dip."

"No thanks," Samuel murmured.

"It's only Wednesday," Everest went on.

"Why do you say that?" Samuel asked, gripping the edge of the table.

Everest raised an eyebrow. "I was going to say that if you're worried about the diet I proposed for the basketball game, it's only Wednesday and the game isn't until next week. Besides, hummus is healthy."

"Oh. Right. I'm not a basketball player."

"But you said you were interested. The offer is still open."

"Yeah, okay," Samuel said breathlessly. "Thanks. Sorry, I—I don't feel very well. In fact, I think I might be sick."

"Should I get a nurse?"

"No, I got it. Thanks anyway." For a very brief moment, it seemed like Samuel was going to break down and start crying right then and there. Instead, he straightened up, feigned a smile, and said, "Well, I better get going. See you around."

"Rajesh texted you?" Charlotte giggled. "Are you guys, y'know, a *thing*?"

"No!" said Ruthie. "Not at all! He just texts me about class projects and stuff."

"Sounds like an excuse," Charlotte teased.

"Charlotte!"

"All right, all right," Charlotte said, sitting up mock-formally. "The jury has voted and I've decided…"

She drum-rolled to build up the anticipation.

"The lemon macarons are the best. I mean, just *taste* that lemon ganache!"

Ruthie giggled. "Charlotte! I wanted to know which dress you thought Layla would like."

"Oh, right. After *much* deliberation," Charlotte added, holding a delicious-looking strawberry macaron and twirling it as she spoke, "I think the red dress is best, with the jewelry you picked out."

Ruthie stared in dismay at the selected dress. "I only have twenty dollars."

"She already has the jewelry and shoes," Charlotte continued. "You just need to pay for the dress. It's not *that* expensive. I mean, it's less than a hundred dollars. Most of my dresses are at least a few hundred."

Ruthie sighed and pulled out her credit card. "I suppose it's for a good cause."

"Layla will *love* it, trust me," promised Charlotte.

"Good point." Ruthie made the payment, then asked, "You mind if I have this macaron?"

"Go ahead. I think I've eaten too many. Then again, no amount of macarons is too many," joked Charlotte. She seemed much more relaxed than before as she lounged in the café, humming along to the classical music in the background.

Ruthie twirled the macarons in her fingers and played with them right above a cake she had ordered for Layla's birthday. Then, oh-so-casually, she drew in the frosting:

I know about VD.

Charlotte stopped laughing.

Ruthie used the end of the macaron to smooth out the frosting. Then she wrote: Security has it under control.

Charlotte still wasn't breathing.

Trust me.

Ruthie held her breath to see Charlotte's response.

The girl with the perfect blond hair stared at the words intently, then looked up and said, "So, you going to finish that macaron?"

Ruthie understood. Someone might be listening. Or watching.

The frosting was smoothed over and the macarons were devoured. Ruthie declared that she still had an appetite and reached over into the box of sweets Charlotte had received. Charlotte watched and said nothing as Ruthie reached for a chocolate in the top left corner, picked it and what was under it up, examined the flash drive briefly under the cover of her hand, and then hid it again under the chocolate. Then she picked up another sweet—some sort of jelly—and shared it with Charlotte. Ruthie's hand reached out and squeezed Charlotte's hand under the table.

Charlotte smiled, and it was like a weight had been lifted off her shoulders. She squeezed Ruthie's hand back and, for the first time in a while, began to breathe again.

"Hey, Sam, give me a second; I need to show you something."

The words stopped Samuel in his tracks and he turned back hesitantly.

Everest used his chip to write in the hummus the same words Ruthie had written. Samuel's face began to crumble as if he was no longer under a crushing pressure. He smiled a little. "Thanks," he said quietly.

"For the hummus, you mean," corrected Everest, quickly writing, Careful, ears everywhere.

Sam nodded. "Of course." Yet for the first time in days, he was smiling again.

Maribel Dwyer did not check her emails that day or night, but she did the next morning. She was late to breakfast and seemed much quieter than usual. While she was walking to class, Layla noticed Maribel in the hallway and invited her to come along for extra coffee later.

"I don't usually drink coffee," Layla admitted, "but I thought I'd try some today. What about you?"

"Yeah," mumbled Maribel. "Sure."

Layla grabbed Maribel's hand and plunged them into the mass of students filing out to get to class on time. Under the loud chaos, she said quietly, "I know about the email."

Maribel gaped at her.

"Trust me," Layla said softly. "Security has it under control."

"But..." Maribel began. She stammered, then finally said, "How?"

"It's a long story. We need to hurry. But I may 'bump into' you again right after you bump into Charlotte." Layla's meaningful smile was not lost on Maribel, who sighed in relief and began to smile as well.

"Oh, shoot!" Maribel shouted, glancing at her watch. "We don't have time for coffee—we need to *run*! We're going to be late for class!"

Right after second period, a small group of girls stopped by the mess hall Thursday morning to get some macarons. They only had a few minutes before class started, but they could be surprisingly fast when it came to getting dessert on time.

While they were walking, Charlotte passed by Maribel in the hallway. Their sleeves brushed by each other. Neither made eye contact as Charlotte's hand passed over the edge of Maribel's jacket pocket. And when Maribel searched in her jacket, presumably for a pencil, she said nothing at the small discovery she found.

Shortly after, Ruthie winked at Charlotte, giving Layla the signal to "accidentally" bump into Maribel. Layla furtively reached into Maribel's pocket and grabbed the flash drive. In one swift move, the drive had been transported from Maribel's jacket pocket to Layla's, and an alternate flash drive that looked the exact same (due to Ruthie's photographic memory) was in Maribel's pocket. If Maribel noticed this, she never let anyone know.

While Layla was taking her seat in one of her classes, Ken came over to discuss *Les Misérables* with her. Layla shrieked with excitement at the thought of the upcoming tryouts and jumped to her feet, grabbing Ken's hand in enthusiasm.

Ken hid the flash drive in her right sleeve. At lunch time, she passed Aiden in the main hallway. She tripped, stumbled directly into his arms, apologized awkwardly, straightened, and went on. Behind her, Aiden couldn't help but wish she would do it again.

He examined the flash drive when safely in his room. Using some software, he was able to discern its purpose.

Immediately, he called an emergency meeting.

When class ended at 4:00 PM, every Hall Monitor reported to the attic. They had each received a note that stated, Code Blue. Right away, they put aside whatever work they had after school. This was a threat to Ravencrest and possibly the world.

"What happened?" said Ken, the first one present at the meeting. Close on her heels was Layla. Ming and Everest stepped in at the same time, having raced each other there. Ruthie slid in right after them as they grouped in the attic, every face alert and worried.

"I found out what this flash drive does," Aiden said grimly. "It is meant to shut down the security system at Ravencrest, but only for one part of the school."

"The dorms?" Ruthie gasped.

"The mess hall?" Everest gasped.

"The dangerous equipment area?" Layla gasped.

"Any entry point to the school?" Ken gasped.

Ming just listened eagerly.

"No," Aiden said. "Worse."

"What could possibly be worse?" Ken wondered. When Aiden didn't answer right away, she snapped, "That wasn't a rhetorical question!"

Aiden admitted, "It's a very long story, and you all need to swear an oath which states that you won't repeat anything you're about to hear to *anyone*. This is classified information, do you all understand me?"

Some versions of *yes* from everyone followed this statement.

Aiden looked from face to face. "Do any of you know the founder of this school?"

"Matthew Ravencrest," Ruthie said automatically. "He was the son of the two most influential people in the world at the time. He grew up with wealthy parents who loved him and raised him well. Furthermore, he received all sorts of scholarships and opportunities because of his extreme intelligence. He was considered the most brilliant prodigy the world had ever seen. By the time he was thirty, he was a leading figure in every field of science and had even invented a few new fields of science."

"Is this the Wikipedia page for this, word-for-word?" Layla whispered to Ken.

Ruthie continued, "He had a heart for kids and wanted others to receive the same opportunities he had as a wealthy, high-class, Caucasian male with plenty of resources and connections. So he saved up his money for years and bought an unoccupied island in the Pacific, then cleared out part of it for the school. Then he recruited the best of the best architects and engineers to work on the school. It was a passion project he worked on for many years and resulted in something he gained a lot of support for."

Ken whispered back to Layla, "I just checked the Wikipedia page. It is."

"When he finally opened it," Ruthie said, nearing the end of her speech, "it made headlines in every major newspaper. He was headmaster of the school for many years before he passed on the job to his oldest son. This tradition of passing on the job to the oldest child or daughter- or son-in-law continued for many years, despite the controversies surrounding it. He died unexpectedly of a sudden heart attack. Hundreds attended his funeral."

"Excellent job with the Wikipedia page," said Aiden briskly.

Ruthie blushed proudly. "Thanks."

"You are wrong, of course," Aiden said, just as briskly.

Ruthie blinked. "But—"

"Now that you've all heard what the press knows," Aiden went on, "it's time for you all to know the truth. As I said, this is classified information, and you are not to tell anyone about it."

Ken burst out, "We already agreed to that, so just hurry up and tell us the classified stuff!"

"It had better be good," agreed Everest. "This is way too much hype."

Aiden sighed. "Ravencrest was originally a cover-up."

"*What*?" gasped Ruthie.

"Yep, that's good," Everest said.

"Elaborate!" Ken insisted.

"Hurry up, you're so *slow*!" Layla demanded.

Even Ming impatiently motioned for Aiden to continue.

Aiden paused in a moment of playful cruelty, then continued, "Most of what Ruthie said is true. Matthew Ravencrest was in fact the most brilliant prodigy this world has ever encountered. He did have a heart for kids and built Ravencrest partially to give more children the opportunities he had."

"*But*..." Ken probed.

"But he did not build Ravencrest solely for educational purposes. He may have originally intended to, but his twin sister persuaded him otherwise."

"Twin sister?" Ruthie said blankly.

"First time I'm hearing about this," Everest admitted.

Layla's eyes were on fire. "Of course, *he* gets talked about, but the girl prodigy gets ignored. How sexist."

"His sister was less famous," Aiden admitted, "but not entirely for the reasons you think. She was less famous because she was more...underground with her talents."

"She was a *criminal*?" gasped Ken.

Layla sighed. "I need some popcorn."

She wasn't a criminal," Aiden said. "Evelyn Ravencrest was Matthew Ravencrest's younger twin sister. They were very different, as most of her talents laid elsewhere. He was more of the bookworm type while she was more of the artistic sort—or so her parents thought. She actually worked for several government agencies as a codebreaker. Brilliant as she was, she kept her talents secret. Her loyalties did not lie with any government in particular; she opted for 'peace above all.' Thus, she prevented terrorist attacks, performed espionage operations that saved lives, and kept certain government secrets secret. She had friends in high and low places alike. The world leaders of that time knew her, yet the public never even heard of her name. To most of the world, she was just a young artist who kept to herself. Eventually, she was forgotten from history. In reality, she worked at a government facility at a time where women were very undervalued. Due to her gender, she was able to operate under many disguises and fool people who underestimated her."

"That is so cool," said Ruthie.

"I want to be like her when I grow up," said Layla dreamily.

"Go *on*," Ken urged.

"Seriously, hurry up!" Everest added.

Aiden was tempted to hesitate or yawn or stretch, but he only smiled in amusement at the vivid interest of the others. He had been the same when he was a child on Mother's little couch in the warm summer heat where she would tell him his true history, and she would tap his nose and call him Raisin—

"Aiden!"

"Right, of course," said Aiden rapidly before his eyes could start burning. "Matthew and Evelyn Ravencrest were only twins yet were always very close. They had a certain special connection that they shared with no one else. Matthew rarely worried about things outside of scientific issues, but his sister was the sole exception. He was always worried about her, as she would disappear for months at a time with no communication, even when she was practically still a child in her twenties. He discouraged her from these dangerous endeavors, but she persisted in believing that this was her calling. She was quite successful as well, though the two often fought about it." Aiden's heart softened slightly. "Simply by reading their letters and hearing about the crazy lengths they went to for each other, one can tell they had a special connection."

Ruthie was sniffling. "That is the sweetest thing I have ever heard."

"You think everything is sweet, Ruthie," Layla pointed out.

"No, I don't!" Ruthie defended.

"Yes, you do!" Layla said. "I bet you think Rajesh is the sweetest person ever. Maybe that's why you like him." She curiously glanced at Ming, who was as stone-faced as ever.

Ruthie was chagrined. "*Layla*!"

Ken came to Ruthie's rescue: "Aiden, what does this have to do with VD's message?"

"There's more," Aiden explained. "Evelyn persuaded Matthew to buy land to build a facility where she could hide government secrets. He always had a dream of starting a school, and she agreed that he should, just so she could cover up her real intentions."

Ruthie gasped. "So there's an underground level of the school that's full of government secrets?"

"There is," Aiden said.

"And Ravencrest was a *cover-up*?" Ruthie said, gasping again.

"Indeed," Aiden confirmed.

Ruthie gasped.

"If she gasps one more time, I'm getting her inhaler," Ken muttered under her breath to Layla.

Everest gasped.

"Oh no, not him too," Layla muttered back to Ken.

"No," Everest said in a rush, "I think I got it: VD targeted that underground part of the school, didn't he? He found some way in so he could get those government secrets?"

"Correct," said Aiden, and Ken and Layla gasped as well.

"So this whole plan was a ploy to find government secrets!" Layla summarized. She jumped to her feet. "We have to stop this!"

"Layla, hold on—" started Ruthie, but Layla had already rushed out of the room. The elevator traveled down to the right floor and she skidded to a stop in the hallway. Sheepishly, she returned to the attic. "Hey, guys, how exactly are we going to stop this?"

"That's what I was about to get to," Aiden said sternly, although he added, "I do appreciate your enthusiasm."

"It's weird that he went from cheating to drug rings to cyberbullying to breaking into rooms full of government secrets," Ken mused. "It's like the stakes are getting higher. What's he going to do next?"

"Cyberbullying is just as bad as breaking into a room full of government secrets," Ruthie pointed out. "Maybe even worse. Governments can adjust their security, but you can't do much about the impact of words after the damage has been done." She shuddered. "Trust me, I know. My temper has gotten me into some bad spots."

"I doubt that—" Layla began.

Everest, who had run out of patience, interrupted with, "So what exactly is our plan?"

Aiden grinned. It wasn't his usual mischievous smile. There was something much darker behind it. "Here is what we're going to do...."

Chapter Twenty

They only had a few hours. By the time everyone had been fully debriefed on their role in the plan, it was already 4:27 PM, even though VD's prescribed time for his plan to take place was 5:07 PM. Ken was sitting on her dorm bed, typing furiously on her computer, rearranging and adjusting the coding for the software on the flashdrive. Ruthie was tracking down Maribel, who wasn't in her room, the mess hall, or the study booths. She ran from classroom to classroom, trying to find her. Layla was in the corner of Ken's room, stretching. She and Everest were the runners. Everest was pacing in the area where the first-floor hallway split into the boys' and girls' dorms. He received some strange looks from nearby porters.

In the meantime, Ming was with Samuel. He attempted to initiate some conversation but mostly said little.

At 4:45 PM, Ruthie called the others. "I can't find Maribel," she said in a panic.

"What?" yelled Layla. "You need to find her!"

"I've checked everywhere! Where could she be?"

"Think," urged Layla. "Where *haven't* you checked?"

"I've checked in every single room on campus besides the rooms where neither of us are allowed!" Ruthie shouted back.

"You checked every room *on campus*? What about—"

"Off-campus!" Ruthie realized. She squeezed her eyes shut and concentrated. When had Maribel ever mentioned a place that was off-campus?

Then she remembered.

Tuesday of the third week of school. Maribel was in the orchestra with Ruthie. As they were leaving, she had spoken briefly with Ruthie. The conversation had shifted from the beauty of music to the beauty of nature.

"There's this place outside," Maribel had said, shifting her backpack. *"It's so pretty. I go there to think sometimes. We're not allowed off campus during the school day or after it gets dark, so I go right after school ends and hang out there sometimes if my roommate's busy. I don't like to be alone in my dorm."*

"Is it far from campus?" Ruthie asked curiously.

"Not that far. It's near the Shed. You know, the storage shed they keep outside? It's kind of near the airport, but south from a bird's eye

view." Maribel shuddered. *"I wouldn't want to go north. That's where the big forest is. I thought I'd want to go, but every time I see the forest, I keep imagining getting lost. No, it's better to stay near the porters when you're outside. And the trees and flowers are so nice. I should take you some time."*

Ruthie bolted outside and ignored the porters' questioning stares. Porter Jimmy followed her from a distance as per protocol while she followed the trail and found herself on the south side of the island. Sure enough, there was Maribel, curled up and sketching something in her notebook.

"Maribel!" Ruthie called.

"Ruthie?" Maribel looked up in surprise. "What are you doing here? I'm working on my art project."

"I can see that. It looks great so far."

"Just wanted to check this place out, huh?"

"Yep."

Ruthie sat next to her. "Are you going to stay here awhile?"

"No, I've got to go somewhere." Maribel checked her watch, and her face grew pale. "Soon."

"Okay," agreed Ruthie. "I think I'll stay here a little." Secretly, she texted Layla and Everest her location. Everest positioned himself near the main hall while Layla walked Ken to the area where the dorm halls split into girls' and boys' dorms on the first floor. All the Hall Monitors lived on the first-floor dorms, though there were second-, third-, and fourth-floor dorms.

Ken's fingers flew as Layla whimpered. She kept glancing at the time. "*Hurry*!"

"Almost there!" Ken said. "I'd be done if Aiden didn't insist VD receive this *exact* information. It's almost like Aiden's going to bait VD or something."

"Just *focus*!" Layla begged. "It's 4:51 PM!"

Ken doubled her intensity.

Finally, at 4:54 PM, Ken completed the program and downloaded it to the flash drive. Layla wiped the flash drive on her miniskirt to get rid of the fingerprints and wrapped her beloved scarf around it. Then she bolted.

Ken called Everest. "Layla's on her way!"

It took barely a minute for Layla to dart into the main hall and pass Everest, brushing the flash drive into his pocket. He handed her a little plate of guacamole and chips, which he had been eating, and ran.

Layla sat down, texted Ruthie that Everest was on his way, and savored the chips with the guacamole. They were good.

Everest dashed outside and followed Ruthie's texted instructions. He moved swiftly and silently, minimizing any noise as he moved through the grass. As Mirabel focused on her art, Ruthie received the text and looked around vaguely. On seeing Everest, she nodded and stretched. Everest threw the flash drive and Ruthie caught it. She gave him a thumbs-up, then inched closer to Maribel. "Is that a smudge?" she asked, and as Maribel peered closer to check, Ruthie leaned in and whispered, "Give me the flash drive."

Maribel looked up in surprise. "But—"

"Here's yours."

"I thought you already—"

"Trust me."

"Is Campus Security—"

Ruthie showed her the security clearance that Aiden had given her. It certainly looked official enough with the badgers and identification.

Maribel hesitated, then said at last, "Should I still—"

"Do exactly what you were asked to do in the email. Don't ask questions. Trust me."

Finally, Maribel stopped asking questions.

A minute later, Maribel rose and left quietly. Ruthie fingered the dummy flash drive that Maribel had returned to her and looked around. It really was a beautiful landscape. No wonder Maribel came here for her art.

It was 5:02 PM. Maribel entered the school. The nearby porters nodded to her, and Layla raised some chips to wave at her. Maribel did not wave back. At the same time, Samuel was robotically going to the same location. He passed Everest on the way, who waved at him. Samuel also did not wave back.

Ming followed Samuel from a distance and joined the elevator with him.

"You shouldn't come with me," said Samuel. "I have something important to do."

"I'm well aware," said Ming. His eyes were straight ahead as the elevator traveled down to the basement of the Residential Hall, where the security office was held.

"Seriously, leave me alone," said Samuel more forcefully.

Ming displayed his security clearance on his phone. "I just want to watch your interview with the Head of Security."

Samuel saw the document. His eyes widened. "You were recruited by Campus Security?" he whispered.

"Of course not," Ming whispered back. On his phone, he typed, Only this once. "Don't be ridiculous. I just want to watch your interview; why would I be recruited by Campus Security?"

"I guess it would be weird if I said no," said Samuel, catching on. "You can come along, but don't say anything or bother me at all."

So Ming and Samuel made it to the office. Samuel used his Cybersecurity pass to enter, getting past any interested porters by showing them the email that the Head of Security had sent him. Upon entering the office, he left the door ajar. He pretended not to notice Maribel walking behind him from a distance. No one dared to speak as they filed into the office together.

By the time they left the office, Ming had a video of Samuel speaking to the headmaster while Maribel switched the flash drives. All three were silent on the elevator.

Ming texted Aiden, Mission successful.

Aiden texted back a thumbs-up, then a message that said, Text it to Ken. She'll make sure Charlotte, Samuel, and Maribel all email VD that same video, supposedly filmed by Samuel himself. He leaned back in his chair with a sigh. Time for phase two of his plan, though this phase would leave him on his own.

Time to go rogue.

At midnight, the many levels of security for the underground floor of the school were hacked.

That is, they were *supposedly* hacked.

In reality, Aiden had spoken with Campus Security and worked with them to give VD the impression that he had succeeded. The cameras kept displaying their recordings from previous nights. The iris scan and fingerprint security procedures were programmed to pretend they worked. And the code Aiden had written displayed the same success messages without any real effect.

Then, by himself, Aiden installed his own cameras. From a distance, he watched VD break in. He knew VD would attack during the night; there was too much security during the day.

Thus, Aiden was prepared for the intruders.

They came, dressed in black, like shadows of the night. There were only two of them, and one was clearly the lookout. Aiden silently descended from the ceiling like a spider. In the next moment, the lookout man was tied and gagged. Aiden pushed up the intruder's mask and frowned at the sight of the face. It was red and the eyes were wide. It was not his attacker from Argentina and it did not look like VD. No, it looked like the face of a bribed construction worker. In fact, Aiden remembered the faces of the construction workers. This *was* a construction worker.

So he let the man be and disappeared into the darkness of the underground facility. He had made Ken add a little modification to the code, something Campus Security wouldn't notice. All he had done was add his mother's credentials back into the security system as an editor of the code. This way, it was doable to use her computer to add himself to the database of people allowed to view and edit the code, all without producing any red flags.

The other intruder passed through the iris scan easily, not knowing that Aiden had just uploaded the identification information to his laptop. The scan revealed that the intruder was a middle-aged man named Xipe Matalon.

Aiden sharply drew in a breath. He recognized the face. This was the man who had attacked him in Argentina!

The file had very little information about this man after he dropped out of school at age 16. *Working for VD, huh? Tried to kidnap me in Argentina? Bad move.* Aiden smirked. Time for part one of his revenge.

Xipe stepped inside the room. The door slid shut behind him, but not before Aiden slipped into the room. Aiden crouched low in the darkness, weapons clutched in his hands, and approached Xipe just as the man pulled out a flashlight and looked around the room.

Suddenly, Aiden attacked. The boy kicked the flashlight out of the man's hands and delivered a strong punch to Xipe's stomach. Aiden punched and kicked and fought with all he had, but Xipe fought back with just as much force. The present darkness was complete and full so that Xipe was blind to Aiden's attacks.

"Let me see your face!" swore Xipe as he ducked. "Coward!"

Aiden didn't answer. He was wearing night-vision goggles and, with a swipe of his knife, had disabled Xipe's goggles seconds ago.

Xipe cried out when Aiden kicked Xipe's legs out from under him. "Feel familiar?" Aiden mocked. He had expected to enjoy this, but felt sick as the man groaned in pain. "It's called getting a taste of your own medicine, so to speak. I hope you like it."

"You'll pay for this," Xipe managed to say in a raspy voice. He lunged for the boy in what was total darkness to him, and Aiden tasered him a couple times. Xipe screamed in pain and collapsed to the floor.

"That's what I thought," taunted Aiden. He waited for the rush of pleasure and delight, which had lasted for almost a second when the man first cried out. Now he felt sick to his stomach. *Too much of Mother in me.* He was too weak. All he could do was stand there while Xipe shook on the floor, face drenched in sweat and pain. Aiden pulled the man over and placed his foot on Xipe's chest. Xipe could only remain paralyzed from the electricity. Aiden leaned in close. "This is what happens when you hurt a Ravencrest. Now we're even after what you did to me in Argentina."

"VD will kill you," cursed Xipe through the pain. "Just wait and see. You can kill me now, but I'm only a martyr—"

"I'm leaving you alive. You'll suffer more that way."

Xipe swore.

Appropriately, Aiden kicked the man in the ribs.

Well, he should have.

He could have.

He just...felt sick. He wanted to throw up as the man trembled under Aiden's foot. This wasn't who he was. This didn't feel natural at all. In some twisted way, maybe with practice this wouldn't feel so uncomfortable. Yet did he really want that?

"I'm not going to beg for mercy," grunted Xipe as Aiden's foot sank deeper into Xipe's chest.

"This isn't mercy, Xipe," Aiden said, taking a step back. The lights were on, alarms blared, and security guards with the training of a SWAT team rushed in. People screamed for Aiden to get out of the way as Xipe was handcuffed. Aiden watched with grim satisfaction as his enemy was dragged away. Before leaving, Xipe spat a mouthful of blood at Aiden's feet.

Aiden looked him right in the eyes and, without blinking, said, "This is revenge."

So that was revenge.

Aiden waited until both men were gone. The guards were bringing them in for questioning. On the way there, Aiden excused himself and went to a bathroom. He threw up in the trash can and leaned against the wall.

What was wrong with him?

When had he become so weak? He was a warrior, a fighter. He had been pursuing revenge every day for weeks now. He had imagined this moment many times. And this was only Xipe—he hadn't even gotten to VD yet.

Aiden retched and threw up again at the mental image of the man groaning in pain under Aiden's foot, twisting and convulsing and screaming in agony.

Perhaps justice had been served. It didn't feel like it. Mercy was an essential part of justice, and even though Aiden had suffered at the hands of Xipe, it didn't mean he was allowed to cause the same kind of suffering to someone else.

For a moment, just a moment, he began to wonder if—suddenly he remembered.

I'm avenging Mother's death.

Then the fierce rush of hatred and anger came back until he no longer felt weak and dizzy. His fists clenched and his mind swarmed. VD would pay. Xipe was only a pawn. VD was the real prize.

Aiden left the bathroom, his eyes cold and his head held high.

"You all right?" Porter Craig asked.

"I'm fine," said Aiden, pushing the man away. "Where's Xipe Matalon? It's time for an interrogation."

Xipe was searched and locked in a soundproof room with nothing more than a bed, pillow, and small bathroom with a toilet and sink. Soap, deodorant, a toothbrush, and toothpaste were near the sink. He had been treated and was instructed to rest. There was also a small, locked door on the wall of his holding cell. It was small enough to slip a plate and a bottle of water through, along with some food, but that was all Xipe got. There was one clear wall between him and the control room, where the keys to his cell dangled between a computer and the door.

Aiden stepped in, Porter Craig behind him on one side, the Head of Security on the other. Porter Jimmy was outside, speaking with a few guards and organizing shifts. Though Jimmy could be frustrating, he hadn't spoken with Aiden ever since Aiden had come back from Argentina. Besides, Jimmy was still good at his job. Here, in the basement of the school, they were holding Xipe hostage. Legally, they were allowed to do so for 40 days, then turn him over to the authorities. But Aiden had a plan.

He stepped into the control room and let the door shut behind him. The moment Xipe saw him, Xipe jumped to his feet and began screaming obscenities.

"I can't hear you," Aiden said smugly into the speaker. The sound system embedded into the ceiling, far above Xipe's head, broadcasted the words into both sides of the clear wall. "I'll unmute if you stop yelling."

Xipe stopped, but Aiden did not unmute. The man would only scream some more.

"As you can see, we are treating you much better than how you treated me," Aiden continued. "We've provided free medical care and a room to stay in. Tomorrow morning, you will receive a change of clothes and even a clean towel. The lights will automatically turn off at 9:00 PM and the ceiling above you will show what position the sun is in the sky, as well as provide Vitamin D. Your food will have all the vitamins you need. Then you will be left to yourself for an entire day with nothing but the sound of the AC running. It's far kinder than how you treated me."

"How long do you plan to keep me here?" Xipe asked calmly, once Aiden had unmuted him.

"As long as it takes to find Vladimir Damon." This was a lie. Xipe would be out of here much, much sooner. Of course, he didn't need to know that.

Xipe pounded his fists against the clear wall and swore. "Let me out of here!"

Aiden's eyes narrowed. "We will. Eventually. We could let you out within 24 hours, on one condition."

"What?" spat Xipe.

"You tell me where VD is. If our security team does not find him, you will not receive food the next day. If they do, you are set free." This was entirely made up. Xipe would soon be released to the authorities, regardless of whether he offered any information or not. He would be completely unharmed. Yet the psychological terror of believing otherwise would hopefully be enough to break Xipe's spirit and give Aiden the location.

Porter Craig's eyes were wide. This was very unlike Aiden to do, and the porter had never seen this side of the boy before.

"What if I go mad?" Xipe shouted.

"Why would we care?" mocked Aiden. This was yet another lie. If they suspected Xipe was insane, an expert psychologist would be called to check on the prisoner.

Xipe gripped the clear wall as best as he could and managed to say, "Whatever you do to me, VD will pay you back a hundredfold. You mess with the bull, you get the horns."

"Perhaps you should have remembered that when you tried to kill me," Aiden said. "Or when you let VD kill my mother using my father. It was a sick, twisted thing to do. Don't expect any kindness from me, Matalon."

"I would gladly do it a hundred times," swore Xipe, "if it would cause you the same pain all over again. Your mother's cries were music to my ears. I've watched the camera footage of her death so many times." He smiled at the grief that rushed to Aiden's face for a brief moment, grief which instantly transformed into hatred.

Blood rushed to Aiden's face. "Well then," Aiden said coolly, "I do hope you enjoy your stay here with us. Let us know when you've decided to do the reasonable thing and tell us where your boss is hiding." He turned to leave.

"Vladimir is not my boss!" shouted Xipe. "He is my brother and I will die for him."

"Your brother?" laughed Aiden. "You think he cares about you enough to risk everything to get you back?" He was at the door now, his hand on the handle.

"Yes," breathed Xipe.

Aiden smiled darkly. It was becoming his new trademark smirk. "Good to know."

Chapter Twenty-One

"Everything okay?" Ken asked Aiden when she saw him in the mess hall Monday morning. He had emailed her with the information that their work had been successful and that he couldn't say more. No Hall Monitor had heard from him since then. She placed her plate down next to him.

"Yes." Aiden ate quickly.

"Why did you come here?"

"What?"

"You normally eat in your room. I get that you like to be mysterious, but you avoid us every day unless there's a mission or something. The only person you see regularly is Everest at your training sessions, and even those stopped after Argentina. We haven't had any Hall Monitor meetings since our last mission, either. I guess we're too 'trivial' for your great mind, huh?" Ken said, half-joking.

"I simply wanted to avoid Jimmy," Aiden said with muted surprise. "I was not avoiding any of you."

"Why Porter Jimmy?"

"We used to not get along very well. Now, it seems as if he is avoiding me, which is why I am sitting here now."

"Oh," Ken said. "So you'll actually talk to us every morning from now on?"

"Most mornings, unless I have another engagement." He cleared his throat. "However, I did hope to congratulate all of you on our most recent success. It truly was most impressive how we stopped VD on his next attempted crime." He smirked. "It was very successful."

Ken squinted at him as she chewed. "Aiden?"

"Yes?"

"What *happened* to you in Argentina?"

"I was attacked—"

"No, I mean..." Ken sighed, frustrated. "I'm not dumb, Aiden."

"I never said you were."

"I can tell when I'm being played."

"Played?"

"You lied to me. You snapped at Ruthie for no reason. You're hiding things. And you never really smile anymore. Ruthie thinks you must have injured a part of your brain and ended up with a change in your personality. Everest thinks you're just stressed out. Layla thinks you've got a lot on your plate that you're not telling us about. Ming never told me what he thinks, but I can tell he's worried. And I think..." Ken shifted uncomfortably in her seat. "I *know* you're hiding things from us that we deserve to know about."

"I'll be the judge of that," Aiden said crisply. "Furthermore, when have I ever lied to you?"

"You asked me to design the code a certain way," Ken explained after swallowing. "And then you added some code to the template I created, just so you could edit the security software illegally, even though you've already been given the right to edit the software under supervision. It's like you want to modify the security software without letting anyone know. I also know you used everything I did to bait VD somehow and, from the way you smiled earlier, you found him or something."

"I didn't find VD," Aiden sharply interrupted. "*Yet.*"

"Then why were you so happy? It wasn't a normal kind of happy, it was a *I just did something horribly bad and it worked* kind of happy."

"I did not do something horribly bad," Aiden said. He paused. "Without my reasons."

Ken pointed her fork at him. "See? We're the Hall Monitors. We did all the hard work. And you won't even tell us what you did about it, even though I can tell it has something to do with stopping VD. Ruthie was right. We should focus on finding VD so we can stop him sooner. Ravencrest students are the ones suffering the most—"

"No, they are not." Aiden's tone warned her to not probe any further.

She ignored the warning. "Yes, they are! They're the ones who're forced to do horrible things, like cheat and transport drugs and hurt the school. They're the ones that're all stressed out and scared and feel unsafe here. They're the victims of what VD's doing."

"Yes, they are," Aiden said quietly. "But they aren't the only ones."

"Who else is VD after?" Ken squinted at him. "What, did VD do something to you?"

Aiden began to laugh. It was a hysterical, bitter laugh that nearly brought him to tears. Ken could only watch as he laughed so hard that he leaned over, his elbows on his knees, gasping for breath. "What has VD done to me?" he said, still bitterly laughing. "Ask him yourself when I'm done with him. See how smart he thinks he is then." His face was transformed into hatred so terrifying that Ken was rooted to her seat.

With that statement still ringing in the air, Aiden grabbed his plate, rose to his feet, and left the room in a few long strides.

Ken watched him in shock. Her hands were trembling. She had never seen such pure hatred in anyone's eyes. This was not the same boy who had fought alongside her the first day Ravencrest was attacked. This was someone completely different. She couldn't help but wonder if the old Aiden would ever return.

Layla came over. "Hey, Ken! Class is starting soon, so we should go. Come on!"

"Wasn't Aiden just here?" Ruthie asked. "I was going to come over, but I didn't want to expose the Hall Monitors or anything."

"Uh-huh." Ken rose to her feet robotically. "He wanted me to tell everyone 'great job with our most recent case' or something like that."

"Case?" snickered Layla. "What are we, private detectives? I could order a couple of trench coats if we need a uniform."

"That would be fun," Ruthie admitted.

"VD's going to lay low for a while," Ken surmised as the three girls gathered their belongings and strolled to the mess hall exit. "That's his usual pattern. He does somethin' big then waits for a little, then strikes again. I think he tries to do it without any pattern so we're not prepared, but we'll be prepared this time. Long story short, he's not gonna strike again anytime soon—"

The words had barely left her mouth when Everest bolted through the mess hall doors with Ming on his heels. "VD struck again!" Everest shouted before Ken could finish speaking.

"What?" gasped Ruthie. "Oh no."

"We don't have time to meet in the attic," Ming said as he caught up to Everest. "The closet will suffice."

"LAYLA!" shouted an angry voice.

"Or not," Ming murmured as Sophia pushed through the crowd, red-faced. "How could you?" she almost screamed. Her eyes found Ruthie and Ken, and her face twisted. "Did *you* tell?"

"I didn't tell anyone, I swear!" Layla promised.

"Me neither!" Ruthie added.

"Same," said Ken. "What happened?"

"This," said Everest grimly. He showed them a picture of the little whiteboard in the area where the hallway split into dorm halls. It stated in permanent marker, SOPHIA MANCHESTER WON'T BE AT RAVENCREST NEXT YEAR. ASK HER PARENTS WHY ONCE THEY'RE FINISHED WITH THAT MESSY DIVORCE. - VD

"Oh, Sophia," Ken said sympathetically and reached out to comfort the girl.

Through tears, Sophia pushed her away. "How could you *do* this? Which of you told?"

"I swear I didn't!" Ruthie begged. "And Layla and I have been inseparable, so I know she didn't tell anyone! And I know Ken keeps secrets!"

"So do I!" Layla added.

"We all keep secrets," Ken corrected.

"Then how did VD find out?" Sophia accused. "I only told you three!"

"Did your parents tell you over a phone call? Maybe someone was listening," Ken pointed out.

"Yes, but I used the new, 'really secure' Ravencrest call app. Everyone uses it now." Sophia's eyes blazed. "It was one of you! You can play all innocent if you want, but I know it was one of you! VD was right—I can't trust anyone here! You're all a bunch of two-faced liars!" She was sobbing now as she shoved Layla hard. "Fine, go ahead and tell everyone! I don't care! No one likes you guys, and I hope everyone sees you for the lying hypocrites you are!"

"That's enough," Ming said firmly as he stepped in front of the other girls. Everest stepped beside him as a warning.

Sophia turned away and ran.

No one saw her, and by lunch, the rumors were flying. The picture of the whiteboard had circulated quite a bit. Everyone knew Sophia had called in sick and was probably crying in her room over the tragic occurrence of her parents divorcing and refusing to pay her tuition fees.

They all agreed to meet after school in the attic, where Aiden would undoubtedly be. Ken was determined to find VD herself now. For once, Layla was quiet for most of the day. Out of all the Hall Monitors, Ruthie was the most hurt. She was found crying in the bathroom during class. The girl who found her—Layla—hugged her and promised not to tell a soul.

Less than a minute after classes ended, every Hall Monitor was present in the attic.

"Okay, I've been thinking about this," Ken said the moment Aiden stepped in, "and I think I know how VD did it."

"*How?* I've been puzzling over it all day and I can't figure it out," Ruthie said.

Layla agreed, "It doesn't make sense. I looked at the security footage Ming sent on the group chat—"

"I uploaded it to Ming's phone during lunch," Aiden explained to Everest, whose phone was being "repaired." Aiden planned to stop by during lunch tomorrow to drop it off with the new security software. He had already "repaired" the other Hall Monitors' phones as well.

Layla continued, "—and it wasn't helpful. I mean, you can't even see the message in the footage because of the glare from the whiteboard. You have to be there in person to see it. I only know that the whiteboard was clean when I left the dorms this morning, but somehow it had a nasty message written on it before breakfast was over. My guess is a student walked by and blocked the camera's view for a second, which is just enough time for another student to slip behind them and write on the whiteboard. Then there would be at least two students in cahoots."

"Yet neither student was emailed," Aiden interjected. "That is, I haven't detected any emails about it."

"And the security cameras would have spotted it," Everest pointed out.

"And that wouldn't be enough time to write it so perfectly," Layla finished. "It doesn't even look like handwriting. It looks like a font."

"It was in marker," Ruthie confirmed. "I went to the dorms during lunch to check it out."

"Ken, what were you going to say?" Everest asked.

"I was thinking during lunch about all these crazy ways VD could have done it," Ken said, "and then I wondered if the solution was much more simple. I thought, what if the whiteboard was just double-sided? A student could have written it earlier, then set a remote-controlled mechanism to flip the whiteboard over. And I wouldn't be surprised if it flipped over at the exact same time that a whole bunch of kids left their dorms for breakfast, hiding the whiteboard from the camera's view. And as for not finding any emails, we already know VD is communicating with some kids in other ways."

"So the message was written earlier," Layla realized. "Does that mean Campus Security has to sort through all of last month's footage to see if anyone wrote on the back side of the board?"

"They could," Ken said. "But it wouldn't do anything if the message was written this week. That's when the banner for *Les Misérables* auditions was put up, covering the whiteboard and allowing anyone to write on it by just stepping behind the banner. We can make a list of everyone who stepped behind the banner, but—"

"That would be everyone," groaned Layla.

"So we can't do anything about it." Everest concluded.

"We can help Charlotte, but the damage has already been done," sighed Ruthie. "Still, we can try to keep it from happening to another student. VD might find some other kid's secret and put it on that board. Aiden, can you get Campus Security to find a way to—"

"I already did," Aiden said. "The cameras have been adjusted so there's no longer a glare from the whiteboard. If anyone writes on it again, we'll know who wrote what on there."

Ken frowned. "What puzzles me is *why* VD is doing all this."

"What does it matter—" Aiden began to cut her off, but Ken plowed on, "I mean, first it was the cheating. Sure, VD got Veronica to broadcast answers from a very lengthy answer key she had to memorize and practice, but who was listening? Was it a reward for something another student had done that we never found out about? Or was it solely intended to hurt Veronica by making sure someone else found out? If so, why did he make her encrypt the answers so much?"

Everest considered this. "The obvious motivation behind the drug ring and the flash drive switch was money."

"Is it?" Ken challenged. "What if it's power, like if he's proving himself to someone else? What if this is VD's way of leaving his mark—by doing crazy, dangerous, horrible things to students of a highly esteemed and supposedly safe academy? It's like saying, *Right now I'm targeting these kids, but soon it'll be world leaders.*"

Layla nodded. "That's a good reason, but there might be more motives behind it. What if he has something against Ravencrest, like a personal vendetta?"

"Who would have something against Ravencrest Academy?" Ruthie naively asked. "I know kids get upset when they don't get in, but you have to be really messed up to start a drug ring and cyberbully students and try to steal government secrets."

Layla sighed. "Oh, Ruthie, do you seriously not realize why people might dislike Ravencrest?"

"It doesn't matter," Aiden snapped. *Another lie.* "You all need to focus on protecting Ravencrest from another attack. If you don't, you're only helping VD. He got away with this because we didn't think he'd do something so soon."

"That's true. Well, we've done everything we could. Poor Charlotte," Everest mused. "I wonder who will be targeted next...."

Everest yawned as he stepped into the mess hall. He could already imagine the simmering, delicious breakfast waiting for him. After he had found out about Ravencrest's incredible menu, he'd decided to try a new dish every day with RAVEN's help. Today, however, he didn't need RAVEN's help. He knew it was time for good old-fashioned scrambled eggs, French toast, and bacon. He was salivating as he picked out his order; he was so focused on his food that he didn't notice how quiet the mess hall had become when he stepped inside.

He searched for a seat and found a grim-faced Ming. It was then he realized how many people were whispering. They were looking at him, then looking away, and then looking back at him.

Anxiety bubbled in his stomach. He sat down next to Ming and whispered, "What's going on?"

Ming was a man of little words. He silently pulled out his phone and gave it to Everest.

The picture had gone viral among Ravencrest students. It was a picture of a whiteboard in the boys' lounge room which stated, ASK EVEREST MICHAELS'S FATHER IF HE'LL EVER STOP DRINKING AND IF HE REALLY DID CHOKE HIS WIFE TO DEATH. THAT IS, ONCE HE GETS OUT OF PRISON. - VD

Everest couldn't breathe. He couldn't speak, couldn't move, couldn't do anything except gasp lifelessly, his mouth opening and closing like a dying fish. "How—that's—" he stammered. Terror and despair pummeled him briefly. He had worked so hard to keep things secret. Then it was replaced by a burning anger. How dare VD do this to him!

"I'm sorry," Ming said quietly. There were no other words of comfort to offer. No amount of sleuthing and punishing VD would fix the fact that now everyone knew what Everest had been hiding for years. Nothing would fix how everyone now looked at him with pity; nothing would fix how his name would now be accompanied by talk of his background. There would be no escape from his past—not anymore, when he had least expected it.

Everest rose to his feet, fully aware of all eyes on him. His face was emotionless. He walked out of the mess hall, went up the elevator, and entered his room. Then he locked the door behind him and didn't emerge for a while.

"I hate VD," Layla muttered.

"Seconded," Ruthie said with a sigh.

The Hall Monitors were in the attic during lunch, and Everest was missing. This was worth missing lunch for. Everest had not been seen all day. To make matters worse, Sophia had emailed the Head of Administration and coldly let them know that she wanted to drop out.

News of this accidentally spread when porters discussed it and students overheard them. Three other students, including Veronica, emailed the Head of Administration with the same intentions; however, after participating in discussions with their counselors and family members, they were just barely persuaded to stay. The shocking news about students dropping out was spreading, and more kids were finding out about the way to escape the terror.

"The frustrating thing is we can't do anything about this." Ken kicked something. "All we know is that it's a boy sending these messages. But the boys' lounge room doesn't have a security camera. Plenty of boys went in and out of the room last night. Any one of them could have written on the whiteboard and left it in a position to be found the next morning."

"Fingerprints find anything?" Ruthie asked Aiden.

"No," Aiden said. His fists were clenching and unclenching, and his eyes were warlike. Everest was his friend. Aiden could only imagine how painful this must be for him.

"I can't believe this," Ken sighed. "I never knew Everest's dad was an alcoholic and had anger issues. He killed his wife!"

"He was suspected of killing her, but he denied it," Aiden corrected. "He always denied that he had anything to do with his wife's death. He agreed that they were not on peaceful terms and that he did beat her, but he firmly stuck to his claim that he did not kill her."

Ming scoffed bitterly. "It matters little here."

Aiden continued, "She was most likely killed by one of her many boyfriends. Neither of Everest's parents were married at the time. Everest was eight. He was in multiple foster homes until he was placed in a group home with people who cared very little about him. That is where he was able to rise up so he could attend Ravencrest."

"How did he get through all that?" marveled Layla.

"Most likely with the help of his older brother," Aiden said. "The two seem to take very good care of each other."

"How do you know all this?" Ken asked.

"I have my sources," Aiden said vaguely. His fingers tapped absentmindedly as he thought. "Where do you believe VD will target next?"

"He seems to like whiteboards. Where are the other whiteboards?" Ken asked, then answered herself just as abruptly, "Classrooms, the girls' lounge room, and the locker rooms. That's a lot of places he could go."

"If it's a boy doing this, you can rule out the girls' rooms," Layla pointed out. "It has to be the same person with the same handwriting, and if it's a boy, he'll be caught going into the girls' lounge room or into the girls' locker room."

"All the classrooms have extra security," Ruthie cut in. "Ever since the drugs incident, they change the classroom security codes every five days now. Besides, a porter is still alerted whenever someone enters or exits the room after hours, even if they're just cleaning the lab."

"Thus, VD's next attack will most likely be in the boys' locker room," Ming reasoned. "We need extra security in that part of the building, along with extra security in general."

"Excellent," Aiden said. "We have a plan. Now, all of you need to go. I know you all are very busy, and there's nothing more you can do."

"That's what we said last time and look what happened," Layla muttered, clearly feeling helpless. "It's not fair. We're supposed to keep going about our lives like nothing ever happened while Everest is..."

"He would want us to," Ming said. "To him, it would be better if none of us knew about this. He wanted nothing more to do with his parents, and we must respect his decision."

"How are we supposed to forget that?" Ken asked. "It's hard to forget something like that on purpose."

"Welcome to my world," Ruthie muttered.

"Pretend you don't know," Ming said. "Please. Everest never wanted anyone to know. He is still the same Everest he was before. He is still a popular, friendly, good-natured, athletic, and very intelligent biologist. He does not deserve to be defined by his parents' actions. Please at least give him that respect."

They all stared at Ming. Rarely had he ever used so many words at once before.

It didn't take long for them all to agree. From now on, they were all going to pretend they knew nothing about Everest's family. It was the least they could do to help their friend.

Chapter Twenty-Two

Aiden hadn't exactly lied. He had simply phrased his words tactfully. Just because he had told the others that they had done all that they could didn't mean he couldn't do something himself. For now, Aiden remained at the gym long after Porter Chan was finished, hoping Everest might show up to fencing practice, even if Aiden hadn't shown up for a while now. It was sad; Everest had been doing well. Aiden had even ventured to teach Everest some self-defense.

On his own, Aiden entered the boy's locker room and wrote out a message on the whiteboard, beginning with the words, DON'T WRITE ANYTHING. TAKE A PICTURE OF THE FOLLOWING MESSAGE AND SEND IT TO VD:

When he had finished, he returned to the main hall and ignored his conscience. He had just willingly passed down an opportunity to find the boy who was being used by VD. Then again, if he found the boy, VD wouldn't be able to communicate in the same way anymore, and Aiden wouldn't be able to bait VD out into the open. *I'll check in the morning before any student wakes up,* he decided. *Just in case.*

It was Tuesday night. Everest usually bought nachos on Tuesday nights and ate them with a few other boys in a lounge room.

To appease his restless conscience, Aiden stopped by Everest's room and knocked on the door. Ming opened it.

"He left," Ming said simply. "He's somewhere on the island."

"Why aren't you concerned?" Aiden asked.

Ming showed Aiden his phone. "I've been tracking him. He's walking around the campus, near the forest. Everest went hiking on previous weekends, so I know he is well-acquainted with nature. There is still an hour before curfew, and he will most likely come in at the last minute to avoid being seen by someone else."

Aiden sighed. "Oh, Everest. Did he tell you?"

"No. It is a part of him that he hoped to hide forever," Ming said. "He succeeded for many years, at his previous middle and high school. It was a cruel thing that VD did."

Aiden began to leave, then stopped. "Did you know?"

"Yes."

"How?"

Ming hesitated, then explained, "Everest's back and arms have scars on them. At night, he has nightmares and cries for his father to stop. When he awakes, he rocks himself back and forth until he falls asleep. It's a common trait in abused or abandoned children to rock themselves when in a painful situation. It was clear that he did not have someone to comfort him and that someone else was abusive toward him. I know of his close relationship with his brother, as seen in their frequent calls. And I know he prefers to never speak about his home life. In the years since his mother's death, he has adapted very well. I understood his intent to begin a new life."

Never had Ming used so many words to express himself. He always chose his words carefully and spoke frugally with little emotion. Yet now, Aiden heard the sorrow in his friend's voice.

"You're worried, aren't you?" Aiden asked. "Do you think he'll drop out?"

"No," Ming answered. "He is too stubborn to do that."

"How can you be so sure?"

"Everest is my friend," Ming said precisely, and that was the end of the discussion.

A few minutes after curfew, Ming called Aiden. "Everest has not returned," Ming said. "I assumed he would return immediately after curfew, but I must tell the porters the truth should they check my room. Would you—"

"Find him?" Aiden was already trekking through the restricted part of the island, where vines covered the ground, trees were overgrown, and animals were scattered around him. He wore a headlight and camping gear should he be forced to stay during the entire night. "I'm doing so now."

Ming paused. "In the forest? It's night."

"I'm well aware."

There was silence. "You are a good friend, Aiden Ravencrest," Ming said at last. "Whether you want to be one or not."

"What's that supposed to mean?" Aiden scowled.

"I think you know." With that, Ming hung up.

"You're not a bad friend yourself," Aiden sighed, long after the chirping of crickets had passed.

Aiden shone his flashlight and used his forensics knowledge to track the path of his friend. Everest had left Ravencrest, seeming to have followed no particular plan or direction. He had been walking, then running, then sitting, and then walking again. By the time Aiden had entered a ten-foot radius of where Everest was, a solid hour had passed and the island was smothered in thick darkness.

While trekking, Aiden half-expected Everest to be on his way back. He also expected to find Everest alive and well, physically speaking.

He certainly did not expect to find him dying.

A snake had bitten Everest; a poison was working through his bloodstream. In the dim illumination, Everest gasped when he saw Aiden. "Aiden! I—I need help—"

"The helicopter's on their way. I just called them," Aiden said, kneeling down next to his friend and examining the bite mark. It was on the side of Everest's leg. He had moved little to slow the spread of the poison and had torn his undershirt, wrapping the rag-like material around the bite to stanch the bleeding. It was excellent work. "Roll over onto your stomach," Aiden instructed, pushing aside the material to see the extent of the damage. He tore off his own shirt and replaced the bandages. "It's bleeding badly, but you've done a fine job keeping the poison from spreading."

"Thanks," grunted Everest. Aiden wondered how long the boy had laid there, waiting, wondering, and hoping someone would come.

"Ming sent me. He was caught by porters when attempting to sneak out to find you." This was true; Aiden had been updated along the way. Campus Security was becoming more and more intense, with little helpful effect.

Everest chuckled. "He wouldn't survive out here for very long. I would've liked the company, though."

Aiden's eyes traveled across Everest's back and arms, and he saw the scars for himself. For a moment, he was sick. Then he regained his composure.

Everest turned. "You know, don't you? Everyone knows now." His voice was bitter.

"VD will pay," Aiden swore. "I promise."

"It doesn't matter. It won't fix anything."

"You're wrong about that," Aiden said.

"I thought I could start over here," Everest sighed. "I thought I could be *me*. I thought I'd never have to deal with it again. But my parents are part of me. I share half my DNA with each of them." He grimaced. "My parents will always be a part of me, no matter how much I try to get away from them."

Aiden was not a man of superfluous words or the sort to hug or cry. Yet at that moment, he felt a heartache not for himself but for someone else. It was a somewhat alien feeling, more so than it would have been before. He was talking quickly now before the helicopter came, almost choking on the words: "Your parents' actions do not define you. You are still Everest. You are not half your father and half your mother. You are *you*."

"Creatively put," deadpanned Everest, and Aiden smiled at the weak attempt at humor. "Don't let what others think of you change who you are," Aiden continued. "Let your merit speak for itself. In due time, your parents won't matter."

Everest chuckled grimly. "It matters to you, now that you know."

"I've always known."

"What?"

"Every Ravencrest student's background is scanned before their admittance," Aiden said. "It makes it more impressive that you've accomplished so much, and it's noble how you tried to hide it so only your merit mattered."

Everest's eyes were wide. "You always knew? But you never talked to me about it."

"You didn't want to. I respect that."

"I don't know what I'm going to do," Everest sighed. "Now everyone will be talking about it."

Aiden didn't contradict him. Instead, he said, "My mother died over a year ago."

Everest gaped at this unexpected statement.

Aiden continued, "I forgot nine months of my life, so sometimes it still feels new and sudden. I don't know if I'll ever make it part of my past."

"I'm sorry," Everest said.

"I remember some of what happened after she passed," Aiden said. His eyes were far away. "I remember how everyone knew and cared. I didn't want it then. So many people came to me and told me what Mother was like, as if I didn't already know. But I liked hearing about her. They made sure I was eating enough and took care of me as best as they could. I didn't want anything to do with that."

Everest said nothing, only listened.

"They cared about me. I see that now." Aiden finally looked back at Everest. "You have friends who care about you. We won't talk about it if you like. We *will* talk about it if you like. We'll be with you no matter what. I promise you our support in whatever you choose. You've been through a lot and—" The helicopter was closer now. Aiden spoke faster: "—we only want to help."

Everest stared at him, studying Aiden's face as the lights from the helicopter flashed above them. Someone said something over an intercom. Everest yelled back that he was all right, and Aiden helped him stand up. As a ladder came down, Everest quietly said, "Thanks, Aiden."

"For what?"

"For being yourself again."

Aiden's mouth became dry.

Everest turned in the half-light. "We only want to help you too."

It was long after midnight when Aiden returned to his room. He had stayed with Everest and made sure the boy would be safe. Everest was exempted from his classes the next day, and Ming agreed to drop off all the classwork. It was admirable that Ming, after having stayed up for half the night, was willing to go to class. It might have been easy at a normal high school to go to school without sleeping enough, but it was extremely difficult to do so with courses as difficult and engaging as Ravencrest courses.

By Wednesday morning, the news had spread regarding Everest's trek into the forest, which involved a snake bite. Friends stopped by the nurse's office to check on him. Darlene stopped by with some flowers and a card, then left, giggling and under the false assumption that no one knew it was her. All the Hall Monitors stopped by and gave their own form of encouragement.

No one mentioned Everest's background.

Everest was as easy going as ever. "I always found snakes fascinating," he admitted. "I suppose it wasn't very smart of me to drop everything I was doing and stare at one right before it got me."

"Couldn't you tell it was about to bite you?" Ruthie asked.

"No; by the time I realized, it was too late. I tried to grab it, and that's why the teeth kind of dragged through the side of my leg." Everest grinned at Layla's grimace.

"I think I'm going to be sick," Layla mumbled at the raw sight of his wound. "I mean, how on earth did you make it through that? Everest, you really are a survivor."

Everest smiled. He had never thought about it that way before.

"Who was targeted next?" Everest asked when the silence stretched thin. "*Did* VD target anyone else?"

"Maybe," Ken said. "But if he did, Aiden erased it this morning before anyone saw it."

Everest was confused. "This morning? But he was with me most of the night. The only way that's possible is if he slept for, like, five hours."

Layla clarified, "It might have been Campus Security. Aiden wasn't clear about it. He just said that 'they' had the issue under control and that nothing was in the boys' locker room anymore. Ming checked, just to make sure." She glanced at the card and flowers Darlene had sent. "Did you like them?"

"You mean the flowers? Did you send them?" Everest asked with a mischievous grin.

"No, I didn't," Layla admitted. "Do you know who did?"

Everest smirked. "Maybe."

Layla read the card out loud: *"Roses are red, violets are blue, I'm sorry about your leg, I hope you don't feel blue!"* There was a cartoon heart next to the words, and the flowers were already beginning to wilt. Layla could barely keep a straight face as she read the poem. Ken was laughing too hard to breathe. Ruthie just pursed her lips and tried to stop smiling but couldn't.

Everest chuckled. "Looks like the next Shakespeare wrote to me, huh?" Ruthie couldn't help it anymore; she burst out laughing.

"Speaking of Shakespeare, are you still trying out for the audition?" Layla asked brightly.

"Who said I was?"

"Come *on*, Everest, you should give it a try," Layla suggested. "You still have two days. The audition is on Friday, and it's only Wednesday. Seriously, give it a shot."

"I'll think about it. What part are you trying out for?"

"Cosette."

Ken interrupted with, "I'm aiming to do the lights, and I know Ruthie's hoping to play in the pit."

Ruthie shrugged. "It'll be fun. Ming's trying out for the same position, too."

"So it'll be fun! All the Hall Monitors will be in it! Well, except Aiden," Layla corrected herself.

Ken looked up from her phone. "I haven't seen Aiden since this morning when he said that they had everything under control. He just grabbed breakfast, said one thing to me, and bolted. I feel like he was hiding something."

Everest winced. "Did you know his mom died a year back?"

"A little over a year," Ruthie corrected. "But yes, I know. I read the Wikipedia page on this."

"Do you know every single Wikipedia page there is to exist?" Layla asked.

"No, but I know a lot of them," Ruthie admitted. "Just the interesting ones, anyway."

Everest continued, "And did you know that he lost his memory for nine months right after his mom died?"

Ruthie was shocked. "I didn't know that. How did that happen?"

"I don't know. He doesn't like to talk about it."

"When I talked to him earlier, he got really weird about VD. I think VD did something to him that made him lose his memory," Ken said. "And I think VD did something else to him in Argentina. Haven't you noticed how much he's changed since Argentina?"

"No kidding," Ruthie agreed. "I definitely noticed."

"Well, if doesn't want to talk about it, we should respect his—" Layla began, but Everest interrupted her, "Actually, I think that's why he doesn't want us to go after VD. He might be trying to protect us, or maybe he wants to go after VD himself. Or maybe it's both of those reasons."

"We don't know for sure," Ken said. "And I'll confront him after the auditions. I think everyone will be busy until then."

"That's two days from now! What if something happens before then?" Ruthie protested.

Ken glanced at her sideways. "What's the most that could happen in the next two days?"

Note from Ken: Looking back on this, I definitely jinxed it.

Chapter Twenty-Three

Aiden was satisfied. He had left a message of his own for VD, daring the man to come out of hiding and warning him that Xipe would be tortured for answers if VD didn't comply. As Aiden had written, he was willing to make a trade: Xipe for answers. VD had to come alone and in person. He was to answer all of Aiden's questions within the span of an hour, and Aiden would hand Xipe over at the end of the hour. Of course, Aiden had been lying. He was not going to hand Xipe over. No, he was going to destroy VD the moment the man stepped out of the darkness.

I WON'T ASK YOU WHAT YOUR PLANS ARE, Aiden had written. BUT YOU HAVE 24 HOURS. I'LL SEE YOU AT MIDNIGHT ON THURSDAY AT THE NORTHEASTERN CAVE IN THE RESTRICTED AREA.

DON'T KEEP YOUR BROTHER XIPE WAITING.

For their own safety, he avoided the others all Wednesday except for a quick update at breakfast. Yet now it was Thursday morning and Ken had just cornered him. He had risen early to avoid her, and apparently, she had anticipated this.

There she was, having woken up ten minutes earlier, impeccably dressed and at the mess hall less than a minute after six in the morning.

"Ken!" he said, trying to sound excited to see her. "How nice to see you! There aren't any updates so I had better be on my way—"

"Really, Aiden? C'mon, you're gonna sit with me during breakfast so I can ask you a few questions." She was clearly enjoying this as she blocked him from leaving. He sighed at last, and she finally sat down, obviously expecting him to sit with her.

Instead, he said, "I've got to go." With that, Aiden ran off.

Ken yelled after him, but he was already gone. She frowned. This wasn't his usual style of avoiding her. Was he too tired to think of something clever? Or was he doing something more important than talking to her? Of course, now he was running off into the distance so she couldn't see him again until tomorrow morning when he would not-so-cleverly outsmart her again, and then—

What if she just followed him?

What a great idea! What could Aiden possibly be doing anyway? It wouldn't hurt, and she was curious. After all, she *was* a Ravencrest student. So instead of getting breakfast, she grabbed a bagel, a packet of cream cheese, a butter knife, a napkin, and a plate, then chased after him.

Aiden was too focused on setting the trap to realize he was being followed. At any other time, he would have thoroughly checked to ensure he was alone. Yet now, time was of the essence. VD would most likely go against his word and find a way to double-cross Aiden. So he had to set the trap now and monitor it until VD arrived. Then he would strike.

First, he found the cave. It wasn't too far of a hike. At times he thought someone was following him, but upon inspection, he found that it was only an animal slithering nearby. After a few repeated findings of this, he stopped checking every time he heard leaves rustling behind him from a distance. He had taken some materials in a backpack, and now he worked hard to set up the trap, tying the ropes and net in their correct positions. He adjusted everything inside the cave and ensured the vegetation covered what it needed to. Then he hoisted his empty backpack over his shoulder, grabbed his duffel bag, and spoke into an old walkie-talkie: "Bring him over."

It took a good ten minutes for a bribed construction worker—the same one who had broken in with Xipe—to arrive, carrying the unconscious Xipe and looking very nervous. "You—you got the money?" he asked.

"I do." Aiden delivered him a bulging parcel. It contained $30,000 in hundred-dollar bills.

"No one will know?"

"No one. Now get yourself out of here and get your mother's medical bills paid."

The man's face paled. "How did you know—"

"Get out. And don't come back."

It took very little encouragement for the man to leave as fast as possible. He was gone within the minute. Aiden dragged Xipe to the other side of the glass and handcuffed him as planned. He locked the glass on the side with a small key and smiled, satisfied.

Aiden left, failing to notice the curious eyes peering into the cave.

The moment Aiden was gone, Ken ran through the shrubbery and curiously squinted into the darkness of the cave. She wanted to call out to whoever was inside, as she had watched Aiden drag an unconscious man into the cave. Why was Aiden setting this up? Was this some sort of meeting place? Why was the other man unconscious?

It was a puzzle, and she loved puzzles.

Ken always wore one of the necklaces from her collection. Each had a tiny little silver gadget dangling off a chain. It might have looked like something small, like a wrench or a mini screwdriver or a small flashlight, but make no mistake, it worked. In her necklace collection, she had a silver little flashlight gadget, a screwdriver, a lockpick, a battery full of wires to use, an antenna, a little pen, and once even a tiny tracker. These techy necklaces weren't just for show; they were extremely helpful whenever she found herself in a tight spot. As a New York City girl who had been in quite a few dangerous situations before, she knew how to take care of herself. Her mother had always thought these necklaces were more of Ken's cute little inventions; Ken's mother was wrong. These necklaces were the only gifts Ken had ever asked her dad to buy for her.

So now she took her little flashlight out from under her shirt and shone it into the cave. It was a small light, as she hadn't thought she would be wandering around in a cave before eating breakfast, and she could only see some boulders and the unconscious man.

Why is the poor guy handcuffed? The unconscious man was chained to something in the wall. He had a faint beard and wore prison uniform-like clothes. *Is he a convict?*

Ken knew better than to wake him up. She saw her reflection and realized there was glass between them. Shifting her position slightly, she saw the keyhole between the boulders on the side. So Aiden had locked an ex-convict behind the glass, then chained him to something in the wall. But why? What had this guy done that was so bad? She studied the man's face. He looked tormented, exhausted, and unnaturally thin.

She hesitated. Her instincts told her that Aiden had a good reason for putting him there. Nonetheless, she could at least get him something to eat. He looked starved. Acting out of the goodness of her heart, she wrapped her bagel and cream cheese inside the napkin and looked for a way to slip it through the glass. She stepped closer to examine it and—

"Hey!"

She yelled in shock as the ground beneath her gave way. *This was a trap!* The ground had been some kind of net covered in mud, and its instability forced her to fall into the pit that lay below. A split second before she hit the bottom of the pit, she stabbed her metal butter knife into the side of the pit and managed to hold herself upright, gasping and thanking God for that father-daughter rock climbing trip in eighth grade. It was true that her mother had guilted her father into taking it and that he ended up leaving halfway through for a business call; nonetheless, she had learned some serious life-saving skills there.

There was a pressure plate at the bottom. She understood; if she hit the bottom, an alert would be sent to Aiden. No way Aiden was going to find out about this. But all she had was a butter knife. She dug her fingers into the thick mud, grimaced, and held the plate in her teeth so it wouldn't hit the ground. Then she did her best to climb up. It was slow, grueling work, and when she hit rock, she almost cried out in frustration. There was no climbing this.

Why would Aiden want to trap someone in here? She was stuck in pitch-black darkness, and it was incredibly frustrating to climb this far just to hit rock. Besides, she was sure something was crawling under her. Bugs swarmed around her, and she thought she felt a faint tickling sensation on her back.

Don't scream. Whatever you do, don't scream.

Okay. She was stuck in a pit with a bagel and cream cheese in a napkin clenched between her teeth, clinging onto mud underneath a layer of rock in utter darkness with bugs and spiders all around her and a tiny thin light from her flashlight necklace slanting downwards into the gloom.

I think I'm going to scream.

"Don't let fear take over," Walter, her godfather, had told her once. "Let it run its course. Then act."

So she let the fear run its course, pounding in her heart, curling in her veins, suffocating her until her gasps became shorter, turning her into living terror.

Walter had been with her then. She was alone now.

Back then, she had been dangling off the side of a cliff, a single rope holding her in place. Walter had stepped in when Dad had stepped out of the trip. Walter had kept her in place and brought her to safety. Walter had taught her how to keep fear from controlling her. She missed him so much. One day she'd take her mother and godfather on a tour of the island and tell them all about this story. She could imagine it now, standing with those who loved her as she laughed and pointed down at the pit. *I can't believe I was so scared back then,* she'd say. *It's just a hole. It's not even that deep.*

That's right. It's just a hole.

A hole with a spider on her neck.

For a moment, the panic was back. She didn't dare to breathe as the spider crawled onto her arm and then into the mud near her. She recoiled away, and in the shaking of her flashlight necklace, glimpsed the unmistakable red hourglass marking.

Why would Aiden do this to anyone? It was horrifying.

If she wasn't a tough New York City girl, she would have started crying and screaming right then and there. But she was Ken. She didn't cry and scream. She acted.

With all her strength, she pushed her way into the mud and crawled through. Something coiled around her hand and bit it; pain exploded as she shoved it away. Red-hot fear was back, working through her system. There was no time to let it run its course.

So she used it.

The adrenaline fueled her as she pulled herself through the mud and kept pressing against the rock until she finally felt something weaker. She broke her head through and pulled herself up, gasping, mentally praying in relief. She wiped the mud off her face.

"Hey, kid," the handcuffed man said. He was standing across from her and had no expression on his face when she gasped. "You mind getting me out of here?"

Chapter Twenty-Four

When Ken returned to campus, Aiden met her at the entrance with a cup of hot cocoa and a towel. She was drenched from the rain, which hid the mud hanging in clumps under her jacket. "Hey," he said, draping the towel around her shoulders as he led her in. She shivered, and he walked with her to her room. "You've got the whole academy looking for you."

"Really?"

"Your friends all got worried when you didn't show up to class," Aiden said. "They checked your room and called you for hours during all your classes. A small army of girls showed up at the office of the Head of Administration and told him you were nowhere to be found."

Ken laughed, then coughed from the cold. "I was gone for three hours. And two of those hours were spent wandering around trying to find my way back."

"I assumed you were out trying to find me," Aiden said as they neared the entrance to the dorm halls. They took a turn, his arm still holding the towel around her shoulders. "Which was a very ridiculous thing to do."

Ken pushed Aiden away and he grabbed her hand, turning it over briefly. Before she could pull it away, his face darkened. "Rope burn."

The atmosphere between them turned chilly instantly.

She knew.

"Why did you set a trap in a cave?" Ken scowled, yanking her hand away. "Why would you do that to *anyone*?"

"Don't tell me—"

"Yes, I fell in, thank you very much!"

For a moment, his face melted into concern, and he examined her other hand before she could pull it away. "Bite marks." His face paled. "There were dangerous animals in there. You need to see a nurse now." Immediately, his pace increased, forcing her to walk faster to keep up with him. Suddenly, he stopped in his tracks. "Why wasn't I alerted?"

"I outsmarted your trap," Ken said proudly. "I climbed up the side of the pit and dug a hole right into the, um, the outside."

He caught her verbal stumble. "You dug yourself into the trap?"

"No, I mean, yes," she stammered.

He blocked her from moving, intent concern in his eyes. "Did he hurt you?"

"No!" Ken tried to say.

"Tell me the truth. What did he do to you?"

"Nothing! Why would you think he would hurt anyone?"

Aiden pulled up his shirt and undershirt. "You see the scars on my ribs? Guess who gave them to me, along with a concussion, some broken bones, and plenty more bruises."

"Argentina!" Ken gasped.

"Yes, it was in Argentina. I was lying about the car accident. Now, answer the question. What did he do to you?"

She swallowed hard. "Why would he—"

"Because he works for VD."

Ken couldn't breathe. "You're joking. I just helped a man who works for VD?"

"You *what*?"

"I mean," Ken managed to slip under his arm and rush to her hall. "You're right, I need to get to the nurse's office. I don't feel well—"

"What have you *done*?" Aiden yelled, running up to her and blocking her from entering the girls' hall. "Did you let him go?"

"Aiden—"

"*Did you?!*"

She felt hot tears prick her eyes. "I didn't know!"

"You *imbecile*!" Aiden shouted. "How *could* you? Do you know how close I was to killing VD?"

"*Killing*?"

"That's right," Aiden said, breathing heavily, burning in rage. "Killing him the way he killed my mother. I was going to make him feel every bit of pain he caused me. I was so close. He was right *there*. And you destroyed everything by letting Xipe go free! See, this is why I don't care for people anymore. They're nothing but weaknesses. Variables. Investments you can never control."

"You don't mean that," said Ken, hating herself for the growing lump in her throat.

"Yes, I do. It's what cost my mom her life. It's what cost me my *revenge*." Who was this boy looking back at her, with eyes so dark and hatred so fierce? Where was the friend who had pulled harmless pranks, who had saved Ruthie from the cheating incident, and who had helped Everest? What was the unrecognizable monster who stood before her now?

"I didn't know, okay?" Ken shouted back. She turned away, brushed past him, and walked down her empty hall. Thankful that the rest of the school was in class, she hollered, "Now leave me alone!"

"Gladly!" Aiden yelled after her. "I don't know what I was thinking, recruiting you—recruiting any of you Hall Monitors. I can handle everything here myself. All you guys do is slow me down."

Ken stopped and spun around, her wet hair tossing behind her. "Now I know you're crazy! We stopped government secrets from leaking out. We created a way to keep VD from hurting more people here. We stopped the drug ring—and you know, we did that one without you. You can be as mad as you want at me, but don't pull everyone else into this! They've all worked so hard to be a part of the Hall Monitors, and you know better than anyone how much we all already have on our plates! We're doing this because we care—"

"And you think I don't? Ravencrest is all I have left." He sounded broken for a moment, his wild eyes on the verge of tears. "I was *so* close to getting things back, I was *so* close, and you ruined everything!"

Despite herself, Ken's heart softened. "Oh, Aiden—"

"Get away from me," he breathed. "You know what? Thanks to you, I'm done with the Hall Monitors. It's over, starting now. You all leave everything to me. It's more efficient that way, more predictable."

A jolt of panic tore through her. "You don't mean that."

"I do. Now get out of here before I have you expelled." He turned and briskly walked away.

Behind him, Ken called, "What if Xipe told me something about where VD is?"

Aiden stopped in his tracks. He didn't turn around.

"He told me he had a friend on this island," Ken said desperately. "I can get the team together and we can find him. Just let us help. Give me another chance. I didn't know anything because you didn't tell me, and now that I know, I want to help. I'm on your side, Aiden. Let me help."

"No," he said without turning. "I think you've done enough damage already, haven't you?" His voice was cold, emotionless, and slightly smug. It was the perfect thing to say to maximize the amount of damage he could cause.

Ken watched him go, tears running down her face the moment his back was turned. "I hate you, Aiden Ravencrest!" she yelled after him.

He didn't break his stride or turn around; he only replied coolly, "Am I supposed to care?"

With that, Aiden Ravencrest left her standing in the middle of the girls' hall, cold and crying. She hugged herself and suddenly longed to go home to her mother and godfather who always treated her like she was special. Then she caught herself. *What am I doing, standing here and crying like a wimp? I'm Mackenzie Robscone, Ravencrest student, inventor, groundbreaking researcher, hacker extraordinaire, and puzzle genius.*

She wasn't going to just stand here and cry.

No, she was going to *act*.

It was time to set things right.

An hour later, Ken emerged through one of Ravencrest's many back doors. She had showered, eaten, and dressed in one of Layla's combat boots, a new pair of jeans, a black shirt, and one of her jackets, the one with all the hidden pockets refilled with her favorite gadgets. She had pulled on her new watch and gadget gloves, then adjusted her technologically-enhanced friendship bracelets. And instead of grabbing her phone, she tucked her own phone (built from scratch and Ravencrest's advanced nanotechnology) into a pouch in the back of her jacket. As she stepped out of her dorm room, she felt invincible. All her tears had been washed off by a cold shower, and she hadn't let herself feel a moment of pity. *It's time to set things right.*

She snuck back into the forest and retraced the path from her memory. She was excellent at directions; by now, she had a thorough and detailed map of most of the island in her head. When she arrived at the cave, she used a more powerful flashlight to look around.

It's not here.

A smile traced her features; her necklace was missing, and with it, the little inactive tracker she had once used to spy on her mom. So the handcuffed man had stolen her necklace, as she'd suspected. It had worked out in her favor after all. For now, she created a hotspot, activated the tracker, and recorded its GPS position.

He's on the island.

He was moving quickly to a position off the island. She tucked her phone away and trekked through the forest. It wasn't safe to be here on her own, not with one of VD's friends roaming around. Why hadn't she listened to her instincts that told her Aiden had a good reason?

Because he was starving, beaten, and didn't deserve to be tied up like an animal.

But he was a murderer! Or working with one, anyway.

Aiden wants to be one too.

She closed her eyes. She could still remember the ferocity in his voice when he swore revenge. How could Aiden swear such a thing? She wanted to help and catch VD, of course, but she didn't want anyone to get murdered. Couldn't VD just go to jail for the rest of his life and his henchmen with him? Why did Aiden want to kill him?

He did lose his mom. She had never known that his mother had been murdered. No wonder he had been so secretive and deceptive lately, or why he was so short-tempered now. He was grieving and seeking revenge. She sighed. Feeling sorry for Aiden wouldn't solve things. He had still treated her badly, and there was no excuse for that.

While Ruthie might forgive easily, it was harder for Ken. No one treated her that way.

No one.

Ken pushed aside vines and shrubbery, then broke into a run as she approached the coast. She crouched behind a tree and peered through the interstices between the low-hanging branches. No one was there. "Where are you?" she murmured, pulling out a pair of glasses with multiple lenses. It functioned similarly to a binocular and helped her scan the nearby environment.

There! A submarine!

Now she'd either bust VD head-on or call for backup. But what if Aiden never answered and VD left? She snapped some photos on her phone, then uploaded them to the Hall Monitors group chat. So some of her friends would know, at least. Maybe they would confront Aiden. For now, she put her binocular lens in their rightful secret pocket in her jacket and cautiously approached the submarine. If she could secretly disable it, she could keep VD from—

A rough hand covered her mouth and muffled her scream.

Aiden was furious. After he had stormed around the building for about ten minutes, he stomped all the way back to his room, shoving Porter Jimmy out of the way.

"What do you want?" Aiden screamed at Jimmy, who stammered back something unintelligible.

Aiden frowned. "Yeah, that's right. Stay out of my way, Eliza."

He pushed past the porter and entered his room. Jimmy caught the door from slamming and stepped in. Immediately, Aiden yelled, "Get out of here!"

Jimmy squared his shoulders and looked Aiden straight in the eyes. "No. I have something to say and I will not leave until I say it."

"What?"

"I saw your fight with Mackenzie."

"So? She deserved it."

"You're pursuing VD?"

"Yes."

"You know about him?"

Aiden frowned. "So what if I know about him and what he did to my family? Don't tell me you knew about him from the beginning." His face darkened. "Of course, you're all keeping secrets from me. Now get out of here."

Jimmy stepped forward. "And I suppose you know about the Society?"

"What Society?"

Jimmy smirked. "Looks like I have your interest."

Aiden glared at Jimmy fiercely. The boy's eyes were on fire as he said, "I have no time for games. Tell me *now*, Eliza."

"I've been trying to get your attention for the past two weeks," Jimmy continued.

"Just tell me!"

"But here's the thing: my information doesn't come cheap." Jimmy was smirking now, and it made Aiden's blood curl. "If you want to know what organization your mother was a part of, you have to step out."

"Step out?"

"Of your security position." Jimmy watched him intently. "I know about the Hall Monitors. If you want to know what organization your mother was a part of, you need to get rid of the Hall Monitors. You've been especially exasperating this year, and if you don't have security clearance, you can't keep getting in my way and trying to outsmart me. From now on, you won't be able to rewrite code and run secret operations and get me into tight spots. I'm asking you to choose between your position and the truth."

"Between my friends and VD," Aiden murmured.

"Correct," Jimmy said with his usual nasty smirk.

Aiden sneered back. "That's low. You saw how desperate I was and used this to get me out of the way once and for all."

"Also correct," Jimmy grinned.

"Why are you doing this?" Aiden said at last. "I haven't bothered you in weeks."

A shadow crossed over Jimmy's face. "That, boy, is complicated. I'll explain only if you agree to resign from your position.

"So, tell me, what's it going to be?"

Chapter Twenty-Five

Aiden studied Porter Jimmy intently. The man was playing another game, another plot that Aiden knew little about. It didn't seem like Jimmy was about to give out answers, either.

"Well?" Jimmy demanded.

Aiden turned away. "I choose my friends."

"But—" Jimmy sputtered. "Your fight—"

"I'm not getting rid of the Hall Monitors," Aiden said. "I might be mad at Ken, but I'm not getting rid of the student union that is accomplishing more than Campus Security could in a year. And while I'll do anything to avenge my mother's death, I'm not going to let her die in vain by hurting Ravencrest. And I'm not resigning from Campus Security, either. I'll do whatever it takes to keep this school safe."

Jimmy's face was growing red. "I offer you the truth, and you refuse it? No one else is going to tell you, Aiden."

"That's probably true," Aiden admitted. He sat down in his mother's favorite chair and powered his laptop on.

"So how do you expect to figure it out?"

"I'm not sure yet," Aiden said placidly. "I have some ideas."

"How can you be so sure you'll find VD and be able to stop him if you don't know any real information yet?" Jimmy scowled.

Aiden smiled his own infuriating smirk. "I'm a Ravencrest, Jimmy. Now get out of here before I ask Porter Craig to drag you out."

Jimmy crossed the room in two steps and opened the door. He hesitated in the doorway, then turned back. "I'm not doing this because I hate you, Aiden Ravencrest, though I very much do hate you."

"That's heartwarming."

"I'm doing this because you shouldn't be involved," Jimmy argued. "The Society has gone on for generations, and I don't want another Ravencrest kid getting mixed up in all of this."

Aiden paused, giving Jimmy a chance to continue. When he didn't, Aiden probed, "Another Ravencrest kid? You mean my mother?"

Jimmy stammered, "Just—just stay out of it. You don't know what you're dealing with."

"I'm a Ravencrest, Jimmy."

"You say that like it means you can get yourself out of anything!"

Aiden laughed. "Who says I can't?"

"Don't be overconfident, boy," Jimmy warned. "That was your mother's fatal flaw."

"What do you mean?"

"I—never mind," Jimmy snarled. "You want that piece of information, you resign."

Aiden shook his head. "You never give up, do you, Eliza? It's admirable. In this case, however, making me resign is just another useless endeavor of yours. Perhaps you might find more success focusing on your job rather than trying to compete with me."

Jimmy growled, and the door slammed shut behind him.

Aiden chuckled briefly. His anger was already beginning to fade, and regret was taking its place. Had he really screamed at Ken, swallowed in the depths of rage? He hadn't been thinking clearly. How could he say that to her? She hadn't known.

He sighed. For the first time, he realized the truth: his quest for revenge was taking over everything.

Even Ken.

It had taken Porter Jimmy's nastiness for Aiden's anger to give way to his senses. He closed his eyes and replayed their conversation in his mind.

I was quite cruel. He'd apologize, of course, but how to make it up to her? Tell her he'd never get rid of the Hall Monitors as long as they were enrolled at this school? Tell her she was an essential part of the team? Tell her she shouldn't be punished for making the same choice he would've made in her place? He was just frustrated by his failure; he had to explain that to her.

"Oh, Mother," he sighed out loud, having stared at his desk for a good five minutes. "I really messed things up."

He'd give her time, and then he'd call her via his laptop. Yes, that was the right thing to do. He couldn't call her on his phone, all because of...well, that wasn't important. For now, he'd focus on his—

BEEP!

The screen of his laptop glitched for a second, and then the vivid image of the island's coast flashed across the display. The camera swung around to show Ken, standing still with Xipe's hands on her shoulders. Aiden stiffened, despite himself.

"Hey, Aiden," Ken said as if she was reading off a script. "VD's got me. He wants to make a deal with you."

"Tell him I'm not interested," Aiden said. "He either lets you go or he doesn't. Either way, he'll be caught soon enough. He has nothing to gain from holding you hostage. I'm staying out of this." This was a lie, of course. He could only pray that VD wouldn't call his bluff.

Ken coughed. "Yeah, um, that's not really an option. I think he's going to kill me."

"How would killing a girl help him?" Aiden scoffed.

Xipe deviously smiled. "Would you like a demonstration?"

"Think logically, Mr. Xipe," Aiden said slowly, like he was speaking to a kindergartener. "Killing a girl—or even mentioning that you have the intent to do so—on camera only adds to your list of criminal charges. And yours too, VD. I know you're there." While he spoke, his fingers danced on a screen under the desk. He had a backup laptop for this very purpose, that is, if his usual technology was hacked. Now he was tracing the video call.

Xipe laughed. "Foolish boy. VD doesn't care for criminal charges. He wants more of those. But he wants you most of all."

"He wants to see you exactly 24 hours from now," Ken recited in a monotone voice, still reading the cards held up behind the camera. "At the cave where you kept Xipe. You need to come alone and unarmed or I'll be killed on camera. Any resistance or tricks and I'll be harmed. For example, about how you're trying to send porters to this location now..." She squinted. "Wait, why does it say *T here*?"

Aiden's eyes widened and he shouted, "Don't!" before he could stop himself.

Xipe smirked and tasered Ken. She screamed once, then fell into his arms as the electric barbs shocked her. Xipe laughed and wrapped an arm around her neck as she silently screamed in pain. "A taste of your own medicine, huh?" he mocked as Aiden's face became carefully hardened once more.

"I'll see you then," Aiden said smoothly. "Should you harm her again, I swear I'll murder you all." He watched, unable to stop himself, as the seizure passed and tears streamed down Ken's face. For her to cry, the taser must really hurt.

Xipe grinned. "Looking forward to watching you try," he said, and the screen went blank as the call ended.

Aiden looked at his reflection in the dark mirror and exhaled. It was time to save Ken.

Ideas came to him right away. He scribbled down thoughts and details of a crazy Ravencrest plan. He could hack, he could break in, he could set a trap, he could double-cross, he could—

Suddenly, he remembered.

He sighed, stood up, crumpled the paper, and threw it away. Then he stepped outside, disarming and rearming his room's security system, and walked down the hallway. Perhaps this time, he'd ask the Hall Monitors for help.

"Ken was *kidnapped*?" Ruthie screamed as she saw the video.

Layla was hyperventilating. "Did you see him taser her?" she shouted. "I hate that guy! Who is he? Is he VD? Oh, man, he's going to *pay*!"

Everest was still. "He's going to kill her," he said quietly. "I knew he was bad, but this..."

Ming was silent, calculating. His eyes revealed nothing, as usual.

Aiden closed his laptop, which had recorded the entire call. "Now, I called you all here and showed you this video without an explanation for a reason. I believe this video explains itself. Still, some background information is essential. The man behind Ken—"

"The one with the taser," Layla snarled.

Aiden continued, "—works for VD. He also happens to be the man who attacked me in Argentina."

Ruthie frowned. "I thought you were in a car accident."

"I knew it!" Everest said. "I knew you were doing some kind of intense training or physical therapy or something like that. And when I saw your injuries in the forest, I *knew* it came from a beating, not from a car accident."

There was silence. Everyone knew how Everest had acquired this information: from experience. No one said anything, except for Ming who cleared his throat and spoke up: "Aiden, what do you suggest?"

"I've got some ideas," Aiden admitted. "But I need your help."

"Finally!" Ruthie said.

"Of course," Ming said.

"Anything for Ken," Layla said.

"Anything to beat VD," Everest said.

Aiden looked from face to face, each determined and blazing with ambition and hope. He was touched. He saw some of himself in each one of them.

No more secrets, he thought. He had been going about this all the wrong way. The Hall Monitors were not his weaknesses. His friends didn't get in his way. No, they could help him. They really cared.

And he knew he'd do anything to help them.

"So?" Layla prompted, impatient as always.

Aiden smiled his old smile. It was a glimpse of his past self. "First..."

Chapter Twenty-Six

"First," Aiden said, "We need to know where Ken is being held. Did any of you notice any clues in the video?"

"I did notice something, but it's kind of small," Ruthie confessed.

Layla nudged her. "Give it a shot."

Blushing a little, Ruthie finally said, "Okay, I might be wrong, but can you zoom into Ken's hand? I thought I saw something, but I'm not sure. Zoom in a *lot*, like as much as possible. And then play the video. There—did you all see that?"

"I do!" Layla said with excitement. "It's a blinking red dot! It's really tiny and faint, and it's blinking so fast. What is it?"

"An infrared light," said Ruthie with a proud grin.

Aiden began laughing. "Brilliant, Ken, just brilliant."

"I don't understand," Everest said impatiently. "How did she get that red light without the goon behind her noticing? And why is it so small and fast?"

Ruthie explained, "Infrared light is light on the electromagnetic spectrum that is undetectable by the naked eye but since its wavelength is so close to the wavelengths for visible light, it can be seen on camera. Ken's a technology wizard, so I bet she created a device where she can tap out a word on her palm and the device will rapidly transmit it in Morse code in infrared light. She's wearing black fingerless gloves, and I know she likes to add all sorts of updates to her clothes, so I bet you those gloves have some sort of technology woven into them."

"Her jacket probably holds a lot of survival gear," Layla said with a touch of pride. "Did you know that she designed a jacket which can transform into a glider?"

"Did you know about the boots that can send electrical shocks through any surface they touch?"

"Did you know about the necklace that can be a magnifying glass, a set of binoculars, or a camera?"

"Did you know about the headband with a tracker and a recording device?"

"Did you know about the—"

"I think we get the point," Everest interrupted. "Ken knows how to take care of herself."

Ming quietly said, "She likes being prepared and doing things on her own, though she doesn't mind working in a team. Even then, she's quite the leader." He glanced at Aiden. "Why was she on this part of the island by herself?"

Aiden winced. "We got into an argument. It's a bit of a long story."

"No secrets, Aiden," Layla warned. "We can't help if we don't know the full story."

At last, Aiden duly recounted how he had lured Xipe, kidnapped him, and left him as bait. He mentioned how Ken had unwittingly fallen into his trap and set Xipe free; next, he described the disastrous argument that had ensued. Finally, he added, "Also, I might have forgotten to mention this, but VD killed my mother, gave me two concussions, and tried to kill me both times."

They all stared at him, mouths hanging open and eyes wide in utter shock.

"Oh, Aiden, I'm sorry," Ruthie said gently.

"And this same psychopath has Ken?" Everest said furiously.

Layla was on her feet now. "We have to act. Ken has a drone in her room that she created, and I bet we can use it to search the island."

"I've already decoded the infrared lights," Ming said. "It says SUBMARINE over and over until Ken was tasered."

"Submarine? Like the picture she sent in the group chat! I thought it was so random, but if she's signaling that...look, I recognized the background in the photo, and I can take you all there now; we don't need a drone," Everest said, restless. "And forget what the doctor said—I don't need to rest. I'm fine."

"Don't push yourself too hard," Layla warned.

Ruthie looked up. "Are we all going to the restricted part of the island or should some of us stay behind? Y'know, in case we need any help?"

"I need to come along to show everyone where to go," Everest pointed out.

Aiden raised an eyebrow. "I know that area of the island well."

"Fine. I *want* to come along. I can't just sit here!" Everest pleaded. Aiden sighed yet agreed. The boy was a survivor. He had always come out alive. Besides, if Ming was by Everest's side, how much harm could come to either one of them? The two were very close, and it was obvious that both were willing to defend each other no matter what.

"I'll stay back, then," Ruthie suggested. "Coordinate things from here. I think we should use the drone anyway, so I'll pilot it for now."

"I'm coming to help Everest," Ming said, and no one contradicted him.

"I'm not staying behind!" Layla said indignantly. "It's time to make that jerk with the taser *pay*!"

"Well put," Aiden joked, and then it was time to act.

Ken grimaced in pain. She wanted to pull the metal barbs out, but her wrists and ankles were tied to the chair. Duct tape was over her mouth, so she watched silently as Xipe and the man with a mask hovered over the submarine controls. They were both speaking in Spanish.

Unfortunately, Ken was not bilingual or multilingual in any way. She spoke one language alone: English. She just wasn't great with other languages.

Fortunately, she did have a little recorder in her necklace, which was recording every spoken word. She was surprised that neither man had put her through a metal detector. Then again, what harm could she do in her barely conscious state, even with a weapon?

Being tasered really hurts, she had to admit. She grit her teeth at the thought of the pain. "Please just take them out," she said through the duct tape, knowing her words were muffled.

Xipe said something back in Spanish, and the man in the mask chuckled. He walked over and pulled back the duct tape. "Do you have something to say?" He seemed smug, as if he knew he had already won. Ken fiercely glared back. "Yes! Could you—" Her voice choked and she gasped when Xipe mockingly pointed the taser at her again.

Surprisingly, the man with the mask seemed to soften. He pulled each metal dart out swiftly and might have even winced when she cried out in pain each time.

"Thanks a lot," she muttered, half-meaning it.

In pulling out the final dart, his hand brushed her jacket, specifically the pocket with her phone in it.

Oh no.

She stiffened, but it was too late. The man with the mask pulled back her jacket and reached inside her pocket to find her phone. The masked man held it up and looked at Xipe, saying something angrily in Spanish. Then he said to Ken, "It seems you aren't as helpless as you look."

"I couldn't use it anyway," Ken said sourly. *VD has a faint London accent.*

Xipe crossed the room and pulled the ropes off swiftly. Ken rose to her feet unsteadily, rubbing the circulation back into her wrists.

Suddenly, she ran to the controls, hoping to send an alert signal out and already reaching for her antenna. Just as quickly, Xipe grabbed her, ripped the antenna out of her hands, and pushed her up against a wall. The masked figure pulled out a gun and placed it at her temples. "Move and you're dead," he said. "Cheeky of you to run off like that, but don't forget that we don't need you alive. You're only breathing because of my reluctance to kill a young girl mixed up in all this. Now, drop all your weapons and tools."

Ken scowled as she pulled out many of the hidden gadgets in her jacket, including her tracker, zip ties, batteries, wires, screwdrivers, extra mini-phones, and a few other emergency gadgets. She threw them all onto the floor, all the while fiercely glaring into Mr. Masked's dark eyes.

"*All* your weapons and tools," Mr. Masked clarified.

Ken sighed and took off her jacket, which had certain wires woven into it. She kicked off her boots, slipped off the fingerless gloves as well as the black sleeves protruding up her arms (both the gloves and sleeves contained embedded nanotechnology), and emptied out her pockets, filling the small pile in front of her even further. Then she reluctantly took off her headband and hairband, both of which were modified.

"*All*," Mr. Masked said menacingly. When Ken hesitated, Xipe pulled out a metal detector.

Sighing, she spit out an engineered retainer, gingerly took off her necklace, pushed off her bracelets, pulled out her earrings, and slid off the laser-producing ring. This was so unfair. She hadn't even been able to use any of her inventions after she was tasered.

Mr. Masked nudged the pile with his foot. "Is that all of them?"

Ken crossed her arms. She was now only in her usual blue jeans, black shirt, and black socks. "What more do you want? I'm not taking anything else off."

Xipe said something lewd in Spanish as he leaned against her. Ken didn't need a translator to tell what his intentions were. A bolt of fear raced through her as she tried to pull away from his strong, vice-like grip on her arms. He began to—

Mr. Masked stopped him. "We are not monsters," he said. He lectured Xipe briefly, who grudgingly let go of Ken.

Shaken, Ken tried not to panic. It seemed like she was at the mercy of Mr. Masked to protect her from Xipe, who was clearly not the innocent, hurt man in the cave. No, despite what Mr. Masked said, Xipe was a monster. A monster who helped kill mothers, who attacked boys, who might have even assaulted her now. It was even more terrifying because she knew who Mr. Masked had to be.

VD.

Being at the mercy of VD was the most terrifying experience of her young life so far, and she had been through quite a few terrifying experiences. But she was Mackenzie Robscone. She wasn't going to let this break her streak.

"What are you going to do to me?" Ken asked calmly.

Xipe suggested something in Spanish to VD, who raised an eyebrow and considered it. From the expression on VD's face, Ken knew it wasn't something good.

"Wait, don't hurt me," Ken said weakly. "Look, maybe we can figure out a deal. You can call Aiden again—"

"The more damaged she is, the more the boy will listen," Xipe interrupted, this time speaking in English.

VD sighed. "She is only a pawn. There is no reason to be unnecessarily cruel."

"Why not?" Xipe joked. At least Ken assumed he was joking. She watched VD's face, her heart pounding. It was horrible to know that her safety depended on the mercy and compassion of a man who had murdered Aiden's mother, mistreated dozens of Ravencrest students, and almost killed Aiden.

Finally, VD began to say, "You may—"

That was all it took. Ken darted past Xipe, pulled out a metal device from her retainer (a part she had kept in her mouth), and aimed it toward the control board, immediately disabling the main controls. The submarine switched into emergency mode, flashing a timer as to when oxygen would run out. It began to surface. Ken inwardly cheered, whirled around to face her attackers, and—

Xipe brutally tackled her to the floor, pinning her to the ground in a steel-like hold. Before she could say a word, he pulled out the taser.

Instinctively, she trembled and tried to crawl away. "No, please—"

He tasered her. Three times.

Unable to stop herself, she screamed at the intensity of the pain that paralyzed her and pulled her under. She was only sixteen; she was too young to be tasered again and again. And even Mackenzie Robscone felt fear. Cold, hard fear as VD stepped forward and kicked her hard in the ribs, sending rays of pain that pulsed through her until she couldn't stop crying. As she lay on the floor, sniffling like a wimp, she suddenly felt a sharp pain in the side of her arm. Someone had stuck a needle into her arm. She turned to see VD straightening back up and disposing of the needle in the trash can, all the while yelling orders at Xipe.

In those terrible moments before she passed out, as Ken saw VD's brutality toward an innocent girl caught in his plans, she understood Aiden's hatred. Now her heart blazed with the desire to make VD pay. She wouldn't stop until justice was served. One thing was for sure:

You messed with the wrong girl, Mr. VD.

The drone, piloted by Ruthie, caught a full view of the northeast region of the island's coast. It was beautiful, that was for certain. She spoke in the old earpieces borrowed from the porters: "You all are nearing the place where Ken was most likely taken, judging by the video's location and the background of the photo she sent in the group chat."

"Excellent," Aiden said. He paused and turned back to the others trudging behind him. Everest and Ming were close by, but Layla seemed exhausted. "Layla, are you alright? Perhaps you should stay back with Ruthie." It was the perfect thing to say to suddenly energize her. Layla sprang to her feet, wiped the sweaty hair from her forehead, and managed to say, "I'm fine. I'm just not used to the heat. And there are so many bugs and animals around."

"Is that a problem?" Everest said, turning back while the others trekked ahead.

"Well, I don't *mind* the animals, and hiking isn't *too* bad, it's just so *hot* and *humid* and I'm not *used* to it," Layla complained dramatically, emphasizing almost every other word.

"You may go back if you wish," Ming offered.

Layla straightened. "No, saving Ken is worth it. Let's do this!" She pulled her leg free from some bushes, then screamed as she lost her balance and nearly fell into a decomposing log swarming with bugs. Everest grabbed her collar and pulled her to her feet in the nick of time so that they were suddenly eye to eye. "Thanks," Layla gasped. "I owe you one."

"Anytime," Everest said, barely able to speak at all.

Layla blinked. "Uh, Everest?"

"Yeah?" he breathed.

"Can you please let go of my shirt collar?"

He blushed and stammered, immediately letting go of her. "Right. Sorry, I—I didn't mean to—"

"Don't worry about it. Thanks for your help!" She skipped around him, hiding the little smile on her face. *How adorable.*

Everest took a deep breath. "Act cool," he muttered to himself. *I've got it bad,* he could tell.

In front of them, Ming turned back and raised a single eyebrow. Everest pretended he hadn't noticed and caught up with the rest.

Ruthie suddenly gasped from the Hall Monitors' headquarters. "Oh! I see Ken!"

"Is she safe?" Aiden asked immediately.

"She's okay," Ruthie said in relief. "I mean, she's unconscious, but she's breathing. And—" She abruptly broke off. When she spoke again, her voice was full of rage. "How dare he! That monster!"

"What did he do to her?" Aiden said fiercely. "Answer the question, Ruthie!"

Ruthie finally said, "She's out cold, but it looks like VD hurt her! She's got blood on her face and shirt. It's like he kicked her in the face and stomach over and over. All her equipment is in this big pile next to her. The man who tasered her earlier is tying her up right now, and there's a man in a mask stepping out of a submarine."

"Get back to Ken," Aiden insisted. "Send me a picture of her now. Get as close as you can. I want to make sure none of her injuries are serious."

"The masked man must be VD," Ming realized.

Layla charged ahead. "Let's go help Ken!"

"She seems okay—" Ruthie began, then stopped after her cell phone *ding*ed in the background.

"Who was that?" Layla asked.

Ruthie seemed embarrassed. "It's my phone. Sorry about that. One second, I'm just telling him I'm busy."

"It's Rajesh, isn't it?" Layla teased as she pushed foliage out of the way.

"Layla!" Ruthie said.

"Oh come on, Ruthie. He's really handsome. I can tell why you like him," Layla said, still teasing. She climbed over a boulder and took out her binoculars.

"So do *you* like him?" Everest asked, trying to sound casual.

"Let's stay focused, shall we?" said Ming, pushing through the vegetation with unusual ferocity.

Aiden chose not to get involved. High school drama wasn't his forte. Rather, he examined the picture of Ken, and a lump swelled in his throat. There were bruises on her face as blood soaked through her shirt. She might need a stretcher if she had broken her ribs, though he *had* brought along a first aid kit just in case anything like this happened. *That monster Xipe better not have hurt her.* Then again, it probably wasn't him; he would have been more brutal. Ken's injuries must have come from VD. Aiden's blood boiled at the thought. He watched from the drone's camera as Xipe roughly tied her to a tree and VD quietly spoke to him.

"Get closer. I want to hear what they're saying," Aiden said. His voice was dark. They had no right to hurt Ken like this.

Ruthie struggled to get the drone closer when suddenly, a gust of wind hit the drone and she temporarily lost control. The man with the mask—most likely VD—looked up at the drone and smiled. He took one of Ken's gadgets, grabbed a rubber band, and slingshotted the drone to the ground in one swift move.

"No!" cried Ruthie when the drone dropped to the ground. VD caught it moments before it hit the sand and rocks.

Aiden winced as VD turned the drone over and pulled out the camera.

"Shoot," Layla muttered. By now, they were all crowding around Aiden as he emerged from the foliage. Faces pale, they watched as VD turned the camera so it was facing him.

VD laughed. "Aiden Ravencrest. I expected more from Molly's son. She was a tough prey to kill, that one. But in the end, she died like the rest."

Layla was furious. "I hate that guy," she seethed.

Aiden said nothing, only withdrew further into his usual mask.

"Now, Aiden," VD said, "I'm glad you sent me your little pigeon. I hope it's not too expensive, as it will be destroyed very soon. Now, your Ravencrest friend did not cooperate well, and thus I needed to teach her a lesson. She sunk my submarine—"

"Go, Ken," Layla whispered.

"—and now I find that this might make my plan easier. You see, Aiden, I only want to talk to you privately. I want to make an arrangement with you, boy." VD's voice grew darker. "I have a deal to make, and I need you *alone*. Now, I hope to see you at your little cave with all its fun traps. I'm leaving this girl here with my friend, who would love to have his fun with her, wouldn't he?" He nudged Xipe, who grinned and sharpened his knife.

"How do we get past him?" Everest asked.

Ming began, "We could—"

"Sh!" Aiden turned up the volume. "VD's speaking!"

VD continued, "Due to changed circumstances, our meeting time will now be in exactly ten minutes. See you then, Ravencrest." He plunged the drone into the salty waters, shutting off its transmission as the current dashed it against the rocks.

Aiden was silent as the group around him erupted into ideas, protests, arguments, and plans. Finally, he shouted, "Enough!"

The rest of the Hall Monitors fell silent.

"Ming, hide behind this boulder," Aiden said, winding back in the video and pointing to the rock. "You brought your poison?"

"Yes," Ming said.

"You know what to do."

"I do," Ming said softly.

"Ruthie will signal you when you must strike," Aiden went on. He turned to the rest. "Everest and Layla, once Xipe is no longer a threat, you will bring this first aid kit to her, untie her, and treat her as best as you can. Together, you'll bring her to the place where Ming will be. Ruthie will ensure everything goes smoothly from the earpieces. Do you all understand what you must do?"

"Yes," they all chorused, but everyone looked uneasy.

"What is it?" Aiden asked impatiently. Better to ask now than to wait until it was too late.

Speaking for everyone, Everest nervously questioned, "What are *you* going to do, Aiden? Are you going to meet him alone, like he asked? Or do you have some sort of plan?"

"I can take care of myself," Aiden said briskly. "Now, resume your positions."

No one moved. Even Ruthie was silent.

"You care about Ken, don't you?" Aiden challenged.

Finally, they all stirred and ran to their positions. In the meantime, Aiden trekked through the forest to the cave, navigating from experience and memory. VD thought he had the upper hand. But he didn't know the island inside and out like Aiden did. Only Aiden knew the dangerous shortcut that involved the cliffs. And only Aiden was crazy enough to face VD alone.

He was a Ravencrest. It was time to fight.

Chapter Twenty-Seven

Ten minutes later, Aiden silently walked into the cave. Pitch-black darkness surrounded him and pressed in, threatening to overwhelm him. In some ways, he had never stopped fearing the dark, the unknown. Now, it was his old friend.

"Aiden Ravencrest," said a cheerful voice, amplified as it echoed off the cave walls. "Please step forward."

"And fall into my little pit? I don't think so," Aiden replied. His night-vision goggles revealed nothing. Mentally, he calculated the positions where VD could be standing based on the acoustics of the cave.

"Oh, but I've missed you, Ravencrest," VD mocked. The friendly tone bounced off the walls, throbbing in the quivering obscurity. "I want you a little closer. I don't think you're in a position to negotiate, are you?"

Aiden obeyed. Rather than stepping forward, he dropped to his knees and quickly adjusted the knot of the net so it wouldn't give out. Then he stepped on each corner of the net, spreading out his weight evenly so he could carefully make it across. As he cautiously crawled, Vladimir called, "That will do."

Excellent. Aiden was alone with VD, struggling on his hands and knees on an unstable net in the dark.

VD called to him, "I'm glad you cooperated. I'm a man of my word; your little friend will go free once our talk is over."

"There was no reason to treat her so badly," Aiden argued.

"I can do whatever I like, Ravencrest," VD scoffed. "You are fortunate I did not kill her."

"What do you *want*, Vladimir Damon?" Aiden said abruptly, his voice rising. "Why do you terrorize children at Ravencrest? Why did you try to kill me in Argentina? And why the heck did you kill my mother?" He used a stronger noun than *heck*.

"You really don't know, do you?" Vladimir said in amazement. His voice continued to echo but with changing acoustics. *He's moving. He's doing something while he speaks.*

"Would you care to enlighten me?" Aiden said, his mind spinning. He clutched to the net and worked on some of the knots.

"Ask your mother about it," Damon snarled. "You'll be seeing her soon."

He's slowly circling me. Why would he—

Then Aiden understood.

VD was untying the rope. He was going to make sure Aiden fell into the pit, and then he would taunt him, possibly torture him, and eventually kill the young boy.

Not on my watch.

Right now, Vladimir was ensuring Aiden wasn't moving. He kept speaking: "Tell me, what did your mother tell you about me?"

"Many things. She told me about your idiocy, your sadistic nature, your cruelty, your hideousness, your obsession with murdering people..." Aiden spoke with his head in the same position so it sounded as if he was perfectly still. In reality, he was untying knot after knot and adjusting his weight so that he didn't fall quite yet.

"So she told you very little," VD chuckled. "Ah, the naivety of youth. You little pig headed fool shouting at me about how I'm a murderer and how your mother was a sweet, perfect angel...oh, you have no idea, do you? You don't know how your mother was a greedy murderer?"

"Shut up, you liar!" Aiden shouted, his voice rising.

"A murderer and a hypocrite." VD was moving again. Aiden calculated: *Vladimir adjusted ⅓ of the circumference and he's moving quickly.* Yet so was Aiden.

"What would make you call my mother a murderer?" Aiden remarked.

"Oh, so now you're interested," remarked Vladimir dryly. "It's ironic how you condemn me yet wish to be a murderer yourself, just like your mother. All Ravencrests are hypocrites, no?"

By now Damon was halfway across the circumference of the circle.

"Us?" laughed Aiden. The poisonous hate threatened to bubble over; his body trembled in pure fury. "No, we mean what we say. When I say I want to kill you, I dream of strangling you with my bare hands, but that would be too merciful to a man like yourself."

"Mercy? You want to talk about mercy?" VD sneered. "What mercy did your mother show to my father when she killed him?"

"My mother killed no one!"

Now VD was two-thirds finished as he spoke: "You really are clueless, aren't you?"

"Then tell me." Aiden was breathing faster now as he worked. He groped for the ropes, prepared himself mentally, and—

In one move, Aiden swung through the air, holding onto the ropes, and connected with the side of the pit. He used his parkour skills to move up the wall, even past the rock, and rolled to his feet. His night-vision goggles sharpened on VD, who also had night-vision goggles and the same mask he was wearing on the submarine. Now that they were face-to-face, VD pulled it off without a second thought. Looking down at Aiden, VD chuckled. "Impressive." He pulled out a gun. "But now you're trapped."

It was true. A trap with broken glass on his left, a hole on his right, a giant boulder behind him, and an armed VD in front.

Aiden chuckled. "It's ironic. You think I'm trapped. Just like you thought you had me trapped in Argentina. Just like you thought you trapped all those kids with lies and threats."

"It's different now," VD replied smoothly. "Now I can kill you. It's what I've been dreaming of for months. You know, when I'm bored, I like to amuse myself by imagining all the different ways you could die." He stepped forward with the gun trained on Aiden. "I was hoping for something more slow and painful. But I suppose this will have to do."

A gunshot exploded.

Aiden's smirk froze on his face as he looked down at the bullet that had hit his stomach. It felt worse than if he had been punched. It was as if an inexplicably large force had torn through his ribs, leaving him gasping and dazed. "Wait," stammered Aiden. "This wasn't supposed to—" He groaned and crumpled to the ground, drenched in sweat and agony.

Vladimir walked forward, shaking his head. "Oh, Aiden. I've been dreaming of this moment for months."

"You already said that," Aiden groaned, clutching his stomach. The red stained his fingers in the vague night vision.

VD was now barely a foot from him. He squatted down so they were eye-to-eye. "How does it feel, Ravencrest? I know your mother will tell you all about it when you meet her."

"You keep repeating that. How unoriginal," Aiden said, still wincing in pain. "Unlike this."

At that moment, Aiden pulled a lever next to the broken glass where Xipe had once been held. The floor groaned and shifted as VD lunged for Aiden, unsure of what was happening. Aiden easily rolled away and VD drew in a sharp breath when the ground under his feet gave way. He crumpled backward into the dark abyss below.

Aiden looked down into the swirling darkness, chuckled, then laughed heartily. "Oh, I never let myself hope it could be that easy," he taunted, calling into the mist below. "How does it feel, Vladimir Damon, to be trapped in your own trap?"

"No need to get cocky, Ravencrest," VD said with utter hate. His voice traveled up from the dark below, only slightly strained. "Bleeding to death on a lonely island in a cave isn't a pleasant feeling either. Whatever predicament I might be in, it brings me joy to know you're in a similar one."

"Oh, but, Mr. Damon," Aiden said mockingly, "I wasn't shot."

There was silence.

"You see," Aiden continued, standing upright and walking along the edge, "I have a friend"—*Layla*— "with quite a bit of nail polish. She had this old red polish, and it was simple to hide it under my clothes near my *bulletproof vest.* I saw your gun in my little drone. And truth be told, I always use this vest now because *you* tried to kill me and succeeded in giving me a concussion. You broke my ribs. Now I always wear a bulletproof vest and it has saved my life numerous times. So I do owe you my thanks." He was smug now, smirking as he spoke and circling his prey. "It's funny, Damon. You were going to trap me down there. Looks like I've got *you* trapped."

For a while, there was silence from the pit. Aiden listened closely, but there was no taunting, no mocking, and no replies.

"So, before I kill you," Aiden said brightly, "anything you'd like to say to me?"

There was still nothing.

"I see," Aiden said as cheerfully as ever. All his usual mischievousness and friendly smiles had completely disappeared. Now his eyes were cruel and sadistic, and his body trembled with the desire to hurt and to kill. He was barely recognizable. "Now, there are so many fun things I can do to you. Which one would my mother have liked?"

"Let's start with the strangling," VD offered. "Your mother enjoyed that. There were red marks all over her neck for weeks when I was through with her."

That pushed Aiden into a total demon-like state. He laughed an evil laugh that rang off the sides of the cave and turned more sinister by the moment. "Oh, that's the death you'll wish for when I'm finished with you."

"You know, Aiden Ravencrest," Vladimir said all of a sudden, making Aiden pause in his pacing. "You do remind me of your mother."

"You keep saying that. Trying to get at me, are you?"

"Let me finish, won't you?" VD mocked. "Your mother was overconfident too. She thought she had won the battle. But that was the day she was killed. You see, Aiden Ravencrest, the battle isn't over until it's over."

Suddenly, VD fired. Gunshots burst everywhere. The bullets sliced through the air around him, and Aiden drove himself backward, pressing up against the wall in the exact same position VD had been in when Aiden first entered the cave moments ago. Aiden held his breath. VD had been quietly calculating too; he must have planned this exact moment so Aiden would be trapped in this position. Now what would happen?

"Enjoy," VD called with a laugh when some mechanism clicked and the rock under Aiden's feet moved. Aiden yelled as he plunged into darkness; VD's pit for him was waiting. Mist swirled above him. At least he had landed on his feet and hadn't broken anything.

Yet it was exactly what had happened to VD moments ago.

Aiden wanted to scream in rage. This wasn't fair. Then the absurdity of the situation caught up to him and he began laughing hysterically, so hard he could barely breathe.

"What's so funny?" VD said from the pit on the other side.

Aiden choked on his laughter. "We fell into each other's traps, and now we're both stuck here."

"That's right," VD said raspily. His breathing grew labored. "But now it looks like your revenge is going to have to wait."

"So is yours," Aiden shot back. His overriding anger was fading and his humanity was returning. Part of him was a little scared of himself. When had he ever been ready to kill another human being? Ever? Mother would've been scared of Aiden herself—

Then Aiden realized the truth.

It was rather surprising that he realized this so late, considering how intelligent he was, but his anger and darkness had blurred his judgment. It had overtaken everything. It had kept him from this realization.

"VD," Aiden said slowly, feeling equally shocked and ashamed, "we're the same."

"What?"

"We're the same. We're both here for revenge. We both used the same methods. We both have no one coming after us. We both—" Aiden nearly choked on the words. "We both lost someone. And we both are here to kill each other. We're the same."

For the first time, Aiden finally understood. He understood why he had been feeling so distant from his mother, from his past, from his old self. He understood and was horrified.

In fighting the monster, he had become the monster.

In fighting VD, he had become VD.

How could he have let his hate take over to the point where the man on the other side was only a grown-up version of him? They were one and the same now. And that was the last thing his mother would've wanted.

Right as always, Mother. She hadn't been weak or foolish. He shouldn't have dismissed her in his mind so easily.

He groaned and clutched his head as he sat down. At last, the rest of himself came back: his clear mind, his heart, and the parts of him that he had gotten from Mother. Life was more than settling the score. He couldn't ignore his conscience anymore. For the first time since he had woken up in Argentina, Aiden Ravencrest understood.

What had he *done*? He was sickened as he saw himself continuing to abandon everyone around him for the sole purpose of hate. Hate that had choked him, changed him, turned him into this. Hate that had crept in through the gateway of grief. What if he had killed VD and Xipe? What if he had tortured them as planned? He would have ignored his conscience even for something as great as this—

And then there would have been no going back.

He would have become VD.

"Oh, Mother," Aiden said out loud quietly. "Oh, *God*. Help me."

"No one's coming to your rescue," VD sneered on the other end. "And you were wrong about one thing. I have a team who's coming after me."

"So do I, and they have Xipe," Aiden wearily replied. Hatred flamed in his chest, but he pushed it away. It would be difficult to not hate someone like VD, but hate was what had almost destroyed him. "My friends went after him. After an hour or so, they'll probably come looking for me."

"I have more backup than Xipe," VD said sharply. "And if your friends lay a hand on him, I'll kill each and every one of them, I swear it."

"More backup?"

"Yes, I've got the whole Legacy after me," Vladimir said confidently. "I'm the Head now since my father was killed by your mother."

"You're the Head of the Legacy?" *What's the Legacy?* He'd pretend to know for now.

"You didn't know who you were dealing with," VD said with pride. "Yes, I'm the Head of the Legacy. It's like the Hydra. You kill one head and more heads emerge. Doesn't your precious Society know that?"

Cleverly, Aiden replied, "So what's the Legacy's mission statement now, being the terrorist organization we all know it is?"

VD barked a laugh. "Ha! You Society members have been saying that for generations. Oh, but our mission is right in our name. We're here to make our own legacy. We're here to outdo the older brother."

The older brother? What—

Aiden's prodigious mind grasped it at last. His heart skipped a beat, and for a brief moment, he couldn't breathe. "Matthew and Evelyn Ravencrest had a younger brother," he said slowly, in shock.

"Stepbrother," corrected VD. "And we all know how he legally disowned himself from the rotten family years later. He isn't even related to them, by blood or law. Oh, and that was my great-great-great-however many greats-grandfather."

"And he established the Legacy while Evelyn established the Society."

"That's correct. What's the purpose of telling me all this? We both already know our history. It's not as if your mommy ever ran out of bedtime stories," VD said. It was clear he kept bringing up Mother to hurt Aiden.

Aiden barely heard this. "And these two societies have been feuding for generations? How ridiculous! Ravencrests are above centuries-long family rivalries that exist for no reason other than spite and jealousy!"

"Don't pretend you're hearing this for the first time," VD snarled. "And for the record, it may have begun as a matter of spite and jealousy, but it became so much deeper over the years."

"Until it became good vs. evil?" Aiden said. "Let me guess: the Legacy are the bad guys and the Society are the good ones." This wasn't an actual guess; he was oversimplifying things in hopes of angering Vladimir to explain more.

It worked. "The Legacy operates to restore the world, whatever the cost!" VD shouted. "We're overturning empires, weakening those in power, letting more worthy rulers rise. We're restoring things to the way they should be. There might be struggles now, but when we're through, the world will be entirely different. There will be a new time where all the problems we face now are gone."

"So the Legacy aims for world domination," Aiden chuckled dryly. "Very original."

"It's not world domination, boy," VD said, breathing heavily. "It's world *restoration*."

"Same thing. And it all started with the little stepbrother who hated his big sister. A little boy who wanted his voice to be heard.

Who wanted the world to be his, just as it was for his big brother," Aiden narrated without emotion. "How dramatic. Meanwhile, the Society is protecting the world from many things, including the Legacy's idiotic moves."

"*Idiotic*? You call mind-controlling the President of the United States *idiotic*?" Vladimir shouted.

"You *what*?"

"We almost succeeded that time. Killing Molly was a tremendous success." VD smirked to himself.

"So it all started with Evelyn Ravencrest's work to protect the world and her stepbrother's attempts to make it his own," Aiden summarized. "And I suppose my mother was part of this Society? It must've been why she traveled so much. And who else?"

"What's your game, boy?" VD said. "Why're you asking me all this?"

"Curiosity. It's a Ravencrest virtue."

"Then it is detestable."

"Then so are the virtues of love, diligence, loyalty, and risk-taking."

VD chuckled. "The Legacy possesses all those virtues themselves."

"Even love?"

"You think my father loved me when he went out to make a name for himself?" VD said sharply. "He entered a hotel room with the intent to kill your mother. In exchange, she killed him."

"In self-defense," Aiden noted.

"The Legacy and the Society have fought before," VD said grimly. "But I am the one who has brought the Legacy close to its first, long-term victory. The Head of the Society was murdered by *me*—"

"You mean *Mother?*"

"—and once I kill you and your father, and burn Ravencrest to the ground—"

"You'll never get that far!" Aiden shouted.

"Watch me," VD challenged. "My team is on its way. You don't think I entered this cave without a backup plan, did you? I kept my little communications device. I have backup. Do you?"

The truth was that Aiden had left his earpiece outside. Yes, he trusted his Hall Monitors friends and they now knew the truth, but they still didn't need to be part of his revenge. *Not anymore,* Aiden decided firmly. *No revenge.* It didn't fix anything. It only changed him for the worse.

Still, it was dangerous for VD and his Legacy to be living free and in the wild. They had to be stopped.

All Aiden had to do was survive this. If VD didn't get away, it'd be like hitting the jackpot. The Head of the Legacy would be gone, and Aiden could use VD to stop the rest of the Legacy.

So he just had to survive.

"They're on their way," Aiden said, not sure if he was lying or not. "Let's see who gets here first, shall we?"

"Or who dies first."

Aiden scoffed. "You think you can still kill me from the other side of this pit? You're relentless, Vladimir."

"It's one of my defining qualities," VD joked. His voice sounded strained.

Suddenly, a gunshot echoed in the darkness.

"You're shooting at me?" chuckled Aiden. "That's—ah!" He howled in pain as a bullet buried itself in his vest, right below his heart. It was clear where VD had been aiming. While the vest protected him, the bullets still hurt. Aiden grimaced and glanced at the wall of the pit. *How did he get the bullet through, aim, and fire from over there?*

Then he saw it.

The small hole VD had made. It was big enough to fit his fist through it. *He must have been working while we were talking.* Clearly, Vladimir would not rest until Aiden was dead.

For now, Aiden calculated the trajectory of any bullets that came through the hole. It was a small hole, but this was a small space. It didn't take much for VD to fire a fatal shot. In Aiden's mind, he visualized the pit, the walls around and under him, and the trajectory of the bullet in proportion to him. Either he could press himself up against the walls and hold his breath, or press himself against the floor and hope the bullet would only graze his vested back. Either way, it would be a tight squeeze.

The Hall Monitors really had to hurry. Yes, he had told them not to follow him. He sighed. Sometimes it backfired to have such trusting friends who assumed you knew what you were doing.

I do need backup. He'd admitted it too few times, and now, it was too late.

VD paused from his shooting and reloaded his gun. "Oh, Aiden," he said. "We can do this for a long time. Or we can take a fun little shortcut. This should speed things up."

Aiden gulped in horror as VD made the hole a little wider and let a small snake slither through the opening. The thin yet quick-moving animal smoothly slid inside. Terror grasped Aiden; his breaths were smothered with fear.

God, help me!

As the snake curled up in the tight space, Aiden realized, *It's a coastal taipan from Australia. It has fangs half an inch long that inject deep into tissues. It releases taxatoxin, which ruptures blood cells and causes major internal bleeding. The venom alone can kill up to 56 people. The wait time between the bite and death is half an hour to six hours.* Every heartbeat shook him. He stood paralyzed in fear watching the snake coil around his ankles. The snake lazily relaxed in the darkness. In his peripheral vision, Aiden watched as VD pulled the gun up again so that its barrel outlined the tiny hole.

"This is going to be fun," taunted Vladimir. "Who would've thought it? I killed Molly by poisoning. I'm about to kill you with venom, then shoot you, and then leave your body to rot. Oh, this *will* be fun." He cocked the gun.

Aiden swallowed hard. He was completely alone. Surrounded by a venomous snake, suffocating in darkness, and shackled in terror.

There was no escape. No clever retort, no quick thinking, nothing.

Nothing he could do.

"Say bye-bye, Aiden Ravencrest," VD mocked. "And tell your mother I said good riddance."

He shot.

The bullet fired. It missed Aiden but bothered the snake, who hissed defensively and turned to the only other living creative in its tiny quarters.

God, help me!

With that, the snake lashed out. Aiden's scream was drowned in VD's maniacal laughter.

"Do you think we should check on Aiden?" Layla said nervously as she filled her bag with all of Ken's gadgets in the pile. "It's been a while."

Ken pushed Everest away. "I'm *fine*, seriously! It's just electricity. I mean, I've electrocuted myself plenty of times by accident."

"Why am I not surprised?" teased Ruthie over the earpiece.

Ken chuckled. "Good to hear your voice again, Ruthie."

Everest raised an eyebrow. "These bruises—"

"VD attacked me while I was unconscious. I didn't feel anything." Ken winced as Everest treated her. "Though now I do. Look, why are we waiting out here?" She was sweating profusely, possibly from the heat.

"Is it difficult for you to breathe?" Everest asked attentively, his eyes narrowed in focus. "From how you were walking earlier, it's as if your muscles were stiffening up."

"I'm fine!" Ken repeated. "Where's Aiden?"

Ming squatted down and examined Ken's hand. "Aiden ordered us to focus on saving you. He claimed to be able to take care of himself."

Ken immediately tried to sit up straight. "He's lying! We need to go after him!"

"Ken, what are the bruises on this hand?" Ming asked as he stopped her from getting up.

"An animal bit me, I think," Ken said dismissively. "It's just a..." Her voice trailed off.

Ming massaged it. "Does this hurt?"

Ken mumbled something vaguely.

Everest snapped his fingers in front of her face. "Ken, can you hear me? Ken?" He looked at Layla grimly. "She's not responding."

Ken slumped limply into Layla's arms as Ming examined the bite again. "The incision is approximately half an inch deep. She didn't show symptoms for roughly four hours, if my calculations are correct. The fangs are thin and tiny. In conclusion, it seems as if her attacker was a snake. Everest?"

"There are plenty of snakes nearby," Everest argued. In one smooth move, he pulled Ken to her feet and wrapped an arm around her shoulders to steady her. "This one was clearly venomous."

"It's the coastal taipan," Layla breathed.

Ming looked up at her. "The deadly snake from Australia?"

"It was brought over for some kid's research project, remember? Ruthie told me all about it. She kept shuddering and—" Layla gasped. "Why wasn't Ken treated when she got back this morning? She needs help!"

Ming was already helping Everest by supporting Ken's other side. "This is Mackenzie Robscone. She, along with Aiden, tends to falsely assume she can handle everything herself."

Ruthie grimly said, "I'm reporting this as an emergency. They'll get a helicopter and everything. Try to make it back to the island. Layla, use a flare gun to send up a distress signal if you hear a helicopter nearby."

Layla wordlessly obeyed for once as the boys hobbled Ken back to Ravencrest Academy. At some point along the way, Ken slumped forward and became completely limp. Neither boy said anything; they only quickened their pace.

Ruthie couldn't take it anymore. "Hurry, please!" she shouted, anguished.

Layla normally would have joked something along the lines of *You probably shouldn't have read all those articles on what snake venom does to you, huh?* if she wasn't so scared. But now she too was silent. She battled the fear of losing another friend to something worse than VD's blackmail.

Death.

Aiden was still screaming when he realized that he had caught the snake's neck. It twisted and squirmed in his grip, its long and pointy tail reaching for Aiden in the pixelated darkness of the night vision.

There was no time to waste as VD cocked his gun. Aiden immediately twisted the neck of the snake, even as it fought him, its head straining to reach him.

He calculated the angle, the trajectory, the—

VD fired again.

In a desperate moment of hope, Aiden held the snake in place and felt the body go limp in his hands as the bullet tore through the snake's body, killing it in one shot.

Aiden gasped in the dimness, then gasped again. He couldn't get enough air.

"Please, let's talk about this," Aiden pleaded, turning to the little hole. He saw VD's eye wink at him, the barrel end adjust, and the gun twitch as it was used yet again. He flattened himself up against the wall as the bullet slid by, missing his nose by inches.

The next shot tore across his chest.

The one after left bloody streaks on his right arm and buried itself in his side.

Aiden cried out in pain whenever a bullet hit his vest. They all hurt. Part of him was searching for some mercy, any mercy, in Vladimir's cruelty. But the man was so saturated by hate that there was no compassion left. The bullets kept coming, each one closer to taking away a limb, some barely missing Aiden's head. "Please?" Aiden tried again, and he groaned in agony as the next shot grazed his shoulder and narrowly missed his neck.

All he could do was lean farther into the cave wall as VD reloaded again and aimed.

There was no surviving this. The bullets would keep coming until he was gone. Even if he could survive, he knew no one was coming after him. It was too late. If anyone had been on their way to save him, they would have come already. By the time his friends would go after him, it would be much too late. And VD's friends didn't sound like a bluff. The man cackled and fired.

Suddenly, he wanted the pain to end. He was tempted to lean forward and let the next shot hit its mark. Perhaps death would be merciful and quick.

No.

Ravencrests did not give up.

Even when all was gone and they were left desperate, grief-stricken, alone, vulnerable, about to lose it all—

Even then.

They held on.

So Aiden just closed his eyes, breathed a prayer, and pulled back as much as he could. The wall burned into his back as the bullets came, raking his stomach and sides. He hid his arms behind him and let his vest take the brunt of each painful, hard impact. He grunted whenever a bullet hit. If he would die, he would die.

But he would die fighting.

The stream of bullets lessened, and as VD was about to reload again, footsteps stopped him. In the sudden pause, Aiden gasped once, cried out, and was cut off by a sharp rise of pain. "Please—" He choked on the words, sunk to the floor, and stopped breathing.

Satisfied, VD straightened. He aimed the gun once more, just to be careful.

"Everything all right in here?" said a familiar, friendly voice.

"Porter Craig!" cried both Aiden and VD at once.

"See, I told you backup was coming!" Aiden crowed. "Toss me the rope, Craig!"

The rope fell into the pit.

But not Aiden's.

Suddenly, something registered in Aiden's mind. A cold feeling slowly crept into him. "VD, how did you know Craig's name?"

Vladimir laughed. "See, Aiden, when you try to be smart, sometimes you fail to notice what's right in front of you. Your friend Craig here works for me."

Aiden couldn't breathe. It was as if he had been punched in the gut. "*Craig*?" he whispered.

He listened as Porter Craig helped Vladimir out of the hole and onto his feet. VD laughed again and fired another shot into Aiden's hole, narrowly missing him. Craig's gruff voice stopped VD from firing again: "Enough. If he's not dead by now, the cave-in will kill him."

The cave-in?

"Why?" Aiden asked with clear anguish in his voice. "My mother respected you! I trusted you all my life!"

"Sorry, kid," said Craig, and he truly did sound sorry. He made no attempt to justify his actions as he led VD away. In the silence that followed, Craig started to say something. He stopped himself, changed his mind, and wordlessly began walking around inside the cave.

Aiden was silent. He was remembering.

He remembered how Craig had been so close to his mother. How Craig had always taken care of Aiden, checked up on him, protected him, and looked after him. He had been the father Aiden never really had. Had it all been a cover-up to keep an eye on the Head of the Society and her young son, the soon-to-be Headmaster?

He remembered how Craig had stepped back while Aiden performed his capers around Ravencrest. He had helped Aiden each time, becoming more and more trustworthy in Aiden's eyes until Craig was an essential part of every stunt Aiden pulled, from sneaking around at night to switching the flash drive for the first-day alarm. It made sense. Craig was a porter; he knew exactly what was happening in Ravencrest at all times. The only unpredictable variable had been Aiden. Now, having gained Aiden's trust, that wasn't a problem anymore.

He remembered how Craig was so willing to turn a blind eye and even aid Aiden's mischief. Craig was so close to the many benefits of retirement. Aiden had believed that Craig chose the academy over his future; now he knew how Craig had actually chosen his future over the academy.

He remembered how Craig had been with him the night Aiden interrogated the intruders who broke into Ravencrest. It was so long ago, practically a lifetime away. Craig had found Aiden in the dark and led him to the clinic. He had stood behind Aiden during the interrogation, claiming to be there to protect him. Yet, the intruder's eyes had widened in fear when he looked past Aiden. Aiden had assumed it was all the needles and possible torture weapons. Had the intruder recognized Craig? Had the intruder been telling the truth all along? Did the intruder know Craig from before the break-in?

Aiden's whole life, Craig had been by his side, supporting and protecting the boy. It had all been a ruse.

Letting Aiden pull his pranks. A ruse.

Allowing the boy to run around the school unsupervised. A ruse.

Caring about Mother. A ruse.

Pulling Aiden out of the way when the intruders broke in. A ruse.

And now, tracking down Aiden and rescuing VD instead.

A ruse of compassion for an act of treachery. That was all Craig had been. Craig was in this for VD alone. All along he had been a traitor; who knew how far back? Aiden understood now. He felt weary, more tired than he had been in all his life. The betrayal stung him so deeply that he made no attempt to say something witty. He just closed his eyes and fought back the tears.

He listened as Craig's boots crunched the rocks and branches, tactfully missing the poisonous animals. There were other crunches too; Aiden listened carefully.

He's dropping something around the cave.

Craig was directly above Aiden now. The porter did not look down. Something dropped into Aiden's lap.

Dynamite.

So Craig was truly blowing up the cave with Aiden in it while VD gleefully watched. There was no escape for the bruised, battered teenage boy who just wanted to go home. Aiden ran his hands over the dynamite and found something strapped to it. A timer, yes, but also a flashlight. He clicked it on and pulled off his night-vision goggles to see the image projected onto the wall next to him.

There was some writing. Craig had hastily grabbed a marker and scribbled something on the clear part of the flashlight so the light would shine through and create shadows which spelled out:

Chapmen, Sebold, García

For a split second, only a millisecond, he was confused. Why—

But only for a second. He was a Ravencrest, and while his mental capabilities weren't the best at the moment, he recovered quickly.

He smiled for the first time all day and shone the flashlight around the pit. He saw the rope attached to the dynamite. The timer on the dynamite was set to ten minutes. Aiden listened as Craig informed VD that the timer was set to thirty minutes and that they might as well sit down. In the distance, Craig began tending to VD's wounds as the man barked orders at him. Aiden used the rope, created a rope ladder, aimed his rope perfectly, and used his parkour training and upper-body strength to climb up the rope and out of the pit. He emerged on top of the side of the pit, still in the middle of the cave, and gasped. Most of the entrance to the cave was now covered by boulders. Aiden used the rope to cross VD's pit, then crouched behind a boulder. It was not safe to travel around outside. VD or one of his team members would find him. No, it was best to wait for help and hope that it would arrive before the dynamite exploded.

He listened carefully, visualizing the others' positions. Below his feet, in the swirling darkness, the black widow spider and the snakes twisted, unaware of their approaching deaths. Outside, Vladimir and Craig argued until Vladimir finally agreed to go with Craig to the submarine to take their emergency First Aid kit. After all, despite his actions, VD was also injured.

"Where is Xipe?" Aiden heard VD say.

"He's out cold," Craig said. "The kid outwitted him. She left him there, grabbed her stuff, and got out. Seems she's at the academy now, being treated. Xipe's still sleeping on the island." "Useless man," VD scoffed, but with the vaguest hint of concern.

Aiden waited patiently. Finally, he hobbled out into the clearing. There were more caves where he could hide. With his flashlight and rope, he could hide until a search party came after him. As he wasn't an official student, and since the Hall Monitors were most likely focused on treating Ken, there was a good chance he'd be out here all day.

That was fine with him. He knew how to survive in the wild.

Thus, Aiden Ravencrest watched VD and Craig from a distance, comfortably sitting in a tree. He saw Vladimir Damon laugh when the cave exploded. Aiden winced at the thought of all the beautiful, rare, dangerous animals inside the cave, some of which were endangered. His actions had put many other lives at risk as well.

I'm not that person anymore.

No, Aiden was not Raisin, the little boy who cheered from the sidelines. His time of watching and waiting was over. It was his turn to fight.

But he would do it the right way, without becoming a monster.

It was what his mother would have wanted.

As Vladimir and his crew packed up and left via their submarine, unknowing of the little tracker that joined their party, Aiden looked at the flashlight. His face softened as he recalled what the writing meant. These last names had one thing in common: they were the last names of some of the most famous double agents in history. It was a quick, three-second way that concealed what could have cost Craig his life to admit.

Things aren't as they seem.

So Craig was working for VD.

But as a double agent for the Society.

Aiden leaned against the warm trunk of the tree. The sun's rays broke through the clouds at last, letting him rest in the warmth. It was a welcome break.

Things would be very difficult in the days to come. He knew the fight would not be easy. He was no longer aiming for revenge, to murder VD. No, he was now aiming to find VD and this Legacy. He would put them behind bars where they could never hurt anyone again.

Yet he would not become a monster.

Things aren't as they seem.

Aiden looked up into the sky, the rose gold stretching across the horizon as the orange sun intertwined with the yawning violet. It was like something right out of a movie.

He missed his mother sorely. He missed her so much.

"I need you," he said softly.

The only answer was the silence as the wind left him. The animals chirped and chattered as the trees creaked and groaned. Aiden closed his eyes and lost himself in the beautiful music of nature.

So he had survived.

That meant he still had a purpose left on this earth. It would most likely not be an easy thing to accomplish. But he had learned. It was time to fight the Legacy. It was time to save the world.

Can I really do it?

Of course he could. He was a Ravencrest, after all.

Chapter Twenty-Eight

The Hall Monitors crowded around Ken, warding off unwelcome students eager for the latest news. When the crowd died down, the nurse forced Everest to rest. In the meantime, Layla refused to leave Ken's side.

Ming had disappeared into the background, as usual, so no one noticed when he briskly pulled his jacket back on and left the room.

He walked quickly and purposefully. As he walked, he noticed Porter Jimmy looking anxious and muttering, "Not him too, not him." He also heard the footsteps he recognized: the sound of Layla's new hiking boots. Wordlessly, Ming followed the sound as it grew more determined.

So when Ruthie walked outside, he stepped out from the shadows and stood directly in front of her. "Going somewhere?"

Ruthie gave a little yelp. "Ming! You—you startled me."

"Where are you going?"

Ruthie hesitated and bit her lower lip, then finally said, "Aiden's still out there. I care about Ken, but no one's out looking for him. Doesn't it concern you that he stopped communicating and no one's seen any sign of him since?"

"You plan to look for him by yourself?"

"I plan to try," she said. "I have the last location his earpiece was transmitting, and I plan on going there. I didn't want to bother anyone or take away from Ken fighting for her life, but..." Her voice trailed off. "Aiden matters too. I just want to make sure he's okay."

Ming zipped up his jacket and stepped into the sun. "Then let's hurry."

"You're—"

"Why would I let you go out there alone?" Ming turned to her, his eyes squinting in the sunlight. "It's not safe."

Ruthie smiled in relief. "Thanks."

As they approached the forest, a set of porters stopped them, seeming to have appeared out of nowhere. "No one is to leave the campus," said Porter Nikolai.

"Apologies," said Porter Julia. "But—"

"But we're looking for Aiden Ravencrest!" Ruthie said.

"You're going back inside," Porter Nikolai said sternly.

Ruthie didn't budge. "Sir, I'm not going anywhere until Aiden gets back safely. He could be dying out there!"

Porter Julia winced. "He is not a student here, so—"

"Does his life matter less because of that?" Ruthie said, enraged. She tried to push past the porters. It was almost an amusing sight: a petite, determined young girl with big glasses trying to push aside a muscular Porter Nikolai, who gently yet firmly took her hand and effortlessly began to pull her back to the academy. She resisted the porter's grip, and it seemed as if he was about to pick her up and walk her inside when Ming ordered, "Wait!"

They all paused.

Ming displayed his security clearance on his phone. "We work for Aiden Ravencrest, who works for Campus Security and the Headmaster himself. If you have any issues with our work, you can take it up with him."

Porter Julia examined Ming's phone carefully. Finally, she nodded to Porter Nikolai, who let go of Ruthie. She glared at him, then smiled gratefully at Ming. As they trekked into the forest, Ming remarked, "It doesn't hurt to have a plan B, no?"

"No," agreed Ruthie. "I mean, yes. I mean, uh…"

Ming chuckled. "I know what you mean."

There was a pause in their conversation as they continued hiking through the forest. "You know, Ming," she said as she pushed aside some branches, "I've noticed something about you."

"Hmm?"

"You don't let people get near you very often, but when you do…" Ruthie turned to Ming. "You don't let anything happen to them. Everest is so lucky to have you as a friend. We all are."

"Thank you, Ruthie," Ming said after a pause. "It is good to know…that you think of me as a friend." He sighed deeply and said nothing else.

"Ming?" Ruthie said. They were walking quickly now, making real progress toward finding Aiden.

"Yes?"

"Why don't you let people get near you often? You always work so hard. Don't you ever spend time for yourself, like with friends or doing something you love?" Ruthie asked.

Ming didn't break his stride. "I love what I do. This is my job. This is what I was born for."

There was silence.

Finally, Ming sighed and spoke again: "You're right, Ruthie. When I know people, I will lay down my life for them. My mother, she…I know her. I know how much she struggled to make it in a world where she was treated so badly. I know how she fought to live, even against a husband who didn't care about his family at all. I know how she gave it all up for me. So sometimes when I feel tired or weary, I think of her. I think of the sacrifices she made." His voice choked. "She barely remembers me now. She is old and nearing death. But I have made her proud." He stopped at a stream and began to climb up the rocks. "Sometimes that is enough." It was the most he had said to anyone in a long time.

Ruthie climbed up after him, letting him take her hand and help her to her feet. "Ming, I..." She looked into his face, which was glistening with sweat.

"I have friends here," he said quietly. They leaned against the next boulder to catch their breaths. "I have met so many people who say one thing but you don't really know them. Ruthie...can you ever truly see someone's soul? Understand them? Trust them in a way—"

"Hey!"

The voice startled them both. Ruthie slipped and Ming's grip around her wrists pulled her back into place. The moment she was on solid ground, Ming turned to find the source of the voice. "Who is it?" he demanded authoritatively as Ruthie pulled out her binoculars and scanned their surroundings.

"Aiden Ravencrest!"

The voice came from the trees. Ruthie gasped as the binoculars focused. "Aiden, what are you doing up there?"

"VD tried to kill me, so I escaped." Aiden jumped down beside them. "I was attempting to wait until they were gone, then return back to campus. I did search for the earpiece, but it seems I've lost it. Honestly, I was rather worried when I heard voices. I'm glad it's only you two."

"Are you all right?" Ruthie asked, leaning forward to see him better.

Ming gently put an arm in front of her, keeping her from stumbling into the river below them. "Let's get to solid ground first."

When all three of them were face-to-face on the ground, Aiden explained, "I'm a bit bruised, but I'll be alright. I don't need any help."

"You're going to the nurse's," Ruthie said firmly.

"There's no need—"

"Ming, you take his left, I'll take his right," Ruthie instructed.

Aiden protested as his two friends helped him limp back to the academy. He found it harder to complain when Ruthie put him down on a comfortable, plush chair and brought him a blanket and a steaming mug of hot cocoa. "Drink," she instructed. Wondering how such a petite girl could be so bossy, he took a sip and his taste buds rejoiced.

Ming placed a plate in front of him. "Fresh from the cafeteria."

Ruthie slipped her phone into her bag. "The doctor's on his way to take a look at you."

Aiden sputtered on his cocoa.

Ruthie sighed and crossed her arms. "The doctor's coming whether you like it or not, so deal with it."

Through the coughing, Aiden managed to say, "No, it's not about the doctor—I just remembered. Is Ken all right?"

"Ken?" Ming said. "Yes, she's fine. She's being treated for a snake bite. According to Layla, Ken's complaining just as much as you are. Everest's the same, too."

Aiden sighed in relief. All at once, he was extremely hungry. He scarfed down the food in a few bites, making Ruthie chuckle. "For someone who doesn't need any help, you sure are hungry."

Aiden stopped eating and looked up at them both. They were both so young, so earnest, and so ready to help. They reminded him of himself. He smiled a little. "Thank you," he said at last. "Both of you. Thank you for everything."

"You're welcome," Ming said softly.

Ruthie smiled a little and looked down at her feet. "Next time, don't mind asking for help. We can't help you if we don't know you need it."

"Right," sighed Aiden. "I'm beginning to understand that."

Aiden knocked on Ken's door at the clinic. It was rather late, so most students were already asleep. He felt guilty bothering her so late, but he wanted to speak to her in private. He felt guilty about a lot of things, come to think of it.

Thankfully, she was awake. "Come on in!" she called. "Layla, is that you? I told you to get some rest already—oh, Aiden."

There was an awkward silence as he stepped in and rested against the doorway, his hands in his pockets. His eyes were on the floor as he asked, "Are you feeling alright?"

"I'm fine," she answered.

"Glad to hear it," he said, and now his eyes traveled up to her. She was sitting on a hospital bed with a bandaged hand. A small workspace had been set up so she could keep working with her right hand. She was wearing a hospital gown and had an IV in her left arm. Her eyes studied him.

The silence stretched on.

Before the atmosphere between them could get any more awkward, Aiden spoke: "Ken...I'm sorry about what I said. I never should have yelled at you. I am so, so sorry. You are absolutely necessary to maintain the safety of this school, and so are the Hall Monitors. I am so grateful I met you and enlisted you. I was angry and wasn't thinking straight when I yelled at you. While that is no excuse, I do hope you can forgive me. I didn't mean anything I said. Thank you for all you do." His eyes were back on the floor now. He kept thinking about the needle in her arm, the poisonous snake that had bitten her, and the awful kidnapping she had just experienced...it had all been his fault. A lump rose in his throat.

Ken replied, "It's okay, Aiden. I knew you didn't mean it. After all, if you really thought you didn't need the Hall Monitors, you wouldn't have sent them to save me. So don't sweat it. I forgive you."

Aiden smiled a little. "Thank you."

"Hey, don't look so down," Ken said, still able to read him well. "I told you, don't sweat it. We all have our bad days, and I can tell you've been having a lot of them lately."

"That's no excuse." Aiden then grew stern. "The same way you had no excuse for following me into a dark cave full of poisonous animals! Ken, you could have been seriously hurt! You *were* seriously hurt!"

Ken shrugged. "No pain, no gain. Besides, now we know about the Legacy and the whole conspiracy against the school. Ruthie updated me on everything. So as far as I see it, all's well that ends well."

"But it hasn't ended yet," Aiden argued back. A smile danced on his lips. "How do you Americans say it? It's not over 'till it's over. And this fight is far from over."

Ken grinned. "You're back!"

"I'm back?"

"You're not that shady, dark guy you were a few days back!" Ken said happily. "I can tell."

"Well, I'm not in this to kill VD anymore or to exact revenge," Aiden did admit. "In fighting VD, I basically became VD. I hated him and wanted to kill him. Now I just want to protect Ravencrest. I'll arrest VD and stop him, but I won't try to kill him unless it's necessary. Killing VD would do nothing to help my mom. It wouldn't set things right or help me in any way. It would just make me as much of a murderer as he is. It took me a while to understand that, I must admit."

"You just needed a little help from your friends," Ken said.

"A reference to the Beatles?" Aiden guessed.

"Yep," Ken said. "My old freshman history teacher loved the Beatles. I know all their songs by heart now."

"Is that a good thing?" Aiden asked.

Ken tilted her head as she seriously considered the question. "It depends on the song."

There was another silence that wasn't as awkward as it might have been a few weeks back. They were comfortable together again, hanging out like old friends.

Aiden stepped a little closer. "Are you comfortable? Do you need anything?"

"You sound like Layla," Ken accused. "I'm fine."

"You need water? Anything to eat or drink?"

"Aiden!"

"All right, all right. Get some rest. You shouldn't be doing homework this late, you know."

Ken rolled her eyes. "I have so much to make up!"

"I could talk to your teachers—"

"Aiden!" she said, outraged. "I don't need you to bully them into giving me special treatment!"

Aiden clutched his heart. "You wound me, Ken. I was only going to explain your situation to them and hint that they might need to be more merciful toward you."

Ken sniffed. "Yeah, right. You were going to bully them into giving me special treatment."

Aiden raised an eyebrow. "And you don't deserve it? You dived into a cave after me, battled poisonous animals, faced off a dangerous criminal, was kidnapped by a criminal mastermind, and then on top of it all, you have way too much homework left to do for class tomorrow."

Ken shrugged. "Hall Monitor life, am I right? I'm not complaining, Aiden. I don't mind." She grinned. "And VD chose the wrong girl to mess with. We are *so* taking him down."

Aiden grinned back at her. Already they were beginning to relax and smile around each other more often. Things were returning back to normal. He was incredibly relieved. "I'll see you around, Ken," he said, staring down at her bandaged hand and gently running his fingers over the fabric. "Get better soon, all right?"

"Thanks, Aiden," she said. It felt as if a weight had lifted off her heart. Aiden was finally back to his usual self. She couldn't have asked for a better ending to a crazy day.

Well, maybe without the snake bite.

By the next morning, most of the school knew how Ken had gone into the forest and emerged with a snake bite. There were varied rumors as to why she had snuck off campus; these rumors included looking for a missing pet, rebelling against the porters, throwing a secret off-campus party in the woods, and plenty of other ridiculous ideas.

Ken only said that she was looking for a friend, which led to much speculation as to why she got off scot-free. No detentions, demerits, or suspensions were headed her way even though she had openly disobeyed the porters. It was difficult to explain how she hadn't done anything wrong, as her Hall Monitor position gave her security clearance to enter any part of the island without adult supervision. After all, the Hall Monitors still operated in secret.

Lately, this was becoming more and more important. If VD had known about the Hall Monitors' involvement, he would have factored them into his plan to trap Aiden. He also would have most likely targeted them.

Now VD knew.

"He's seen my face," Ken said miserably as she spun around in her swivel chair.

Last night, Aiden had called all of them into the attic for an impromptu meeting. He had declared that he was finished with secrets and went on to explain everything he had hidden from them previously. He told them about Xipe and VD, about the Legacy and the Society. He made each of them swear it all to secrecy. He never mentioned Porter Craig, for their safety as well as Craig's. Finally, Aiden asked them for their help in stopping the Legacy. After the thrill of the past few days, and thanks to their never-failing passion for protecting Ravencrest Academy, the Hall Monitors were all in.

During that meeting, he had wondered if he was too trusting with this carefully guarded information. Yet when he saw their determined faces, he changed his mind. Ken, Layla, Ruthie, Everest, and Ming all had a passion burning in their eyes.

Now it was time to gain more information about the Society. It was the next morning, and they all were a bit sleepy as they waited for Aiden to show up.

"VD hasn't seen my face just yet," Ruthie said slowly, "Or Layla's or Ming's or Everest's. But he's tried to blackmail me and he's...well, you all know what he did to Everest."

Everest bluntly said, "Yeah, he definitely exposed me. But it's fine. No more secrets."

"No more secrets," agreed Layla.

Ken frowned. "Yeah, if you don't count the ones we have to keep from those outside of the Hall Monitors. It's been the worst not being able to tell my mom or godfather that I got bitten by a snake."

"Walter, right?" Ruthie asked. "You mentioned something about him before."

"Yeah. He's the best. I miss him so much," Ken reflected.

When the silence had stretched thin, Ming spoke up: "Why do you think Aiden called us here for a meeting this morning? It's rather early."

"No kidding," yawned Ruthie. It was 5:45 AM. Last night, Aiden had requested via notes under their doors to meet fifteen minutes before the cafeteria opened. The cafeteria opened at 6:00 AM. Then again, all the Hall Monitors were dedicated enough to sacrifice twenty minutes of their sleep. All five had brushed their teeth, washed their faces, and staggered upstairs. After having stayed up late last night because of makeup work, everyone was sleepy.

"Today is busy," Layla admitted. "There are auditions for *Les Misérables* after school."

Ruthie shivered in excitement. "I know. Musician auditions are after the acting auditions. Ming and I are both trying out."

"Good luck to you both," Ken said. "And good luck to Everest and Layla. I know you two are going to try out for acting positions."

"That's exactly why I called us here at this time," Aiden said, entering milliseconds before the clock turned to 5:46. "Apologies for the early wake-up call and the late entrance. I'm well aware that today's a big day for you all. That includes you too, Ken, even if you're not auditioning for a music or acting position."

Ken grinned as she spun around. "Actually, I'm already guaranteed to be the tech person. It's by application. And I already showed them my tech skills for the show."

"Good to know." Aiden turned to the others. "Now, as you all well know, I didn't just call you here to wish you good luck before your auditions, though I do wish you all the best of luck."

"Thanks," Layla said nervously. She had spent all week practicing and reviewing her lines with Ruthie.

Everest shrugged. He had skimmed over the audition script for one of the minor characters. "Let's hope I can make it in time for sports practice right after."

Ruthie hummed to herself the audition portion and Ming gave her an encouraging smile. There were dark circles under her eyes from how late she had stayed up to practice.

Aiden winked at them. "You know, if you ever needed me to adjust the casting list..."

Outraged cries and indignant "Don't you dare!"s met this statement. All the Hall Monitors were immediately on their feet, glaring fiercely at Aiden.

He put his hands up in surrender. "My apologies, I thought I should ask."

"Honestly, after all that's happened, it's offending that you'd think we'd cheat," Ruthie grumbled as they sat back down.

Aiden paused. "Now to business. We need to find out more about the Society. Porter Jimmy isn't going to tell us anything, so it's time to take matters into our own hands. Let's start with the intruders." He forced himself to remember that horrible conversation in the clinic. "Their leader claimed that they were trying to 'protect Ravencrest.'"

"They must have been Society members," realized Everest.

Ken frowned. "Then why did the headmaster lock them up? Isn't he part of the Society, since he's the headmaster and all?"

"I don't think he's part of it, but he must know about it," Aiden said slowly. "He must have found out after Mother died."

"So why didn't the intruders just ask him for help?" Ken pointed out. "They didn't need to break in if they had the headmaster as an ally!"

"I'll ask him about it," Aiden said. "And perhaps you should come along as well. The last time I interrogated my dad, things got...intense. If you're with me, he might be more trusting and less likely to call for backup."

"And about the intruders," Ruthie said, "whatever happened to them? Since they're in prison, can't we visit them and ask them about it too?"

"I'll stop by there as well. Ken, I'll need backup," Aiden hinted.

Ken grinned. "I'm in."

"But what about the rest of us?" Layla whined. "You two are going to interrogate the headmaster and the Society members and do all this cool stuff while we're busy trying to get into the school play!"

"I'll keep you all updated," Ken promised. "On the group chat. The one Aiden hasn't joined yet...."

Aiden quickly changed the subject: "And once we find out what the Legacy and Society are trying to do, we'll let you all know. Keep your weekends free. There might be some traveling involved."

Everyone erupted into excited exclamations.

Aiden finished with, "Now, get some breakfast and go to class. I can't write a note to excuse you if you're late."

"You know, this meeting could have been a quick video call if you had joined the group—" Ken started.

Of course, Aiden was already gone by then.

"Darn it. Aiden Ravencrest, I'm getting your phone number for the group chat, whether you like it or not," Ken muttered under her breath.

Chapter Twenty-Nine

Classes flew by as everyone grew more and more excited about the auditions. Everyone was trying out, and it was clear that only the best actors and musicians would make it in. The practice rooms were completely booked, and more than one student walked into a wall as they furiously muttered their audition lines under their breath.

The moment classes ended, Ken met with Aiden to go after the headmaster. "Let's hurry," Ken advised. "I want to make it in time to cheer on Layla and Everest at the auditions."

"We have time. Don't worry," Aiden replied, adding a few minor edits to his paper before sending it to one of the Ravencrest Academy professors. The professor would grade Aiden's paper as if he was the professor's student, something Aiden truly appreciated.

As they walked up the stairs to the headmaster's office, they passed by Ruthie and Rajesh talking in the hallway. "Are you trying out?" Ruthie asked.

Rajesh sighed. "No. I was going to be the tech person, but the people in charge were idiotic enough to choose someone else. Don't they know about my experience?" He rolled his eyes. "I'm the best person they could have chosen. The moment the cast list comes out, I'm going to make sure that whoever did get that part is well aware that they got lucky."

Ruthie felt uneasy. "Maybe they were just better? Like, their program was more advanced or something? It is merit-based—"

"Don't be ridiculous. I'm the best there is; my program was perfect for the show," Rajesh replied bitterly. "This is clear favoritism. I bet whoever got the position had a wealthy guardian or well-connected relations."

Ruthie hesitated. "I don't know, Rajesh. I feel like you're just upset you didn't make it in."

"No, I always get what I want. This time, it had to be some other reason, I know it. I'll have my parents call the directors and pull some strings." He quickened his pace as Ruthie gasped, "But you just said that wouldn't be fair!"

"I never said that," Rajesh pointed out with a sly smile. "Sometimes you have to do what it takes to get what you want."

Ruthie stared at her feet. "Rajesh—"

"Are you trying out?"

"Well, yes, but—"

"For which part?"

"Musician."

"Oh." Rajesh frowned. "I'm not into music."

"Oh." *I am.*

Rajesh glanced at her sideways. "Do you have any plans for tonight? What about the weekend?"

"Um, I'm busy this weekend."

"With what?"

"I—I can't say—"

"You're busy all right," chuckled Rajesh. "You're going to be busy with me."

"What?" Ruthie asked, stopping dead in her tracks. She could sense what was coming.

Rajesh turned and looked directly into her eyes, leaving her tongue-tied. They were now near the study café, the same place they had first met outside of class. "Ruthie, I've been trying to ask you this for weeks, but I've always lost the courage."

"Um, I'm kind of—" Ruthie tried to say, but he pushed on: "You're the most intelligent, beautiful, and kind person I've ever met."

Ruthie forgot everything she had been about to say. "Wait, really?" she stammered, caught off-guard. "Uh, thanks."

Rajesh took her hands in his and instantly she was very uncomfortable. "There's a formal NASA dinner tomorrow with some of the leading figures in astrophysics. I was invited to come, and I told them I was bringing someone special."

"You mean me?"

"That's right," he said. "You."

"Thank you for the invitation, but I can't," Ruthie stammered, pulling her fingers away as gently as she could. "I have something important then. I already made a commitment. I'm sorry, Rajesh, maybe another time."

"What?" Rajesh repeated in shock as if he hadn't heard her correctly.

She stared at her feet. "I told my friends I would be there this weekend. I can't say no to them."

"But you're okay with saying no to me?"

"I—I already told them—"

"Come *on*, Ruthie," Rajesh pleaded. "I want you to meet my parents."

Ruthie swallowed hard. She had no experience with these kinds of situations. Was she supposed to be coy or make a joke? How was she supposed to respond? Layla would know what to do—but she wasn't Layla. So she chose to be herself. She chose to be honest.

"Rajesh, I can't go this weekend. I have an important commitment I've already made and I'm sorry I let you down. And to be honest...I don't think we should be in a relationship. I barely know you and...I'm not interested anyway." She squeezed her eyes shut, terrified of his response.

"What do you mean, you're not interested?" Rajesh scowled. She knew he was used to getting what he wanted. "We've been dating for weeks."

"Dating? We just studied together!"

"Oh, please." He was getting angry now. "Don't tell me you were that clueless."

She was getting a little nervous. She had never seen this side of him before. "Look, I have enough on my plate. And I'm really not ready for this. Can we please just stay friends?"

"Ruthie, I already told everyone I was taking you along."

"You shouldn't have done that!"

"Are you telling me I made a mistake?"

"Yes!" Ruthie was getting angry now too. "You made a mistake! You were wrong! You were wrong to say I was coming without asking me! You were wrong to expect me to say yes instead of giving me a choice! You were wrong not to let me know ahead of time what your intentions were! Rajesh, I really thought we were just friends!"

"I didn't think you were the type of person to lead me on or to bail on me last minute!" Rajesh shouted.

"I didn't mean to lead you on!" Ruthie was on the verge of tears. "And it's not my fault you didn't just talk to me about this earlier!" She took a deep breath. "Look, Rajesh, we're both really angry right now. Why don't we just—"

"God, I can't believe I ever liked you!" Rajesh said, stepping away from her like she was acid.

She felt pressure building up in her eyes; she was about to cry. "Rajesh, the answer is no. I never said I liked you like that. I thought you were just my friend. I'm sorry if you're hurt by this, but it's the truth." She swallowed hard. "And I know people think I'm nice, but I'm also wise enough to know that it would be worse for us both if I pretended I was interested in you when I'm not."

"Are you...breaking up with me?" Rajesh said slowly.

"We were never together in the first place," Ruthie said firmly. "And if I may give you some advice, Rajesh...if you ever want a girlfriend, be honest and clear with your intentions from the start. I liked you when you were my friend. But now I'm not sure who you are."

Rajesh only stood there in shock. He watched mutely as she turned away. "Goodbye, Rajesh," she said at last, leaving him standing in the hallway.

Behind her, he called, "You're going to regret this, Ruthie!" He sounded absolutely furious. With a pang in her heart, Ruthie realized that for him to get this mad, he must be really hurt. For a split second, she wanted to turn back around and apologize for hurting him this much.

But she forced herself to keep walking forward, her eyes ahead. She refused to look back.

As she turned in the hallway to head to her room, she brushed by a familiar face. "Sorry," she muttered reflexively, her voice on thin ice. She didn't notice who it was as she trudged down the hall, wiping her eyes.

Ming said nothing and only moved out of the way.

Layla was still practicing when the dorm door flung open. "Oh, hi, Ruthie—" Then she noticed the tear stains on Ruthie's face. "Wait, what happened?"

Ruthie buried her face in her pillow. "I don't know. Rajesh hates me now. I think we're not friends anymore."

"Why? What happened?"

"I said no."

"What? He asked you out on a date?"

"Should I have been nicer or something?" Ruthie asked, raising her head. "We really were just friends, Layla. I guess I confided in him and he told me all about his plans, and we joked together and hung out and all, but I never thought for a moment that we were dating. Layla, you have to believe me!"

Layla sat down next to her. "I do believe you. What a jerk."

"Me?" Ruthie asked.

"No, of course not!" Layla said. "Rajesh. If he really respected you, he'd understand a no."

Ruthie leaned her head against Layla's shoulder. "I don't think I ever want to have a boyfriend," she confessed to Layla. "Guy friends are complicated enough as it is."

Layla put an arm around her friend. "Agreed." Her eyes were far away and sad.

"What's wrong?"

Layla sighed and stared out the window. "My sister learned the hard way about guys who can be jerks."

"Divorced?"

"It's a long story." Layla stared at the floor. "Just...know that I've learned the hard way that guys are stupid until they're 21. And you know what? Even after that, they're still stupid sometimes."

"Layla!" Ruthie giggled through her sniffles.

Layla chuckled. "Well, whatever happens with Rajesh, know that we're still friends, okay?"

"Okay." Ruthie exhaled. She closed her eyes. "Sorry to bother you. You can practice all you want; I know the auditions are in an hour."

"You matter way more," Layla promised.

Ruthie looked up at Layla and realized how much the older girl had changed; earlier in the year, Layla wouldn't have even bothered talking to Ruthie unless Ruthie was popular enough. Now, Layla made a genuine effort to reach out to quieter, less well-known girls as well. It was as if she was learning how to be selfless through Ruthie's example. For the first time, Ruthie realized how much they had helped each other; Layla had taught Ruthie how to stand up for herself, and Ruthie had taught her how to be less selfish. Ruthie's eyes filled with tears again. "Thanks, Layla. Really."

After a brief hug, Ruthie pushed Layla away. "Now, time to practice! Here, tell me your audition lines. I'll pretend to be the judge."

"Are you sure you're okay?"

"Layla!"

Chapter Thirty

While Layla was becoming Cosette, Ken was becoming more impatient by the minute.

"Why does your dad have such long meetings?" she grumbled. "What could be so important that would keep him busy for eight hours straight? I mean, he can't even meet with his son for ten minutes?" She had joined him right after classes ended and had waited for nearly an hour to no avail.

"It's actually been ten hours since I asked him this morning for a quick meeting," Aiden said with a sigh. "It's plausible that he forgot about me. We could just interrupt whatever meeting he's in, though that might not be a good idea."

Ken frowned. "Whatever meeting he's in, how important could it be?"

It was then that the door to the headmaster's office opened and none other than the President of the United States strolled out, his bodyguards close behind him. "Glad we came to an agreement," Headmaster Ravencrest said.

"Of course, sir," agreed the President. He didn't see the two teenagers observing this exchange between ceiling tiles.

Gawking, Ken turned to Aiden and gasped, "What's your dad doing with the President of the United States of America?"

Aiden shrugged. "He's had more important meetings."

"How could—"

"Quick, there's an opening!" Aiden pushed aside a ceiling panel and threw down a rope. Both slid down right after the President and his bodyguards stepped out of view and right before Headmaster Ravencrest headed back inside.

The headmaster could only blink in surprise as Aiden cheerfully said, "Father! Glad we could finally meet."

"Oh, right, you wanted to meet with me," Father mumbled. "I forgot about that."

"Now's as good a time as any, no?" Ken said brightly, then remembered to add, "Sir."

"I think I need my bodyguards behind me," Father said meaningfully, looking straight at Aiden. "Just as an extra level of protection. And I need you both to empty your pockets and pass through this metal detector before coming inside."

Ken sighed and began taking off her jacket, shoes, and jewelry. She knew the drill.

"Don't worry, Father," Aiden assured him as he stepped through the metal detector. "Hopefully this meeting won't require any protection. No one's bringing any—"

"Is that a pen stun gun?" Father gasped as Ken added it to her pile.

Ken shrugged. "I wanted to be prepared after last time."

"What do you mean by *last time*?" Father asked.

Before Ken could answer, Aiden quickly interrupted, "So, Father, we may be discussing some...*classified* information in this meeting. Could you please ensure no one is listening?"

Father slowly nodded. "I'll consider it."

By now, Ken had finished her pile and had already grumpily walked through the metal detector. "What's the point of having backup gadgets if you never get to use them?" she muttered as she fell into the plush chair where the President had been sitting moments ago.

Father whispered to his son, "Why is she here?"

Aiden whispered back, "As a promise that I will not do anything to harm the school or threaten your safety."

Father looked at Aiden, and then at Ken for a long time. At last, he dismissed his security and sat down at his desk, looking very alert and cautious. It was clear he had learned from the last time Aiden had interrogated him. "What did you want to discuss with me?" he asked politely.

"The Society," Aiden said.

"And the Legacy," Ken added.

Father tried to control his surprise, but Aiden caught the widening of the eyes and the quickening of the breathing. "I'm sorry?"

"We know about both organizations," Aiden explained as Ken flicked a piece of lint off the chair. "Vladimir Damon personally told me about them both. I have to say that it would have been better to hear it from you, but I suppose you were sworn to secrecy, so I can't blame you."

Father sputtered, "Damon was in contact with you?"

"Almost killed me. It's funny, really," Aiden continued calmly. "I think I would have been in less danger if I had known the truth beforehand. It's almost as if keeping me in the dark is putting me in more danger."

Father leaned back with some resignation. "So you know."

"Yes," Aiden said simply.

Father motioned toward Ken. "Does she—?"

"I know," Ken said just as simply.

Father ran a hand over his face as both students waited patiently. Finally, Father sighed. "How did your mother do it?"

"Keep the Society a secret from me?" Aiden said.

"Perform her duties as the Head of the Society so well." Father looked down at the desk with clear dark circles around his eyes. "The Society was thriving before she was killed. I knew it would be hard, but I never thought it would be *this* hard."

"Being Head of the Society?" Aiden guessed. He was really asking, *Are you the Head of the Society*

"Yes. It's hard to be both the Head of the Society and the headmaster at the same time," admitted Father. "We had such a fine system: your mother would run the Society while I would run the school. We both performed our duties well. Things ran so smoothly. The Legacy was kept under control. You were safe, protected, and well-raised. The school was safe, protected, and well-run. Now..." His exhaustion made it clear that he was not lying.

Just to be careful, Ken casually let out a sigh. Via an earpiece, Ruthie informed Ken, "He's not lying."

(When Aiden had been talking to Father earlier, Ken had passed through the metal detector with a small pouch. She had quickly thrown it into the air and briskly caught it on the other side of the detector while Aiden kept eye contact with the headmaster. Now, she had an earpiece in her ear, a camera in a small necklace, and a few other just-in-case materials grasped in her hand.)

(Ruthie, who was watching from the necklace camera, added, "He really is tired."

Distantly, Ken could also hear Layla singing, *I know a place where there's no one lost...I know a place where no one cries....* while practicing for the auditions.)

To let Aiden know that Father was telling the truth, Ken tapped her fingers on her chair's armrest.

Father's tired eyes jumped from Aiden to Ken. "Why did you tell her?"

"He didn't," Ken clarified. "I found out the hard way. It's a long story."

"There's a lot of information we know and a lot we don't know," Aiden interjected. "So we would all appreciate it greatly if you answered our questions in a straightforward manner."

"Even if you don't tell us, we're taking a trip to interrogate the intruders," Ken added. "Don't you think it'd be better if we heard the truth from you instead of them?"

Father snapped to attention, suddenly straightening up. "You're going to the prison where the criminals who broke into Ravencrest are being held?"

"We'll find the truth somehow, no matter what it takes," Aiden said firmly.

Father hesitated.

(Ruthie spoke up again: "He's deciding whether to trust you two or not.")

At last, Father muttered, "What's there left to lose? You'll be in more danger if I don't tell you."

No one gloated or prodded for answers. Aiden held his breath and Ken waited.

Finally, Father slumped back in his chair and said, "I will answer all your questions on one condition."

"Which is?" Aiden asked.

"You don't interrogate those intruders. I don't know what lies they're going to put in your mind or how they plan to manipulate you to their own advantage."

Ruthie immediately said, "He's lying—no, wait—he's half-lying. He was telling the truth at the end but lying when he was talking about the lies." (In the background, Layla sobbed fiercely as part of her practice.)

Ken was quite confused. "What?" she hissed to Ruthie, hoping for clarification.

Father glanced at her and repeated, "I mean it. Take or leave my offer. Either I answer all your questions now or you can have those manipulative criminals plant whatever lies they want in your mind. It's your choice. Aiden, you're a smart boy. What will it be?"

Aiden nodded obediently. "Neither of us will interrogate the criminals who broke into Ravencrest."

Father frowned. "That was very specific."

Aiden held his gaze. "I was. I might have broken my agreement to be honest on my last visit here, but I will not do so again. From this time onwards, neither I nor Ken will interrogate any of the criminals who broke into Ravencrest Academy." He did not break eye contact with Father. Under the table, Aiden used Ken's phone to text the others that they had better pack their bags after the auditions; they would be the ones interrogating the intruders this weekend.

Finally, Father threw up his hands. "Laissez-faire!"

"The free market?" Ken asked, confused.

"My hands are clean," Father said. "I cannot control, stop, or protect you in any way as you refuse to let me. You are forcing me to tell you what I do not believe is safe for you to know. But you are an adult now. You're fourteen—"

"Fifteen," Aiden said offhandedly.

"Fifteen?" Father paused. "Really?"

Ken turned to Aiden. "Wait, seriously?"

"My birthday was a few weeks ago. I forgot to celebrate it. I had more important things on my mind." Aiden dismissed the matter with a wave of his hand. "Continue, Father."

Ken wasn't ready to change the subject. "So no one celebrated your birthday? Aiden, that's horrible! When is it?"

"This isn't a good time, Ken," Aiden said through clenched teeth.

Ken pursued her lips. "Well, fine, but I'm not going to forget this. Or the group chat."

"What group chat?" Father asked.

"Focus!" Aiden commanded. "Father, tell me. I made a promise. Now keep your side of the deal: what is the Society? What are its values? What does it strive to accomplish? How did it begin? How was my mother involved? Then explain all those things for the Legacy. Start at the very beginning."

("A very good place to start," agreed Layla over the earpiece. Right away, Ruthie cried, "Shush, Layla! Get back to practicing!")

Father exhaled, closed his eyes, and began with, "Almost seventeen years ago, I met your mother."

("That's a good start," Layla said admiringly.)

"I always thought she was beautiful," Father said. His eyes were far away. "Apparently, she thought I wasn't too bad myself. I knew how to make her smile. We dated for a while, and I gained her parents' blessing once they saw my sincere care for her. We were together for quite a while before she told me that she was the only person who could become Headmaster of Ravencrest Academy. And as she did not want to, her fiance was to become the headmaster himself.

"Contrary to what you all might think, I did not date her with the intention of gaining that position. In fact, sometimes I wonder if she dated me with those intentions herself. I mean, I loved this academy. I once studied here myself. This is where I met her, where we started dating. However, four years later, when I found out that her husband would be the headmaster, my intentions changed. I no longer wanted to be her boyfriend and eventual husband because I loved her. I just wanted that position.

"So I used every gesture, every dinner together, and every single idea I could conceive to convince her and her parents that I was the best person for her. I poured all I had into making her believe I loved her."

"Did you love her?" Aiden interrupted.

Father looked at his hands for a long time. "I did," he said quietly. "I did love her. At first. Then...then I loved the idea of being headmaster, one of the richest people in the world and one of the most respected scholars of all time. I loved the idea of being headmaster more than anything else. So I manipulated her. I told her I loved her and did everything I could to show her I meant it. It took time before she truly believed it. When she did, I pressured her to rush things, which is why we were married relatively quickly."

(Layla was furious by now. "What a jerk!" she hissed. "Aiden, your dad is like the villain in a soap opera! No offense."

"How is Aiden not supposed to take offense to that? This is his dad!" Ruthie pointed out.

Layla replied, "Yeah, but—"

To cut them both off, Ken cleared her throat and coughed loudly. Father glanced at her strangely, but continued to speak:)

"I immediately jumped into the role of Headmaster of Ravencrest Academy. I loved my position here. It took over everything else in my life. It was one of the greatest mistakes of my life to put my job before my family, I promise you that. Your mother jumped into her role of the Head of the Society with just as much excitement, yet somehow managed to keep you as the highest priority in her life. She balanced it all so well; raising you while running the Society was quite the feat. But I wasn't like her. It took much too long for me to realize where my heart was. So I took steps to set things right. I came to visit her. I underestimated Vladimir Damon and thus I was forced to poison your mother." Now Father drew in a sharp breath as if it was becoming more and more painful for him to speak. "So he used me to kill her. After her death, I was grief-stricken and bewildered. I knew little of how the Society functioned; she always hid things so well. Yet I knew she would have wanted me to run things until a proper candidate—namely you, Aiden—rose in her place. So I took the reins.

"At first, it wasn't too bad. But I learned quickly how running a school and running a secret agency are two very different things. On top of it all, VD wanted to kill you, Aiden. Your first concussion was really a failed murder attempt. I thought then—" Father's voice broke. "I thought I had lost you. I couldn't go through that again, not after what happened to your mother."

(Ruthie sniffled in the background. "This is so sad!"

"Shh!" Layla shushed. "I want to hear the next part!")

"Thankfully, you survived," Father said. "But you forgot what you had witnessed. I thought it was for the best. I decided to keep you safe and out of harm's way. I underestimated you as well, Aiden. I thought one day you would understand."

"I do understand, Father," Aiden said.

Father barked out a laugh. "Then why do you keep putting yourself in harm's way?"

"Because I want to be Head of the Society!"

This revelation startled everyone, including Ken, who turned and stared at Aiden in shock. Father was amazed. "*You?*"

Aiden's eyes blazed. "I cannot stand by and let the Legacy destroy this school. I want to do something. I want to be the new Head of the Society."

Father chuckled humorlessly. "Do you know what you're getting yourself into?"

"Yes," Aiden said.

"You'd have to contain VD, stop the Legacy, and protect the Society's secrets," Father pointed out. "All while continuing your education."

Aiden did not waver. "I can do it."

Father rubbed the back of his neck. "You're fifteen years old. Can't you enjoy your childhood? Hang out with your friends? Have some fun?"

"This is his way of enjoying his childhood, hanging out with his friends, and having fun, sir," Ken said.

"True," Aiden had to admit.

Father sighed. "Well, the answer is no."

"*No*? But—"

"Your mother agreed that you should be the next Head of the Society, if you are willing," Father said. "However, you are not of age, as per her will. Once you are eighteen—"

"Due to external circumstances, couldn't that be waived?" Aiden cut in.

Father frowned. "I would not advise it, and I am the current headmaster."

Aiden stiffened. "I see."

"Then we have reached an agreement?" Father seemed to think the conversation was over, already starting to stand up.

"Hold your horses!" Ken called, then remembered to add, "Sir."

Aiden explained, "You haven't answered a single one of my questions. I want a little history lesson right now. Tell me about the origins of the Society and why it exists. And then repeat all that for the Legacy."

Father glanced at his watch. "I've thirty minutes to spare before I have to leave for another meeting...ah, well, I suppose you know about the third Ravencrest sibling?"

"Stepsibling," Aiden corrected.

Ken nodded in agreement. "That scum wasn't good enough to be considered part of the Ravencrest family."

Father raised an eyebrow at this, but continued, "The third Ravencrest sibling was named Vincent Darien."

("VD!" Ruthie gasped.)

Father added, "Yes, his initials were VD. It's a tradition in the Legacy to change the initials of the new Head to VD. I suppose this time it was Vladimir Damon. But I digress. Vincent Darien was the biological son of the man who married the mother of Matthew and Evelyn Ravencrest. They became stepsiblings and, very soon, rivals. Vincent became jealous of Matthew's achievements and attempted to outdo his older brother. His jealousy turned to bitterness, which turned to hate until one day Vincent Darien attempted to kill Matthew Ravencrest and publish Matthew's works as Vincent's inventions. Evelyn found out about this attempt and saved her older brother's life. From that day on, the sides were made clear. Matthew went out to academically advance the world. Evelyn went out to protect the world. Vincent went out to destroy his older siblings and the world for his own gain."

("What a jerk," Layla muttered.)

Father went on: "The Society was formed by Evelyn Ravencrest to uphold her values after she passed; the Legacy was founded by Vincent Darien in the same way. The Society operates to protect the world and preserve world peace as much as possible. It's a humanitarian organization that has rescued refugees, prevented world wars, and stopped several terrorist operations. It also protects the secrets of Ravencrest Academy, some of which I cannot say in front of Mackenzie here. The Legacy operates as a terrorist organization, with their end goal as world dominion."

"What do you mean by Ravencrest's secrets?" Aiden asked. "Vague answers are fine, but I would like some examples."

"I can't say," Father said, looking directly at Ken.

Ken stood up. "I can leave."

Father admitted, "I couldn't say it in front of Aiden either."

Aiden frowned. "Do you want me to find out the hard way?"

Father's face twisted as he looked between them. (Ruthie added, "He's thinking about whether to trust you both. Also, he hasn't lied at all in the story.") It took a good thirty seconds before Father sighed again, leaned forward, and softly said, "Armageddon."

"You mean the Biblical Armageddon?" Ken asked.

"No," Father said. It was clear that it pained him to give up the secret. "There is a device that could bring about the end of the world. It is called Armageddon."

"How does it work?" Aiden asked.

Father clenched the sides of the chair. "It can manipulate spacetime."

Ken fell silent as Aiden sucked in a breath. She would later make him explain. For now, she understood that this device was very, very dangerous.

"Matthew Ravencrest developed a prototype years ago. Should this device end up in the Legacy's hands, the world would very well be brought to its knees." Father closed his eyes. "The entire situation would be disastrous."

"And this is relevant because...?" Aiden probed.

Father sighed for what seemed like the hundredth time. "Your mother was killed on her mission to find Armageddon."

Aiden was still. For a moment, the world swam before his eyes. So this was what his mother had died to protect. It was time to hand the responsibility to him. He sat up straighter in his chair, his heart pounding.

"You see, about ten years ago, she decided to go after some of the older missing items Ravencrest protected," Father explained. "Armageddon was the most dangerous item on the list. Matthew Ravencrest sent it away to protect it. Your mother thought she knew Armageddon's true location, yet was unable to find it on her first trip. However, on that trip, she came face-to-face in a hotel room with the assassin who happens to be Vladimir Damon's father. It was a brutal fight to the death, as Damon's father is a very vicious fighter, but in the end, your mother survived. She had to kill him out of self-defense. Afterward, she returned to Ravencrest straight away and didn't revisit the idea of finding Armageddon until years later. The entire trip was a horrifying experience, but it set an even more sobering reality in place for all of the Society, as Vladimir Damon swore revenge. Damon was utterly ruthless in rising to his position, as you all well know. He has worked until now to earn his place as Head of the Society. After he killed your mother—" Father hesitated briefly, almost choking up yet pushing on to say, "—he earned his position as Head of the Legacy."

"And now he's here to destroy Ravencrest and the Society once and for all," Aiden said slowly. "Out of revenge."

Now Ken understood. "They targeted students to weaken Ravencrest Academy and to refocus the Society's efforts on protecting the students instead of defending the world."

"That's right," Father said grimly. "And they're not quite finished yet."

Chapter Thirty-One

Ken slumped back in her seat as the full ramifications of what had happened this year hit her hard. "Sophia Manchester. She pulled out of Ravencrest this year and she's, like, the only student in a lot of the school's history to drop out of Ravencrest Academy. The rest of the students didn't, but...she's not coming back."

(Ruthie and Layla were silent here. Sophia's permanent disappearance was painful for them both to think about; she had been a loyal friend and now she no longer spoke to them. She had been brilliant, yet all that talent had been wasted. It was tragic. No one knew what had happened to her.)

"And they didn't just target her. They started pushing perfect-seeming, elite students to do horrible things. She just cracked faster than the rest under all the pressure and pain," Ken realized. Her stomach hurt just thinking about it. "It's all so horrible. I hate VD."

"Was Operation Injection the plan to target students?" Aiden asked.

Father recoiled. "Where did you hear about Operation Injection?"

"Just answer the question, please," Aiden said.

Surprisingly, Father obeyed. "No, Operation Injection was an attempt to hypnotize the most elite students in the world. Vladimir Damon had a master hypnotizer with him. He planned to mind-control Ravencrest students, at least before I found his hypnotizer friend and ensured he wouldn't be able to do so."

"See, you aren't doing so bad as Head of the Society, sir," Ken said encouragingly.

Father smiled a little at her. "It was a great relief when the hypnotizer was finally taken care of. I felt as if I had dodged a bullet."

"So why is VD cyberbullying these kids and turning them into criminals?" Aiden inquired. "Is it simply a way to weaken the school's reputation?"

Father straightened some of the files on his desk while he talked. "He's proving himself as Head of the Legacy. He's not just hurting the school's reputation, he's pushing students to their limit until they leave the school or end up in a much worse position. He's also trying to make a point by showing us that he can get to them. It's as if he's saying, *I'm doing this to our future world leaders now, but soon, I'll be doing this to our current world leaders.*"

"I was right!" cheered Ken. "See, I knew it was a prestige thing!"

"It's also a very tactful move," Father conceded. "As trust in Ravencrest's security diminishes, despite our increasing security measures, fewer kids feel safe. That means fewer students are able to truly benefit from their experience here. Students can't learn well if they don't feel safe here. If Ravencrest students suffer, the whole school suffers, and if we're so busy trying to help our students by looking inward, we can't look outward and focus on whatever plan he's about to execute."

"What plan?" Aiden asked.

"We think he's about to do something big," Father said. He lowered his voice as he explained, "His attacks are increasing in intensity and impact. We think he's pushing us to help these kids so we don't see what's coming next. I think that at any moment soon, he's going to switch from attacking kids to attacking the physical school itself."

"Why do you think that?" Ken asked.

"We have intel," Father said carefully, and immediately Aiden thought of Porter Craig. "VD is soon going to target the building of Ravencrest Academy once he's finished making these students miserable. At least your Hall Monitors have really helped these students through all of this."

"No," sighed Ken. "We've only helped stop VD after the damage has been done. We have to be faster and stop him beforehand."

("How are we going to do that?" Ruthie asked. "I definitely agree, but I don't know how. It's not like we have our own intel or double agent working for us."

"I could be a double agent," Layla offered.

Before they could start arguing, Ken coughed and they both fell silent.)

"I appreciate all you've done," Father said. "It's been a great help to Campus Security, and it's the only way we've been able to protect the school from VD. At this point, every bit of help counts."

Ken was not yet satisfied. "What about the intruders? If you really are Head of the Society, and if you really did stop Operation Injection, then why did they break in and try to stop it themselves? And why did you send them to prison if they were just Society members?"

Father admitted, "Some Society members felt the need to take matters into their own hands. They splintered off and created a smaller, extremist version of the Society called the Union. I suppose they felt breaking into the school and attempting to kidnap all Ravencrest students was the safest way to protect them from

Operation Injection, which I dismantled shortly afterward. They still committed a crime, and if I don't send them to prison, how else am I to stop the Union?"

("So the intruders were part of the Union, which is a mini-Society," Ruthie realized. "Except they were more extreme in protecting the school."

Layla added in a menacing voice, "Like, *We'll stop the Legacy all right...at all costs.*")

To check if Father had been lying at all, Ken sighed loudly. Ruthie picked up on the coded signal and updated Ken, "He wasn't lying at all before, but I'm getting mixed signals when he's talking about the Union. It's like he's sort of telling the truth, except there's something he's not telling us."

Ken tapped her fingers in the pattern that meant Father was telling the truth, then slowed down in tapping them, which meant he was now telling half-truths.

"Why don't you want us talking to the intruders?" Aiden questioned.

Father frowned. "I told you. They're desperate extremists. They'll lie and do whatever it takes to manipulate you into helping them. I want you to stay away for your own safety, so they don't plant any lies in your minds."

(Ruthie excitedly shouted, "He's lying, I can tell! He's definitely hiding something!")

To signal that Father was lying, Ken yawned.

Aiden leaned forward and held Father's gaze without blinking. "Is that the only reason you don't want us to see the intruders?"

"Yes," said Father firmly, glaring back at Aiden without blinking. "Now please obey the only order I have given you."

"As promised, I will," said Aiden, leaning back in his chair. Ken's phone buzzed with news from Ming and Everest: they would be free this weekend to interrogate the intruders. Ming could also observe whether people were lying, though not as well as Ruthie, and Everest knew how to make people relax. No one in the Society or Legacy had seen either of their faces. Thus, they would be excellent interrogators.

For now, Aiden and Ken could sense that the Headmaster was not about to give away any information regarding the real reason why he didn't want them to speak to the intruders. It was time to move on to other questions.

"Do you have any leads on how VD is hacking into student accounts?" Aiden asked.

Father groaned in exasperation at the mere mention of VD's hacking. "I've tried to figure it out! I've reviewed countless security reports and enlisted the best programmers in the world to study our code. There's simply no way an outside force could hack into these students' email accounts."

"So it must be an inside force," Ken realized. "An inside job."

Father frowned. "Young lady, our porters would never do such a thing. Every one of them is a member of the Society. Most of them are doing assignments that extend off-campus. Besides, even if a porter wanted to hurt Ravencrest students in this manner, they wouldn't be able to. Student credentials can only be found in a highly encrypted and protected flash drive."

"So it's not the porters and it's not normal hacking," Ken said slowly, the gears in her mind turning, "There's some other internal force that's allowing VD to send messages to students from their own email accounts."

"Correct," said Father. "And what other internal force has access to student credentials?"

"Students." The idea came instantly to Ken. "What if there are students tasked with finding other students' credentials? It would explain why it's so hard to find a common factor in all the students that were targeted. VD could have some other way to communicate with the students that are helping him, maybe at their home on weekend trips, and he could force them to send him other students' credentials so he can log in and write those emails."

There was a silence as Father gaped at Ken. He had consulted several security professionals, hired way too many software developers to strengthen the code, and personally gone over every single possible way VD could get into those kids' email accounts. And yet this junior had figured it out so quickly. The Headmaster was speechless.

Even Aiden was amazed. He grinned at his father's shocked face. "I know, right? She's brilliant."

Ken blushed. "Aiden! It's just a puzzle."

Aiden laughed. "Right, a puzzle that an entire security team couldn't solve."

"It makes sense," Father said to himself, in shock. "Vladimir hasn't been hacking us at all. He's simply been logging in and writing these emails himself."

"The only questions remaining are which students and how are they getting everyone's credentials?" Ken wondered out loud.

Aiden looked at Father and leaned in, his elbows resting on the table, his eyes locked on the Headmaster. "Father, if the Hall Monitors catch VD before this year is over—"

("Aiden!" gasped Ruthie and Layla at the same time as Ken raised an eyebrow at the magnitude of this challenge.)

"—will you make me, Aiden Ravencrest, the Head of the Society?" Aiden asked. His eyes never left his father's face. "And would all the Hall Monitors become members of the Society?"

("Woah!" Layla gasped as Ruthie muttered, "There's no way he'll say yes to this unless he's desperate enough to stop VD.")

Father groaned. "Aiden, you really do put me in tight spots, don't you?"

"He does it a lot," grumbled Ken.

Aiden shrugged. "It's a talent."

For the next minute, no one spoke. Both Ken and Aiden barely dared to breathe as Father thought so hard that he developed a headache. He closed his eyes and deeply contemplated whether the risk was worth it.

After a good minute had passed, Father opened his eyes. "If you fail, you will stay away from all matters pertaining to the Society and the Legacy. You will also report to me before you perform anything even remotely dangerous. The rest of your Hall Monitors will only monitor the halls of Ravencrest Academy and not one of you will ever get involved in any of the dangerous and actually relevant parts of protecting Ravencrest, am I understood?"

His tone could not have been more patronizing. It was clear how high the stakes were; if they did not fulfill their end of the deal, they would never be able to truly protect Ravencrest. They would be banished to doing nothing more than leaving the hard work to the grown-ups.

Father seemed amused by the horrified looks on Aiden and Ken's faces, which had grown pale at the mention of abandoning the true purpose of the Hall Monitors. "You two should learn to enjoy your childhood while it lasts. Focus on your studies. Make friends. Live your life to the fullest."

"Saving the world is how we do that, sir," Ken said.

Father chuckled. "Would it really be that horrible to be a couple of little kids again, leaving all the scary stuff to the adults?"

(He sounded so patronizing that even Ruthie muttered, "Let's do this."

"Definitely," agreed Layla.)

"I couldn't be on the sidelines if I wanted to," Aiden protested.

"You mean I couldn't make a difference, couldn't actually do something with my life?" Ken said angrily. "No way."

"There are other less dangerous ways to make a difference," Father pointed out.

Ken agreed, "Yeah, and I'll get to them later. But this is what I'm good at, so I'll stick with it for now."

Father exhaled. "So this is the only way I can get either of you out of harm's way for good?"

"Yep! It's the only way you can keep the most effective security team there is from helping Ravencrest Academy," Ken said.

Aiden admitted honestly, "I wouldn't call us the most effective security team, considering how we are all high school students, but we're certainly the cheapest yet most highly qualified team you could put together, Father."

Father closed his eyes to think. When he opened them again, they were serious and decisive. He had come to a decision. Slowly yet surely, the Headmaster of Ravencrest Academy nodded and said, "It's a deal. You have the next few months to find and stop Vladimir Damon. I suggest you get started now."

Chapter Thirty-Two

While Ruthie and Layla were erupting in cheers, Ken was wincing at how loud they were and Aiden was sitting back in satisfaction. He shook his father's hand and left the room with Ken right behind him. Meanwhile, Ming practiced his violin while Everest endured a brutal basketball practice.

When Ming and Everest met in their dorm room, both were sweating profusely. Everest wiped his brow. "I'm done," he sighed, putting down his water bottle. "I've been working so hard for the past hour that I'm barely alive right now."

"I doubt you mean that," said Ming. "Your endurance is incredible."

Everest shrugged. "I could handle a little more, but don't tell Coach. I'm about to drop dead if he makes me do another drill."

Ming rubbed some circulation back into the red mark on his neck where the violin had pressed into his skin. He had been practicing nonstop for the past hour. "The auditions will begin in half an hour," he said. "You may freshen up in the restroom first. I can help you with your lines."

"No, you focus on your own auditions," Everest said. "It would be nice if I made it into the play, but it's not going to kill me if I don't get in. I know you're crushing all the musical achievements, though, so don't let me stop you."

Ming smiled gratefully at his friend and said, "While I appreciate your encouragement, I truly need a short break."

Everest laughed. "I thought the great Ming never took breaks."

Ming was about to respond when his phone *ding*ed with a new notification. It was an audio recording of the entire conversation between the Headmaster, Aiden, and Ken. While Everest showered, Ming listened to the entire conversation, neatly picked out his clothes for the week to save time, and finished some homework. By the time Everest emerged, somewhat refreshed, Ming only had to hand him the headset.

So while the boys were walking to the auditorium for the auditions, they were silent, their minds reeling from this new information and buzzing with ideas on how to proceed.

Ruthie and Layla met them in the hallway. "You heard the recording?" Layla said eagerly.

"Shh!" Ruthie said nervously, glancing around.

"We did," Everest agreed. "And all I can say is *woah*."

"That's what I said!" Layla said.

Ming spoke loudly, silencing them all with his stern tone: "There are so many other people here as well. We'd better hurry if we want to make it to our auditions on time."

It was then that Ken and Aiden joined them in the crowd of students on their way to the auditorium. Both Ken and Aiden were thoughtful and quiet, yet still smiled and wished the others good luck. They had come to watch and cheer their friends on. As they all entered the auditorium, they were met with a general chatter of voices as kids prepared to audition. Layla fervently muttered more lines under her breath just as she came face-to-face with Veronica.

"Madame Thenardier!" Layla gasped, meaning to say, "You!"

"You!" Veronica gasped at the same time.

"Don't forget me," Ruthie said, trying to lighten the mood.

There was an awkward silence as Layla's gaze traveled to the audition script Veronica was holding. "You're trying out for Cosette?" she said in amazement.

Veronica's eyes narrowed. "You're trying out for Cosette too, aren't you? Just to beat me? For your information, my family is actually from France, so I've been singing to this musical since I was six."

"Not everything is about you, Veronica," Layla sniffed aristocratically. "And yes, I *am* trying out for Cosette. Though I do know French very well, it doesn't matter. This musical is in English. Besides, today's audition covers singing *and* dancing *and* acting."

"Well," said Veronica with dignity, "let the best actress, singer, and dancer win."

They glared at each other until Ruthie intervened and a possible altercation was avoided. As the Hall Monitors finished checking in and prepared to separate to their respective positions, Ruthie suddenly found herself face-to-face with Rajesh.

"Rajesh," she said with a dry mouth.

Rajesh's face hardened at the sight of her. He pretended not to notice her, brushing past her roughly as if she did not exist.

Ruthie sighed and hugged herself. "I made a permanent enemy."

Layla shrugged. "Better that than a terrible boyfriend."

Ken interrupted with, "Excuse me, what just happened? I thought you two were, um..."

"They broke up," Layla explained.

Ruthie's eyes flashed. "We weren't together in the first place! Why does everyone think we were a couple?"

"You weren't?" Everest asked blankly.

Ruthie threw her hands up in the air in exasperation. "No! Just—ugh!"

Aiden wisely intervened: "Ken, let's find a seat to watch the auditions." They all heard the silent words which followed: *So we can discuss ways to fight VD.* "Ming and Ruthie, your auditions are in an hour; if you wish, you may sit with us until then."

"Sure," mumbled Ruthie. "And Rajesh and I were never together in the first place." She glared at the others defiantly, daring them to contradict her.

The auditions ran smoothly. They were long and exhausting, ending at around 8:00 PM. Aiden had been mostly quiet while watching the auditions while Ken spouted idea after idea. Layla was entirely focused on her audition; on the other hand, Everest was too busy cheering on his friends to spend much time on his audition. Ruthie and Ming played well and did their best, knowing full well that due to the lack of musicians who had volunteered to play for two hours straight every day for several weeks in a row next semester, Ruthie and Ming would both most certainly get in.

At exactly 8:15 PM, the Hall Monitors dispersed after agreeing that Ming, Everest, and Layla would leave on an early flight tomorrow morning to interview the intruders. In the meantime, Aiden, Ken, and Ruthie (who had a hunch she wanted to check out) would continue investigating on their own. Despite their excitement, a good night's rest was required for an eventful day tomorrow, and they all still had plenty of work to do. The commitment of being part of the Hall Monitors took a notable amount of time—time they were still learning to use carefully due to the intense course load all Ravencrest students faced.

So while Layla was showering before bed, Ruthie chatted with her sister online. They had gone their separate ways after the audition; Layla to their room, Ruthie to the study café.

I miss u so much, Ruthie texted her little sister. She texted her sister often on this computer. The computers in the study café were popular because of their advanced softwares and features that most computers didn't have. For one thing, it could send and receive texts at a higher speed and accuracy than most other messaging softwares, regardless of how strong the WiFi signal was.

Has anything happened since we last talked?? asked her little sister.

So much! Ruthie hesitated. There were so many things she wanted to say but couldn't.

What happened???

Ruthie wished she could tell her little sister about Rajesh, the Legacy, and Vladimir Damon. She wanted to tell her about joining the Hall Monitors and maybe the Society, and about how she now protected Ravencrest Academy. She had always been so close with her little sister and brother. But now, all she could muster up was, A lot of ppl aren't feeling so well.

Is everyone sick?

No, I mean, everyone's super stressed out. It's rlly competitive here.

Well, yeah, it's Ravencrest Academy! typed Bella. Can u come home for the weekend?

Aw, I wish I could, but I told my friends I'd help them with something this weekend.

Oh.

Through the screen, miles and miles away, as electrical currents zipped through wires, Bella stopped typing and stared at the keyboard wordlessly. Somehow her older sister knew her well enough to sense this.

What's wrong? Ruthie asked.

Ur so busy now!! We never get to hang out anymore. :(

A lump grew in Ruthie's throat. When this is all over, I'll hang out with u as much as I can!!!

When what is all over?

Oh, oops. When this semester is all over, Ruthie quickly replied, trying to sound casual. In 2 months, after Winter Break, I'll do all sorts of fun stuff with u.

K, fine, Bella sighed. Well, c u, Ruthie—Daddy's calling me. I'll txt u later.

Cya!

Ruthie leaned back from the computer and slowly sighed. She and Bella had been so close for so long. They used to tell each other everything. Now, she missed her so much. Mechanically, Ruthie signed out of her computer account and began to stand up. Something itched at her mind.

What? Am I missing or forgetting something?

No, there was something right in front of her, something very important that she was overlooking, something she had to figure out right now. What was it?

Ruthie stared long and hard at the computer. She finally scratched the side of her head, stood up fully, and pushed her chair back under the table. Whatever it was, she wasn't going to remember it anytime soon. She turned to leave and bumped into Darlene Dickens on the way outside.

"Sorry," Darlene apologized at the same time Ruthie did. Darlene added, "Didn't mean to startle you. I thought you saw me."

"How long were you waiting?"

"Only a few minutes," Darlene said, and Ruthie immediately understood that she was lying.

Ruthie winced. "Oh, I'm so sorry, I didn't notice."

"It's okay," Darlene brushed it off sincerely. "These computers are always busy. Besides, I know you missed some classes 'cause of Ken, so seriously, don't sweat it."

Ruthie smiled and said something nice in reply, then left the room. Darlene was a sweet girl, always super friendly—

She stopped.

An appalling idea had struck her so suddenly that she could barely breathe. The itch at the back of her mind swelled. The past three months swirled around in her mind, memories streaming uncontrollably. She took a deep breath and told herself how ridiculous that idea was. There was no way it could be true. She took another step forward as her mind filtered through the memories. Slowly, carefully, she recounted each situation, each scenario, each simple yet obvious truth. Had it been possible that they had all missed something so clear all along? It had been right in front of her this whole time.

Her newly discovered theory was an incredible breakthrough. She had finally figured out how VD was getting into students' accounts. She simply didn't understand which student Vladimir Damon was using to do it. And besides, she was tired from all the hard work and longed to curl up on the little comfortable chair in her dorm and maybe read a good book....

Yet she was a Hall Monitor, wasn't she?

Sighing, but not reluctantly, she turned around and waited patiently for Darlene to finish printing. As Darlene rose and exited, Ruthie stepped into the nearest closet and listened to the footsteps receding. Then she left the closet and entered the café. For once, the study café wasn't heavily populated, most likely due to how late it was. Checking to make sure no one else was watching, she sat down at the same computer as before and called Ken.

Ken answered on the first ring. "Ruthie?"

"I have this huge idea. I need you to come to the study café."

"I can't. I'm about to have a video call with Professor Radiff. I'm going to ask him for an extension, since I've got way too much to do."

Ruthie sighed. "Fine. Then can you send me a log of who used this computer this past month? It's Computer #6."

"Why?"

"Just trust me."

"Fine. I just sent you some login credentials that will let you see a log of everyone who's used that computer." Ken hesitated, then added, "Aiden told me this was highly classified stuff. If it gets out..."

"I'll delete your message after I use it," Ruthie agreed. "Also, just to make sure, a person would need these credentials in order to view the log, wouldn't they?"

"Yes. They could also view the student's search history and see a recording of their screen, but all the passwords are blocked from view." Ken paused. "It's why it makes no sense that someone in Campus Security could be the mole."

Ruthie scrolled down. "So if someone had access to this log, they could find out a tremendous amount of information about anyone who used this computer, correct?"

"Yes, but they couldn't find out other people's passwords—"

"Couldn't they?"

"What do you mean? Passwords are student-generated, are required to be fifteen characters long, have multiple—"

Ruthie interrupted, "At the beginning of the year, passwords were very basic. I guessed sixteen different people's passwords and got them correct on the first try—"

"Wait, what?"

"It's a pastime. I never actually use these passwords, of course. I just like to guess other people's passwords for fun," Ruthie admitted. "Just by gaining access to all this information about each person, VD could easily guess the passwords."

"But the password security got updated, remember?" Ken interrupted. "We all had to make new, more complicated passwords, and everyone gladly did so. But even then, VD's emails continued anyway."

"True," Ruthie admitted. "But what about keylogging software?"

"Software that records every key pressed? Okay, how would someone download keylogging software to a study café computer? There's a lot of routine security at the beginning of the year, so it would be impossible!" Ken said. "Ruthie, explain yourself."

Ruthie was getting excited now as she impatiently tried to explain. She tried to start from the beginning: "Look, Ken, I figured out the pattern: every single person VD targeted used this computer! I finally figured out the common factor of people who received these emails! I thought about every single person who was targeted, and I realized that they all used this computer, including me!"

"Ruthie, I don't get how that's helpful," Ken said bluntly.

"Our mole somehow gained security clearance to this log. They watched the screen recordings of all activity on this computer, and they gathered personal information about each individual. Then they sent it all to VD! They *also* downloaded keylogging software that I just found in the coding," Ruthie continued. "This software can detect the passwords used!"

"There's keylogging software on the study café computers?!" Ken gasped as she understood. "You're right, and so was I. We *do* have a student mole."

"With security clearance. I mean, they must have some sort of security clearance to have access to the log in the first place," Ruthie said.

Ken disagreed. "No, VD could have contacted this student with the credentials needed. Remember, Porter Craig, or any other mole here at Ravencrest, must have had access to Campus Security credentials too. They couldn't have gotten the full list of passwords, but could have supplied the credentials for some security clearance, just enough to see that log. Our mole could have figured out the passwords through keylogging software, and might've even sent VD a bunch of information about each student. Then VD could use those credentials to log into the accounts of students. Now the biggest question is who's the mole?"

"Can't we figure it out somehow?" Ruthie asked. "I thought I'd look for someone who used this computer frequently and for long periods of time, but every single person on here has been targeted. I've checked and double-checked."

Ken massaged her temples and thought hard. "Okay, there should be a recorded history of whenever that log was opened," Ken finally said. "Open it up, send me a picture, and I'll cross-reference it with security footage of who used that computer then."

"That's going to take a while. What about your video call with Professor Radiff?"

"Rescheduled it while we were talking. This is more important."

"Ken—"

"Ruthie, just send it!"

It took a few minutes for Ken to figure it out, which was just enough time for Ruthie to log off the computer and get some snacks for tomorrow. She was still replenishing her snack stash when she heard Ken gasp.

"What?" Ruthie said with excitement. "You found them!"

"I did," Ken said quietly.

"Well?" Ruthie demanded. "Who is it?"

"Ruthie..." Ken didn't know what to say. "I...I don't think you should know..."

"Why not? Who is it? It can't be a person who was targeted, and...."

"Actually, it *is* a person who was targeted," Ken said. "He must have just pretended to be another victim. I can't believe he would do this. I knew he was a bit messed up, but this..."

"Who?" Ruthie shouted. "Ken, who?"

There was a terrible silence as Ken said, "This changes everything. I'm sorry, Ruthie." *This is the worst betrayal I've ever seen,* Ken reflected grimly.

"Ken, tell me! Who's the mole that's been helping VD?"

At last, Ken spoke, just as the door swung open. The mole himself stepped inside and gaped at Ruthie standing there. Ken miserably answered, "It's Rajesh."

Chapter Thirty-Three

"Ruthie? What are you doing here?" Rajesh asked. Then he seemed to remember he was angry at her. His face darkened and he added, "Whatever, I don't care. You should go. I've got stuff to do." He slumped into the exact chair Ruthie was in moments ago and pretended not to notice her as he clicked on the *Login* button.

Ruthie could only gape at him as she processed this new information. *Rajesh?*

He tapped the keyboard but not the keys. Without looking at her, he said loudly, "I would greatly appreciate it if you left me alone right now."

Ruthie staggered backward. "No, that can't be right," she said. "He wouldn't do that." No, even if Rajesh was controlling and selfish and arrogant, he could still be nice and friendly and he wouldn't push Sophia Manchester to drop out or expose Everest or mentally torture students for months—

"What?" Rajesh scowled.

Ruthie tried to calm herself down as every single memory of Rajesh flooded her brain. She grabbed onto the side of a desk and gasped for breath when the memory rush became overwhelming. She closed her eyes briefly. She knew the drill; she knew how to calm her mind when needed.

Ruthie barely was aware of Rajesh's concerned exclamations and questions until he was standing right next to her and shaking her. "Hey! You need me to get a nurse?"

"I'm fine," Ruthie muttered, pushing him away. She rubbed the side of her head as Ken stayed silent and texted for help.

Rajesh glanced at her. "What happened? Your asthma flaring up?" He sounded genuinely worried about her, despite their fight. "You look kind of sick. Stay here; I'll get a nurse." He guided her to a chair, and she wobbled along, still in shock.

As she looked into his face, she realized the horrible truth: Rajesh really did care about her. It was why she had believed him for so long. Her psychology skills proved with absolute certainty that this boy cared about her and, despite his selfishness, wanted to make sure she was okay. She felt very weak.

And yet...there was the truth. He was the mole.

If there had been any doubt before, it evaporated. Rajesh had just given himself away without knowing it. Now she knew for sure that he had to be VD's student correspondent. Sudden rage flooded through her. She no longer felt weak, only very, very angry. *He* did this?! How could he?

She shoved him away. "Get your hands off me," she said with such fury that her voice didn't sound like her at all. "You—you—you—*you*!" She couldn't think of a bad enough word.

"What's wrong with you?" Rajesh said, bewildered. A shadow crossed over his face. "Oh, I get it. You think you're so high-and-mighty—"

"How could you?" she screamed in his face.

(Over the earpiece, Ken's mouth dropped open. She had never heard Ruthie lose her temper before, but she knew from what Ruthie had told her that it was about to be very, very bad.)

"What?" Rajesh blankly said.

Ruthie stamped her foot. "Don't even. You spoke to VD."

"You mean the sender of the—"

"Vladimir DAMON! You know him pretty well, don't you, Rajesh?" Ruthie yelled. "You've been helping him hurt Ravencrest students all semester! It's because of you Sophia quit! It's because of you everyone here is so stressed out and scared! It's because of you Everest can't start over! It's because of *you*! And you hid it so well!"

Rajesh raised an eyebrow and crossed his arms in faint amusement. "Are you done?"

"Yes!" she shouted.

"Ruthie," sighed Rajesh. "Let me get this straight. You think I'm working with VD?"

"I *know* you are!"

"Why? What makes you so sure? Because I broke up with you?" Rajesh shook his head mournfully. "Ruthie, I didn't think our break-up would push you over the edge. Come on, let's get you to a counselor." He took her arm.

She pushed him away. "Get away from me! You can drop your act, Rajesh. I know you're guilty."

"Oh boy," said Rajesh, putting his hands in his pockets and leaning back against the table as he surveyed her. "You really believe this, don't you?"

She was amazed—there was no sign of remorse, of surprise, of anything. For a split second, she doubted herself. Then she remembered. "If you have nothing to do with this," she said at last, stepping closer to him and scrutinizing him carefully, "then how did you know about my asthma?"

"What?"

"You said my asthma was flaring up. But I haven't had an asthma attack in years. Only my family knows about it. I haven't even told Layla or Ken or anyone." Ruthie narrowed her eyes. "How could you know?"

For a split second, it seemed as if he was going to talk himself out of this one as well. Rajesh confidently rolled his eyes and said, "Well, obviously..."

His voice trailed off.

"Obviously what?" Ruthie demanded.

Rajesh closed his eyes. When he opened them again, they were anguished. His smooth, double-faced charade had disappeared. "Ruthie, I had no choice."

"No choice? You could live with yourself after hurting everyone else here so badly?" Her voice cracked. "You pretended to be a friend...you pretended to be *my* friend when you sent me those emails earlier this year, didn't you?"

Rajesh grabbed her hands. She swiftly pulled away again as he spoke: "Ruthie, I didn't know you then. VD wanted more information on you, but I didn't want to hurt you. I gave him some info on some other kid instead because I cared about you. Doesn't that count for anything?" His eyes pleaded with her for a shred of understanding and compassion.

Yet she had seen too much pain in the eyes of Ravencrest students. Too much fear and stress and agony. For some, it was nearly unbearable.

Ruthie clenched her fists. There was only disgust in her eyes. "So you did it. You got the information on Sophia Manchester, about her parents divorcing."

Rajesh lowered his eyes. "She searched for legal documents about getting money after her parents' divorce. She even chatted with a lawyer online and explained her situation. When he declined to help her, well..."

"Everest too?"

"Not too long ago, he had a heart-to-heart conversation with his brother. They hadn't spoken in some time, I guess, so they spoke about their past. I did some digging to find the records and then sent them to VD."

"Do you choose the victims or does VD?" Ruthie asked coldly.

"VD. I have to feed him as much information as he wants. If I don't give him enough, he'll expose me. Ruthie, please, I didn't have a choice," Rajesh wheedled.

Ruthie paused. "Expose you? How?"

Rajesh groaned. "I can't tell you."

"Fine. Wait until the Dean finds out about this." She turned to walk away.

Rajesh called out from behind her, "Fine! I'll tell you."

Ruthie paused, refusing to turn back. "Well?"

"I...I cheated."

"Cheated?" She spun around. "On what?"

"My Ravencrest entrance exam."

(Over the earpiece, Ken gasped again.)

Ruthie could only stare at him in shock. "You...cheated on your Ravencrest entrance exam? How? It's practically impossible to cheat on that thing."

Rajesh shrugged. "What can I say? I even made it in. I wanted to give it a shot and...it's a cool place. I figured it wouldn't matter in the end. My essay, interview, and extracurriculars were pretty good too, so—"

"How close was your score to the cut-off?"

Rajesh looked away. "It was barely above the cut-off score."

Ruthie breathed slowly, hoping to regain control of her temper before it got the best of her. "So let me get this straight. You cheated."

"Yes."

"You cheated on a test that's practically impossible to cheat on."

"Yes." He looked rather proud of it.

"And if you hadn't cheated, you wouldn't have gotten past the cut-off score and couldn't have made it in. In other words, you stole another student's position here, and if anyone finds out, you can't be a student here."

"Yes."

"So you cheated your way into Ravencrest and VD used that to blackmail you into bullying all the students here?" She was shouting again. The deep breathing was clearly not going to help.

At least now he looked a little sorry. "I felt bad about it at first, I really did, but I didn't have a choice."

It was the lamest excuse in the history of excuses.

If Ruthie was the sort to hit people, she would have shoved Rajesh as hard as she could. Instead, she gave a frustrated, angry grunt. How could he stand there, so...so...*selfish*? "You're such a...a...a really horrible person!"

He was truly hurt now. "I told you, I had to do it."

"You had to cheat?" Ruthie said, walking to the door quickly so he couldn't see the rage on her face. "Cheat and lie and steal?"

"Yes! I had no choice!"

"Rajesh, this *was* your choice—a whole slew of bad choices."

"Vladimir Damon manipulated me! He told me he had a friend in Admissions who let me in just so he could use me since I'm good at sneaking around and stuff!" Rajesh called after her as she made it to the door. "None of this is my fault—it's *his*! Can't you understand that? Come back here—Ruthie! Ruthie, I order you to come back here!"

Ruthie wordlessly walked out the door and did not return.

Every single Hall Monitor was astonished. "Rajesh," Aiden repeated. "Rajesh, a student mole planted by Vladimir Damon himself." It was slowly becoming more and more clear that people were not who they seemed to be. But Rajesh, Ruthie's almost-boyfriend? No one had seen that coming.

"Ugh, don't remind me," Layla said, shuddering. "This is definitely a case where good looks do not equal good character."

"Is Ruthie okay?" Ken asked.

"She's fine," said Layla. "From the way she screamed at him, I can tell she's more angry than anything else."

"Everest is with Rajesh," Ming interrupted. There was a coldness in his eyes that chilled them to their bones. "He dragged Rajesh into a closet. He just texted me asking what to do now since he has Rajesh alone with him. I suggested making him suffer, but Everest declined and requested that I ask the rest of you."

"Sue him," Layla said. "I have a lawyer in mind already."

"No, interrogate him and find out how VD's contacting him since it can't be over email," Ken said. "See if he knows if there are any other student moles like him."

(Ruthie was not present at this meeting. She was kicking something downstairs and pretending that the object she was kicking was Rajesh.)

"Well, which is it?" Ming asked.

Aiden interrupted with, "I have an idea. We can use this to our advantage. What if we use our new contact with VD to bait and trap him?"

They all fell silent. Speaking out against VD was one thing; trapping him was another entirely. Could it be done?

If they failed, the consequences would be great. They had to find VD within two months or else the Hall Monitors would just become another student organization, except without any real purpose, which meant VD would be able to hurt Ravencrest students for months to come.

"Let's do this," Layla said with determination, and right away everyone was in.

Everest circled Rajesh as slowly as a shark circles his prey. "You claim VD contacted and manipulated you?"

"Yes!"

"How did he contact you?"

"I visit my parents on the weekends," Rajesh explained. "My first weekend back, I met VD at the airport. Now I have to do what he says or he'll tell."

"He's expecting you to contact him tomorrow?"

"Yes," Rajesh said.

"What time?"

"Saturday morning, when I land at the airport."

"Where?"

"The Delhi airport. My parents pick me up at the boarding area about an hour after I land since the airport's far from where they live. They think I use that time to do homework," he confessed. "They have no idea. They have no idea about a lot of things, actually."

"VD speaks to you in person?"

"No. He did the first time. That's when he gave me a phone. He's been using it since to talk to me."

"Where's the phone?"

"I hid it."

"Where?"

"I can't tell you."

Everest took a deep breath. Then he said very calmly, "I want to make something clear to you, Rajesh. Right now, I am in contact with Campus Security. I can easily tell them what's going on and get you expelled. Or you can cooperate with me and I can help you while getting VD out of the way for good. I'm working with a branch of Campus Security that wants to do just that."

"So it's true then?" Rajesh asked.

"What?"

"Security's recruiting students?"

"What—where did you hear that?"

"It's a rumor."

"No, well, yes, but it's temporary," Everest fumbled. "Look, you tell anyone about my helping Campus Security and you're expelled, got it?"

"No, I think it's cool. You got hit, so you're rising above the ashes to fight back. And I get it. My lips are sealed." Rajesh smirked.

Everest immediately understood. "That's the look you get before you add something to your little notebook of what to tell VD, isn't it?"

Rajesh's smile disappeared.

Everest concealed his disgust as best as he could. "Anyway, it's either your cooperation or your expulsion. Make your choice."

Rajesh glanced at him sideways. "I think I already did. I mean, who's the winning side right now? VD or Ravencrest Campus Security?"

"Look, think of your parents," Everest pressed, not answering the question.

Rajesh scoffed. "They do whatever I want. All I have to do is say I was framed and they'll sue the school."

Everest resisted the urge to hit Rajesh right then and there. As someone who had been deprived of loving parents, it sickened him to see how Rajesh used his parents so remorselessly. "Fine," Everest said. "Think of Ruthie."

This actually seemed to get through to Rajesh. "She thinks I'm garbage now, doesn't she?"

She's right about that, Everest thought.

Rajesh sighed. "Fine."

"Good," Everest said. "Go pack. You'll need to see your parents this weekend. It'll be a normal trip for you, except this time, someone will accompany you. Someone with this seal." He showed the Campus Security seal on his phone to Rajesh. "If you see this seal, do exactly as you're told."

"Or what?"

"You're expelled, and that'll be the last you ever hear from Ruthie. You know how angry she is, don't you?"

Rajesh's face darkened. "I didn't want to do this at the beginning, Everest. I didn't want to hurt anyone or help VD blackmail them. I used to feel sick when I did all that stuff."

"And now?"

"It's another thing I need to stop feeling guilty about. Life is about getting ahead. You have to know how to shave the dice, manipulate the variables, make the right investments—"

"By investments you mean people," Everest could tell.

"Look at where I am now compared to the thousands of kids back home," Rajesh hissed. "You think I got this far by being a nice little boy who always obeyed the rules? No, Everest. You work the system. You work the people. Then you get what you want." Now there was no more kind, friendly, yet slightly arrogant Rajesh. There was only his true self glaring back at Everest. "So stop judging me. I'm just being smart. That's what Ravencrest is all about, isn't it? Being smart?"

Everest couldn't think of an adequate response. There was nothing he could say that would make the other boy understand.

Suddenly, the door tilted all the way open and Rajesh heard the footsteps behind him. Without looking at him, Ruthie said quietly, "What does it profit a man if he gains the whole world yet loses his soul?"

"What?" Rajesh asked.

"What does it help you if you gain the whole world but lose your soul?" Ruthie replied. "It's an old saying. I want you to answer it."

Rajesh couldn't answer. Finally, he muttered, "I'll see you two tomorrow."

"You won't if everything goes as planned," Everest answered. Ruthie stepped beside Everest, her face emotionless as he finished with, "Good luck. Let's hope we all end up on the winning side." With that, Everest stalked out of the room, half-expecting Ruthie to follow him. Instead, she remained still, leaving herself alone with Rajesh. Everest hesitated in the doorway but changed his mind when he saw the fire in her eyes. He left, leaving the door open a crack.

Rajesh was nervous yet hid it well. "You hate me, don't you?"

"How can I not?" Ruthie shouted. "Don't you feel sorry for what you did? All these kids suffered because of you!"

"Ruthie, I didn't have a choice!"

"You had the choice to cheat on the entrance exam! That must have taken a lot of planning, didn't it?" Ruthie yelled.

"Lower your voice!" Rajesh whispered. "And what do you want me to say? I'm sorry?"

"No," Ruthie said. "I know you wouldn't mean it. So instead, I want you to turn yourself in to the Dean."

Rajesh recoiled. "*What*?"

"I mean it."

"What about the plan for tomorrow? All that stuff with—"

"I won't let you get away with this, do you understand me?" Ruthie screamed. "You *used* me! You used everyone here! I thought you were my friend but instead you're this...this...monster!" She was hardly aware of the tears piling up in her eyes. "For months I've wanted to stop VD, to stop all the pain here, and I didn't even know I was friends with the person who caused it all!"

Rajesh paused. "Just friends?"

"Agh!" Ruthie yelled in frustration and kicked the wall. "See what I mean? You're so—so—selfish and—"

"So what do you want me to do to make it up to you?" Rajesh said briskly, getting straight to the point.

There was no mercy in her eyes; she was too angry for even that. "You're coming with me to talk to the Dean."

"*What*?"

"They'll expel you right away, but you can still carry out our plan tomorrow. This way, justice will be served." She crossed her arms.

"How could you expect me to do that?"

"Think of the thousands of students who applied to this school and got rejected. You took someone else's place wrongly. It's not fair."

"Life isn't fair!"

"Rajesh, you know you were wrong! I'm trying to set things right," Ruthie said.

Rajesh glared. "You didn't set things right with the other kids that VD blackmailed. Why me?"

"Because of—because—" Ruthie sputtered.

Rajesh smirked. He knew her too well. "Answer that. Why do you want me expelled? Because you were actually starting to like me before you found out? I mean, does this really have to change anything?"

"Do you know how much it hurts that I cared about you when you were another person entirely?" Ruthie burst out. "Do you know how much it kills me that I could have stopped all this somehow—that all the students who could have had an incredible time here ended up dropping out, crushing their dreams, being pushed to unspeakable ends, all alone and scared because of someone like you? *And you don't even feel bad about any of it?*"

Rajesh stepped back. "What are you going to do if I don't tell?" he said coldly.

She glared at him, chin high. "I'll turn you in myself."

"You wouldn't." He met her glare.

She smirked back at him. She didn't look anything like herself as she stepped out of the closet and quickly walked down the hallway.

Rajesh tried to laugh as his throat went dry. He raced after her and grabbed her arm menacingly. "Ruthie, let's talk about this—"

"Good night, Porter Liberty!" Ruthie called behind him.

Rajesh let go of her as the porter nodded to them. Ruthie innocently smiled back and continued walking ahead purposefully. Behind her, Rajesh felt his world tilt. "Please," he pleaded with her as they crossed the garden and entered the Staff Residential Hall. "Ruthie, I'll lose everything. You can't."

Ruthie hummed to herself as she walked up the stairs.

"Ruthie!" yelled Rajesh. "Ruthie, stop!"

She broke into a run. Rajesh swore under his breath and began chasing her. He was far behind, but he was fast, especially when panicked. He was close behind her, and when she slowed down to catch her breath, he finally grabbed her arm right outside the Office of the Dean of Education.

"Listen to me, Ruthie," Rajesh begged.

"I listened to you all semester," Ruthie replied, trying to pull free. "Now let go of me or I'll make sure you get in a *lot* of trouble."

"Ruthie!"

"Let go."

"Ruthie—"

"Let go of me!"

"I NEVER WANTED THIS!" Rajesh yelled as she shoved him away. "Okay? I don't know who I am now! Did you know I threw up after the first time I reported to VD? I hated this! It's easier now, but that's only because I learned to do what I had to! I didn't want to and I still don't!"

Ruthie glared at him. "It doesn't change anything. The damage has already been done."

Rajesh clenched his fists. "Don't you see? I couldn't change if I wanted to. I took a path and there's no going back. It's like you said." His voice was bitter. "What do you want me to do for you? I can't change. This is who I am. I do what I need to do. I don't let myself have regrets."

"You can change," Ruthie said. "There's always a way out."

"How?"

Ruthie hesitated. "You really want to change? Not just for me?"

Rajesh looked up, and she saw the pain in his eyes. She understood. She had opened his eyes to the despicable person he had become. It was the truth he had known all along and yet refused to hear.

Her heart softened. Yet only for a moment.

"Well, justice still needs to be served," she said briskly. "We can talk later."

"No!" Rajesh yelled and fought with her, keeping her from opening the door. She struggled past him, pressing the doorbell button, and he slammed her back against the wall, unintentionally pushing her against the hard windowsill. The metal blades were pulled down and covered the window. One gashed her cheek, drawing blood, and she cried out.

The Dean of Education opened the door to his soundproof office and gasped at the sight of the blood on Ruthie's face as the young man stood next to her in shock. "Jocelyn?" he repeated. "Oh my, what happened to your face? Do I need to call a nurse? Did this young man hurt you?"

Rajesh couldn't move.

Triumphantly, Ruthie opened her mouth to accuse Rajesh. She met his eyes once before speaking. In them was pure, clear anguish. Guilt. Shame. He had never meant to hurt her.

So he had meant what he said. He wanted to change.

And he did care for her.

And how could she show justice without mercy? It went against everything she believed in.

She remembered all he had done. All the horrible things that had hurt the school. How he had cheated his way into such an amazing place. How he was a manipulative, remorseless monster. How he only thought for himself.

It was time to make a choice that would impact the course of Rajesh's future forever.

Ruthie swallowed hard, unsure of what to say. Her heart pounded.

"Well?" the Dean asked. "Is everything all right?"

"I'm fine, thanks," Ruthie said at last. "I got hurt when I fell against this wall. I'm trying to be less clumsy." She did her best to avoid lying. "I'll take care of it."

"Well, I have a First Aid kit in my office," the Dean said. "Come on in. Why are you here? And who's this young man?"

Rajesh staggered after them, then stopped at the doorway and said, "Maybe I should go." He didn't say it, but Ruthie heard the words which followed: *Before I cause any more damage.*

"All right," said the Dean, and Rajesh left. His footsteps were slow and quiet as he walked down the hall and stairs, his gaze pointed to the floor.

She applied the cotton to staunch the bleeding and placed a bandage over the small cut. Then she apologized to the Dean of Education for the intrusion, claimed she had to go, and left as fast as she could. As she walked down the stairs, she picked up speed and called, "Rajesh!" She wanted to talk to him one last time to answer his question about a way out.

But he was gone. The stairwell was deserted.

Ruthie stood in the middle of the stairs for a long time. She sat down and hugged her knees. Her head and heart hurt. She closed her burning eyes.

"You okay?"

She looked up to find Rajesh looking down at her in concern. He had come back to check on her.

Ruthie nodded as he sat down next to her. "Why didn't you tell me?" she said at last. "I could have helped somehow."

"I was wrong to think of you as a variable to be controlled," he confessed. He looked at his fingers. "I don't mean to manipulate my parents or friends, you know. It just comes naturally now."

"You said you wanted to change."

"I do. I just don't know how to."

"That's the first step, you know. Wanting to turn your life onto the right path." She fully turned to him. "Rajesh, we're never going to be a couple. I want you to understand that."

"I know," he muttered.

"But that doesn't mean I can't forgive you. And it doesn't mean you can't change. It just means you have to change for yourself, not for me."

"I got that too," Rajesh said. "So what's the magic formula?"

Ruthie looked down at her feet. "I experienced a supernatural love I've never experienced before. It was deep and strong and firm. It gave me hope, peace, and certainty. It was and is and will always be more real than anything else."

"You mean God?"

"Yeah."

"No offense, but we all know God was a story made up by our ancestors to explain scientific principles not yet discovered," Rajesh pointed out.

Ruthie glanced at him. "Actually, science supports the existence of God. The Bible supported the Big Bang five thousand years before astrophysicists discovered it. And no one knows why it happened. So, tell me, since you're an astrophysicist: why *is* there something rather than nothing?"

Rajesh seemed a little interested. "Your answer is God?"

"He created us," Ruthie explained. "He's the uncreated Creator and the undesigned Designer. You know, looking at the Second Law of Thermodynamics, it's obvious that the universe has an end. And we all know it has a beginning. Just like the Bible said before anyone found evidence for a beginning and end for the universe."

"I guess that's kind of interesting."

Now Ruthie was getting into it. "And why do you think there's order? Order to the laws of nature, to the mathematical beauty of the world? Did you know the first scientists—like Kepler and Newton—were scientists who believed God would want us to study His creation? I mean, how can you look at the complexities and intricacies of the human body or the particles of the universe or any aspect of science and claim it just happened due to billions of years of random chance? It's like seeing a hundred-story, intricately carved sandcastle and believing it just happened due to billions of years of erosion!"

"Well," said Rajesh. "I never thought of it like that."

"How do we have free will to choose good or evil? What even is our concept of good and evil? As C. S. Lewis once said, 'How can I know a line is crooked if I don't have an image of a straight line to compare it with?'. Since evil is a corruption of good, how do we all even have a shared concept of goodness?" Ruthie continued.

She explained, "There are some variations of certain ideas, but in general, there *are* universal moral truths in all cultures and societies—I mean, all cultures might disagree on stuff, but there are underlying assumptions and rules everyone agrees on. I don't think any culture would say that a guy killing the people kindest to him is okay. Everyone might disagree on who to be unselfish toward—your family, your country, everyone—but everyone agrees that you shouldn't always be selfish. Even kids have an idea of what's fair and what's unfair, no matter the society or culture they grew up in."

"True," Rajesh admitted.

"The fact that we have our own beliefs and can reason about things points to the existence of a Creator. You could look at the fine-tuning of the universe and the incredibly improbable chance of everything existing by accident—"

"Incredibly improbable chance?" Rajesh interrupted. "We exist, don't we? That's not improbable, that's a fact."

Ruthie chuckled. "Would you mind if I quoted a renowned Oxford University mathematical physicist named Roger Penrose?"

"Go ahead."

"Try to imagine the phase space of the entire universe. Each point in this phase space represents a different possible way that the universe might have started off. We are to picture the Creator, armed with a 'pin'—which is to be placed at some point in phase space. Each different positioning of the pin provides a different universe. Now the accuracy that is needed for the Creator's aim depends on the entropy of the universe that is thereby created. It would be relatively 'easy' to produce a high entropy universe, since then there would be a large volume of the phase space available for the pin to hit. But in order to start off the universe in a state of low entropy—so that there will indeed be a second law of thermodynamics—the Creator must aim for a much tinier volume of the phase space. How tiny would this region be, in order that a universe closely resembling the one in which we actually live would be the result?"

"I don't know."

"According to his calculations, the 'Creator's aim' must have been accurate to 1 part in 10 to the power of 10 to the power or 123, that is 1 followed by 10 to the 123rd power zeros. As Penrose put it, that's a number that would be impossible to write out in the usual decimal way, because even if you were able to put a zero on every particle in the universe, there would not even be enough particles to do the job."

Rajesh didn't have a response to this. He was quiet, processing everything she said.

"We didn't occur by random chance," Ruthie said softly. "We were created. We are loved. God exists. There is overwhelming evidence for the existence of God, but people choose to ignore it."

"That's deep," Rajesh said quietly. "But why are you telling me all this? Are you trying to prove your faith to me or something?"

"I want you to know the proof behind why I believe what I believe," Ruthie said. "But sometimes logic and science and math isn't enough. In fact, I had to experience it for myself. All the wrong things you've done lead to dark places, and God loves you—"

"So hold on," Rajesh said. "You believe in a God."

"Yes."

"And you believe this God loves you? Why?"

"He said so Himself. Besides, He sent His only Son to die an excruciating death in our place so we wouldn't be in those dark places. That takes love."

Rajesh sighed and stood up. "Well, that's nice, Ruthie. I know you're passionate about what you believe. It's sweet. But do you have any actual evidence for what you're saying? I get your logical reasoning for the existence of God, but how does that have anything to do with Jesus?"

"Christians believe Jesus was God."

"But didn't He die?" Rajesh pointed out. "Historians all agree that Jesus existed, lived, and died."

"Exactly! And over 500 people witnessed Jesus after he was resurrected from the dead. Those people went on to lose everything for their beliefs. They were persecuted, burned, and killed. It was awful. Do you think that many people would be willing to lose everything for something they knew was false?"

"True," sighed Rajesh. "Fair point."

"There is so much evidence that the Bible is real and true—historical evidence, archeological findings, its unity, its endurance and timelessness, its influence on people and nations, and its many fulfilled prophecies. Jesus fulfilled over 300 specific prophecies in the Bible. Just fulfilling eight of them has the mathematical chances of one in 100,000,000,000,000,000, according to mathematician Peter Stoner."

Rajesh stretched. "I understand all you're saying, and you make really good points, but to be honest, I'm not religious. I don't really think about any of this stuff."

Ruthie glanced at him. "Why not? If you don't have God's love as the foundation of your life, what is the foundation of your life? Do you know why you matter?"

"Why should I care?"

"Because everyone keeps saying stuff like '*You matter*' and '*it's important to do the right thing,*' but they don't say why. That's because, if everything is random and meaningless, nothing matters. People think life is all about finding pleasure and avoiding pain." She looked up at him. "But life is so much more. We matter because there's a God who loves us and gives us worth and meaning. What do you think makes us different from animals, huh? Our ability to reason, to appreciate beauty, to understand the world—it's all because we were made in the image of God."

"Look, Ruthie," Rajesh interrupted, but Ruthie persisted: "He loves us so much more than we could ever imagine. He *died* for us to save us, then rose up from the grave. And now he protects us and provides for us and looks after us—"

"Ruthie, are you trying to convert me or something?"

"I'm just trying to help. God's love for me is what gave me hope through some of the darkest times in my life." She looked away.

"I know you're just trying to help and all but I don't believe in that stuff. Besides, I'm an atheist. You know about colonization, how people forced the world to believe in Christianity for their own profit?"

Ruthie tilted her head at him. "You would correlate the colonizer's religion with the colonizer? You know, there were many other

Christians of different races and backgrounds. There are a lot of distorted, twisted, and messed-up versions of the truth, just as the Bible predicted thousands of years ago. It doesn't change the everlasting truth I've personally experienced."

Rajesh sighed. "I don't know. It sounds complicated."

"It's simple. Love God and love people. Know He loves you and excruciatingly died for you so you could be with him forever instead of in eternal misery. Accept what He's done and let Him come into your heart so He can change you into His image—someone loving, good, and selfless, like Him. You won't be perfect, but He'll keep working on you. He will forgive you for everything you've done wrong if you just ask Him. God is Love, and He's the only One who can truly change us." She hesitated, seeing his thoughtful face. "Think about it, would you?"

"I will."

"Honestly, I know all the facts, opinions, arguments, and experience are important for you to consider," Ruthie admitted. "But at the end of the day, it all comes down to your faith. Just know that God and His love is more real than anything you can imagine. That's one thing I know with absolute certainty, and I hope it's something you can understand one day. It's the only thing that can save you, but it's all up to you."

"Maybe." Rajesh turned. "Sleep well, Ruthie. I'll see you soon—or, as Everest said, it might be better if I don't."

"Right," Ruthie said. "Please let me know if you need anything, okay?"

"Okay. See you around."

She watched him leave, knowing that as he walked down the hall, he was really walking out of her life. She could only pray that she had said the right thing.

Chapter Thirty-Four

"So let me get this straight," Layla said. "You tried to get Rajesh to turn himself in, but you changed your mind once you saw he meant what he said about changing, so you gave him a big sermon?"

"I was trying to help him," Ruthie defended herself.

Layla rolled her eyes. "Man, you are a saint. I've never met anyone more religious than you."

"I'm just more open about it," Ruthie said. "And I'm not a saint."

"No, you're so perfect that none of us dare to compare," Layla muttered, half-mocking her as they walked. The Hall Monitors had agreed to meet up before bed, just to review the plan one more time. "Geez, I don't get why it matters so much to you."

"I was depressed a long time ago. I felt trapped and hopeless, and I even considered ending it all. God was my way out." Ruthie hesitated. "I just want others to find that way out. Just because I'm more open about what I believe doesn't make me a saint or anything, you know."

"Well, I'm doing just fine," Layla said. "I don't need a way out."

"You need one more than you know." Ruthie glanced sideways at her as the elevator doors swung shut. "Look, you can still consider yourself a good person, but you're not perfect. No one is or was, except—"

"Let me guess, Jesus?" Layla sighed. "Look, Ruthie, right now, all I care about is taking down VD. I don't care about all that philosophy. I'll deal with it later."

"One day it might be too late to deal with it," Ruthie quietly said.

"Seriously, not now," Layla urged. "Please?"

Ruthie sighed. "Fine. I won't mention it again for now."

"Deal. And in exchange, you be your super awesome self and help us take down this cruel monster named VD." Layla cracked her knuckles as the doors opened. "I am so ready for this!"

Ruthie smiled a little. "So am I."

They entered and found the rest of the Hall Monitors lounging around. Together, they reviewed their plan one final time. "It's a lot to remember," Aiden cautioned, "and we will be performing multiple objectives at different times."

"We got this," Ken said, and the others cheered as she continued, "We're on our way to becoming future Society members."

"Taking down VD."

"Protecting the secrets of the Society."

"Saving the world."

"Let's do this thing!" Layla yelled and they all cheered.

"Guys," Ruthie interrupted their cheering. "It's kind of late. We can't do this thing if we don't get some sleep first."

Ken checked her watch. "It's nearly eleven. Ruthie's right."

"I'll finish this homework first," Everest said, getting comfortable.

Ruthie sighed. "I finished almost everything. I just have chemistry left." She grimaced.

"You don't like chem?" Ming asked sympathetically. While his major was chemistry, he understood how difficult RA Chemistry was.

"I do, it's just hard! Normally I wouldn't mind, but I just have so much going on at once that it's just so overwhelming and stressful!" Ruthie admitted.

Ken sat up in mock amazement. "Wait a moment. You feel overwhelmed and stressed out?"

"A Ravencrest student feeling stressed out?" Layla repeated in the same pretend shock.

"That's a new one," Everest agreed. "Never heard of it before."

Ruthie groaned. "Guys, you're not helping."

"Ravencrest coursework is supposed to be challenging," Ming reassured her. "You're not alone in struggling with how difficult the coursework is. What's important is that you're willing to work hard to overcome those challenges."

"I am! It's just...I love all my other courses so much, and I don't mind working through all the challenges. It can be kind of fun, you know?" Ruthie admitted. "It's just so hard for me to do well in RA Chem. I have to take tutoring for it a lot, but tutoring is so long that by the time I get it, our class is, like, three topics ahead. I feel like I'm always falling behind, and I have to do my violin and Hall Monitor duty too."

"I could help you," Ming offered.

"That would be nice," Ruthie said. "But I know you're busy too."

"I don't mind. Chemistry is one of my favorite classes," Ming said.

Layla giggled. "You know, all the scary kids are chemists. Like Norton, who started a drug ring. And all the guys could probably blow up the school if they wanted to. Really, every single person in the chemistry fan club is a little scary. After all, if you're a chemist, you have the ability to do a lot of crazy things."

"True," Ken admitted.

Ming raised an eyebrow. "Are you saying I'm scary?"

Ruthie tried not to laugh. "We could be."

Everest chuckled. "I'm a biologist. Am I scary?"

Layla cocked her head, seriously considering the question. "I don't think so. I mean, is being able to determine the species of trees scary?"

"I love nature," Everest offered. "To the point where I ended up getting bitten by a snake and nearly died. That's scary."

"I don't know, Everest," Layla said. "That's more brave than scared."

Everest tried not to blush. He did his best to act cool. "Really? Well, I'm glad you think so. I mean, I don't care. I mean, I might."

(He failed miserably.)

Ming saved his friend and interrupted with, "Whether frightening or not, your research is incredible, I will admit. Everest, tell them about that groundbreaking extra-credit project you did last week."

"I think I heard about this," Ruthie grinned.

"Wait, so how did the experiment work?" Layla asked eagerly. Aiden tried not to laugh. Ravencrest was so academically focused that even students of different majors liked to hear about each others' projects. Even now all the Hall Monitors were listening with muted interest. It was rather humorous to him, considering how most teenagers their age would not spend their free time excitedly talking about what they learned at school.

As the conversation traveled on, Aiden leaned back in his seat and watched with faint amusement as the Hall Monitors leisurely talked about what scientists would discuss at their work. These students were incredible, and so was Ravencrest. He was very relieved to find that while VD had made Ravencrest feel unsafe, he had been unable to destroy the heart of Ravencrest—the heart to learn at a level most people could only dream about. The only question was, could they stop VD from destroying all of Ravencrest before it was too late?

As the Hall Monitor girls walked back to their rooms at around eleven, they were each very excited and nervous, showing it in different ways. Layla couldn't stop talking, Ruthie was alternating between bouts of rambling and thoughtful silence, and Ken was fidgeting with her gadgets. Everest and Ming had left via a separate route to their own dorms, also barely hiding their excitement and nerves.

"We should go to bed soon," Ruthie said as she unlocked the door and entered their dorm. "I'll see you tomorrow, Ken."

"Tell you what, I'll bring my sleeping bag over and we can have a sleepover," Ken said. "It'll be easier to get together tomorrow morning when we have to split up."

Layla bit her lip as she took out her toothbrush. "I know it's weird for me to be the one saying this, but shouldn't we all take this seriously? It feels like we should go to bed early, wake up super early tomorrow, and be super focused the whole time."

"We are doing all that!" Ken defended. "Except for the 'going to bed early' part. We'll get our rest. I just really dislike how my dad paid extra for my single room. It gets so lonely there sometimes."

"Why did he do it, then?" Ruthie asked as Layla began brushing her teeth in the bathroom.

Ken shrugged. "He wants to show my mom how well he's being a dad. He does stuff like this all the time. He's really rich, you know, and by buying unnecessarily expensive stuff for me or only the 'highest-quality products,' he's trying to show my mom that all I need is his money. He's way too busy. I mean, he loves his job, but..."

"You feel like he loves it more than you?" Ruthie said sympathetically.

"Well, obviously he does, but it's not as if I care," Ken pointed out. "I have a pretty awesome mom and godfather. Mom isn't super rich or anything, but she loves her job and she works hard at running her own bakery in New York City. She's the best mom ever. She gets me, y'know? We're pretty close."

"That's so sweet," Ruthie said as Layla spit in the sink. "What about your godfather?"

"He's my dad's assistant. His name is Walter and he's the best. We talk a lot." Ken grinned. "I think I might have told you about him before."

"You have," Ruthie admitted. "But it's still sweet how close you are with them. I'm sorry about your dad."

"Don't be. I've learned a lot from him." Ken kicked off her shoes and slumped onto Layla's bed. "I've especially learned that I'm never going to have a boyfriend or get married. Ever. The amount of my dad's exes says a lot about what guys are really like."

"Not all people are like that, you know," Layla said, entering their room. "My sister's had a pretty rough time with that stuff and she's sworn off it too now, and my brother's definitely not the romantic type, but my parents really love each other. They get each other and it's a give-and-take kind of thing. Like, neither one feels like they have to do it all. And they're the sweetest couple I know, even if my dad is literally a US diplomat while my mom's from London. I will say that my family is way too overprotective of me, though."

"What do you mean?" Ruthie asked. It was her turn to brush her teeth, but her eyes were so heavy she could barely keep them open.

"Well, let's just say the Writcroff family reputation is spotless," Layla said, leaning back on her elbows. "My parents and older siblings are all entirely dedicated to their work, and they're all really good at what they do. They're all smart, incredible people, you know..."

"Just like you," Ruthie finished.

"No, trust me, if you knew how smart my sister is, you wouldn't even try to compare me to her. And don't even get me started on my brother. He's a *neurosurgeon*, and one of the best ones in the field at that." Layla rubbed her arms. "On the other hand, I couldn't read on my own until I was four, even with the best tutors. I got diagnosed with dyslexia pretty early. And I'm all right at math and science, but nowhere near as amazing as my sister and brother. And I'm okay with all that. I've got my own talents, and I don't have to live up to the rest of my family. They've made it clear that they love me no matter what. Still, sometimes I wish I was a prodigy like the rest of them. It's like the Writcroff family legacy skipped me somehow." She chuckled bitterly.

Ken hugged Layla. "Well, we think you're awesome just the way you are."

"Yeah, and you think you aren't as great as the rest of your family?" Ruthie said angrily. "That's ridiculous. You're incredible. I mean, you know *fourteen languages*. That should be a world record. And you're an incredible code-breaker. And you write in this shorthand no one else can decipher. And you work really hard. And you're an amazing actor. And you're—"

"I get it," Layla said with a grin. "You guys sound like my parents. Well, like my mom, anyways. It's not like my dad would sit down and compliment me for a long time. Don't get me wrong, he's the best too. I mean, he's not exactly verbal with his love, but he shows it in a lot of other ways. He's kind of like your dad, Ken, with how much stuff he gets for me. Like, if I ever need any money or really anything at all, I go to him. But he does understand me a lot. He would definitely never buy me a single room since he knows how much of an extrovert I am."

"What about your parents, Ruthie?" Ken asked. "I remember you told me you have a big family. How many siblings, again?"

"Two younger ones," Ruthie said. "A little sister and a little brother. I'm close with them both."

"That's not that big," Layla said.

"In Ravencrest students, that's a big family," Ken said. It was true. Most Ravencrest students were only children or maybe had a single sibling. It was simply because so many resources had been invested into them that most parents would have saved some for their other children as well.

Ruthie shrugged. "My sister and brother both want to come here someday." She hesitated. "My parents aren't as rich as your parents, but they work hard. They're amazing, and I'm really close with them."

"I forgot about that," Layla said. "I'm guessing everything here is expensive for you, then."

Ruthie half-smiled. "It's true. Everything here is so pricey. But I'm not poor or anything. I have enough money to get by and if I ever need anything, I can call my parents. I just don't have my own private jet like your dad does, Ken."

Ken laughed. "What can I say? I told you my dad's real extra when it comes to money."

Layla blinked. "Wait, that's expensive? My family has several."

"Seriously?" Ruthie said, her mouth dropping open.

"No," Layla told her. "My parents are smart with how they spend their money. We do get a lot of airplane bills every month since everyone in my family travels so much."

Ken crossed her arms and yawned. "I'm so sleepy. This bed is way too comfortable. What kind of mattress is this, Layla?"

"It's a personalized version of memory foam. My dad had it specially ordered for me," Layla said. "What? Stop looking at me like that. Sleep is important."

Ruthie grinned. "Your dad really loves you, doesn't he?"

"Yeah. So?" Layla asked.

"And you like to use that to your advantage, don't you?" Ken giggled.

Layla frowned. "Oh, come on, guys, it's not like that! I just ask him for things once in a while, and it's only for important stuff. For example, yesterday, I asked him to buy this designer coat since it's getting cold here, and the day before I sent him a few online shopping links for some new clothes, and a few weeks ago I asked him for a business-class airplane seat when I was on my way home, and..." Her voice trailed off until she sheepishly muttered, "Okay, maybe I do ask my dad for a lot of things."

Ruthie shook her head in mock disdain. "Oh, Layla. Now it makes sense why you have so many clothes, shoes, jewelry, and just...stuff."

"Mom did give me a spending limit for each month!" Layla defended.

"Which is why you go to your dad for money, I presume?" Ken teased.

Layla rolled her eyes playfully. "Fine, it's true, I guess I'm a little spoiled. Look, I'm working on it."

Ken sighed and rolled over on her bed. "I don't blame you. This place is so nice. I could fall asleep right...now..." She yawned.

Layla chuckled, then said seriously, "That's funny, but you should get your sleeping bag. I'm about to collapse from exhaustion right now."

Ken mumbled sleepily and hugged the pillow. "I can't...get up...looks like I'll have to sleep here..."

Layla raised an eyebrow. "I see what you're doing here, Mackenzie Robscone. Now, we can do this the hard way or the easy way." She threateningly raised a pillow.

Ruthie yawned from the other bed while a pillow fight ensued. She rolled over as her mind traveled to Rajesh. High school drama was the last thing any of them needed. So that night she decided that whatever was going to happen in the days that followed, she would forget about Rajesh. She might have forgiven him, but she wasn't naïve enough to ever trust him again or let him into her heart. So she wouldn't dare think about him ever again.

Even she could tell that she was lying to herself.

"Ravencrest Academy is certainly not an easy school to attend," Ming mused as Everest pushed their dorm door open, kicked off his shoes, and collapsed onto his bed. More neatly, Ming removed his polished shoes, placed them in the corresponding location, and took out his toothbrush. While he did so, he added, "I suppose I'll tutor Ruthie once all this is resolved."

Everest looked over at his roommate. "You like her, don't you?"

Ming sighed deeply. He looked at his reflection in the mirror. "I do."

"And she has no idea?"

"No. She considers me a friend."

Everest stared at the ceiling. "Well, she just broke up with Rajesh. That guy is some jerk. He had us all fooled all year."

As Ming brushed his teeth, he pondered Everest's words. Between mouthfuls of toothpaste, he asked, "I thought you despised Ruthie."

"Despised is a strong word," Everest corrected. "And I guess she's starting to grow on me. She's small, but she's smart. I have to say, I'm glad she's on our team. Besides, she's my friend now. No one treats my friends like that."

His voice had the trademark fierceness of a Hall Monitor. All six of them had grown incredibly loyal to one another. Somehow the Hall Monitors had become more than a group of high school kids. They were more than a team now. They were close friends.

Everest stretched and forced himself to stand. "I haven't done my usual evening routine in a while," he said, half-yawning. "I'll just do extra tomorrow. Have you seen my toothbrush?"

While Everest rummaged through his lone suitcase, Ming washed his mouth, changed, and turned out the lights. As he lay awake in bed that night, he thought about all the drama. Was any of it necessary? They were up against some serious enemies, and clearly, the fight was bigger than any of them could have imagined. The last thing they needed was high school drama getting in the way of teamwork. After all, he was sixteen years old and as knowledgeable as an official mathematician. He had his school's future resting on his shoulders. They all did. So there was the truth. No more drama. They were all going to remain friends until everything was all over. Anything from that point onward...he would deal with that when he got there. He sighed, not sure if he was lying to himself or not. It was time to focus on VD.

Big day tomorrow, he thought. He knew full well what an understatement that was.

Chapter Thirty-Five

At five the next morning, Aiden met Ruthie at the entrance to the Residential Hall building. He offered her a brisk smile and motioned for her to follow him. She obeyed silently. They had two hours before the planes left. The rest of the Academy was fast asleep.

Together, they traveled outside. Campus Security had alerted the porters beforehand that Aiden would be taking a student with him into the restricted part of the island. They soon reached the small building known as the storage shed, which was called *The Shed* by most students. It contained outdated or malfunctioning technology that the staff had yet to fix and probably never would.

Aiden entered with Ruthie, allowing the computer to capture her security information (her iris scan, fingerprint, facial recognition scan, etc.) while they stepped inside. He pushed a small lever and allowed the computer to scan him. Once he had stepped in, he took about twenty minutes to modify the programming so Ruthie could also enter. She too suffered the same ordeal.

It was about 5:40 AM when they finally entered the small, dumbwaiter-like shaft. As the shaft sped downwards, Ruthie yawned and Aiden patiently waited, a rush of excitement filling him. He had only been here once before with Mother.

She must have been here more often than she let on, he realized, feeling rather bittersweet at the thought. *Now I'm following in her footsteps.*

Ruthie had unintentionally memorized the entire procedure to enter this area. So now she, Father, Aiden, and a select few of the Society were the only people who knew the location they were heading to. This was knowledge which had to remain secret for the safety of the Academy and the world.

Finally, the shaft stopped, and the rough, rusting doors were half-opened. Aiden pushed them the rest of the way open and Ruthie stepped inside. Another round of security procedures passed, taking with it ten precious minutes.

"We will have to hurry," Aiden said quietly as the machine left Ruthie grimacing and clutching her finger. "Wear these gloves and this hazmat suit."

"It's as if I'm about to deal with something so dangerous it could kill me," said Ruthie, half-joking.

Aiden didn't chuckle or laugh or even smile. He simply helped her put on the suit and then slipped into one himself. Then, together, they walked into the room. First, they approached a very, very old wooden desk with a frail matching chair. Aiden reverently slid the chair back and knelt before the framed drawers. He winced as he carefully pulled one out, sending a mist of dust into the air. Ruthie sneezed.

"Adjust your helmet," Aiden instructed. "You shouldn't have smelled that."

He waited until she obeyed, then he gingerly shuffled through the tea-colored parchment-like paper in the back of the second-lowest drawer of the desk. It was one of the few places his mother had prevented him from looking at. Names of classified projects jumped out at him: *The Next Level of Nuclear Weapons, Galaxy Destroyer (Manipulator?), Making Another Planet Suitable For Life, DNA Targeter, Mother's Recipe for Scones, Planet Imploder, Assassin Automation (Killer Robots?) Ideas...*

"This is where all his dangerous ideas went," Ruthie realized, squinting to read the names. "I guess all his less dangerous ones are the ones in the front and everywhere else."

"Shh, lower your voice," Aiden whispered.

"Why? Is someone else here?"

"No, it's just...respectful." Aiden knew full well that he made no sense. He couldn't explain the awe he felt in the presence of this desk. Matthew Ravencrest was his hero, after all.

It comforted him to realize that Ruthie understood. She really did have the uncanny ability to understand others very well.

Aiden double-checked every single file. Slowly panic and frustration crept into him as a vicious terror rose. "It's not here," he said in disbelief.

"What?" In a flash Ruthie was kneeling near him, triple-checking his work. "Then where else would it be? These are where all his dangerous files were held!"

"Mother must've hidden it." He miserably rose to his feet and closed the desk. "Just not in this room."

"Why would she—"

"Mother never did things like this unless there was a strong reason behind it. Perhaps the room was compromised. No, she would have taken the rest as well." He closed his eyes. "Why would she take the files out of the room? They're the safest here."

"We're jumping to conclusions," Ruthie interrupted. "We don't know if or how your mom smuggled the files out of here. It could still be somewhere in this room. What if it was never placed in the desk?"

"No, all of Matthew Ravencrest's files on his classified inventions are in here. Armageddon was classified," Aiden pointed out. "At least, that's what I gathered from what Father told me...unless there was something he was hiding from me."

Ruthie recalled the conversation. "I guess Headmaster Ravencrest *was* very uptight and withdrawn when talking about Armageddon." She groaned. "We have to search the whole room now."

"We do not have much time, and it will take quite a while to exit this study. We need to hurry," Aiden said as he looked around the room. Various inventions and prototypes designed by Matthew Ravencrest were scattered around them. "We'll have to split up. You take that side and I'll take this side."

"No, wait," Ruthie stopped him. "Maybe there's a shortcut. How could your mother have discovered its existence if it was hidden so thoroughly?"

"There's something we don't know that she did. Unless we discover it—"

"Listen, Aiden, I've been thinking," Ruthie interrupted him again. "Armageddon can manipulate spacetime, right?"

"Yes," Aiden said. "That's what Father told us, anyway."

"So that would mean Armageddon could change gravity, physics, time, everything, right?" Ruthie asked.

Aiden considered this. "Theoretically, though it depends on your definition of everything."

"Why would Matthew—"

"Dr. Matthew Ravencrest," Aiden interrupted.

"Sorry. Why would Dr. Matthew Ravencrest create a device that could manipulate spacetime?" Ruthie asked. "I'm still learning physics, but Ming's an expert when it comes to this stuff. I talked to him about it after the auditions and he thinks it has something to do with time travel."

Aiden nodded. "That is a possibility."

"So why would Dr. Matthew Ravencrest create something about time travel?" Ruthie probed.

Aiden sighed. "There are various possible reasons, some of which include his innate curiosity and his desire to venture into the unknown when it comes to science. Time travel was another testable theory, I suppose. Now, we—"

"Aiden, please, just listen for a minute," Ruthie pleaded.

Aiden glanced at her. He trusted her, knowing she would not waste the little time they had. "All right. Tell me quickly."

"The question isn't 'where would Dr. Matthew Ravencrest hide a possible time traveling device?' The question is *why* would Dr. Matthew Ravencrest hide a possible time traveling device." Ruthie's eyes shone as she examined the desk. "You said it was dangerous, but if that's the reason he wanted to hide it, he would have put it with all his other dangerous ideas. No, he didn't hide it because it was dangerous. Dr. Matthew Ravencrest hid his own time-traveling device creation because it was personal."

Aiden couldn't remain quiet any longer: "It's a plausible theory, but I doubt its legitimacy. Dr. Matthew Ravencrest had little of a personal life. He had a close relationship with his sister, but that is all there is to it. Furthermore, we have little evidence that Armageddon is a time-traveling device built for personal reasons."

"Where would Matthew—*Dr.* Matthew Ravencrest—put his personal things, stuff he didn't want anyone else to see just because it was personal?" Ruthie pressed.

"Why would you think he'd hide a time-traveling device because it was personal?" Aiden asked instead of answering. He knew she probably had a good reason, but generations of Ravencrests hadn't been allowed to see Matthew's diary in honor of the man. Aiden needed a good reason to show her now.

She had one. "Listen, Aiden, what year did Evelyn Ravencrest die?"

It was a startling question. Now Aiden understood. "Three years before Matthew Ravencrest did," he answered. His heart ached as the sudden realization flooded him. He had forever known of Matthew Ravencrest's great achievements in the scientific world, and he had known how Matthew Ravencrest had risen from his parents' death to utilize the many resources at his disposal to become the incredible hero he was, but Aiden had never known how much Matthew Ravencrest must have grieved his little sister's death. They had been so close. She had been all he had. For him to lose her must have been as painful as it was for Aiden to lose Mother. A fire of recognition and an invisible bond of sympathy passed from Aiden to the long-deceased man whose secrets they were seeking.

"Dr. Matthew Ravencrest might have created a time-traveling device to deal with his sister's death," Ruthie said with excitement. "So where *were* his personal things?"

Aiden moved like a robot as he guided Ruthie to the little drawer in the top right corner. He mechanically pushed the small button and entered the code in the rusted lock—it was Evelyn Ravencrest's birthday, interwoven with the Fibonacci sequence—and the secret compartment was revealed. He couldn't stop thinking about

Matthew. Had the great hero really been so grief-stricken that he was willing to manipulate time just to get his sister back?

Aiden remembered his darkest nights of grief. He knew better than anyone how far someone was willing to go to make it go away. *I just wanted Mother back.* Matthew Ravencrest and Aiden Ravencrest were truly very similar, in more ways than either of them knew. Aiden was only just beginning to realize this.

For now, Ruthie found the small notebook. Due to the lack of time, she flipped through page after page, her eyes resting on each page for a fraction of a second—long enough to create a mental snapshot—until she made it to the end of the book. She put the book back in its place, and the two silently made it back to the shaft, which scanned them for hidden documents and artifacts. They undressed their suits and gloves, leaving both in the right positions for future Society members. As they traveled back, no one said a word.

Ruthie's eyes were closed the entire trip back, so Aiden kept ensuring she didn't get hurt, grabbing her arm whenever she almost tripped. He walked her back to the Residential Hall as she skimmed each page of Matthew Ravencrest's diary.

Finally, her eyes flew open. "I got it!" she cried triumphantly. "Aiden, I was right!"

"I knew you were," he admitted. There was no other explanation that made such perfect sense. Besides, even if she had been wrong, there was nothing they could do about it. They had to make it to the plane, and it took a while to enter or leave the restricted area.

"He does write about inventing it," she said eagerly. "And he really did create it to see his sister again. Oh, Aiden, it's so tragic when his sister dies. But it's so hopeful when he says he will see her again one day. Oh, how sweet!"

Internally, Aiden winced. No one had been allowed to read Matthew Ravencrest's personal diary except for a select few people. It was a merit-based honor. He had broken that rule due to how badly they needed to know where Armageddon was. And here Ruthie was, calling it sweet and tragic like some theater show. It displayed a great hero's life, throughout its highs and lows.

Ruthie plowed on: "In his despair, he decided he would find a way to travel through time to tell her goodbye, no matter what it took or who he hurt. He just wanted to say goodbye. So he worked hard for about a year and created it."

"Created his mother's recipe for scones?" Aiden said loudly as they entered the school. A bustle of activity greeted them. Ruthie got the message. "Yes! Ming did get his mother's recipe for scones, and it was delicious," she ad-libbed, caught off-guard. "He, um, gave some to me."

"Did he?"

The voice startled them both. They spun around to find Charlotte, struggling to carry several suitcases of clothes. Despite this, her eyes were full of gossip.

"You and Ming aren't a couple or anything, are you?" Charlotte teased. "You two do hang out often."

Ruthie glared furiously.

Charlotte chuckled. "Just teasing, Ruthie dear. I know Rajesh holds your heart."

"Where did you hear that?" Ruthie roared. "I never said that! Why does everyone think we're a couple? We're not a couple!" She stormed off to her room, presumably to pack.

Aiden winced. Rajesh had plenty of influential friends and had worked the rumors to his advantage, making it clear to everyone they were together. When they had broken up, he had said some angry things about her. Much of the gossip about them was misinformed, and it had to be hard on Ruthie.

Charlotte looked wounded. "I guess I hit a sore spot." She seemed rather worried as she added to Aiden, "Personally, I don't think it's a good idea for them to be together. He's not right for her at all."

"I agree," Aiden said. "Perhaps that's why she called it off before they could ever be in a relationship."

"She did? Where did you hear that?"

"She told me. He invited her to dinner, and when she declined due to a commitment she had already made, he yelled at her. He also got very angry when she told him she wasn't ready for a relationship. Since then, he's been rather cold to her," Aiden narrated this without any emotion. "I don't know what he told everyone else, but I'm assuming it wasn't the truth."

Charlotte's mouth hung open. "What a jerk! Poor Ruthie! And why didn't I hear about any of this?"

"Truthfully, it's none of your business," Aiden pointed out. "It's Ruthie's alone."

Charlotte grimaced. "Touché. You're one of the most honest and upfront people I've talked with around here. Sorry, I don't remember you. What's your name again?"

He winked at her and walked away.

"Wait, did you just mysteriously wink at me?" she called after him. "You realize I can just look you up in the student registry, right?"

He didn't look back, smiling the whole time.

A flurry of activity ensued as each of the other Hall Monitors scrambled out of bed and swiftly packed what they would need. Ken took all the gadgets she had salvaged from last time and, a little smugly, took some of her newer gadgets.

She was feeling pretty good about it until a porter informed her that she couldn't take all those weapons onto a plane. "There's a process involving a lot of paperwork," he added. "So I need you to remove all your weapons for now."

Ken growled. "What? But some of these aren't really weapons!"

"Do they have the ability to hurt another person?"

"Everything has the ability to hurt someone else!" she protested vainly. "It just depends on how it's used! I can turn anything into a weapon!"

"That's comforting," the porter dryly remarked. "Now, I'll rephrase. Please remove everything that has the intention and ability to inflict harm on another human being."

Ken glared and stepped out of line, turning back to go into the building.

"Where are you going?" the porter called.

"I have to get changed!" Ken shouted back. "Thanks to you."

The porter scoffed. "It's not as if she's programmed weapons into her clothes." He glanced at his clipboard, hesitated, then looked up after her. "No one could do that," he said to another kid. "It's not possible."

The other kid, Aiden, tried not to laugh. "I don't know," he said. "It might be."

Chapter Thirty-Six

Everest, Ming, and Layla boarded the same flight to a maximum-security prison in America. It was an eight-hour flight and they would arrive at 3:00 PM that day (for them—in America, it would be 2:00 AM when they landed). Meanwhile, Ken and Rajesh were headed to the Dubai airport on a flight that would take five hours, arriving at noon (again, for them—in Dubai, it would be 9:30 AM when they landed). Aiden was headed elsewhere as per Ruthie's instructions.

Each one of them boarded the plane, sleepy and energized at the same time. Little was said. It was game time, as Everest put it.

Ken and Rajesh landed first in Dubai, five hours later. Ken had finished much of her homework while Rajesh had been mostly silent. When he disembarked with his Ravencrest credentials and waited at the airport, he said nothing about Ken's distance. On the plane, she had shown him the seal of Ravencrest Campus Security.

At 9:50 AM, Rajesh's phone rang. He looked at Ken, who nodded and tapped a key on her laptop. She had already made some security adjustments to Rajesh's phone that would allow her to record and trace the call, even though it was from a blocked number. Rajesh swallowed hard and held up the phone to his ear. "Hello?"

"A wise man has many friends," said a distorted voice.

Rajesh automatically replied, "But it takes a sly one to have friends on the winning side."

"A sly one?"

"I mean, a sly fox," Rajesh corrected himself. "Sorry. It's been a while."

"Well, my sly fox," said the voice, "I'm expecting an update."

Rajesh straightened. "Right. So—"

"Before you begin," the voice interrupted, "I'm sensing there's something wrong about this call. In fact, I think someone is trying to trace this line. Are you trying to trick me, my little fox?"

"Trick you?" Rajesh's mouth went dry. "I don't know what you mean. I'm calling you like normal. Are you saying someone hacked into my phone? I can call you from a different line." He had endured months of lying practice and thus sounded genuinely nervous.

The voice laughed. "That won't be necessary. I think I know who our little visitor is. Aiden Ravencrest, did you miss me?"

Rajesh sounded truly confused as he asked, "Who's Aiden? There's no one here with me. Why would I want to get myself caught? I'm not working with anyone, VD—you have to believe me!" He did his best not to look directly at Ken, who was sitting several seats away but was still in his line of sight.

"Keep your voice down and don't call me anything other than *friend*," VD hissed, cutting him off. "And I believe you. Your phone has been compromised."

"I was hacked?" shrieked Rajesh. "Are you kidding me? I'll call you somewhere else right now. Send me your number."

"Not so fast," VD said. "I think I want to talk to our listener. And I'll find another way to contact you, my little fox. For now, Aiden dear, I have a message for you."

"Actually," Ken interjected, speaking in her own distorted voice, "I believe I should intervene."

"What—who are you?" screamed Rajesh.

"Lower your voice, fox," Ken muttered. "No need to draw attention."

"For once, Aiden and I agree. Now, shall we get down to business? Fox, your only responsibility is to keep this line open. Should you fail to do so, well, I can't be responsible for the news that reaches the Headmaster, can I?"

Rajesh was silent.

"Well, my fox?"

"Fine," Rajesh muttered. "I'm on your own side. You don't have to keep threatening me."

"Don't I?" VD taunted. "Aiden, we have much to discuss. I was very disappointed to hear that you are still alive. I had to remove one of my best agents, dear Porter Craig, from your academy. But don't you worry. In about a few months, you'll lose everything."

"You're so sure of that, aren't you?" challenged Ken. "But what if I know a way to make *you* lose everything? Your precious Legacy? Your revenge against my mother and my bloodline?"

"Oh? And what way is that?"

"I have Armageddon."

It was as if she had dropped a bombshell. Silence descended over the phone line. Finally, VD spoke, softly and dangerously: "You're lying."

Ken chuckled. "You think I'm lying? You must be desperate."

"Then tell me: what is Armageddon?"

"A device to manipulate spacetime, designed by Matthew Ravencrest in an attempt to time travel so he could see his sister again after she died," Ken quickly replied. "It's sitting right here in my backpack. I must say, the craftsmanship on his design is exquisite. It's exactly according to Matthew's drawings in his diary."

"What do you intend to do with it?"

"I have many options. You see, VD, I know you want this machine. If you stole Armageddon, you would really create your own legacy, so to speak." Ken smirked. "And your precious Legacy could do whatever it wanted with Armageddon. *However,* I also want something from you."

"My life?"

"Oh, that's too much to hope for. No, Damon, I know you won't give me your life. But I know that you might be willing to hand over your friend's life."

"Who?" VD asked. "Whoever it is, it's done."

"Xipe Matalon."

There was another shocked silence. Ken smiled even though she knew she shouldn't. VD had one weak spot, one person that he truly cared about. This was the one person he couldn't hand over in exchange for anything. Aiden was correct: after losing his father, VD hadn't let himself grow attached to anyone except for Xipe. *After all,* Aiden had said, *Xipe is a murderous, horrible henchman VD uses to do the dirty work for him. Since VD considers all good things as weaknesses, it makes sense that he would respect and actually care about someone as twisted as Xipe.*

Finally, VD spoke again: "All right." It was so obvious to anyone intelligent that VD was planning to double-cross them. It was fine; they knew that VD could tell they were planning to double-cross him. Yet they would meet, and that was what mattered.

"There's more to the exchange that I need," Ken continued. "I want one hour alone with you. You can't touch me and I can't touch you. I want no lies, no half-truths. I just want the whole truth and nothing but the truth about my mother's death. I want to know what really happened."

"Now that I *can* do," said VD, and Ken could almost hear his evil excitement. She knew what kind of ideas were brewing in his mind to cause Aiden the most pain. "I'll tell you what you need to know, boy, and then I'll hand over my friend. In exchange, I need something else besides Armageddon from you as well."

"What?" Ken asked blankly, a little nervous. They hadn't anticipated this.

"Give me Matthew Ravencrest's diary."

"No."

"Then the deal's off."

"Fine. I have Armageddon and you have Xipe. We're back where we started and perhaps better off because of it."

VD must have scowled. "Think clearly. I only want to read Matthew Ravencrest's diary, nothing more. I'll return it in perfect condition if that's what you're worried about."

"So it's information you seek. Well, there's nothing valuable in there."

"Then give me the diary."

"I can't."

"Oh, why not?" Now the tone was mocking.

"Because I burned it."

"You're lying."

"I'm not, I swear it on the fact that my name's Aiden Ravencrest."

VD muttered under his breath, "What a revolting last name."

"You're one to talk! Vladimir? What are you, a vampire?"

VD rolled his eyes. Ken could hear it in his voice as he spoke through gritted teeth, "It is a name of honor and respect."

"And Damon? Like, what kind of surname is that? It must be hard to find names that fit the initials V and D. Your options are pretty limited, I must say. What kind of tradition is that, anyway? I know the Legacy is messed up, but to make you swear your life to a cause your dad died for is more messed up than—"

"Shut up!" It was clear she had hit VD's weakness.

"We're squabbling like children," Ken said.

"You are a child."

"If you know that, why are you holding me accountable for my mother's actions? *That she performed in self-defense*?"

"Self-defense?" VD screamed. "Was stealing a treasure that rightfully belonged to the Legacy and hiding it *self-defense*?"

"Killing your father was in self-defense! Murdering my mother and constantly trying to kill me and my father is not self-defense."

"It's called revenge, boy."

"You think that will do anything? Revenge only hurts you more."

VD chuckled. "Did fairy tales teach you that? Revenge is sweet."

"A sick kind of sweet. It makes you as bad as the person you're up against. It changes you into a total monster."

"A monster like your mother."

Ken couldn't help herself now. "You think she was as bad as you? She never tried to torture or murder children!"

"Do you know what kind of life I lived without my father, left to the mercies of the Legacy? All that matters here is to climb up and make something of yourself. Any life less than that doesn't matter." His voice grew darker and more bitter by the moment. "So imagine what it's like, dear boy who has lived in the lap of luxury all your life. Imagine what it's like to lose everything so young and then be thrown around by half-hearted members of the Legacy. I was a little boy then, quiet, and observant. I never fought back. Until one day, my dad died, and I swore I would fight back. I took revenge on every single member that wronged me. Now I stand as Head of the Legacy, and I will complete my last act of vengeance to set things right. Then I will prove my true worth to the Legacy and rise up in ways I've only dreamt about until now. So yes, dear Aiden Ravencrest, I believe your mother was as 'bad' as I was. She was also making a legacy for herself. She was also rising up in rank. The only difference is that she had everything so easy for her every step of the way and that she killed people—" His voice broke. "She killed people who didn't deserve to be killed. They simply did their job and had people who cared about them, a kid who...who needed them." The voice managed to control the vulnerability that had briefly emerged. "I'll kill you one day, Ravencrest. I'll destroy everything you stand for and care about. Just wait and see."

The line went dead.

Ken hesitated, unsure of what to do next. A notification lit up Rajesh's screen:

The exchange will take place tomorrow night at exactly 8 PM in Society Headquarters in the United States, the one nearest the old, adorable house that's so white. You will give me Matthew Ravencrest's diary as well as Armageddon and I will deliver to you Xipe Matalon. We will have one hour to communicate once the exchange is complete. Neither one of us will be in any danger during that hour. The very second the hour is finished, I make no promises. Oh, and there may be a small surprise for your little girlfriend, just to ensure you understand the consequences should you break our deal and attempt to double-cross me in any way. Have a nice flight.

Her heart skipped a beat. *A small surprise for Aiden's "little girlfriend?"*

It's nothing. What's the worst VD can do to me? she asked herself, trying to stay calm as she emailed all the Hall Monitors a recording of the conversation with a picture of the text message. Aiden immediately called her via his laptop: "Where are you?"

"Still in the Dubai airport. Rajesh is on his way to talk to his parents."

"Are you safe? Stay where the security cameras are. There should be a porter present near the Ravencrest Campus Security area since they're required to stay there for a minimum of half an hour after all the students disembark. They always have to make sure you get to your destination safely. There should be one keeping an eye on you."

"There is one," Ken admitted. "I never knew that. So that's why the porters always take forever to leave the airport." She scanned around her. "There's three, actually."

"Excellent. I ordered a few others to ensure you were safe. Stay with them for the next few hours. Once we receive intel from the others, I'll have them bring you to the location for Phase B as fast as possible. If we don't receive intel, we'll ensure you return to Ravencrest as quickly as possible."

"How? The Ravencrest plane here doesn't leave until Sunday."

Aiden smiled. "I've made arrangements."

She checked her email and gasped at the screenshot of a first class ticket. "Aiden! First class! No way. That's way too expensive! Pay them back!"

"No, it's free."

"You're hilarious."

"Let's just say I have a friend who told me they have room for an extra first class seat, and that friend happened to owe me quite a few favors, so…" He let his voice trail off.

Ken grinned. "Wow, thanks." She paused. "What surprise do you think VD was talking about?"

"An attempt on your life, most likely," he answered. "No need to worry. I have everything under control. Enjoy your flight. Prepare for Phase B."

"I will."

"Also, no worries about your failure to trace VD. Mistakes happen to the best of us. It's best to move on and focus on the mission."

Ken frowned. "I don't know what happened. My software should have been able to trace the call. It just doesn't make sense. I used state-of-the-art Ravencrest technology and even had security experts check my work. I even have an invention based on this design!"

"So why didn't it work?" Aiden asked curiously.

"I don't know." She examined Rajesh's phone. "Hold on, I'm going to try something."

She plugged the phone into her laptop and uploaded all the phone's coding, typing furiously for a few minutes. She groaned once she understood. "Aiden, this phone was given by VD to Rajesh, right?"

"Yes."

"And Rajesh only uses it for communication with VD, right? So that means—"

"The phone must have had backup code on it to ensure if it was ever traced. It even had a false front to make you think you were successfully tracking him." Aiden sighed. "In fact, he's most likely tracking your position right now. Destroy the phone."

With excellent aim, Ken threw Rajesh's phone into the trash can on the other side of the room. She chatted with Aiden for a while, then continued her homework. After a few hours, Ken was on her way to Phase B: Finding Armageddon.

Chapter Thirty-Seven

While Ken was baiting Vldamir Damon, Ruthie was writing down the clues she had found in the diary. Layla, Everest, and Ming, however, were busy talking with the intruders.

All three of them had explained their fake purpose for being there (to gather information regarding the break-in for the Ravencrest school newspaper), and dutifully shuffled through the security protocols until they were standing in front of a handcuffed and resigned prisoner. Layla took a seat in the back of the room, pulled a hood low over her eyes, and pretended to be writing. She was going to jot down the entire conversation into her notebook in her shorthanded form, as they weren't allowed to bring any electronics or recording devices into the room.

The prisoner was the leader of the criminals who had broken into Ravencrest Academy. He wearily watched Everest and Ming sit across from him on the other side of the glass.

"Hello there," said Everest cheerfully as Ming sat as still as a rock. "My name is Everest and I'm a student reporter for the Ravencrest newsletter. This is my friend, Ming."

Ming nodded his greeting.

"I'm here to ask you about the break-in. I would have come earlier, but for some reason, the Headmaster never let us." Everest hesitated, then added, "The Headmaster doesn't actually know about this visit. We do have the Head of Campus Security's permission to be here, though."

For the first time, the prisoner showed a hint of a smile. "That man might still have some loyalty left in him," the intruder mused.

"Your name is Simon, correct?" checked Everest.

"I prefer to be called by my middle name: Wolf."

"Wolfe? Is that spelled with an E?" Everest asked.

"No. W-O-L-F." The fierce eyes glimmered.

"Oh-kay," Everest said, noting that on his paper. "Why Wolf?"

"It was my code name."

"You had a code name?" Everest chuckled. "What, did you belong to a secret organization? The Agents of the Neverseen?" he added in a deep movie-trailer voice. He laughed at himself.

The prisoner was silent.

"Why did you break into the school with guns?" Everest said at last. "You could have killed someone."

"We would never."

"Then why the guns?"

"They were only to intimidate. They weren't even loaded." The prisoner's appearance was ragged. His beard was unshaven, and he stared at the floor distantly, as if the man behind those haunted eyes had withdrawn far into himself.

"I know you were in solitary confinement for some time," Everest said, trying a sympathetic approach. "That must have been terrible."

Again, the prisoner made no response.

Everest looked down at his paper. "So Mr. Wolf, tell me, why did you break in? Were you really going to kidnap Ravencrest students?"

"We were."

"We? You were the leader, weren't you? According to the trial—"

"My lawyer was paid by your headmaster to send me and my team to jail," said the prisoner. For the first time, strong emotion surfaced in the intruder's eyes. He snarled and his fists clenched at the mention of the word *headmaster*. "Your headmaster is a liar and cheater. He charms his way into his position and then takes over. You think he's sincere until he ends up murdering his wife and driving us to ruins."

"Murdering his wife?" Everest yelped. "That's—you think Headmaster Ravencrest murdered his wife?" He was really wondering, *How do you know about that?*

"Ask him that, why don't you? Go ahead and tell him to his face. Ask him if he killed his wife." The eyes burned. "Then ask him what the heck he's doing takin' over her position. He might not be entirely evil, but I'll tell you one thing: he's a thief."

"What do you mean he took over her position?"

The prisoner was silent again. "I can't tell you that."

"You're not making any sense."

"That's because you don't know the full story."

"Then tell me what the full story is," Everest countered. "Please. Listen, you're going to be in jail for the rest of your life, so you may as well get the truth out now, while you still can. I want to help. Please?"

The prisoner glanced at him for a long time. Finally, he spoke: "It's a secret. You can't print it in your newspaper."

Everest bit his lip. "I'll make you a deal. You tell me what I can and can't include, but you still tell me the full story."

The man barked out a laugh. "No way. I know reporters. You'll be hinting at it in your article, and then a centuries-old secret will be destroyed. No, I will not destroy the cause I was imprisoned for." He folded his arms and leaned back in his seat, catching Everest's gaze. The eyes were playing with him, beckoning at him. This was some sort of game, and there was something Everest was missing. He tried to play along.

"Do you want money? Some kind of bribe? I mean, I already know one side of the story. I just want to hear your side as well," Everest tried.

The man tapped his fingers on the table wordlessly as he shook his head no. His eyes spoke *Wrong answer.*

Everest looked vainly at Ming, who was supposed to alert him when the intruder was lying (Ruthie had trained Ming in the art of catching deception). Instead, Ming was studying the man closely. Suddenly, Ming spoke: "We are lying."

Everest almost dropped his paper and pencil. Behind them, Layla barely stopped herself from gasping in shock. Yet Ming did not flinch or waver. Still making eye contact with the intruder, Ming said, "We are not student reporters, and I promise you we are not here to find a story to tell everyone at Ravencrest Academy. We are here to find the truth. We were sent by Aiden Ravencrest."

The corners of the man's mouth twitched. "I knew that the moment you walked in."

"Aiden wants to know the truth."

"Why would he care?"

"He found out the truth about his mother's death."

There was still nothing on the prisoner's face as he continued to speak in a raspy, haunted voice: "So Headmaster Ryan finally 'fessed up, did he? Guess he didn't have a choice. So what's Aiden gonna do about it?"

"He's hunting VD."

A streak of emotion crossed over the intruder's face. "That's ridiculous. You need to stop him before he gets himself killed."

"He almost did die, twice," Everest admitted. "Look, he wants to know the truth. He's heard most of it from his father, but he wants to hear it from you. You have the other side of the story, and we need to know it."

"We?"

"If we succeed, we will be part of the Society," Ming pressed on. "More importantly, Ravencrest Academy will not be destroyed by Vladimir Damon and Aiden's life will be saved. So please, tell us the truth."

Behind them, Layla's pencil scrambled to write the dialogue in her shorthand notation. She was almost sweating from the rigorous effort of recording everything. They hadn't been allowed to bring in any other recording devices. Now she paused to take a breath as the conversation halted. Neither side said a word. They both knew that whoever would speak first would lose.

Finally, Simon Wolf said, "You must swear never to tell anyone outside of the Society."

"Or about to enter the Society," Everest added. "I swear."

"I swear as well," Ming added.

Simon's eyes traveled behind them to the slouched Layla scribbling the notes. "Your recorder must also swear."

Layla said, "I swear."

Simon leaned forward and put both elbows on the table, resting his chin on his clasped hands. When he spoke, he spoke cautiously, as if he had prepared for this very conversation: "The Society fell apart when Molly Ravencrest was killed. No one knew what to do. She had always run things so smoothly. Right away, the Headmaster stepped into the role of Head of the Society. He said he had things under control. Yet he failed miserably at stopping the Legacy's attacks. People died. Systems were infiltrated. We were desperate. So we took matters into our own hands."

No one responded. So far they already knew all this information. Layla's pencil was poised, ready for more.

Simon's eyes focused on Everest, peering deeply into the young man's gaze. "You must already know all this."

"The Headmaster told us," Everest said.

"He left out some crucial information, however," Simon continued. "For starters, he killed his wife."

"Already know that," Everest countered. "He told us the full story. He was forced to make a choice between his wife and the world—"

"Lies."

"He was not lying," Everest said. Ruthie would have known.

"Fine. He made the honorable choice. But the murder was intentional. It must have been. How else could he have been so ready to take over the Society? No, the Headmaster was greedy and took his wife's life. They were not on friendly terms, you know."

Ruthie would have told them if this was true. She had promised that there was real grief present when the Headmaster spoke. He truly grieved his wife's passing, and had told them the truth. That, or he was a psychological expert himself, if he really could outwit Ruthie. Thus, every Hall Monitor knew better than to believe what Simon had so willingly assumed.

"So you believe Headmaster Ravencrest killed his wife," Everest summarized flatly. "Did you break in to declare revenge?"

"We would never endanger children for something like revenge," replied Simon. "No, some of the Society decided to branch away and create our own society. We call ourselves the Union."

"Like in the US Civil War?"

"No. It's a temporary truce until the Society is back on its feet. The Union heard about Operation Injection, a plan to hypnotize every single student in Ravencrest Academy. We stepped in to rescue the students. They would be in more danger staying there. We were forcing the Headmaster to take action and to do something to save them."

Everest stifled a yawn. Like the others, he was beginning to feel disappointed. They had come all the way here to have a conversation full of information they already knew. Perhaps Ruthie had been wrong. Perhaps Father wasn't really hiding something. Ming patiently waited for more while Layla's shoulders slumped in the same realization.

Simon paused, looking straight at his fingers. "Now, that mission was not successful."

"The Headmaster did stop Operation Injection," Everest pointed out reassuringly.

"True. But at the cost of all of our freedom. Now the Society is either jailed or living in fear of the Headmaster's tyranny. They have no say in what to do. He's the one pulling all the strings in the Legacy and Society."

This jolted Everest. "What do you mean? How can he pull all the strings in the Legacy?"

"Oh, didn't you realize? Ryan's a fraud. He's working with VD."

Layla's mouth fell open and Everest dropped his pencil in shock. "Are you serious? Do you really believe that?" He glanced at Ming, who grimly nodded. Simon truly believed Headmaster Ryan worked for VD.

Yet every one of them had seen the pain glistening in Father's eyes, the anguish behind the old, hardened face. There was no way Father could have faked that.

"So you think the headmaster..." Everest couldn't finish.

"Ryan stopped Operation Injection because he saw how the Society was turning against him. He painted himself as the hero, but everyone knows he's a fraud. The Union is the only part of the Society left. We'll do whatever it takes to protect the school and the secrets it hides." The prisoner slammed his fist down. "Even kill Headmaster Ryan, if that's what's necessary!"

The air turned tense. "You'd kill him?" Ming said quietly.

Simon's shoulders slumped. "No. None of us would kill Molly's husband. No matter what he did, she loved him. No, but we would find him and send him behind bars. We would have overthrown him already if he wasn't the Headmaster of Ravencrest Academy and the only guardian of Molly's son. Too much would be lost if we stopped him. Ravencrest would have to close until another Headmaster was found. Aiden would be in the foster care system or sent to an orphanage, and the Legacy would hunt and kill him. Ryan might be a double-minded liar, cheater, thief, and murderer, but he does look after the school and his son. In the end, we couldn't stop Ryan. That's why I'm here. Behind these bars."

"You really do believe you are a martyr," Ming observed.

"I am." Simon's eyes traveled from face to face. "None of you believe me."

"Do you have any evidence to back up your claim that Headmaster Ryan has been working with the Legacy this whole time?" Everest asked calmly.

"I don't need evidence if I know the truth!" Simon spat furiously. "Why can't any of you understand? He's evil! He's got it all in his hands and he's going to throw it all away! There's no hope unless someone stops him!"

"VD or Headmaster Ryan?" Everest asked.

"Both!"

Well, this was a waste of time, Everest thought as Simon faced him, panting. His eyes were wild and crazy, like a rabid dog. As Everest rose to his feet, briskly thanking Simon for his time, he remembered to smile politely and grab his paper. Layla also stood up, disappointed as she shoved her stationary away. Clearly, Father had not wanted them to see Simon because Simon was somewhat insane. Also, Father probably hadn't wanted Aiden to ever work with the Union. *He doesn't have to worry about that,* Everest mused. *We'll never work with the Union unless it's absolutely necessary.*

Only Ming did not get up. Instead, he asked, "Tell me, what do you know about Armageddon?"

Everest was almost at the door. He stopped, hardly daring to see Simon's reaction. Layla froze as well. Simon caught his breath. "That's the device Molly was looking for when she was killed."

"Armageddon?"

"Yes. If handled incorrectly, Armageddon could destroy all the physics on earth. Could kill us all. She thought she might as well find it and get it back." He shrugged. "She had performed more dangerous, high-stakes missions. We all figured she had it under control. She already had found it a long time ago, but I suppose she forgot about it for ten years. When she went back for it...none of us thought..." Simon looked down at his hands and closed his eyes briefly at the mention of her death. "Now Armageddon is still out there, and neither the Legacy nor the Society has it. Everyone wants it. But only Molly knew where it was."

"To find it..." probed Ming.

"To find it you'd have to follow in Molly's footsteps. The only thing I know about Molly's plans to find Armageddon is this: the first time she was looking for Armageddon, she killed the father of the man now known as VD. Oh, and she did so in India."

"India?" gasped Layla across the room, despite herself. "Why *India*?"

Simon shrugged again. "Who knows? My guess is that Armageddon was hidden somewhere in India. To be more specific, she killed VD's father in the closest hotel to the Taj Mahal. That's all I know about it."

"Thanks for your help," said Everest kindly. "If everything goes well, maybe you'll get out of here soon. You never know." He was just saying this to be nice, but for the first time, a spark of hope brightened the prisoner's eyes.

They left quickly, not looking back. All three waited until they were outside to discuss the interrogation. "So, this was a bust," sighed Layla. She winced. "Poor guy, the headmaster. He's got to deal with stopping the Legacy, running the school, raising Aiden, grieving his wife, and on top of it all, keeping an eye on the Union. Maybe that's why he locked them away in prison."

"How could they be so extreme?" marveled Everest.

Ming answered, "Lack of transparency and communication on the headmaster's part. Considering how he is handling two full-time positions at once, it is an understandable mistake on his end. Of course, natural suspicion rises any time someone holds that much power."

Everest called a taxi and they entered. "Well, the Union isn't entirely evil, although it does have a few extremists in there who want to kill Headmaster Ravencrest. Speaking of extremists, did you see the passion in Simon's eyes? He really thinks he's a martyr."

"He's definitely an extremist," Layla sighed. "Which can be a problem, even if it's for a good cause."

Everest pointed out, "We did find out that Molly Ravencrest killed VD's father in the hotel closest to the Taj Mahal."

"India is a big country," Layla muttered. "It's not like we can just send out a search party to find Armageddon. And what if she didn't stash it there?"

"We can at least try to follow her footsteps like Simon said," suggested Everest.

Layla scoffed. "Now we're following the advice of Simon, the martyr of the Union?"

Ming interrupted, "Sorry to interrupt, but I'm receiving a call from Aiden. I suppose he would like an update."

"I do," Aiden said briskly, calling them through his laptop. "Any new information?"

Speaking in lowered tones, they relayed the information to Aiden: the intruders were exactly as Headmaster Ravencrest had portrayed them to be (that is, crazy), except they happened to also believe that the headmaster was a murderer and traitor. Also, Molly Ravencrest had killed VD's father in the hotel closest to the Taj Mahal.

"That's a random yet helpful bit of information," Aiden mused. "I have the rest of the team listening in. From what I can tell, Phase A has been mostly successful. Ruthie has found and memorized Matthew Ravencrest's diary, you all have found the helpful information we need, and while Ken could not trace VD's location, she was able to set up the exchange with him for tomorrow night."

"Tomorrow night?" gasped Layla. "That's not enough time to find Armageddon!"

"Phase B will have to be executed quickly," Aiden admitted. "However, I believe we can do it. I'm already on my way to the old Society headquarters in the United States. It's the responsibility of the five of you to find Armageddon and deliver it to me before the meeting tomorrow."

Ruthie hesitantly said, "You know, Aiden, I originally thought you had the easiest part of the plan since you were just waiting for the meeting. But to be honest, you probably have the most dangerous part of the entire plan. You're going to meet VD alone."

"You know I'll be careful. I've got a good plan, an excellent team, Ken's weapons and gadgets..." Aiden smiled, but the others weren't comforted by this.

"Phase C is pretty dangerous," Everest said. "Trapping VD is going to be scary. I mean, he knows we're not just going to hand over the diary and Armageddon."

"He does know that we're going to double-cross him," said Ming quietly. "The trick is to fool him while he's trying to fool us."

Ken interrupted, "Okay, enough chit-chat. We don't have much time to find and deliver Armageddon to Aiden. Also, I'm guessing Ruthie's not at the Academy anymore since she's hunting Armageddon, so we can't get Dr. Matthew Ravencrest's real diary for the exchange. We'll have to make a fake one."

"Correct," Aiden confirmed. "Speaking of Ruthie's recent travel—Ruthie, you are on an airplane to the UK right now. Care to explain to everyone why?"

Ruthie replied, "Because Matthew Ravencrest wrote about giving Armageddon away for safekeeping. He said he gave it to a 'dear old bird and loyal friend' that he wouldn't dare to mention in the book. Now, I knew Matthew Ravencrest had a lot of 'loyal friends,' but 'dear old *bird*?' So I did some research and made a list of Matthew Ravencrest's closest friends, and I found one who happened to be an ornithologist. From there, it was pretty easy to find the last living relative of that family. Her name is Wren Adams. Now, since I found her address..."

"...you're on your way to visit it," Everest finished. "Great work!"

"Thanks," blushed Ruthie.

"So you hope to ask her about Armageddon?" Layla cut in. "She's not just going to give it to you, you know. And the UK is not India."

"True," Ken interrupted, "but I think Aiden's mom went on a little treasure hunt and traveled to both places. It could be at either of those locations. Aiden, you looked at some old flight records and found where your mom traveled right before she passed away, am I right?"

"Correct," said Aiden, his voice sounding a little distant at the mention of his mother's death.

"And tell them what you found!"

"I found out that she made a trip to the UK. Looking at the records, I also see that the trip took place right before she traveled to India, presumably not to meet up with some old friends." He humorlessly chuckled. "I wonder how many times she lied to me like that."

"Oh, Aiden," Ruthie said sympathetically. "You know your mom just wanted you to be safe. She didn't want you to get mixed up in any of this."

"Too late now," said Aiden quietly. "I would have appreciated less lying."

"She might not have been lying about all her scientific expeditions," Ken said. "She was a scholar as well as Head of the Society. No doubt she multitasked all the time. She was an incredible woman, and the life she showed you was genuine. I know you think she was living a double life, but just because she was secretly running operations to save the world doesn't mean she didn't love you."

"She probably was going to tell you one day," Everest added. "I bet she just wanted to keep you safe until it was the right time."

"You must have suspected something," Ming said.

Aiden mumbled, "I didn't. I trusted her completely. I never thought she would hide something this big from me."

"She had a good reason for it, Aiden," Ruthie said. "How many times has your life been threatened ever since you found out about it?"

Ken burst out, "Aiden, how many times have you almost been killed since she died? She must have worked hard to protect you on top of everything else."

"She was an amazing person, Aiden," Ming said. "And I don't say such things unless they're true."

"She really loved you," Layla said. "If she was Head of the Society *and* a scholar, she must have been very busy. The fact that she still raised you and even took the time to ensure you were raised *right* proves that she really did love you."

Aiden smiled a little. "Thanks. But it doesn't matter, we need to focus on—"

"It does matter," Everest interrupted. "Trust me. You matter a lot more than finding Armageddon."

"Or beating VD," Layla added.

Aiden felt a lump in his throat. He had some incredible friends. Still, he forced himself to add, "Nonetheless, we need a plan. Ruthie, you may go ahead with your interrogation. I'm splitting you all into two groups: Everest and Ming to India, Ruthie and Layla to the UK. Ken, I need you to be at the halfway point from India to America, at an airport where the boys in India can quickly give the device to you so you can fly over and give it to me in America."

Ken's fingers flew over her keyboard. "Would Germany work? I'm booking the tickets now. Oh, and who knew? They have a few extra first class seats."

Aiden smiled to himself. "I'll ensure my friend allows you to have those seats—for free, of course. Take a porter along with you on trips to and from the hotel. Your job is to get Armageddon from Everest and Ming once it's found, then travel to give it to me, as I said. You can also coordinate things from both flights as well as your hotel."

"Fine," sighed Ken. "Though it's almost like you're trying to keep me out of all the action and excitement so you can always keep tabs on where I am."

Aiden cleared his throat and changed the subject: "Ruthie and Layla, you two will meet up in the UK sometime tonight, I suppose?"

"Yep," said Ken. "I'll send you the link to book your flight, Layla."

"You two know what to do to retrace Mother's footsteps. Everest and Ming—"

"We're headed to India," said Everest in a thick Indian accent. Layla burst out giggling.

"Yes, and once Ruthie and Layla find something, you'll retrace Mother's footsteps from then on," Aiden continued with only a trace of a smile in his voice. "Does everyone understand their jobs in Phase B?"

Versions of *yes* from everyone met this statement.

Ken sighed. "All these time zones are so confusing. I'm beginning to understand why people who travel a lot have multiple watches—one for each time zone."

"It is quite confusing," agreed Aiden. "I know too much travel can be exhausting. Truly, it's amazing how strong your dedication to the Hall Monitors is. I just want to say thank you all so much. Once we catch VD, hopefully by tomorrow night, I will ensure you all are well rewarded."

"We don't need any reward," Layla said defensively. "The world will be a much safer place without VD, and knowing that we protected a lot of people is definitely enough."

"And joining the Society is going to be awesome," Everest said excitedly.

"I can't wait," agreed Ken. "The Hall Monitors are amazing and all, but the Society? Wow!"

"We don't know for sure if we'll even succeed…" Ruthie began, then finally said, "But whatever happens, I'm glad to have worked with all of you. You're all amazing and incredibly talented. Together, we can do this."

"That's right!" cheered Layla. "Let's do this thing!"

Even Ming smiled as they cheered. He leaned back in his seat and looked up to watch the taxi driver, who was silently driving. His eyes were focused forward, but Ming knew the man had heard every word. There was nothing they could do about it. They had to keep moving for the plan to work.

Nonetheless, they could only hope the driver had nothing to do with the Legacy. Otherwise, their entire plan might have been doomed from the start.

Ming watched the man tap his fingers. His stomach clenched when their driver pulled out his phone. He spoke too quietly for any of them to make out the words. To his shock, Ming heard the name *Ruthie* mentioned.

The car stopped as they hung up. Layla bounced out, Everest paid the driver, and Ming crawled from the backseat to the passenger seat. "What are you doing?" Everest called as Ming took the driver's phone and held it out the window.

"Hey!" yelped the taxi driver. "What's your problem, man? Gimme it back!"

"What do you know about Ruthie?" Ming said ferociously. "Answer me!"

"Ruthie? I don't know anyone named Ruthie!"

"Don't lie to me. I heard you say her name. You heard every word, didn't you?"

"What?" gasped the taxi driver. "No, dude, look, I have earbuds in." The man brushed back his long, shaggy hair. "I was listening to music, see? Here:" He pulled the earbuds out and rock music blasted in the car. "I did tell Siri to play music by a singer named Ruth E. Rocker, but I didn't think it was illegal!"

Ming looked at the man, then at the phone, and then at the earbud. With dignity, he handed the phone back and briskly left the car with a quick, "My apologies."

As they left, Layla began giggling.

"It was an honest mistake," Ming said defensively.

"Of course. Done purely in the name of protecting the Hall Monitors," agreed Everest, struggling not to laugh.

Layla turned away to hide her laughter.

"What is so funny, Layla?" Ming asked.

"Nothing. I just figured something out that was so obvious from the beginning. I can't believe I didn't realize it before," Layla said to herself, still giggling, as they entered the airport.

"What?"

"It's nothing related to our mission, don't worry," Layla said, her eyes twinkling. "And your secret is safe with me."

"What secret?" Ming snapped, blocking her from moving.

"Come on, Ming," said Everest, "I think all of us know what she means."

Ming glared at them both. "Neither of you will say a word, do you understand me?"

"Relax," Layla said. "I won't say a thing. I know about a dozen different crushes at school and I've kept them all a secret."

Everest saluted. "You've got my word, general."

Ming clenched his fists. "It's not funny. If he had known about her..."

"You're as worried about her as Aiden is for Ken," Layla teased. "Don't worry, she'll be fine. I'll look after her in the UK. I bet she's just as worried about all of us."

"No, that's not what I meant," Ming said, his face tense with hidden anguish. "Think, both of you. Ruthie has a perfect memory, doesn't she?"

"And?" Everest probed.

"Wouldn't that be dangerous if VD discovered it?"

They were silent as the full implications crept in. If VD or anyone in the Legacy knew about Ruthie's perfect memory, they could use that to their advantage. They could use her as a human camera: a girl whose mind could hide pages of national secrets.

Layla's face grew slightly pale and Everest sucked in a breath. The giggles and laughter faded away. Ruthie was in danger simply by getting involved in these types of organizations. Knowing Ruthie's loyalty, she could easily store thousands of secrets in her mind and withstand interrogations in order to keep them secret. She had to be kept safe.

Then again, didn't they all? Layla's family legacy was enough to make her a target for any kidnapper looking for a wealthy girl to hold ransom. Everest may have seemed like he had nothing to lose, but his lack of familial relations meant that only his brother would notice if he went missing. Ken had a wealthy father and her inventions put her in direct danger with her competitors, which included large, powerful organizations. Ming was always ready to give up his life for his friends, and Aiden had VD after him.

Not for the first time, they understood the danger they were all in. They truly had to be careful.

Chapter Thirty-Eight

All six of them spent the night either traveling or sleeping in a hotel room. Ruthie and Layla were both transported to a hotel by porters and stayed the night there. Everest and Ming spent the night in an airplane on their way to India. Everest fell asleep the moment he had enough food while Ming worked hard to finish his homework. Meanwhile, Ken enjoyed a smooth flight to Germany. She completed the rest of her homework and even had time to watch a movie.

Aiden paced around in the United States of America, monitoring each one of his friends' positions as well as checking to ensure everything was set in motion for Phase C. He couldn't help but feel personally responsible for both the safety of the Hall Monitors and the success of this mission. He slept restlessly that night, plagued by the terrible sense of impending danger while wondering about his mother's double life. His stomach twisted and his anxiety refused to let him breathe. He closed his eyes, took a few deep breaths, and did what his mother used to do when she was stressed: whisper a verse to herself. "Be still and know that I am God," he muttered and obeyed it. Slowly his anxiety receded and he was able to sleep a little more easily than before.

The next morning eventually came. As Aiden rose out of bed, remembering last night, he wondered about his faith. It had wavered over Mother's death. She had been so firmly a believer, even during her parent's death and during all the craziness of her life. How could God have let her die?

He remembered seeing her early in the morning, face twisted, eyes closed, fingers clasped, praying fiercely for her son. He had watched her lips move too fast to make out the words. Every morning she had risen early to pray for him. Father had never cared much for her faith. He attended church occasionally to please her, Aiden knew, but that was all there was to it. For Aiden, the belief that she was in a better place now was what had pulled him out of the darkest nights. The hope of a distant afar with heavenly choirs waiting for him was what nudged him into the future.

Now he was face-to-face with reality. Mother was gone, everything was upside down, and he could only trust his friends. Soon they too would leave, he had to remember that. Soon they too would leave like Denver and forget all about him. They had their own wonderful lives ahead of them and the last thing he wanted was to jeopardize their futures. He would never ask them to stay back or remember him; no, he would nudge them into their own lives, safe and sound, doing great things for the world. He wanted only the best for them.

So what if he was alone? Why did the pain feel so real and strong? Was it because of the thought that his death wouldn't matter, that no one would mourn him? Yes. He would feel so alone if it weren't for his friends. Yet they would leave or change. Everything left or changed. Except God.

Where had He been when she had been killed?

So there was the question. *Answer that,* Aiden challenged into the darkness as he stood on the balcony of his dimly lit hotel. *Where were You then?*

There was no response, save for the wind whistling through his hair. He wondered about that verse: *Be still and know that I am God.* Hadn't Mother taught it to him years back? She had told him her own story about it too, what was it? She had once said—

Oh no.

Aiden clenched the balcony windowsill. He knew what was coming. Whenever he felt this way, whenever he reminisced for too long on his times with Mother, the memories would return. Here they were now—

No.

He waited.

Nothing.

Nothing?

Were they gone? He opened his eyes in amazement. No more flashbacks, no more memory rushes, no more temporary losses of consciousness? His mind rushed back to the months erased from his mind. They were slowly returning. He remembered struggling with grief while investigating the truth. The last month before he had ended up in the hospital was the haziest. He didn't remember much of anything. It really would take time for all the memories to fully return.

The world was eerily still. Not a sound could be heard. No crickets chirping, no noise whatsoever. There was utter, pure darkness around him, save for the distant lamplights he could barely make out. Aiden wasn't used to this. Even at Ravencrest, there were the low, distant murmurs of porters and the vague rumbling sounds of the AC. No, here everything was so silent. Deadly silent.

He heard the faint movement, the faint *click*, and the slight aiming of the gun. Instinctively he dropped to his knees.

Bullets shredded the glass above and around him. The darkness exploded into white. A scream was ripped out from his throat as the gunshots echoed. The bullets paused and did not resume.

Aiden worked quickly. He packed his things, including his monitoring of his friends, and left the hotel room via a back entrance few employees knew about. When a figure kicked down the door, they found no one inside except for a small note which read: See you tomorrow night. Don't be late.

As he darted through the darkness outside, Aiden muttered to himself, "Idiot!" What had he been thinking, stepping outside onto a balcony like that? He had been practically dangling bait in front of the enemy. Of course, he had to admit, he hadn't expected them to find him so quickly. It was his fault for needing the Internet and thus putting himself in a trackable position.

So he found an alternative shelter for the night and powered off his monitoring devices. Tomorrow, he would enter a public library with a hood blocking his face from the cameras so he could use those computers to keep an eye on his friends. Should anyone trace him afterward, he would be long gone.

"Should I ring the doorbell?"

"Of course!"

"Can't *you* ring the doorbell? I don't want to be the one to explain why we're here."

"Ruthie, you don't talk to people enough," said Layla, exasperated. "You're the one who's going to explain why we're here."

"Layla, please—"

"No, I'm serious! My personal goal before the end of the year is to get *you* to come out of your shell!"

"I don't have a shell!"

"Yes, you do!"

"Just because I don't know the life history of every person I meet does not mean I'm shy!" retorted Ruthie. "It just means I'm not *you*!"

Layla paused. "Touché." They stared at the doorbell a little longer until Layla added, "Why don't you want to?"

"I always stammer and forget what I'm going to say when strict-looking people glare at me."

"How do you know Wren Adams is strict-looking? She could be a nice person who bakes cookies and gives them to orphans, like some old grandma."

"I bake cookies and give them to orphans!"

"You do?"

"That's literally what my nonprofit organization is about! And it's not just cookies! So did you just call me an old grandma or what?"

Layla just rang the doorbell. "Forget it."

Before Ruthie could reply, the door swung open. "Oh, hello!" said the young woman on the other end with a big smile. "Who's this?"

Ruthie immediately began stammering, "I, um…"

"I'm Layla," Layla said confidently.

"I'm…my name is…" Ruthie mumbled. She turned to Layla and whispered, "What's my name again?"

"She's not even strict-looking or old," Layla said in frustration. "You really are a turtle!"

Ruthie glared. "I am *not*!"

"What?" asked the woman.

"I'm sorry," Layla said. "My friend Ruthie here has trouble talking to people sometimes. We're here because we need to talk to Wren Adams."

"And why do you need to talk to her?" asked the young woman.

Ruthie bit her lip. "It's a long story, ma'am, but it's kind of personal."

"Do you know her?"

"Yes," Layla admitted. "But she doesn't know us."

The young woman hesitated, then said, "I'm Wren Adams."

"But Wren Adams is fifty years old!" said Layla in shock. "You look like you're thirty!"

"Why thank you," said the woman with a smile.

"In that case, we should come inside. This is confidential information," Ruthie told her. "Is that okay?"

"Of course! Come on in, dear."

"Do you have cookies?" asked Layla innocently.

Ruthie hissed, "Layla!"

Wren laughed. "Of course I do! I have a great big cookie jar for children such as you two. Come in, come in." She receded into the kitchen.

Ruthie glared. "Layla, you don't ask people for cookies! Where are your manners?"

"She's the cookie-baking type, I could tell," Layla replied.

"How could you—" Ruthie broke off as Wren returned with a plate full of cookies. "I'm going to heat these up for a moment, okay, girls? They taste much better that way."

"Sure!" they chorused.

Behind Wren's back, Layla whispered, "What do we call her? Mrs. or Ms. or what?"

"She was married," Ruthie whispered back. "But now she's trying to get a divorce since her husband left her. So I don't know."

Wren returned and set a delicious-looking plate of cookies in front of them. The scent of freshly-baked cookie batter and melted chocolate made even the normally health-conscious Ruthie grab one. They tore through four in three minutes.

"They're delicious, thank you, M—" Layla started, then coughed and finished smoothly with, "Adams."

"Thank you, dear," said Wren kindly. "Now what were you two coming here for?"

Ruthie wiped the crumbs from her mouth and tried to seem professional and business-like once more. "Right. Do you know anyone named Molly Ravencrest?"

Wren thought for a moment. "No, I don't believe I do."

"Are you sure? She visited you some time back," said Layla. Ruthie kicked her lightly under the table and Layla looked up in indignation. "Hey, Ruthie, what was that for?"

"Why don't I make us some tea?" Wren suggested and left as Layla rubbed her sore leg.

Ruthie whispered, "She's lying! She recognized the name."

"So what do we do?"

"I don't know! I was hoping she would cooperate. I don't want to threaten her."

Layla grinned. "So can we do bad cop, good cop? I call bad cop."

"No interrogation techniques," Ruthie said firmly. "We'll be honest with her."

"That only works if the other person is a good person," Layla said. "We don't know if Wren Adams is a good person. She could do something to us."

Ruthie sighed. "Fine. Just follow my lead."

At that moment, Wren Adams returned with three steaming cups of tea. She placed one in front of each girl and sat across from them. "Now, what was it you were saying?"

"Have you heard of Ravencrest Academy?" Ruthie asked. "Or its founder, Matthew Ravencrest?"

"Why, yes, I have. I believe I have a friend with a lawyer whose son got in some time ago," said the woman cheerfully. "It's a nice school, isn't it?"

"It is," Ruthie admitted. "Matthew Ravencrest invented a very dangerous device and entrusted it to one of his friends. The name of the device is Armageddon, and the friend was your *very* great-grandfather, several generations back. You're his last living relative."

"Am I?" Wren Adams' eyes widened. "So you believe I inherited this device from him?"

"You must know *something*," said Ruthie desperately. "Don't you have a box or something? Please, we need to have it. The device is very dangerous, and Molly Ravencrest's son's life depends on it."

Now that last sentence had an impact. "What do you mean?" asked Wren, and the anguish rose in her eyes. "Is Molly all right?"

Layla's mouth dropped open. "What? You haven't heard?"

"What do you mean?"

"Molly died!" Layla said bluntly, much to Ruthie's dismay.

Wren dropped her teacup, which shattered and sprayed hot liquid everywhere. Layla yelped and Ruthie jumped to her feet. "Nobody move, I'll clean this!" Ruthie shouted. "Anyone hurt?"

"No, but look at my dress!" complained Layla. "Do you know how much this cost?"

"Dead?" repeated Wren distantly. "That can't be."

"She died protecting Armageddon," Ruthie said. "And earlier, she killed a man in self-defense when she was searching for it."

Layla paused. "Wait, even I'm confused. First she killed VD's father and then after ten years, she was killed too?"

"Essentially," Ruthie confirmed. "First, Molly Ravencrest went to India to find Armageddon, and killed VD's father in self-defense. Ten years later, she was killed when searching for it again." She turned to Wren. "Do you have any paper towels?" It was then she noticed Wren's hands, which were shaking badly. "Oh, you poor thing! Layla, get a chair. She needs to sit down."

"No," Wren Adams mumbled. "I'm perfectly fine. Let me be." She kept turning away from the girls, and Ruthie couldn't see her face. "What do either of you have anything to do with this?"

"Oh, we're helping Molly's son," Layla explained. "He'll be in serious trouble if we don't have Armageddon soon. Do you see why this is so important?"

All either girl could see was Wren's back. "Drink your tea," said Wren as she rose and walked to the door. "I'll clean this mess."

Ruthie sighed and picked up the drink, raising it to her lips.

Suddenly Layla, who had been so relaxed, uttered a scream and knocked the cup from her hands. Again, the porcelain cup shattered and the hot liquid soaked the carpet. Layla pushed her tea away in horror.

"Layla, what—" Ruthie sputtered.

"Poisoned!"

"What?"

"The tea is poisoned!"

Ruthie spun around to the kitchen, a growing sense of dread pulsing in her chest. "So that means…"

Wren Adams stood in the doorway, holding a long, serrated butcher's knife. She held it up and pointed it at Layla. "I have a gun," she said, and now her voice sounded very different. "It's just in my bag over there. Ruthie, dear—that's your name, isn't it? Nice gold name tag you have—get me my purse."

Ruthie managed to squeak out, "I can't. You'll kill her."

Wren Adams turned the knife toward Ruthie. "I suppose you want to be the first? My contact tells me to kill one of you and keep the other alive. Questioning purposes, I assume. Now, which of the two should I kill?"

"Me," Ruthie said.

Layla shouted, "Don't you dare!"

Ruthie stepped forward with absolute calm. "If it's going to be anyone, it better be me."

"Your wish," smirked Wren. She reached for the young girl.

"Please, don't do this," Layla begged. In that split moment of distraction, Ruthie grabbed Layla's cup of tea and threw the hot liquid into Wren's eyes, scalding her face and causing her to scream. Ruthie twisted the knife out of Wren's hands and threw it onto the other end of the room. Layla ran forward and grabbed Wren's shoulders, shoving her into a seat. Working together, Ruthie and Layla tied Adams' hands behind the back of the chair seat with a zip tie Layla had kept for this very purpose.

For once, Ruthie didn't tease Layla about carrying random spy materials. She simply helped Layla. Once they were finished, Ruthie stepped back, visibly shaken. "She almost killed you," she said to Layla, still a bit in shock.

Layla shoved Ruthie so hard that she was nearly pushed off her feet. "You *idiot*!"

"Hey!"

"How could you do that? Try to sacrifice yourself for me?" Layla was livid.

Ruthie stared at the ground. "I'm not afraid of death. You are."

"How can you not be scared of death?" Layla said. Her anger was fading and an old hollowness was taking its place. "My parents don't even want to write their will; they don't want to think about that word."

"Well, I'm a—"

"Do you have a death wish or something?" Layla shouted in fury.

"No, I'm just not scared of—"

"We can talk about this later," Layla cut her off. She turned back to Adams. "You monster! I thought you were a sweet old lady with your tea and cookies! I didn't think you were a *freakin' assassin*! Some jerk you are, Wren Adams!"

Wren Adams laughed. "You think I'm Wren Adams? Oh, no, Wren Adams is dead. I killed her. No, I'm the Legacy employee sent here to catch anyone looking for Armageddon by pretending to be Wren Adams. I simply played my part well, with my pretending to hide a friendship with Molly." She smugly smiled. "So it's true then. Aiden Ravencrest does not have Armageddon."

"He almost does," Ruthie said quietly. She rose to her feet. "We'll have the authorities put you in jail for murdering Wren Adams as per this recorded confession I just took, and then we'll be on our way."

Layla grimaced. "This was a total failure. We didn't even get a clue to find Armageddon. Instead, we almost got killed, plus we tipped off VD that we're still searching for it. Wonderful."

Ruthie didn't reply. She felt the same way.

Finally, Ruthie spoke: "Keep her still. I'm going to call the police. The reception might be better in the kitchen." It wasn't until after Ruthie had disappeared into the kitchen that Layla realized the absurdity of those words. The reception was fine here. So why...?

Using her compact mirror, Layla was able to catch a glimpse of Ruthie's activity behind the shelves of ingredients. She was searching through drawers for something, then started up the stairs.

There's no way she could possibly find it, Layla thought glumly.

"I found it!" Ruthie slid down the stair railing and jumped off exuberantly. "Layla, I got what we need, so let's get out of here!"

"What about the authorities?" Layla pointed out. "We're not getting this person behind bars?"

"If we're voting, I like this plan," the hostage piped up.

Ruthie glared at them both. "No, we'll send an anonymous tip-off to a neighbor. Hurry!"

Chapter Thirty-Nine

"How did you figure out that the tea was poisoned?" Ruthie said at last. Everest and Ming had settled into their hotel and were eagerly waiting for updates on what to do next, though neither girl had opened the files yet. They were still walking under the beautiful trees in a park, licking some ice cream to calm their racing hearts.

"Smelled like almond," Layla sighed. "My nanny taught me. She was from Norland College and was trained to defend me. Mother made her teach me a few tricks while she was at it."

"Oh," Ruthie said. "Of course. Silly me."

Layla grabbed Ruthie's arm and pulled her around, almost pushing the cone out of her hand by accident. "Before we start looking at all the stuff you found, I need to talk to you."

"About what?"

"You almost gave yourself up so I could be okay," Layla reminded her. "That was the dumbest thing ever. Why would you get yourself killed?"

"It's not like I wanted to!"

"You don't ever sacrifice yourself for me, okay?" Layla said. "I'm not worth it."

"Stop right there!" Ruthie said. "You are totally worth it, Layla. I did it—"

Layla rolled her eyes and threw the rest of the ice cream away in one swift move. "—because you're not afraid of death, right? You've told me this over and over."

Ruthie stammered, caught off guard, "Well, I—"

Pacing down the sidewalk, Layla continued, "When I say I don't want to talk about something, I mean it. I don't like to think about death. My mom takes a pill at night to avoid thinking about that stuff. Do you understand what I'm saying? I don't like to think about that stuff and I would like it if you would just respect my decision, *okay?*"

Ruthie was shocked at Layla's fury. So far she had been so tolerant of Ruthie's views.

"Okay," Ruthie said in surprise. She remembered to casually lick her ice cream as if she wasn't hurt. She hadn't meant to make anyone upset. "Are you feeling alright? I feel like there's something you're not telling me—"

"It's none of your business, so shut up and leave me alone."

Now that hurt. Ruthie blinked rapidly so she wouldn't cry.

Layla groaned, disgusted. "Geez, you're so sensitive! Grow up already, you're sixteen!"

"Fifteen," muttered Ruthie. She had begun school in India at age three and moved to America shortly after. Now she was a year ahead of her grade. But it was not the time to explain that. "I'm sorry. I can go figure out the files myself and maybe we can meet at the airport."

"Of course not! I want to know what you find!" Layla slumped onto the seat of a nearby picnic table. "So spill it. The guys are getting restless. We shouldn't have wasted our time getting ice cream like you suggested," she snapped at Ruthie. "And if you start crying because I raised my voice at you, I'm going to pick up these files and figure them out myself."

"I'm not crying," Ruthie said as tears burned her eyes. She rubbed them quickly and pulled out the documents, spreading them over the table. "First I found Wren Adams' diary—"

"Always helpful," Layla said sarcastically.

"—and then her last will and testament," Ruthie continued. "Since, you know, she had to figure out what to do with Armageddon."

"VD must have traced Molly's discovery back to poor Wren, which is why he killed her," Layla mused. "I don't get why Molly had to take two trips to India to find it. She seems like she could have grabbed it in one shot."

"Maybe she was looking for something else the first time?" Ruthie tried.

"Just read the diary and I'll get through the will," Layla said briskly. "Maybe we'll find something. I bet you I'll find something first."

"Did you find something?" Aiden said the moment he had established an online connection between the remaining Hall Monitors.

"Yes!" Ruthie said. "I found something first in the documents! In the entries dated over ten years back, Wren Adams spoke about a visit from Molly Ravencrest. She wrote that Molly came searching for a treasure which had been passed down through generations. According to Wren, though, the treasure had never been given to the Adams family."

Everyone groaned. "So it was all useless," muttered Ken dejectedly. "We're toast."

"No!" Ruthie said. "The treasure *itself* had never been given to the Adams family, but guess what *had*?"

"Don't guess," Layla said without a hint of a smile. "She's going to tell us."

"A clue to *find* the treasure!" Ruthie told them excitedly. "And Layla saw that in Adams's will, the clue would be given to a family friend named Benjamin Wilkins, along with an explanation. I did some research and he's also an ornithologist. But since Adams died recently and no one knows she's dead yet, he doesn't know! Only we know about the clue!"

"Tell us the clue!" Everest yelled. "Hurry up! VD knows we're after Armageddon and if he gets to it first we're *really* toast!"

"The burnt kind," Layla was quick to add.

"Here it is," said Ruthie, and she cleared her throat to make it sound more formal. Then she read:

"Thou art the ruler of the minds of all people,
But where the Crown of the Palace slept,
Lies the irony of the dark truth:
Our life here can never be kept.

Matthew's failure lies near still,
In the arms of glass men.
In their eyes glimmer the fear,
Of the coming world's end.

One day they'll meet their Maker,
One day the truth will be known,
One day there'll be no more hiding,
But until that day comes...

Remember the truth:
Nothing gold can stay."

"It doesn't even rhyme," Layla said, breaking the silence. "And it's ridiculously easy for a centuries-old hidden secret. *Thou art the ruler of the minds of all people* is the first line of the Indian anthem. *The Crown of the Palace* refers to Mumtaz Mahal, and the Taj Mahal is her tomb. So 'Matthew's failure'—obviously Armageddon—lies 'near still' the Taj Mahal."

"Yes, but 'in the arms of the glass men?'" Ruthie asked. "And the abrupt ending must be important. *Nothing gold can stay*? That's another poem, written by—"

"Robert Frost," finished Ken.

Everest jumped in, "Got it! So we wander around the Taj Mahal looking for glass men who might be hiding Armageddon, and if we see any gold, we know it can't stay!"

"Great plan," said Layla mockingly. "Yep, we're really going to catch VD. Let's try not to kill ourselves along the way, shall we?"

Aiden interrupted, "Actually, we have made excellent progress and I am proud of you all. Ruthie and Layla, job well done. Lay low while Ming and Everest try to find these 'glass men.' Ken, I need you to help us figure this out."

"What are *you* doing, Aiden?" Ruthie asked. "I'm sensing you're about to do something risky."

Aiden hesitated, then admitted, "I'm going to look for information about VD's father."

"For revenge?" asked Ken in dismay. "I thought we talked about this."

"No," Aiden corrected. "The reason behind all this is VD's grief over his father's death. It turned him into a monster. There might still be a boy's heart in there, a heart like mine. Perhaps some information about his father could give him a change of heart."

"Never going to happen," Layla said cynically. "Ever."

Aiden sighed. "It's worth a shot. The only way to really win is to save the bad guy, you know."

For a moment, they were all silent in reflection.

"Ming and Everest," Ruthie spoke up abruptly, "keep yourselves safe, okay? This not-Wren person almost killed us. VD wanted to keep one of us alive and kill the other, most likely to send Aiden a message while keeping someone alive for an interrogation." She shuddered. "So please be super careful. Trust *no one* until this is all over. Okay?"

"We got this," said Everest. "We're just looking for glass men. What are the chances we're going to get ourselves killed along the way?"

"Don't say that," Ruthie warned. "It might happen."

Everest chuckled. "Naw, we'll be fine. What's the worst that could happen?"

Ruthie groaned.

"Let's do this!" cheered Everest the moment the sun rose over the horizon. The sky was a beautiful blazing red as Ming packed his small backpack. "Remember, we are here to find 'glass men,' but to the rest of the world, we are student reporters writing about the Taj Mahal for Ravencrest Academy."

"Should we be in uniform?"

"No, that is too dangerous after what happened to Ruthie," Ming said quietly.

"And Layla," Everest reminded him.

"Of course," Ming remembered. "Poor girl. She sounded very shaken."

"I could tell. She was pretty grumpy and short-tempered, and Layla only acts like that when she's going through something rough. She must have been through a lot, being almost killed by that Wren Adams murderer," Everest anxiously said.

Ming glanced at him sideways. "And Ruthie as well."

"Of course," Everest remembered. "Her too."

Ming's eyes twinkled despite his usually hardened face. "You were truly thinking of them both?"

"Come on, don't be like that," Everest argued. "Are the bags done?"

"Almost. Everest, listen." Just as quickly, Ming became very serious. He held up a small black rectangular item with a white handle-looking part. "This is a stun gun. In order to use it against an attacker, you would touch the attacker with these prongs. It will send enough energy into the person's bloodstream at a high pulse frequency so that the muscles will turn all blood sugar into lactic acid, thereby depleting energy resources and causing instant energy loss. It will also stop the neurological impulses from the brain from reaching their destinations at various points around the body. This effect, along with the instant energy loss, will leave the victim dazed and confused."

"Does it hurt?" Everest asked, his own playfulness fading away.

"Yes. It is very painful." Ming wrapped Everest's fingers around one, then threw one into his own small pack. "I'm putting one in each of our pockets as well as our bags." He turned back to see Everest still standing there, staring at the stun gun. Ming sighed. "It may have a high voltage, but it also has a low amperage, so there will be no permanent damage to any vital organs."

"But it will hurt."

"Yes."

"Why do we—"

"Better safe than sorry. That's what the Americans say, right?" Even Ming's slight attempt at humor had no effect. Everest tucked the stun gun in his pocket.

Ming zipped up his bag and continued, "As a general rule, a one-half-second contact with the prongs will be enough to daze and repel the attacker with pain and muscle contraction. Holding it to the person for one to two seconds will lead to more muscle spasms and a dazed mental state. Any more can cause a loss of balance, muscle control, mental confusion, disorientation—"

"We don't have to be cruel."

"No, of course not," Ming agreed. "I would never want to use this. I'm only equipping you in case of danger."

Everest stared at the ground. "I hope we'll never have to use this. I don't want to have to hurt anyone like that."

Ming turned away. "Neither do I," he said quietly.

"At least it's a stun gun and not a real one," Everest said with some relief.

Ming nodded. "May we leave?"

"Let's do this," Everest said again, with less enthusiasm and more focus. He took a deep breath and stepped out of the room to go to the Taj Mahal. He watched the doors swing shut behind him as he and Ming stepped into the bustling streets of Delhi. Motorcycles raced by. Stray animals ambled around. Open market vendors offered alluring prices.

Now it was time to find these "glass men" while trying not to die along the way.

Rajesh drummed his fingers on the wooden table in the small dining room as his mother set down another bowl of spicy chicken lollipops, his favorite meal. He politely thanked her and avoided her questions. He felt unwell. After his meal, he wandered up to the roof and sat on the edge, his feet dangling three stories above the ground. He watched the city below until he felt rather sleepy. Perhaps he would go back down...

His phone buzzed, jolting him awake. He looked down. *Blocked number.* As a new rule of habit, he declined the call and rose to his feet.

The same number called again. Rajesh sighed and picked up the phone. "Hello?"

"My little fox."

Rajesh hung up immediately, his heart thumping. The phone rang again with the same number and now Rajesh flung it over the rooftop, gasping in panic. He flew down the stairs and burst into his room. "Amma, I don't feel well," he called as he curled under his blankets like a child. He felt like one, frightened and trapped.

Strangely, Amma did not rush in and fuss over him. In fact, there was no response to his calls.

The eerie silence frightened him. He distantly heard the familiar cacophony of car honks, planes flying, and city noises; inside the home, there was nothing. He slowly rested the covers in front of him and stood on his feet, eyes alert, body tense. Holding his breath, he stepped forward and peered around the edge of his door.

Losing all his bravo, he cried, "Amma!" to see his mother on the couch, the knife pressed against her neck. A man in a nice dark suit and black ski mask was patiently waiting, holding the knife. Rajesh instinctively knew it was either VD or one of VD's friends.

"Please," he begged, avoiding his mother's frightened gaze. "This has nothing to do with her. I was the one who made the wrong choice."

"You did," said the man in the dark suit. "Oh, but how I admire you, my little fox. You remind me of myself: young, naive, but with the right talents. You know which side to pick. Sometimes we all have our bad days and make the wrong decisions." VD sighed. "Such as when you agreed to let Mackenzie Robscone infiltrate your phone right after you failed to make your usual update."

"Mackenzie who?" Rajesh lied. His mouth was dry.

"Another bad move," sighed VD again. "Oh, my little fox, you'll grow with practice. Whyever would you help the losing side?"

"You mean Mackenzie? Oh, that Mackenzie," Rajesh improvised. "Maybe she wanted my phone on the plane for something, but how was I supposed to know she was going to download something on there?"

VD ignored him. "You indicated that you did not see her when she was clearly in your line of sight according to our cameras. Now, it's almost as if you were working with her to catch me. *No*, I thought. My dear fox wouldn't make such an obvious mistake. Sadly, I was mistaken. Dear Mackenzie forgot about the existence of many wonderful cameras present in the room, designed to keep an eye on *you*, my fox. You see, after the call, I thought to check on the cameras. I was quite shocked to see that Mackenzie seems to be working with Aiden Ravencrest. I knew their acquaintance due to how she visited him in Argentina, but, well…" VD clucked. "It is a shame. She was such a nice girl. I seem to keep underestimating her. Now that I know of her true involvement, I know I'll have such fun with her."

"Fun?" Rajesh repeated. "What do you mean by fun?"

"Oh, I've already made her mother disappear," grinned VD. "The girl only has her mother left, you know. I'll let her imagination run wild. Then I'll bait her in and capture her too. Dear Aiden may find himself rather upset when he sees the darling girl and her mother in my hands. Now, I was rather annoyed to find that a girl who I believed was unrelated to my work had been working against me this entire time—so annoyed that I might let my friend Xipe have some fun with her, as much as he really wants." VD was enjoying Rajesh's crumbling stony exterior.

Rajesh was now aware that he was in the presence of terrifying, absolute evil. "Tell me what you want."

"Information. Who is working with Ravencrest Campus Security?" VD probed. "Aiden must have recruited students."

"I don't know anything," Rajesh lied. Normally he would have spilled about Everest's involvement and Ruthie's accusations, but he was not about to hand Ruthie over to this man. She might hate him forever, and she certainly had the right to, but he was not going to let this man hurt her.

"Layla Writcroff has been confirmed to be involved," VD continued lazily. "And Ruthie Jocelyn."

This jolted Rajesh. "Why would you think that?"

"You recognize those names," VD remarked. "Especially the second one."

"What does it matter to you?"

"Well, my fox, I've got my little eye on both girls. They're staying at an adorable hotel in the UK. I have men ready to take them out when I call. I could have ordered their executions, you know. I still can. I just need to hit this button and send this text message, as you can see here—"

"Stop," Rajesh begged. "They're only kids. We all are."

It was as if VD hadn't heard him. "I want to send a message to them. I'll kill one and keep the other alive. No, perhaps I'll kill them both."

"Don't!" Rajesh shouted.

"Why, my fox?" VD was amused. "Oh, you seem agitated. Don't tell me you want me to keep them alive. No, no, dear, they turned in one of my best operatives. This will certainly send a message to Aiden Ravencrest."

"Don't kill them," Rajesh pleaded.

"Give me one reason to keep either of these girls alive," VD offered.

Rajesh's mind went blank with terror. Did the lives of two young girls really rest on his shoulders? Fear choked him. "Ruthie," he mumbled.

"Ruthie Jocelyn?" VD's voice sent a shiver through Rajesh.

"She could help you," Rajesh said. "She...she has a perfect memory."

"A perfect memory."

"Photographic. Superior Autobiographical Memory. She can memorize anything. You could give her pages and pages of information, and she would memorize it." Rajesh held his breath. "It would hurt you to kill her. She could help you."

"Interesting," mused VD. A glimmer was in his dark eyes. This was valuable information, and it would be very helpful in the future. "And the other girl?"

"She's a Writcroff. If she goes missing, nations will know," Rajesh said bravely.

"Excellent. And Mackenzie?"

Rajesh was silent as he racked his mind for reasons. "Her father is a millionaire," he blurted. "He would raise a fuss if she was killed."

"Nice try," laughed VD. "Her father barely knows the girl exists."

"How—"

"If Aiden Ravencrest has a girlfriend, of course I'll learn more about her. Why do you think I kidnapped her all that time ago?" VD pointed out. "It was no mere coincidence. My intelligence officer told me about Aiden's crush on her and so I used it to my advantage."

"So do you have a thing for targeting young girls?" Rajesh asked dryly. Perhaps if he could distract VD long enough, a neighbor would call the police when they came by for their daily talk with Amma. His heart pounded.

"Oh, no, I just use them along the way. Don't worry, I target children of both genders. I wouldn't dare discriminate," VD chuckled. "For example, that dear boy Everest. He's been through so much struggle. It would hurt him so badly if I made him lose one more thing. That brother of his in the military—did you know he's coming home for Christmas? Or maybe he won't be after all. It's going to be a fun surprise for Everest."

"You're despicable," Rajesh said, surprised to find his voice.

"Oh, you're only an untrained younger me."

"I'm nothing like you," snarled Rajesh. "And I never want to be like you. Maybe I make a lot of wrong choices, and I'm working on that, but I'll *never*, ever be the horrible psychopath you are!" He shouted this and clenched his fists. Suddenly, he cared about everything Ruthie had told him. If this was on the path he was on, he would do whatever it took to get off it.

VD smiled coolly. "Lower your voice."

"No!" Rajesh shouted.

Amma gasped as the knife scraped the bottom of her chin. Her eyes watered from the sudden sting.

"Fine," Rajesh muttered. He tried not to look at his tearful mother as he quietly asked, "What do you want?"

"Information, as I said. Which students are working with Campus Security at Ravencrest Academy?"

"I don't know."

VD's fingers curled around Amma's neck.

Rajesh's eyes burned. "But I'll find out."

"Better," VD observed. He smiled and let go of the woman, who recoiled and stumbled away from the man. She reached for her phone. "Ah-ah-ah," VD said playfully, knocking the phone out with one quick move. "No police or else your son will suffer. After all, some things must remain secret, am I right?" He winked at Rajesh, who went as close to pale as he could get. "Have a nice day, you all. Rajesh, I'll be back in twenty-four hours. I want answers." With a gracious smile, he rose to his feet and left swiftly.

Rajesh fell to his mother's side. "Amma..."

"Who was that man?" Amma gasped. Her fingers were shaking. "What was he talking about?"

Rajesh closed his eyes. He couldn't bear to see the emotions on Amma's face. He knew it was time to tell her the whole story. Fear and shame choked him as he mumbled, "Amma, there's something you need to know...."

Chapter Forty

"We're being followed."

It was a casual-sounding observation. Everest kept his voice low as he scanned their surroundings through binoculars in the back of the taxi. Ming nodded and continued drumming his fingers, his eyes focused outside. "Of course we are."

"You knew we were being followed?" Everest asked.

Ming shrugged. "After Ruthie and Layla were discovered, the Legacy must know that Aiden is sending out operatives around the world to find Armageddon. They want to get it first before tonight. So they must be following every Ravencrest student around the globe until they find the true student members of Campus Security." He spoke in a low tone. "We must be very, very cautious."

"We're just student reporters," Everest reassured him. "We have nothing to do with this."

"Of course," Ming agreed. "We're on a Seven Wonders of the World tour."

Everest grinned. "And we can say we're trying to find the Eighth Wonder too. It's the perfect excuse for more traveling."

Ming smiled. "It's not an excuse if it's true." He gestured at the clearly eavesdropping taxi driver. Everest nodded silently and returned his gaze outside, pretending not to notice the following car.

"Can we talk?" Ruthie asked, sitting next to Layla on her bed. Her eyes were downcast as she kicked the wall. Trying to be friendly, Ruthie asked, "What are you listening to?"

"It's none of your business," Layla muttered.

Ruthie caught a glance. It was a Shakespearan tragedy, a grim and horrific one.

"Fine, it is your business," Layla said abruptly, shoving off the headphones. "It's just...you nearly killed yourself for me, which reminded me of something I really hate to think about."

"What?"

Layla kicked the wall much too hard for Ruthie's comfort.

"Kick this instead," Ruthie suggested, handing Layla a pillow. "Or throw this. Just remember that this belongs to the hotel, not our room."

Layla threw the pillow so hard it knocked over a lamp and shattered the bulb.

Ruthie managed to stammer, "Oh-kay. I'll pay for it."

"No, I'll pay for it!" Layla shouted. "I broke it, I pay for it! You don't have to do stuff for me! No one has to!" Her face crumbled. "No one." She slumped onto her bed and tears pooled in her eyes.

"Can I ask what's going on?" Ruthie asked kindly. "I know there's something you're not telling me."

Layla buried her face in her pillow and did not respond.

Ruthie began picking up the shards of glass. She was halfway finished when a hand bumped hers. Their eyes briefly locked. Then Layla wordlessly helped her.

"I was really little when it happened," Layla said all of a sudden. "My parents said I didn't know any better. But I did know better."

"What happened?"

"My first nanny died. Car accident," Layla said. She was rearranging the pieces. Her face twisted. "Everyone said it wasn't my fault. It doesn't matter that it was my fault I left my books behind at home and wanted to throw a fit. I was nearly six and spoiled out of my mind. I felt like throwing a tantrum since I didn't feel like going to lessons, so I purposefully left them behind and went crazy over them, forcing my nanny to have to drive home. I was such a jerk about it too." Layla clenched a sharp piece so hard she drew blood. "She died on the way home. Hit-and-run. My parents hired a new nanny, but she had been my nanny since I was four. She had been with me through it all, loving and patient the whole time. And I took a lot of patience." She sucked in a breath. "My parents went to the funeral and tried to get me to go to counseling, but I pretended I was fine. I wasn't."

"Oh, Layla, I'm so sorry…" Ruthie began.

"No, let me finish. It was a long time ago. My parents don't even know I still remember it. But it was my fault, and that's a cold, hard fact, no matter what everyone says. She died because of me, because of my mistake. For many nights I wondered if she was in Heaven, just watching me and thinking about me. Thinking some not-so-great things, I'm guessing." Layla tried to bitterly laugh but couldn't. "It just forced me to think about stuff I didn't like thinking about. I don't want to die, you know. I don't want to lose anyone I care about. But everyone dies one day. Everyone. There's no running from it."

"You don't have to fear it," Ruthie said comfortingly.

"You don't fear it because you're Ruthie," Layla said in frustration. "You're perfect in every way. If there is an afterlife, I know where I'm headed. And if there's not, then nothing really matters, because that stupid poem was right. Nothing gold can stay. Nothing that matters lasts forever, you know."

"That's not true," Ruthie said. Her own eyes burned with compassion. "Layla, listen to me. God loves you no matter who you are or what you've done, and it's a love that lasts forever. He doesn't want you to have to be scared of death or the future. He wants to give you hope, peace, joy—"

"It's not for me, Ruthie," Layla said, resigned. "And if you don't mind, I'd rather not talk about it."

"Layla, please listen!" Ruthie cried, desperate.

"Ruthie!" Layla said firmly. Her eyes were red. "I *don't want to talk about it anymore.* Please."

Ruthie wanted to speak. She wanted to explain to Layla, to make her see reason. This was something that could save Layla's life the way it had saved Ruthie's. But now wasn't the right time. Ruthie held her tongue, so many words piling up inside her to say.

As the broken lightbulb was cleaned and discarded, neither said a word. The silence was suffocating yet enough. Finally, Layla said, "I'll pay," and left the room. Ruthie slumped onto the bed despondently. *Will she ever let me tell her the Good News? God, please let her understand.*

They were leaving soon. It wasn't as if...

Ruthie rolled over and grabbed a brochure from the pile of places Layla had said they should visit before they left, just for fun. Ruthie had shouted her down due to the risk of danger, but maybe a trip would give Ruthie a chance to speak to her. What would Layla be interested in? Anything expensive, anything interesting, anything with some history behind it...

An auction!

Perfect! They could stop by the auction, visit a theater afterward, enjoy an expensive meal at a high-class restaurant, go shopping, and then stop by the airport for the return trip home. Layla would love it.

Ruthie immediately began making plans. She didn't have much spending money, but there were few limits to how far she was willing to go for her friends. She began the calculations, not noticing the darkness settling outside.

"It's beautiful if you like this sort of stuff," Everest sighed. They had finished some vlog videos about the Taj Mahal. The gardens had stunned them both, and they had been in awe of the intricacy and wonder of their surroundings. However, the failure of their missions hung over their heads like a dark cloud. Now they were dejectedly waiting outside the Great Gate, the exquisite entrance to the Taj Mahal gardens. "But no *glass men*."

"We can buy some Indian sweets," Ming offered. "As a gift."

"I think I know for whom," Everest teased.

Ming frowned. "I meant for my sister. She has quite the sweet tooth."

"You have a little sister? How sweet. You never talk about your home, you know," Everest mused as they traveled to a small nearby bakery.

"I have a younger brother and sister. I'm the eldest." Ming placed a thousand-rupee note in front of him and ordered some sweets as Everest pondered this. "Can I see a picture?"

Ming relented and pulled out a small pocket picture containing an image of his family.

"Your brother looks a lot like you," Everest said, studying it. "And your mom looks so pretty. And your sister...oh." His voice caught. "I mean..."

"She has Down Syndrome," Ming confirmed.

Everest stammered, "Oh, I didn't know."

"It's quite severe, actually," Ming said casually as he took the sweets and thanked the vendor. As they left, he added, "She took a while to learn how to say her own name."

Everest could only imagine what it was like to have a brilliant prodigy like Ming and then to have a severely mentally disabled child. "Your mother deserves a medal. Three kids, and one like you?" he tried to joke.

Ming didn't smile at the attempt at humor. "But my sister is brilliant in her own way."

"She is?"

"Oh, yes. Only I have noticed it."

"Well, how old is she?"

"Six, and she already can count. I've taught her." Ming did not falter as he spoke and walked. "I'm proud of her, you know. In my opinion, she is just as smart as anyone here at Ravencrest. She tries just as hard and loves to learn just as much. She knows she is loved, which is more than I knew for years. She is braver than I, and while things may be harder for her to grasp, it does not change who she is." His voice wavered for the first time Everest had ever heard. "We are particularly close. I do not believe anyone has ever spent as much time with her as I have, except possibly my mother."

"That's...wow," Everest finally said. In a school like Ravencrest, it was easy to forget that intellect wasn't everything when it came to people. "Smarts aren't everything. Everyone can succeed, no matter if they're a prodigy or not."

Ming smiled. "Exactly."

Together they stood again in front of the great building, watching tourists stream in and out of its doors.

"Do you think it could be an anagram?" Everest asked, breaking the silence. "*Glass men.*"

"Excellent idea," Ming commended. "*Manless, angels smn, mangless...*"

"What if we heard it wrong and it was actually *grass men*?"

"*German SS...*" Ming paused.

Everest frowned. "We can't give up! Come on, *glass men.* What could it be?" He groaned in frustration. "Agh...glass men." His eyes lit up. "I have an idea! Let's try this:" He pulled out his phone and typed in *glass men.* "We have a band named *The Glass Men*, products of actual glass men...do you think there might be some glass-blowing people nearby who can make us glass men, and the glass men might have clues engraved in it?"

"Molly Ravencrest was able to find the glass men," Ming said. "However brilliant she was, she proved that it was possible. Now, what glass men could she mean?" His own eyes traveled from person to person. "Perhaps..." He stepped forward to one of the officials near the entrance and asked, "Excuse me, sir?"

"Yes?" said the man.

"Do you know where the glass men are?"

"The glass men?"

"Yes, sir," Ming said as Everest winced. He was about to speak up and apologize on behalf of his friend when—

"Yes, I know where the glass men are. I can have a friend drive you—for a fee." The official smirked, obviously thrilled at the idea of charging these two foreigners quite a bit of money. "How about $50?"

Everest's eyes lit up. "Of course!"

Ming nodded and handed the man five crisp ten-dollar bills. The official checked twice to ensure it was enough, then motioned for them to follow him. Behind them, Everest whispered, "I can't believe this! We found the glass men!"

"We didn't find the glass men," Everest muttered in dejection as they stood before the nearest eyeglass store, which was called *Glass*

Men. The official lingered and added, "If you would like some advice..."

"No, thank you," Ming said. "I'm not giving you any more. Fifty dollars is certainly sufficient."

The man laughed and left, still counting the money with a satisfied smirk on his face.

"Well, unless you need new glasses, we've hit a dead end," grumbled Everest. He slumped against a wall dramatically. "I guess that's it. We let down the others. We've let Armageddon slip into the wrong hands. We can't be Society members. This is the last—"

"Hello, sir," said Ming as he stepped into the air-conditioned room. The young man, not much older than Ming, looked up in surprise. His name tag read *Prasan*. "Prasan, my name is Ming. I am here to ask you about finding glass men."

"That is us!" said Prasan brightly. "How can I help you, sir?"

"No, not your store," said Everest. "We're looking for *glass men*." He said the words meaningfully.

"I'm sorry?" Prasan asked. "Please say that again?"

"Glass men," Everest pronounced, standing next to Ming. He spelled it slowly as Prasan wrote it down.

"Glass men? I'm sorry, I don't understand."

Everest tried again: "You heard us correctly. Do you know anything about them?"

"No, I'm sorry," Prasan said in confusion. "We do have many different eyeglasses and types of spectacles. Perhaps I can find this brand you want."

"It's not a brand," Everest said, frustrated. "It's something we're looking for, just like Molly Ravencrest was. Do you know her?"

Ming held his breath.

Prasan did not seem to even recognize the name. "I'm sorry, I don't know anyone named Malee Ravencrest, but I will ask—"

"Molly," Everest corrected. "Not Malee."

"Mali?"

"Molly."

"Mallie?"

"Close enough," Everest finished.

Prasan nodded. "I will ask my supervisor if anyone named Malee Ravencrest has asked for a Glassmen eyeglass brand, and if she has any information, I will let you know. May I know why you are looking for Malee Ravencrest or this Glassmen brand?"

"We're not—" Everest began, but Ming interrupted and said, "It's a matter of life and death. If we find the glass men, we find something called Armageddon which could save our friend's life. Furthermore, our friend happens to be Molly Ravencrest's son."

Prasan scratched the side of his head, looking absolutely bewildered. "I'm sorry, could you please repeat that? There's a friend who is Malee Ravencrest's son, and she is looking for spectacles?"

Everest smiled politely. "Never mind. We should be on our way."

"Actually, my friend Everest here would like some glasses," Ming said. "Would you mind getting some for him to try on?"

"Of course," Prasan said. That he knew how to do. "Wait right here, please, and do not move."

The moment Prasan disappeared into the closet, Ming leaped over the desk, knelt, and ruffled through the contents under the desk. Everest peered over excitedly and whispered, "You think he was lying?"

"No," Ming replied. "He is completely clueless. This is one last resort."

Everest sighed. All he had wanted was to find Armageddon. Why was it so hard to find a centuries-old secret which had led to the deaths of two different people and the rise of both VD and Aiden? But he was a Ravencrest now and Ravencrests did not give up. So he swallowed his pride and went to the backroom to get his eyes checked for glasses.

Ming was still looking through the papers when he heard the sudden breathing, the slight rustle of movement, and the quick catch of breath. Someone was standing behind him. Ming slowly and calmly rose to his feet, placed the papers back on the desk, and transitioned his stun gun so it was in his right hand. The person behind him stepped closer until he could feel their breath on his skin. He brushed off some dust off the mouse casually, as if that had been his purpose from the beginning. Suddenly, he spun around and held up the stun gun, shouting, "Don't move or I'll shoot!"

The old woman standing there gasped. "I—"

"Sorry," Ming apologized, lowering the stun gun. He stepped around the counter and back to his rightful position. "I was looking for papers regarding Molly Ravencrest or glass men. Would you know anything about that?"

The woman was badly shaken. Her eyes looked wild, frightened. "I'm sorry, I can't help you," she said, almost begging him. "Please leave."

"Her son's life depends on finding Armageddon," Ming continued. "And I noticed that this store has been here for several years. I know it's not centuries old, but it doesn't have to be. Someone could have added or replaced a verse of the riddle to update it with Armageddon's new location."

The woman, whose name tag read Aditi, said again, "Please..." She may not have understood every word, but the words *Armageddon* and *riddle* terrified her.

Prasan stepped protectively in front of the old woman. He had just returned. "Is everything all right?"

"Yes," said Aditi, her terror still clear. "Please, Prasan, would you leave us for a moment?"

"But—"

"Please," Aditi said.

Prasan left grudgingly, glancing back occasionally to ensure nothing had happened. The moment he had stepped behind the doors, Aditi leaned forward and whispered, "What is it you want?"

"Armageddon," said Ming.

"The glass men," said Everest at the same time. "Or any information about Molly Ravencrest."

"She came here to say hello whenever she stopped by India," said Aditi in a quivering voice. "Her first visit was ten years ago. Shortly after I spoke with her ten years back, a man came in and demanded to see Armageddon. He was killed that night. I was told Armageddon held the keys to destruction and death. I have seen with my own eyes that everyone who has hunted for it has died."

"Yeah, but that's only two people," Everest pointed out. "What's the worst that could happen to us?"

Aditi's eyes haunted him. "If this is to help Molly's son, I will tell you what happened to Armageddon, but I will say it with a warning to be careful."

A centuries-old secret she's willingly giving away? Ming glanced at Everest. Both were on high alert. Something wasn't right here.

Aditi took a frail breath. "Molly Ravencrest took Armageddon with her when she came here ten years ago."

Now it made sense. Of course she was willing to tell them what happened to it—she didn't know where it was now. And it made perfect sense—Molly Ravencrest needed two trips to find Armageddon because she had found and hid it the first time, then attempted to get it back the second time, which was when she had been killed. She must have wanted to hide the device somewhere safer and then return to find it once things had quieted down in the Society.

Everest looked ready to scream in frustration. "Are you kidding me? *Another* dead end? Molly Ravencrest stole it from under our noses and hid it somewhere? Agh, it could be anywhere! You've got to be joking."

"I am not joking," said Aditi. "Now I ask the two of you to please leave. I do not want whatever this is to affect my other customers. Please, go!"

"Do you know where she could have kept it?" Ming asked. "Any information would help."

"No!" Aditi shouted. She grabbed a broomstick and pointed it at them. "I need you to leave before I call for help!" From the fierceness in her eyes and the way she was holding her broomstick, it was obvious she did not need to call for help.

Everest raised his hands in surrender as Ming politely excused them. They left quickly.

Together they strolled to a busy street where cars honked. Then Everest yelled as loud as he could and kicked a trash can. "Are you *kidding* me? Molly Ravencrest *hid* it? Why?"

Ming turned away. "She had had multiple attempts on her life. Perhaps she was already making preparations in case something happened to her. It was a safety net which, tragically, ended up being used."

"The tragedy is that we can't find Armageddon. We have no clues, and tonight Aiden will meet VD empty-handed. All our planning was useless," Everest ranted. "Ruthie and Layla were almost killed in England. Ken's over in Germany with nothing to do because we didn't do our jobs. And here we are in India. All that time and money wasted. And worst of all, VD's going to win!" Everest kicked so hard that the trash can fell on its side and the trash spilled out in great clumps, carried by the wind. Wincing, Everest pulled it right-side up, but not before a few passengers in passing vehicles shouted obscenities at him.

Ming said little. Yet from his eyes, it was clear that he was well aware of the depth of their failure. Together, they finished the trip back to their hotel in silence.

"How much worse can this day get?" muttered Everest as he slumped onto his hotel bed.

Hundreds of miles away, Ken began to panic. Her mother was not picking up her calls and, worse, she couldn't track her mother's location. They hadn't spoken for a while now. "Mom, pick up," groaned Ken as the phone rang. "Finally!" she cried when the ringing stopped. She eagerly snatched up her phone and held it to her ear. "Mom, where are you?"

There was no reply.

"Mom?" Ken repeated, her voice beginning to waver.

Silence. A deep, low laugh started on the other end of the line, a horrible sound which rose and fell steadily. Pure evil resonated over the phone.

Suddenly, she remembered VD's words: *I have a little surprise for your girlfriend....*

Terror struck her. "Mom!" Ken screamed. "Where is she? VD, you monster! Where is she?" No, this couldn't be happening. Mom was all she had left. No, no, no—

Laughter rose. The line went dead.

Ken dialed it again anxiously. When a mechanical voice told her the line had been disconnected, she couldn't help the tears. "Mom," she said through the sobbing. "This isn't fair." She pulled in every single old tracking gadget she no longer used. Everything told the same story: her mother had left yesterday and had disappeared the moment her car made it to the main road. Ken didn't need to guess to know what had happened.

She stumbled to her feet, feeling hollow. It didn't matter what it took, she was going to find her mother. She was going to hunt to the ends of the earth. She would search every continent, every corner. She was going to find Mom.

She was going to find her before it was too late.

It was the wrong thing to think. She found herself crying again as she staggered into the hall, having shoved her clothes into her suitcase. She checked out, called a taxi with a brave, trembling face, and made it to the airport where she booked her own ticket. Her phone rang; it was Aiden (via his laptop—*he's probably still monitoring us all*).

"And where do you think you're going?" Aiden asked the moment she picked up.

"Have you been tracking me?" Ken accused him angrily. "You creep!"

"It was for your own protection," Aiden defended himself.

Ken felt the tears swelling again. Something in her choked out, "Mom's missing. VD has her."

There was silence on the other end.

"Did you hear me?" Ken repeated. "My mom's missing. VD has her."

"I heard," said Aiden quietly. He drew in a breath slowly, then said, "Listen, here's what we're going to do. I'll get some porters looking for her and alert the local authorities with an anonymous tip. You stay safe in your hotel—"

"What? No!" Ken shouted. "You're going to try and find her from your cozy laptop in your cozy hotel room, aren't you?" she accused. "Well, Mom could be in serious trouble!"

Aiden spoke carefully, like he was coaxing a small child or taming a wild animal. He knew he was treading on thin ice and the wrong words would break her. Delicately, he said, "She may be, but we will find and help her. In the meantime, she would want you to stay safe." It may have been the best thing to say, but it did not help. Ken slumped back. Her eyes were very red.

"Ken, are you there?" Aiden said, worried. His heart pounded. "Are you there? Answer me!"

"I'm here," Ken said wearily. She sounded quiet, defeated, and very unlike herself.

"I'll recheck you into your hotel—"

"No."

"Ken," Aiden tried, but Ken cut him off: "I didn't like being kidnapped. It wasn't fun having a monster like *Xipe Matalon* deciding what he wanted to do with me or how many times I should get tasered. It wasn't fun having *VD*—that's right, *VD*—protecting me whenever he felt like it. If he was feeling gracious, maybe it wouldn't be so bad, but do you know how cruel he was when he was angry or annoyed?" She started crying again. "I hated it! I acted all brave and macho but I never want to go through something like that again—and do you know what it's like knowing my mom is at the mercy of VD while I can't do anything about it?" She descended into sobs.

Aiden couldn't answer. On the other end of the line, he closed his eyes and swallowed back the pain. He himself was on the verge of tears. "Oh, Ken..." There was nothing more he could say.

Ken took one trembling breath and pulled herself together enough to say, "So that's it. I'm going to look for my mom and you're not going to stop me, Aiden. I'll do whatever it takes to find her and you're just going to have to deal with it." With that, she hung up.

"Ken, no!" Aiden shouted, but it was too late. He immediately called her again, only to have her decline his call. He tried twice more before she blocked his number.

Fine. I'll track you from my other devices.

Aiden felt himself drop and descend into his own internal abyss as every single tracking device and way to keep an eye on her dropped off the grid. Ken was a technological expert. She knew how to cover her digital tracks. He tried to calm his racing heart. This was exactly what he had been afraid of. Now Ken was out, alone, refusing to let him help her, and if VD got his hands on her...

Aiden clenched the sides of the tables. His head swarmed with fear. Everything was going so wrong at once. He couldn't imagine things getting any worse.

Chapter Forty-One

"You want us to go to an auction?" Layla repeated. "*Now?* While Ken is missing and the guys have found nothing and our mission is crashing faster than a burning spaceship falling back to earth?"

Ruthie blinked. "That was very vividly described. And, yes, the auction will help us get our minds off things."

"Fine," Layla muttered. "Whatever."

An hour later, after a guided tour of the museum and the historic site, even Ruthie found her eyes beginning to close. Layla was openly yawning. "This is boring," she complained. She had been complaining for the past hour to the point where Ruthie struggled to keep her patience. Layla could be very irritating when she wanted to be.

Ruthie felt her face getting hot. "It was supposed to be interesting. I thought you liked history."

"I do! But looking at a bunch of old antiques is not my idea of a good time," Layla snapped. She stretched. "Can we get ice cream? I like ice cream."

"We just *had* ice cream," Ruthie responded.

Layla smirked. "You're getting annoyed. I can tell."

"It's just...you could at least say thank you," Ruthie muttered. "It was a lot of work putting this together."

"But it was boring, and you were way off in your idea of a good time, and I'm hungry, and I'm tired, and I just want to sleep," Layla whined. She slumped into a very comfortable couch conveniently nearby.

"Fine! You're worse than a three-year-old!" Ruthie shouted, finally losing her temper, and stormed off into the crowd beginning to gather for the auction.

Layla groaned. "I'm going to have to go after her." She rose to her feet, then changed her mind. "Nope. She's going to have to come back for me." With that, Layla slumped back into her seat, sighed contentedly, and fell asleep.

It took a few minutes for Ruthie's temper to cool off. Ten minutes into the auction, she decided to return and go back for Layla. However frustrating Layla could be, she was still Ruthie's friend. Ruthie looked after her friends, especially when there were operatives around the world searching to kill them. "Layla," Ruthie said, nudging her. "Layla, wake up."

"No, give me five more minutes," Layla mumbled.

"You can't always get what you want, you know," Ruthie said with growing frustration. "We need to go. The auction is starting, and there's this shady-looking guy who keeps staring at me."

"He's probably some random guy who's checking you out," Layla replied with her eyes closed. "Now let me rest in peace."

"That's even creepier," Ruthie said, and her eyes locked with the man. There was a split second of recognition. Then she half-screamed, half-gasped.

"What?" Layla yawned.

"Xipe Matalon!"

"WHAT?" Layla's eyes flew open and she bolted to her feet. "Here? But he's supposed to be with VD in America...no, no, no! This is bad. This is really bad."

"Vladimir double-crossed us," Ruthie groaned. "And we're the first to be eliminated."

"We need to run, like, now."

"That's what I've been trying to...oh, never mind," Ruthie agreed. Together, they began shifting through the crowd to get to the exit. Xipe Matalon followed from a distance, also shoving through the crowd. His eyes glinted with a very terrifying and sadistic desire to watch the world burn.

"That guy is so creepy," Layla muttered as she pushed aside an older man. "Excuse me, sir."

"Excuse you," said the man roughly, and he locked his fingers around her wrists. Another hand stifled her scream as her feet left the ground.

"Hey!" screamed Ruthie. "Put her down!" Her voice was lost in the roar of the crowd. The man wrapped his arm around Layla's neck and swiftly strangled her, choking her screams.

As Layla kicked and struggled in the suffocating grip, Ruthie reached into her pocket, steeled her nerve, and shoved the stun gun into the man's shoulder. He tried to yell but only drew in a breath as his grip slacked and Layla kicked him away. She pushed him as hard as he could and he crumpled to the floor, dazed and completely stupefied.

Layla gasped, recovering. "This was a set-up!"

"What?"

"Look around!"

Ruthie spun around. While most of the crowd seemed genuinely there for the auction, she spotted at least three others making their way toward her. Another casually leaned against the exit and another at the entrance. They were completely trapped. Ruthie pushed her glasses back and grabbed Layla's hand.

"Don't touch me!" Layla shouted, pulling her hand free.

"No, we need to stick together! Come on, let's stay near the security!"

"What security?"

"There are guards in uniform over there!" Ruthie shouted back over the crowd's cries. "Let's stay with them. As long as we're in their sights, we should be okay. Come on!"

Together they struggled to make it there as numbers flew over their heads. "Sold!" cried the auctioneer as Layla stumbled right next to the guard standing there, who observed her with a raised eyebrow. Layla looked back into the crowd for the small frame. "Ruthie?"

"I'm here!" Ruthie pushed by a larger figure and stood next to Layla. "I'm okay. Are you okay?"

"I'm fine. Are we just going to wait here?"

"I knew this was a bad idea," Ruthie said. Her eyes were filling quickly.

"What?" Layla asked. "Standing by security?"

"No! Coming here, in public. I thought it was worth it since you seemed so upset and now..." Ruthie sniffled.

"Yeah, it definitely wasn't worth the risk," Layla said bluntly. She was too tired and frightened to try to make her friend feel better. "But we can talk about it later. Right now, let's try to get out of this alive."

"The orders were to kill one of us and to keep the other alive," Ruthie said, swallowing back the lump in her throat.

Layla glanced sideways. "If you go all self-sacrificial..."

"I won't. We're in this together. Neither of us has to die," Ruthie said firmly.

Layla nodded. "Agreed."

The security guard rolled his eyes. *The make-believe games kids play these days are ridiculous.*

Above their heads, the crowd was fully immersed in the auction. The auctioneer continued, "And now, a box donated by the Ravencrest family, which originally belonged to Molly Ravencrest, the deceased wife of the Headmaster of Ravencrest Academy. It is said to hold 'a dangerous treasure' and requires an eight-digit alphabetic combination. After her death, this box was donated from her room and thrown around as person after person struggled to pry open this lock to find the mystery held inside. Who will be next? I will start the bidding at 25, will I have 25?"

"No way," Layla whispered.

"You have got to be kidding me," Ruthie said in shock.

Even as the auctioneer's voice sped on ahead, every single Legacy operative in the room turned to look at the man on the podium.

Layla and Ruthie looked at each other. *GLASSMEN.* It was the perfect, eight-digit, alphabetic combination.

"Get that box," Ruthie whispered.

"One step ahead of you," Layla said under her breath, then called out, "50!"

Xipe called, "500!"

Every eye in the room turned to him. That was quite the jump in price.

"So much for inconspicuous," Ruthie muttered.

"550," Layla called.

"Two billion!" Xipe yelled.

Now murmurs circulated. "He doesn't even belong here!" Ruthie shouted above the swirling noise. The man on the podium quietly said something to the person next to him, and then Xipe was searched and forcibly escorted out.

"We will resume with 550," said the auctioneer. "575, any takers? Going once...going twice..."

Another Legacy operative raised his hand.

The man on the podium called, "600!"

"1,000!" Layla shouted.

"1,500," cried another operative.

"We're not going to get it," Ruthie realized. "They're going to outbid us no matter what."

"We'll have to take matters into our own hands," decided Layla. She grabbed a chair, dragged it under her, took off her coat and hat, and handed them to Ruthie.

"Oh no," said Ruthie as she understood what Layla was thinking. "This isn't a good idea."

Layla had a militant look in her eyes. "I wasn't asking. You have one job: be confident."

Ruthie gulped, put on the coat and hat, stood on the seat, and said, "1,501!" in a quiet, shy voice.

Layla winced. "You are definitely not the right person for the job."

Ruthie awkwardly fidgeted as others called numbers. She adjusted her hat and the auctioneer shouted, "1,550 for the little lady on the chair! Can I hear 1,575, I've got 1,575, what about 1,600?"

"I didn't even—" Ruthie began, jerking her head up in surprise and realizing that even the slight movement indicated she wanted to buy.

The man shouted, "1,600 for the little lady, can I hear 1,650, going once, going twice—"

"How much can we afford?" Ruthie asked as another called for 1,700.

"A lot on my dad's card. Trust me. Just keep driving it up."

"No, please," Ruthie whispered, but Layla was already gone.

Already Layla was working through the crowd as Legacy operatives called out numbers and Ruthie nervously pushed up the price. One operative opened his mouth to shout out a number when a look of surprise appeared on his face before he slumped to the ground, dazed. Ruthie's heart dropped into her stomach as two more operatives were taken out. *I should never have given her the stun gun.* Another operative managed to whirl around and bring up his hand to defend himself, but just a touch with the prongs made him collapse.

"Two thousand," shouted the final operative, who had dark blond hair, a smiling face, nice blue eyes, and a gun cocked at waist level. When Layla snuck up behind him, he put his gun to her ear, held his arm around her neck so she couldn't breathe, and made eye contact with Ruthie.

"Going once," cried the auctioneer.

Ruthie felt her heart twist.

"Going twice," said the auctioneer.

Layla made eye contact with Ruthie, pleading with her. *Bid, please!*

"I can't," Ruthie whispered. "You're worth more than an old antique." She said this softly, of course, and looked straight at Layla with her own pleading eyes.

Layla's face lit up as the auctioneer interpreted the slight shake of the head as Ruthie's next call and continued, "Can I hear 2,200?"

Ruthie froze up as the man holding Layla called out again and suffocated her, pressing his wrist into her windpipe. She choked out loud and struggled in his gasp. Suddenly, the man on the podium yelled "Hey!" and the guards broke through, tearing the man away from the girl. The shaken crowd erupted into frenzied movement. Ruthie was nearly knocked off her chair. Someone lifted her off her feet and said, "Stand on my shoulders."

She gaped at the guard. "But—"

"It looks like you two need that box," said the guard, nodding at Ruthie's Ravencrest tag, which she had yet to take off. "I'll help you." There was a friendly twinkle in his normally gruff eyes. His tag read *Justin*.

She grinned at him and stood high on his shoulders, shouting with newfound confidence as she saw her friend helped to her feet by a security guard, "Twenty-five hundred, take it or leave it!"

"Going once, going twice...sold to the little lady!" said the man on the podium. He wiped his sweaty brow. Clearly, his job never got boring. "Next up, we have..."

As he rambled on and the chaotic crowd clamored for more antiques, Justin safely got Ruthie through the crowd. She happily accepted her prize and put it in her backpack. She locked eyes with Layla, who emerged from the crowd and stood next to her. "You got it?"

"I did, with some help." Ruthie smiled gratefully at Justin. "Thank you so much. You have no idea how grateful we are for your help."

"Do you girls have a safe ride home?" Justin asked.

"I was going to call a taxi," Ruthie began, but Justin interrupted her: "No, I'll organize a ride." He took out his phone to make some calls.

Layla was no longer grumpy. Her face was shining. "We did it!" she gasped to Ruthie. "We got Armageddon, beat the bad guys, stayed alive, and now we're getting a police escort home! This is incredible!"

Ruthie couldn't help but smile at the abrupt change in Layla's mood. "Well, at least someone's back to normal." She hesitated, remembering how moments earlier Layla had taken out all her rage and frustration by stun gunning five different people across the room. One very resilient woman was groaning and struggling to get to her feet. The rest remained motionless and dazed. Ruthie grimaced at the thought of the pain they must be going through.

"We did it!" Layla cheered, dancing in excitement. "We got this, we did it, whoo-hoo!"

"At the cost of all those people," Ruthie said. "Did you have to be so brutal?"

"It was just a stun gun. Police do it all the time."

Ruthie frowned.

Layla sighed. "I do feel a little bad, inflicting pain like that," she admitted. "But those guys were literally assassins sent to kill us and grab Armageddon. I guess it was for a good cause." She paused, then said again in a less enthusiastic tone. "I won't do it again unless I ever have to. But they were going to kill me or you, so..." She shrugged, revealing that hollowness again. "It was necessary."

"And now 2,000 for the little lady in maroon," called the auctioneer, and with a start both girls realized he was talking about them. "Can I hear 2,100?"

"Wait, I didn't even move," Layla started to say, jerking her head up in surprise. The man called out, "3,000 for the little lady, can I hear 3,100?" He was speaking so fast that they could barely make out what he was saying.

"Don't move," Ruthie cautioned. "Or else they'll think you want to buy something."

"Yeah, I got that," Layla said, frozen in place. Offers flew. The moment there was a break between the auctioning, they bolted outside and cheered. They had finally won. Just wait until the others found out! They would be so happy and relieved. Everything was going to be alright.

"No," Ruthie whispered. The flush of the excitement faded from her face. They were sitting on the comfortable hotel bed. After entering the code *glassmen*, they had found...

Nothing.

Absolutely nothing, except for a cute little globe with a note which said *For your birthday, to the greatest Head of the Society. Xoxo, Mom.*

"This is 'a dangerous treasure?'" groaned Layla. "How?"

"It's a record of everywhere she traveled," Ruthie said half-heartedly. "I guess it probably has some secret locations on there, too. But since it's from Molly's mother, it's not a map that leads to Armageddon. It's probably something else equally dangerous, like a family heirloom or something." She slumped backwards onto the bed. "It's not Armageddon."

"We *didn't* find it? But...the auction..." Now Layla deflated. "We went through all that trouble for *this*?" She kicked the box and tossed herself onto the bed as well.

"Careful," Ruthie said without emotion. "We could need it."

For one miserable moment, both girls lay on the bed, staring at the ceiling.

"How could we have been so misled?" Ruthie said, rolling over and burying her face in a pillow. "We must have been desperate."

"Twenty-five hundred dollars wasted, not to mention all these traveling expenses," Layla said. "I give up. We went all over the world looking for Armageddon and found nothing but dead ends. Our plan crashed and burned."

"Like a burning spaceship falling back to earth," Ruthie agreed.

Layla sighed. "At least one good thing came out of all this."

"What?" Ruthie asked.

Layla smiled and took Ruthie's hand. "I know I've got a friend who's ready to go along with my crazy plans and risk her life to make sure I'm safe. You didn't desert me, even when I was a total jerk. I was angry, but I'm glad you respect my views. I know we disagree on a lot of stuff, but I can tell you really care about me no matter what." She sighed. "I'm sorry I was so cranky. The history was kind of interesting and I like spending time with you. I can tell you really tried. Maybe one day I'd like to hear what you were trying to tell me earlier." She shrugged. "I mean, there's something different about you and…maybe I want that."

"Thanks," said Ruthie with a small smile. "And thank you for being my roommate. If nothing else came from this, well, I have another sister now."

Layla rested her head on Ruthie's shoulder, looking at the old box sitting on the bed. "Well, you know what they say. It's all about how you deal with failure. If you learn from it, you could…" Her voice trailed off.

"You could what? I don't know, tell me the rest of the quote," Ruthie said. "I don't think I've heard that one before."

Layla sat up straight and gasped, "Shoot!"

"You could be shot?"

"No, it's a saying, just—listen, we can still do this!"

"Do what?"

"The Legacy doesn't need to know we didn't actually find Armageddon. They think we did, since they saw us at the auction." Layla picked up the little globe and spun the small sphere around. "Instead of offering the real Armageddon, we can make our own little fake Armageddon. In fact, we can double-cross them the way they tried to double-cross us."

"But there's no way we can get a fake copy of Armageddon to Aiden," Ruthie pointed out, sitting up as well. "Ken's off the grid, and Ming and Everest are on their way home. And just because I have the original design memorized doesn't mean it will be easy to recreate it."

"We're in England and Aiden is in the US. If we take into account the time zone changes, we could totally make it!" cried Layla, her face flushed with excitement once more. "Let's get this to him! I need a laptop, my dad's credit card, some scissors, glue, tape, coloring markers, and an ice cream milkshake!"

"It's all in your backpack," Ruthie said. "There's no way this will work. If VD finds out we double-crossed him, we're done. And it's going to be really tight getting this to Aiden on time. And will our imitation even fool anyone?"

"We have to try, don't we?" Layla said, looking at Ruthie hopefully.

Ruthie agreed at last. "We do. We're not going to give up."

"We're Ravencrests now, and we never give up," grinned Layla back. "That should be the Hall Monitors' motto."

Ruthie crawled forward on the bed, completely focused on what they had to do. "Okay, hand me some paper. I'll sketch the design from what I remember."

Chapter Forty-Two

"The girls found Armageddon," said Ming, hanging up and slipping his phone in his bag. He had been told it was the real Armageddon, just in case the line had been tapped. Now, he, Everest, and Aiden all believed that the real Armageddon device was headed their way.

"Yes!" Everest cheered. "Victory in sight!" He did his own little victory dance, then stopped abruptly. "Wait a moment. How did they find it?"

"It was at an auction," Ming explained. "Apparently a box from Molly Ravencrest was being sold, and it happened to contain Armageddon. They managed to evade Legacy operatives and find Armageddon, and now both girls are on their way to hand Armageddon over to Aiden in the US."

Everest hesitated. "Part of me cheers them on, of course, but...how is this possible? Isn't it weird how the box just happened to show up for them? The chances of that are pretty low."

"Well, that is what happened," Ming said. "The girls most definitely have Armageddon, and Aiden will most definitely have it in time for his meeting tonight."

"We still did our best, and in the end, we're going to crush VD so hard," Everest said. "All six of us are the best security team there is."

"That is an exaggeration," Ming said as he finished packing.

"Not too much," teased Everest as he zipped up his bag. "Shouldn't we be on our way to the airport?"

"We should," Ming agreed. As he walked over to the door, his step did not falter. The moment Everest was about to push the door open, Ming whispered to Everest, "Did you leave the window open?"

"No, of course not! It's been locked since the moment we got here," Everest whispered back.

"Then why is it slightly open?" Ming asked in a low tone.

Everest casually looked around the room. "One last time for the memories," he said loudly as he raised the camera to snap a picture. As he examined the picture, he saw a small figure in the background of the photo. Zooming in, he saw a smiling American woman looking up at them. "It's just some tourist," he said, showing the photo to Ming. "Still, we should be careful."

"She knows we see her," said Ming in surprise. "She just winked at me."

"Tourists," said Everest lightly. He reached for the door.

Ming grabbed Everest's arm, locking eyes with Everest and communicating an unseen message. "Hold eye contact with her."

Everest obeyed as Ming dialed the number for Guest Services. "Excuse me? We have an issue in room 3252. Please come as soon as possible." He hung up without further elaboration. Everest whispered, "She's still staring right at me. It's kind of unnerving. Oh wait, she just winked at me too. I think she's flirting with me."

"We may be paranoid," Ming admitted.

Everest held the woman's gaze a moment longer, then said, "We probably are. Let's go." He opened the door just as Ming shouted, "Wait, don't—"

Suddenly, an explosion erupted and knocked them both off their feet. The floor in front of them flew up in pieces and smoke billowed, flames licking the air. It was in the exact position Everest would have been if he had stepped forward instead of pausing to look back at Ming. Both boys immediately turned to look out the window.

The woman was gone.

"It was a distraction," Ming realized. "She planted the bomb. She must have broken in!"

"She could probably hear every word we said," Everest said. "That's how she found out we were part of Ravencrest Security!"

"She's an assassin!" Ming was now at the window, pushing it open. "We'll escape this way. She must be coming up the stairs to kill us."

"To *kill* us?" Everest gasped as he followed Ming to the window. "Are you sure? Remember, they were going to keep one of the girls alive for interrogation purposes. Maybe the bomb was designed to scare us, not kill us."

"Do you want to stay behind to find out?" Ming yelled. "Get up this window!"

"Why me first?"

"Because I said so!" Ming was usually soft-spoken and gentle. Now his voice was harsh and furious. Everest glanced back to Ming's face and glimpsed the fear in his eyes. *He's scared,* Everest realized. *Terrified that he might lose me.* Doing his best to stay calm, Everest grabbed the side of the window and hoisted himself up with excellent upper body strength. He climbed up a little farther with great precision and rolled onto the roof, which was scalding hot. "Ouch," Everest winced as he stood and looked down the side of the building to aid his friend. "It's hot up here!"

"About to get hotter," said a female voice as something shoved him off the side of the roof, down eight floors to his death.

Except Everest had incredible reflexes. He grabbed the arm of whatever tried to push him off and used it to swing around above the road eight floors below. Just as easily, he was back on the roof, twisting the arm of the woman who had just tried to kill him. Now he saw her face and was surprised to see that she was beautiful and young. She couldn't have been much older than him.

"Hey!" he said in surprise. "Who are you? Why are you trying to kill me?" He let go of her arm.

Rather than answering, she delivered a strong punch to his ribs which had him reeling.

"Guess my brother's advice about never hitting a girl doesn't apply to the ones trying to kill me," he muttered to himself. He dodged her next blow and sent a kick that was supposed to knock her legs out from under her. Instead, moving so fast she was practically a blur, the girl flipped him over and had him landing face-first on the concrete roof. Thankfully, he brought his hands up in time and rolled out of the way.

The girl smiled flirtatiously, looking as beautiful and innocent as ever. She held up a switchblade. "Guns were overused," she said in a sweet, melodious voice. "I thought I'd be a little creative this time."

"You're working for the Legacy," Everest said, ignoring his burning hands and trying to make sense of the situation as they circled each other. "They must have some youth recruitment team."

"Oh, no," she said with a sadistic smile. "The Legacy adopted and trained me. Rescued me from the asylum I was put in. They call me the Black Widow. My brother's known as the Black Recluse. We make a pretty good team, I think." She tossed her bouncy, wavy hair over her shoulder and offered him a dazzling smile. "This is my first assassination mission. How am I doing? A plus?"

"Extra credit for the knife," Everest agreed as he found himself back on the edge of the roof. "But you lose points for what you forgot."

"Oh? And what's that?" She batted her eyes at him as she raised her weapon and twirled it, practically salivating at the thought of running it through him. For the first time, he realized the cute little red shape in the corner of her black dress. It was a black widow symbol. This girl—she was older than she looked, so maybe a young woman—was dressed to kill.

"I have a friend," Everest said as Ming, standing behind her, sent a stun gun shock to the Black Widow that had her reeling. She gasped, suddenly limp in his arms. Ming gently positioned her on the roof so she wouldn't fall off or get burned. He looked up at Everest. "Are you all right?"

"I'm fine," Everest said as he stepped away from the edge.

Ming frowned and stared at the ground, eight floors below. "How will we get down? I was hoping for a staircase leading up here, but it seems unused."

"You forgot something too, Everest," said a voice behind him. They spun around to see the Black Widow back on her feet, this time with two glistening knives in her hands instead of one. "I told you I have a brother."

Ming found himself silently screaming in pain as a stun gun shocked him. Electrical impulses shot pure agony up his veins and he could only crumple into his attacker's arms as the anguish became too much to bear. Another equally well-dressed man let go of the boy and let him fall roughly to the ground. The man, clearly the Brown Recluse, laughed. "Always fun to push this thing to the highest level," he said, toying with the stun gun. He pointed it at the frozen and horrified Everest. "Looks like you're next, little boy."

Everest couldn't stop looking at the still Ming, whose face was clenched from the pain of the stun gun and the burn of the roof. "You monster," Everest said, barely able to breathe. "That kid wasn't going to kill either of you!"

Now the Brown Recluse offered his own evil smirk. "We know. So weak."

"But we're not weak," added the Black Widow, standing behind Everest. The two circled him like vultures circling their prey. "After plenty of practice, we know how to ignore the effects of stun guns. The two of us happen to have incredibly high pain tolerances."

"You know why we name ourselves after dangerous spiders?" the Brown Recluse continued. He was also disguised as an American tourist. While he was older and somewhat more experienced than the Black Widow, he also seemed young and handsome. "Come on, you're a biology major. You can figure this out. Why do we name ourselves after poisonous spiders?"

"Because you're another dumb criminal with nothing better to do," Everest spat back. How dare they do this to his friend! Rage overrode his terror at being cornered and surrounded by two assassins.

"Not quite," said the Black Widow. "Recluse, turn up the gun a little higher. I want to make sure it hurts."

"It's already at the highest," the Brown Recluse replied.

"Higher."

"That's not possible."

The Black Widow temporarily shifted her eyes into a glare, transforming her once-pleasant smile into something despicable. "Turn it up, I said! You never do what I ask you to do!"

"How am I supposed to do that?" scowled the Brown Recluse.

"You just move this button!" the Black Widow instructed, shoving it. "I don't care if it stops working, I just want him to suffer!"

"He—where is he?" said the Brown Recluse, looking up all of a sudden. There was no Everest in sight. Both assassins rushed to the edge to find Everest slipping through an open window on the side of the building. "You've got to be kidding me, you *idiot*!" shouted the Black Widow. "You lost him!"

"Not for long." Already the Brown Recluse was sliding down the side of the building and jumping through the window, but not before he shouted up one last time, "Take care of the other one."

The Black Widow turned to the semi-conscious Ming and smiled evilly. She kicked him once in the ribs and he groaned. "Does this hurt?" she mocked before wrapping her arm around his neck and half-strangling him as she brought him to his feet. "Well, it's going to hurt a lot more soon. Looks like you're the lucky one. You're going to be staying alive. But don't worry, when the Legacy is through with you, you're going to wish you were your friend. We'll give him as much of a painful death as you deserve." She laughed, a terrifying noise.

Ming kept his eyes closed and remained limp. Fighting back would only make everything hurt more, he knew.

"Come on, *Ming*," taunted the Black Widow as she wrapped a rope around him that would keep him attached to her when she climbed down the side of the building. "You know, you don't have to worry. You're going to have company soon."

Ming did not respond.

"A really sweet little girl named Ruthie Jocelyn," said the Black Widow cheerfully, landing and untying Ming before half-dragging him to a car. "She's my next assignment."

Now Ming managed enough strength to convulse and rasp out, "Don't you dare."

She *tsk*ed. "That wasn't very smart. Now it hurts more, doesn't it? Poor thing."

Ming tried to tune out her psychotic voice and focus. He had to recover, escape, and save Everest, Ruthie, and the others. Their lives were in even more danger. So he didn't fight as he was dumped into the backseat of a car. He listened as his captor impatiently called her partner and waited for Everest's dead body to arrive.

Everest raced down the hotel's hall, heart pounding, eyes alert. He had one goal now: to survive. It would be hard with a trained killer on his trail, but if he could conquer the world of biology, he could definitely conquer the Brown Recluse.

Suddenly, he felt something sharp skim over the surface of his arm. Poison darts. *The Brown Recluse is really living up to his name,* Everest thought grimly as he threw himself into the next room, shut the door, and locked it by sliding the small bar in place. He turned to find himself in the breakfast area of the hotel, where waiters stared at him blankly.

Instead, he raced down to the patio side and pushed the door open, ignoring the calls of inquisitive waiters. He dashed outside, his eyes darting around the busy Delhi area. They focused on one item in particular: a man unlocking his motorcycle. He had a child with him.

Everest truly felt bad about this later when he thought about the fear in the father's eyes when Everest came running in with his stun gun buzzing with electricity and pointing right at them. Everest grabbed onto the motorcycle and began driving, leaving the man yelling behind him. "I'll pay for this!" Everest yelled back. The man shouted something rude about Americans that Everest felt no need to respond to. The one comfort was that this was India, so no one would notice or mind if he drove like a madman.

As he picked up speed on the already too-fast motorcycle, he heard the faint sound of thunder. Soon it was drizzling. *Just what I needed.* As water blurred his vision, he looked up to find the Brown Recluse leaping from roof to roof. *How is he—?* Then Everest saw the little safety nets that the Recluse quickly created and used between the longer gaps. Even his ability to climb up walls rivaled Aiden's. *This guy is good.*

The motorcycle sped even faster and dotted around autobuses and honking cars. It darted into thin alleys, hitting a speed bump—and Everest nearly fell off his bike from how high he was thrown into the air. The bike jerked upward but gravity kept him from flipping over. Gasping, Everest realized he had no option but to continue at this speed; otherwise, the potholes he was narrowly avoiding would kill him, especially since he was now at a steep uphill climb. Every muscle strained, every breath a struggle, every bit of trained focus—it was now or never. He spun his motorcycle around to park right outside a building, jumped off, and ran inside. He had stopped at a busy mall where it would be much harder to find him and even more difficult to kill him in public. He did his best to lose himself in the crowd, even grabbing a hat on a display to cover his head. Finally, he found a nearby storage closet where he managed to get past the lock, rearrange the box full of beautiful clothes, and bury himself inside with the lid pulled over. He would hide in here for however long it took before it was safe to come out again.

Now that he was alone in the dark, still room, the full terror of the situation caught up to him. His killer was prowling outside, waiting for the right moment to strike. He might be stuck here for days. And Ming—oh, what would happen to his friend? Everest had run off due to his flight-or-fight instinct, but now he remembered his unconscious friend who had taken a terrible hit on Everest's behalf. He gulped at the thought of these psychopaths tracking down all his friends and murdering them. As he curled deeper into the rustling sheets, he heard the sound of whistling.

Shock. *No, it can't be...*

With a smug smile on his cruel face, the Brown Recluse swung the tampered door open and switched on the lights, flooding Everest's vision with blinding light through the small hole in the box. Everest watched as the boy reached down and picked up a small tracking device that must have fallen off Everest's clothes in the mad rush to escape. "Hello, Everest," said the Recluse, looking delightfully at the many boxes of clothes. "Are you really going to try to hide? I'll give you a less painful death if you come out now."

Everest didn't move. He could barely breathe.

"Last chance," said the Recluse in a sickly sweet voice. He began counting down, "Five...four...three...t—" Suddenly, he pushed over a large metal sewing machine and completely crushed the first box, destroying whatever was inside. The Recluse dragged out the remains of the first box, lit it on fire, and threw it onto the second box, catching it on fire as well. There were a total of eight boxes, some stacked on top of each other. Everet was hiding in the last one.

"It's all right," the Brown Recluse added, "I wasn't going to give you a less painful death anyway. Come on, you don't have to be so scared. It will all be over so quickly."

Three more boxes were brutally destroyed, the Brown Recluse laughing and making casual remarks the entire time. First, he would do something painful, such as throw sharp objects in or flatten it or catch it on fire, before pretending to save it by pulling out the arrows or dragging the remains out or putting the fire out briefly. Then he would only destroy it even more brutally.

Two left...

Everest was vaguely aware of how much he was shaking as his body trembled with fear so hot and intense it was alive, squirming through his veins, convulsing through him, descending him into a barely human-like state. *I'm next, oh God, I'm next.*

Last one...

The man plugged something into the wall and watched as the entire box shook with repeated electrocution. He then drizzled the box in some kind of liquid before setting it on fire as well. In a few moments, all that remained was a pile of charred ashes after the fire died out.

It's my turn.

The Brown Recluse began giggling when the last box was annihilated with no trace of blood or human life. He kept chuckling, then began full-on laughing as he stood in front of the last box where Everest could clearly see him. There were no words, only laughter—pure, terrifying laughter. *He is a madman,* Everest realized with cold, dark horror.

Finally, the laughing stopped. As the Brown Recluse was so close that Everest couldn't see his whole figure, he could only see black fabric as the lid was lifted. Thankfully, Everest had hidden well. He held his breath as the Brown Recluse hummed and closed the lid again.

He began speaking: "You know, everyone needs a friend in life. Sometimes they have a perfect person to manipulate. Sometimes they have a teammate they plan on killing one day. Sometimes they have people around them that just drive them crazy, and so they imagine different ways of ending their life one day." As he spoke, he strolled around the box lazily. "Sometimes you have a pet. Now, Everest, remember when I asked why I call myself the Brown Recluse?"

No.

Please, no.

Finally, Everest understood. As a biology student, he struggled not to panic as he felt the slight, tingling, prickling sensation as another tiny living organism in the shape of a cranky Brown Recluse spider began its journey through the box searching for him. There was no way out. He was totally and utterly trapped with one of the most venomous spiders in the world.

"Can I give you a fun little lesson about my buddy here?" continued the Brown Recluse. When Everest didn't give him the satisfaction of answering, the Recluse went on anyway: "When he bites, it hurts." Everest closed his eyes as the Recluse went on to lecture about necrosis, the way the venom would kill the tissue at the site of the bite. He went on about how painful the bite was and how the necrosis was extremely toxic, causing blood clots and eventually causing the system to shut down.

"You criminals are all the same," Everest said once the Recluse had paused to catch his breath. It was the first thing he had said. "This same thing happened to Aiden. Vladimir Damon had him cornered in a small space in a cave. He sent him a poisonous snake. He shot at him."

"And what happened?" said the Brown Recluse with amusement.

"VD underestimated him," said Everest. "The way you just underestimated me. You see, I know spiders better than you do. I know many animals better than you do. And I know that this spider is definitely a venomous, dangerous Brown Recluse spider." Everest rose to his feet calmly, standing in the middle of the box full of clothes and staring at the Brown Recluse while holding the spider. "I also know that this little spider is very non-aggressive unless it feels threatened. Now, I happen to have a way with animals, and this spider seems to care a lot more about finding a place to rest rather than killing me." Now Everest smirked. "However, it does hold grudges when it has been mistreated. For example, now it doesn't like you. See how it's crawling toward you?" Everest held the spider closer to the Brown Recluse, who took a step away.

"You can drop that," continued the Recluse, "or I'll shoot you."

"Oh you don't know much about this spider, do you?" Everest asked. "It has friends. It hunts you down. It won't leave you alone. In fact," Here Everest threw the spider forward so it landed directly on the Brown Recluse, who tried to jerk it off and found the spider clinging to him. "In fact, I think you're going to enjoy its company very much."

The Brown Recluse pointed a finger at him, which had a small poison dart gun attached. "Don't think about moving."

Everest acted calm as his confidence faded. This was as far as he had figured out. All he could do now was pray in total desperation. *God, please help me...*

"This will be fun," grunted the Brown Recluse. He shot.

Everest felt the pinprick and a slow, agonizing paralyzing pain crawl up his body. He had time to breathe a prayer before he slid to the ground, helpless at the feet of the monster.

That was what should have happened.

What happened instead was completely different. The Brown Recluse gasped unexpectedly as the spider bit down on him.

Everest frowned. "He must not have liked your threatening, sharp weapons. He's usually pretty friendly, but he fights back hard if you hurt him. A lot like me." He stepped closer to the door.

"Don't move," said the Brown Recluse with rage in his eyes. He tried to shake off the spider, who held fast with a tenacious grip. "I'll kill you faster if you stand still."

"Hard pass." In one swift move, Everest was out the door, a poison dart skimming the back of his shirt and burying itself into the wall. He slammed the door shut as the Brown Recluse rushed to it and threw his weight against the frame so hard that Everest could feel the shock waves. He locked the door behind him, sliding the metal into place, and ran to the nearest shop assistant, gasping, "Hey!"

The older woman turned to him in surprise. "Yes?"

"Do you know how to get out of here?" Everest said, breathing too fast to speak clearly. "I can't use the front door since it's too crowded."

"We have an alternate back exit and a stairwell to the roof," she said slowly in accented English. "But you can't go to the roof unless I—"

He pulled out fifty dollars.

She immediately stopped speaking, led him down the aisles of jeweled clothes, and unlocked the door to the roof. He briskly handed her the money and started upstairs, ignoring her curious gaze. Wherever the Brown Recluse was now, he would not rest until Everest was dead.

As Everest ran up the stairs, he sighed once in relief. He had accomplished several things: half-lied to the Brown Recluse enough to hopefully scare him away, trapped him in the closet, and shortened the amount of time Everest needed to keep running before the Recluse was permanently silenced. He had 2-8 hours before the Recluse showed symptoms and began to die. There was a slight chance the Brown Recluse might develop some common sense and go to a hospital, but Everest doubted it. He had seen the fury in the Recluse's eyes.

He pushed open the door to the roof and pulled himself up onto the gleaming, sand-like surface as it reflected blinding light all around him. For a moment, he was awestruck with beauty as he looked into the rugged, busy streets of Delhi. He walked to the edge and looked down to the jagged, rocky road three stories below. *I'll wait and watch if the Recluse leaves from here,* he decided. *There's no way he would—*

Scarcely had he conceived the thought when the door was punched off its hinges. Rising out of the cramped stairwell was the spider-like man himself, silent yet furious as he slipped out of the hole and smoothly rose to his feet. Standing in the midst of the fighting heat wave, the Brown Recluse stepped once to Everest and took off his gloves.

"Hey, Spiderman," Everest said weakly as he backed up to the roof's edge. He had completely and totally run out of options.

"I know sixteen different ways to kill you," said the Recluse without emotion. "But I've decided it would be more fun to do it without weapons." With that terrifying statement, he bolted toward poor Everest, who instinctively stepped back into the air, lost his balance, and found himself flying backward, yanked down by the fierce pull of gravity. His scream died in his throat as he hurtled limply toward the ground.

Chapter Forty-Three

Halfway through the fall, Everest managed to flip himself over in midair so he was falling feet-first. The terror had fully taken over now, electrifying every cell in his body. He lunged forward with the precision of milliseconds and his hands caught a sign sticking out of the side of a building. The burning metal dug into his flesh as the momentum swung him forward, then released him so that he dangled ten feet above the ground. His arm was nearly torn out of its socket by the sudden agony. For a brief moment, he hung there and slumped his head back so he could see the Brown Recluse looking down at him from the roof. With that, Everest looked down once, steeled himself, and let go.

He landed on his feet and never stopped moving, using the momentum to propel him through the alley and into the fast-moving street. Car honks screamed at him and he threw himself onto the little patch of grass between the lanes, narrowly avoiding the vehicles rushing past him. For a few seconds, he lay on his back on the dirty grass, the sun directly above him. *A few more hours*, he told himself, panting. *I need to avoid him for a few more hours.* The future looked so bleak. He was already barely in one piece, and an hour hadn't even passed.

He heard the familiar click and forced himself to his feet, staggering and then running between the fast-flying motorcycles and speeding cars. Everest turned back to see the Brown Recluse land safely on the ground, curling up a rope from behind him. The spider still clung stubbornly to the man's shoulder, refusing to let go.

Maybe I can call the police? It would have been a great idea if he hadn't left his phone in the side pocket of his backpack in the hotel room.

He ran through alleyways and dark passageways until he skidded to a stop in front of the same exact eyeglasses store. Behind the counter, Prasan continued his daily job as he polished the counter. Like a lightning bolt, a thought struck Everest so suddenly that he was immediately across the table from Prasan.

"You again!" Prasan managed to say before Everest begged, "Help me. I will pay you. I need to hide."

The man stared at the young boy for a moment and looked behind him to see the spider-like man cross the street. He looked back to find

Everest emerging from the nearest storage closet and wearing a store uniform, a Covid mask, and some dark-colored glasses. Prasan was still blinking when the door swung open and the Brown Recluse jovially waltzed in. All the hate and cruelty had disappeared from the assassin's face and had been replaced with a good-natured, friendly stranger's smile. "Hello! Prasan, is it?"

"How can I help you?" asked Prasan robotically, still struggling to comprehend the situation.

"I'm here looking for a boy who entered your store a moment ago."

"He's here," Prasan agreed as Everest continued closely examining some glasses with the store jacket covering his trembling fingers. Keeping the hat firmly adjusted and his head low, he knelt down to put the box back in its place so that his back was facing the Recluse and Prasan, though he could see the reflection in the glasses. Prasan added, much to Everest's relief, "He left through the back door. Why are you chasing him?"

"He's my son," the Brown Recluse explained. "If I find him, he will be in a lot of trouble for running off."

Prasan nodded. "I understand completely. Follow me."

As the Brown Recluse was led to the backroom, he brushed by Everest, never once looking down at the store help who continued polishing new glasses on display. Everest breathed a wordless prayer of thanks.

When Prasan returned, he found the store uniform neatly folded on the counter, the new glasses perfectly polished and placed on display, some money waiting for him, and the mysterious boy missing yet again. Prasan scratched the side of his head and took up his place at the counter. Aditi had a lot of explaining to do.

Ken slept restlessly. When she landed in America, she rushed to leave the airport as fast as possible and managed to outwit the porters waiting for her at the airport. No doubt they were all sent by Aiden. She ditched a porter who managed to tail her until she reached the swiveling doors; then she lost herself in the crowd. With a single small suitcase and a backpack, she could easily hide. Once she was outside, she found a willing Lyft driver with a much-too-strong cologne and spent the last of her money getting to her home. From there on she knew how to trace her mother's footsteps.

She had powered off her phone so Aiden couldn't track her, but privately she wondered about any updates regarding the search for Armageddon. Their mission was a bust. They had really failed badly.

It's not over yet, she wished she could tell Aiden. However miserable they all must be, he must be taking the worst of it. She wanted to call him and tell him that they still could do this. The meeting was tonight and it looked as if Aiden would have to double-cross VD, which would be difficult since VD was double-crossing him in return. She sighed and rested her head on the car windowsill.

It was strange. One would think she would've started seeing the familiar landmarks by now. It wasn't as if she could trace her journey on a GPS. Unfortunately, she really did have to "power off."

After a while longer, she began to suspect something was amiss. But she had slept so little on the plane ride and the car seat was so comfortable that the next thing she knew her eyelids were sliding down and she was dozing lightly in the backseat of the taxi. She thought she vaguely heard her Lyft driver speak something mentioning the arrival of something important into his Airpods, but perhaps it was nothing.

What are you doing, falling asleep like a wimp? Mom's out there, and she could be hurt!

Ken jolted herself as awake as she could but found that something was keeping her in a feverish daze. She could barely keep her eyes open. The car suddenly parked; the door swung open and Ken couldn't muster the energy to take off her seat belt. Through the slanted haze, she saw the bright sky above her. She heard the car doors lock as the Lyft driver walked away. Something was in her peripheral vision...a sign of some sort...a sign from one of the windows...

It was so hard to stay away. Drowsiness gently yet firmly tried to pull her into sweet slumber, but her restlessness was enough to move her head slightly to see the inscription on the sign.

Railroad crossing.

She tried to sit upright and found that her seat belt held her tightly. She was too exhausted to do anything. *The Lyft driver's cologne.* No wonder he had been wearing a Covid mask the whole time. It took all she had to move her head.

Panic tried to rise but fell short; her body was too hijacked by the drug to even feel fear at this point. She was in the backseat of a car in the middle of railroad tracks. She was completely and totally alone. But why would VD order this? If he wanted her dead, why didn't he kill her instead of ordering a "surprise for your little girlfriend?" *Surprise,* not *surprises,* she pondered. Mom was kidnapped; why did he have her?

It's not for me, Ken realized. *This is for Aiden. To scare him. I'm the damsel in distress. I'm the bait. I'm what will make him talk, what will make him give up!*

She hated this. *I am not some damsel in distress, needing some knight to swoop in and save me.*

So prove it. She imagined her godfather's teasing voice as he playfully placed down the winning card and watched her mouth drop open. *You really think you can beat VD? Show me.*

With strong determination—and she allowed no other emotions to clutter her already lethargic mind—she channeled all she had into trying to move...

...and nearly made it a whole centimeter forward.

A car's coming right next to me.

She was still and limp again. A car door slammed shut. Voices followed. The doors were unlocked, opened briefly as a person stumbled inside, and then slammed shut again with another locking noise. Her eyes were closed, but her ears were taking it all in. She was unable to keep herself from gasping when she heard the sound of her mother's voice, asking her if she was all right.

Ken's eyes flew open right away. "Mom?" The fresh air helped; she was beginning to breathe easier now, and the fog was slowly lifting.

"Ken!" In a moment they were in each other's arms, embracing in the backseat of the car as it remained firmly locked on the train tracks. Ken buried her face in her mother's shoulder, hiding the tears of relief. So her mom was all right. They were going to be fine. For a few moments, they stayed like that as Ken recovered.

"Oh, honey, we have to get out of here. I don't know who these people are, but they seem very bad. We need to call the police."

Ken sighed, her head clearing, as she looked out the windows. She began exploring the car, studying the buttons, and using her general powers of observation to analyze the situation as she spoke: "Not gonna happen. My driver is watching from over there. If we somehow get out of this locked car, they'll ambush us. There's no way out, and I bet a train's coming here soon."

"No, of course not," her mother argued. "They won't hurt us if they get the ransom."

Ken stopped and turned. "What ransom?"

"They must be contacting your father for money. That's what this is all about. I overheard them talking. There's a man in charge named—"

"VD," Ken finished for her. "He's not after money. We're the damsels in distress."

"What?"

"Aiden has to do what VD says or else VD will kill us." Ken sighed. "I guess I owe you an explanation. I may not have been entirely honest with you about staying at Ravencrest. In fact, I left out a lot of stuff. It's a really long story."

"We have time."

"Well..." Ken braced herself for the predictable reaction. "I joined the Campus Security team at Ravencrest Academy and I ended up putting myself in a lot of danger."

"Your Campus Security puts kids in danger?"

"No! I chose it for myself."

Her mother frowned. "Ken—"

"Mom, I helped people, and I'm not sorry for it. I *will* find a way out of here. I promise."

Mom sighed. "I told you never to make promises you don't know if you can keep."

Ken grinned. "What if I knew for absolute certainty I would keep them?"

"How would you—"

"I just found a way out."

"What?" Her mother brightened. "You found a way out of the car?"

"No," Ken conceded, "but I found a way to contact the outside world. See here? This button connects us to the car's emergency system. We can call 911 right now or connect to a GPS and get out of here." She frowned as she pressed the button and nothing happened. "That is, if we had a key in the ignition. But if we hot-wired the car..."

"You are not hot-wiring the car, young lady," Mom said authoritatively. "It's much too dangerous without the appropriate equipment."

Ken shrugged. "You just need a screwdriver, wire scissors, and gloves."

"You don't have any of those things."

"Actually..." Ken took out a necklace with a small screwdriver and lengthened it to form an even larger screwdriver. She took two metal shards from the inside of her jacket pocket and twisted them in a practiced way to make scissors, then wrapped them in thin sheets of rubber from scratched and molded erasers in her pockets. Finally, she took off her jacket, wrapped the sleeves around her hands, and used the covering as gloves. With hope, she looked up at her mother, who was trying not to smile. This was the Ken she was used to. The woman sighed. "I suppose this situation warrants your hot-wiring skills. But never again, am I understood?"

"Yes, Mom," Ken obediently chimed, having no idea that she was lying very, very much.

Armed and ready, Ken began working, her face twisted in concentration, already imagining the victory in her head. Soon they would be out of here, safe and sound.

As she worked, time passed.

The moment the flight ended for Ruthie and Layla, they rushed off the plane and left the airport as quickly as possible.

"It's already 7:30," groaned Ruthie. "We'll never make it in time."

"We have to try!" Layla insisted. She had ordered a car to drive her and Ruthie to the convention center by planning ahead of time on the plane and using her father's credit card.

By the time they reached the destination and ran to the glass elevator of the connecting building (a hotel), it was already past eight. Both girls bolted across the Sky Bridge to the old headquarters that had been transformed into a convention center for businesses to rent. The Sky Bridge between the buildings was entirely made of glass, except for the ground and ceiling. On the other end was a large door that remained disappointingly locked.

"Are you kidding me?" cried Layla indignantly as she tried to get past the metal lock, then pounded on the door and yelled, "Hey, is someone in here?"

There was no response.

"They must be closed," said Ruthie as she turned and surveyed the situation, looking into the world beyond the glass. "This was the shortcut, but there's a longer way there."

"We'll never make it in time," despaired Layla as she gave up on the stubborn lock.

"We have to try," reminded Ruthie, and they rushed back to the other door, pushing it open—

Except it didn't open.

"Don't tell me this locks automatically," Layla said angrily, pushing against it. "Maybe we should have gotten someone who works at this hotel."

"I saw a phone number attached to the front desk when we were running by there," said Ruthie, already remembering the number. "I'll call it now." She pulled out her phone. "No signal? Weird. It's a Sky Bridge. Why wasn't there some kind of warning at the hotel if the doors were locked or if there wasn't a signal up here?" For some reason, her phone seemed to be acting much slower than normal, slowly loading to create a hotspot.

"Does it matter? We're trapped!" In utter frustration, Layla kicked the glass. It was so thick that the kicking didn't do much.

"Layla, I think someone locked us in here," Ruthie said. "I vaguely heard footsteps when we were running across here. The door locked behind us a few seconds after it closed. Someone was waiting to lock us in here."

"They knew we'd be here? How?"

"I don't know! We went over our plans in the back of the car..." Ruthie groaned. "Layla, our driver."

"Earl's a family friend!"

"Everyone has a price," grumped Ruthie, which was so unlike her that Layla fully turned and saw that Ruthie was holding back tears. "What do we do?" she said at last. "We failed. All of us did! It's past eight. There's no way to get Armageddon to Aiden. We're doomed."

She slid to the floor, her back against the glass. In a few seconds, Layla joined her. Neither of them wanted to say what they both knew was true.

The Hall Monitors failed.

Aiden could not believe this. He faced unmitigated failure. He had so incredibly failed in every aspect and in every way.

Ken was officially off the grid.

Ming and Everest were also missing and officially off the grid, which was very unlike them.

Ruthie and Layla were nowhere to be found with Armageddon. They too had dropped off the grid.

And now, as he stood before the mirror one last time, he caught the dark bags under his sleep-deprived eyes. He grieved his mother. Entering a conversation with VD while thinking about his mother was not a good idea. Yet he had no choice. It was now or never. The deal had been made, the plan gone astray, but...

A Ravencrest sees it through 'till the light of day. That old saying from his mother came back to him, and he smiled a little, despite everything.

He stepped away and strode to the exit, ready to—

He was forgetting something. He stopped, closed his eyes, and prayed.

Whatever was about to happen, he was alone with no options left. All he could do now was show up at the meeting, bluff, and most importantly, pray.

God, please help me.

Whatever would happen would happen. One thing was for certain: it was going to be an eventful night.

Chapter Forty-Four

Aiden found himself entering the closed convention center to come face-to-face with VD. He bypassed the security controls by using clearance granted by [redacted] [censored for security purposes] and stepped into the dark yet grand hall. He flicked on the lights to see each hallway slowly light up, but only halfway so that an eerie dimness was cast over the room. He sat at the desk in the center of the room and turned to face the double doors, crossing his legs and leaning back with a disinterested expression, feigning confidence.

He felt everything but confident. He was choked with worry for his friends. They were all he had left. He couldn't lose them like he lost...

I'm not thinking about Mother tonight.

He steeled himself. VD was about to use every dirty trick possible to cause as much pain as possible to Aiden. Mother was certainly the greatest weapon VD could and would use.

At 8:00 PM in Eastern Standard Time, the doors swung open and in stepped none other than VD himself, smirking, arms crossed, eyes glimmering already. "Aiden Ravencrest," he said as he strolled casually to the front desk.

"Vladimir Damon, how nice to see you," said Aiden, sarcasm dripping from his voice. "Did you have a nice flight?"

"I did," agreed Damon. "But it pales in comparison to what a nice night I'm about to have." Vladimir drew his gun and shot Aiden point-blank, aiming right at his temples. There was a smoking gunshot and silence, and then Aiden smiled back at Vladimir Damon placidly. "Vladimir Damon, how nice to see you," he repeated. "Did you have a nice flight?"

Confused, Damon lunged and grabbed the boy by the neck. VD's hand melted through. Now he understood. The image of Aiden sitting behind the desk was a hologram. The boy must have cast the lights in a certain way to ensure the effect was realistic.

VD straightened and noticed the speaker under the bottom of the desk. He picked it up and said to it calmly, "I'll give you ten seconds to come out before I get out of here."

"But then you can't kill me," Aiden whined. "That's what you want, isn't it?"

VD laughed. "I have thousands of years to kill you and hundreds of ways to do it. This is only a shortcut."

"But then you won't get Armageddon!"

"You can't possibly have Armageddon," VD chuckled. "Otherwise you would not send your operatives dashing throughout the world. We have caught and killed every one of them."

There was silence on the other end. Aiden suddenly found himself short of breath, as if the life had been knocked out of him. He could barely breathe or think or move.

"That's right," grinned VD. "Mackenzie Robscone has a train headed her way. She and her mother are in a locked car. The train comes at 8:00 PM; it looks like she should be dead right about...now."

"You're lying," Aiden begged without meaning to.

"Oh, no, I wouldn't lie to you, little Aiden. Don't you want to hear about the rest of your friends? What about Everest Michaels? Or Ming Xingshi? I send some of our most vicious assassins after them. From my reports, they both were disposed of earlier today. I'll have their bodies shipped to the Academy."

Aiden was still. He could no longer breathe. The world was blacking out, patches of gray everywhere.

"Or Layla Hawthorne and Ruthie Jocelyn," continued VD lazily as he sat in the chair himself and put his feet up. "Brilliant girls. It's too bad I had them trapped on a Sky Bridge ten minutes ago, right when they were supposed to meet you here. Right now my finest operatives are in that Sky Bridge. I have instructed them to severely injure but not kill both girls so they will be weak enough for interrogation purposes. However, if I find Armageddon on them, well, they will both be disposed of."

The walkie-talkie slipped from Aiden's hands. As the world turned bleak and numb, he felt himself losing all hope. *God, please, no...please let him be lying....*

"So, Aiden Ravencrest," continued VD cockily, "if you don't come out in the next few minutes so I can finish you off as well, it looks like I'll just have to wait until I finish Ravencrest Academy. I have a friend there who's going to be of great service to me. He's the sort to finish you off if I give him the word, though he's feeling a bit squeamish at the moment."

"We know about Rajesh," Aiden said, gaining his strength. Though his emotions were overpowering—he felt as if he was sinking into a dark hole—he knew he had to focus on his mission. This was their last-ditch attempt to salvage their plan. Ken, Ming, Everest, Layla, and Ruthie would have wanted him to.

Not "would have." They "do" want me to.

They were alive. They had to be. He couldn't...*dear God, please let them be alive!* He was shaking now, his throat burning, the world growing more feverish by the moment.

"Oh, Rajesh? My dear fox," said VD with feigned affection as he rose to his feet and crossed the room. "He's entirely disappointing, that one. He holds such great potential. And yet he too tried to double-cross me recently. Rather than giving me the intel I requested after twenty-four hours, he tried to stall me with lies or half-truths." He shook his head mournfully. "So I kidnapped him. Some interrogation, some threats, some mind work, and I'll make him one of the Legacy yet."

"You are pure evil." *It's what happens when you let hate take over you.* Despite his grief, Aiden found his voice and managed to say, "You are a hateful, sadistic *monster*. Look at yourself. Killing six teenagers, preparing to torture another, making plans to kill kids who'd never hurt you. Is this what your father would have wanted you to be?"

It was one last chance. One last way to try and make this monster see reason.

For a split second, VD wavered. Yet it was only for a millisecond.

"My father would have certainly wanted me to go after you," he agreed. By now, VD was checking all the hiding spots, inside every closet and under every piece of furniture. "And your mother? Oh, she would have loved to see me destroy you. Didn't you want an hour with me so I could tell you the truth about your mother's death? I've got quite the story ready."

"I have my own story ready," Aiden said, steeling himself even though his whole self felt like jelly. He was absolutely and totally destroyed already. All he wanted to do was fall to the floor and sob. VD had killed all Aiden had left.

He has not killed you.

I won't let your deaths be in vain, he swore mentally to his fallen friends, the ones who had been with him through so much and had ended up dying, dying because of their loyalty....

Through the overwhelming pain of the tragedy, Aiden continued, "You see, VD, I know you're here to talk to me about my mother, but there's something about your father you don't know."

VD laughed. "Trying to get at me, are you? That's not how it works, boy. I already know the full story."

"Do you? Your father was killed ten years back. That's ten years of hate brewing, anger eroding at all your reason, and cruelty being fostered by the Legacy." Aiden stood up. He felt as if he had aged a hundred years; his knees wobbled so that he could barely walk. *Don't think about them, just keep following the script.* "You believed what you were told. You didn't search deeper for the truth. That's not what Ravencrests do."

"I'd rather die than be a Ravencrest!" swore VD, punching a fist against the wall. All at once, all of Damon's rage caught up to him. "And you know what, Aiden Ravencrest? I'm done with your mind games. If you want to talk to me, come here yourself." With that, VD dropped the small speaker into a flower pot, not bothering to watch it fry in the water.

"Fine." Aiden Ravencrest stepped out on the other end of the hallway.

Vladimir Damon smirked. His entire facial expression changed to that of a hungry, greedy predator eying his new catch. "Oh, Aiden Ravencrest. At last. Face to face." He took out his gun, but Aiden stopped him by shouting, "This is your father's!" He held up an old piece of paper, folded neatly. "It has his handwriting and was written moments before his death. It is addressed to *you*."

VD was momentarily taken aback.

Encouraged, Aiden continued, "When your father died, my mother took this note and kept it safe and sound, hiding it in a safety deposit box which only opened to a certain individual named *Vladimir Damon*. She couldn't track you down, but she wanted to make sure you eventually received it. I didn't know until I asked her lawyer if he knew anything about you. He met me earlier today and gave it to me. This letter explains everything."

"You think I'll believe you?" VD raised his weapon again. "I'll just take it over your dead body—"

"And the lawyer told me the full story!" Aiden continued.

VD paused. "You have thirty seconds," he said at last, the gun still held in place, his grip never wavering.

"Your father was assigned to kill my mother. He was an experienced assassin, a professional," Aiden explained, looking straight into VD's eyes. He felt sick doing this, but he knew he had to. He owed it to them all to tell the truth. "When he died, it was not of his own error or my mother's expertise. She did not kill him."

"She said she did. You're going against your mother's own—"

"She swore my lawyer to secrecy unless he had the password, which was your name. The truth is, she went along with your father's scheme. She didn't have a choice."

"What scheme?" VD demanded. "Where are you going with this story?"

In the most gentle voice he could, Aiden said, "Vladimir, your father killed himself."

VD dropped the gun as if lightning had struck him. His eyes were wild. "Liar!" he shouted. "I'll kill you!"

"I have evidence!" Aiden held up the paper. "This letter was addressed to you. He left it on my mother's windowsill. She reported the body. She would have stopped him if she could've!"

VD wasn't listening to reason. He rushed toward Aiden with mad abandon, eyes only focused on the target—

All of a sudden, the world shattered. He had thrown himself against a thin layer of glass so that his entire frame fell onto the tiny, sharp pieces. Looking up past the blood, he saw Aiden dart into the passageway. VD looked up to see the convention center's last defense: the thin layer of glass between rooms, installed to protect the artifacts. Normally, an alarm would have gone off, if Aiden had not disabled and reprogrammed the security controls earlier. He had been very busy that day.

Damon staggered to his feet and followed Aiden through the passageways and around corners, chasing the faint footsteps up the stairs, up to the top where—

Where was he?

The man kicked open door after door, threw over furniture, and screamed threats, but found no one. He pressed a button on his phone and Legacy operatives ran into the building. Finally, on top of a fireplace in the last room laid the little note, still folded. Vladimir Damon crumpled it instinctively, then hesitantly opened it again. The first line read in the handwriting Damon knew all too well: ***My dear Jabez...***

No one else on earth knew Vladimir's real name.

Damon was very still. He was past swearing, past screaming, past running into the darkness. Suddenly, he threw the rest of the letter into the fireplace without reading any more and looked up at the rest of the operatives with a dangerous fierceness that terrified even them to their cores. "Kill him," he spat. "I want every single Legacy unit on this earth to be looking for Aiden Ravencrest to kill him!"

They rushed out of the room as the manhunt began to find Aiden Ravencrest. Only Damon stayed back, staring into the fire, the fire that reflected in his eyes. He turned away to find the door locked. He threw himself against the door to break it down, but the door did not budge. He tried twice more, and to his mounting frustration, realized that metal bars had descended and locked him in. Damon turned to the window to find it barred as well. Aiden had drawn him in here and then trapped him.

For a split second, Vladimir regretted throwing away the paper, considering the truth he had now discovered, almost wondering if...

But after ten years of all-consuming hate, evil was not ready to release its grip. Again, a tidal wave of fury consumed him. He shouted and went nearly insane, foaming at the mouth as he threw himself against the metal again and again. He heard the faint whirring of a helicopter and rushed to the window, looking through the metal bars. Navy SEALS were already opening the doors of the building. He could hear a voice through a megaphone.

He was trapped.

So VD did not say another word. He allowed himself to be handcuffed and dragged away. He said not a word during the interrogations and never called for a lawyer. That day he withdrew so dangerously deep into himself that even the guard to his holding cell felt uneasy near him. In the silence that followed it all, he swore he would take his revenge on Aiden Ravencrest. Maybe now Aiden held the victory, but VD would utterly kill him. The battle was not yet won. Let Aiden think it was. Let the boy believe he had done it, that he had truly defeated VD.

That night, Damon's prodigious mind calculated the plan. Before the next year was over, Aiden Ravencrest would be dead and VD would once again be Head of the Legacy.

It was only a matter of time.

Chapter Forty-Five

Maybe Aiden had succeeded, but it didn't feel like it. Not at all.

For starters, his friends were all missing and presumed dead. Also, everyone was looking for him. He was constantly running and hiding. Most of all, he couldn't shake the feeling that this was not the end of VD. No, Damon's reign was only beginning. The battle was far from over.

Aiden had to find a way to the airport. There were too many Legacy operatives near the SEALS, so they weren't an option.

Normally he wasn't the sort of person who cried, but he kept fighting the lump in his throat. His friends couldn't be dead. *God, please,* he begged, praying to the One who loved him stronger than he could imagine. *Please let them be alive.*

He made it to the street and bought a small phone in cash as soon as he could, knowing full well he was automatically making himself a target for every Legacy operative ready to kill him. All that mattered was if his friends were alive. He called all five of his friends in one giant merge call, holding his breath and praying furiously as the phone rang on all ends.

Ken picked up first. "Please tell me this is Aiden!"

Thank you, God, Aiden couldn't breathe as gratitude filled him so deeply that his eyes almost blurred. "Yes, it is," he managed to say. "I bought a temporary phone."

"Aiden, you won't believe it!" Ken said in a rush. "My mom and I were kidnapped and left us on train tracks to get you to talk but I hot-wired the car and drove it out of here and found a way to call 911 in the process and the Legacy came after us but I squealed the tires and pulled a donut—"

"Isn't that illegal?"

"Don't interrupt with irrelevant information," Ken said. "And so I was like this heroine in a car chase movie and my mom was screaming the whole time and we made it out! Since the car has an installed GPS, we're on our way to Washington, D.C. since I know you're near the White House. It's about four hours, and my mom's driving now. Can you stay alive until then?"

"I certainly can, though it will be a challenge," Aiden countered once she had come up for a breath.

"Why?" Ken asked, concerned. She had half-jokingly asked that last question.

Before he could answer, Everest picked up the call. Once more Aiden's eyes almost blurred with enormous relief as Everest said, "Aiden! I'm on the run for my life. I've been hiding for a while now. There are these assassins after me with the corniest names you can imagine. The *Brown Recluse*—I mean, seriously? It sounds like some bearded hermit. Anyway, he almost killed me, and I've been hiding for a long time. A *long* time. I just disguised myself and slunk into an alleyway, eating a coconut. The coconuts here are *amazing*. Did you know they crack them open and scrape off the jelly inside? It's delicious."

"Why isn't Ming picking up? Isn't he with you?" Aiden asked quickly before Everest could continue.

Everest grew serious. "He was kidnapped by the Black Widow. I don't know where he is. I wanted to track him down, but every time I tried to leave, I saw the Brown Recluse nearby. I powered off my phone so I couldn't be tracked, but since I was chased at night and spent all night in an alleyway, I thought I should turn it on when I leave at dawn. I ended up forgetting because I was finding a way to get some dinner—or breakfast in this time zone—without getting caught, and so I just remembered and noticed that you were calling me. Is this your phone number? Also, what happened?"

"This is a temporary phone I just bought. Do you know where Ming is?" Aiden pressed.

"No! I've been seriously worried about him all night." Everest swallowed hard. He didn't want to think about his friend. "But I know he can take care of himself. If there's anyone who can survive being kidnapped by a sadistic assassin, it's Ming."

"What about Ruthie and Layla?" Aiden continued, his mind spinning. "They're not picking up."

"They're not?" Everest repeated in shock. "They were supposed to give you Armageddon! You haven't seen them?"

"Maybe they just don't have a signal," Ken suggested. "Or Layla forgot to charge her phone."

"No, Ruthie would still answer her phone on the chance that it could be me. She wouldn't forget to charge her phone." Aiden tried to calm his racing heart. "All right. Ken, you're safe since your mom is driving—"

"I take offense to that," Ken interrupted.

"And Everest, you stay in hiding for now. I'll track down Ming, Ruthie, and Layla." He hung up, cutting off their queries for more information. Aiden peered around the side of the building. His Smart Lens detected the gun in a pedestrian coat. He immediately pulled himself back into the dark alley. In a flash, he had crossed the street and entered a bar, where he distracted the bartender and slunk behind the counter into the closet full of glass bottles. He slid behind a shelf full of drinks. No one his age was allowed in the bar, and he knew that if anyone asked, the bartender probably would assume he had left. It was not a comfortable fit; he had to push himself up against the wall to ensure the shelf properly covered him and he held his breath whenever the bartender entered the room. Nonetheless, it was a much better fit than being left for dead in an alleyway.

Normally he would have thought of something more clever, but all he could think of were Ruthie, Layla, and Ming. He was glad Everest and Ken were alive, but Ming was in the hands of a professional assassin, and Ruthie and Layla were to be tortured for information, according to VD.

All he could do was wait, search for information on his phone...

And pray.

While Aiden was facing VD, Ruthie and Layla were pacing around in the Sky Bridge, occasionally kicking the glass, screaming for help, or simply yelling in frustration. Layla's phone had died, and Ruthie's phone was strangely unable to get a signal or work at all. It was as if some sort of phone-disabling device had been placed on the Sky Bridge beforehand.

"I think that car stopped!" Layla said hopefully. She had used tinted lip gloss to write *SOS* in giant letters on the glass, but since it was so late, it was too dark for any car to see.

"That's nice," said Ruthie despondently. "It's probably someone else dropping coins into the hand of the homeless guy three sidewalk spaces away from the crosswalk. The one with an old baggy green shirt who looks really desperate in his gray sleeping bag."

Layla glanced over at the girl sitting with her back to the glass. "Did you even try memorizing that?"

"What?"

"You glimpsed the outside, like, once when we were screaming," Layla said with some amazement. One would think she'd be used to this by now. "You really are something, you know that?"

"Doesn't matter if we're stuck in here. Aiden could be fighting for his life right now, and we can't even give him Arma—" She stopped and did not continue.

Layla sighed. "Don't lose hope!" she said encouragingly, though she was too exhausted from all the screaming and failed signaling attempts to really believe it. "We can still—"

Ruthie jerked her head up suddenly and whispered, "Quiet!"

Layla paused, hurt. "That was rude." Then she caught the expression on Ruthie's face, one of both anticipation and dread. "What?"

"Someone's coming."

Layla glanced at the door. She had used the long, thin straps of leather on the sides of her coat to ensure it remained closed in case whoever had trapped them returned. She assumed a martial arts fighting stance while Ruthie crawled over and peered under the door. She squinted, then gasped and pushed away, stumbling to her feet. "Polished black boots, and they make the same sound walking down the hall as the boots we heard earlier! It has to be the guy who trapped us in here earlier!"

"Or girl," Layla corrected.

Ruthie was panicking. "What do we do? They have to be after Armageddon!"

By now, Layla also could hear the footsteps until they were outside the door. Ruthie was too panicked to do anything other than shout warnings and stagger backward until her back was pressed to the other door at the end of the hallway. In horror, she watched as the man on the other end unlocked the door and tried to push it open, though the leather kept it firmly in place. He jiggled the handle as the door remained stubbornly closed.

For a split second, Ruthie began to feel relieved. Maybe they would be fine. Maybe this person wouldn't hurt them.

It was then that bullets tore the door apart. Ruthie screamed and covered her head, bracing herself for impact as the remains of the door were thrown open and the figure stepped inside. It was impossible to discern anything about them, as they were clad in black, complete with a ski mask. Ruthie, still gasping, straightened and gazed into the figure's eyes. She thought she saw a smirk as the figure raised the gun.

Suddenly Layla, blocked by the swinging door, rushed forward with a perfect roundhouse kick that connected with the figure's head, sending them reeling as her heeled boots ached. She deftly knocked the gun out of their hands so that it clattered across the ground, and then she raised her fists as the figure got back up and rushed at her. The figure began to strangle Layla, who choked and struggled. As the two fought, Ruthie stepped forward, dropped to her knees, picked up the gun, pointed it at the figure, and said calmly yet fiercely, "Let go of her."

The figure smirked and continued to strangle Layla. Their eyes dared Ruthie to shoot.

She started crying. "I don't want to hurt you, but please don't kill her!"

Layla's lips were turning blue. She was gasping, her eyes pleading for Ruthie to shoot. The figure laughed once and wrapped their fingers even tighter around the young girl's neck, causing Layla's knees to give out.

I have to do it.

Trembling, Ruthie raised the gun and aimed. Her face was streaked with tears and she squeezed her eyes shut as she pulled the trigger.

A gunshot preceded Layla's scream.

Ruthie opened her eyes to see that she had aimed correctly: the bullet had hit the glass and shattered the entire surrounding tunnel of glass so that they were now standing on a ledge above the street, broken glass all around them and crashing into the street below. An alarm screeched and cars pulled over, drivers stepping out with their phones to call 911. The figure let go of Layla, backing up once they saw the drivers taking pictures of the scene. Just as quickly, they were gone, racing into the hall and leaving the remains of the door swinging behind them.

Layla was on her knees, gasping for breath. Her eyes were glassy as she desperately wheezed for as much air as she could breathe in.

Ruthie rushed to her, but Layla waved her away. "I'm fine. Let's get out of here." She started after the figure, but Ruthie held her back. "We need to stay in public view."

"Are we just going to wait for the fire truck?"

"No, we can make a rope!" Ruthie peered below her and gulped. They were two floors above the road. "Or not."

"So we're just going to wait for the fire truck?" Layla repeated, exasperated. "Aiden's never going to see Armageddon!"

"We've got bigger problems," Ruthie said, nodding to the distant police cars headed their way.

"They were fast," Layla said, turning pale.

Ruthie tried to act casual as she said under her breath, "We thought this was a shortcut to the convention center, which we need to go to for a school project. Since we couldn't get out of here, we got scared and thought we would just wait for help. Someone blew the door open and shot at us. After the glass shattered, they rushed off. We didn't catch a glimpse of their face."

"You're not very good at lying," Layla worried.

"Everything I said was the truth."

As they waited for the fire truck to drive in, people shouting at them from below, Ruthie gasped. "Aiden! I see him! He's hiding in an alleyway!"

"What? Aiden!" Layla shouted, but Ruthie clutched her arm. "Don't! See how he's hiding? He's in danger. Thank God, it doesn't look like they hurt him."

"He disappeared down that alleyway," Layla said, biting her lip. "Ruthie, I say we run after him."

"No! We have to stay in public view! What if the Sky Bridge murderer is waiting for us?"

Layla glanced at the adjoining buildings. "No, too many people saw us for him to risk it."

"We need to be careful."

"We need to take this risk. Aiden's life could depend on it!"

They glared at each other, fists clenched. Layla suddenly broke away, running past the remains of the door. Ruthie cried out in frustration, then reluctantly followed her. "Layla!"

Layla darted down the stairwell, Ruthie fast behind. Together they burst out the back doors and melted into the crowd, ignoring the people who showered them with questions. Layla pushed them away and took Ruthie's hand. They managed to enter the alleyway as the sirens neared. In response to the sirens, they rushed through the darkness to the other side.

"There's a bar," Ruthie pointed out. "We should go in."

"I never thought in a million years you would say something like that," Layla said, swiveling to stare at her little friend. "You? A bar?"

"What's that supposed to mean?"

"You're just...so..."

"So what?" Ruthie demanded, face red. "So little you just ignore me? So wrong that you just do the opposite of whatever I say? I'd stomp off right now into the bar myself, but I'm not leaving you here with an assassin on the loose, so you're coming with me." She grabbed Layla's arm and half-dragged the older girl with her.

"Wait, just explain why you're dragging me in here!" Layla shouted, trying to pull free, but Ruthie's grip was surprisingly strong.

"Why? You're not interested in doing what I say, so why should I explain myself?" Ruthie challenged. Before she could step forward, the bartender blocked her. "Sorry, miss, but you're underage."

"Did my friend come in here?" Ruthie asked.

Layla scoffed and said, "There's no way—" just as the bartender interrupted, looking surprised: "Young boy, a little older than you?"

"Do I really look that young?" Ruthie asked, taken aback.

"He came in, but he must've left," the bartender finished. "Whatever the case, you two need to leave."

"Do you know where he went?" Layla asked, catching on.

"No, ma'am, didn't even see him leave. Now I'm going to need to see some ID stating that you're at least eighteen," said the bartender as Ruthie's face grew redder in rage. *I'm a 'miss' but she's a 'ma'am?' I'm underage but he needs to see her ID? Do I really look that young?* She glanced at her reflection in the mirror as Layla started to go back outside.

"What are you doing?" Layla asked. People were beginning to stare.

"Nothing! Let go of me."

"Well, if it's nothing, come on."

"Wait, there has to be some way we can track down Aiden," Ruthie said. "Are you sure, sir, you don't know where he is?"

"No, ma'am, I don't," he said.

"How did you even know he went in here, out of all the other shops?" Layla asked.

"This is the only place where they wouldn't look for him," Ruthie explained in a low tone. Then she shouted suddenly, "Aiden! Are you hiding here?" Her voice traveled throughout the entire bar, causing even more people to look up at her.

"You need to leave," the bartender repeated firmly. "Now."

Scarcely had he finished talking when a voice gasped, "Ruthie? Layla?"

Out came Aiden Ravencrest, face pale, looking like he'd seen a ghost. For a split second, Ruthie thought she saw his face fill with relief and gratitude. But only for a second. Then he was himself again, looking completely calm and composed as the bartender sputtered in rage. "Girls, we should go."

"Good idea," Layla agreed, and they all quickly left. Outside, the crowd was looking for the missing girls; the moment someone saw them, they rushed over.

"Should we run?" Ruthie wondered. "Aiden, don't you need to stay hidden?"

"You have the police with you," Aiden replied. "I'll be much safer with you two. How did you both get out?"

Ruthie and Layla glanced at each other. All the tension, anger, frustration, and fear faded as the simple realization hit them both: they were somehow still alive. Somehow, despite the assassins and the near-kidnapping and the betrayal and the double-crossing attempt...they were alive.

They had no time to swap stories as the crowd surrounded them. Firefighters came over, and the police ushered them into a car. As the car drove away, Aiden saw a Legacy operative watching them leave. The sunglasses revealed nothing as the figure turned away and pulled out their phone.

Aiden's heart sank. The battle truly wasn't over.

Where is Ming?

Chapter Forty-Six

Everest was asking himself the same question as he paced back and forth nervously. He was still hiding in the same alley, too terrified to emerge. Constantly shuddering with nightmares of the Brown Recluse stepping out into the street and looking around with unfortunate timing, Everest feasted on mangos from a street vendor. He had stayed in the alleyway all night and was now exhausted from the confusion of the jet lag, the action of the previous day, and the simple fact that it was getting dark in the Ravencrest Academy time zone. His eyes struggled to stay open. Around him, vendors called out deals.

Ming, where are you? He desperately hoped his friend was all right as he faced the overpowering guilt of leaving Ming behind to the nonexistent mercies of the Black Widow. *Come on, Ming...*

Finally, he checked his watch. To his relief, a full eight hours had passed since the Brown Recluse had been bitten by the spider. Since it took two to eight hours for the poison to set in, either the Brown Recluse was dead or in a hospital. Now it was relatively safe to emerge, though he was still on the lookout for the Black Widow and Ming.

He called a taxi, handed the driver the remaining twenty dollars he had left, and instructed him to drive to the airport. The car rocketed across the road, narrowly missing debris, breaking speed limits, ignoring lanes with reckless abandon, and barely missing other vehicles. "Are we being chased?" Everest asked, glancing back.

"No," said the taxi driver, annoyed. "I'm driving normally. Why would you be chased?"

"Never mind," Everest said, afraid that a moment of distraction would spin the car out of control. He was beginning to think this taxi ride was more dangerous than hanging out in a dark alleyway.

As the taxi pulled into the airport, Everest slunk low in his seat and tried to scan his surroundings in case anyone was watching him. He stepped out, thanked the driver, and walked into the airport. Thankfully, he had his flight ticket and ID on him. Once he could talk to a porter at the airport, he'd organize a way for someone to find Ming and ensure he was safe. For now, Everest passed the customs and security checkpoints. He waited until he was in the boarding area with other Ravencrest kids visible near him. Now that he was in public and thus safer, he approached the nearest porter and prepared to question him about Ming. Just as he opened his mouth to speak—

"Everest!"

The voice, full of pure desperation, came from behind. Everest spun around to find Rajesh standing there, gasping. His face was streaked with sweat, and there were dark bags under his eyes. He seemed completely out of breath. The younger boy swayed on his feet as if he was on the verge of collapsing, but Everest reflexively caught him and pulled him to a seat. "Sit."

Rajesh sat and wiped the hair from his eyes. "I looked for you everywhere! They have your friend Ming!"

"I'm well aware," Everest said coldly. He hadn't forgotten that Rajesh was a traitor.

"They tried to use me to find out where you all were, but I kept stalling them because...because I heard Mackenzie talking with VD about someone dying, and I realized that this was serious and that your lives were in danger." Rajesh closed his eyes at the painful memory. "I mean, this wasn't about winning or climbing my way to the top. This was *murder*, and I could tell these guys were really dangerous."

"Congratulations," Everest coolly replied. "You're supposed to be smart. Would've thought you'd have figured this out by now."

Rajesh ignored him. "And then they broke into my apartment and held my mother at knifepoint—"

"Wait, what?" Now a flicker of surprise flashed on Everest's face.

"Yeah, I know," Rajesh bitterly said. "Jerks. VD, specifically. He was there, holding a knife to my mom and trying to get some info out of me. I convinced him to keep you all alive, and then I tried to send him on a wild goose chase."

Everest was touched. He began to soften. "Thanks, man. You saved our lives."

Rajesh snorted. "I wish I had. VD saw right through me!"

"It's the thought that counts," Everest said comfortingly. He paused. "And he didn't kill you right away?"

"No, he just kidnapped me," Rajesh said. "I escaped. I came here to warn you. You need to help me. I heard them talking—they're going to kill Ming. Come on, I'll show you where he is."

Everest almost followed, but he had already been betrayed by Rajesh once. He lingered back. "How do I know you're telling the truth?"

Rajesh rose to his full height. "Everest, trust me," he implored. "Trust me like you trusted me with Ruthie when you first found out we were dating."

Everest kept his face still, but on the inside, he was reeling in bewilderment. When he had found out Rajesh was dating Ruthie, he hadn't trusted Rajesh at all. In fact, he had taken Rajesh aside and had specifically warned him. *She's my friend, and if you treat her like you treat half the people here,* Everest had said, his tone rising in anger as Rajesh looked on, mildly amused, *I will personally make sure you regret it. Do you understand?* Somehow Everest had grown to think of her as a friend and, in some ways, like a little sister. Of course he naturally felt protective of her.

He hadn't trusted Rajesh then. What did Rajesh mean? *Trust me like you trusted me with Ruthie?*

But I didn't trust you.

At that moment, he suddenly understood. Rajesh was saying, *Don't trust me.*

It had been a gamble. Everest was supposed to question Rajesh's legitimacy so Rajesh could slip him this hint. Now it made horrifying sense. They were being watched, and Rajesh had been planted to draw Everest out of the careful gaze of the porters into a trap farther ahead. If Rajesh messed up, Ming or Rajesh's mother would be hurt.

Everest pretended to think long and hard, letting his gaze travel around. He saw no one watching him, but there could easily be cameras nearby. "You know where Ming is?" he said at last.

"Yes!" Rajesh cried.

"Can I ask a porter to come along?" Everest tested.

Rajesh reacted correctly. "No! You can't! Then the porter would be caught and they'd be onto us. Please, Everest, you have to come *now*!" It was perfect acting, almost as good as Layla. There was no way anyone could accuse Rajesh of lying.

Everest sighed. "Fine. Take me to him."

"Now?" said Rajesh uncertainly. He met Everest's eyes, forming an unspoken agreement. Everest had a plan.

"Let's go before the plane leaves."

"Right. Come on!" Rajesh motioned for Everest to follow him, and then led the way around the side of the airport to a back door. They stepped out into the morning air and walked away from the airport. An old, beaten-up car was waiting for them both outside. The moment Everest was close enough, a man lounging by leapt to his feet and grabbed Everest in a powerful bear hug, lifting him off the ground. Rajesh miserably looked away as another man stepped out of the car. "Everest, is it? Pleasure to meet you. Rajesh, would you kindly introduce me to your friend?"

"Everest, this is VD," Rajesh said, not looking anywhere.

"You're lying," Everest said. "VD is in America with Aiden Ravencrest." *If he didn't double-cross us.*

Rajesh jerked his head up. "Then who are you?"

"Another Legacy leader. I go by Voldemort Devon. Earlier, I had a camera and speaker underneath my mask for Vladimir Damon to speak with Rajesh. Vladimir left this part for me, though." Devon smirked.

Everest snickered. "Your name is Voldemort? Like Harry Potter? He-who-shall-not-be-named?" Even Rajesh cracked a smile as Everest continued, "You guys need to get more original."

"Shut up!" Voldemort Devon shouted. He flicked his wrist, and suddenly there was a crushing pressure against Everest's ribs.

"You're trying to break my ribs," Everest noted, his voice growing more strained by the moment. "That's a violation of the Ravencrest Student Handbook for Traveling."

"Sue me," Devon said sarcastically.

"I will." Everest shouted out, "Porters!"

Before anyone could even blink, two armed porters stepped out from behind a nearby street vendor's stall. Both approached Everest. Porter Carter kept her weapon trained on her target and instructed, "Drop him."

Everest was roughly dropped. He bounced back to his feet, unhurt, as Devon lunged for Rajesh and held the trembling boy in front of him. "No one move," Devon replied. "And no one gets hurt."

"I don't think so." A third porter opened the car door and stepped out.

"But—my driver!"

"On his way to jail," the man smoothly replied. He winked at Rajesh, who was still frightened. Voldemort let go of the boy, shoving him forward so that Rajesh stumbled. The driver caught him and added, "Now I suggest you put your hands behind your head so I can handcuff you."

Devon put up his fists. "I'll fight back. You can't keep a gun on my man while keeping an eye on me."

The driver chuckled. "We're doing this the old-fashioned way?" There was a twinkle in his eyes. Everest tried to remember where he had seen the driver before. He looked vaguely familiar.

"I suppose not." Devon pulled out a handgun and aimed it between the driver's eyes.

The driver didn't even flinch. He simply flipped out a sleek, black device that looked similar to a phone. "I don't think so," said the driver, pointing it to Voldemort Devon.

In interest, Everest squinted at the driver's device. He had never seen it before. Or had he? It looked similar to a device Aiden had described, a device hidden behind Headmaster Ravencrest's desk. What was it? Whatever it was, it was enough to cause Voldemort Devon's face to pale before he placed the gun at his feet and put his hands behind his head.

In less than a minute, Voldemort and his assistant were handcuffed and led away to jail. Porter Carter took both boys gently by the shoulders and brought them back to the boarding area, but not before Everest thought he glimpsed an unconscious Black Widow slumped in the backseat of the car. *Could that mean—?* Everest dared to hope as he scanned the boarding area.

His shoulders slumped. No Ming.

As Everest robotically moved to his seat, he tried to find the words to explain to the porter what had happened to Ming. Before he could compose something, he felt a tap on his shoulder. He froze. *It can't be. Don't get your hopes up.*

It was too late. He spun around and cried out.

"Ming!"

In a moment, Ming was engulfed in a giant bear hug. "You're alive!" cried Everest over and over as Ming quietly pleaded with dignity to be released. When Everest finally let go, Ming chuckled. "I'm perfectly fine, I assure you."

Now Everest looked his friend over. Ming did look perfectly fine, albeit rather exhausted. "How did you get out? Were you rescued or did you escape?"

"Both."

"You must have had an interesting eight hours," Everest remarked as Ming led them to his own smaller seat in the back of the boarding area, where they were less conspicuous. He was sitting with the regular passengers and held both backpacks from the hotel room.

"I did," Ming agreed.

Everest waited. "Would you care to elaborate?"

"I would, but perhaps I should take a small nap, I do feel rather exhausted." There was a rare twinkle in the boy's eyes. He was really saying, *I was worried about you too.*

Everest lightly punched his friend. "Tell me!" He was really saying, *Don't ever do something like that again. You had me worried sick.*

Ming began telling his story in a droll, narrative-like fashion, "When the effects of the stun gun wore off, I simply opened the car door while it was speeding, leaped out, and applied the right amount of pressure to the right parts of the body, thereby knocking out the Black Widow when she attempted to attack me. Then I utilized her weapons to create an emergency SOS radio signal. Subsequently, a police officer approached me and arrested the Black Widow. We were brought to a police station. A porter came to my rescue and took care of the Black Widow. Then I took a very long nap as the porter searched the area for you. He failed to find you, though he returned our bags. I must say, you worried me quite a bit." His smile failed to reach his eyes. Ming had been just as helpless, worried, terrified, and panicked as Everest, as seen by how much he had just spoken, which was out of character.

"Well, we're all safe now," Everest said in relief. "Do you know if Aiden's all right?"

"I was asleep for most of the past several hours, but the signal reception is very bad here." Ming grimaced. "I haven't been able to reach him. How did you rescue Rajesh from VD?"

Rajesh intervened: "He must have signaled the porters to follow us."

"I did," Everest agreed. "I used American Sign Language to sign '*HELP*' to Porter Carter on the way out."

"That was smart," Rajesh admitted. His voice trembled ever so slightly, and the others noticed.

Everest caught Rajesh's gaze. "You were also very smart, signaling me like that."

"That was murder," Rajesh said, his voice hysterically rising. "VD, I mean. He almost killed us."

"Let's just say the VD terrorizing Ravencrest is part of a bigger organization that's just as sadistic, sometimes even more so," Everest admitted.

Rajesh was shaken. "And there's no one to stop them?"

"There is."

"Just a bunch of kids? You, Ruthie, Ken, and Ming? That's it?"

"No, there's more of us," Everest argued. "People who secretly help protect the world."

"And I...I was..." Rajesh looked away. He was clenching and unclenching his fists. "I'm going to change. I swear. No more cheating, no more lying, no more manipulating, nothing. From now on, I'm going to be different. I'm not just going to try; I'll do what Ruthie said."

"What did Ruthie say?" Ming asked.

"Never mind that," Rajesh exhaled, his mind racing ahead. "What's more important is getting you all to contact that Aiden person. You said you needed to see if he was okay. I've got an allowance, so I can buy a phone. Just stay here. I'll be right back."

"That won't be necessary," the driver interrupted. "I have a phone." He dialed the number.

"How do you know Aiden's phone number?" Ming asked as the phone rang. "He hasn't given it to any of us."

"Good question. It's not his phone number. I simply called the police station where he is currently held—"

"A police station!" they gasped. Everest was the first to add, "How'd you know where he is?"

The porter winked at the boy as the link clicked. The man quietly said, "It's me. Put me on the line with Aiden Ravencrest, please."

After a moment of silence, Aiden cautiously asked, "Who is this?"

At the exact same time, all four said their name.

Aiden paused and tried to recount what he had just heard: "Everest, Ming, Rajesh, and…I'm sorry, who's the other person?" His voice hinged a little as if he was holding his breath.

"Nothing more than a spy," said Porter Craig in a gruff voice.

Aiden drew in a breath sharply, then said nothing. When he spoke, his voice was on thin ice: "You could have killed me in the cave."

"I took precautions to ensure you'd be safe."

"VD thinks you're dead."

"Good."

"How did you survive?"

"Tales for another time."

"Are you still running?"

"For now."

"Is this line secure?"

"Relatively, but not enough."

"Are the others safe?"

"On their way home."

"Do you know about…"

"Yes."

"And…"

"I'll be fine."

The cryptic conversation paused. Aiden said in a hollow tone, "You'll take care of yourself, then?"

"More than you know."

"I'll see you around?"

"You will."

The line clicked dead, and the boys stared at the phone, perplexed. It had almost sounded like Aiden was on the verge of tears. But everyone who knew Aiden knew that he never cried.

"Who *are* you?" Everest asked at last, speaking for all of them.

Porter Craig—no longer a porter, no longer called Craig—rose to his feet as the boarding call came over the speakers. "That's confidential." He slipped away into the rush of people, and instinctively they all knew he would never let them see him again.

"I was afraid he'd say that," Everest grumbled as they watched him leave out the side doors.

"We never even said thank you," Ming mused.

"I think he knows we meant to," Rajesh said, leaning back. "We should go. They just called us. If we don't leave now, we're going to miss our flight."

Ming and Everest looked around one last time. In some ways, their trip had been a failure: they hadn't found Armageddon, they had almost been killed multiple times, and they had been chased by assassins. In other ways, their trip had been a resounding success: the Black Widow had been captured, the Brown Recluse was probably dead, they were all still alive, and best of all, another Legacy leader had been caught. More information on the others would not arrive until they had boarded the plane. Until then, they could only wait. And pray.

Chapter Forty-Seven

When Father heard the news, he was incredulous. "Excuse me?" he repeated, staring at the six teenagers on the other side of his office desk.

Aiden, Ken, Ming, Everest, Ruthie, and Layla stared back at him innocently.

"You all—" Father sputtered.

"Didn't you receive a call that VD had been taken care of?" Aiden asked. He drummed his fingers on the side of the desk.

"Yes, but I dismissed the very idea that you six had actually..." Father stammered. "You caught him?"

"Yes, do try to keep up, Father," Aiden said with faint amusement as his father coughed.

"I just—I never expected—" Finally, the headmaster fell back in his seat and looked from student to student in admiration. "That is one incredible story."

Layla resisted a yawn. All six students had been called to the headmaster's office the moment the plane had landed. Their luggage was still being brought to their rooms, and they had spent the last ten minutes telling the headmaster what had happened, their voices overlapping as they finished each other's sentences and added their own accounts.

"You don't believe us?" Ken said.

"No, I do. I just...how could six children capture VD?" Father repeated. "I gave you the order on Friday and now it's Monday. It took you all one weekend to accomplish what we have all been trying to do for months."

Everest was already fast asleep in his chair. Ming nudged his friend with his elbow, and Everest mumbled, "Five more minutes."

"Excuse me?" said the authoritative voice of the headmaster, and Everest bolted awake. "Ah, sorry, sir, I'm just so tired."

"Is there a reason you brought us here, Father?" Aiden asked. "We did, in fact, perform a service to this school, and we are all very tired. We also have a surplus of homework to accomplish as we missed a day of school, so we would greatly appreciate it if we could have some rest."

"He means we wanna sleep," Ken added. Even her eyes were struggling to stay open.

"These chairs are too comfy," Layla complained. "And we've been in so many life-threatening situations that we really just want a nap."

Father looked once more in disbelief at all of their exhausted faces. Finally, he began chuckling, then outright laughing. "Aiden Ravencrest, I never thought it would take a simple challenge to get you to accomplish something only your mother could do. Do you realize how incredible this is? The six of you"—he gestured to them all—"saved the school. VD is behind bars. Assassins were caught. And you did it all in three days. This is something that the Society, the trained Ravencrest Campus Security force, and the military services from three different countries could not accomplish."

"And we survived," Ken agreed.

"Biggest accomplishment of all," joked Everest.

Father snapped his fingers and pointed at him. "That's right! All of you are richly deserving of a reward, of recognition. I'll call an assembly—"

"No!" all six shouted at the same time.

"The Society needs to stay secret," Ken said firmly.

"We can change the details so you are all still awarded—" Father suggested, but the others cut him off again.

"That would be lying," Ruthie said, her arms crossed.

"Besides, we all just want one thing," Layla added.

"Something you promised," said Everest, staring hard at Father.

"Something you said you would do before we even began this mission," Ming added, speaking up for once.

Slowly Father's face transformed into surprise. Then he smiled and nodded. "Of course."

Aiden hardly dared to breathe. "You mean..."

"Jimmy, stand outside and lock the door behind you," instructed Father, and Porter Jimmy, who had been silently standing in the corner, was forced to comply. Father reached under his desk and took out six gold seals, each with a beautiful gold engraving that stated: *The Society of Ravencrest Academy*, curved around an image.

"Woah," Ken said in amazement.

"Dude," Everest said, echoing their sentiments.

"You're joking," Layla said in shock.

"He's not," Ruthie affirmed as she studied Father's face. Her mouth dropped open. "He's not! We're going to become members of the Society!"

A smile slowly stretched across Ming's face.

And Aiden grinned broader than he had ever grinned before when Father began the official ceremony: "Do you, Mackenzie Robscone,

Ming Xingshi, Everest Michaels, Layla Writcroff, and Ruthie Jocelyn, solemnly swear to become members of the Society of the Ravencrest Academy?"

"I swear," they said in unison.

Father stood, and so did all the Hall Monitors, except Aiden. One at a time, the Headmaster formally fixed the seal to their shirts until they all wore the golden seal of honor. Ken's eyes were wide. Everest was shaking his head in amazement. Ming was solemn and serious, his eyes full of excitement. Layla was giggling and grinning. And Ruthie was bouncing up and down, too happy to say anything else.

And now it was time.

Everyone smiled in excitement as Father slowly turned to Aiden, who was still seated. "And now, to Aiden Ravencrest," he said. "There is a much more formal ceremony for this with a much more official oath. We can plan for it later. For now..."

In awe and excitement, Aiden rose to his feet as his friends grew misty-eyed. Father cleared his throat gruffly as if he was holding back tears. "Aiden Ravencrest," said Headmaster Ryan Ravencrest, "do you solemnly swear that you will faithfully fulfill your duties as the Head of the Society?"

"I do," said Aiden.

Aiden's face shone with pure joy as the seal was fixed in place. For a moment, his father caught his gaze and Aiden saw the pride in his father's eyes. Father quietly whispered, "Your mother would be so proud of you, my son."

At that moment, Aiden felt something in him blossom, something so filling and satisfying that he knew he had been seeking it his whole life. His father really loved him. He had made his mother proud. It was his turn to add to the Ravencrest legacy. There was a swelling feeling of total relief, contentment, and joy between the six of them. He looked around to see the glowing faces of the others.

They had done it.

The Hall Monitors of Ravencrest Academy were now official members of the Society.

Chapter Forty-Eight

Despite the overwhelming crush of homework and makeup classes, the Hall Monitors were mostly back on track by the middle of the week. By then, they had found out who had made it into Ravencrest Academy's *Les Misérables*.

"Whoo-hoo!" cheered Layla, dancing in her dorm room when her phone uploaded the casting information. "I'm Cosette! I did it! Take that, you no-good, egoistical, backstabbing Veronica!"

"Uh, Layla?" Ruthie tried.

"That's right, I did it!" grinned Layla. "World tour, here I come!"

"Layla?" Ruthie tried again.

"It's time for my dream of being an international star to come true!" swooned Layla, twirling in excitement. "I can't believe I did it!"

"Layla!"

"*This is the best day of my life,*" Layla sang cheerfully. "*My li-i-i-i-i-i-i-ife!*" She hit every single note perfectly.

"LAYLA!"

"What?" Layla snapped, a little annoyed that Ruthie had cut short her victory dance.

"Veronica was cast as Fantine!"

There was a moment of silence. "Wait," Layla said in slow realization. "That means Veronica and I are going to have to pretend to be family."

"Yeah," Ruthie agreed.

Layla slumped against her bed in growing dread. "We have to pretend to like each other."

"That's right," Ruthie agreed.

"Oh boy. This is going to take some major acting skills," Layla said, already looking exhausted at the thought. "What did you get? I mean, *did* you get a part?"

"I'm a musician," said Ruthie with a bright smile. "Exactly what I was hoping for! Thank God. Ming is a musician too and Ken's doing the lights. Maribel's doing set design, Charlotte's doing costume design, Darlene's the director, Amika's the assistant director—"

"What about Everest?" Layla interjected.

"Uh…" Ruthie squinted. "He's not here."

"Oh, poor Everest!"

"Not really," Ruthie admitted. "He didn't really try. I don't think he wanted to get in. A lot of the performance dates coincide with when he plans to meet with his brother."

"Then why did he try out?"

"Because you wanted him to."

"So? Why does he care what I think?" Layla asked blankly.

Ruthie glanced at her. "Wait, seriously? You don't know?"

Layla blinked. "Know what?"

For a moment, Ruthie could only stare at Layla in disbelief. Then Layla burst out laughing. "Don't be ridiculous! I'm an expert at this stuff. Of course I know he likes me."

"What are you going to do about it?" Ruthie asked anxiously. She hadn't realized until now that Everest truly was her friend; she didn't want him to be hurt, and sometimes Layla could be a bit callous with other people's feelings.

Layla shrugged. "Pretend I have no idea! Maybe he'll change his mind. Give it some time."

"You don't like him?"

"He's my friend. I don't know how I feel about him. Maybe I do like him. I don't know and I don't care." Layla plopped down next to her. "I told you, I'm not interested in any of this stuff anymore. After what happened to my sister, I don't want anything to do with it for now. I'll wait until I'm older, or until I know I've definitely found the right person. But I'm sixteen, and I have way too much to deal with to care about drama."

"That's...surprisingly mature of you," Ruthie commented. "Are you feeling alright, Layla?"

Layla threw a pillow at her playfully and Ruthie shrieked in mock dismay.

Ken spun in her desk chair and suppressed a sigh as her mother continued, "...and if anything like this ever happens again, you need to tell me, understand?"

Ken paused. "So this might not be the best time to tell you that I'm now a member of the Society?"

"Ken!" Her mom gasped. "You joined the agency that puts children in direct danger?"

"We're the only children put in direct danger! And for that matter, I'm 16 now, so I can choose this for myself!" Ken argued. "I know how to be careful."

"Which is why you were kidnapped *twice*," her mother interjected. "Is it too late to resign?"

"Too early," Ken countered. "I really want to do this, Mom. Why can't you see that?"

Her mother hesitated for a while, then finally sighed, "Fine."

"Fine?"

"I can't stop you. I don't want you putting yourself in danger, but I can't do anything about it. That is, except..."

"Except what?" Ken tensed. Her mother's tone was getting smug.

"Except tell him."

"Dad?" Ken asked. "So what? He wouldn't care."

"Not your father." Her mother hesitated, then added, "He might care more than you know."

"Yeah, right. And if not Dad, then..." Ken suddenly realized who her mother was talking about, and she bolted upright in her chair. "You wouldn't."

"Walter's a retired military general. I'm sure he'd—"

"Mom, you can't tell him! He'd get as overprotective and worried as you," Ken sputtered. "You just can't tell him!"

"Who says?" her mother teased.

"The government of three different countries," said a voice behind her, and Ken whirled around with a yelp. "Aiden! I'm talking to my mom!"

"Well aware," Aiden agreed as he pulled up a chair. "You've got the volume quite loud, and this *is* the Hall Monitor headquarters. Though if you would like privacy..."

"No, it's fine. Mom, Aiden's here."

"Aiden? The boy who got you involved in all this?" Her mother's voice took on a steely edge. "Could I speak to him?"

Aiden's eyes widened and he stood up quickly. "On second thought, there are other places to study."

Ken paused. "Well, at least stay so I can add you to the group chat," she hinted, and just as she'd predicted, he was gone in a flash. She smirked to herself. "Works every time. I wonder why."

"What was that?" her mother asked.

"Oh, Aiden left. I don't think he wants to talk to you."

"Oh, well, at least give me his mother's number. I don't have any of your friends' parents' numbers, and how can I stay in the loop without a parents' group chat?" her mother joked. "Seriously, though, send me his mom's number."

Ken didn't answer.

"Ken? Are you there, honey?"

"Yeah. Mom, Aiden's mom died about a year and a half back."

"Oh my goodness!" her mother gasped. "Oh, I'm so sorry. That poor boy." Her tone, which had sounded like she wanted to strangle him moments ago, turned mournful and sympathetic. "How horrible."

"He's been going through a lot lately," Ken continued in a low tone. "He's getting better. I think he's turning back to his normal self but...pray for him, you know?"

"I will. Poor kid," her mother mused.

"So you're okay with me joining the Society?" Ken asked, getting the conversation back on track. "I promise I'll do my best to stay out of harm's way. Please, Mom, this is so important to me! I'm actually making a difference in the world!"

"You always have and always will," sighed her mother. "Fine. I want updates."

"Always," agreed Ken.

"And as for your friends' parents' phone numbers?" probed Ken's mom, and so Ken agreed and complied. When she had finished, she was hungry and ready for a break. While leaving, she failed to notice that she had accidentally pressed a button on her computer that recorded all the sounds in the room. Even after she left, the little red recording light continued to flash and glow.

"So I didn't get into the play," Everest surmised as he threw the basketball in. "But now I'm captain of the basketball team, so I'm alright with that."

"I'm still absorbing the fact that you're alive," said Ming. "You gave me quite the scare back in India."

"Shh," Everest reminded him as he went after the rebound. "We're in the gym. We can't talk about you-know-what business here."

"Why not?" Ming asked. "No one else is here except for one person."

"We still shouldn't—wait, one person? I don't see anyone." Everest powerfully shot the ball so that it made a perfect arch in the air.

"He's waiting outside," Ming explained as he rose to his feet, taking his books in his arms. "He just arrived and he's very eager to see you."

"Who?" Everest caught the ball and turned to his friend, curious.

Ming was already at the door. He pushed it open, saying, "You can come in now."

The ball dropped from Everest's arms. "No way..."

"Heya, sport," smirked Everest's older brother, Maverick.

"Rick!" Everest cried, and in a moment, the brothers were together. Rick messed up Everest's hair and teased him. Ming watched the reunion with a small smile and silently left before anyone noticed his absence.

"So your little friend told me about what you did," Rick said as he picked up the basketball. "Saving the world."

"Was he allowed to?"

"I have military clearance. Gotta say, little bro..." Rick dodged Everest's attempts to steal the ball. "You're a lot like me."

"Oh no," Everest said as he strained to knock the ball out of his big brother's grasp. "That's concerning."

"No, I mean...you're destined for great things, you know that?"

Everest glowed. After having battled his past for so long, this was exactly what he needed to hear; somehow his brother knew that. With a smile, Everest said, "Let's just hope I don't have your humility."

Rick scoffed. "Who, me? I'm proud of how humble I am." He spun the ball in the air above Everest's reach. "Captain of the basketball team, is it?"

"You're taller than me, and you have military training," Everest pointed out, leaning back, arms crossed.

"You give up that easily?"

"No, I just wanted to distract you."

Before Rick could comprehend this, Everest grabbed a soccer ball from a bench nearby and threw it past his brother. The ball bounced off the wall and, through Everest's mental calculations, hit Rick on the back of the head, stunning him enough for Everest to snatch the basketball and race past him. Rick laughed, shouting "You little cheat" playfully as he ran after his brother. At the last moment, as Rick tackled him, Everest managed to slam-dunk the ball. "Ha! I won!"

Ming watched from the doorway as the brothers wrestled, and he walked away with a smile. He had called Rick earlier and organized this little surprise.

"Hey, Ming," Aiden said, appearing next to him. "What have you been up to?"

"Homework."

"Of course," agreed Aiden. "Good call on the surprise for Everest. After hiding in an alleyway for over seven hours, he deserves a medal."

"Joining the Society is enough for him. How did you know about my surprise?"

Aiden winked at him. "I have my own surprise for you."

Ming chuckled. "I doubt that. You would have to drag my brother here, kicking and screaming, if you want him to talk to me. My mother needs to remain heavily medicated at her home. And my sister needs someone to take care of her at all times."

"Such as a trained porter or Ruthie," Aiden finished just as Ruthie turned the corner with Ming's little sister on her shoulders.

Ming couldn't breathe, couldn't move. "You mean..."

"If it were up to me, you would all receive medals of honor," Aiden finished. "This is the best I can do."

From across the hallway, little Bai Xingshi saw her brother and gasped "Mim, Mim!"

Ming embraced his sister. The little girl squealed and jumped up and down. "I learned! Learned!"

"You did?"

"Three, six, nine..." Her eyes squinted in concentration. "twelve, fifteen, eighteen, twenty-one, twenty-seven, twenty, a hundred!"

"That's excellent. I'm so proud of you."

She grinned, her face glowing, and buried herself in his shoulder. He lifted her up and his eyes traveled to Ruthie and Aiden. He mouthed, *Thank you*. He couldn't describe the joy he felt. After his acceptance into Ravencrest, he was rarely given the opportunity to see his sister. In fact, this was the first time he had seen her in months.

"Anytime," said Ruthie, getting teary-eyed at the scene.

"Anytime," agreed Aiden. "Ruthie, would you like to take a walk with me?" Her little sister and brother were waiting in the loading dock, having already left the plane. They were with Layla's sister as her brother had a conference overseas. It was only Ken whose family couldn't come. She was an only child, like him.

He'd figure out something for her one day. Something really special.

That night, Ruthie packed her violin and trudged over to her reserved practice room. She peered in, her heart sinking, and saw what she knew she would see: Danke, still at the piano.

Gathering all her courage, Ruthie timidly knocked. Over the swell of the majestic music, her barely-perceptible knock went unnoticed.

Again, louder, she knocked. Still nothing.

Finally, she cracked the door open, stepped inside, and called, "Danke?"

The boy glanced up just as the beautiful music abruptly stopped. There was a glazed look in his eyes. "What?" he snapped.

In the past, Ruthie would stammer and melt away, stepping back outside with a stuttered apology. Now, she channeled her inner Layla, straightened up, and said in a voice as quiet as a mouse, "I reserved this practice room from 9-10?"

"You're kidding, right? I have a recital this weekend. You don't."

"But I was accepted into the musical, so I need to practice."

Danke gave her the fiercest glare she had ever seen in her life. She reverted back to her old self, melting out the door with a slight apology, even quietly closing the door behind her. She heaved a sigh. Her violin practice time had diminished greatly due to how often Danke was there. Somehow the lanky boy with a "don't waste my time" vibe always kept her from practicing as much as she wanted. She slumped against the door as the practice music began again. The boy simply loved his piano. She respected that.

So she clutched her violin case and traveled to her other practice room, where she could secretly practice. She checked both ways before sneaking up the elevator into the Hall Monitors attic, swiping the keycard scanner Ken had recently installed. The doors silently slid open and she stepped inside, her mouth dry. This space was to be reserved solely for Society purposes now that they were official members of the Society. Nonetheless, she knew if she asked Aiden, he would be perfectly fine with her practicing here. But to ask Aiden would mean she would have to admit she was too insecure to stand up to Danke, and then that would be a big deal. All of the Hall Monitors seemed to treat her like a little sister; they were all so protective, kind, and friendly to her.

It wasn't just her. Somehow Layla had become the fashionable, comfortable one of the group, like an bold, witty older sister. She knew fourteen languages, was an expert in world history and cryptography, and had traveled the world. Ken was the puzzle-breaker, the problem-solver, the technology expert, the leader, and also a loyal sister in her own way. Everest spent so much of his time training as an athlete while keeping his love of biology. He was always exploring the science of the world around him. In a way, he was the little brother of the group with his eager, competitive ways and jokes. Ming was his usual self, withdrawn yet fiercely loyal and protective, with a passion for math and music. Despite his constant seriousness, his heart was always good, and he truly was the eldest brother of the group. And Aiden? He was the heart of them all.

The doors automatically slid shut behind her. She propped up the music on Ming's chair (it was the only non-comfortable chair that would hold up the music), lifted the violin to her chin, and began to draw the bow over the worn, dusted strings. Her eyes strained as she mechanically practiced her scales and stepped through each of the notes. When she worked on the music for the school musical, she found herself getting frustrated. Her music was flat, dull, and uninteresting. There was little interpretation, little finesse. Maybe it was because she was so exhausted. It was frustrating. She knew she wouldn't get a chance to work on her music like this again; when meetings resumed, anyone could be in here.

Eventually, she gave up with an exasperated sigh. *I need inspiration. A spark of creativity. Something.*

Miserably, she raised the violin to her chin again. It was getting late.

Suddenly, a movement out of the corner of her eye caught her attention. She turned to see Ming stepping into the room, carefully placing his case onto a chair and gently taking out his old violin. In a moment, he was next to her with his violin and bow poised and ready. "From the beginning," was all he said, and together they played.

At first, they played politely as they ran through the first sheet of music. Yet Ming's tone was so rich and deep, the sound waves reverberating under her skin, that she found herself lost in his music, her notes growing quieter and quieter. In response, he grew quieter until she understood. Together, the music swelled and fell in total harmony. At some point, Ruthie closed her eyes and stopped sight reading, freestyling based on impulse. Ming never wavered, transitioning into a simple accompaniment.

Her sweet, gentle melody and his deep, unfaltering rhythm symphonized perfectly. They were both lost in the beautiful music, the rest of the world fading away as they played.

Finally, the bow came to a slow, gentle stop and the air rang. Neither spoke to break the spell.

That was beautiful.

Ruthie thought it and turned to tell Ming. She stopped short when she saw there were tears in his eyes. She was just as surprised to find tears in her own.

Suddenly, a striking flash of color flickered in the corner of her vision. Her eyes darted to the doors, which were silently sliding shut. Strange, as Ming had entered much earlier and no one had entered since then. Brushing past Ming, Ruthie made it to the doors and tried to keep them open. "Hello?" she called as the elevator doors slid shut, giving her a glimpse of someone inside, standing with their back to her.

"I'm checking the cameras," Ming said, typing the security code into Ken's computer.

"Who is it?"

"Do you recognize this hat and coat?"

Ruthie gasped. "No way."

"Who?" Ming asked intently as Ruthie dialed and called. On the other end of the line, Layla picked up. "Hey, Ruthie!"

Ruthie could not believe what she was seeing. "It doesn't make sense," she said, confused. "Layla, where are you?"

"With my sister! I'm giving her a tour of the island and school. Say hi, Melanie!"

"Hi!" said the cheerful, friendly voice of Melanie Writcroff.

"But there's no one else on the elevator," said Ruthie, her eyebrows scrunched in confusion.

"Why do you think it's Layla?" Ming asked in a calm tone.

Layla interrupted their conversation with, "Wait, what are you talking about?"

"I'll explain later, Layla," Ruthie said dismissively as she hung up. Then she turned to Ming. "That's Layla's hat and coat! I'd recognize her black designer coat anywhere. It's Layla's third favorite winter outfit, and she said her father had it personally tailored for her last birthday. Sometimes she wears that hat when she misses him. All her family's signatures are on the inside tag."

"Could it be another hat?"

"No! See that stain? That's from the time I accidently spilled coffee on it, and instead of getting mad, she told me that now my signature was on there too. She said it was perfect since we were practically family anyway." Ruthie's eyes misted slightly. "What are they doing with Layla's hat? Layla never lets anyone else touch her clothes without her permission!"

"They must have broken into her room," Ming said, already calling someone.

"Who are you calling?"

"Security."

"Why?"

"To stop the elevator." Ming's face creased in frustration. "Voicemail."

Now the elevator neared the second floor.

In a rush of impulse, Ruthie pushed Ming aside, clicked on the small microphone button, and recited, "[redacted]." Stop the elevator."

Her words override all security measures and gave her immediate control over everything. The elevator froze, the doors only slightly open. The figure strained to pry the doors apart.

But Ruthie wasn't finished. She recited, "Put me on the speakers." The speaker control was transferred, and Ruthie said through the hidden speaker in the elevator, "Step away from the doors. We're closing them now."

The person on the camera jerked back in surprise. For a moment, they paused. Then they pushed more fiercely.

"Did you hear me? We're closing the doors in five..."

No response.

"Four...three...two...two and a half..." Ruthie frowned. "Please move! We don't wish to cause you any harm."

"They know that," observed Ming quietly. "Because they know you. They must know who you are. That's how they knew how to react."

Ruthie huffed. "Seriously! I'm sending Campus Security and you're trapped anyway so..."

Her voice died away as the figure reached into the coat and pulled out a small crowbar that they wedged between the two doors, forcing them apart.

"Stop them!" Ruthie cried, pressing several different buttons. For a moment, the doors tried to close on each other, the crowbar holding them in place. Then the doors backed open and the person smoothly strode away, much to the frustration of Ming and Ruthie. She quickly put her violin away before rushing to the doors. Ming clicked the button to return the elevator back to normal, then followed on her heels.

Once the elevator was on the right floor, Ruthie dashed down the hall as fast as she could, her eyes searching for the coat. She found the corner of the right color of fabric darting to the Walkway between the Academy and the Residential Hall. She followed through the bridge, down the stairs, and into the main entrance of the Residential Hall. She triumphantly turned the corner to find...

An empty coat.

It was positioned neatly on a chair. The hat rested on the chair seat.

Ruthie clenched her fists in frustration. She reached into Layla's pockets and found Layla's keycard. *That's how this person got up there.* What was in the other pockets? Ruthie scrambled through the empty pockets until she found a small picture. Her eyes widened and she gasped again.

Ming was now behind her. "We lost them."

"No," Ruthie said slowly, sinking into another chair in shock. "I mean, yes, we lost them, but they left us a major clue."

"What is it?"

"You can't tell Aiden."

"Why not?"

"You can't." Ruthie pleaded with her eyes. "Tell me you won't."

Ming studied her, then said, "I won't."

"You mean that?"

"I always mean what I say."

Ruthie took a shaky breath and added, "You can't tell anyone else either."

"I won't."

She pulled out the small picture and looked at it one more time. Her heart pounded and she bit her lips. Ming waited patiently until she finally looked up at him, her eyes wide and worried.

"It's a mugshot." Ruthie showed Ming the picture, her fingers trembling. "Of Molly Ravencrest."

Chapter Forty-Nine

"I need to talk to you in secret," Ruthie said to Ken as they waited in the breakfast line. Ken held up a finger and tapped her earpiece. "RAVEN, give me something I haven't tried yet. Oh, and make sure I can't spill it."

"Would you like an egg salad sandwich with a napkin?" the robotic earpiece chirped. "Ask the nearest porter for dish #13302."

"Thanks, RAVEN." Ken turned back to Ruthie. "Why didn't you text me?"

Her eyes pleaded with Ken. "It's a secret."

"Can it wait? We have ten minutes until class starts, and I'm hungry."

"Please, Ken," Ruthie begged. She hesitated, then leaned in and whispered into Ken's ear, "It involves Molly Ravencrest."

Ken immediately understood. "We don't have time now, but during lunch, I can 'tutor' you in the Hall Monitors' headquarters. Can it wait until then?" Ruthie nodded.

"After all," Ken continued in a louder voice, "I needed some help with my homework earlier in the year too. I don't mind helping you out."

"Thanks, Ken. You're the best."

Layla walked by, chattering with her friends. "Hey, Ken! Oh, and Ruthie, Charlotte says she saw this picture and wants to try something with your hair at lunch."

"At lunch?" Ruthie repeated. "I can't, sorry, Ken's tutoring me during lunch."

"Yeah," Ken agreed. "Maybe later."

Layla paused. "What subject?"

Ken said, "World History" at the same time that Ruthie said, "Chemistry."

There was an awkward pause. Ruthie repeated, "Chemistry. That's what I need help the most in." She glanced at Ken, who played along. "Sure. Yep. Chem. I could totally help with that."

"Oh-kay," Layla said slowly. "Well, see you guys around."

"See ya!" Ruthie chimed, quickly stepping away. She reached into her pocket and fingered the photo. It was all she could think about.

"What do you need?" Ken asked the moment Ruthie entered the Hall Monitors headquarters. They were alone, which is exactly what Ruthie wanted. The older girl neatly finished her sandwich while Ruthie spoke: "I need you to run facial recognition software on this and tell me if it's Molly Ravencrest."

Ken sucked in a breath when she saw the picture. "Woah. That's...."

"A mugshot of Aiden's mom in an orange jumpsuit," Ruthie finished. "But we have to make sure it's actually Aiden's mom before we tell anyone."

"*Are* we going to tell someone?" Ken asked.

"No!" Ruthie corrected herself. "No one can know."

Just then, an alert flashed on the computer screen. Someone was in the elevator, riding up to the Hall Monitors headquarters. The screen switched to a live video of Ming standing in the elevator. "Oh, yeah," Ruthie sheepishly added. "Except for Ming. He was there when I found out."

"Found out what?" Ken asked.

Ruthie hesitated while Ming stepped into the room and nodded to Ken. "I suppose Ruthie enlisted you to assist us in solving this."

"Where did you find this, anyway?" Ken probed. She sensed they were hiding something.

"Around," Ruthie answered vaguely at the same time that Ming answered, "In the coat pocket of the person who stole Layla's hat and coat, then broke into here."

Right away, Ruthie knew the gig was up. She sighed and recounted everything to Ken: practicing with Ming, being absorbed in the music, suddenly noticing someone dart out of the attic into the elevator, discovering that the mysterious person must have stolen Layla's hat and coat, and finding them on a chair with the picture and Layla's keycard. "I returned the hat and coat to Layla's room," Ruthie finished. "She has no idea about any of this. I want it to stay that way for now."

Ken looked at the photo for a while, lost in thought. Finally, she said, "Here's what we'll do. I'll run a facial recognition program on this photo plus some other software which'll tell us some more stuff. I won't tell Aiden about this for now because, well, you know."

They did know. Every one of the Hall Monitors cared deeply about the prodigy. It was clear to them that Aiden was still recovering from his mother's death; something like this could destroy all the progress he'd made. So Ken continued, "However, I do have to tell him about the break-in. I'll talk with him, maybe install some security software..."

"You could check the recordings," Ming suggested.

"What recordings?" Ken said in surprise.

"The red recording light on your computer has been flashing this whole time," Ruthie explained. "Ming and I thought it was just another security protocol."

"That wasn't intended," Ken said, her fingers flying over the keyboard. "It says here I turned on the recording when I left yesterday. Huh, it must have been by accident. One sec, I'm looking through the record of people who entered this room...looks like no one came in here after I left until you and Ming entered...then it says Layla came in, but that must have been her keycard." Without turning, Ken wondered, "Ruthie, do you remember anything about the dude who broke in?"

"Could be a girl," Ruthie corrected automatically. She closed her eyes and recalled the exact piece. She played it again in her mind, absorbing every note. "I'm sorry, Ken, but my Superior Autobiographical Memory only works on memories of what I consciously notice. Usually it's not a problem since I notice everything, but this time I was lost in the music."

"No worries," said Ken. "We have a recording." She pulled it up on her screen and clicked *play*.

They listened to the recorded sounds: Ken's breathing and humming as she strolled to the doors, the slide of the doors as they swished open, the faint mechanical hum of the elevator before the soundproof doors of the attic closed and cut it off, and the silence which followed. The silence stretched on for hours, according to the recording's spectrogram, so Ken skipped ahead until the sound waves on the spectrogram rose again.

Now the three listened even more carefully to the recorded sounds: there were the doors sliding open, Ruthie stepping in, Ruthie breathing and humming as she set up a temporary practice room...

"Why were you here anyway?" Ken asked, pausing the recording. "There are practice rooms for musicians in Student Life." She was referring to the Student Life building on the other side of the garden and the mini-greenhouse in the center of all the buildings.

"It doesn't matter," Ruthie mumbled.

Ming sighed. "Someone was in your practice room, I presume?"

"Danke," Ruthie admitted. "He loves his piano."

"Why didn't you ask him to leave?" Ken asked more pointedly.

"I did, but, um..."

"He refused," Ming said with a frown. "Even though you needed to practice."

"He has a concert this weekend, so he needed to practice more than me," Ruthie reasoned. "It's fine. It all worked out anyway. I think he had been practicing for two hours, so he was on a roll. It was kinda rude of me to interrupt, I guess."

"It *was* your time slot to practice," Ken said. "You should have said something."

Ruthie was uncomfortable. "It doesn't matter."

"Has this happened before?" Ming suspected.

Ruthie bit her lip. "Yeah," she said. "A lot."

"That's not right," said Ming. "Perhaps we should talk to Danke. He needs to respect your practice time as much as you respect his."

"Well," said Ken. "I'll put it on my to-do list. In the meantime, Ruthie, you need to learn to speak up for yourself. We're not always going to be there to yell at people for you. You know, if Layla knew about this, she'd berate Danke until he'd drop everything and run whenever you walked into the room."

"Speaking of Layla, can we get back to the recording?" Ruthie changed the subject, her face red. "Someone stole her hat and coat, snuck in here, snuck back out, and basically gave us a mugshot of Molly Ravencrest. We need to know who it was and what they wanted."

"Fair enough," sighed Ken, reluctantly switching the recording back on. In the recording, Ruthie dutifully took a deep breath, set her violin on her shoulder, and began playing. They listened as she went through the scales, then began practicing the pieces for the musical. It wasn't until lunch was halfway over that they heard the sound of Ruthie pausing, preparing to play again, then stopping as the doors slid open. By now, Ming and Ruthie had pulled up chairs, sat down, and finished their lunch. They all stopped eating and held their breath as they heard Ming pull out his violin and stand near Ruthie in the recording. Ken turned up the volume even louder.

As the beautiful music flowed from the speaker, Ruthie and Ming closed their eyes to concentrate. Right at a trill—

"There!" shouted Ruthie, jolting Ken. "I heard something!"

Ming paused the recording and rewound a second back. Together, they listened again to the faint, practically silent noise of the doors sliding open as the trill ended. As Ruthie descended down a scale, the person softly stepped inside, and the doors slid shut behind them. Then, as the melody rose and fell, there was the slight noise of a camera snapping. The sound of the camera snapping pictures ended right before Ruthie's melody came to a gentle resting point. Ruthie had lifted her bow, letting the note ring beautifully. They heard the brief moment of silence. Then they heard the faint, rushed steps as the doors slid open and shut. In the recording, Ruthie ran to the doors to call out—

"We know what happens after that," said Ruthie, pausing the recording. She stood up and paced, swallowing the last of her food. Thinking aloud, she said, "So we know this person stepped in while we were playing. They walked behind us, took some pictures, and left. Pictures of what?"

Ming stood as well to reenact what had happened. "We were facing this corner. The person must have darted in directly behind us and stood at the opposite corner, which is—"

"Layla's corner," Ruthie and Ming said together, and they rushed to her corner. Propped on Layla's headset was a small notebook.

"The notebook's in a slightly different position than when I first came in," Ruthie remembered. "They must have opened the notebook and taken a picture. But there were multiple quick and quiet snapping noises. It must have been done with an official camera, not a cell phone."

"Those can still be traced," Ming said, nodding.

"So they must have opened the notebook to take pictures of each page," Ruthie said, recreating the scene mentally. "Then they probably closed it and backed up. That's when I stopped playing and they just made a run for it."

"Let's see what this book holds," said Ming, carefully picking up the book.

"Ken, come over here," said Ruthie, glancing at her unusually quiet friend. "Ken, are you okay?"

Ken was sniffling. "Sorry," she said, wiping her eyes. "I'm just in shock."

"Because of what happened?" Ruthie asked, confused.

"No, it was just...the music. It was so beautiful," Ken croaked out. She didn't know how to describe it, but she managed to say clearly, "You guys should start a duet. You two are *perfect* together, y'know?" She swallowed, cleared her throat, and stood. "Right. Layla's notebook."

She joined them and gingerly took the book from Ming. Holding her breath, she opened it to the first page. In unison, all three of them either groaned, gasped, or muttered, "Oh no."

Every page contained a little snapshot of a member of Layla's family along with their phone number, email address, occupation, preferences, quotes, and picture. The handmade book included Layla's parents, siblings, and grandparents, and included a half-finished page for Ruthie with only her name, number, and photo. Obviously, this was some sort of family scrapbook Layla had put together. Yet this book contained the address for the family's 'home base.' It had information on every single member of Layla's family.

"Now they can stalk her," said Ruthie, who grew more terrified by the second. "Oh no, what do we *do*?"

"I'll talk to Aiden about this," Ken said assertively, closing the book and slipping it inside her bag with brisk efficiency. "I'll inform him of the break-in and whoever this person is. He's currently setting out security details for all of our families, but he really needs to focus on Layla's safety."

Quietly, Ming wondered *Why is this person so interested in Layla?* as the girls agreed on not telling Aiden about the mugshot. "And we can't tell Layla either," Ruthie added. "It would scare her. I don't want her to live in constant fear. She should be protected." Ruthie turned back to the computer. "You already installed stuff in our phones so you'll know where we are at all times, right? Can you send, like, a protective ring around Layla or something?"

"I'll do what I can to protect her," Ken conceded, "but Layla is very intuitive. It'll be hard to keep a secret from her."

"Trust me, I know," Ruthie mused. "She knew how the truth about Rajesh hurt."

Ken sighed. "I know you two weren't a couple, but you really trusted him, didn't you?"

"With my life," Ruthie said sadly. "I was so stupid. I told him *everything*, Ken." Her eyes burned. "He was just so nice, and you could tell he cared. He's a really good listener, you know? Maybe that's how VD found out half the stuff he did, because people directly told Rajesh stuff." She sighed. "My earlier emails were most likely because of him. Not counting my family, he's probably the closest guy friend I've ever had."

Suddenly, Ming stood up. "I need to go," he said with an unreadable expression on his face. Before Ruthie could ask him why, he was gone.

Ruthie reached for her backpack. "We should go too. We still have a while left before class starts, but it doesn't hurt to be early."

"Ruthie!" Ken shouted all of a sudden, causing Ruthie to jump. "I just realized something! Remember the first email you got from VD?"

"When I was accused of being a cheater." Ruthie nodded. The entire ordeal felt like a lifetime ago.

"VD told you to make sure Veronica didn't get expelled, right?"

"Yeah?"

"Why do you think he did that?"

"I don't know..." Ruthie muttered. "Probably to ensure Veronica could keep working with him."

"So she could keep broadcasting the answers."

"Yeah?" Ruthie said again.

"But who in that class would have benefited from that? Veronica sure didn't, since she had to convince everyone that she didn't cheat. You didn't. No one else in that class did either...or maybe not." Ken swallowed hard. "Ruthie, *Rajesh* is in that class."

Ruthie gasped. "Are you saying—"

"Veronica's answers were Rajesh's *reward*!" Ken said in a rush. "Rajesh's reward for helping VD! They must have made a deal or something. And then when you were both caught—"

"The cheating stopped, but I had to make sure Veronica didn't get expelled so that—"

"Rajesh could keep cheating so he'd keep his side of the bargain."

Ruthie could hardly believe this. "Does this mean Rajesh has been cheating this entire semester?"

"We'll have to ask him," said Ken, sitting down again. "Or I could check his grades in that class."

"He did tell me he hated English," admitted Ruthie quietly. She recalled the first time Rajesh had spoken to her. He had wished her luck and told her he knew she hadn't cheated. Now she understood how he could have known. Maybe he had felt guilty about how she was unfairly accused. Or maybe he had planned to use her to find out more about other Ravencrest students. She had really trusted him, hadn't she? And as she was Layla's roommate, she knew the secrets of plenty of girls. She miserably realized how valuable of an asset she must have seemed like to Rajesh.

Her eyes burned, blurring her vision as Ken pulled up Rajesh's past test grades and recounted, "Wow, he did pretty well in that class at the beginning of the year. In fact, he's been doing well for most of the semester." She swallowed hard as she scrolled through the scores. "He's been cheating for most of the semester in that class."

Ruthie couldn't help it. She felt the tears roll down her face as she remembered all her past conversations with him. How much information had she given him? How much of the blackmail had she caused? She quickly turned away and rubbed her eyes. "Poor Veronica," she said in a choked voice, then cleared her throat. "Since she must have been doing this all semester."

"Not the entire semester," Ken noted. "She transferred classes halfway through the semester. It was right before..." Her mouth dropped open. "Oh, no! It was right before her father was fired!"

Ruthie slumped into a chair. "So VD coerced Veronica into cheating so Rajesh would offer him more information. When she finally refused, he had her dad fired. Then what happened?"

"Rajesh's scores went down," Ken noted. "And so did the level of VD activity."

"Less incentive for Rajesh, less information for VD," said Ruthie miserably. "And then it went up again? Correlated with an increase in test scores, I presume?"

"Actually, that's not true," said Ken. "Rajesh didn't seem to cheat again. His scores seem pretty low, but not too low. I think he really tried on all the tests after she transferred. Maybe since her dad was fired, he felt bad about what happened."

"Or maybe he was too scared of what VD would do to him," said Ruthie, recalling her conversation with him. "Especially after seeing what VD did to Veronica's father."

"Whatever the case, VD activity went up again after that," exhaled Ken, leaning back in her chair. "Though it looks like the emails VD sent you decreased near the end of the year while his emails to other kids grew worse. Rajesh must have given VD less info on you in exchange for more info on other kids—" Just then she spun around in her chair to see Ruthie's face streaked with tears. "Oh, Ruthie!"

"I'm sorry," Ruthie said, sniffling. "It's just...it's all my fault. I trusted him. Do—do you think the only reason he asked me out was so he could have a permanent source of information on other kids? Do you think he was just manipulating me the entire time?"

"He really liked you, Ruthie," Ken said, giving her friend a hug. "I could tell. Maybe it *was* manipulation at first, but somewhere along the way, it wasn't anymore. When he asked you out, he meant it. I could tell. Besides, you keep other people's secrets to the grave. I'm guessing you didn't tell him a lot of stuff."

"Not about other people, but about me," Ruthie confessed, openly crying now. "He knew basically everything about me, you know?"

"See?" Ken said. "He knew about *you*, but you were loyal to everyone who trusted you. Since you're so tight-lipped about other people's secrets, he couldn't have gotten much from you. I think he was genuine about liking you. I mean that. Besides, you are not responsible for what he did. *He* lived a double life, not you."

Ruthie took a shuddering breath. "I hope he's going to change."

"I think he will," said Ken gently. "The Dean went easy on him since VD coerced him into doing all this, and no one knows he cheated, but he's going to have to live with that for the rest of his life. It's worse than any punishment he could have received. Besides, he's on a better path now.

Ruthie wiped her tears one last time. "It's for the best that Rajesh and I never talk again. I don't know how I feel about him but..."

There was a solemn silence.

"We'll be late for class if we don't leave right now," Ken said at last, checking the time.

"Right," Ruthie sighed. "Are my eyes red?"

"Just splash some cold water on them," said Ken, turning her computer off. "We'll stop by a bathroom, but we need to hurry. Come on!"

Ruthie instinctively clutched the mugshot as Ken ran a hand over the notebook's spine one last time. Together, they left, anxious and silent. It wasn't time to think about Rajesh; it was time to act. After all, it was clear that Layla and her family were in remarkable danger.

Everest was kept in the dark about all this and that's why, when his tennis ball was caught in the rafters, he was nearly suspended.

The story was longer than that and soon, through many rumors and versions of the story, Everest became very infamous for what had happened. The truth was this: when Everest was talking to Matthew Welsh, he had cut through the performance hall because Matthew had lost a water bottle there during the auditions and Everest had bet he could help find it. So, while the performance hall was about to be filled by actors ready for the first practice, Everest and Matthew scoured the aisles. Everest casually threw the ball up while he asked Matthew where he sat, and unfortunately, on his third throw, the ball went much higher than usual and hit the ceiling, descending to the rafters and thereafter remaining immobile.

Everest had gulped as he and his friend stared up into the ominous darkness of the rafters. It was a tennis ball signed by a famous tennis player and had been given to Everest as a gift. Now it was in the ceiling and could not be detected. That was when Matthew's shin hit metal and he found his water bottle. Everest joked about it, but he kept thinking of the ball. Thus, when Matthew had left, Everest snuck to the attic, ignored all Aiden had told him earlier, and used the secret entrance to travel through the rafters of the school. He crawled cautiously to the boards above the performance hall. On the stage below, Layla was reciting lines and the director was giving feedback.

Meanwhile, Everest used his phone's flashlight and checked the rafters. *Oh, shoot.* The tennis ball was right above the third-row seats, where the background actors were sitting. It happened to be precariously close to the stage as well. Gulping yet resigned to his fate, he crawled slowly and carefully until he was on the single board nearly a hundred feet above the chairs below. He picked up the tennis ball and placed it in his pocket. His eyes caught on Layla, shining under the spotlight. His gaze began to travel when his peripheral vision noticed the movement. In a moment his eyes caught the figure standing above Layla, aiming a phone-like device directly at her.

In that split second, Everest's mind shot to the black, phone-like device the driver had held when they were apprehending Voldemort Devon. It was the same device—and now it was about to be used on Layla.

He acted instead of thinking. Immediately he was throwing himself forward, lunging for the figure with an angry shout of "Hey!"

The figure looked up. Everest couldn't make out their face in the darkness; he only caught the fact that their eyes were lens of utter blackness. *Sunglasses.* Or night-vision goggles. Whatever the case, the figure began to run. Everest was too enraged to allow that to happen. No one was going to kill Layla or do whatever that device did to her, not on his watch. He chased the figure farther ahead until his common sense caught up to him. He was now right above the stage, standing on a board that squeaked with the sudden large weight of a lanky Everest. He looked back up to see that the figure had disappeared into the shadows.

Now he had no time to worry about that. He had to get back to safety. He tried to step back, but the board gave way and suddenly he was hurtling through the air, amid screams of actors below. The director jumped to her feet and yelled in surprise as Everest fell about a hundred feet through the air.

At the last moment, Everest grabbed the side of the curtain to slow his fall and managed to swing through the air like Tarzan. In a move which looked planned, he used the momentum to leap through the air, then rolled to his feet on the carpet. The effect was somewhat ruined when he stumbled back, overwhelmed with the rush of adrenaline. Everyone was staring at him, mouths open. Then all at once, they all started yelling at him.

"Valjean, are you out of your *mind*?" Layla shouted.

"You could have died!" shrieked Darlene.

"What were you thinking?" hissed Veronica.

"What were you even doing up there?" Amika asked.

Amid all the yelling, the adult in the room—Drama Director Mrs. Drillian—stepped forward and said in a very authoritative tone, "Quiet, please!" As the room grew silent, Mrs. Drillian ushered Everest to the door.

Everest gulped. "Where are you taking me?"

"To the Dean of Education."

"But I didn't do anything wrong!"

"You interrupted our limited time for our rehearsal by falling through the ceiling. Not to mention that the area above the rafters is very off-limits." Mrs. Drillian's voice never faltered. "You are in serious trouble, young man. You could have gotten yourself or someone else seriously hurt."

"But I was trying to help!"

"Help who?"

"There was someone above the rafters, and they were going to…" Everest now realized that he couldn't say much without compromising the secrecy of the Society. Guiltily, he finished with, "Well, I just had to stop them so I chased them over the boards, and then I fell."

"Why were you up there in the first place?" said Mrs. Drillian in exasperation.

"Because I threw my tennis ball up there!"

"So?"

"It was signed by—"

"I don't care who it was signed by, but I do care that you put the lives of my students at risk, not to mention *your own life.*" Mrs. Drillian never broke her pace. "Now hurry; you've already interrupted my class because of your recklessness."

Everest reluctantly followed; he had no choice. Along the way he pressed a button on his watch which sent an alert to Aiden Ravencrest. He would need backup in facing the Dean.

Predictably, all it took for the Dean to let Everest off easy without a note in his permanent record was some not-so-gentle persuasion from Aiden Ravencrest, an impassioned testimony from Everest, and a promise to board off that area of the school even to Campus Security. Yet the moment Everest stepped out of the office and saw four girls wanting his autograph plus six other boys quizzing him on if he was really disabling a bomb up there, he knew right away it wasn't over. He fibbed about how he had ended up there, claiming that he thought he saw someone and tried to run after them but fell. From the glints in his audience's eyes, he knew that many more dramatic retellings would push the story even farther from the truth. There was nothing he could do about it.

The moment he got through the crowd, he hid in a closet and let the rush of students pass by. A hand grasped his shoulder while another stifled his shriek.

"Do you want me to tell Layla you scream like a girl?" Aiden said.

"Sure, tell her," Everest replied in the darkness. "She'll be insulted that you accused anyone of 'screaming like a girl.'"

"Fair enough," Aiden conceded. "No more talking. Follow my lead."

Everest obeyed. Aiden slipped outdoors to the garden at the center of all the buildings. He led him directly into the office of the Head of Campus Security. Inside, Ken was patiently waiting, her notebook ready.

"Wow, you really have everything set up," Everest said in amazement. The Head of Security and a few important-looking officials were standing in the corner, watching him intently.

"Please sit down," said Aiden without a smile.

Everest sat.

"Start from the beginning." Ken's pencil was poised. "What really happened?"

So Everest explained about losing his tennis ball and seeing the figure point something at Layla. The description of the weapon made one of the officials suck in a breath. A little unnerved, Everest continued to tell of how he chased the figure, fell through the air, and was screamed at by a bunch of teenage girls. "Now they all want my autograph," Everest joked, but no one else smiled. Even Ken looked grim.

"Someone's targeting her now," Ken said to Aiden, her pencil eraser pressed against her chin. "You have security measures for our families, but what about her?"

"She'd protest to a bodyguard," Aiden pointed out. "I thought we agreed she wouldn't know."

"But she needs a bodyguard! Now they know all about her and her family—"

"Wait, who? What happened?" Everest interjected.

"You're dismissed now," said the officer behind him, and Everest was led by the arm to the door. Aiden signaled to Everest not to tell anyone. In a few moments, Everest was escorted out. He made his way to his room and finally slumped on the bed, his phone ringing. It was Layla.

He glanced at his phone. *I can't tell her.* So he let it ring.

Unfortunately, Layla was persistent. She called him six more times before she finally sent Ming over to fetch Everest. Everest pretended to be asleep until Ming left, but he knew Ming knew he was only faking it.

Why is Layla in danger? Are we all in danger? And there was another nagging question that had been bothering him for a while: *Why doesn't anyone know that VD's in jail? Shouldn't there be cause for celebration? But no one knows. Why is that?*

He rolled out of bed and pulled out his phone to Facetime his brother. "Hey, Rick!"

"Heya, sport. How's it been?"

"Great. You?"

"Eh. Won't be able to talk to you for another month or so. You know how it is."

"Yeah." Everest was glum for a moment. "Hey, Rick?"

"Yeah?"

"If someone you know is in danger—a friend of a friend—and if they had no idea but you weren't supposed to tell them, and if someone else thought they had it under control when they probably didn't, should you do something about it?"

"That's a lot of *if*s, sport," Rick said. He paused. "By danger, you mean..."

"If someone tried to kill her." Everest's voice quivered a little at this.

Now Rick grew very serious. "I would call the authorities. Right now."

"But—"

"Any time a person's life is in danger, you need to get the authorities involved."

"What if the authorities already know, but you don't think they'll do a good job of protecting her?"

Rick seemed to relax. "If the authorities already know, then they have the situation under control. However, if you still feel unsure about your friend's safety, you can generally keep an eye on her and report to the authorities if you have any other concerns or see anything suspicious. At the very least, you'll have peace of mind and she'll be a little safer."

"Yeah. Okay, thanks, Rick."

"And Everest?"

"Yeah?"

"*You're* not in any danger, are you, sport?"

Everest paused a little too long before replying, "No, I'm fine."

"If you are, call me. If I'm on one of my missions, call Uncle Jeremy. You remember him; he's the old SEAL who looked after us that time we ran away from the McRalisons back in ninth grade. I'll text you his number."

"Sure, Rick," Everest replied.

He was already on his feet, reaching for the door. So that was it then. It was time to find out who her attacker was and solve this problem on his own, like Rick had said.

Perfect. What could go wrong?

Chapter Fifty

Layla was beginning to feel paranoid. Four times now she had caught Everest nearby every single time she turned around. Weird, considering how shifty he had acted when she had stormed over and questioned him concerning how he fell from the auditorium rafters. Then he had tried to stick close to her despite her many hints to leave her alone so she could study. Why was it that when she had finally left the room in exasperation, he still followed her from a distance? The whole situation was creepy, so she decided to consult someone to talk to Everest for her, someone trustworthy and reliable who was good at keeping secrets.

"Ruthie!" Layla gushed the moment she stepped into the cafeteria. Ruthie glanced up, and her eyes widened at the sight of Layla. She immediately jumped to her feet. "Layla! Come sit over here with me!"

"Sure, I was just about to," Layla agreed. "That looks delicious. Hot pasta with ricotta cheese? I prefer Mexican food, but I'll say, this looks so good I want to scarf it down right now."

"You should take a picture of it," Ruthie said. "In case you want to look at it later."

Layla blinked. "Why would I want to—"

"Here, I'll take it for you." Ruthie took the phone out of Layla's hands and snapped the picture. "One moment, let me work on some editing. I'll make it look really nice. You'll thank me later."

"Oh-kay," said Layla slowly, feeling very weirded out. "I take it you're interested in photography now?"

"Um, yeah. Sure." Ruthie's cheeks turned red and the color flushed through her face. She fidgeted uncontrollably. It was very, very obvious that she was lying. As Layla reached to get her phone back, Ruthie moved the phone away.

"What are you doing?" Layla asked.

"Just editing this." Ruthie quickly finished and gave the phone back. "Doesn't it look better now?"

The picture looked the exact same, but Layla played along. "Uh, sure. Anyway, can I ask a favor?"

"Sure!" Ruthie agreed, fidgeting even more so. Her breathing was more rapid than usual.

"So all day I've been followed by—"

"What?" gasped Ruthie. "Who? Oh, God, I was afraid this would happen." Already Ruthie was on her feet, pulling out her phone. "I'll call Ken. You have to come with me; I'll explain everything later. We can work with the Witness Protection Program—"

"Ruthie! *Everest.*"

"What?"

"*Everest* has been following me all day! I don't know why! Ever since he fell from the ceiling—"

"Wait, *what*? Do you mean Aiden Ravencrest falling from the ceiling or just normal falling from the ceiling?" Ruthie asked, sitting back down. "Layla, I thought you were in real danger. If it's just another Hall Monitor..." Suddenly, she froze. "Wait a moment. It could have been a Hall Monitor with your coat."

"What about my coat?" Layla was defensive. "Did something happen to my coat? Is that what this is all about?"

"No! I mean, yes, but no. I mean—never mind." Now Ruthie was clearly lying again.

"Ruthie, I know I'm missing something. What happened?"

Ruthie stammered again and looked across the room desperately. "Oh, look, it's Everest! He should come over here. Everest!"

"No, wait," Layla whispered urgently. "Ruthie! I just told you he's been following me all day! Why would you call him over?"

"Oh, sorry," blustered Ruthie. "I forgot."

Layla only stared at Ruthie in amazement. Never in her life had Ruthie ever forgotten something. Again, the color rushed through Ruthie's face. Obviously, Ruthie was lying. But Ruthie did not lie, not unless there was a very good reason. This was so strange. Ken would sort things out, that was for sure.

"Did you call me over?" Everest asked casually as he put his books down on the table. "Oh, that looks delicious. I might have some. I'm kind of hungry."

"Well, I was leaving anyway," Layla said, already at her feet.

"I'm actually not hungry after all," Everest said, also rising to his feet. "I might just, you know, walk around a bit."

This is so weird, Layla thought. *At least I can rely on Ming. I can ask him what's up with Everest.*

So in a few moments, Layla was walking outside and into the Student Life building to find Ming at his usual destination when he wasn't in his room: at a study booth with intense focus in his eyes. It took a few tries before Ming finally looked up. "Oh, my apologies, Layla, I didn't hear you."

"What, are you reading the newest cool math textbook?" Layla teased. "With the latest theorems?"

Ming paused. "Something like that." His hand covered the title, but Layla caught a glimpse: Extreme Security Measures That May Save Your Life. Strange, but most likely Ming was just feeling as paranoid as her. Layla crashed on the chair next to him as Everest lounged a few seats away, subtly alert. "Ming, do you know why Everest has been following me around all day? Or why Ruthie has been acting so weird? I figured at least *you* would be honest with me. So what's going on? Is there something I'm missing?"

Ming shrugged, too-casually gathered his belongings, and rose to his feet.

"Where are you going?" asked Layla in astonishment. *Et tú, Brute?*

"Homework."

"That's not an answer."

Instead, Ming departed with a quick, "To my dorm."

Layla was left in total bewilderment. *Well, the only person left to call is Ken, and if she gives me another half-truth, I'm going to get mad.* With this furious declaration in mind, Layla called Ken, who answered on the first ring to say, "Layla? You all right?"

"I'm fine. Why is everyone so concerned about whether I'm all right?!" Layla half-shouted in frustration as she sat at the study table, music drifting around her. She stopped and sighed. "Sorry, Ken, today's just been weird."

"No problem. Have you called your sister lately?" Ken asked with a much-too-casual voice. "I know you guys like to talk, right?"

"Uh, yes, but she's busy with her work."

"What about your brother?"

"Him as well."

"You don't want to check on them? Or your parents?"

"Why would I need to? They're fine."

"I know, it just wouldn't hurt to, you know, make sure everyone's having a great day. About that, what do you mean you had an odd day? Has anyone been following you or trying to kill you?" Ken held her breath.

Now Layla stared at her phone. Jokingly, she deadpanned, "Yeah, I think I'm being stalked by an assassin."

"WHAT?" shrieked Ken.

"I'm joking!" Layla tried. "Calm down! Geez, why is everyone so jumpy today?" Already she knew she wouldn't get an answer. She frowned and, before her temper caught up with her, snapped, "Forget it. Bye."

Layla hated to be left out of things. Right now, she felt like everyone was in on a secret while she was left out. She hated that. Speaking of things she didn't understand…

"Hey, Rhonda," Layla called to a random girl two seats away who was immersed in some history homework.

"Yeah?"

"Have you heard any news about VD?"

Rhonda paled. "Don't say his name! He could still be out there, listening to us."

"But he's gone."

"No, he isn't."

"You mean, people have heard stuff from him?"

"Not recently, but we all know he's still lurking out there." Rhonda shivered. "This school is incredible, but those emails…I have to admit I was thinking about dropping out too. A lot of kids were. Have *you* received any emails?"

"No." So now nothing made sense. No one knew VD was behind bars? What was this? They had traveled internationally, stopped criminals, used real stun guns on people, and almost died several times—yet everyone here still thought VD was at large! Now she knew for sure that all the Hall Monitors were keeping her out of things.

That was it. She was going to march up to Aiden Ravencrest and make him explain everything to her. Layla left the cafe, took out her phone, and called Ken again, who once more anxiously answered before the first ring. "Yes? Layla, is everything okay?"

"I'm perfectly fine!" Layla shouted. "Where's Aiden? I need to talk to him. At least *he'll* tell me the truth."

"Aiden?"

"Aiden Ravencrest, son of Molly Ravencrest, a total prodigy, who acts like James Bond and who likes to pretend to be mysterious?" Layla didn't even care how loud her voice was. "The guy who is obviously in love with you?"

"Layla—wait, what? You think Aiden's in love with me?"

"KEN!"

"Fine! I'll get him. In the meantime, you need to calm down." Ken was firm. "And for the record, Aiden Ravencrest does *not* like me like that. We're friends, trust me."

Layla scoffed. "Sure. Now put me on a line with him."

"See, I can't do that."

"Why not?"

"Because he's in a very important meeting."

"With whom?"

"With, um...it's confidential."

"Ken, if you don't tell me right now who Aiden is talking to, I'm going to stop right where I'm standing and scream!" Now Layla was losing her cool. "Right here in the hallway!"

"Layla—"

"Three..."

"Layla, please, calm down!"

"Two..."

"No, stop!" Ken urged. "The people in the library might hear you!"

"One!" Layla finished triumphantly. Then she froze. "Wait a moment. How did you know I was next to the library?"

"Um...background sounds? Or rather, the lack of them?" Ken tried.

But Layla was at Ravencrest for a reason. She was a smart girl. In a moment, she was scrolling through her settings. "Would you look at that! Ruthie activated some weird thing on my phone that's telling you exactly where I am right now—and it says here you're monitoring my location at all times!" Layla clenched the phone. "Which is almost as creepy as Everest following me all day! Or Ruthie lying to me! Or Ming just abruptly leaving the conversation with a guilty look on his face! OR AIDEN IN A MEETING WITH SOME CONFIDENTIAL—"

"Fine, lower your voice! He's talking to your dad!"

"*WHAT?*"

Ken massaged her temples. "Why don't we all calm down?"

"How can I calm down? He's talking to my dad!" Layla yelled. Now people in the library were beginning to stare. "And for the record, why hasn't the information about VD been released yet?"

"What information?" mouthed one girl in the library to a nearby boy, who shrugged.

There was silence. Then Ken quietly said, "Layla, why don't you sit down and take a deep breath—"

"Ken, I nearly died putting VD behind bars!" Layla shouted. "I am an official member of you-know-what and I deserve an explanation!"

"VD's behind bars?" whispered someone in the library as a porter began walking over.

"Fine!" cried Ken. "I'm sorry. You're right. You deserve an explanation and I'll give one to you, I promise."

"Thank you," said Layla, satisfied. "So? Where?"

"The explanation? Um..."

"No, where are we meeting? I want to hear everyone's explanations for today. *Now.*"

Ken sighed. "I'll text everyone in the group chat."

"And find Aiden."

"I will." Ken couldn't resist adding, "But he doesn't like me."

"We'll see," smirked Layla as she hung up. She looked up to see the entire library staring at her, whispers circulating. "Is it true VD's in prison?" asked Rohal, a boy in one of her classes. She shrugged and left calmly, finally satisfied. At least now she would get some answers. After all, she deserved an explanation.

"You all deserve an explanation," sighed Aiden as the last attendant of the hastily-called Hall Monitors meeting entered. Each of the Hall Monitors retreated to their corner, dragged a chair out to form a circle in the middle, and faced each other, eyes beaded in suspicion.

"We do," Layla said curtly. "Especially me. Can I go first? Great," she answered before anyone else could. She pointed at Everest. "Why were you following me around all day like some creepy stalker?" She turned to Ruthie. "Why did you, *you*, Ruthie Jocelyn, lie to me?" She faced Ming. "And you were acting all weird, avoiding me like that!" Then Ken. "And you had Ruthie install something in my phone to follow me around!" Now she crossed her arms, glaring at them all. "All of you are terrible liars...at least when you lie to me." Her face softened a little. "Seriously, I hate it when I'm left out of things."

"We were trying to protect you," said Ming quietly.

Ken seemed focused on the floor. "I'm sorry, Layla. We should have told you. We just didn't want you to worry."

"It's just that—" Everest began, but Aiden interrupted, "I'll tell her. I don't want to tell her too much startling information at once."

Ruthie burst out, "Layla, there's this person who stole your clothes and tried to use your keycard to break into the attic and they took pictures of your scrapbook so now they can stalk you and your family and we're all just really worried about you!" in one long breath.

Aiden sighed. "So much for limiting startling information."

"Oh, and they tried to kill you back in the performance hall," Everest finished. "That's why I fell from the ceiling—not like Aiden Ravencrest falling from the ceiling, more like just terrified, screaming falling from the ceiling."

"There's a difference?" Ken asked blankly.

Aiden frowned. "There's clearly a difference."

"I'm just kidding," Ken said with a laugh. "Just trying to brighten the mood, y'know?"

"Wait a moment," Layla said slowly. "So someone's been trying to kill me?"

"Yeah," said Ken.

"That's why you've been following me?" Layla asked Everest. "Not because you like me?"

Everest's face turned red and he began to sputter. "Me? Like you? No, no, of course not—"

"He means no," said Ming, coming to his friend's defense. "That was not the reason he followed you. He was hoping to protect you as a friend. I believe he hoped to intercept the attacker if they tried to hurt you again, so he could discover their identity and protect you at the same time. He was only trying to help."

"And you were too," Layla said, touched. "Even Ruthie lied for me. That's a lot, coming from her."

"I'm sorry I didn't tell you the truth," Ruthie said regretfully.

"So am I," said Ken, finally looking up at Layla.

"It's all true," Aiden confirmed.

"It's okay! It's fine," Layla said in relief. "Now I know why you guys are all so freaked out. Well, guess what, you don't need to worry. I know who the person in the rafters is." With a smug smile, she plopped back down into her seat and crossed her arms.

"Who?" almost all of them shouted at once.

"Guess," she said with a grin.

They all groaned. "Layla!"

"Seriously, guess!" Layla asked. "Come on, guys, I want to hear what you can come up with!"

Ruthie bit her lip. "You-know-who?"

"Voldemort?" Layla said in confusion until Ken whispered into her ear, "She means Rajesh."

"Oh!" Layla said in surprise. "Oh, no, not him. I haven't heard from him in a while."

Everest tilted his head. "A younger or newer porter?"

"No, but you're closer," Layla encouraged.

"Veronica? Any of the actors from the musical?" Ming guessed. "Or perhaps a photographer you hired?"

"No, but good guesses," Layla admitted.

Aiden stood. "Sophia Manchester."

Now a sudden silence fell over the group. All the other heads swiveled to see if the guess was right. Layla's mouth dropped open. "How on earth did you guess that? Everyone here was told that she dropped out. How could you have...unless..."

"That's the real reason I called everyone here today," Aiden finished. "I found out the truth." He walked to the doors. "And now you will too."

The doors slid open soundlessly, revealing Sophia Manchester dressed in Layla's hat and coat, tipping the end of the hat at them with a little flair. "Missed me?"

Chapter Fifty-One

"You didn't drop out?" Ken asked in astonishment while Ruthie jumped to her feet, exclaiming "Sophia! You're okay!"

"Hey, Ruthie," said Sophia, melting a little at Ruthie's reaction. "Nice to see you too."

Layla remained relaxed in her chair as she turned to the rest of the Hall Monitors. "You see, I lent Sophia Manchester my hat and coat because she needed to blend in while staying here so no one else recognized her. My keycard was in her pocket because she needed to come up here. I knew where she was all along. In fact, she was worried about my safety too. That's why she was in the auditorium ceiling."

"So…I almost died, but it wasn't because of a dangerous assassin, just some girl?" Everest said in disgust.

"Excuse you," Sophia interjected. "I'm much worse than a dangerous assassin. And as for the 'some girl' part, my existence on this island is a secret to everyone except for the Society, so I need to just be 'some girl' for now."

"Why didn't you tell us?" Ming asked Layla. "You must have known about this ever since we got back."

"Because Sophia told me it was a matter of national security," Layla said. "The first day I got back, I glimpsed her and went running after her, and then she convinced me to keep quiet about it. Besides, she has her own story. Sophia?"

"I'll take it from here," Sophia said, regally strolling into the room and casting her hat and coat onto Layla's chair with a flourish. She tossed her hair back and grinned at them all, suddenly looking like a normal teenage girl. "Guess what? I'm an honorary member of the Society!"

"What?" the rest repeated in shocked unison, except for Aiden, who hid a smile.

"You see," Sophia continued, "after I dropped out of Ravencrest, I wanted to find out who told. Pretty soon I realized that you guys really were innocent. I returned home, and my parents kicked me out." Her smile faded. "But my brother took me in for a bit. Since I had to wait for the next semester to continue my education, and since he was busy with his jobs, I had some free time on my hands. I was still pretty down about being the first RA dropout—"

"Why did you drop out?" Ruthie blurted.

Sophia looked down at her feet. "It wasn't just the rumors. It was the constant anxiety and terror that I was being watched and studied. It just got worse and worse, and my parents' self-absorbance didn't help, and then you guys supposedly told people my secret...and it just broke the last straw." She looked up. "I swear I know now you guys didn't do it."

"What happened next?" Ken probed.

Sophia glanced at her. "I'm getting there. I was so miserable and depressed that my brother was really worried about me. We couldn't afford counseling or a therapist. After all, he was working two jobs to take care of us both, so we didn't have the money or transportation available for me to regularly get professional help. So he read off a mental health website and told me to write out my feelings. Anyways, I went ahead, but the more I typed, the angrier I got. I wrote this seething, horrible email to Ravencrest Academy, but I couldn't work up the nerve to send it. The email just sat in my inbox for days while the Academy kept emailing me, asking me to change my mind. I didn't think VD would contact me since I was kind of out of the way, but he did. Apparently, he read the email and thought I might be helpful because of how much I seemed to hate Ravencrest. He basically sent me a job offer."

Even Everest was absorbed. "Did you accept it?"

"Yep."

Layla inhaled sharply. "That was a very—"

"Stupid thing to do," Everest finished. "VD would just use you to hurt more kids and turn you into his henchmen, er, henchwomen. You shouldn't have done it."

"—stupid thing to do," Layla finished as well. "But not because of what Everest said. You could have gotten yourself killed. These people are dangerous; you know that!"

"But you had a plan," Ruthie observed.

"Finish the story!" Ken yelled.

Sophia tried not to laugh at their eagerness as she continued, "Well, I didn't accept the offer because I wanted to work with VD. No, I'm smarter than that, believe it or not." She paused. "That was a joke." Everyone shouted at her to finish, so she hurriedly continued, "See, I knew who VD was. When he said I should join him, I immediately hated the thought. I realized I didn't hate Ravencrest; I hated all I had gone through there. It wasn't the school's fault; it was this monster's fault. So I decided to go after him instead, just not out of revenge—"

"Smarter than me," Aiden quietly said under his breath.

Ming overheard and added, "You lost everything. It's understandable."

"But not justifiable. Wrong is wrong." Aiden sighed. "And my actions would have been irreversible."

Sophia coughed. "Am I interrupting you two?"

"Go on," Aiden said with dignity as the others screamed at them.

So Sophia went on: "I joined him because I thought I could be a sort of double agent and keep him from hurting anyone else."

"Did your brother know?" Ruthie anxiously asked.

"No, but he did know something was up. See, I already basically graduated high school before coming here. That's why I'm trying to graduate college while I'm here," Sophia continued. "While I was at Ravencrest, I was one of the top students, and I scored a deal with an Admissions Officer to go to their school after I graduated. I talked to them, and they're still giving me the scholarship. According to the officer, I can start school there next year. I'm pretty excited."

"That's great!" said Ruthie, relieved that Sophia still had a wonderful future ahead of her.

"So I have the rest of this school year plus summer break to just do whatever. The problem is, I'm not used to...well, not doing anything. I'm usually always working, you know? So not having anything to do was weird. I was lounging around at my brother's place, thinking of getting a job since he was behind on the rent, and then I got the email. I had a new mission, and my brother definitely noticed the change in me."

"And then?" Ken asked impatiently.

"I snuck out and met with a Legacy member at a café. I ordered the one-day special of dark chocolate bubble tea with black pearls and whipped cream." Her nose wrinkled. "That was the code. I was the only person to order it. It tasted awful, and boba tea is never supposed to come in contact with whipped cream, but at least I followed the directions in the email."

At this, Everest interrupted: "What kind of code is that? Bubble tea, really?"

"It's boba tea," Ming and Ruthie automatically corrected at once.

"Finish!" Ken cried.

Sophia chuckled. "So he told me to come with him. I followed him until I saw a car. Then I knew I'd made a mistake. I tried to run, but he just picked me up and threw me into the backseat. So I was kidnapped and seriously freaked out...until I met VD and he was basically like, 'Sorry about kidnapping you and stalking you and putting you through all that, but hey, at least you get to be a Legacy member now! You start training tomorrow or else we kill you to keep you silent.' Of course, I was laughing nervously and was like, 'Sure!'" Now her smile was gone. "I had no idea what I was agreeing to. They faked my death and sent an empty car off a cliff. My parents and brother were told that I was dead, and the funeral was postponed as people searched for my body." She shuddered. "So there I was, trained to be a Legacy member. Trained to defend myself, to use weapons, and to kill. I learned how to decode letters, how to disarm bombs, how to pull off heists..."

"That sounds *so* cool," Layla said enviously.

"There was psychology training too," Sophia said, shuddering more. "It was awful. We learned how to torture people, how to manipulate and gaslight others—oh, and my personal 'favorite' was how to numb yourself so you feel nothing and can resist any human need."

"I take it back," said Layla. "You had me horrified at 'torture.'"

"You did all that training in, what, a month or so?" Ken asked in amazement.

"No, I just learned the basics. Thankfully, we never got to the darkness class, but I heard plenty of stories and saw the effects," Sophia said. "I considered escaping, but that attempt led to me finding out about my faked death. That was when I realized I had no choice. If I escaped, the Legacy would hunt me down until I was dead."

"There's a darkness class?" Everest said. "What, to keep you from being afraid of the dark?"

"No," said Sophia quietly, "to teach you to become darkness." There was a haunted look in her eyes that said she didn't want to talk about it. "I'm just glad I got out before that."

"How did you get out?" Ming asked softly.

"Well, I worked out a plan to escape, but I had to wait for a good opportunity," Sophia said, resting now in a comfortable chair. "So I skipped some classes and waited. At the beginning of my training, there was this one supervisor there who seemed familiar, and I recognized him as Porter Craig. He had a pre-bought ticket in his pocket to get to Ravencrest Academy for a mission. It was easy to swipe it during our conversation and trade it in for a ticket with my name on it."

"So you snuck out and found a way to Ravencrest," Layla finished triumphantly.

Ruthie grinned. "Porter Craig was on our side, Sophia! He was probably letting you get away."

"Seriously?" Sophia gaped. "Huh. Who knew? He was a good actor."

Ken grumbled, "And now Legacy operatives are actively looking for you. Wonderful."

"She made it here shortly before we did," Aiden explained. "The porters kept her safe until our return. Then I intervened. I've been secretly corresponding with her. All the secrecy is for her own safety, of course. She is now an honorary, unofficial Society member."

"Working on the unofficial part," Sophia said cheerfully.

"Then why'd you take pictures of Layla's stuff?" Ken asked.

"Because Aiden wanted my help in arranging protection for you all since he was catching up on his schoolwork. I promised him I had it under control, but then I remembered Layla's scrapbook and thought I could use it to provide protection for her family," Sophia answered.

Aiden added, "Sophia and I have had limited communication to keep her safe, so I didn't find out about the misunderstanding until recently."

Sophia added, "Oh, and it's so cute that Ruthie was in Layla's scrapbook. It looked like it was only for your family, so you must think of Ruthie as a sister now."

"Really?" Ruthie said, her eyes misting.

"You're practically part of my family," Layla said with a smile. She glanced at Sophia with a slight frown. "It was supposed to be a surprise."

"Oh, I'm sorry," Sophia apologized. "I didn't know. Oh, and Ruthie, while I'm apologizing, I'm sorry about sneaking in here behind you while you were practicing with Ming yesterday. By the way, you two sound *incredible*. I had tears in my eyes. It was perfect harmony."

"I know," Ruthie agreed. "We really did play in perfect harmony."

"Not just the music, I mean—" Sophia began, but Ming interrupted, "What about Everest?"

"That's right!" said Everest. "What were you doing in the auditorium aiming stuff at Layla? You were going to kill her!"

"No, I wasn't. I was going to see if I could set up a camera system so I could keep an eye on all that was happening in the auditorium without bothering anyone," Sophia replied. "Aiden kind of hired me as the Hall Monitors' unofficial bodyguard, at least until my first term at Harvard starts next year. As I said, they offered me nearly a full scholarship, which is very cool."

"The remaining money will be covered by the school," Aiden added.

Sophia groaned. "For the last time, Aiden, I don't need payment! I *want* to help."

"Very well, but with your inability to earn money and the unlikelihood of your family supporting you once you begin your term..." Aiden hinted.

Sophia frowned. "My brother might help."

"I thought you said he thinks you're dead," Layla pointed out.

Sophia smiled a little. "I have my ways. I've sent him a few inconspicuous messages that I'm still around."

"Is he looking for you?" Everest asked. "I know my brother would." Ming glanced at his friend. They both knew Rick would search the ends of the earth to ensure Everest was safe. Then again, Rick had enough resources to do so. It didn't sound like Layla's brother did.

Sophia sighed. "I hope not. Then again, my brother is a lot smarter and more resourceful than he thinks."

"Hold on!" Ken interjected. "Let me get this straight. You were never in any danger, Layla?"

"No," Layla admitted, looking a little disappointed.

"That's not true," Aiden interjected.

Layla's eyes brightened. "Really? Who's after me?"

"All seven of us have Legacy members searching the globe for us," Aiden summarized. "Our only mission right now is to lay low. Until we know that the Legacy is no longer the Society's highest concern, we need to keep quiet about VD's capture as well. Until then, none of you can leave this island unless I organize a highly certified team to watch your every move."

"Think 'Secret Service for the US President' kind of security," Sophia clarified.

"So we just do homework and wait?" complained Everest. "Can't we do *something*?"

"Staying safe *is* doing something," Aiden said firmly.

"Don't tell me you're complaining about being a Ravencrest student," Sophia said sternly. "There's a lot I would give up to be in your place."

"Fair enough," agreed Everest.

Layla sighed. "Honestly, I guess we've got enough to do here."

"It can get a little overwhelming," Ruthie agreed.

Layla slumped in her chair. "Tell me about it. I underestimated how much work the musical would be. It's totally worth it, but..."

Before the conversation could dissolve into small talk, Aiden cleared his throat and ended with, "That should conclude our emergency meeting. I hope you all are at ease now. Is there anything else anyone wants to add?"

"Tell me the next time you all want to stalk me," said Layla. "I don't like being left out of things."

"Don't worry about me," said Sophia. "I can take care of myself. I'll be fine."

"Sorry about being so creepy, Layla. Oh, and glad to see you're back, Soph," Everest said.

"Don't call me Soph," Sophia scowled.

"Anything else?" Aiden said, getting them back on track.

There was a pause. Ken had been strangely silent the entire time. Her eyes kept darting to Ruthie, then back to the group in an attempt to look casual. Only Ruthie picked up on this; well, so did Aiden, but he trusted Ken enough to believe that it wasn't anything that needed to be brought to his attention. So when Ken stood up to go down to use the bathroom, Ruthie followed after a reasonable interval. Ming noted her absence as the rest caught Sophia up on all that had happened on the Hall Monitors' end. No one seemed to notice him as he slipped out of the attic and down the elevator to follow the girls.

Chapter Fifty-Two

"What is it?" Ruthie asked Ken in a low tone as they quickly walked down the hallway.

"I'll tell you in the bathroom," answered Ken without looking at her. In a moment they were inside the deserted girls' bathroom, the door closing behind them. Ken cranked up the water faucet until the water was rushing as loud as it could go, all while Ruthie waited patiently. Finally, Ken whispered in Ruthie's ear, "I found out more about the picture."

"What did you find?" Ruthie whispered back. Her heart was pounding as she eyed the door. She was terrified that someone would burst in and catch them standing there so guiltily.

"I ran some facial features software and found that the picture was taken when the subject was approximately sixteen years old," Ken said. She swallowed hard. "She has the right facial feature ratios. The woman in the picture is definitely Molly Ravencrest."

Ruthie processed this. "That doesn't make sense. At sixteen, Molly Ravencrest was under the care of her parents. She was a legal minor; this had to have been her third offense, and she must've done something really bad to be put into jail at such a young age. I mean, if she committed a crime at sixteen, she should have been in juvenile detention, not jail."

Ken continued, "That's the weird part. There are no records of Molly Ravencrest ever being sent to jail. *Ever*. I searched everywhere on the Internet, and I even used top-secret clearance. She was never, ever sent to jail in her entire life. She's visited jails before, but she was never an inmate."

"Then what about the picture?" Ruthie said in confusion.

"I highly doubt it was photoshopped, though it could be a deepfake. But now that I know it's Sophia and that she's here to protect us, I can't help but wonder why she would photoshop this. It doesn't make any sense."

Ruthie was bewildered as well. "So Molly Ravencrest never went to jail. Then how did Sophia find a mugshot of her in a prison uniform?"

"We have to ask Sophia," Ken summed. "Can we tell Aiden? It feels so wrong to keep this from him. I mean, it's his mom."

"I know what you mean, but we can't," Ruthie said. "It'll crush him if this really is his mom. If he knew that his mother could have been a criminal and hid it from him, he might not handle it well. And he's doing so much better now."

Ken sighed. "True. Also, speaking of people doing better now, how are things with Rajesh?"

Ruthie stared at her feet. "Things are okay. We haven't talked in a while, though I did see him recently. I thought things would be tense between us, but he's a lot more honest now. He's starting to change for the better, and I'm glad. I'm praying for him."

Ken was relieved. "If you need anything, just let me know, okay?"

"I will. How are things with your godfather?"

"What?"

"You feel guilty about keeping all this a secret from him, don't you? Just like you feel guilty about keeping this photo a secret from Aiden." Ruthie squeezed Ken's hand. "I get it. It's got to be hard since you're so close to both of them."

"Do you psychoanalyze all your friends?" Ken asked, a little startled.

"Usually," Ruthie answered honestly. "It's become a habit."

Ken leaned back and crossed her arms. "What about me now?"

Ruthie studied her. "Using my powers of observation, you are...currently missing your godfather...wanting to talk to your mother...and feeling guilty about keeping a secret from Aiden Ravencrest."

Ken's mouth dropped open. "How—"

"Oh, and you're in love with Aiden Ravencrest," Ruthie finished with a sneaky grin.

Ken scowled. "Now I know you're not serious. You heard that from Layla."

"I did," Ruthie admitted. "I just wanted to see your reaction."

"How did you get all the other stuff?" Ken asked in amazement.

Ruthie mysteriously winked. "I can't reveal my secrets."

Ken was getting suspicious. "Wait a moment. I see that look in your eye. All those observations about me...didn't I tell you all that stuff earlier?"

"Yep."

"Ruthie!"

"What? You were so excited to see my 'powers of observation,' remember?" teased Ruthie good-naturedly. By now they had switched off the water faucet and were pushing the bathroom door open. It was then that they found Ming lounging at the water fountain directly outside the girls' bathroom. Both girls froze at the sight of him. Then Ken said casually, "Oh hi, Ming! Did everyone leave already?" at the same time that Ruthie blurted, "You heard everything, didn't you?"

Ming only smiled. "I saw you leave and brought Sophia."

Sophia had been standing behind them in the shadows. Now, she stepped out where they could see her. Ruthie yelped at her sudden appearance as she spoke: "To answer your question, Ruthie—yes, we heard every word. I put a tracker on you when you left the room."

"What?" Ruthie frowned. "You tracked me?"

"Like it or not, I am your bodyguard as well," Sophia said. "You two aren't as discreet as you might think. Aiden, Ming, and I all noticed your absence; even Layla asked where you two had gone, and Everest was pretty surprised to see that Ming had disappeared."

"He noticed my absence?" said Ming in surprise. "People rarely do."

"Oh, he noticed it the moment you left. He was the only one of us who caught it, though," Sophia said with some embarrassment.

Ruthie crossed her arms. "What if I really needed to go to the bathroom?"

"Then you wouldn't have looked at Ken like that or left at the precise time you did," said Sophia. "Anyway, I take it that you all found my photo? I left it so you could do some of the fact-checking for me. Now we know that Molly Ravencrest, the once-esteemed—"

"Shh!" Ruthie and Ken said at once. Even Ming was alarmed.

Sophia lowered her voice. "My apologies. But Ken just confirmed it. There's no other explanation. We have to tell Aiden. He still idolizes his mother, you know. He thinks she's perfect."

"This would crush him," Ruthie said in a quiet voice. "Please don't."

"Then what do we do?" sighed Sophia. "Forget about it? If his mother was once in prison, and there aren't any other records of it, she must know some way to destroy legal documents or change history however she likes. Besides, if she can make her crimes disappear, how many other unrecorded crimes did she commit?"

"Wait a moment," said Ken abruptly. "You know that there aren't any records of her imprisonment? Then where did you get this?"

"VD had it under his desk," Sophia explained.

Ruthie groaned and slumped against the wall miserably. "So it *is* Molly Ravencrest. There's no denying it."

"Aiden will eventually find out. He may as well hear it from us," Ming said.

"No," Ken said.

"Ken—" Ming began.

Ken cut him off, her eyes widening as she said, "No, wait, I have an idea. It's the craziest idea in the history of ideas. Let's go back upstairs. I need you all to distract Aiden or get everyone out of there or *something*. If you give me ten minutes alone with my computer, I can figure this out."

"Ten minutes?" said Ruthie skeptically.

"Ten minutes," Ken said. "You need to distract five of the smartest teens in the world for ten minutes. You guys think you can do that?"

They all stared blankly at her.

"I could sing," Sophia volunteered. "It may have some rather disastrous effects, but it will certainly get the job done."

"I could recite the first million numbers of Pi," Ruthie volunteered.

"I could present an unsolved mathematical problem," Ming volunteered.

"Or," Ken said, "we could celebrate a birthday."

"Whose birthday?" Ruthie asked. "I don't—oh!" She spun around. "Sophia! It's your birthday in three days!"

"Oh yeah," Sophia reflected. "I forgot."

"We'll throw a surprise party!" Ruthie said excitedly. Her mind raced ahead. "Sophia, can you act really surprised? You need to fool everyone, and that includes Aiden."

Sophia smirked. "After my Legacy training, I can fool anyone with any emotion."

"Then we have a plan. I'll get Layla; she's an expert at throwing surprise parties," Ken said. "Let's hurry. I need to check out my idea as soon as possible. If I'm right, this could change everything."

"—and then I sauntered up to VD without breaking a sweat," Everest continued. "Voldemort, that is. I was like, 'Hey, he-who-shall-not-be-named, what d'ya think you're doin' with my friend?' and then I went all ninja, with roundhouse—"

"More accurately, you were restrained and nearly killed," Ming finished as he entered the room.

Everest chuckled. "Hey, Ming! Where'd you go? We didn't even finish our meeting."

"The meeting adjourned a while ago," Aiden countered. "I simply let you all stay so we could catch up, so to speak."

Ming shrugged and sat next to them. "I went to the bathroom."

"Hey, guys," said Ruthie with a mischievous grin on her face as she skipped into the room, Ken on her heels. "Sophia isn't here? Okay, great. Listen, Ken and I remembered that it was almost Sophia's birthday, so we organized a surprise party for her. Aiden, can you bring Sophia to one of the study booths? I pulled a few strings so we can celebrate her birthday right now."

Aiden paused. "What strings?"

"I had a key lime pie ordered for Sophia and grabbed some birthday decorations from our room," Ruthie explained. "Ken helped."

"I ordered the pie," explained Ken. "We really should have planned this out better."

"That's so sweet," said Layla, touched. She jumped to her feet. "You should have told me."

"It'd be too suspicious if we all left the room at once," Ruthie said, motioning for them to follow. "Come on! I have the study room reserved."

Aiden didn't fall for any of this. He said nothing as he wondered, *Why didn't they just call it up here instead of making us all go to the study booths in the Student Life building? Why are we celebrating today instead of on her actual birthday in three days? Perhaps they're just excited to see her again.* While suspicious, he didn't think too deeply about it.

The surprise party was well-played. Sophia had her favorite key lime pie. She didn't have to act to look touched by the others' meager, last-minute gifts. The party was quick and held in secret; Sophia kept Layla's coat and remained hidden in the secluded study booth with her friends. In about twenty minutes, it was all over. They all helped clean up before going their separate ways. Ken left the earliest; a whole ten minutes passed before Ruthie finished talking to Aiden and let him leave as well, relieved when she saw him go in another direction.

Ruthie returned to the headquarters to "grab her bag," which she had intentionally left behind. Inside the attic, Ken stared at the image of Molly Ravencrest on the computer screen. Then she looked back at the photo, her eyes wide. "Well?" Ruthie asked, looking over Ken's shoulder. "Did you find what you were looking for?"

Ken nodded numbly.

"Are you okay?" Ruthie asked, concerned. "You look like you don't know whether to laugh or cry or maybe just sit there in shock."

Ken looked up as if through a haze. "Is Aiden with you?"

"No, but he's coming." Ruthie noticed Aiden's half-open laptop left in the attic.

"He is?" Ken immediately came back to life, erasing her history, deleting her backups, and shutting down the computer. It was then that Sophia bounced in. "Ming's in his room with Everest to avoid suspicion. Was our little plan successful?"

Ken could barely breathe as she looked at the two eager faces. "It was successful, all right. It turns out that I was right after all."

"Don't sound so shocked," Sophia teased.

"What is it?" Ruthie asked. "I've got stuff to do, Ken. What did you find?"

"Don't keep us in suspense," Sophia added.

Ken robotically stood up. She walked to the doors, checked inside, tapped a button to stop the elevator, and allowed the soundproof doors to close behind her. Finally, she turned to the two expectant faces. "I did find something."

"No kidding," Sophia muttered.

"Ken, tell us!" Ruthie pleaded.

Ken closed her eyes. "I found out about Alexia."

"Alexia?" the other two chorused.

"Alexia Ravencrest, twin sister of Molly Ravencrest. They were separated at birth." Ken opened her eyes to see two stunned faces. "And guess what? She's a criminal."

Chapter Fifty-Three

"I don't understand," Ruthie said in shock. "Why have I never heard of her? Why hasn't *anyone* heard of her, for that matter?"

"She's in the Witness Protection Program," Ken said. "Er, was."

"Is she dead?" Sophia bluntly asked.

"No. She just...disappeared." Ken exhaled slowly. "Before she was in the program, she was in jail for manslaughter."

"You mean she killed someone?" Ruthie gasped.

"Yep. She was sixteen."

Ruthie couldn't believe this. "Wow, that's horrible."

Ken slumped into her chair. "No kidding. She pleaded guilty to it, too. Something about a gang fight. After she got out of jail, she entered the Witness Protection Program. They erased her existence while she stayed in hiding. After a few years, she disappeared."

"So no one knows if she's still alive?" Sophia asked.

"Not exactly. Law enforcement thinks she's alive. They even think she was behind some of the most terrifying heists in history. They found evidence that she stole the last living strain of the smallpox virus. No one knows where it is today since it's jumped around in the criminal underworld. If someone drops it in a subway, it could change history, you know? She stole a bunch of other valuable stuff, too. A lot of people think she's working with Rolyn Radcliff."

"You mean the art thief who graduated from Ravencrest?" Sophia said in an amazed, hushed whisper. It still felt illegal to mention the infamous, incredibly skilled Ravencrest graduate who had gone on to pull off some of the most astonishing heists in history.

"How did you find out about all this?" Ruthie questioned.

"Ah, you know," Ken said vaguely. "You can find out anything by using this computer, even classified stuff like Alexia's existence."

"Wow," Ruthie exhaled, dropping into the nearest chair. "That's...wow."

"Seconded," Ken said. "We can't tell Aiden."

"Why not? If it's not about his mom, it won't hurt him!" Sophia argued. "Besides, he deserves to know. I mean, he *is* Head of the Society now, isn't he? Or are we keeping this a secret until he officially becomes Head through a big, fancy ceremony?"

"We're keeping it a secret," Ruthie answered. "But you offer a good point. Now that Aiden's the Head of the Society, he kind of needs to know this. It's literally about his *mom*."

Ken rubbed her eyes. "See, and that's the worst part: Alexia Ravencrest tried to steal Aiden as a baby."

"*What*?" the other two shouted in unison.

"She's messed up!" Ken said. "She surfaced again and argued with Molly Ravencrest about who got to raise Aiden. Something about keeping up the family legacy since Molly Ravencrest had her own job to worry about. I guess Alexia wanted kids, so she tried to steal her sister's only child. According to Molly Ravencrest's diary entries hidden in cyberspace—"

"You mean she deleted them?" Ruthie clarified. "And you somehow found them?"

"Yes," Ken said. "I don't think anyone has read those entries out of respect for Molly, and that's one of the reasons Aiden would kill me if he knew I read them. But what was I supposed to do when the computer detected Alexia's name in there? Molly Ravencrest specifically said that when Aiden was born, they fought over who got to keep him."

"But she's Aiden's mother!" Ruthie said. "That's ridiculous!"

"Unless..." Sophia said slowly. "Wait a moment. What if Molly Ravencrest *wasn't* Aiden's biological mother? What if Alexia Ravencrest was?"

"I don't know!" Ken said in exasperation. "I have no idea! This whole thing is so confusing and complicated! Molly's parents kept Alexia a secret, so it was a shock for Molly when she found out. Apparently, the sisters were kind of friends for a few years. Then Alexia went to jail and everything just went downhill from there."

"You found all that from the Internet?" Sophia questioned.

"So you see? We can't tell Aiden," Ken finished at last. "This has to be kept secret."

Ruthie looked up. "But there are so many questions. How can we tell if Aiden is really Molly Ravencrest's child? If Alexia Ravencrest is still alive, what if she tries to contact Aiden?"

Sophia spoke up: "You guys can't find out, but I can. I'll do my own investigation."

"We can't tell Aiden," Ruthie repeated Ken's words dully. "If he finds out..."

"I won't tell," Sophia promised.

"Neither will I," Ken agreed.

Ruthie stood up. "I won't promise, but...from now on, we're never talking about Alexia Ravencrest again unless Sophia finds something."

"No. If you find something, don't tell us. I want to pretend I never heard about any of this," Ken finished. "You need to be the only person who knows about this stuff. The rest of us will do our best to forget it. Okay?"

"Okay," agreed Sophia.

Ruthie bitterly laughed. "I can't forget it."

They solemnly stood in silence, knowing full well that they were on the verge of discovering something that could change everything for poor Aiden.

Suddenly the doors were pushed open in one swift move and in walked Aiden Ravencrest with his usual smirk, startling them. "Are you all having a secret meeting up here?" he teased. His smile disappeared once he saw all three of their faces. "Why did you all disable the system? I was just alerted. I had to restart the elevator and push the doors open to get back in here."

Ken opened her mouth and couldn't find the right words. Ruthie stammered. Sophia tried to smile casually, though it didn't work.

Aiden studied their faces. "Is something wrong?"

"I'm late," Ken managed to say as she ran past him. He grabbed her arm and suddenly twisted the photo out of her hand, despite her attempts to pull it away. His eyes widened at the sight of Molly Ravencrest in the orange jumpsuit. "Where did you find this?" he said, not laughing anymore. "My mom was never in jail."

"No, she wasn't," Ruthie said, and he knew she wasn't lying.

"Then...?"

"An experiment," Sophia said, thinking fast. "An application of the newest photoshop technology. That's what we *think* it is."

"She found it on VD's desk," Ruthie added truthfully.

Aiden frowned. "Well, get rid of it. I don't want any lies about my mom spreading. She wouldn't keep something like this from me, you know? Even the Society was something she'd tell me about someday." He glanced at their faces. "Don't tell me you all believe this. VD's just trying to spread some lies about her, probably to draw me out." He tossed the photo to Ken. "Burn it or something."

Ken nodded and scurried away.

Sophia left quickly, leaving Ruthie alone with Aiden. Her eyes were big and sympathetic, and she decided she would at least try to tell him the truth. "Aiden, what if your mother wasn't really...you know..."

"She would have told me. She was a good person, you know?" he said, a little distantly. "Sometimes that's what keeps me going: knowing that I'm part of the Ravencrest family and that I have a legacy to uphold. My grandparents were Nobel Peace prize winners. My mom was incredible in every way. She had the kindest heart I know. My dad...well, I'm warming up to him." He chuckled. "I've got this awesome heritage and I'll do what it takes to live up to it. Sometimes it's a lot of pressure, but in the end, it's all worth it." He sounded younger, almost like a little kid as he spoke. Ruthie realized she was seeing a raw part of him. "I miss my mom a lot, but I know she'd be proud of me, as proud of me as I am of her."

Ruthie had been about to say something, but now she couldn't. She paused. "You're right, Aiden," she said at last. "Your mom *would* be proud of you."

He smiled at her. "Run along now. You've got homework."

"How'd you know?"

"I saw those textbooks."

"All right, I'll go. See you later, Aiden." Ruthie lingered in the elevator, looking back at him once more. His eyes were far away as he looked at the ground, smiling sadly, as if he was still grieving yet healing. She knew he was thinking of his mother—if Molly Ravencrest really was his mother.

"Bye, Aiden," Ruthie said softly, and she watched the elevator doors slide shut on the image of him standing there, still looking lost. He was only beginning to be found.

The next day was a beautiful moment in Ravencrest history.

That morning, over the intercom, the Head of Security cleared his throat and stated, "We have news regarding the status of the hacker known as 'VD'. Last weekend, our security team caught VD and put him behind bars."

The rest of his statement was lost in cheers as kids from all over the school cheered. Students rushed into the halls. A few were crying in relief since the anxiety and terror were finally gone. Some danced in the hallways while others called their parents and told them the good news.

The truth had been blurred; the story given to the students and the press was that VD, the infamous man who had blackmailed and coerced many Ravencrest students into doing terrible things, had turned out to be a hacker living in America. He had been arrested and would be in prison for life. All his methods of getting past Ravencrest

Campus Security were recorded and dismantled. Neither he nor any other hacker would ever be a threat to Ravencrest Academy again.

There was a noticeable change in the atmosphere for the rest of the week. Someone suggested they have a party, and soon most of the entire student body assembled in a lounge or one of the "just-for-fun" rooms. Just for a day, they were kids again, teasing each other, playing board games, swimming, relaxing, and just celebrating their freedom from all the fear VD had caused. They were safe now. Every one of them was reassured, relieved, and excited.

None of the Hall Monitors were ever awarded or praised for their achievements. No student knew of the role of the Hall Monitors in capturing VD, except for Rajesh and Sophia, who had both been sworn to secrecy. Yet all the Hall Monitors agreed that just the sheer joy of that day was enough reward for what they had done.

Chapter Fifty-Four

The days blurred into weeks, then into months, and before any student knew it, the semester was over. Sophia had obediently stayed out of sight after making sure the security measures were all in place. On the last day of the semester, all six Hall Monitors lounged in the attic, meeting up one last time that year. They had completed a few Society cases here and there after catching VD; ever since the Head of the Legacy had been dismantled, the Legacy had basically fallen apart. Thus, the Hall Monitors had been able to fully focus on their exams, which was quite a relief. Now, it was as if the adrenaline rush had passed; the stress was gone, and as the six of them met up one last time before dispersing to their families for Winter Break, there was relief and joy in every one of their faces.

"This was the coolest semester of my life," said Ruthie happily. "I accomplished almost all of my goals for this year, including all the nonprofit organizations I began and the cutting-edge psychology papers I published."

"I know, right?" said Ken excitedly. She smiled lovingly at her computer. "I love all the new nanotechnology advances I made. I worked with a few of the leading people in the technological field, and let's just say I made a lot of friends in high places, including an MIT Admissions Officer. I even have an internship at one of the biggest tech companies in the world! Apparently, some of my inventions are really making an impact."

"This semester *was* pretty cool. I think Madame Kate really likes me. It's awesome that I'm the lead of the musical *and* got onto the Varsity Dance team *and* have won medals as a gymnast! Plus, I learned another language while staying here, which is *potryasayushchiy*! That's Russian for *awesome*." Layla grinned. "And guess what? I'm going to intern as a United Nations translator! My dad's super excited about it. He's booked me business class tickets and everything!"

Everest wiped the sweat from his brow. He was completing another exercise routine. "Our team won first in the highest league for basketball *and* my biology research papers are about to be published, which is pretty cool. I gotta admit, this was an awesome semester."

Ming smiled. "I've accomplished quite a bit myself." He bragged little, but the truth was that he had won another Menuhin Competition as well as the international MATHCOUNTS, AMC, and AIME competitions. He had also contributed significantly to the field of physics and mathematics.

Aiden enjoyed seeing his friends so happy. He didn't offer his own accomplishments, though they were many. He had made significant progress in his academics; in fact, he was close to earning his PhD. Despite the setback of losing his memory for nine months, he had been able to make up for all the time he had lost. Regarding his memory, most of it had been fully restored except for the last month, which still remained murky. Strange, but he dwelt little on it. The greatest achievement, of course, had been his recent inauguration as Head of the Society. Father had planned to host the inauguration ceremony in January of next year when they all returned from Winter Break. For now, he was still the unofficial Head of the Society and continued to fulfill those duties.

The Legacy had been stopped at every turn. Its leader was gone and its rogue operations were all dismantled. The truth was clear: as long as VD was behind bars, there was no reason to worry. Even Simon from the Union was soon to be on parole. Father had been gracious enough to help him and other Union members leave prison faster.

"Did you know Veronica and I are starting to get along?" Layla said, making a face. "We still dislike each other, but we're getting better at pretending to be a family, just for the musical."

"Speaking of friends, Norton and I are gonna hang out together over Winter Break, just like old times," Everest added. "He's not a bad kid. I've talked to the Dean, and he's not putting any of this in Norton's permanent record due to VD's influence. The kid's gonna come off Scotch-free, and I'm glad. He's gonna be alright."

"You mean the guy involved in the drug ring?" Ken recalled. "Wow, that was so long ago. I wonder if Isabel's all right now too."

"She is," Layla confirmed. "Her family's in a much safer place now. Didn't you see her glowing in the halls? The Dean let her off without even a note in her record. In fact, she just received an internship at her dream job. She's definitely going to be okay."

"I'm glad," Ruthie reflected, hugging her knees. "Madeline just texted me. All the girls in our hall are getting together for a pre-Winter-Break celebration."

"More cake?" Layla teased.

Ruthie blushed. "The cake here is delicious. All the food is."

"You're right," Everest admitted. "The sundaes they serve at the café are the best."

"I disagree," said Ming. Normally he didn't get involved in small talk, but even he was feeling very relaxed. "Asian sweets are my favorite."

"I'll remember that," said Ruthie with a grin.

Layla glanced at her suspiciously.

"I remember everything," Ruthie reminded her. "*Including* the fact that it will be Darlene's birthday in a week. You want to throw her a surprise birthday party when we get back?"

"Alright texting Charlotte and Amika," said Layla, her fingers flying.

Everest stretched. "More partying? I'm not used to not doing anything for so long."

"It's only for a few weeks and you all deserve it," said Aiden. He rose to his feet. "Speaking of things you all deserve, I suppose a smooth flight home would be one of them?"

"You booked first class tickets, didn't you?" summarized Ken. "Got your 'friend' to pull a few more strings?"

"Perhaps," Aiden admitted.

"We're taking Ravencrest planes," Ruthie pointed out. "That's first class enough."

Layla chuckled. "Oh, Ruthie, there's first class...and then there's *first class.*" She and Ken shared a grin. They were probably the only kids in all of the Hall Monitors who had ever traveled via a first class flight.

Ken added, "Are the Ravencrest planes going to drop us off at one of the nearby airports that have exceptionally good first class service?"

Aiden smiled. "That's correct."

Ken leaned forward and rested her chin on her folded hands. "Maybe I'm a good guesser. Or maybe I just know you pretty well. So well that...I could get your number for the group chat?"

The conversation halted. Everyone turned to Aiden, who immediately made some excuse about needing to speak to a porter regarding the flight tickets. He was almost in the elevator when he found that they were jammed shut due to a technical error caused by Ken "accidentally" resting her elbow on her keyboard. Just as calmly, he strode across the attic to the restricted area and found, to his dismay, that Everest suddenly decided to take up his residence there, preventing Aiden from passing.

"Come on, Aiden," Ruthie pleaded. "It would be so much easier for us to contact you and for you to contact us. I mean, we don't usually check our email every few minutes. What if there was an emergency?"

"Why are you so against it, anyway?" Layla asked. "It's just a group chat."

Aiden suavely glanced back at them. "I like to keep an air of mystery."

"We've noticed," they all said in unison.

"You can still be mysterious if we have your phone number," Ken reasoned.

Aiden sighed. "You realize I have access to seven different weapons right now?"

"Please?" Ken begged. They all joined in, pleading with him. Even Ming added, "It would be a wonderful gift from you for the holidays."

Aiden groaned. This made it too difficult to decline. "It's only a phone number."

"That you keep hiding for some reason!" Ken finished. "So go on, give it to us!" Half of them already had their phones out.

Now it was clear that he truly had no choice. Aiden sighed. "Goodbye, dear dignity." He slumped into a chair and stared at his shoes. "The truth is...I don't have a phone."

There was a shocked silence.

"Wait, what?" Ken repeated. "*You*? Aiden Ravencrest?"

"The guy who jumps from ceilings?" Layla clarified.

"The guy who knows everything about everyone?" Ruthie checked.

"The guy who is a total prodigy and masterminded the plan that took down VD?" Everest asked.

"The guy who is Head of the Society?" Ming concluded.

"How can you not have a phone?" Ken said in shock. "Every single teenager has a phone. How can you not—"

"I've been grounded, at least until I turn 21," Aiden confessed.

"What did you do?" Ken said in awe.

Aiden dismissed it. "It doesn't matter. All that matters is no one was seriously hurt, all the reptiles were safely returned, and it was all chalked up to my young age. Besides, social media has a negative impact on mental health and can interfere with daily life. I don't need to be a teenager. I have enough important work that I enjoy doing. That's all there is to it."

"Yeah, yeah, yeah," Ken said, dismissing his excuses. "We get that, cool, but what did you do?"

Aiden groaned. "Please. Enough of my dignity is already gone."

"No, tell us!" implored the rest. Everest added, "Come on, it's got to be something good if it got you grounded this long!"

"No," said Aiden firmly.

"Wait a moment," Ruthie called. "Does it involve Porter Jimmy?"

"How could you—" Aiden began, but Ruthie finished excitedly, "Is it the reason he always flinches whenever someone says *giant lizards*?"

With that, Aiden was back on his feet. "I think I better go now before you all coerce me into doing something else."

"Wait!" Layla called. "Aiden, hold on. I think I speak for all of us when I say...that's cool. We don't care if you don't have a phone."

"You don't?" Aiden repeated. He normally did not repeat things others said, but he was caught off-guard.

"No! You're still Aiden Ravencrest!" Ken said.

"The guy who jumps from ceilings," Layla clarified.

"The guy who knows everything about everyone," Ruthie added.

"The guy who is a total prodigy and masterminded the plan that took down VD," Everest repeated.

"The guy who is the Head of the Society," Ming concluded with a smile.

"You're the coolest person we know," Ken finished. "And what if you're not a 'normal' teenager? It doesn't matter."

"Thanks," said Aiden stiffly. He felt the urge to leave immediately. There was a tingling sensation in his throat and his eyes were beginning to mist. He cleared his throat. "Have a good Winter Break, everyone."

Everyone cheered at this. Suddenly, Layla bounced to her feet and asked, "Group hug?"

"No way," said Aiden firmly, but the next thing he knew, they were hugging and laughing and talking excitedly. Soon they were leaving, ready to grab their suitcases and go home to their families. Ken to her mother and godfather, Ming to his little sister and mother, Layla to her internship, Everest to his brother, Ruthie to her family, and him to his room. Even Porter Jimmy gave him a half-hearted, "See you soon...or, even better, never" before leaving, to which Aiden had responded with a pleasant, good-natured, "Likewise." They had exchanged a single look of mutual respect before they went their separate ways. Many of the porters were assisting with the departure of the entire student body, planning to leave after the students were gone.

The Hall Monitors had one last rather tearful goodbye, with the girls hugging and the boys promising to call. Then the plane was flying off the runway. Aiden melted into the background as student after student boarded. Within hours, the school was deserted.

Aiden walked through the now-empty hallways. His footsteps echoed in the silence. The feeling was vaguely familiar. Suddenly, a memory rushed back to him from before the concussion: Mother, walking with him after a busy semester. Her presence was so real that he could barely speak. For a moment she was smiling at him, smiling brightly with eyes full of joy. She stopped and knelt so she was eye-to-eye with him. He was still, frozen. "Mother..." he whispered, unable to move.

"Aiden..." she replied, tracing his cheek one last time. "I'm so proud of you, Raisin." She kissed his forehead and he closed his eyes to fight the burn.

When he opened them, she was gone.

The hallways were long and silent. The sky was dimming and the sun was setting. The melancholy choked him and loneliness crept through his heart. He ran his fingers over the edge of his mother's portrait. Somehow he was in his father's bedroom. Footsteps tinted the silence. The door creaked open. Without looking, Aiden began, "I was just—"

"Your mother's portrait," Father said, standing behind him. "She was beautiful, wasn't she?"

Aiden nodded. He had no idea what Father would say or do next. This area was strictly restricted.

Father also traced his fingers over the outline of the portrait, a deep sadness in his eyes. "I do miss her. We were not on the best of terms, but I hope that one day, we will be. She was right about a lot of things. It's because of her that I know where she is now." He turned to his young son and Aiden saw that his father's eyes were red. "I've never been much of a father, but I promise you this, Aiden."

"Yes, sir?"

"I am so proud of you." Father's voice choked as he, for the first time, hugged his son. His grip was strong and sincere, and it took only a moment for Aiden to hug him back.

Then they were standing and talking and laughing (Father! Laughing!) as they walked outside together, his father's arm around his shoulders for the first time in a long time. Father's gaze promised that he would do better, that things would change.

In the distance, the stars shone as Aiden showed the Headmaster how to climb to the restricted part of the rooftops for the best view of the stars. Together, they leaned back onto the cool material and pointed at the constellations. They spoke well into the night. Aiden fell asleep the fastest. He woke up the earliest, finding his head resting on his father's shoulder. The sun was beginning to rise, its magnificent rays spreading across the sky like beams of joy lighting the horizon.

It was a new day. The storm was gone; the night had passed. The light of dawn was coming.

Aiden smiled and sat in the coolness of the early morning. Birds chirped and the melodious sounds of nature played their harmony. As he looked up to the heavens, he knew where his mother was. For the first time in a long time, he was at peace.

Goodbye, Mother.

A cloud lingered in the sky once, then pulled away. In that slight breeze, Aiden knew his mother was waving her final goodbye to him.

Goodbye, my son.

Goodbye.

Epilogue

The chains clanked in the darkness. Someone coughed. Someone else sighed deeply. Men with black holes for eyes and numbness for their souls lay listlessly on the cots as guards chatted. One prisoner vomited, on their hands and knees, gasping for breath. A guard gently turned him over to see the bloodshot eyes. There was another groan, and then the inmate convulsed in pain. The guard helped the sick man to his wobbling feet. He pressed the back of his hand to the inmate's forehead: high fever. Guard Antonio Vilski shouted something to his colleague, and the inmate was put on a stretcher and brought to the prison hospital.

Antonio Vilski had served as a prison guard for eighteen years. He had seen the roughest of men and the cruelest of prisoners, men with horrible pasts and even more horrible futures. They could smoke a cigarette and laugh in one breath, then strangle another to death in the next minute. Suicides were common, and more than one prisoner had lunged at him with clear murderous intent in their eyes. Vilski knew how to respond. He would keep his eyes locked on his attacker as he calmly slammed his inmate over the head with his steel baton, effectively giving the prisoner a concussion. Brutal yet necessary to lay down the rules. He had fought for his life before, protecting his face while blocking every blow. He knew seven different martial arts and had been specifically trained, always equipped with sixteen different types of weapons, including pepper spray, tasers, stun guns, batons, handheld guns, and more military-grade material.

Yet despite his experience dealing with the darkest of humanity, he was surprisingly gentle with the prisoners. No matter how they jeered and cursed, he never provoked or spoke back to them. He was firm when needed and only fought in self-defense. Outside of his work, he was a kind-hearted, gentle father with a wife and two sons, a third on the way. Now as he brought the inmate to the prison hospital, he recognized the desperate, racking pain which seized the prisoner mercilessly. The inmate groaned in agony, sweat beading his forehead. The doctor frowned upon examining the prisoner; "Poisoned," he said. "Possibly a suicide attempt. You need to be more careful with what kind of gifts you let family members give prisoners. This is serious."

Vilski sighed. "Will he survive?"

"Unlikely."

"We will try," said Antonio Vilski firmly, and that was the end of the discussion.

The inmate was dressed in a hospital gown and stripped of everything he owned. His room contained only a bed, a mattress, a pillow, and a blanket. Cameras monitored the room, and a guard was assigned to keep an eye on the unstable prisoner at all times.

The system was duly notified and, as expected, no one showed up to speak to the prisoner. The inmate clearly had no close family or friends. Antonio glanced at the shivering figure one last time, who was gritting his teeth in pain. The man did not seem like he would survive the night. Antonio crossed the room briskly and took out his phone. Within a few minutes, he was the arranged supervisor of the watch. Free coffee was the sole reason he gave for watching the inmate over the security cameras. His job was to alert prison security if the prisoner tried to escape. He was the only one to see the man sob pathetically and crumple onto his bed, entirely destroyed.

The sick prisoner was different from other prisoners. He was skinny and unaccustomed to the harshness and roughness of prison life. He treated the guards with respect and obeyed the law dutifully, refusing to cheat or steal. Of course, one could assume he simply wanted to get out of prison faster; that is, until one noticed how the prisoner intervened and called for peace in fights. The man wasn't one of the hardened criminals that the prison was infested with. No, this man seemed utterly defeated.

Vilski checked his watch. Four days had passed since the inmate had been assigned to this hospital room, and there was still no sign of recovery. In fact, the inmate seemed to be getting worse. Antonio's shift was almost over; another guard was on his way and would be here in about five minutes.

Antonio cautiously entered the hospital room, his hand on his gun in case the prisoner responded. The sick man just looked up at him lifelessly, all the fight in him gone.

"You're not trying to get better," Antonio Vilski said.

The man continued to stare without emotion.

Vilski gestured to the room around him. "This isn't forever. Keep up your good behavior, and you'll get out of here soon."

Still no response.

Vilski sighed. "Look. I'll make you a deal. You recover, and I'll send you to a nicer prison."

The patient stirred a little, but it was enough. There was a flash of surprise, and so Antonio pounced on it: "Yeah, I can do that. You've been on good behavior so far. You just need to make it a few more months."

"You mean a year?" the prisoner rasped. His eyes were empty. "Nothing matters anymore."

"You've got a way out—"

"No." The inmate turned away. "They took them."

"What?"

"My girl and kid. Murdered."

"You're not married," said Antonio Vilski, startled. He had read the man's file.

The prisoner closed his eyes. "The kid was two. *Two*. Killed because of me." His voice was sorrowful. "My stupidity. Thought I could take down the Legacy single-handed. Do you know what happened? I lost everything. They found me, erased my existence, and destroyed me. Pushed me to horrible ends by torturing my kid..." He shuddered. "They tried to make me go too far. They wanted me to burn down a school with a thousand kids in it. I stopped at that. So they set me up."

"Why didn't you fight back? Legally?"

"Too many charges, charges I had to plead guilty to or else they'd kill my kid. I had no choice."

"You had a choice," Vilski said, his heart burning. "I can help you. I have a lawyer, resources, and connections."

"Why do you care?" the inmate rasped.

"Because you don't belong here. I work for the law, and I don't like to see people put in this kind of place for things they didn't do."

Now the prisoner turned so he was facing the guard. "I deserve being here. You know my charges. What they made me do...and I lost everything anyway. I thought I could fight back. But, oh God, I lost everything. I don't know why I kept trying." His voice broke. "Please, they're gone now. You have a gun. Just make it quick."

Antonio Vilski stepped forward. "I'm not going to shoot you, I promise. Listen, you haven't lost everything. There's still hope."

The inmate slumped onto the bed, staring at the ceiling blankly. "There's no hope."

"There's always hope."

"Not for me."

"Hey," said Vilski, now standing next to the bed. He looked sternly at the man. "Look at me."

The prisoner reluctantly did.

"We'll find a way to help you. I promise." Vilski's face softened with compassion. "Trust me, I'm getting you out of here if it's the last thing I do."

"Don't," said the prisoner.

"Don't what?"

"Don't move."

"What do you—" Antonio Vilski stopped mid-sentence. Something faintly stung his arm. He looked down to see that it was bleeding.

The prisoner looked at him. "You're hurt."

"It's strange," Vilski said, suddenly woozy. "I was fine a moment ago...."

"Did you know there are cleaning supplies in the bathroom over there?" The inmate's tone was different now. "Including bleach. Deadly. And the doctor had an IV in me for a bit, but since it gets changed so often, it was easy to grab a needle from a nurse. All it takes is a little poke. Oh, and a good sob story to get you close enough. You can't even hear me now, can you? Or understand anything I'm saying? Oh, don't look so confused."

"But..." mumbled Vilski, sliding to the floor, "I thought..."

Now the prisoner rose to his feet and stretched. "Acting is exhausting. Can you imagine? All those nights, being the poor, persecuted criminal who didn't deserve to be here. All I had to do was make you feel sorry for me. Whichever guard gave in first, well, that was a fatal mistake."

Antonio choked on his own blood. His eyes rolled into his head and the entire world grew hazy.

"The trick is to mix truth with fiction." The inmate knelt and pulled the keys out of Vilski's belt. He released his own handcuffs, pocketed the gun, and swapped his orange jumpsuit for Vilski's guard uniform, talking all the while. "My poor wife and kid. You know, I've got an army waiting for me to take command. Looks like they won't have to wait long."

Vilski slipped deeper into unconsciousness. Barely alive, he mumbled, "My kids..."

"Oh, they'll survive," said the inmate, buttoning up his suit. "Unlike you." He grabbed Vilski and dragged him onto the bed, positioning him in the same place. The IV was reinserted, the rugged blanket was strewn over the bed, and the body was positioned so that the left hand dangled off the side, just as before. The inmate fingered the name tag. "Antonio Vilski. Hmm. I like your last name. Vilski. Has potential, don't you think?"

There was no response. Vilski no longer heard anything said by the patient; no, his face was shining as he looked into a beautiful, bright glory, a glory he would be enveloped in for eternity.

"You were right, Vilski," chuckled the man as he strolled to the door. "You *are* helping me get out of here. Looks like it's the last thing you'll do."

With that, he pushed the door open and shut it behind him. The security pass allowed him to freely walk down the halls until he was outside. The man dressed in Vilski's clothes left the prison building and used Vilski's pocket phone to call an unknown number. "Hey, honey," he said in a voice loud enough for the other guards to hear. "Shift's ending now. Can you pick me up? We'll get dinner at that place you love."

The car pulled up barely a minute later. The escaped prisoner stepped briskly into the backseat and crawled under the seat and into the trunk after the car passed security inspection. After they were safely on the highway, the car pulled back onto the parking lot of the movie theater where it had been stolen, as no security cameras were around. The man stepped out, having changed clothes in the trunk, and now discarded the uniform in the backseat of the car. Still in the back of the parking lot, the man and his driver entered another car. They left, and no one noticed.

At last, the escaped prisoner spoke: "Thank you for the poison."

"Don't mention it. The Council is eager to see you."

"How have they done without me?"

"Not very well."

"Excellent." He smirked. "They need me."

"Why else did they invest in your escape?" scowled the driver.

He chuckled. "Excellent point. Oh, and how is our little friend Aiden Ravencrest doing? On his holiday vacation, I presume?"

"We have our eyes on all the Society members, including the newly-enacted ones," the driver answered.

"Good, good," the passenger observed.

"Do you have a plan?"

"What?"

"Do you have a plan?" the driver repeated. "The Council expects much of you. They've just helped you escape, so they have high expectations. If you show up to their meeting with nothing but a 'Thanks for helping me escape!', you're finished."

"Oh, no need to worry," mused the passenger, his dark eyes fixed outside the window as his mind worked. An evil smile spread over his face. "I do have a plan," he said. "A plan to destroy Ravencrest

Academy. A plan to take away everything from Aiden Ravencrest the way he took everything from me. A plan to make every one of those Society members pay. They think the battle is over; no, it's only begun." His cruel laughter rose until he was cackling, the malice in his eyes unrestrained.

When the car came to a stop, he and his driver stepped out. The passenger surveyed the building in front of him and didn't break his stride as he stepped past the other offices, reciting the required security codes until he was standing in front of the Legacy Council.

"Vladimir Damon, I trust you have an explanation? A *plan*?" accused a Legacy Councilor, his sharp eyes narrowed.

"I do," smirked Damon as he stood in front of some of the most devious criminal masterminds in the world.

"We'd like to hear it!" insisted another.

Damon stretched leisurely. He had all the time in the world. Every detail of his plan had been perfectly plotted and intricately planned. With every moment he had spent forcing kindness in that rotting cell, he had envisioned hundreds of ways to make Aiden Ravencrest pay. This was the plan that maximized the most revenge. Every word made the Council's scowls slowly turn into evil smiles. Soon, they were excitedly discussing his ideas, their grudging respect rising. The plan was set into motion; phone calls were made, documents were forged, and certain people were discarded while others were recruited.

VD smirked as he watched his plan unfold. "Oh, it's good to be back."

www.ingramcontent.com/pod-product-compliance
Lightning Source LLC
Chambersburg PA
CBHW051508250626
47156CB00001B/5
* 9 7 8 1 5 0 6 9 1 1 6 2 5 *